For Lauro

Who can swear that there will not come a pope
so imbued with God's spirit and that of our
time . . . as to raise the flag of freedom on
the towers of Castel Sant'Angelo?

N. Tommaseo to R. Lambruschini,
November 1831

Without the Pope, there can be no true
Christianity.

Joseph de Maistre, *Du Pape*

Acknowledgment

I am grateful for the assistance of
the Arts Council of Great Britain,
and for that of the Rockefeller Foundation which
granted me a residency at Bellagio.

NOTE

Pope Pius IX – Pio Nono (1846–1878) – took to polemic as salamanders do to flame. His invective was biblical, and his enemies gave back as good as they got. Caught between their cartoons and his anathemas, the Catholic world was pushed ever further towards polarisation. The Right loved him for his torments, his piety and his charisma, and he has long – oddly long? – been a candidate for canonisation. The Left came to hate him.

I have tried to imagine what it was like to be a moderate dependant of his and, to give myself freedom, have invented several characters. I hope that the climate in which they move is close to that which prevailed in the Papal State during its final decades.

J. O'F.

SWITZERLAND

SAVOY

AUSTRIAN EMPIRE

Milan
LOMBARDY
VENETIA
Venice

Turin
R.Po
PIEDMONT
PARMA
MODENA
Ferrara
Bologna
Ravenna
Imola
Cesena
Rimini
Sinigaglia

FRANCE

Genoa

Lucca Florence
Leghorn
R.Arno
TUSCANY
Perugia
Castelfidardo

NICE

Nice

(KINGDOM OF SARDINIA)

Elba
Spoleto

CORSICA
(French)

Viterbo
Civita Vecchia
Mentana
ROME

Caprera

Gaeta
Naples Benevento
Portici

NAPLES

SARDINIA

The Papal States
① Romagna (or Legations)
② Marches
③ Umbria
④ Patrimony of St. Peter

Palermo
Messina

SICILY

0   50   100 miles

LIST OF THE PRINCIPAL CHARACTERS

Amandi, Cardinal: Friend of the Pope and patron of Nicola.
Andrea: Cardinal Girolamo Marchese d'.
Antonelli, Giacomo Cardinal: 1806–1876: from 1848 Secretary of State.
Bassi, Father Ugo: chaplain in papal armies of 1848 and later with Garibaldi.
Blount, Edward: Nicola's companion in Paris during Bloody Week.
Bonaparte, Louis Napoleon: becomes Napoleon III.
Bonaparte, Napoleon Louis: his brother, dies of chickenpox in 1831.
Cesarini, Duke Flavio: earlier known as orphan called Diodato.
Cesarini, Donna Geltrude: Flavio's mother.
Chigi, Flavio: nuncio to Paris.
Darboy, Archbishop Georges of Paris.
Diotallevi, Costanza: a spy.
Döllinger, Ignaz von: German theologian.
Dubus, Father: priest whom Amandi meets in Savoy in 1847.
Dupanloup, Bishop Félix of Orléans.
Gatti, Maria: girl whom Nicola falls for in 1849.
Gatti, Pietro: her son.
Gavazzi, Alessandro: a nationalist and Liberal preacher and chaplain in army.
Gilmore, Augustine: a classmate of Nicola's at the Collegio Romano.
Giraud, Maximin: child visionary who sees Virgin in 1846.
Grassi, Father: a Jesuit.
Lambruschini, Cardinal Luigi: Secretary of State to Pope Gregory XVI, and
    right-wing favourite to succeed him. He lost to Mastai.
Lambruschini, Raffaello: a nephew of his, who keeps a diary.
Lammenais, the abbé: a Liberal Catholic thinker.
Langrand-Dumonceau, André, later Count: Catholic financier.
Manning, Cardinal Henry of Westminster.
Martelli: classmate of Nicola Santi at Collegio Romano.
Mastai-Ferretti, Giovanni Maria: later Pope Pius IX.
Mauro, Don: an unfrocked priest.
Mérode, François Xavier de: Chamberlain, then Minister for Arms.
Mortara, Edgar: Jewish child kidnapped by papal authorities.

Nardoni: police lieutenant in Imola, spy.

Oppizzoni, Cardinal Count Carlo: Archbishop of Bologna.

Passaglia, Carlo: a Jesuit theologian at the Collegio Romano.

Paola, Sister: nun who first appears as unnamed girl during revolution of 1831.

Reali, il canonico: dissident priest.

Randi, Monsignor Lorenzo: papal minister of police.

Rossi, Count Pellegrino: Pio Nono's chief minister, murdered in November 1848.

Russell, Odo: unofficial agent of British Government.

Sacconi, Monsignore: nuncio to Paris.

Santi, Nicola: later Monsignore.

Stanga, Prospero: later Monsignore.

Stanga, Count: his father.

Stanga, Contessa Anna: father's second wife.

Verità, Don Giovanni: a Liberal priest.

Vigilio, Don: a spy.

Viterbo: Edgar Mortara's uncle.

One

After midnight a funeral took place with furtive pomp. It was an event likely to puzzle any stranger who chanced to witness the defiant advance of the red-draped, four-in-hand hearse and the throngs of trudging mourners who growled out angry prayers and held tapers up like spears. Behind them, a two-hundred-strong cavalcade of carriages bore prelates and members of the city's papal ('black') aristocracy. Houses were lit up and flowers thrown from windows. But the mob was there too, stationed all along the way from St Peter's to San Lorenzo Outside the Walls. At first its mood was uncertain. Then a song rose jeeringly: '*Addio, mia bella, Addio*!' Scuffles broke out and the police had to stop demonstrators seizing the corpse. 'Long live Garibaldi!' was the cry. 'Death to the priests!' and 'Pitch the swine in the Tiber.'

'*Carogna*! Into the river with his carcass!'

Driving through the whitewash gleam, which had transformed their grimy old city into a whited sepulchre, disheartened the prelates. They were burying an epoch with their last Pope Prince. Pius IX, having reigned for thirty-two years, had set a record for longevity which left his predecessors' in the dust. His reign had been riven by paradox and this funeral was its last, for when he died three years ago, his household had not dared cross the hostile city and bury him where he had asked to be laid. How come, marvelled watchers, that the three-year-old corpse didn't explode? Mummified, was the answer, like the papacy itself. Embalmed and boxed in.

Reports of police connivance – only six demonstrators had been charged! – reached the provinces in the high colour of parable. Pope Pius, when alive, had been inclined to wrap himself in the seamless robe of Christ,

I

and the robe, a metaphor for papal power, had been rent when the Kingdom of Italy seized his state.

Two principles had clashed: a people's right to determine its destiny and the Pope's to territorial independence. This latest Italian failure to defend papal dignity fuelled arguments afresh. The robe had been spat on and Christ vilified in his Vicar's person! The new pope protested angrily. Clergy, up and down the country, stiffened their opposition to the regime and men who had tolerant leanings shelved them. This was no time for give and take. Even personal loyalties must be sacrificed.

Father Luca, who had been hiding the diary of his dead benefactor, the abate Lambruschini, inside a wrapper entitled *Experiments in Crop-Rotation*, now lost his nerve. What if it were found? By friends who would reproach him with not destroying it – or, worse, might want it published! The abate had been a Liberal priest. A great but sad man, born out of his time, he had hoped that, after his death, his diary might safely see the light of day. But now he had been dead seven years, and Father Luca worried lest, somehow – the devil had his ways – it should fall under some dangerous and alien eye. He himself couldn't sit in judgment on it. He was a simple priest, a labourer's son educated at the abate's expense. But reports of the mob's insults recalled older ones about how, many years ago, at the start of his reign, Pius too had been a Liberal and been worshipped by that same Roman mob. Lambruschini had described him walking in among them in his white robe and how, as he passed, they sank to their knees in the dung-wet streets. 'Long live the Angel pope!' was then their cry. Father Luca, his curiosity piqued, took down the book.

From the diary of Raffaello Lambruschini: *Rome, 1846*

In Rome, just after his election, I glimpsed the new pope. I was on a balcony with my uncle, the defeated candidate, who was scanning the crowd with the eye of a man who knew the odds. For ten years he had been Cardinal Secretary of State and, in practice, the most powerful man in the realm – which was why *he* was not elected pope. Cardinal Secretaries rarely are. Being too visible, they rouse resentments. He should have known this. Yet loss of power shocked him and I, who had not been on terms with him, felt a surprised impulse of pity.

'*Viva Papa Mastai*, the people's friend!'

It was half-prayer and half-cheer. 1846 looked to be a miraculous year for we had, or thought we had, a Liberal pope. Political and religious hope fused in that cry while my uncle, Luigi Cardinal Lambruschini, sat still as a pillar of salt.

I disdained his doubts. To be sure the new pope's love-transaction with the crowd was hazardous – but how can men who have not defied their limitations conceive of God?

Once a fritter-vendor, scrambling onto the roof of his booth, came so close that we smelled frying oil of incalculable age. He cradled his balls in a – pagan? – gesture of celebration and I saw my uncle wince. Anarchy, he clearly felt, had been unleashed and his own handiwork undone, for Pius was releasing conspirators whom it had taken *his* spies miracles of ingenuity to catch.

All around us, seminarians in bright cassocks – scarlet, white, purple, black – craned and flexed as if turning themselves into human flags. Only when His Holiness exchanged jokes with our fritter-seller did I see a pulse tremble in my uncle's neck. A particle of flesh, by defying his will, reminded me that our new pope's was more wayward. I knew this because I belonged to a group which had secretly worked to get him elected. Mastai-Ferretti knew nothing of our reasons for choosing him to succeed to Peter's throne. These can be summed up in one word: humanity. Like Peter, he had proven fallible, flexible and, we hoped, open to change.

My uncle was not. Sitting beside him, I was aware of having betrayed my kind for – kinship apart – he and I were men who put principle above personal ties, and I knew that if he could have understood my disloyalty, he would have condoned it. So there I sat, inwardly twisting like Judas on his rope. Once he pressed my hand. '*Sursum corda*,' he whispered. 'Let's raise our hearts.' But I, his Judas, thought of the schoolboy pun, 'raise the rope' – *corda* – and feared he had seen inside my head.

It was only later, in the gaunt cavern of his dining room, that I thought I saw tears. The candelabra, however, were inadequate and the light too dim for certainty. A year later, at the time of the so-called Jesuit plot, I wondered if he had had a hand in that, but guessed him to be too shrewd.

*

3

The words 'Jesuit plot' made Father Luca blench and so did the reference to the dead pope as a 'Liberal'. The abate had been writing in and for happier times and Father Luca felt a pang of nostalgia for his patron's lightness of spirit. Maybe it was as well he'd died when he had.

Moving to a window, he watched fork-tailed swallows wheel. The air was still. Sounds carried across surprising distances and, down valley, a skipping rhyme was being thrummed on some threshing floor. Sour words reached him with painful clarity.

> Pyx! Pax! Pox! St Peter's on the rocks!
> His leaky boat won't float!
> Pyx! Pax! Pox!

The abate's great fear had been that of adding to the boat's distress. This was why he left Rome. He had liked to joke that this Tuscan retreat was like the islands to which the Emperor Augustus had exiled adulterers and that he, rather than adulterate honest certainties, had embraced silence as well as exile. And indeed, after the débâcle of '49, he had published nothing more contentious than a treatise on silk worms. He had gone on writing, to be sure, but 'for the drawer'. But now, thought Luca, let it be some other drawer than his! The abate's trust weighed on him and, remembering that he knew a dependant of the Cardinal Prefect of the *Congregatio Indicis*, he determined to send him the diary and get the matter off his conscience. Surely the abate would have understood?

From the diary of Raffaello Lambruschini:

Controversy stifles charity. I learned this as I watched my uncle meet *his* Calvary. That evening, he talked of a universe of pain through which humanity must struggle in search of lost unity.

We must have sat up later than usual for the footmen were visibly falling on their feet when he leaned towards me and whispered: 'Revolution is part of God's plan. The French one was a punishment and we too shall soon be tested. Blood will flow here! *Sangue!*' he hissed with such relish that I was amazed. 'The *popolo*,' he gloated, 'will get more than they bargained for.' Then he pursed his old man's mouth

4

until it looked like a chicken's anus and went red with malice. My revulsion shocked me. In the end a distrust for zeal – my own included – led to my renouncing public office. Yet what I had already done by promoting the candidacy of Mastai-Ferretti was to have long-tailed consequences.

People who remember papal Rome tend to talk of a paradise or a prison. My own recollection is of a sleepy little place choked by rotting brocade with a population – in the year of Mastai's election – of 170,000 souls, few of whom knew much about the world outside their city gates which were kept timorously locked at night. It had its own system for telling time. A twenty-four-hour day ended at the Ave Maria, half an hour after sunset, and so varied with the seasons.

Memories differ and so do maps. I have two of the old town before me as I write. On one the Tiber flows down the left while on the other it festoons up the other side, carrying a sailboat upstream from Ripetta to Ripa Grande: a draughtsman's whimsy intended no doubt to show that, even after the advent of steamers, trade was plied at a sluggish pace – as indeed it was. Weed-webbed and gilded – in memory – by the sun of a perpetual siesta, Rome droused to the flap of wet laundry and the chomp of oxen chewing the cud in 'the Cow Field' which was how citizens called the Forum. At night it slept through antiphonies of caged nightingales, disturbed only by the odd clopclop of a carriage fetching guests home from a *conversazione* in some noble palace. Productive activity was rare. Strangers came to dawdle and dabble, and in the margins of memory there is always an Englishwoman with an easel. Pyrotechnists prospered as did stage carpenters. Rome, in short, was a stage on which we learned to exhibit ourselves, and my first moment of revulsion came when, as a very young cleric, I saw a senior prelate go down on his hands and knees, bark like a dog and entertain Pope Gregory by waggling his reverend rump. His influence with His Holiness depended, I was told, on the alacrity with which he was prepared to play the buffoon.

Gregory was my uncle's pope, and his need for such solace may have been due to distress at the harsh measures which my uncle persuaded him to adopt. Our regime was doomed. Our government knew this, but could not agree to diminish God's sway over His state. In moments of unrest it appealed for help to the Austrian Army.

It was in this climate that some of us began to gather data about possible candidates for the succession: *papabili*. Transitions are risky and the last bad disturbances had erupted just before Pope Gregory's

5

own election during the *sede vacante* of '31. How had our candidates behaved then? One had been in the very eye of the storm: Archbishop Mastai-Ferretti whose record we now proceeded to scan. I still have documents whose existence might surprise him.

1831

PROCLAMATION

by Giovanni Maria Mastai-Ferretti, nobleman of Senigallia, Ancona and Spoleto.

By the Grace of God and the Holy Apostolic See, Archbishop of Spoleto, Commendatory Abbot of Santa Croce in Sassovivo, Domestic Prelate to H.H. Gregory XVI and Assistant at the Papal Throne.
  Following our provinces' happy restoration to their lawful Sovereign and trusting in the pious submission of our flock, we wish to make known our concern that respect be shown to all rebels who hand in their arms in token of their intention to return to the paternal embrace of the Supreme Pontiff . . .

30 March 1831
Spoleto, Palace of the Archbishop

Archbishop Mastai-Ferretti reread his old proclamation where the words 'paternal embrace' had split apart. Had someone . . .? No, just wind and weather. The thing had been rained on then, no doubt, split in the May sun. He thought of the May procession and the play of light on embroidered banners. The Austrian High Command had questioned the wisdom of holding it so soon after the disturbances, but the archbishop had prevailed. Last spring he had been a bit of a hero.

Passing a café, he nodded an acknowledgment to risen hats. A hen scuttled under his feet and a woman darted out to collect it, then withdrew with a movement not unlike the hen's. In a garden another woman was throwing water to keep down the dust. Shutters slapped open. The siesta hour had passed and, up in the *Rocca*, a bugle announced some changeover in the prisoners' routine.

The archbishop's stroll had brought him to a palace which he should have remembered to avoid. Here too shutters had opened and a liveried servant was hanging out a bird cage. Now the sensitive, tapir's nose of the old marchesa slid into sight and her eye caught his.

6

'Afternoon, Monsignore.'

'Afternoon, Donna Maria.'

He walked unhappily on. They had been friends, but not since Easter.

Trying not to speed his step, he remembered, with residual pique, how a mutiny at the *Rocca* had been used by local notables to worm permission from him to recruit a Civic Guard. The marchesa's son had led the delegation. After all, said Don Gabriele, His Eminence the Legate was known to favour mobilising the citizens.

'Arm the people against the people?' The archbishop could not openly criticise the legate's judgment.

It was Ash Wednesday and there was a smudge of penitential ash on the delegates' foreheads.

'General Sercognani's force is approaching,' Don Gabriele argued.

'*General* Sercognani?'

'He's been promoted.'

'By?'

Don Gabriele had the grace to look embarrassed. 'The people,' he said. 'The Provisional Government in Bologna.'

In recent weeks town after town had been appointing such governments and the one in Bologna had declared the popes' temporal dominion to have ceased '*de facto et de jure*'. Posters, blossoming in the night, announced plans to march on the capital and 'separate the sceptre from the tiara'. More worryingly, the rebels were opening prisons to recruit the riffraff inside.

'There are six hundred prisoners at the *Rocca*.' On Don Gabriele's forehead, sweat made runnels in the Ash-Wednesday smudge. 'If they're let out, who's to guard the citizens' property?'

'And who's to know,' mused the archbishop, 'that a Civic Guard, *if* I let you raise one, will not turn its arms against the Church?'

'Are we to take it,' challenged Don Gabriele, 'that His Holiness's government is unwilling to permit its subjects to defend their homes?'

Cornered, the archbishop had given in. 'Form your Civic Guard,' he yielded. It was putting foxes in charge of the hen run – but what choice had he? 'I'll review them,' he decided shrewdly. 'I'll be their chaplain and say a few words.'

Don Gabriele could not object. However, when the archbishop came to review the recruits, he could feel their hostility. Allegiances had grown volatile and indeed it was later to turn out that, elsewhere in the province, relatives of his own had been compromised. Later still – now – this made it difficult to be hard on men like Don Gabriele. Yet, if the archbishop let bygones by bygones, loyal citizens would take it amiss. His social life was in ruins.

Plucking a verbena leaf from a garden, he inhaled its fragrance and set off on a detour so as to avoid returning by Don Gabriele's palace.

'Monsignore!'

Two peasants had moved their cart aside to let him pass. Whittled faces. Deferent eyes. Few of their sort had joined the rebels and the few who had, had been armed with halbards stolen from museums. Friends in Rome, tittering over this, failed to appreciate the danger which had been averted.

'Beloved sons!'

Those were his words to the guards when exhorting them to take an oath of loyalty to the freshly elected pope.

'Will you do this, *diletti figliuoli*?'

The silence was sullen. Suddenly – if there was a signal he missed it – they whipped tricolour cockades from inside their coats and shouted as one man, '*Viva l'Italia!*' *Viva* – this was rebellion, a repudiation of papal rule. Italy though! *Italia mia* . . .

The archbishop kicked a stone. He disliked remembering what he had done next which was to burst into tears. The stone hit a dog which limped reproachfully away. To his surprise, the tears had been triggered less by the guardsmen's treachery than by an urge to shout '*Viva l'Italia!*' himself. Treachery had got inside his head, which went to show how hard this new nationalism would be to check. It was, as he had since argued with Monsignor Amandi, quite unlike the godless anticlericalism of the last century. Sercognani's manifestos declared that he respected the pope as pope, but not as king: *papa si, re no*!

Back in his palace, the archbishop had summoned the captain of the papal garrison and advised that, to avoid trouble with the new Civic Guards, he should disband his troop.

As a result, Sercognani's men passed through without incident while his Grace lay low and meditated on the notion of change which a mentor of his had called the essence of temptation. Monsignor Marchetti had lived through the years of the French Revolution.

'What *is* temptation,' he used to ask, 'but an overweening appetite? Its ultimate lure is the hope of becoming God!'

All through Lent, the archbishop prayed on his knees before faceless statues bundled in purple cloth, and felt his mind rave as he tried to distinguish between prudence – avoiding bloodshed – and sympathy with the rebels. From outside the church windows came smells of spring

8

blossoms and the lilt of young men singing late into the night. In his youth he had hoped to wield a marshal's baton rather than a crozier and, but for his epilepsy, would have joined the Noble Guard. He had written Latin odes too: some on liberty, a classic theme.

'Fool!' would have been Marchetti's comment. '*Every* skirmish is part of the long war between God and Satan!'

'Could we not,' the archbishop argued in his mind, 'win them by paternal persuasion?'

The line of his mentor's clamped lips cancelled half measures. No! Austrian troops must be called in to restore order. This state was God's.

'But men like my brother and Don Gabriele only want a few reforms: lower toll charges and the like. They're not Jacobins!'

'Toll charges are the thin end of the wedge!'

The argument had the monotony of a wheel and the archbishop's stroll too had come full circle. He was back at the café. A man approached: Count Bernardo Montani, the former Gonfalonier who had not been reappointed after the Easter troubles.

'Monsignore, if I might have a word?'

The archbishop's hands rose in an exasperated flutter. 'My *dear* count, I sent a most reassuring report of your conduct to Rome. It is uncharitable to remind me of my lack of influence!'

The count did not believe him. The archbishop saw it in his face. Together they walked past the old proclamation, put up when contact with Rome was lost and Spoleto was on its own: a brief interval. Within days Austrian 'liberators' would be overawing the townsfolk with the glory of their white uniforms, rebel leaders fleeing to Paris or Corfu, and Rome reneging on promises made by men on the spot.

'It is true,' Mastai had since written to friends at court, 'that I granted a safe-conduct to the defeated rank and file and paid their back pay. If I had not they might not have laid down their arms.' He wondered if he had fatally jeopardised his career.

'Even my letters in support of my brother,' he thought of telling Montani, 'are getting short shrift.'

'It's Donna Maria's name day.'

'Ah, so it is!'

This evening her *palazzo* would be lit up and cake and sorbets served. Another year he would have been the guest of honour.

The ex-Gonfalonier smiled. 'You know you would be more than welcome.'

The archbishop looked him in the eye. 'Giovanni Mastai would enjoy being with you. The archbishop cannot.'

'Has the Church cast us out then?'

'If you'll remember, count, it was your party which tried to cast out the Church.' Then, smiling, with a hand on Montani's shoulder: 'Why are we arguing? I'm the one who'll miss a pleasant evening.'

The ex-Gonfalonier went back to the café.

'Well?' he was asked as he sat down.

'Monsignore plays his cards close to his chest.'

The archbishop circled back towards the cathedral. He was thinking of a letter he had received from Monsignor Amandi.

My lack of charity is grown notorious. A certain bishop having lately ruled that all members of his flock must carry lanterns after dark, I remarked, while watching a play in which an actress was carrying one: '*Fiat lux*!' She must be one of Mgr X's sheep!' Can you believe that I received a reproof within days? His lordship is to be congratulated on his spies! Blessed are those tormented by trivia. Clearly our fright of last spring is quite forgotten. I have two items to impart: (1) your conduct then has at last been recognised as judicious, and (2) there has been gossip about the three days you spent in the mountains. Odd things are being said. *Fiat lux?*

What was being said? Oh God! thought the archbishop and rushed into the dusk of the cathedral where a sacristan was removing wilted flowers from the altar. Kneeling down, he began to bargain with God.

Back in the café, Count Montani and his friends were discussing the archbishop. A level-headed prelate like that, said a lawyer, was a boon.

'If he *hadn't* conciliated the retreating rebels, they'd have sacked the town, and if he hadn't made himself scarce earlier by running off to Leonessa, they might have taken him hostage. Then, when the Austrians got here, *they*'d have wreaked havoc.'

'So you think he was trying to preserve the peace?'

'What else?'

'His own skin.'

The lawyer grinned. 'There are other versions of the thing.'

*

The sacristan had left vases of stale water in the track of a draught and the smell reminded the archbishop of hung meat. Looking at a statue of the Virgin, he said: 'It's a message, isn't it? All flesh is meat and prone to rot? Well,' he harried, 'is that it?'

The statue looked like the girl they had brought to Leonessa. Plaster-pale at first, the visible bits of her skin had later broken out in a raw rash.

The archbishop had known her name from the diocesan records. There had been some awkwardness there a year or so earlier.

Orphaned by cholera, she had been adopted by an uncle, a parish priest who unwisely kept her by him until she was thirteen and nubile. The case came to notice during one of Mastai-Ferretti's campaigns to moralise his mountain parishes. What he had been after were priests who were cohabiting with their housekeepers, but, once the girl's uncle had been denounced by some tattletale, she had had to be put in the care of a community of nuns living at a prudent distance.

Monsignor Amandi's letter nudged back into the archbishop's train of thought. 'Your policies have at last been recognised as judicious.'

Christ's kingdom might not be of this world, but the pope-king's was, and archbishops could find themselves dealing with things temporal. Last February, when the apostolic delegate, who should have seen to these, have fled from Spoleto, Mastai-Ferretti had been confronted by some thorny choices. The Bonaparte brothers, for instance, neither of whom was much more than a schoolboy, had fallen into his grasp like a pair of snared ferrets. What was he to do with them? They had well-connected relatives all over Europe but had fought with the rebels. Arrest them? How? The Civic Guard was not reliable and the Austrian Army not yet here. Meanwhile, here were these two who had possibly raped the girl.

Again her face slid into the archbishop's memory. Root-pale and taut as a muscle, it was not the sort of face which had appealed to him in his secular years. Gracious, no! Impossible to imagine *her* in Donna Clara's salon.

She was a wincing little thing: touching in an odd way and had, in her innocence, stumbled into the very thick of trouble.

On hearing of the disturbances, she had slipped from her convent and arrived at her uncle's to find him dying of a heart attack and Bonaparte bravos living in his presbytery. They were a scratch collection who, having billeted themselves here, were nervous about being blamed if he died.

Ironically, she arrived on a mule supplied by Napoleon Louis, the elder brother, who, on finding her limping along a mountain trail, offered help. *He* had been foraging. Two hams swelled the mule's panniers and he promptly cut her a piece. It was that sweet ham which peasants hang from their rafters in good times and bury in bad. This time they hadn't moved fast enough.

The archbishop imagined the young pair – Napoleon Louis was twenty and she fifteen – picnicking in the pale spring sun. Later, she denied having met him at all. Why? What had happened? Did Napoleon Louis tell her what he and his brother were after? Of course he did. All Bonapartes were obsessed with their destiny. What they were after were hostages: apostolic delegates, bishops, legates, any stray prelates who might have fled their palaces and be masquerading as country priests. If the Bonapartes could take even one such hostage, General Sercognani would surely have them back. He had earlier let them enlist, then, on reflection, asked them to leave lest a Bonaparte connection be miscon-strued by France in whose help the rebels put their trust.

Desperate to be let fight, Napoleon Louis and Louis Napoleon had recruited a band of men and set off to scour mountain presbyteries for fugitive prelates. They had imagined – Napoleon Louis later admitted this – that the girl's uncle could be the archbishop in disguise. There was, it seemed, a resemblance. Besides, his Grace had been seen making his way with some stealth from Spoleto towards these very hills.

'Forgive us, Monsignore. It was a sort of carnival: a great masquerade.'

'And you,' reproached the archbishop, 'threw in your lot with the ragtag! What would your uncle, Cardinal Fesch, have to say about that?'

The young man was already feverish with the nursery malady which was to carry him off: chickenpox. 'My late uncle, the Emperor, would have approved! General Sercognani was echoing his words when he spoke of abolishing the popes' temporal power.'

'You'll have no luck,' said Mastai-Ferretti who knew that Bonapartes needed luck. 'You believe in nothing,' he reproached.

'On the contrary, Monsignore,' said Louis Napoleon, the younger brother, 'we believe in the cause of Italy.'

'Children! Children!' admonished the archbishop, but gave them passports to get them past the Austrian lines.

Calling them that exonerated him. It was the excuse he had ready in case of trouble with the troops of H.R.I.H., the Emperor of Austria, which were even then marching to defend us and as apt as not to be a band of right royal imperial ruffians.

'I'm doing this,' he told the brothers, 'in the name of peace. Remember that when next you're tempted to oppose the Church.'

As it happened, he saved only one brother. The elder had already contracted the chickenpox which was to lead to such scandalous conjecture. Rape? *Stuprum?* The girl's visible slivers of skin – face, neck, wrists – had erupted in pustules budding with the same disease.

The archbishop looked at the Virgin's plaster face and thought it mulish: like *hers* when he tried to question her.

'Can't you remember?' he had kept asking.

She had looked at her shoes which were furred with dust from the mountain roads. The cracks in the leather were white.

'When you met on the mountain, did you know who he was?'

Her foot jigged.

'Did he tell you his name?'

They were in the Capuchin monastery parlour at Leonessa: a grimy place. Capuchins were the Church's rabble.

More silence. Out on the mountains the last rebels were burying their weapons. Some, hardly older than this girl, had been seen sitting by the roadside sobbing and wiping their eyes with their sleeves.

The archbishop summoned patience. He needed to know just what accusations might be forthcoming against the Bonapartes whom he had let escape. The horse of history, he reflected, passes this way every fifteen years and men leap on its back. Last time was when Giacomo Murat proclaimed himself King of Italy and nationalists marched with him to Rome. People were always marching on Rome. It had started when Napoleon, avatar of a secular religion, took over the Holy City. Now, again, the Bonaparte seed was active.

The word recalled him to the matter in hand. He tapped the girl's knee.

'Look at me.'

She didn't.

'You told the nuns you were pregnant. Why?'

Silence.

'You do know, that . . . you wouldn't know yet, even if . . .' Foundering, he changed tactics.

'What happened?' he barked.

Abruptly words spurted: 'He was dying when I got there. He'd had the last sacraments . . . He was trying to tell me something, only she pulled me away.'

Who? Ah! Her uncle. He hadn't been asking about *him*.

She wailed: 'Is he dead?'

'But surely you knew? I was told you'd seen his body.'

The girl reddened. 'You mean naked? *She* said that, didn't she?'

The interrogation was booby-trapped.

'If he's dead he was killed!'

'By the Bonapartes?' What if it were to come out that he had given passports to men guilty of the death of one of his own priests? 'He died in his bed. The housekeeper . . .'

'*She*'s a liar!'

Ah, so that was it. Two years ago, then, it must have been the housekeeper who anonymously denounced the priest for keeping his niece in the house. Whereas the real intrigue . . . The archbiship marvelled at his own slowness. These mountain presbyteries!

Let sleeping dogs lie had been his predecessor's maxim. It wasn't his. 'She said it was his heart.'

'Is that what she calls it?' Her mouth twisted with contempt.

'So you think it was not the rebels who killed him, but . . .'

'It was she! She!!' Hatred hammered at the word.

The archbishop thought of the housekeeper. A lustreless woman with quick, subservient eyes, she was waiting in the corridor at this moment.

'He told me,' the girl insisted, 'what brought on his attack. She let the rebels fornicate with her.'

'Rape?'

'Not rape. They'd had a fight, you see. It was to do with . . .' Again that look of contempt. 'Property. A will he wouldn't sign. So she started drinking with the men . . .'

'The Bonapartes?'

'No. Hangers-on. Riffraff.' She was sobbing now and he couldn't make out her words.

Never mind. He knew all he needed to know. There would be no accusations from this quarter.

'I'll give her to you,' he told the Virgin. She needed containing. Gossip said so, the gossip of those who hoped to deflect attention from their own conduct during the troubles. Opting for neither side, most of his flock had stayed prudently at home, sewing cockades for their hats with papal colours on one side and the tricolour on the other. How blame them? *He*, after all, had kept dark the business of the Bonaparte passports and only to his friend, Monsignor Amandi, did he ever say how the beleaguered child had flung herself on him with the hungry impulse of misdirected passion. Abashed, he supposed that this was how

14

she had flung herself on the uncle who had, according to Napoleon Louis, borne a startling resemblance to himself.

In that season of reversible cockades, that hug had been a last flicker of the madness which was unlikely to flare up again in this part of the peninsula for another fifteen years.

'That,' he told the Virgin, as he left the cathedral, 'is why *you*'d better keep her.'

Outside the leather-lined door, a five-month-old poster was still exultantly announcing in the name of the then newly elected Pope Gregory that all civic militias were to be disbanded, civil servants who had taken office under the rebel government hereinafter suspended from employment, and persons found to possess cockades or other seditious items gaoled as enemies of the state. A corner of the poster had curled to reveal an earlier one signed by the rebels who had held power in February. This threatened anyone who appeared *without* a tricolour cockade with equally summary penalties.

The archbishop reflected that it was a wonder he had not caught the chickenpox. Perhaps he had had it as a child?

In the café, gossips were trying to pump the lawyer about the scandal he claimed to know touching the archbishop, but he would not be drawn.

When the group broke up, Montani linked an arm in his and walked him home. If he had information, said Montani, it was his duty to put it to use. Sooner or later patriots were going to have to overturn the priests' government. Bernetti, the new Cardinal Secretary, was a savage reactionary, and mild men like Mastai were propping up an intolerable regime.

'Our cause might be stronger today if there *had* been a massacre,' he began, but, seeing that he had shocked the lawyer, dropped this line of talk. 'Seriously though,' he urged, 'if you know anything to his discredit . . .'

From the notebook of the noble abbot
Raffaello Lambruschini:

When my uncle was 'Cardinal Nephew' to Pope Gregory, I, who did not share his opinions, could not honourably play the nephew's nephew. So

15

I exiled myself. That was when I first began to devote myself to pedagogy – I have, over the years, educated a number of village boys – agricultural experiments, and my own thoughts. These I scrupled to publish but did discuss in letters, with the result that men who had been formed by their correspondence with me were later able to mediate between the world and my retreat. Among them was the young Monsignor Amandi, then a diplomat for the Holy See, who kept me posted about shifts of policy in France and the German principalities as well as at the papal court. We did not neglect gossip and one of his stories was about how a girl distantly related to himself – small nobles in the Legations are all cousins – had been made pregnant, possibly by a Bonaparte, and how the local bishop was refusing to adopt the usual remedy and marry her to some needy 'St Joseph'. We joked that if St Joseph was good enough to father the Son of God, a 'St Joseph' was surely good enough for a Bonaparte. Later, when I learned who the bishop was, the item went into the file I was keeping on Mastai-Ferretti.

The girl, dressed in a smock provided by the nuns, had a belly like a watermelon but denied she could be pregnant.

'I'm a virgin,' she told the Reverend Mother. 'I'm like a mare that's eaten wet grass. They swell up.'

'We've had cases like that before,' the Reverend Mother told the archbishop. 'They dream away the memory.'

'Yes, I do know where babies come from,' the girl had told her. Then she had talked of her uncle's housekeeper, a real Magdalene, fornicating with him, naked as a potato, under the black cloth of his cassock. She said she had seen this through the crack in a shutter and that the strength of their joining was like potato-tubers bursting through storage sacking. No, no, she had not performed the act herself. Never. She wept indignantly.

'Maybe she imagined the housekeeper in her place? The uncle,' said the Reverend Mother, 'could be the father.'

The archbishop asked if the girl might be weak in the head and was told no. She was clever, devout and happy in the convent but wouldn't want the baby. 'We'll send it to an orphanage right away,' decided the Reverend Mother. 'To the Holy Innocents or the Holy Ghost Orphanage in Rome.'

But the archbishop, who had had experience of such institutions, said most of those babies caught fever and died on the journey south. There wasn't money to feed wet nurses and, lamentable though it was, there was no stopping the bearers using the trip to smuggle contraband goods across the border. They packed these under the infants who were left to lie in their own ordure until a sufficient number had accumulated to make the journey profitable. This girl, said His Grace, was of good family and distantly related to Monsignor Amandi. Something better must be done for the child.

'Do you want to see her?'

The archbishop did not. Later, he said, when she was delivered, he might accept her as a penitent. He knew her to be an innocent if impetuous creature for she had bared her soul to him in Leonessa. She had bared more than that and the hot throb of her fever haunted him who, unlike her, could not dream away memory.

'When do you think it was conceived?' he asked. 'Her previous trip home would have been Christmas. Could it have been then?'

The abbess was unsure. 'We think,' she said, 'that she's due in November, so you can count back.'

In October the archbishop arranged to meet Monsignor Amandi at a spa. Although Mastai-Ferretti was older, the two had studied together in Rome where he was said to have proven such a dunderhead that his chief merit, in his teachers' eyes, had been his lack of all claim to intellectual pride. Since *that* had led to the upheavels of '89 and brought the brigand Bonaparte to Rome, dunderheads were in better standing there now than men like Amandi, whose cleverness unsettled people. *He* was not thought likely to do well at the papal court.

The two bishops, however, were fond of each other and, as they strolled, ate, worshipped and took the waters, observers noted a distinct liveliness to their colloquies and, in the archbishop's case, some agitation. As a result, a rumour got about that his epilepsy had again begun to trouble him. It was known, as a doctor at the spa informed the interested, as 'the sacred disease' – *morbus sacer* – and also, according to Pliny, as 'the spitting disease' because, if caused by the evil eye, one could rid oneself of it by spitting it back. Due to some garbling of this, the notion now gained currency that Mastai had the evil eye. A spa is a place for gossip, and in no time people were collecting evidence of small mishaps occurring in his vicinity which proved so amusing that his reputation as a *iettatore* was soon unshakeable.

*

That November, Cardinal Odescalchi, Prefect of the Congregation of Bishops, and H. H. Gregory XVI received letters from the Archbishop of Spoleto humbly craving permission to lay down the burden of an office which would tax even an angel's shoulders – '*angelicis etiam humeris formidandum*'. The supplicant drew attention to his lack of proficiency in sacred studies and the difficulty of governing a diocese where, in the wake of the recent troubles, he was faced with a choice between scandalising the staunch or embittering the compromised. There was more in the same strain.

'What is this about?' Cardinal Odescalchi had summoned Monsignor Amandi for consultation.

'Why not believe what he says, Eminence?'

'Scruples? Doubts?' Odescalchi shrugged them away. He knew Giovanni Maria Mastai-Ferretti for a sound element. Two uncles in the prelacy! And in his youth he had paid court to the right sort of woman. Donna Clara Colonna had, after her young admirer donned the cassock, seemed to take more pleasure in promoting his career than she had in whatever mild dalliance had preceded it. It was she, observed his Eminence, whose influence at court had got Mastai his bishop's mitre and almost certainly she who had provided the cash for his elevation. Given the finances of the Mastai-Ferretti – they were petty and penurious nobility – one could presume as much. Why not? Very commendable. Such women were as rubies – when they didn't become busybodies. It might indeed be wise to call for her help. It had proven useful before when she put the necessary stiffening into the young Giovanni Maria who, shortly after his ordination, had had tender notions of devoting himself to the poor. Indeed he had done this for a while as director of an orphanage and later of San Michele, that great labyrinth on the Ripa Grande where he first came to notice by making the place pay. It was an epitome of the papal state itself, comprising as it did an asylum, a reform school, an old people's home and a refuge for fallen women; and he had turned it into a going concern by selling its workshop products at a profit. Well, a man who could do that had an obligation to put his talents to work in a wider arena. As Mastai's spiritual director was promptly requested to let him know, there were very few men who could stop the state losing money let alone help it make any. Money was a bleeding wound in the Church's side and it would be sinful self-indulgence for a man who could staunch it to waste his time playing at being St Francis of Assisi.

'What bee has he in his bonnet now?' Odescalchi inquired. Laicisa-

18

tion? Retreat to a monastery? Did he not know – if he did not, would Amandi kindly inform him – that the first was unthinkable and the second justifiable only if he was irredeemably maimed by sin or epilepsy. *Was* he? If he was, should he not atone for this by service? Reluctance could only prove worthiness. Paradox was the Church's climate. While mediating a higher reality for the world, it was itself stuck in some very particular mud with which its servants must occasionally dirty their hands.

'Does he imagine he's the only one tempted to devote himself to his own salvation? asked Odescalchi. 'You may tell him from me that I wrestle with the urge on an average of once a fortnight. Tell him too that we're praying for him.' Then he advised Amandi to stress spiritual fellowship when talking to the archbishop. In time of need your fellows could provide support, and he and Amandi now held Mastai up, or anyway back.

They presumed him to be a prey to scruples more precise than those mentioned in his letters. A temptation of the mind or, less importantly, of the flesh? Patriotism? Heresy? The excessive charity which leads to heresy? The cardinal knew that only a deep disarray could have made Mastai grind out the letter to His Eminent self and the one to Pope Gregory which ended: 'Permission to withdraw would, Oh Most Holy Father, be the greatest expression of your love and I would be grateful to you always . . .' Permission was not forthcoming, but Mastai was to receive more tangible grounds for gratitude when the following year – Donna Clara again! said the monotonous gossips – he was promoted to the Diocese of Imola. This was a major see, though not an archbishopric, so it was with a purely apparent loss of rank that he became for a while plain Bishop Mastai. He was forty now, and though he would not recover from the emotional disorders left by the epilepsy of his adolescence, had for years been judged sufficiently free of it to say mass unaided. Was he still beset by scruples? Perhaps, for he was unusually susceptible to signs and wonders and sent assiduously to solicit the prayers of the visionaries who, being numerous at this time, were thought to have been sent by God to comfort His people after the ravages of revolution. They must have comforted Monsignor Mastai, for the following year he received letters from Odescalchi and Amandi congratulating him on his new serenity. Amandi, who had been on missions to Paris and Brussels where he sharpened an already keen political sense, was particularly pleased at his friend's elevation to a key diocese.

Two

Now that you are back I warn that you may get more letters than you
might like. While you've been away, I have been struggling to come to
terms with my translation to this great see with its stipend of nine instead
of three thousand scudi, and do not doubt that, after my protests, I must
look in some quarters like a shrewd contriver.

The same divisions prevail here as in Spoleto. Did I tell you that my
first invitation was from a gentleman whose wife is a connection of yours,
Count Stanga? This happy discovery was a trifle marred by a subsequent
one that the count is held to be unsound. But then I am sometimes
considered so myself by, among others, His Holiness who likes to quip that
in my family's household even the cat is a Liberal! I take this to mean that
I am on the Church's reserve, to be used only if it should one day need to
show a Liberal face. Having, thus, little to lose, I dine fearlessly with the
unsound Stangas. At first we were always *en famille*. Then I met their
friends. I fancy the aim had been to sound me out because no sooner was
the ice well broken than a young guest began to praise my mildness during
the Spoleto troubles. I told him that this had been due rather to charity
than to partisan feeling, whereupon he remarked that charity was precisely
what was bringing some priests to make their peace with Liberalism. He
was unabashed by my saying that, being unacquainted with the ideas
current in fashionable drawing rooms, I could not discuss them. His name
is Gambara. He is greatly exercised by His Holiness's condemnation of
freedoms of thought and the press and by the new encyclical which, he
fears, must drive Liberals from the Church. Did I know, he asked, that
there is a secret movement for reform within the Church itself? I said I
did not and marvelled at his knowledge. He claims he has it from his
spiritual director, whose name he will not divulge, since the secret of the
confessional should cut both ways. I took this to mean that I too might
speak my mind without fear.

This was impertinent but I own to some curiosity about his clerical friends – Tuscans, would you not guess? – who espouse unorthodoxies, some of which go back at least fifty years to the Synod of Pisa which, as we know, was declared a non-event. This shadow-Church is, I suppose, the equivalent of the *Carbonari*, who equally secretly elaborate plans for an alternative form of civil government. The count is thought to be one of *them* and his young friend, a layman with a curiously clerical cast of mind, must, I suppose, aim to recruit me. To be prudent, I should delate him but am reluctant to do so – except now to you. In our conversations I am the soul of discretion and beg you to be the same by destroying this, which I shall not send by the public post.

*From the same to the
same*:   *April 1835*

Gambara continues to tease me. I ask the count about him and am imperfectly reassured by his replies. I fear that he too is rash and that his wife worries about this. She is a quiet, pretty woman and devoted to their small son who is about four. I suspect her health prevented her having another.

Gambara's spiritual directors talk, it seems, of abolishing mass stipends, confessions, benefices and, to be sure, ecclesiastical courts. Priests and laymen should be equal before the law! Parish priests should be elected by the laity and the clergy be of and with the people. It is a farrago of generous contradictions, not the least being Gambara's status as a layman. On my saying so, I was surprised to see him redden like a girl.

'Forgive me,' he begged. 'I don't want to insult you – but neither do I want the privilege of being a priest. In this state, you see,' he explained gravely, 'the privilege is a worldly one, since only the clergy enjoy high stipends or qualify for high office.'

I have decided not to visit the Stanga villa for a while.

Amandi saved these letters. Later ones were peppered with sideswipes at the chronic absurdity of those around Mastai who was as easily roused to humour as to indignation. Both bristled in the margins of a pamphlet which he sent on with a complaint that someone was circulating it among his diocesan priests.

It praised the *Centurioni*, a militia founded to 'defend the godly against French doctrines', and urged priests to keep an eye on free-thinking landlords and forbid labourers to work for them. 'That,' triumphed the pamphlet-writer, who signed himself 'the water-sprinkler of truth', 'will teach these proud gentlemen that they need the people more than the people need them!'

'Who writes such things?' marvelled Mastai. 'They undermine people's respect for their betters. Our zealots don't need a guillotine. They'll cut off their own heads!'

He had failed to hit it off with local conservatives who were alarmed by his hobnobbing with the Stangas. The count, they warned, was a *Carbonaro* and the Devil knew what heathen mumbo-jumbo went on in his villa after dark. Had Monsignore himself seen none of this?

Lieutenant Nardoni laughed. 'Well, no, I suppose Your Lordship wouldn't!' A squat man, dense with muscle, Nardoni kept his fists in a half clench and his knees bent as though ready to spring. 'They have tunnels and secret entrances,' he explained.

He had come to the sacristy one Sunday. Would it be presuming, he wondered, if he were to invite his lordship to lunch at his humble home? There were devout members of his flock who had not had a chance to meet him. This sounded like a challenge, so the lunch became an armistice. The other guests made it clear that they, though less well-born than the Stangas, were loyal and that loyalty was insufficiently prized. The *Centurioni*, for example, were the true salt of the earth and *were needed* to defend property. Vagrants had been cutting down fruit trees and the roads were unsafe.

Mastai, lest his presence seem grudging, accepted second helpings of boiled beef and caper sauce.

'It's a local speciality,' said his hostess.

A communion? Eyes winked in the grease.

'Some,' said the Signora, 'think they're above the law. It's not the common folk who conspire.'

'And some,' said her husband, 'get puffed up by reading the likes of Babeuf! *Boeuf*,' he joked as the meat came round again. 'Ba!' An ex-customsman, who knew the names of forbidden authors, he was silly with pride at having a bishop at his board. 'Sometimes,' he reminisced, 'we would find subversive papers like *The Morning Chronicle* wrapped around travellers' shoes. You had to be alert for such tricks. Or they'd line suitcases with it. Gentlemen were the worst! Expecting to get away with it. Nobody is above suspicion.'

The bishop was reminded unpleasantly of the girl whose baby, it was now clear, could not have been sired by her uncle, although – he hoped cravenly – *she* might think so for she had called him by her uncle's name.

'Were you,' his confessor had asked delicately, 'quite yourself?' Referring to the epileptic symptoms which could still cause mental confusion. Maybe he'd dreamed the episode?

'Expecting to get away with it,' repeated Nardoni. 'But that didn't work with me. I'm in-corr-up-tible, Monsignore!'

The bishop blushed.

'No point dwelling on it,' the confessor had decided. 'The thing now is to deal with the consequences.'

The girl had been moved to a convent at Fognano in his new diocese. Best for her, the Reverend Mother had agreed, to be where nobody knew her story. The Abbess of Fognano must, of course, be told. But she, an old friend of Monsignore's, would be discreet.

He had already visited to ask how things were. Had the girl mentioned the child at all? No. Or her past?

'Not really. We gave out that the reason she left the other convent was because she'd been ill and the air here was healthier.'

'You think she has managed to forget . . . everything?'

The abbess looked from under her coif at the bishop who had once held her longer than was strictly necessary, during a game of Blind Man's Buff, when they were both fifteen and living in the town of Senigallia. 'Who knows?' she said. 'We all forget things.'

He saw that she had been hoping to reminisce with him about their youth. They had belonged to big, friendly families, and she loved recalling long-gone carriage drives and cheerful gatherings at New Year. Today, though, his mind was on the girl.

'Oblivion,' he told her, 'is a grace. Better relinquish the past.' He made a chopping gesture with his hand. Tac! Cut it off.

The abbess insisted that he honour the convent by taking a refreshment, though her mood had changed. They had been young together and now here she was, a woman of forty with nothing further to expect, whereas time moved differently for Monsignore. In the end, the same thought struck him and he became affable as people do when made aware of an inequality. He even listened to some of her gossip. Her girlhood friends were now grandmothers and she had crocheted caps for their children's children. The thought returned them to the girl and her baby. Monsignor Amandi had sent for it. It had seemed wise to give it to a wet nurse straight away.

'I know you'll be kind to her,' he said as he left.

He was right. The abbess had entered the convent to escape a tyrannical, bedridden father who was still tormenting two sisters left behind. In gratitude for her escape, she made the lot of other refugees who came here as happy as she could.

Monsignor Amandi wrote to Gambara that Monsignor Mastai had lunched with a spy who worked for the office of the Cardinal Secretary of State. 'Be prudent,' he recommended. 'Keep away and let his lordship get his fill of the Zelanti once and for all.'

Amandi, a man whose energies found insufficient outlet in the diplomatic missions at which he showed such tact, relished the sly exercise of influence over a man like Mastai who, being shrewd, pious, ailing and charming, was likely to rise higher than he would himself. People pitied Mastai – and how distrust a man you pity? Besides, he still had the support of Donna Clara.

Summer. Imola dozed among its brick arcades. Pigeon's-foot pink, amber, plum and tawny were blanched to a sparkling pallor – pigeon-droppings – until sundown when a cardinal tint blazed then dissolved in a dusk sweet with eddies of tobacco smoke, as old men hauled straw-bottomed chairs into the streets and began to gossip.

The rumour was that Monsignor Mastai-Ferretti . . . Shush! Sounds carry! What about Monsignore? . . . a row with Monsignor Folicardi of Faenza. Really? Why? He wants the Abbey of Fognano to be under himself and Folicardi says it's always been in *his* diocese which is true. Maybe Monsignore wants the *abbess* under himself! Shush! They say that she . . . What's all this whispering? What? How old is she? *No*! Well, have it your way. Anyway what's sure and certain is that Monsignor Folicardi sent a protest to Rome but Monsignore has friends there and the convent has changed dioceses. Yes. Oh, he's a powerful bishop and will soon have a red hat. An attractive man too. No smoke without fire.

The lieutenant crossed the cathedral square with the bandy gait of a horseman. Guessing that secret gawkers had him in their sights, he squared his shoulders. Authority needed to impose itself. Every so often, as he'd told His Lordship, you had to fire off your gun. Jacobins were getting too confident. 'With respect, they've been raising their heads since Your Lordship's kindness to them. They think now they have licence to meet openly. Oh, nothing to put your finger on, but we can smell their mood. Around here you get a feel for that. Bologna law school is close and turns out pettifoggers who would argue the leg off an iron pot. That young fellow, Gambara, thinks he has Your Lordship's protection.'

The bishop had given him a look of lordly detachment. 'Oh?'

Feeling squat – he wore boots with heels – the lieutenant recognised the lordliness as a secular and resented it. The Mastai-Ferretti were small nobility and as pugnacious as bantams. Men like that – the lieutenant knew – expected men like us to fret our guts for them and, if it came to it, fight. Nardoni had a wound near his groin – a bit closer and *buona notte*, he'd be a eunuch! The thought haunted him. He dreamed frequently that he was being gelded and woke sweating – or, worse, only thought he'd woken up, so that when he touched himself to make sure, he found nothing there and heard his voice whimper in a falsetto. Wrenching himself from sleep's sharp practices, he would bite himself, touch his balls and waken his wife. 'Open your legs. Yes. Now! I don't care if you do get pregnant again! Move, can't you! Oh Jesus! oh God, God, GOD!' Well, at least he had proven his manhood – if he was awake! *Was* he? He never enjoyed it now. Not any more and all because of a skirmish on the Tuscan border! All to keep fat prelates safe – men who themselves had no use for balls and used their safety to encourage agitators who might one day. The lieutenant's hand crept unstoppably to his groin and he saw the bishop look fastidiously away.

'He's a tout, Monsignore. A spy.'

'Who?'

'Gambara, Gianmarco.' Despite himself, it came out like a police report.

'For whom?'

The lieutenant planned to find out. For now, all he could say was: 'He gets letters by private courier. And his talk in cafés is too free.'

'Too free for a *spy*?'

'He could be a decoy – sent perhaps to provoke others.'

That, Nardoni saw with satisfaction, upset the bishop. Somehow he'd hit home.

'He,' said Mastai surprisingly, 'says you're one.'

'Me? A spy?'

'Or decoy.' His lordship laughed as though this were a joke. In the lieutenant's experience, jokes were rarely just jokes. 'The talkative,' said

25

Mastai, 'in your book are all decoys and the rest are spies. So you too must be one or the other. Provoke *what*, anyway? Talk of what?'

'In the café yesterday,' said Nardoni, 'the topic was Your Lordship's tiff with Monsignor Folicardi.'

Mastai's ringed hand flashed a benediction and he leaned towards the door. A flunkey opened it and Nardoni found himself outside.

Since then he had been reviewing the conversation. 'He says you're one,' could have been a chance bull's-eye. Had he flinched? The crux of the matter was that Nardoni was on the payroll of Vienna as well as Rome and Rome mustn't know it. If Gambara too was working for Austria . . .

Now, standing outside the bishop's palace he pulled the bell-pull and realised too late that he had prepared nothing to say. Never mind. He'd feel his way. Discover just what Gambara had said about him – if he'd said anything. The bishop might have been chancing his arm.

Frighten him, he thought. 'We're worried, Monsignore,' he might warn. 'Conspirators are in touch with Vienna. There's a move to detach this part of the state from the Holy Father's dominions and attach it to the Empire. Has nobody mentioned Austria lately in your lordship's hearing? Her enlightened policies? How much better off her subjects are? No? Not even Signor Gambara? I ask because we have reason to believe . . .' That would do. Again and with greater assurance the lieutenant pulled the bell.

The footman who finally came to the door said that Monsignore was in Fognano conducting a retreat for the nuns. He wouldn't be back for three days.

Three days! The lieutenant walked back across the square. Three nights! Pausing at the apothecary's shop, he decided to buy a bottle of laudanum.

They were hot days and the bishop returned from his journey in a paste of dust and sweat. His clothes clung to him and his mind was dizzy with the scruples of women. Yet he was good with nuns, being much in demand as a confessor, and had improved the health in the convents of his old diocese by insisting on better food and hygiene. Medical certificates must, he had ruled, be supplied by all new novices. Too many families used the religious orders to rid themselves of sickly daughters. Consumption was rife. Deaths upset survivors and in the

26

midst of all this, the foolish quarrel over jurisdiction with Monsignor Folicardi was the last straw.

On reaching his palace, he told his vicar-general who had come to meet him to go back in and wait. 'I want to say a prayer in the cathedral,' he said. 'I won't be long.'

It was cool by the main altar and he was enjoying the shade and occasionally shaking the neck of his cassock to get air on his skin, when a man sprinted up the nave followed by two others. The first one vaulted over the altar-rails and shouted 'sanctuary!' Then he turned and shouted it again. There was a panicked tremor in his voice until, seeing the bishop, fear visibly fell from him. 'Ah, Monsignore!' he cried. 'Thank God!' It was Gambara.

His pursuers were now on him but he didn't try to resist. 'Sanctuary,' he reminded them more steadily and, as they started to pinion his arms, his protest had an almost pedantic assurance. 'This is the high altar . . .' he was arguing when his voice expired in a strangulated gulp. The man holding his arms had jerked his head upwards while the other one slit his throat.

Mastai felt these images explode into flying shards and for seconds could not put them together: blood, Gambara, violated sanctuary . . . They wouldn't coalesce. And then he thought: murder, while something prickled on his skin and his vision blurred as though gnats had got in his eye.

He started to scream but couldn't, and when he took his hand from his locked throat it came away bloody. Then he was breathing again and lurched beseechingly towards the altar, howling 'Oh God, my God!' It was at once prayer, query and reproach.

The men were now gone and Gambara's body had slithered down the steps. Clutching his own chest, the bishop found it soggy with the dead man's blood. No question but that Gambara was dead. Blood was spreading from the crooked heap which lay before the altar like some savage offering.

A few old women and a priest who had been hearing confessions in a side chapel gathered round. A boy was sent for the police. The priest whispered in Mastai's ear. 'Come, Monsignore.'

'No, no. I knew the victim. I must testify.'

The old women buzzed and whispered and the priest – a small man in a stained cassock – hovered a while longer then plucked at his superior's sleeve.

'Monsignore, with respect, it would be better if Your Lordship weren't

27

here. The killers were *Centurioni*, you see, and the police can't arrest *them*. Well, strictly speaking, they can, but it could cause trouble and if your lordship denounces them, the police won't know what to do.'

Mastai turned on him. 'What do you mean? What do you know about this?'

'Nothing, Monsignore.' The small priest backed fearfully away.

Later, people would agree that the priest had given wise advice, for the two *Centurioni* disappeared, spirited off, no doubt, to a part of the state where the corps was clandestine, whereas here it was expected to take responsibility for its acts. A representative of the *Commissario Straordinario* – a State of Emergency was still in force – told His Lordship that, regrettably, nothing could be done. Better not give scandal. The *Commissario*, you see ... The dead man was thought to have been a – well, there had been denunciations. The Cardinal Secretary of State himself ... But this was guesswork, for the gossips relied on footmen for their information and the crucial conversation took place out of doors, where there was nowhere for a footman to hide, and only gestures could be vouched for: evasive on the part of the *Commissario*'s envoy, incredulous on that of Monsignor Mastai. Lip-readers – at a distance – recognised a recurring word which might be 'Rome' or 'no' or '*morte*'. The bishop looked stunned. As for Padre Cassio – the wise little priest – nobody thought he had played much of a role, although it was of interest that he was the confessor of Lieutenant Nardoni's wife who had recently grown thin and agitated and was going to confession as often as others to the café.

From the notebooks of the noble abbot
Raffaello Lambruschini:

Monsignor – later Cardinal – Amandi is my source for the story of Gambara's murder by *Centurioni* and, while I do not doubt his veracity, I note that he was abroad at the time and that an equally good source has it that it was Gambara who killed the *Centurione*, then fled the country and ended up in California where he grew rich in the Gold Rush. According to this version, Monsignor Mastai-Ferretti helped him escape and, decades later, when the Church was in dire need, a providentially large and anonymous donation arrived from Sacramento. A parable? Perhaps. Pious parables are much alike and it is worth noting

28

that Mastai's having helped Louis Napoleon escape the Austrians in 1831 is sometimes linked to the help the future emperor was to give the future pope. Men who inspire gratitude do better in life than those who don't.

Common to both versions of the murder-story is the account of the bishop being splashed with a dying man's blood: a baptism which leads to his looking differently thereafter on the world around him. What is unquestioned is that for years after this he shunned politics and that, although, in 1840, he duly received a cardinal's hat, he continued to live as quietly as a *porporato* could.

Naturally, he continued to receive news from the capital where, apart from spies and manufacturers of lace-trimmings, the most active citizens were those who hoped to topple the regime and men like my uncle who were labouring to prop it up. The latter were regularly lampooned in squibs stuck on the broken marble torso known as 'Pasquino', the 'protester's patron', which stood outside Palazzo Braschi.

> Black beetle, black beetle,
> You live off the people!

The pasquinade, never a subtle genre, grew crude towards the end and I am bound to say that the fault lay with the regime which by now suffered from a touch of rigor mortis. Panic stiffened it. Respect was on the ebb and on the via Pia, at the hour of the promenade, irreverence could be detected in many of the looks cast at the eminent *porporati* who descended from gilt-trimmed carriages to read their breviaries and stretch their red-stockinged legs.

'What's needed,' murmured the disaffected, 'is a dose of a different sort of red.'

Outside, ecclesiastical hatters, swinging replicas of behatted heads, stirred bloody associations and so did the trunkless wooden forms inside the shops on which red skull caps were displayed.

Few, to be sure, gave thought to such signals, and hatters went on doing a thriving trade with men whose enthusiasm for violet and red *zucchetti*, birettas, damask mitres and hats trimmed with cords appropriate to rank was as lively as any lady's in the latest plates from Paris.

The loftiest headgear was naturally that of the popes whose triple-tiered tiaras manifested claims over heaven, hell and here, realms which some of them seemed unable to distinguish, such as Pope Leo XII, who, hoping to force his subjects to live like angels, closed the Roman wine shops. Naturally, when he died, they danced like demons and drank his successor's health so copiously that the Almighty must have been displeased for He took him to Himself the following year. The next pope was Gregory who, being elected during the disturbances of 1831, ruled harshly and fearfully – or so everyone said, including the poet Belli, who later worked as a censor preventing others doing the same. Oh, life fizzed with irony in those years! Citizens joked and preachers preached and when agents began coming from the north to stir up rebellion, the jokes worried them more than the sermons, for they saw them as proof of a Roman incapacity for belief. 'Cynical,' they called our citizens. 'Servile!' And it was true that most of the lay population were servants and maybe they *were* cynical. 'See Rome and lose your faith!' The old tag worried the Jacobins for a new faith can founder as fast as an old one. *Roma veduta, fede perduta*! It worried them. At least, they thought, the priests believed in *something* and for a while they tried working with priests against priests and tried to enlist me. But I said that I would not work against the Church but only, if it could be done, help reform it from within. So off they went, leaving me to wonder if posterity would ever be able to imagine how *la Dominante* was in those years. Rome. The *caput mundi*. It was strangling in bureaucracy and privilege. Impoverished. Undeveloped. Idle. Its aristocracy had been ruined when the French forced them to divide their fortunes by abolishing entails. Nobody knew what to do and under my uncle's rule it was difficult to find out since it was illegal to travel abroad to attend a scientific congress – too many free-thinkers there, you see – and illegal to discuss the reforms which we all knew were needed. Even goodwill tended to get bogged down. As the future censor put it in one of his secret jingles:

> Here every day they say that soon
> We're all to have the sun and moon.
> But when enforcement's due to start
> We're fobbed off with an empty fart.
> In Rome when any rule's proclaimed
> Immunities are quickly claimed.
> When half the town is proved exempt
> The law itself invites contempt!

Contemptus mundi was the great temptation, but Mastai-Ferretti did not succumb to it. Instead, he stuck to his last and ruled his diocese with an iron rod, ferreting out laxness until his priests dubbed him Bishop

Nosy and prayed for his transfer. Their prayers were half-answered when a disaster at the Villa Stanga diverted his attention from their peccadilloes.

Count Stanga's wife had been murdered in their own garden when a patrol of *Centurioni* mistook her for one of her husband's *Carbonaro* confederates. An appalling thing. It seems that she had been wearing a long winter cloak and playing with their small son. It was dusk. Visibility was poor and when she darted, in what the intruders later described as 'a suspicious manner', behind some trees, they shot her.

It was an accident. This was established. But the similarity with Gambara's death drew the survivors into a combustive alliance.

It is not hard to imagine their colloquies or how those counter-elixirs, Liberalism and piety, must sometimes have curdled as the pair took sips at each other's sustaining faith. I picture them fevering over winter fires and over the mazy flicker of fireflies on summer nights. Friends from both factions disapproved of their friendship and Mastai, shaken by this, begged the nuns at Fognano to pray for him. He was still an assiduous visitor there, for one or two of his penitents had mystic tendencies with which a less sensitive confessor might have found it hard to deal. Indeed, evidence that he found them hard to deal with himself turns up in his letters to Monsignor Amandi.

One of these penitents was the girl from Leonessa, now a novice, whose name in religion was to be Sister Paola.

Amandi wrote a rallying letter ending:

Pax tecum. Though if you cannot be tranquil, it is no great matter. Do not dwell on things past and gone. There is so much to do now. The faith is what matters and the Institution which preserves it for 139 million individuals needs men like you. Its endurance is under threat. Should it adapt? Perhaps the best memorial to Gambara would be putting his ideas into practice. Or don't you think this possible?

Cardinal Mastai to Sister Paola:

Pax tecum. Live every day as if it were to be your last. You'll know the maxim. It is by St Francis of Sales. Yes, burn my letters. Advent is a season for forming great wishes: such as that the baby Christ be born in your heart. Try and prepare a crib for him in it by putting away human affections.

Either you do or you don't want to take final vows. It is a generous move worthy of a noble soul to give yourself totally to God. Remember that in

31

order to make it Sainte Françoise de Chantal had to pass over the body of her son, who had lain across the threshold of her door to prevent her leaving. If you do not feel the same courage in your heart, then it is clear that God wants you to return to the world. After all, you have had ample time to decide.

Some sins are better banished from the mind. Scruples over past confessions are an effect of pride. Try to be tranquil – though if you cannot it is no great matter. But do not ponder over things which are past and gone. If you must ponder, ponder over the passion of Christ.

Mastai to Amandi:

I am harsh with her. It is kinder. What would she do or be in the world? It is cruel and needs the sanctuary of the Church.

Mastai to Amandi, 1845:

Rome, I'm told, is negotiating with the prince of worldlings. Czar Nicholas, whom the abbé Lammenais calls 'the Satan of the North', is to have an audience with His Holiness who must receive him by the rules of the etiquette books while extolling those of the gospel! Not easy!

The same to the same:

The departing Russians – had you heard? – distributed seven little boxes: a perfect number and perfectly suited to the recipients. Their Lordships, the Governor and Treasurer, got fine ones; the Major-domo a good one and four *inferioris notae* went to lesser hands. They say H.H. is ailing.

From the diary of Raffaello Lambruschini:

Interesting to reread those letters and note the tart, easy irony of the man on the sidelines! His Holiness, Pope Gregory XVI, was not ailing but dying. Shortly after this, His Eminence and his fellow cardinals met in conclave to elect a successor. After some haggling, Mastai-Ferretti was himself picked as a compromise candidate to the surprise of everyone except Monsignor Amandi, who claimed to have had a premonition of his friend's rise.

It was not, of course, a premonition at all. Amandi was a pope-maker.

For years he had been haunting antechambers and dropping hints in influential ears. Then, when his efforts succeeded, he began to wonder whether, after all, his friend had the stomach for the job. Mastai was a good administrator but there is more to politics than that – especially in times like ours.

I have a letter which Amandi wrote at the time, justifying himself. 'Stomach maybe not,' he wrote, 'but head yes.' Mastai had a head for figures and *that*, as Amandi must have assured half the conclave at one time or another, was what was needed with the Treasury in the state it was. I can just imagine him: 'Your Eminence didn't *know*! About our near-insolvency! The lack of balance sheets! The public debt!' He must have seriously unsettled his hearers. 'Remember,' he would add, 'how he handled the disturbances in Spoleto! He's a man to build bridges between factions and what else should a pontiff do?'

His hope was that Mastai could reconcile the ideals of 1789 – the ideals only: liberty and fraternity, not the guillotine! – with the gospel's message, and the Church with a world it had shunned for fifty years.

'If he succeeds,' wrote Amandi, 'it will be by blind instinct which is the only safe way.' Pius, as we both knew, had no grasp of the abstract and this, argued Amandi, was all to the good. Theory frightened more people than practice and had sunk the chances of Cardinal Gizzi, who went into conclave with the reputation of being 'the reformers' candidate', just as my uncle, Cardinal Lambruschini, was known as the champion of the *status quo*. In the end, as so often happens, it was the third man, the dark horse, whose discretion won the votes of the timid old *porporati* who were fearful of extremes but eager for a change.

Three

Returning from Paris after the conclave – as he was not yet a cardinal, he had not returned for it – Monsignor Amandi picked up garbled news. Along the route, the new pope's name was being mauled beyond recognition. In the north nobody had heard of him. Mastai-Ferretti? They tried it on their tongues. Bishop of *where*?

Closer to Imola legends had begun. A white dove had been seen to land on Mastai's carriage as he left for Rome and had refused to leave the carriage roof. A link boy, while lighting Amandi to his lodgings with a torch of pitch and tow, swore that he, personally, had seen the dove hover. Dazzled by the boy's exclamatory torch-waving, Amandi was soon seeing hovering doves himself. Also tongues of fire. A hot drop burned his hand.

In Rome the great topic was the new pope's first political move. Pius IX – this was now Mastai's title – had granted an unusually generous amnesty to political exiles and prisoners, and Liberals were collecting money to pay for their return. Some, already back, were said to be advising the Pope about prison reform.

Grey-faced men with skittish eyes were received in the Quirinal, and prelates were scandalised that fellows fresh from studying subversion in Swiss cafés or the prisons of the realm should have the new pope's ear. The city was filling up with dangerous elements.

The Caffè Nuovo, the spice shops and the Sapienza University were hives of Liberal agitation and who could doubt but that counter-intrigues were being hatched in the gloom of certain great palaces?

Monsignor Amandi was alert to the danger posed by quondam power-brokers and by the underlings who, having worked for them as bravos, would now be frightened for their lives. Rome was a town inured to intrigue and he guessed that the Gregoriani – this was the name being given to those who hankered back to the late pope's reign – would not

34

easily throw in the sponge. Dispatches from Vienna warned that Metternich was aghast.

Absorbed by these dangers, Amandi nearly missed a subtler one to which his first meeting with the new pope should have alerted him. Mastai did not smile at his friend's teasing reference to the white dove. All in white himself, he seemed as awed by his regalia as a bride on her wedding day.

Amandi asked about another anecdote he had heard. Was it true that the cardinals had been about to blackball the amnesty when Mastai, taking off his white skull cap, placed it over the voting counters and said: 'Brothers, Pio Nono has turned them all white'?

'Ah!' Mastai softened. 'The people like that story, don't they? I play to the gallery a little – under inspiration.' Fluttering a wing-like hand, he mimed a hovering paraclete. 'I *have* to believe that. You, better than anyone, know the meagreness of my human powers.'

'But you were elected because of them.'

Pius gave a shrewd laugh. 'I was a compromise candidate. But now the stone the builders rejected is on the top of the arch and I must have confidence in God's choice, must I not?'

As Amandi described them afterwards, the pride and humility were absolute. 'But now you are Peter. Peter and Pater.'

'By God's grace.'

And mine, thought his friend, and wondered if it might have been safer for Pius to rely more on human advice. 'Let me,' he offered, 'be your ears and eyes for a while.'

'Oh, I have the eyes of Argus working for me now.'

It was hard to tell whether the snub was deliberate.

'And the people's hearts are good.' Pius had a sweet, exalted smile which Amandi didn't remember from before. It was a held a little too long, as though for distant viewing.

'Holy Father ...' Amandi's mind divided. Part of it monitored the delivery of a warning about the enemies of reform who would find it all too easy to create trouble. Already this year there had been bread-riots in the provinces. One third of the inhabitants of Bologna were indigent and poor cereal harvests all over Europe had exacerbated their misery – but there were also those who *used* the mob. 'Holy Father ...'

The other half of his mind was marvelling at how this title had reversed relations between himself and his old protégé. 'Holiness,' he practised, while a bounce of memory recalled the sorry figure the young Giovanni Maria had cut after being rejected by the Pope's Noble Guard.

He had used his epilepsy to avoid being drafted into Napoleon's Grand Army to fight the Russian campaign, and later the excuse, staying on his record, closed off all hope of a military career. For a younger son, there was nothing for it then but to don a cassock. Had Mastai forgotten the mundane source of his vocation?

'Let me at least take a look at the police archives,' Amandi pleaded, 'now before they start hiding things.' He was thinking: they may have files on us both.

The man in white was twice the size of the rather wispy youth who had been Amandi's fellow guest at the Colonna palace a score or so years before. Damascened vistas flickered in memory as Amandi recalled draughty hangings, smoky oil lamps and the charcoal foot-warmers supplied on evenings judged unbearably cold. On others, the only resource was to persuade one of the princess's pug dogs to sit warming one's lap. The malicious claimed that, when her other guests had gone, Donna Clara sometimes performed the same service for Giovanni Maria.

Turning from old scandal to new, Amandi asked whether gaslight was at last to be installed in the city?

'Yes,' said Mastai. 'A Jesuit adviser,' he confided, 'warns me that this makes me the second Lucifer or Light-bearer since it will encourage adultery and conspiracy and people's staying up when they should be asleep. I asked if sleep was the Christian ideal. He doesn't want us to build railways either.'

'People should stick to their station in life.'

'*Chemin de fer, chemin d'enfer.*'

The old jokes drew them together.

Mastai did not, however, want to leave his friend with the impression that the Jesuits were hostile. Quite the contrary. Why, after his election, pupils from the Collegio Romano had untackled his horses, harnessed themselves to his carriage shafts and pulled him in triumph up the Quirinal Hill.

'Showing you their stamina perhaps?' Amandi feared that the Jesuits must be smarting under their loss of power for, during the last reign, they had been consulted at every turn. It was said – and he saw no reason to disbelieve it – that all the cardinals resident in Rome had gone every evening to the Gesù to receive instructions. Yes, they must be smarting, for Liberals were making much of the fact that Mastai had not taken a Jesuit confessor. He should beware of them, Amandi warned. But Pius was euphoric with optimism. He was not a Liberal, he assured. He loathed Liberalism – but neither did he care for conservative fanatics.

36

The people, he insisted, understood him. The people were his and he could rely on their support. He began to talk about a fritter-seller whose stall had been moved by the police and who had appealed to him for help. Seeing the look on Amandi's face, he laughed and acknowledged with his old, shrewd charm that, to be sure, statecraft was not a matter of pleasing fritter-sellers. No! But, since half our troubles came from insensitivity to trifling abuses, he planned to overhaul the police, improve the penal system, dissolve the *Centurioni* and . . .

Amandi was appalled. 'Holy Father!' The title rang like an oath. 'You'll stir up a hornets' nest! You'll unite your enemies against you!'

'But,' Mastai skirmished, 'I'm not thinking of *reforms*! Only improvements.' Then, taking Amandi by the elbows, 'You'll help me tame the hornets, won't you? Gently, as St Francis tamed Brother Wolf?' Rocking slightly on the balls of his feet, he added: 'Tell me who they are.'

'They're everyone!' And Amandi tried to explain the dangers of tinkering with a crumbling edifice. 'First the bureaucrats . . .'

'Well, tame them for me then.' Mastai kissed him on both cheeks.

So Amandi went forth to take the bureaucratic pulse.

He was not sure whether Pius had thought up the task so as to rid himself of an intrusive old friend's concern. Mastai was changing in office and proving, if proof were needed, that power made men volatile to the point of femininity. Exalted and excitable in his new white gown, he was in manifest need of protection from competing suitors – mob, Jesuits, reformers – and perhaps most of all from the pride he took in seeing his election as a miracle from God.

Amandi wondered whether to tell the pontiff of his own electoral machinations on his behalf, but decided that this would look like the presentation of a bill. Still – Pius's exaltation was worrying and it was hard not to feel alarm at his talk of overhauling the police and dissolving the *Centurioni*.

'Away with them!' he had said, flicking his palms. '*Via!*'

And to be sure the *Centurioni* would be no loss. On the other hand, once disbanded, might they not *plot*? Might they not hire themselves out to the reactionary faction whose leaders were now despondently brooding in their palaces? Mastai's ingenuousness was worrying and so was his gusto: that irruption of private feeling which clerical celibacy was designed to minimise.

So off the devoted Monsignore went to Palazzo Madama to disarm the fears of the Treasury employees whom he found, as he had expected, in a panic at the news that a New Broom was to sweep through their offices. They were men whose most daring concession to novelty had hitherto been the occasional use of an iron pen.

'Monsignor Amandi, have you forgotten your friends?' The festive voice came from a carriage inside which sat an old cardinal with whom Amandi's acquaintance was slight. Two horses, three lacily liveried footmen and a coachman waited and so did anyone else who needed to get past, while His Eminence, bobbing like an affable puppet in its booth, blocked the narrow lane and paid court to the new pope's friend. Today, he told Amandi, he had learned a new word: 'Gregoriano! Have you heard it? The Contessa Spaur tells me that that's what they're calling the old guard who regret the days of the lamented Pope Gregory. Well, there will always be some who can't change: *Codini* who'd like to keep on powdering their hair and tying it in a tail! Nostalgia ferments. It can also explode. I don't have to tell you.'

Laughing inside his red-trimmed window, the cardinal had managed to transform the fetid lane into a drawing room – or was it a confessional? 'Whisper here to me!' His own hair could not have been whiter if he had powdered it. 'Why don't you come round for a chat? I'm a tomb, you know. Nothing you say will go further. When will you come?'

Amandi was about to excuse himself – he had no time to visit the old man – when the cardinal's hand drew him close. 'Those who have something to hope for,' said His Eminence in a lower, brisker tone, 'are less dangerous than those who have not. His Holiness must not drive the Gregoriani to despair. Even a tamed beast fights when cornered.'

Amandi was speechless. 'His Holiness,' he managed after moments, 'is a man of peace.'

'To be sure!' The other man's tongue flicked like a lizard's. 'But those he has pardoned are not. They want revenge on the men who condemned them – or the Gregoriani think they do, which is just as bad! Fear, Monsignore, can unleash the worst catastrophes!' Amandi's hand was released and the face in the window gave him a social smile. 'Come and see me, Monsignore. We'll toast your future which I'm sure is rosy! Come tomorrow,' called the cardinal as his carriage lurched off and the dung, churned up by its wheels, released a sweet, pungent blast.

Lifting his skirts, Amandi walked on and soon came to the meat-market, where iridescent flies hovered. Dodging a cart fresh from the shambles, he passed San Eustachio Church where stags' heads – carved ones – displayed crucifixes in their antlers.

The incongruity of such an emblem in a butcher's quarter was a sample of the city's contradictions. Who had sent the old cardinal to talk to him?

At Police headquarters rumours had preceded him. Clerks, with forearms encased in false sleeves of shiny cotton, popped from cubby-holes and desks. Their concern was to know whether laymen were to be brought into the service.

Was it true, Monsignore? What sort of laymen? Did that mean men so blatantly lay that they wouldn't wear a cassock? For, if it came to that, most of them were lay too and only wore it from respect for usage. Were they now to be penalised? Turned out of their jobs? No? Really, Monsignore? Could they count on that?

Reassured, they told him that he was, of course, welcome to look at any records he liked, although finding them would take time. They, said the archivists, were not to blame for this. Speaking with respect, Monsignore, the worst complexities were the results of efforts at reform. The truth was that to change anything you would have to change everything since the system was a network of exemptions and privileges.

Whose?

Those of certain families, Monsignore. Of religious houses, parishes, chivalric orders, cardinals . . . Pleased to connive, they flung open doors and cupboards, vying with each other to show this representative of the new authority the ways of the old. Come, come and see. And up and down they led him, through smells of mice and mildew, to a vestibule where boxes of ledgers were being packed for removal.

To where?

Appeasing him – whom they had perhaps led here on purpose – they shrugged and laughed so that the pens stuck behind their ears trembled like antennae. 'It's as you say, Monsignore,' they exclaimed, although Amandi, had said nothing. 'To change anything one would have to change it all!' Amused at the enormity, they tapped their papery foreheads. Here was where the indexes were, Monsignore. All in here! Tap, tap! Indexes to indexes! They held St Peter's keys – or the keys to his keys, which was why they were hard to get at and hard to turn. They laughed and their laughter had the creak of rust.

What were these boxes? asked Amandi. Where were they going?

The clerks stared. Boxes? Ah, those boxes? Someone must be moving them. The former minister perhaps? Or one of the senior employees – all prelates – might be taking them into safe-keeping. The new appointees had not yet come but if Monsignore wanted these files himself, they had no authority to stop him.

'It's a miracle,' said Pius, when Amandi showed him the police file on himself. 'You say someone was about to take it away? Just as you came? What's that but a miracle? God must have guided you!'

In the file which Amandi had had transported to his lodgings were boxes full of letters copied by Cardinal Lambruschini's spies: letters to himself, notes, reports of Mastai's movements and – Mastai picked up an envelope marked 'Leonessa 1831' then dropped it. His eye met, then dodged, Amandi's.

'Astonishing!' he said. 'Do you suppose he kept files on *all* senior churchmen? Here's a note from me to you.' He read: '"1845. Rome is negotiating with the Prince of Worldlings! Czar . . ." What trivia! Why should he have kept that?'

Because, Amandi could have told him, I was promoting you as *papabile* and he knew it and wanted to be pope himself.

'*Oremus!*' Pius dropped to his knees. 'Let us give thanks.'

Amandi, robbed again of gratitude, dropped willy-nilly to his knees. Pius had been known to do this even in cabinet meetings and one of the new lay ministers told how, on one occasion, pressing business had been interrupted and the whole cabinet required to prayerfully salute a comet visible from the palace window.

A letter awaiting Monsignor Amandi's attention was marked 'confidential' and spotted with a number of large capital letters.

Monsignore,
Yesterday while waiting in Yr Lordship's antechamber, I burned so ardently to place my life in Yr Lordship's gracious hands that when at last my turn came to be admitted to Yr Lordship's presence, my strength forsook me, I grew faint and, believing myself to be on the point of death, was obliged to rush away. If Yr Lordship could but read in my heart you would surely feel compassion for me.
Do not think of me as a spy, Monsignore, but as a man whom Zeal had destroyed. Having repeatedly risked my life for what I held to be a Sacred

40

Cause, I find, after a lifetime's devotion to the Security of This Realm, that men like me are now vilified and our Zeal seen as a crime. Colleagues have been cast from their posts or assassinated; the police dare not take action; while the Enemies of Order, now fresh released from gaol, glory in their impiety and return rejoicing to the embrace of their families.

I, Monsignore, have had to take leave of mine and come to Rome where I am in hiding for fear of the poniard. So fierce is the intent of the amnestied men that if Yr Lordship will not extend your protection to me soon, I fear that I shall not have another chance to request it.

May Yr Lordship take pity on the unfortunate man who kisses your hand, etc.

Luca Nardoni

The letter came with a note from Father Grassi SJ informing Monsignor Amandi that the spy hoped to buy protection in return for a set of files which he had amassed over a lifetime's police-work in the Romagna: an astonishing achievement. 'A man like that spies from passion,' wrote the Jesuit. He invited Amandi to do him the honour of calling at the Collegium Romanum on any day convenient to him about an hour after the Ave Maria.

Father Grassi was a sinuous man with soft, blackberry eyes. 'It is good of you to come,' he told Amandi. 'We had begun to feel like pariahs.'

Amandi assured him that he, like His Holiness, had a high esteem for the Society of Jesus.

'Which,' said the Jesuit, 'is an epitome of society itself. We have our differences, although it suits our opponents to say we have less autonomy than a colony of polyps. *I* had the temerity to write His Holiness a rather bold letter and would not like penalties due to me to fall on my fellows. I wrote sincerely but – well, you see my dilemma.'

From outside the window came the sound of boys' voices and from further off the cry of a melon-vendor praising his pyramid of freshly cut pink-fleshed fruit. Amandi had just passed this in the square and the sweet melon-smell floated in on the breeze.

'. . . your ward,' Grassi had been saying. 'The boy in whom you take an interest is fifteen now. Nicola Santi. It would mean a lot to him if you were to let me call him here for a few minutes. He's an orphan, as you know.'

To be sure, thought Amandi: the boy! His mind slid back to the spy. 'Your cousin sometimes gives him lunch.'

Amandi had a slightly eccentric cousin. Poor boy, he thought. Perhaps I should see him? The thought faded. He asked: 'Is Nardoni here?'

'Of course. You came for *him*.' Father Grassi was now all business. 'I'll bring him.'

Left alone, Amandi glanced down at the game in the courtyard. He could distinguish two teams, each with a home zone, from which players kept running out, challenging opponents to catch them as they rescued captured members of their own side. It struck him as a typically Jesuitical game.

Nardoni too could hear the boys whose game struck him as mirroring his plight – except that he had no rescuers.

He had left the Romagna in a cartload of pigs which had pissed all over him while the cart jolted over rutted roads, rattling his bones until he felt as if he had been soundly beaten – as he would be, the carter assured, if Liberals were to catch him. Nardoni, an ex-policeman, had helped convict some of the amnestied prisoners, hadn't he? Testified against them? Rigged evidence? Well, said the carter's grin, what could he expect? A beating would be the least of it.

He didn't know what to expect. He had trouble marshalling his thoughts. Mastai-Ferretti was wearing the triple tiara. His mandate ran in heaven and earth – so where could Nardoni go? He understood as little of what had happened as the pigs did when they shat on him because they had nowhere else to shit. How long would he be on the receiving end of shit?

A long time, said those who claimed to know.

He couldn't see where he'd gone wrong. A man chose his side and stuck to it. That was what loyalty meant. But now the side itself had dissolved. Even his friends were turning coat – or dead. Theirs had been the party of property and order – and now all the men of property were joining the gaolbirds!

'Possibly not all,' the Jesuit had said. 'Possibly not for long. Monsignor Amandi is a man of influence: clever and moderate. I'll talk to him first. You needn't say much at all.'

Nardoni's plans kept unravelling in his mind. 'Are we *against* the pope?' he had asked the Jesuit during one of their elusive and, to him, deeply opaque exchanges.

'We hope to enlighten him,' said the priest and left before he could be asked to enlighten Nardoni.

42

He had got the Jesuits' address from a friend. '*They*'re not happy either,' said the friend. 'They're your best hope.'

But he was too dispirited to hope. Being cooped up here could turn a man's wits! He needed movement – exercise to bring the blood to his brain. Why not try a handstand?

When Father Grassi opened the door, the spy's face confronted him at foot-level, while his feet waved like those in a fresco showing the damned with their heads thrust downward into pots of boiling oil.

Nardoni thrust a paper at Monsignor Amandi. It was a summary of the advice reaching Roman Liberals from London. The Monsignore ran his eyes over it and Nardoni, watching their movement, remembered what he'd written: '(1) seize all pretexts – cheering the pope, etc. – for assembling the people; (2) let them see our strength; (3) let sympathetic priests and nobles think each move will be the last; never reveal the revolution's final aims; (4) repeat the words "freedom, rights, progress, brotherhood, equality", also: "despotism, privilege"; (5) encourage all those who will come some way with you; later, if they try to retreat, they will be isolated.'

The Monsignore looked upset. Good, thought Nardoni: sweat a bit in your turn.

'Who prepared this?'

'We did, Monsignore. Ex-policemen.'

'But this is new material – written since the amnesty.'

'We continue to work. From loyalty.'

Amandi crumpled the paper. 'What do you want?'

'To serve the state, Monsignore, and save us all. Dangerous infor-mation could reach the wrong hands.'

He watched that register. Message received, he saw and went limp with relief which grew as talk turned to the Romagna. A maligned province. A place you could come to love, with its high skies and hard-working people. Nardoni, seeing that he was being soothed, joined in reminiscing about cafés and great players of bowls and billiards and it was in these coded terms that the two made their pact, agreeing that to reach an understanding could never be difficult for those who had the Holy Father's interests at heart.

*

An after-image caught up with Amandi as he left the Collegio. At an upstairs window, a cluster of pale, young faces gleamed, as though blanched in the dim enclosures where the Jesuits kept their charges. Too late now to see the boy. Besides, he was not in the mood. Diplomatic politeness had given him a cramp in the mouth.

Reaching the Caffè Venezia, he sat down to read the other paper in his pocket: a copy of Father Grassi's letter to the pope. The date was old. Hence Grassi's anxiety. The wind, he must feel, had changed and it was time to trim sail.

> Most Holy Father,
>   I pray that Yr Holiness will disdain neither this humble expression of joy at Yr Holiness's elevation . . .

Amandi's practised eye, skipping some pious courtesies, landed on the word 'reforms' and Grassi's plea that Pius resist those pressing for them.

> . . . since reforms, oh most Holy Father, would open the way to a pluralism incompatible with the States of the Church. No compromise is possible with modernised forms of government since these take their mandate from the people's will which is no substitute for truth, because:
>   men do not understand their own needs;
>   universal suffrage delivers them up to the frauds of demagogues;
>   the sole safeguard for human happiness is order;
>   order depends on institutions and especially on the one now in Yr Holiness's keeping.
>   Since dynasties incarnate the unity and continuity of creation, princes are symbols of the Supreme Being and, since it is on this mystic harmony, not on changeable constitutions, that human society is based, it follows that it is the duty of all princes to preserve the powers they inherit and pass them on intact . . .

And so forth. Several more pages warned against introducing such 'instruments of communication and conspiracy' as the electric telegraph, and climaxed in a request for indulgence for Grassi's forthrightness. Then the writer prostrated himself with veneration to kiss His Holiness's feet.

Amandi folded the letter. He marvelled that Mastai – whom he knew to be easily swayed – had resisted the warning. It was true that others were pushing him the other way.

*

Sister Paola had not burned His Holiness's letters and was glad because, now that he had been translated to a higher sphere, they were all she had of him. He had sent a last note to say he would not write again and she must choose a new confessor. His tone was cool. 'I am making time to write,' said the note, 'so as to encourage you to detach yourself from creatures and fling yourself with greater resignation into the arms of Divine Bounty.' That phrase cropped up as often in his letters as the ones professional writers copied from the manual. As a small girl, in her uncle's parish, she had enjoyed hanging round their tables on market days when they were one of the chief attractions.

'Tell her the cow calved,' a client might say, 'and that we've planted the tobacco and my leg is better.'

'Put in something fancy,' a listener was sure to suggest. 'Something from the manual.'

'It's to my daughter,' the client would argue. 'She's in service in Forlì. She'll want the news.'

This was always a disappointment. Letters to daughters were rarely interesting. 'My daughter,' began the ex-confessor's letters because we were all part of God's family and must love and see God in each other – which meant, did it not, that to fling yourself into the arms of God was also to fling yourself into *his*? But he didn't like that sort of thinking.

'Your last letter,' ran one of his old ones, 'is hard to understand, but I warn you that the mind's dwelling on certain sorts of temptation comes from our nature's having been corrupted by Eve's sin and weakened by our own. Close your mind to such fantasies ... Don't yield to anxiety. That makes things worse. Say humbly to Jesus Christ: see how abased and vile your bride is now! Despise these temptations. No matter what happens in them or what shapes they assume, victory will be yours so long as your will refuses its consent ...'

But her will did not refuse and – could he even imagine what happened in what he called her 'temptations'? She blushed to think he might. Some seemed as real as memories, and sometimes she was ready to think that that was what they were. Mad, she scolded herself, you're mad.

'Pray to St Gregory,' instructed another of his old letters, 'that he may defend the Church and assist our own Pope Gregory who is governing it among tribulations ...'

Now he was governing it himself. Yet he had thought of her one last time. She wondered whether he had a picture of her in his mind: Sister Paola, the one who needed rallying. '*Calma*' was his great word when

45

writing to her. It was one her uncle had used when running his hand down the necks of carriage horses which had not yet learned to be staid. '*Calma, buono!*' Picturing the hand on a horse's coat, she felt her skin shiver in sympathy.

The abbess did not inspect cells. If she had, Sister Paola could not have hidden the letters. You were supposed to keep nothing personal. Everything belonged to the community and even the property her uncle left had become her spiritual dowry without which she would have had to become a lay sister and do menial work. Hearing that her uncle's housekeeper was without provision, she had asked whether it would not be right to give her the money and for her, Sister Paola, to become a lay sister.

'No,' said Monsignor Mastai, adding that excessive humility was a form of pride.

'Detach yourself from creatures.' But could one not serve God in creatures? 'I,' she told the abbess, 'did a little nursing in my uncle's parish. Should we not concern ourselves with people's bodies so as to help their souls?

The abbess said we must raise the matter with our new bishop. 'How are you getting on,' she asked, 'with the new confessor?'

'I think I frightened him.'

The priest had been baffled by Sister Paola. Had she not been His Holiness's penitent, he would, he told the abbess, have thought her unstable.

'Would you say the saints were all stable?'

'But they were saints!'

'Do you think those around them could tell?'

The abbess looked at the chubby face in front of her. Twenty-five years old? Twenty-six? 'Father,' she gave him the title without satiric intent. However, he blushed. 'You should know that Sister Paola's instability is due not to herself but to history. Shocking things happened in '31. His Holiness used to discourage her dwelling on them. You may have your own ideas . . .'

Again the priest reddened and within days word came from the bishop that a new confessor would be sent. The first one wasn't, it seemed, up to being a secular priest at all and was now thinking of becoming a monk. The bishop expressed regret.

'What,' the abbess asked Sister Paola with curiosity, 'upset him?'

'He asked me to confess a sin from my past life. I told him about the child.'

46

'Ah.' The abbess had been led to suppose that Sister Paola was suffering from a lapse of memory with regard to the child and that this was a mercy.

'I have the evidence of my senses to remind me,' said the nun. 'Marks on my stomach.'

'Do you worry about the baby?'

'No. I was promised that it was being looked after and would be better off without me. I should like to help people who have nobody to look after them.'

Sister Paola was now thirty-one years old and knew her own mind.

Shortly after this the abbess arranged for her to study nursing with a French nun who claimed a connection with the Bonapartes and talked of them eagerly, especially of Louis Napoleon, who had so much of the family ambition that he had wrecked a plan to marry his cousin by embarking on a *coup d'état* which failed. Princess Mathilde – the cousin – had had to learn from the public press that her betrothal was off and her intended leaving for an enforced exile in the United States.

'What a shock,' said the nun, 'for a young girl. He's back, you know. Now. In Paris. He may yet come to power.'

'Show me how to make a plaster.'

'You haven't an ounce of romance!'

Sister Paola did not mention her own meeting with Louis Napoleon but found her mind returning to that time and to her uncle's death.

Coming in from the glitter of noon, she had sensed rather than seen him in the gloom of his curtained, walnut bed.

The housekeeper had warned: 'He's raving. The Bonaparte riffraff did for him.'

'No,' whispered the dying man and the whites of his eyes were phosphorescent. 'It was her! She fornicated with them!'

The woman pulled at the girl's arm and both saw a gleam of malice in the dying eyes.

'He's dead.'

'No!'

But he was. The malice was the fixity of death.

Again she brought up the idea of giving money to the housekeeper. But the abbess said, 'My dear, leave the poor wretch alone. Don't go piling coals of fire on her head and shaming her. She has probably made some sort of life for herself. Forget her. You're ashamed of hating her . . .'

'I don't . . .'

47

'You do. It's jealousy. I do think you were right when you said we should work in a practical way – nurse, help the poor and so forth. His Holiness expected so much and we were so eager to satisfy him that we've had a tendency here to *imitate* the spiritual life. Practical charity is easier to measure . . .'

'You mean we've been lying? To him – and to God?'

'I don't think that's as rare as you think,' said the abbess tranquilly. 'I suppose the housekeeper was your uncle's concubine? Well, the truth may be that they were both saving him from incest. Think of him as wanting to protect you. Think of her as helping him.'

'I suppose I do hate her.'

'That's your sin: the one you never told His Holiness.'

'Maybe women's confessors should be women?'

Four

The boys stared after Monsignor Amandi. They were bored. Rain had prevented their going to the open ground outside the city, where they could have played ball or watched the games of seminarians whose cassocks swooped like shuttlecocks. Just past Porta Pia was their place. It was near the priests' promenade where you could see cardinals stroll, while their carriages lumbered behind and footmen clung to them like grasshoppers. Towards sunset, the red of Their Eminences' wraps could seem to run like dye and sounds turn tinny in the air. The grass in summer went as dry as plush.

'He didn't ask for you, Santi!'

A slim boy mimed mock despair: hands folded, chin on chest. He had picked up tricks like that from being regularly cast as an angel in the Christmas play where, until recently, his weight had been no strain for the flying-machines. The Jesuits were famous for their amateur theatricals. Nicola's tactics, when teased, were evasive and even girlish, but this went unremarked at the Collegio where masters, after all, wore skirts which they tucked up to play games and the laybrothers who looked after the boys' domestic needs were described as having 'motherly hearts'. Clerical Rome, on excluding women, had borrowed their characteristics.

'Didn't you say he was a cardinal?'

No, said Nicola, but a priest, *confusing* Monsignor Amandi with Cardinal Amat of Rimini, had tried to get Nicola to intercede with him for a favour. It had been the day the old pope died. Last spring. They'd gone on an excursion to the Villa d'Este and Tivoli.

It had been a luminous drive. The sky had throbbed with larks and the villa had been like a vision: a place of rainbows where terraced fountains foamed in celebration of the insubstantial. Cardinal Ippolito d'Este, making the most of his mortal span, had had it built in the sixteenth century and now five hundred fountains played for forty black-hatted adolescents in rusty uniforms. News of Pope Gregory's death reached them there and impromptu prayers heightened the sly voluptuousness of the place, while moss dampened the knees of their trousers.

News kept coming from the city and the school party mingled more with others than the Jesuits would normally have thought fit. Some secular priests and foreigners joined in conversation. What, asked the foreigners, would happen now? They were told that there would be a conclave and the college of cardinals elect one of themselves.

· 'His patron's one.' A boy pointed to Nicola Santi who, as talk raced on, had no chance to clear up the error. The priests were hoping for a pope who could handle change. A young, fresh-faced one pointed at the fountains. Only ice could arrest *that*.

Disapprovingly, the Father Prefect moved his charges away and, when the others caught up, talk turned to other matters. Tivoli had been the Tibur of ancient Rome and the fresh-faced priest lowered his voice to say that this was where Propertius's girl was buried. Nicola, pleased to show off, quoted:

> Midnight, and Cynthia's urgent note to say
> I'm here at Tibur: come without delay . . .

The urgency pleased him and so did a glimmering guess as to what had made the poet ready to brave his fear of brigands and set off on the road to Cynthia – the very road which the Collegio charabancs had taken this morning.

The one braving things just now was Nicola, for the poem was not on the school curriculum. I'm here at Tibur, he thought. Yearning for urgency, he could not decide whether to think of himself as the imperious Cynthia or her lover.

The young priest's name was Padre Rampolla. His party was turning back to Rome and, as he regretted missing the cascades, the Father Prefect offered him a seat in a charabanc. The sound of the great natural falls was audible long before they could be seen. *Praeceps Anio!* Here it was: plunging from its altitudes with a white tumultuous flourish. Its water possessed petrifying properties and a descent into the caves led past rocks hung with stony vegetation.

The horses' heads were now turned towards Rome and the Father Prefect took his place in the leading charabanc, whence choruses of Ave Marias were soon floating on the breeze. In the second vehicle, however, where Padre Rampolla was sitting next to Nicola Santi, things were different, for he kept the boys entertained all the way with jokes and poems. They were dazzled.

Next day when Nicola was called to the parlour, he was elated because he scarcely ever got visits. Padre Rampolla was sitting, with a lively smile, under the cheese-coloured bust of some forgotten cardinal. For some minutes, he chatted about their meeting yesterday, quoted some lines from Propertius and, just as he was starting to win Nicola's ready and vulnerable heart, got down to business. He wanted a favour.

'Our acquaintance,' he apologised, 'is recent, but . . .' The priest's sudden diffidence amazed the schoolboy. He hoped, he said, that Nicola could see his way to asking his patron to let Rampolla make himself useful to him during the coming conclave. 'He hasn't been living in Rome and will need men to fill temporary posts. These are ephemeral appointments but draw attention to the men chosen. If you could drop my name . . .'

'With my patron?'

Rampolla looked put out. Nicola must not think he was moved by personal ambition. No, what he wanted was to be in a position to *serve*. Evil forces were mobilising. Father Rampolla's tone grew hectoring, then, remembering that he was here for a favour, he stopped, smiled, then began to explain himself with pleading sweetness. Soon, however, he was excited again and began to walk about so that his cassock swished with eloquence. Zeal, he concluded, was needed as never before and he didn't want his to wither while he wasted his youth performing trivial tasks.

'Will you speak to the cardinal?'

'I don't know any cardinal.'

The priest looked hurt.

'I don't know why you should think I do.' Nicola had forgotten the misinformation given by his schoolmate yesterday. 'My patron is Monsignor Amandi.'

'Not Amat?'

'No.'

Martelli roared with mirth. 'Ah, the scheming priest! I wish I'd seen his face. What had he hoped for anyway? Did you find out?'

Nicola had. It seemed that, since conclavists must stay locked up until they had chosen a new pope, each needed a priest to bring him meals and the job was hotly sought.

'Sacred scullions!' quipped Martelli, who was a newcomer in Nicola's line, having been in the senior one until he got sent back as a bone-head – which he wasn't. What he was – and this amazed his classmates – was contemptuous of the Collegio curriculum whose excellence nobody, until now, had challenged in their hearing.

The Collegium Romanum thought of itself as the brains of Rome and was housed near the Pantheon in a great, barracks-like, sixteenth-century building which smelled of chalk, mutton fat, boiled greens and unwashed boy. It contained a boarding school, a day school, a famous observatory and the Gregorian University, and catered for twelve hundred youths whose waking hours were taken up with the study of dead languages and pious practices, wholesome games, and the pursuit of gentlemanly accomplishments. It was the only home Nicola had and he was pleasurably shocked by Martelli's irreverence.

Martelli's chief claim to fame was that last year he and another boy from a Liberal family, having been found doing nobody knew what, had each received fifty strokes on the buttocks from the school janitor on whose behalf each of their families had then been presented with a bill for five solidi. The other boy's family had forthwith withdrawn him from the school and sued it for battery, a doomed manoeuvre since all courts were run by the Church.

When the litigious parents' case had been duly quashed, the Father Minister had delivered a sermon castigating their failure to understand their son's true interests. Martelli's father, by contrast, was praised and Martelli acquired a halo of merit as though the strokes on his backside had ennobled him. He was now allowed more leeway than anyone else.

'Well,' he teased Nicola, 'the would-be scullion muffed his shot because your patron is the Pope's best friend. Cardinal or not, he's a man to keep in with – and so are you!' Laughing, he flung his arms around Nicola, then jumped away as he saw a priest hover in the corridor. Touching was forbidden. Even at football it was a foul to put a hand on another player and the word oozed contagiously through other prohibitions. Thus gestures took on force. Not linking arms became a link in itself.

This time, though, there was no reprimand. The priest had moved off. Something was changing in the Collegio. There had been other signs, small slacknesses which registered in that well-regulated place, as dust might do in the mechanism of a clock. Lately, some priests had grown stricter and others more affectionate. Hoping, perhaps to bind their community close? Accounts, read at meals, of the Society's times

52

of heroic trial, described a beleaguered exaltation which might start out like this.

Pope Pius was to visit here shortly and preparations were in full, bustling swing. Did that mean that rumours of a rift between him and the Society of Jesus were false – or so true that a visit was necessary? Yesterday a Collegio boy had been spat on by a woman shouting, 'Jesuit vermin!' He had been the last in a group to file down one of those dark lanes canopied by laundry, and when they reached the sun there was a sparkle of saliva on his black uniform. Nicola, reliving the scene in his mind, imagined the spittle landing on his own trouser leg and experienced the pleasure he sometimes felt when checking a tantrum. He was quick-tempered but, somewhere in his body, an opiate, triggered by stifled rage, could procure a strangely soothing languour.

Just now there were plenty of occasions for turning the other cheek. Mobs had been throwing dung at the Collegio windows. One of these nights, they yelled, they would burn it down. Why? The Collegio pupils, who studied no modern history, could not imagine. Their teachers had kept them in ignorance of today's world and the mob too was ignorant. Now, like baffled zoo creatures, the two herds confronted each other.

Nobody knew why – except, perhaps, for Martelli who had raffish connections and got secret news. Shrugging and putting his hands in his pockets – another forbidden act – he sauntered off.

Over the next few days, preparations for the papal visit speeded up, as borrowed tapestries were delivered, half-moon-shaped portraits of past pupils who had achieved distinction inserted into the courtyard arches, and chalk and string lines drawn where, at the last moment, mosaics of fresh flowers would be arranged. Into these would be incorporated Pope Pius's initials and coat of arms – a gold-crowned lion rampant on a ball – and various emblems indicative of Jesuit loyalty to the Holy See. Martelli claimed that secret preparations were also afoot and that it was not only the mob which engaged in nocturnal sorties. Jesuits had been making trips to a graveyard where one of their most revered bretheren had been buried, a man who had struggled to save the Society from Pope Ganganelli's dissolution order in 1773.

If the corpse were to be found intact or, better, smelling of roses, this would show him to have been a saint and Ganganelli wrong to have given in to the pressures of free-thinkers. Those now attacking the Jesuits would receive a set-back and the Pope turn a deaf ear to their arguments. That, said Martelli, was the plan.

How did he know? He laid a finger to his nose. Attar of roses, he

53

assured, had been sprinkled on the grave after Father Grassi had been seen leaving here in a carriage with two muscular novices and a bag of picks and shovels. However, the corpse, or rather skeleton, had proven putrid and had to be reburied fast. The attar of roses was cover for the stench. The trick had not come off.

'Martelli, you're a little rat! Here we are besieged by a rabble and you . . .!'

'Have you no loyalty?'

But his stories held them. Among fifteen-year-olds there are always some who hope to discover that the world is full of surprises. Martelli, a Prince of Darkness, went so far as to sneak candles into his friends' cubicles at night, open locked doors and lead forays to view the besieging mob. Nor did it stop there. One thing led to another and soon they were rolling dice and accepting dares. This was how Nicola, one evening after lights out, found himself in a forbidden part of the Collegio whence he must, by the terms of the dare, bring back proof of his incursion. He was dodging down a dark corridor when he heard the Rector's voice and, stepping backwards, felt himself pulled into an alcove. The Rector and another Jesuit passed by.

'Sh!' whispered a voice. 'Spies must stick together.'

When the coast was clear, his rescuer pulled back a curtain and, by moonlight, Nicola saw a balding man with hard, close-set eyes. 'You were spying?' supposed the man.

'No. I came for a dare.'

'Ah. Well, I saved you from trouble anyway. Will you post a letter for me?'

'I can't go out alone. We're not allowed.'

'Give it to someone who can. Milk boy. Day boy. There's always someone. Well, will you? Or are you the timid sort? A rabbit?'

'I'll take it.'

'Good. Wait.' The man disappeared, then came back with a letter. 'I've been wondering whom to give it to,' he said. 'Stroke of luck. That's a good sign. Once luck starts it stays a while. Don't tell anyone you saw me. Hurry now. They'll be at their prayers for a bit. Go.'

Nicola went.

'But I promised,' he cried, as Martelli broke the seal. However, his protest already seemed part of a world of scruple which was now childishly obsolete.

'This is in code!' Martelli read: '"Resurrection urgent!" I have friends who'll be interested.' He had a Liberal cousin who was said to be close to the Pope.

'We can't post it with a broken seal.'

'We are not going to post it.' Martelli put the letter in the lining of his jacket.

Next morning the two had the task of helping hang a very large tapestry which smelled of the sooty, private palace from whence it came. It had been rolled into a cylinder and so tightly roped that at first they couldn't undo it. At last a stretch of it uncoiled and motifs became visible – a border of grotesques whose bodies, like tadpoles, tailed off below the bust. Then the thing stuck fast. A third, more muscular youth, a day boy from the Irish College, was summoned to help, but the roll remained jammed between islands of immovable furniture.

'It's heavy,' said the Irish boy. 'I think there's something inside it. Something hard.'

'Nonsense!' rallied the priest who had given them the job. 'Three strapping fellows like you can manage that. Hanging it will be trickier. We'll have to rig up a pulley. I'll get some ropes.'

He left. The three gave a concerted heave and . . .

'*Oddio*, what . . .'

'Cover them! Quick! Roll it up!'

'Shouldn't we . . .?'

'No. *No*! Best pretend we never opened it!' Martelli kept watch while the other two rerolled the stiff parcel. Grotesques, embowering greenery and their awful find, were re-enclosed and the ropes feverishly reknotted as the three recoiled from unmanageable knowledge.

When the priest came back in consternation to say that this particular item should have gone elsewhere, his charges' red faces could be ascribed to vain efforts to pull off the ropes.

'Those guns . . .'

'Shsh!'

'Listen! Either they were brought to make trouble for the Society or else a few firebrands *here* are planning trouble for . . .'

'Who?'

'The Pope!'

Martelli's listeners goggled.

55

'I won't listen,' said the Irish boy whose name was Gilmore. He was big, slow and pious.

Martelli was impatient. What they should know, he said, was that there was some very desperate plotting going on among men who would do anything to get this pope to change his policies. 'The Jesuits are thought to be in the thick of it and if they're *not* then something could be done to make them come in. This is just the sort of thing – plant guns on them and let them be "discovered", maybe during the Pope's visit! Can you imagine the scandal!'

'But why?'

Austria, Martelli explained, needed an excuse to send in troops and a disturbance here in Rome would serve perfectly. Troops would 'rescue' the Holy Father, then dictate terms to him and stay until they had restored the old Gregoriani to power.

'These tapestries will be hard to get rid of. For the Collegio's sake we should let one of the moderate ministers know.'

The other two were out of their depth. Could the Jesuits truly be against the Pope? And if they could not, what harm could come of doing what Martelli said?

'We can't tell anyone here,' he argued, 'because we don't know who knows already. It could be dangerous to tell the wrong person.'

Unexpectedly the Irish boy nodded. Yes, he agreed, remembering stories of Ribbon men back home.

So, decided Martelli, they'd tell the police. The minister in charge of them was a friend of his cousin. They could come in discreetly to look about – after all, with His Holiness expected here on the 27th, what could be more natural? They could take the things out the way they came in. No scandal.

'Gilmore can take a note out on his way home to the Irish College.'

'No,' said the Irish boy. 'Not me. Sorry, no.'

'Oh all right then. I'll manage myself – but you two hold your tongues. Will you?'

'Yes.'

What Martelli could not know was that Gilmore, returning every evening to his own college, escaped *his* influence and surrendered to a nervous hysteria brought on by starvation. For some time now, the Hibernici had been eating very little in order to save and send money to their country, where a famine was raging.

Hunger gave Gilmore insomnia and insomnia scruples, and after three nights of staring at the small, screened window above his bed, he became convinced that it was his duty to denounce Martelli.

'Cleanse my heart and lips, oh God,' he prayed, 'who didst cleanse the lips of the prophet Isaiah with a live coal.'

Then he went to see the Prefect of Studies at the Romano.

The Prefect was not in his study and Gilmore was put to wait in an ante-room lined with bookcases. Nervously, he examined the books behind the wire netting. There were several copies of one by the late pope entitled *The Triumph Of The Church And Holy See Over Innovators*. Outside in the courtyard, work had begun on the floral mosaic and containers were being set in place. Light ricocheted off glass and made Gilmore sway. His hands shook with hunger. Perhaps there was a harmless explanation for the guns? On the 27th, the papal guard would accompany the Pope. Could they have been delivered for their use? Treachery had a queer repellent attraction. Gilmore savoured the thought of hurting Martelli and Nicola whom he liked. It was because he did that the thought appealed. He wanted to get close and hurt them so that he could then succour them or at least share their hurt. Missionary tales of martyrs were his source. You suffered torture together. Your blood mingled and your bodies opened. The mind was blasted into extinction and you were freed from your beastly separate self.

Outside, the sun abolished edges. Its glitter fused the figures of black-uniformed boys. Gilmore's eyelids blazed when closed and, when he opened them, red flames floated like those in a devotional painting.

Coming in, the Father Prefect found him with his head between his knees.

'Well?' The priest, visibly in a hurry, was carrying papers and his old soutane was rubbed shiny in several places. The boy saw this with unusual clarity.

'You wanted to see me?'

'Father, I . . . wanted to report someone.' The boy felt as though he had been taken over by a part of himself which he didn't wish to know. A traitor? A spy? The shock of these names jerked him awake.

'Who?'

'I'm sorry. That wasn't what I meant to say.'

'Well, you've said it.'

'I'm sorry, Father. I've been ill. Dizzy. There's nothing really to report.'

The priest looked keenly at him. 'You've lost your nerve!' he accused. 'You don't like to denounce a fellow pupil. Yet might it not be for his good?' He paused. 'You may rely on my discretion.'

'I know, Father.'

'As I have explained to you all, it is your companions' souls you should consider . . .' The priest spoke rapidly. He was busy. The building was being metamorphosed; images of harmony must be laboriously invoked and an effort made to show that the Society could work with this dangerous pope. Now here was this boy, not even one of our own boarders, but clearly in need of attention . . .

'Father Prefect.' Someone stood at his door.

'One moment.' He told the boy, 'Come to confession to me tomorrow.'

'It's Martelli,' said the youth in a nervous rush. He spoke as if racing himself and was ungainly, all knobbly wrists and with feet like fetlocks under his outgrown cassock.

'A delivery!' The messenger at the door made urgent gestures. Downstairs, carriages were arriving in a stream, workmens' drays making deliveries and the square outside in such a tangle that . . .

'Yes,' said the Father Prefect. Then, to the boy, 'Tomorrow then. Now I have to go.'

The boy walked down the stairs.

Outside, a party of papal guards waited while their officer explained something to the porter. As Gilmore passed, the officer took back a paper which the old man had been studying and ordered his men to enter the building.

The porter shook his head. 'An inspection, if you please. As if there wasn't enough confusion.'

Gilmore rushed off into the hot afternoon.

'Can you believe he's blown the gaff?' Martelli was caught between mirth and indignation. 'Half-blown it! He started to snitch then stopped. Who? The Irish testicle and testifier: *testis Hibernicus*! It seems he mentioned my name, then lost his nerve. Anyway, it was too late. I'd already reported *them*.'

Nicola was horrified.

'*Et dimitte nos . . .*'

They were in chapel. The rector, Father Manera, had, said Martelli, summoned him but was being cautious. 'My cousin's going to be on the

Pope's Advisory Council, so . . .' Papal guards, he confided, had removed you-know-what after dark.

'*Pax domini sit semper vobiscum,*' sang the choir hopefully.

Scurellus was Nicola Santi's nickname and there were two stories as to how he got it. One turned on a small spiritual swindle and the other had a whiff of the midden. It happened in that same summer of '47. There had been food riots in the northern Legations; half Rome was living on charity and he and some classmates were sent with alms to an orphanage. This institution caricatured their own. It was a vast, draughty place with outsize pilasters and pediments and peeling baroque flourishes and, in its vestibule, between grubby busts of dead cardinals, a braided whip, made of ligaments from bullocks' necks, hung prominently on a nail.

When Nicola entered one of the workrooms, a boy was kneeling in the middle of the floor. The overseer motioned him back to his place and Nicola saw that he had been kneeling on dried beans.

The alms were received politely but there was mockery in the recipients' eyes. These were boys from the streets. Driven off them by the bad times and dearth of foreign tourists, they must know more about life than the Collegio pupils could imagine.

Shyly, the donors delivered their message. At their request, the orphans were to have a half holiday. All were to meet in chapel and celebrate with a Te Deum. Impatiently, the monk in charge of the workroom cut in with a roar. Work tools must first be put away and if he caught anyone stealing any, he'd personally flay the hide off him. Then all must proceed in an orderly manner. He barked this out with the domineering relish of a non-commissioned officer and it struck the Jesuit boys that that was precisely what monks like this were: low-level bullies in the Church's army. It shocked them, for their own teachers were gentlemen and they watched with shame as the tools were accounted for under the monk's grudging and suspicious eye. Hammers, awls, waxed thread, and needles were locked up and the key secured to his rosary beads.

Nicola, who was an orphan himself, shuddered to think he might have ended in a place like this. Just then, the boy who had been kneeling on beans startled him with a wink. On the way out of the chapel he whispered, 'Is that your livery?' pinching a fold of Nicola's sleeve. 'It's dangerous nowadays to wear it. Did you know that in the Legations men won't wear black ribbons in their straw hats. Guess why?'

'I can't.'

'Because black and yellow are the Pope's colours. He's not as popular as he was. Nothing lasts, you see. I had a pretty livery once. Covered with gold lace. I was working for an English milord who called me his Roman monkey.'

The exit from the chapel had halted. Too many people were trying to squeeze through.

'What sort of work did you do?'

'Monkey work.'

Nicola was offended. The boy put a hand on his. 'It's myself I'm making fun of. I was his toy. He had funny ways.'

'Why didn't you stay with him?'

'I got consumption and he was afraid he'd catch it. Couldn't get rid of me fast enough. He used to kiss me, you see, and *that* carries the disease.' The boy lowered his voice: 'Would *you* kiss me? Would you be afraid?'

'No,' said Nicola with defensive scorn. 'No to both questions.'

'Do I disgust you?'

'Of course not.'

'If I had my gold livery I'd swop it for yours. I like yours. It's austere. Are you a Jesuit?'

'How could I be? I'm only a boy.'

'You think I'm ignorant, don't you? I'll bet I know things which would surprise you!'

'I don't doubt that.'

The crowd had at last started to move. Nervously, Nicola began to elbow his way forward.

'They say,' his companion's breath was hot on his ear, 'that the Jesuits will be thrown out of Rome any day now. Thrown out or burnt out. So it's as well you're not one, isn't it?'

'I couldn't be!' Nicola was relieved to have something specific on which to concentrate indignation. 'I told you. I'm only fifteen! A boy! Like you.'

'I'm seventeen. I know I don't look it. It's the feeding. My mother – if she *was* my mother – was undernourished, so . . .' He made a gesture to indicate his own dwarfishness. 'My name is Flavio.'

'Santi!' The Collegio group was being rounded up. 'We're leaving.'

Outside in the sunlight there was the tail-end of a commotion and Nicola's friends began to tell him what had happened. A drunken beggar had shouted insults at them and mocked their slimy charity. 'Keep the best back, don't you!' he had cried. 'Keep it for yourselves!' Then he put his finger on a gold medal which one boy was wearing. He had probably meant to do no more than touch it, but the boy snatched at the chain and, somehow, the medal flew through the air to land in one of those middens which citizens persisted in leaving in the middle of the most elegant squares. These heaps of rot, excrement – equine and human – old cabbage stumps and the occasional dead animal were often left to ferment through the dog days so that they gave off a smell like gas and, when finally carted off, steamed as though on the point of combustion.

'I'll get your medal,' Nicola told its owner.

'No,' called the priest in charge, but already Nicola had a foot on the heap which was piled around a fountain. The stink caught his throat, bringing tears to his eyes. Balancing against the fountain's statuary, he put his other foot on the rim, leaned into the muck and picked out something which was gleaming in the sun, the medal.

'I'll wash it,' he called, aware that the boy from the orphanage must be watching. It was unclear to himself why, but he felt as though he had recoiled from a challenge and was doing this to make up. Turning, he lost his footing and fell in the filth.

On the walk back, a mock debate started as to whether his act should be castigated or admired. This was the sort of topic which, worked up into Latin verse, could win you a prize in the Collegio. His stink, however, offended the debaters' nostrils.

'*Self*-sacrifice, my foot. *We* have to smell him.'

'Keep to the leeward, Santi! That beggar called us slimy. Santi's like a drowned rat!'

'Rat's harsh. Let's say squirrel: *Sciurus, scurellus, scoiattolo*! Sounds slimy enough!'

'*Scurellus stercoratus*!'

The outing turned out to be the last for quite a while. Shortly afterwards the boys left for the Society's villa in the country and when they returned the streets had become so precarious that they were hardly let out at all.

The other reason for Nicola's nickname was connected with a jar of white stones.

Emulation was encouraged at the Collegio whose pupils belonged to two rival armies. It had been especially keen just before the Pope's visit

61

and, as marks for athletic and academic performance drew even, it was Nicola who persuaded the Father Prefect that spiritual acts be counted too. Anyone performing one was to drop a white stone in a jar. Since such acts were private, honour had to be relied on and, at the final count, his own was put in doubt. He was the custodian of his army's jar which, filling suddenly, tipped the balance for his side. Challenged, he swore to his good faith and, although the losing army protested, teachers turned a deaf ear. Hush! No grousing. Here we were all one big family. Testing times were upon us and our enemies at the gates.

This was true. A five-volume work maligning the Society had been printed in Switzerland and smuggled into the peninsula and the Pope had not condemned it. It looked as though his visit, seen first as a sign of support, had instead exhausted his goodwill. The worst sign of all came when in July the Austrians crossed the Po and occupied his city of Ferrara. The Pope protested and immediately rumours spread of an 'Austro-Jesuit plot' to assassinate him.

'My dear sons and brothers in Christ,' said the Society's General, Father Roothan, in a special address to the community, 'what sane, sober mind could believe such fancies?'

It seemed that few minds just now were sober or sane, for many did believe that a disturbance had been planned to furnish Metternich with a pretext to send troops to Rome.

'But even if this were so, why connect it with us?' asked the General. 'What possible shred of evidence . . .'

Nicola, remembering Martelli's note to his cousin, now began to get nightmares and awoke whimpering in the night. Was he a traitor? Were the Jesuits? The mob had taken to screaming that they were. '*Traditori*' was the shout out in the streets as lumps of dried dung were hurled against the Collegio windows, along with crumpled broadsheets showing Jesuits armed with phials of poison and bloody daggers. They had murdered Pope Ganganelli with slow poison when he condemned them in 1773. Beware, warned the broadsheets, lest they do the same to Papa Mastai! Cartoons, showing Jesuits with foxes' tails sticking from under their soutanes, were pasted on walls, torn down by the police, then stuck up again. The Society's claim to be politically neutral fell on deaf ears and expectations in Liberal circles were that the Pope would soon banish it 'to prevent bloodshed'.

It was Flavio who brought this gossip which the Collegio pupils would not otherwise have heard.

'I'm Flavio. From the orphanage. Don't you remember?'

At first Nicola didn't. He had been summoned to the porter's lodge with his congregation's basket of supplies for the deserving poor and had not recognised the orphan who was taller now and better dressed.

'I brought these,' he told Nicola, as they packed clothes and foodstuffs into bags. 'Here.' He slipped folded broadsheets into Nicola's now empty basket. 'Thought you'd be interested. Tell me, is it true the Jesuits brew up slow poisons which leave no trace?'

'I don't think you should take our charity and then spread idiotic tales like that.'

'Who says they're idiotic? Everyone believes them. I go out to work now and I hear a lot. I've been apprenticed to a bag-maker.'

'What's all this whispering?' The doorkeeper, an ancient laybrother in a black bonnet, was standing over them. 'Pishpishpish!' he mimicked.

This old man was the Collegio's link with the outer world. His nickname – as key-keeper – was Brother Peter. 'Well,' he sucked in his draw-string mouth, 'hearing each other's confessions, are we? There are professionals for that.'

'Brother, is it true that the Fathers might get sent away like they were before?'

The doorkeeper, proud of being the last man alive to remember this event, was easily roused to reminisce. The Jesuits, he droned, were the Pope's first line of defence and if there was, once again, a move to persuade the Holy Father to be rid of them, there was no need to ask who was behind it. Brother Peter's finger was a divining rod blasted with old knowledge.

'Satan!' he quivered. He was as thin as sticks.

Flavio nudged Nicola. 'Satan?' he encouraged.

'Satanassa,' confirmed the old man. The fiend had started wreaking havoc after Pope Ganganelli suppressed the Society in 1773. In no time they'd had a revolution in France. Then Napoleon Bonaparte had come here to take a pope prisoner. A pope! The old man's speech was asthmatic with excitement. 'Pius the S-s-sixth. He wasn't a day under eighty and paralysed in both legs but off they trundled him regardless. In February. Over the Alps.' Brother Peter's tremulous hands scaled peaks.

'You're older than that yourself, Brother, aren't you?'

'I am. But I'm not being bumped over icy roads and hope not to be. Do you know who the Holy Father's companion was on his Calvary? An ex-Jesuit. Father Marotti! His *Maestro di Camera*. Yes. "Faithful to the faithless" should be our motto. Have you packed your stuff? Well, off with you, then!'

As Flavio was leaving, another old Jesuit appeared. A transparent man with white hair-tufts in his nose and ice-pale eyes, he was known as 'the Russian' because, having lived in Russia when the suppressed Society had found refuge there, he could sometimes be persuaded to tell stories full of frozen, snowy wastes.

Flavio, who had been walking with his head turned to hear the doorkeeper's last remarks, bumped into this frail man who might have fallen if Nicola had not steadied, then helped him to a chair.

'Are you all right, Father? Well, we'll be off then.'

'Wait!' The Russian stared at Flavio. 'Who are you? he wanted to know. 'What's your family name?'

'Rest yourself, Father!' said the doorkeeper and whispered, 'He's nervous. A stone flew in his window last week. Stones they're throwing now.'

He was herding Flavio out the door when the Russian asked again: 'What's your name?'

Flavio was clearly tempted to tell some magnificent lie. Instead, looking mortified, he admitted that his was a foundling's name, Diodato, meaning God's gift.

Well, the Jesuit persisted, did he know who his father was? No? Nor even his mother? Flavio, sulkily, shook his head. And how old was he? Seventeen. The old Jesuit nodded. 'I *may* know something about you,' he said. 'Don't start hoping. It's a long shot, but worth looking into. Come and see me tomorrow – no, the day after. What time do you stop work?'

Flavio told him.

'Good,' said the old man. 'Come and see me then.'

For some time after that, Nicola did not see Flavio, but the thought of what had happened kept running through his mind. He had dreamed of something like it happening to himself and felt Flavio had stolen his luck. Could this be a punishment for his initiative in the matter of the white stones? What had happened there was this. Nicola's side had so fallen behind in the contest as to have no hope of winning by work or sport. It was also too late to catch up by spiritual acts but, since *their* currency was outside time, he decided that they could be counted in advance. There and then, he filled the jar with unearned stones and

64

now, months later, was furtively and single-handedly paying off the debt. It was a sort of spiritual slavery.

His patron's feast day was coming up and Nicola had been encouraged to prepare an address in Latin verse. Will he be coming to hear it? he wondered.

But it seemed unlikely that Monsignor Amandi would come. There was a curl to the Father Prefect's lip. Fair-weather friends were keeping their distance, for the Pope, whose policies had led to an impasse, seemed likely to sacrifice the Society. Last Sunday our preacher at the Gesù had thundered, 'One cannot make a pact with the devil!' He meant the Constitutional Liberals with whom Mastai was on dangerously good terms. There was a pent silence while the preacher's eloquent eyebrows rose, then descended. 'Even,' he whispered piercingly, 'to defeat a greater devil!' The hush was now breathless. The Party of Revolution was the greater devil.

The church had been crowded and several great families had turned out to show their support for the Jesuits. Silken bonnets and jet-bordered mantillas caught the gleam of votive candles, but the Civic Guard, which was on duty, had to restrain students from the Sapienza University from assaulting the preacher. Another time – this was on everyone's mind – the guards might fraternise. They had been freshly recruited from among the citizens and were dangerously forbearing with the blackguards who continued to disturb the peace outside the Collegio windows.

Sometimes the boys caught glimpses of these. Dark mouths nuzzled the air and the mob's faces seemed stunned by a conundrum. On his election, eighteen months ago, the Pope had promised to improve their lot and now it was worse.

With diminishing optimism, they varied their cry: Long live Pius the Ninth *only*! Down with bad advisers!

So now the advisers were looking for scapegoats.

This was no sillier than their other notions. Take 'progress': a sad trick, said the Prefect of Studies, whereby unbelievers consoled themselves for their loss of faith. It related, he said, to the presumptuous anarchy of Protestantism and other -isms which meant as little to his pupils as the contagions afflicting sheep: Indifferentism, Pantheism, malignant pustules, Febronianism, carbuncular fever . . . 'Ism, -ism,' he lisped and his mouth puckered. Eczema, rabies, mange . . . The Prefect's

65

face was the colour of bone. His hands hung like damp napkins. Was it not clear, he asked, that as mankind had fallen from grace and Rome from greatness, decline, not progress, must be nature's law? How, in this metropolis, which had shrivelled and shrunk within its walls, could that be put in doubt? Did the walls' marooned circumference speak of improvement? Did the fact that ancient Rome had covered three times the present city's site? Cows now grazed in the Forum. Vineyards smothered the approaches to the Colosseum, navel of the ancient city.

'Alas, my sons,' and his damp-damask hands dangled with limp grace, 'we come too late to plot the way our enemies suppose.'

His martyred melancholy caught at their hearts, and they longed to rush out and thrash these enemies – but the essence of martyrdom was *not* fighting; so dreams of giving back as good as you got had to be quashed.

There is comfort in passivity too, and Nicola sometimes surrendered to it during services in Saint Ignatius' Church, where perspectives drew the eye towards the brown vortex of its cupola. The cupola was false. The Jesuits had never got around to building a real one, so torpid reveries were apt to liven into speculation about the technicalities of *trompe l'oeil*. Most of the Prefect's colleagues would have thought this a good thing. Boys' minds should be kept busy and the school day was a system of vents and checks designed to prevent any overheating of their inner life.

Unmixed feelings were dangerous – even family affections. Indeed, to the priests' minds, families, though a necessary source of supply, were propagators of moral contagion for youths who had been insufficiently hardened. Like seedlings, it was a risk to remove them from shelter, and visits home were discouraged. Only during the annual vacation, starting in mid-September, were pupils supposed to go home and, even then, many were persuaded to go instead to the Society's villa where sporting events, picnics and other wholesome activities were on offer. Thus Nicola had not suffered much through being an orphan. That is, he had not until now. And now there was talk of pupils being sent home. Home? To him it was unknown territory. Friends, when questioned about it, mentioned getting up late and eating pancakes. Indolence and gluttony seemed to sum up their nostalgia, as though they too were apprentice travellers in that foreign sphere.

Sometimes, at the end of a vacation, he had glimpsed one of their mothers through a carriage window, crushing her bonnet as she hugged her son goodbye. Then, off she would be driven and, for months, be as

66

remote as the Virgin Mary. 'Queen of Heaven, Lily of the Valley . . . pray for us!' Women were mediators and ambiguous. Real lilies of the valley were modest blooms sold by ragged vendors in the spring: girls from the Agro Romano who wore long gold pins in their hair with which, if you trifled with them, they would, it was said, unhesitatingly stab you through the heart.

Where, if the Jesuits were exiled, would Nicola go? Monsignor Amandi was his only connection outside the Collegio, so Nicola planned to use his Latin address to remind him of himself and, citing the old anagram for Collegium Romanum – *angelo mirum locum*, a place wondrous to an angel – invite him to visit.

It was, surely, time that Amandi told Nicola who his parents were.

The reasons for his lordship's reticence might be painful. Nicola was braced, especially as everyone else was reticent too, including his confessor, Father Curci.

'My son,' he had answered when Nicola brought the matter up. 'You have a family right here.'

'I know, Father, and I'm grateful. But I must have had a real one too.'

'What do you mean by "real"?'

'Blood . . .'

Blood, said the confessor, was a mere animal link. 'If your natural father turns out to be a Turk, will you become a Muhammadan? No? Well then . . .'

Cornered, Nicola admitted that he hoped to be – the word was hard to bring out – loved. This upset the confessor, who asked whether Nicola believed that a man who unthinkingly scattered his seed loved the fruit of it better than the one who chose to devote his life to the care of the young. 'Why,' he asked, 'do you think we are called "fathers"?'

Nicola, dismayed, again mumbled the word gratitude. But Father Curci, now feverish behind his grille, seemed to want more. He leaned so close that Nicola could feel the hot blast of his breath and asked if Nicola wanted to be loved for nature's sake or for God's? Nicola wanted to be loved for his own, but was afraid to say so lest he further upset Father Curci who had excitedly embarked on a discussion of love which managed to be, from Nicola's viewpoint, depressingly arid. 'After all,' said the priest, 'it is the capacity for loving which matters rather than the lovableness of the object. God is the most deserving love-object, yet is often badly loved. Is this not so?'

The topic was hopelessly off course.

Nicola's anxiety swung off at a tangent. 'I'm not the son of the public executioner or someone like that, am I?' Anxiously, he began to recite prayers, bunging them, like stoppers, into a crack which was yawning in his head. Not the headsman, he prayed. Please! *Confiteor* – what sins? Treachery – no, better not mention that one. Intermittently, behind the porous screen of prayers too well known to block him off, he heard the confessor quote St Paul who had, it seemed, told the Galatians that spiritual fathers went into labour to give birth to Christ in their children.

The voice behind the screen rose zestfully and was undoubtedly audible to penitents awaiting their turn. '*Filioli miei*,' it cried, '*quos iterum parturio . . .*' Nicola hoped a destiny was not being thrust on him.

The Jesuits were girding themselves for persecution, one of their specialties. Accounts of their gruesome and gallant deaths in Tudor England and Japan had been dinned into him and, having eaten their bread for years, it would be shameful to admit that, now, when things were again getting hot, he'd like to leave. Especially if he was, as Father Curci claimed, peculiarly theirs. If only he had a family somewhere!

'*Fili mi . . .*'

The confessor's appeal was hard to deal with because he wasn't acknowledging it as an appeal at all. He seemed to be offering some awful sort of love.

Amandi, clearly, was Nicola's only hope. On his last visit, his lordship had actually suggested that Nicola should soon leave the Collegio and spend some time in the world. Later, if he did enter the Church, he would have help in making his way. He need not become a *priest*! Amandi's smile had seemed to mock his own status, but you knew it was mock mockery, meant to make the prospect seem cosy, which it did. The prelacy, said Monsignore, was a true democracy since all a man of merit need do was to put on ecclesiastical dress. No need to take vows even. There were cardinals who had not.

Smiling, he blessed Nicola with two fingers, then turned away. The encounter had been festive but brief, being fitted into the gala occasion of the Pope's June visit, when pope and Jesuits had seemed so pleased with each other – yet, even so, Monsignore had let slip the suggestion that Nicola leave. There had been no chance to ask him anything about this.

In the end the papal visit had gone off like clockwork with just one eruption of emotion when the *Schola cantorum* sang *Tu es Petrus* and the old doorkeeper was heard to weep. Pius had duly distributed the communion wafer to chosen students and Nicola had his three-minute meeting with Amandi. Now neither pope nor bishop looked likely to return.

Seen with hindsight, the display had been an appeal. 'Stick by us,' was its gist. 'You are Peter and we are your brothers in Christ. Don't drop us on the say-so of your new friends.' At several points during the proceedings, the papal guard – brought for security or show? – had sunk to their knees with a ring of metal and a leathery creak.

Five

Nicola had been called to the parlour. It was now almost winter and the sun was low in the sky. His visitor was his milk-brother, Ciccio, on whom he had not set eyes in eleven years.

'Nicola!' Light smeared thick spectacles. The stranger was thin as string. 'Remember me? You must have heard that our foster-mother died. Tata.' Nicola was pinioned in a knobbly embrace. 'I wouldn't have known you. I suppose they'll find you a gentleman's job? I've been working since I was twelve. Pen-pushing. Now even that's dried up.'

Ciccio's coat, pinned at the throat, could be holding in untidy bones. One shoulder rode high and he looked like a damaged specimen from one of those books of fables which show insects dressed as men: the grasshopper perhaps or the ant? Timidly, he paused, as if pondering an oblique approach, then asked if he could see the Rector. Nicola told him that *he* could not arrange this. Disappointed, Ciccio talked again of their foster-mother, as though hoping to tighten their bond. She had died three years ago and, no, he hadn't attended the funeral.

'She used to say that you'd come back one day in a fine carriage and take her for a ride. With emblazoned door panels! You came in one, you see. She was proud of that.'

Nicola could hardly remember the milky woman. She was a blur: warm and slightly sour like an ooze of old cushions. After leaving her, he had spent some years with nuns.

'She said you had a good heart.'

This shamed him. 'How could she know?'

'She put a lot of children through her hands.' Ciccio lowered his voice. 'They didn't pull it off, did they?'

'What?'

'You can trust me, Nico! I had a position of trust. In a ministry. Now newcomers are as thick as fleas, so I left before I was pushed. We took boxes of stuff with us. It's why I wanted to see the Rector. We thought

70

the section would be reformed and we'd be in work again. There were bigwigs interested. Your Rector would know – but it looks as if it's come to nothing, eh?'

'I don't know what you're talking about, Ciccio.'

Ciccio looked downcast. 'Ah well, it was good to see you, Nico.' No longer hoping for help, he had lost his nervousness. Yet his forehead was damp with sweat and he refused to open his coat. Perhaps he had pawned his linen? Nicola had an impulse to detain him. He wanted to ask 'What else did Tata say about me?' Instead, he asked: 'About those rumours . . .'

Ciccio stood up. 'It's not my place to tell. Tata used to say "Ciccio's limited but reliable".' Sadly, his smile accepted this.

'I'm sorry I can't help.'

'I understand. The fathers are preparing you for big things.'

'You're making fun of me.'

'No. Why? I thought you'd be a man now. But *they*'re holding you back. Reserving you. You'll be the better for it.'

Nicola was piqued. He felt that the innocent one here was Ciccio. How *could* he have expected to walk in and get a meeting with the Rector? Why not with the General himself?

'Maybe I'll come again when you're a bishop!'

'That might be a long time!'

'Oh, I've copied letters about babies getting appointments before they're out of swaddling clothes. Drawing salaries!'

Nicola, who saw him to the front door, was ashamed when Martelli stepped from a carriage and stared. He had been home for the autumn vacation and was no doubt making worldly comparisons. As Ciccio crossed the square, he looked more than ever like an insect which had been crushed by a careless foot.

Martelli was full of news of the arguments going on in *clubs* and cafés. Their topic was whether the Pope, whose most recent concession was to set up an Advisory Council composed of laymen, could truly be weaned away from the zealots. Ciccio's hints interested him. 'It *proves* they're plotting,' he cried and Nicola was sorry he'd passed the chatter on. Martelli, at the time of the 'tapestry' – their code word – had claimed to be thinking of the Jesuits' own interests. Now he seemed to have forgotten them.

He denied this. 'Don't you see that to prevent the really wild men

71

from taking over, we must anticipate them. Bring in reforms, take the wind out of their sails!'

'Who's "we"?'

'Santi, we're nearly sixteen! If it wasn't for my shitpot of a father, I'd be active already!'

Nicola was shocked.

'He doesn't want me to see my cousin because he was in gaol. In Bologna, anyone who's been in gaol is a hero. Don't look like that, Nicola. Are you going to be a Jesuit? Even if you are, you'll have to pick sides.'

Would he? The Jesuits themselves denied this. It consoled them to know that, even now, aloft in their Observatory, Father Vico, famous for having tracked Halley's comet, was oblivious of things terrestrial, as he got on with describing the entire visible sky. The Father Prefect had made much of this in his last talk.

The Prefect, said Martelli, had his head in a bag.

The text at dinner was by a man who had opposed the Jesuits until he saw how the Church's enemies united against them. Then: 'A conviction took root in me that there must be some mysterious explanation for the amazing unity among those odd bedfellows, their enemies. Hidden in that intuitive hatred is a conviction that by striking at *them* one strikes the Church at its heart.'

That, said the reader, was from a speech made in the French Upper House three years ago, when our schools in France were being forced to close. The reader then sat down to his cooled meal.

Martelli at once began a voluble conversation and Nicola, who was too far away to hear, was exhilarated by the flash of his eye. Yet the reading too had appealed. Like moths to light, their teachers seemed drawn to fatality. It was an abyss into which they felt enticed to plunge. Sometimes, just before falling asleep, Nicola imagined sliding into it with them and the thrill of surrender crossed over into his dreams.

In more energetic moments, these fancies gave way to ones in which he rushed out into the mob and laid about him with a stick.

Martelli was idly rearranging meat-scraps on his plate. He's reading the entrails, thought Nicola, and felt relieved to find his friend's challenge reducible to a joke.

*

'Souls for God . . .'

'Holiness, you win them!' Amandi meant this. 'Something extraordinary happens between your flock and you.'

Mastai sighed. 'They ask for material things. I fear they'll soon start to see me as the representative for Railways and Lower Customs Tariffs!' His smile was cheerless. 'You and I were accustomed to follow orders.'

'Now you give them.'

'And the advice I get is contradictory. Grassi's, Gizzi's . . .'

Cardinal Gizzi, the Cardinal Secretary, had resigned on the grounds that Mastai lacked fixity of purpose and was impossible to work with. The gossip was that Chancellor Metternich had used Austria's secret veto to stop Gizzi himself becoming pope and was now sorry. Warnings about the Chancellor's state of mind came thick and fast from the nuncio in Vienna, but Mastai disregarded them.

'Why,' he had greeted Amandi today, 'has the Austrian eagle two heads? To gobble its prey faster.' Jokes restored him. 'The dove,' he quipped, 'won't speak through eagles' beaks.' But did the dove speak at all? Advice blasted Mastai's ears. He needed a new St Joan. 'Maybe we should pray for one?'

This was seriously meant. Like a fairytale king, he had asked for news of the visionaries of his realm and was now hoping to learn what was on God's mind – which mattered more than Chancellor Metternich's – from the testimony of two children to whom the Virgin was said to have appeared shortly after his own election.

It seemed that God, like the Chancellor, was angry. Recent crop-failures were a warning and worse would follow unless people renounced blasphemy. 'She said,' Mastai told Amandi, 'that her Son's hand is raised to smite the world and she has been holding it back, but her arm is tired.' The vision had occurred near a small Alpine village and this in itself was a message. God had chosen to speak to the simple. A rebuff for our intellectualists. Mastai relished it. 'We must believe,' he said, 'as little children do.' 'Blasphemy' meant the whole baggage of modern presumption. He agreed with this. His Liberal mentors were insatiable and he would have liked nothing better than to turn his back on them and drive to where the Madonna had appeared to two French cowherds aged eleven and fourteen. She had been floating over a ravine, by a stream whose waters were now healing the sick.

'I said we needed a St Joan. Well . . .' Mastai smiled. What a trial, thought Amandi, if he turned out to be a saint. The thought shocked

73

him. I'm forgetting his shrewdness, he decided. This is a way of extricating himself from the Liberal grip. For a moment, he closed his eyes. Opening them, he found Pius watching him.

'I know what's on your mind. Politics. But I won't use you there.' Mastai's grin split his aimiable currant-bun face. 'I have enough men of reason there. I want you to go to France.'

Two weeks later, having journeyed up the leg of Italy and over the Alps, Amandi reached the parish of La Salette in the diocese of Grenoble. He was dazed by a repetitious effulgence of pale precipices and cataracts as white as horses' tails. Snow, crisp as salt, stung the air, and at one point the travellers had had to leave their carriage, as its horses were harnessed to a sled.

He had removed his violet insignia and dressed like an ordinary priest, even adding the neck bands peculiar to French ones. The local bishop favoured the local miracle and Amandi did not want reports reaching him that Rome had sent an observer. Bishop Philibert de Bruillard, ordained in 1789 – a year to mark a man – had gone into hiding during the Terror, then been spiritual director to Madeleine Sophie Barat, foundress of the Sacred Heart nuns who were widely known as 'Jesuitesses'. Their proclaimed aim was to teach the future mothers of well-to-do France how to keep revolutionary notions from entering their sons' heads, and it looked as though the new miracle's aim was to prevent them burgeoning in those of the starving.

There were plenty of these. The potato crop had failed again and so had cereals. All along the way, Amandi saw fields of rotting stalks and, when his carriage sank in mud and broke its rear axle, he was himself mistaken for a victim of the times.

He had managed to hire a cart to convey his baggage to the nearest inn and, as he walked ahead of it, was surprised by the approach of what looked like a mirror-image of himself. Another priest, wearing a tattered soutane, walked beside a cart piled high with furniture. The winter sun dazzled, and for moments Amandi wondered whether he, like the cowherds, was seeing a mirage.

The other priest raised a hand in salutation. 'Are you another of us, Father?'

The man's face looked tear-stained and now, as though triggered by the thought, wails burst from behind his cart where a woman was

74

hobbling along. She had furrowed skin and darned clothes: a priest's housekeeper or mother? He was young enough for that.

Amandi, sensing a misunderstanding, said he'd had an accident.

He wasn't the only one, said the Frenchman. Thirty-five accidents had happened today. Thirty-five letters had been sent from the episcopal palace, throwing priests from their parishes with scarcely more ceremony than if they'd been thieving footmen. 'We're lucky to be spared the kick in the bum! We'll end sweeping the streets. In the old days we'd have had redress. But since the church courts are gone, bishops are all-powerful. Oh, mother, *stop*! You'll have me crying too.'

The young man's voice had an edge of hysteria. While he tried to comfort the old woman, Amandi observed their possessions. A bucket hung from the cart's tail. There were bedding rolls, pots and a painting of St Aloysius Liquori. All had the humiliated look of objects which need to be arranged just so to hide their blemishes. There was one padded chair. Who got that? The mother? Yes, for her son was fond of her. He was rubbing her hands now and gently shaking her as though in the despairing hope of infusing a little spirit into her.

'I'm making a list.' He turned back to Amandi. 'Will you let me put your name on it, Father? Since the Church denies us recourse, we can try the state. Go to law. After all, we're on its payroll. This is no time for turning the other cheek. The poor depend on us. You *are* one of us?' The youth was seized by doubt.

His mother knew better. Alert as a dog, she had been plucking at his arm to warn that there was something not right about Amandi.

The young man's muscles froze. Then the blood rose in his face. 'I'm a fool,' he acknowledged as he took in the good cloth and cut of Amandi's dusty clothes. 'You,' he supposed dully, 'must be an observer for Monseigneur de Bruillard? His . . .' the word slipped out, 'spy?'

'No.' Amandi felt awkward. He *was*, after all, a sort of spy.

Suddenly, the young priest began banging his forehead with his fist, to the scandal of the two carters who stared reprovingly at this unpriestly behaviour. 'Fool!' The boy banged his forehead.

'Stop!' Amandi caught his arm. 'It's not what you think. On the contrary, we may be able to help each other.'

Later, in a private room in the nearest inn, he and le Père Dubus – the young priest's name – became allies. Dubus had to be wooed from his suspicions; but Amandi, after all, was a diplomat, knew France, knew men, and disposed of the excellent argument that the other had nothing to lose. Neither had the French Church which, for reasons to do with chance and history, needed outside help.

'Outside?' Dubus' mind was slow. He had been up early, packing his depressing possessions, and had just put his mother to bed after feeding her bread soaked in broth.

Now he and Amandi, alias le Père Roux, which was the name on his papers, sat burning their shins at a fire whose heat was mostly escaping up the chimney – like the Church's energies, said Dubus, who believed in applying these to the needs of this world and had on this account fallen foul of his bishop.

Amandi, to establish his independence from the tyrannical Monseigneur de Bruillard, claimed to be a preacher answerable only to the provincial of his order. Which? The Barnabites, a liberal body of men. He was, he said, returning from their house in Rome where a new wind was blowing.

Giving that a chance to sink in, he ordered dinner. He would pay for it and for their rooms, being allowed, he explained, to spend a portion of what he earned from preaching on charity. So a table was brought in and laid with the linen and silver which he, as a seasoned traveller, always carried. In that famine year the meal of thin soup and boiled chicken was a banquet to the French priest. In his parish, he began – then remembered that it was no longer his. He had not been a tenured priest, could be removed at will and, when he organised charity for indigent parishioners, was. His bishop, terrified of organising the poor, saw him as a gamekeeper who had sided with the game.

The two men sat late over their wine and Amandi learned about Dubus who had been brought up near here by his widowed mother. His early childhood had been blissful and his memories were all of streams, clear skies and of fresh branches being carried in feast-day processions, so that the woods seemed to come into the church to pay homage. Then, when he was nine, his mother told him that she had lost a law suit and with it their farm and must go into service in Paris.

The shock stunned them and so did Paris, where they slept in an attic with windowpanes so grey that you could never tell whether the grime was on the glass or in the sky. The streets smelled sour. His mother had to wear livery and when they went to a park, the trees were in wire cages and someone stole her purse.

Months passed. Then one day he heard a hymn. It was the Corpus Christi procession. For some reason – perhaps religion didn't seem part

76

of their new life – neither he nor his mother had been to church since leaving home. Yet here, down in the street, were banners billowing like sails and gleaming crosses and the hymns he had always known.

'It was a vision,' said Dubus. 'I closed my eyes and saw the Alps and three months later entered the seminary.'

It was a satisfying tale. Even the bishop would have liked it. After that, to be sure, there had been a long wait, before Dubus could be ordained and take his mother from her dingy surroundings. The seminary was not in Paris and they hardly met from the day he entered it until his ordination at the age of twenty-four. *That* was the climax of their hopes: that and his assignment to a parish, in their native place, where she could be his housekeeper. This was their Eden and behold they had returned to it. Bliss! Dubus had been two years in his parish.

'You know the rest.'

And had he no prospects? No. His seminary friends were as poor as himself. Did he, Amandi asked casually, know anything of what was happening in the parish of La Salette? Oh, said Dubus, the whole diocese was talking of its miracles and of how the Royal Prosecutor had sent two magistrates incognito to spy. Sighing, he reviled politics, and Monsignor Amandi had to remind him that it was contempt for them which had blinded him to the way men of substance would see his own activities! He should have guessed that they would denounce him to his bishop, an impolitic man himself whose acceptance of the new miracle had led to the Royal Prosecutor's having similar doubts of *him*. The Minister for Justice and Cults disliked popular movements of any sort.

'The people,' Amandi told the young ninny, 'are, in political terms, a powder keg and regimes which ride in on revolution, as this one did, fear it. *Our* function, in the minds of the ministry, is to check this combustive potential by snuffing out any spark which could set it alight. Even religious enthusiasm frightens them. You may not like this, Father Dubus, but you should know it. Christ said "My kingdom is not of this world." He sends us into it as missionaries and we owe it to Him to learn its ways – else how shall we preach His message?'

Father Dubus was despondent. It was that hour when a man's cheeks grow stubbly and his failures loom.

Amandi spoke of a new era and of the Pope who was rousing hopes south of the Alps. He could help men like Dubus. After all, railways and the electric telegraph were here to stay. The world was now smaller and the Pope's reach longer. 'He could defend you from your bishop. Make an appeal and I will see that it reaches him. Give up hoping for help

77

from the state, which has no jurisdiction over your case and sees men like you less as shepherds than as guard dogs.'

Outside the window, a crystalline glitter sugared the Alps. Dawn. Amandi said he would pay the priest a stipend.

'I shall only rarely ask you for services. For now I want you to go to La Salette, stay there a while, make friends and become acquainted with the nuns in the nearby village of Corps, where the two visionaries are being educated. Find out who has access to them and through whom their public statements are made.' All this, said Amandi, was to be written and posted to him with maximum discretion. He gave Father Dubus an address in Rome. It would be a good idea if the priest gave it out that his mother had inherited a legacy and they were living on that. The secret messages – there were known to be two – which the Madonna had given the herders were of especial interest. The herders were saying that she had told them not to divulge these.

'Well,' said Amandi, 'so long as they stay secret, well and good. But suppose Monseigneur de Bruillard were to tamper with them? Put his own ideas into the children's heads and so into others? He could have an incalculably powerful impact. Not just here but in Rome. And we both know what Monseigneur's ideas are.'

When Monsignor Amandi left in the public diligence which was to take him to where he might hire a private carriage, Father Dubus' mother seized his hand, wept, kissed and then dried it with her skirt and said that he was her son's benefactor and she would pray for him as long as she lived.

Amandi retrieved his hand and raised it. The carriage door closed and they were off.

A gentleman in a greatcoat half rose from the seat opposite and introduced himself. Amandi gave his false name: le Père Roux.

'So you know that priest, Father?'

'Not really. We met by chance and dined together at the inn.'

'Dined!' The other man's nostrils quivered. 'On what money? He must be in the pay of the Jacobins! I'm from his old parish. He and his mother are jumped-up peasants of the sort who use the Church to raise themselves from their ordained station in life – ha, ordained is right!' The man's laugh was a gulp of surprise at his own pun. Dubus, he told Amandi, had organised food collections and a co-operative shop. 'Gave the poor ideas. We know the dangers of that! Besides, we guessed from

78

the first that he was stealing half the proceeds *and* teaching them to do the same. He was quite brazen about it. In the public pulpit he said it was no sin for a starving man to steal food. Just think of it! He was issuing a licence to brigands. Anyway, the outcome was that shortly after that a householder fired a warning shot to scare an intruder who was climbing along his roof, and the thief took fright and fell. He was a child: the sort thieves use to send through narrow apertures. His neck was broken. There was bad feeling in the village – but whose fault was it? You tell me, Father. You're a priest.'

Amandi shook his head sadly.

'The evil counsellor's, that's whose,' said the man in the greatcoat venomously.

'Were you the householder?' Amandi risked. 'Did you denounce him to the bishop?'

The man's face tightened. 'Ah, so he told you that? I thought he might have seen me.'

'No, no. I guessed it. I can see how your anger is tormenting you. Underneath it, you must be feeling something quite different.'

'Feelings,' said the man, 'don't come into this. The Church has too much truck with feelings. It's a fad and a weakness.'

Nicola Santi had begun to visit the apartment of a priest who needed a clever student to assist his secretary. The visits were forays into a world of singularity and possible loneliness. For Don Eugenio, unlike the Jesuits, had his own household. Nicola observed it with a zoologist's care.

In its hall were two crackled, smoky portraits of Don Eugenio's parents wearing black dresses and powdered wigs. They were got up like this because the father had been a papal employee who, though free to marry, was, according to the convention of the day, expected to wear clerical dress. The wife may have thought of herself as belonging to the prelacy in a subsidiary way.

The apartment was almost as dim as the portraits. Its windows were made up of small panes of beer-coloured glass. To Nicola, the tinted air seemed thick with domestic promise for it was the colour of the cake which he was sometimes given on arrival. The walls were hung with yellow damask which yielded pleasantly to the touch. Sometimes, surreptitiously, he tried on Don Eugenio's three-cornered hat.

It was in the study, under the eye of a grimy bust of Pope Pius VII,

79

that the secretary, Don Federico, briefed him on what he must know before he could be put to work.

Today Don Federico's lesson was about sealing wax: mode of application, removal of stains therefrom, and dimension of seals. There were six sizes in use at the Secretariat of State to which Don Eugenio was attached. Of these the largest was for official use, the next for letters to a correspondent of a rank below that of the signatory. The third was for a correspondent of almost equal but still inferior rank, the fourth for equals, the fifth for superiors, while the smallest was for letters to a pope or king.

'One makes oneself small when dealing with the great,' explained Don Federico, who was stirred by the order typified in these distinctions. He left Nicola to memorise them.

Picking up a quill pen, Nicola began instead to sketch a letter to Bishop Amandi.

'*Illustrissimus et Reverendissimus,*' he wrote. An earlier lesson with Don Federico had turned on the distinctions between men eligible to be so addressed and those who could be called *Excellentia Reverendissima* or, more grandly, given all three titles at once.

> Despite my reluctance to importune Your Excellency with my humble concerns, circumstances oblige me to ask who I am. Insinuations have led to the perhaps presumptuous conclusion that I might be related to Your Exc . . .

Here his pen made a bashful blot which he at once made into a doodle, thus spoiling the letter which was a doodle too since he would never dare send it. Folding it up, he tore it into bits.

In this bachelor establishment, everyone petted Nicola who was greedy for affection and sought it with shy, thrusting moves. Even small kindnesses encouraged his hopes which throve on very little, just as eggs can be warmed and hatched in an invalid's bed.

He felt able to talk openly to Don Eugenio.

'Your father was a married abate then?'

'Yes.'

'I don't know who mine was. I'm sure it wasn't Santi, the notary. I think he must have been paid to let me have his name. He's dead now. But he never showed any interest in me. Never visited.'

Don Eugenio did not contradict this.

'I've wondered if my father was a bandit or a headsman: someone people think I wouldn't want to know about.' Nicola waited, then: 'Or a priest. I'd be an embarrassment then. And I wouldn't be able to be one myself. They don't want the illegitimate.'

Don Eugenio didn't answer and Nicola began to wonder whether he might be thinking that Nicola thought *he* was his father! *Oddio!* How mortifying! Nicola pretended to examine his shoe. Embarrassment over his error deepened with the thought that it might not be one. After moments of shy, suppressed turmoil, he shot a look at the man's face and was relieved and disappointed by his smile.

'I shouldn't worry,' said Don Eugenio. 'Innumerable illegitimate men have become priests and bishops. Besides, you have Santi's name.'

'You think I should stop wondering?'

'Just be ready to accept what comes – or doesn't. It will matter less soon. You're at the age when young men leave their families, at least in spirit. They fly with their own wings.'

Rome, 1848

It was spring. The Feast of the Epiphany had come and gone. Its lights had smudged the sky with a reflected radiance, and a din of tin whistles floated teasingly into the embattled Collegio. Were they omens? Perhaps, for within days a plague of revolutions was sweeping Europe. First Palermo revolted, then Paris, then Vienna, and when Milan followed suit it appealed for help to rid the peninsula of Austrian rule. Inflamed by example, an invigorated *mobile vulgus* was soon enjoying the mild weather in the Roman streets. Threats to burn the Collegio were again flung in. They were written on scaps of paper wrapped around stones.

'They'll do it yet.'

The porter spoke with zest. A martyr's death offered a man in his nineties the best of both worlds. 'If Austria sends troops to restore order, that lot out there will make a real revolution!' With the side of his hand, he guillotined himself in mime. 'What *we* are is bait.'

'Hark at them.' Martelli cocked an ear. 'They've no idea why they're shouting. The *piazze*,' he said, 'are controlled from certain *palazzi*.' He was disillusioned. It seemed his cousin's friends might be outflanked. Rival groups were fighting for possession of a revolution which had not yet happened.

81

A number of pupils had been withdrawn from the school, but this only made the Father Prefect more exalted. He spoke of those left as 'the faithful'. 'Blessed are you,' he quoted, 'when men persecute you and, speaking falsely, say all manner of evil against you for my sake.' It did not occur to him that this blessing might not appeal to the families of young boys. Once, he raised the knot of his hands to intone: 'Oh God whose only Son annihilated himself to help a world in perdition, should we not accept your will if you decide to annihilate our Society?'

His pupils were shocked. This, surely, was going too far?

Another time, he raised a face bleared with enthusiasm to share 'a cheering thought'. It was this: 'Joseph would never have had to flee with Mary into Egypt if Jesus had not been with them! Is it not the same with us now and an occasion of the most exalting joy?'

'He's soft in the head,' said Martelli.

What had happened to the Church's elite corps? Had it lost all backbone? Even rebellious pupils were disappointed. Their pride was invested in the legend of cunning, powerful Jesuits.

The hope was that the Society's leaders were holding secret talks with the Pope. And when, in mid-March, a Te Deum was sung in the Collegio chapel, everyone guessed that he had promised them support. On the 19th, which was St Joseph's Day, Nicola's division was taken on an excursion outside the city walls. We could not, said the Prefect, stay cooped up forever.

The outing became a celebration. Sweet St Joseph's fritters were selling at open-air booths and the Prefect bought some for everyone. Then the boys wore themselves out playing the strenuous games they had been missing. They were in high spirits, and even the walk back was a pleasure for the air was fizzing with smells from hidden gardens and from the hayricks which were still numerous in the city's heart.

A crowd blocked their way through piazza Venezia, and word went down the line that they were, at all costs, to stay together.

A priest stood on a cart in front of the Austrian Embassy.

'See there!' A woman pointed at a pale patch on the wall behind his head. 'That's where the Austrian eagle used to be. It was torn down when news got here of the revolution in Vienna. The crowd dragged it the length of the Corso, beating it with sticks.'

A man laughed.

'What's there to laugh at?' She was offended. The eagle had been burned in the piazza del Popolo. 'From patriotism!' she told the mocker.

'Well, if that's the extent of their patriotism,' said he, 'the Austrians can sleep on both ears.'

'Austro-Jesuit!' The patriotic woman spat.

Nicola and his friends edged away from her, then found that they were no longer with the rest of their group.

'Who's the preacher?' they asked and were told that he was the abate Gavazzi, a Liberal priest who had the ear of the Pope. But, a dispute arose about this. Some contended that the Pope had imprisoned the abate who had only just been released.

'But if Gavazzi's one of his advisers why would he lock him up?'

'Because the Holy Father's shillyshallying.'

'And has advisers who think differently.' A young man looked askance at the Collegio uniform.

Clutching Martelli's coat, Nicola found his nose being rammed into breasts and backs. An elbow caught him in the ribs. His hat tilted over his eyes. No touching was countenanced in the Collegio and now here was this smothering flesh. At moments, he was pushed out like something newborn only to be reingulfed. This, he thought, is the secular world.

'Stop shoving, you boys!'

But Martelli, propelled by the buttress of his friends, forged forward until, breaking through to open space, they fell to the ground. The crowd commented disparagingly. Hands yanked at their collars. Members of the Civic Guard were lined up around the speaker's cart.

Aloft on it, the preacher loomed full-blooded and muscular, like a creature which could have stood between its shafts. His nostrils dilated. His role was to link God and man, and the movement here was clearly from below. He spoke soothingly. These, he said, of the Collegio boys, were only children. Let them listen now that they were here.

So, with the Guards' grip on their necks, the six had to stay put while the abate used them to instruct his audience. Italian youth, he said, must be helped shake off a bad old heritage. 'Young men,' he exhorted, 'free yourselves from dead ways of thinking lest you be like the corpses who walk our streets pretending to be alive. Try to live as God meant so that we may all be brothers instead of plotters and spies!'

Nicola felt queerly hollow as if what had been most secret inside himself had been pulled out for public display.

'*Sì!*' yelled the *mobile vulgus*, whose embrace was disconcertingly seductive.

So were the abate's arguments as he challenged the Jesuits to stop plotting with Austria. 'I challenge them!' he cried and his eye roamed.

83

'Let them not say that this would be to pander to the world, for the world is no longer the corrupt old world we have known. It has become new, young and hopeful. This, my friends, is truly a time of hope!'

There were cheers. Martelli joined in and Nicola too, though reproaching him with a dutiful nudge, felt exhilarated by the prospect of a young, hopeful world waiting for them both. It was sad, of course, to think of the Father Prefect and Father Curci as corpses and corrupt – meaning, surely, no more than soft like decaying fruit – but how deny that an aura of doom clung to these good, unmanly men?

Meanwhile the preacher was promising an end to poverty. Cheers. More promises. Then shouts so deafening that he had to use the full resources of his lungs and it was as if he were inhaling his listeners' energy with his black, pumping nostrils. Nicola lost track of the sermon which mentioned war and tariffs. The preacher, glowing with sweat, managed to look both bull-like and heroic, which might well have been how Zeus had looked when he took the shape of a bull to woo Pasiphae and beget the Minotaur.

'As God created light by naming it,' cried Gavazzi, 'so shall the cry of this generation restore life to a nation which was once the light of Europe and the world!'

This, though obscure, glowed in the imagination like old coal. Nicola was stirred and so was the piazza which went silent for a pent moment. Then someone called '*Bravo!*', someone else cried 'Now!' and from all sides the word '*Italia!*' began to explode. Mouths jutted. Lips trumpeted and, like birds volleying from cover, the syllables whirred. It was impossible not to join in. Nicola, caught off guard, was like someone whose foot taps to an enemy tune.

'By God, young man!' A floppy old face leaned into his. 'I've prayed for the day I'd hear a Roman crowd shout that! Ten years the Austrians kept me in gaol.' The old man's eyes watered and his jaw shook. 'Ten years of eating soup with cooked worms floating in it! But today,' he touched Nicola's shoulder, 'I feel as young as you. God bless your youth, boy.' The gummy smile was impossible to snub.

'God bless you too,' Nicola answered and wondered whether God or he had turned coat.

'*Viva l'Italia e Pio Nono!*'

Drunk on this man's vision, the random collection of gawkers, agitators and – possibly? – paid demonstrators felt the touch of history. *They* were the Roman people.

Then, disappointingly, it was over. The speaker was whisked off and

84

his admirers faced an empty afternoon. 'Can *we* go too?' Perversely, Martelli defied the exultant mood which the crowd was still savouring.

'It's over, isn't it?' he insisted.

A guard – still dazed – continued to hold him and several people gave him black looks.

Abruptly, Martelli wrenched free. The guard reached for and hit him, possibly by mistake. There was a hubbub.

'It's the Jesuit boys. They've attacked the Civic Guard.'

'To think that at this moment in Milan young fellows are fighting Austrians while these . . .'

Someone hit Nicola on the nose and blood began to flow.

'You,' Martelli harangued the guards, 'are meant to keep the peace . . .'

Nicola wished he would pipe down. A squad of fellows, older than they, hemmed them in between the cart and the wall of the Austrian Embassy. With faltering authority, the guards cautioned everyone and the newcomers began amusing themselves. Slow banter was tossed about like a knife in the hand.

'But I agree with you!' was Martelli's response to a comment about Jesuits. He did too. He was the least 'Jesuited' of their pupils.

But agreement was not wanted. 'Sneaky, eh?' said one of his tormentors. 'Trying to pass for one of us. That's what the Jays teach them,' he told his friends in mock surprise. 'That,' addressing Martelli, 'is how we *know* you're spies.'

Suddenly, the boy next to Nicola was knocked down. There was a lull. Any move now could trigger a free-for-all and the Civic guards were refraining from making one.

The man who did came from nowhere, and, before anyone knew it, had an arm around the throat of the chief lout. His other hand grabbed and held the lout's knife. Astonishingly, he wore a cassock.

'You,' he told the guards, 'look sharp about doing your duty or I'll report you for fraternising with troublemakers. Escort these gentlemen to their school party which is by the Corso. These buffoons,' he tightened his arm around his prisoner's throat, 'aren't worth locking up.' Releasing his victim, he prodded a knee into his spine. 'Disperse. Now. Fast, before I change my mind. And that,' he told the bystanders, 'goes for you all.' Still holding the confiscated knife, he climbed onto the cart to supervise their retreat.

He was a lean man, a bit ungainly with a crooked eye, a long nose and the face of a stone crusader. 'Quick!' he chivvied. Jumping down, he

85

caught up with the six boys as they reached the Prefect of Studies and introduced himself. He was Xavier de Mérode, a novice who until three years ago had been a serving officer with the French in the Sahara. He smiled and the Father Prefect did too, pleased to recognise a man of his own sort in this champion. Mérode? Surely, he must be related . . . And indeed it was soon discovered that they had a distant but definite connection.

Rain, rattling down like staves, now drove everyone into a covered courtyard where the conversation quickened. Nicola, brimming with the stimulus of the day, felt his imagination enticed in a new direction: the Sahara!

The Prefect too had been ignited. Cousinship drew him back to the world: an odd region of it scattered through France where grandmothers tended the flame of memory, prayed for relatives guillotined sixty years ago and turned their châteaux into shrines. 'They mourn their dead saints,' sighed the Jesuit. A class had been consecrated by blood. 'Your maternal grandmother – a Grammont, was she not?'

'Yes.'

Rain lashed the ground outside, and golden horse droppings frothed and leaped. If you squinted they could have been flames.

The Prefect began a game of naming families, matching them like cards in a suit. Had Mérode an ancestor who had died at the siege of Maestricht? Or was it that of Landres?'

'Both! Both!' The novice's ancestors' deaths had conferred panache on half the battlefields of Europe.

The guards stared morosely at this heraldic creature in the crumpled cassock who, it emerged, was also descended from the royal saint Elizabeth of Hungary. One thought of all the church statues which, during this Lenten season, were hidden under lumpy purple cloth. Mérode too could have descended from some niche. He had, he said, attended today's sermon, for a purpose.

'If we,' said the ex-officer, 'do not listen and report what we hear, how will princes keep informed?'

The Prefect looked nervously at the guards and Mérode told them curtly that they could leave.

'Gavazzi,' he said then, 'is dangerous. Last month, as you know, the Holy Father used the words "God bless Italy" in a public speech. Harmless words, one might think. But Gavazzi has been twisting them to mean that to bless Italy is to curse Austria whose presence in this peninsula makes a free Italy impossible. Arguing that the Pope has thereby launched a crusade, he recruits young men to fight in it and then tells the Pope that it would be dangerous to check the tide of patriotism which he himself has unleashed. He's viperous! A snake!'

'I heard,' said the Prefect, 'that they're calling him Peter the Hermit.'

'It's only half a joke. People are enrolling to fight and giving money for his "crusade". A crusade against a Catholic country! Launched by the Pope! It's demented,' said the novice, 'or deeply cunning. Because, such a ragtag army could only fail – and out of failure comes revolution. We in France have seen what the Gavazzis do. They pit the Son against the Father and the Sermon on the Mount against the Ten Commandments. They smuggle revolution inside the Church.'

Six

A breeze blended street smells into something as poignant as a pot-pourri while the ex-ambassador paused to eat cheese-stuffed rice-fritters with his fingers. This gave him intense pleasure. Just now, on the Gianiculum, he had seen a cardinal descend from his crested carriage, refuse the services of three footmen and do the same. Roman noncha-lance! The ex-ambassador had never been able to indulge it until now.

An exile watches his step and His Excellency Count Pellegrino Rossi had been moving around Europe like a journeyman for thirty-four years! Minding your step lest the ground shift was sound strategy, but now it was too late. The shift had taken place and his replacement had been installed in the Palazzo Colonna with a tricolour over the door.

His Excellency whisked crumbs from his waistcoat and tried to remember whether in childhood he had ever eaten fritters in the street. Probably not. Prodigies do not have true childhoods and he, though in his sixties, was aware of a fund of boyishness still rash and urgent in an untapped part of his soul.

The word drew him up. It was much in use these days. So were 'free' and 'fight': buoyant words which revived memories of three and a half decades ago when the prodigy kicked over the traces and bolted. He soon learned to keep his soul well in hand.

The fritter crumpled. Its batter was bubbly like condensing air. He had got his teeth into the radiant Roman day.

Weeds coloured the crannies of monuments and a foreign woman, having set up her easel, was dabbing in watery approximations of this anarchic brilliance.

He moved along. Idleness was alien to him and he had already killed time at Merle's bookshop. It was a meeting place for the lettered whom he had no longer any reason to avoid.

Vacating the ambassadorial appartments had cost him few regrets. His wife, a Geneva Protestant, was not *persona grata* to the papal government, so his three-year residency had been something of a bivouac. Charlotte, obliged to keep out of the way, had claimed not to mind and probably hadn't. Being French ambassadress to the Holy See would not have suited her. Few could be less fit for the role. Watching her, you saw how the Reformation had come about. Not only did she get things wrong, she saw wrong everywhere – even in a cardinal's companionably accepting snuff from his footman's snuffbox.

'It's not what you think,' Rossi reassured. But her mind was no more negotiable than a ledger. 'The cardinal,' he explained, 'does not need to insist on status as a *bourgeois* might.'

'What's wrong with being *bourgeois?*' asked his *bourgeoise* on whom their recently acquired title sat oddly.

'Only that people here are more intimate with their servants.'

To Charlotte 'intimate' meant lewd. She got homesick and, despite remissions – springtime, carnival – only recovered when back in her wholesome Geneva. Rossi understood. One became a hybrid, missing Swiss cleanliness in the scrolled and golden Roman cafés, yet – in his case – yearning, when in Geneva, for Roman ease. Charlotte did not. She complained querulously when here and had not acquired the nous of Roman ladies who knew how to feign abstraction when a gentleman was emptying his bladder into a potted shrub. Her delicacy was as vulnerable to a urine splash as demons to holy water. Thank God she was now enjoying Northern hygiene in the company of their second son. There had been one appalling occasion when some drops bounced onto her dress. At the Princess Colonna's. Memory quailed. He shook his head.

Theirs had not been a love match, so he had no reproaches to make. She had been the companion of his cautious years.

He reached the Caffè Nuovo. Marco Minghetti, one of the new lay ministers, invited him to his table and Rossi sighed at the smeared marble. 'Would you think I was being Swiss if we asked one of these fellows to clean it?'

They took up their usual debate, pausing only when the still smeary table – the waiter's flourish had merely rearranged the dirt – was approached by a cleric whose stoop sagged into a bow. Dottor Vigilio was off his beat in this Liberals' café.

'Bad news, Minister,' he greeted Minghetti. 'A man has been

murdered in Ancona under the windows of the British consul whose daughters witnessed the knifing. It seems he hoped for sanctuary.'

Minghetti looked put out.

'The victim was the unfortunate Lucarelli whom I had the honour to recommend to both Your Excellencies some time back.'

'Lucarelli the spy?' asked Rossi.

'A sincere man who craved the consolation of kissing both your Excellencies' hands.' The cleric granted him ten seconds' silence. Then: 'There are others for whom something may yet be done. Archives have been opened stripping away the mystery which should protect such men. If we use them, can we then deny them?'

'I,' said the minister, 'used nobody.'

'Not you personally, Minister.' Dottor Vigilio smiled mossily.

'I find,' said Minghetti, who had not asked the cleric to sit, 'that half the Treasury's revenues go to parasites who disgorge its vital substance to lesser creatures of their own. Your clients, Dottor Vigilio, probably belonged to the best-paid category we have. We now need money for arms and are at a loss where to look. Will they pay the state back what they milked from it?'

'Count,' the agent turned to Rossi, 'I appeal to you . . .'

'I am a private citizen, Dottor Vigilio.'

'Oh Excellency, that is unlikely to last.'

The young minister was impatient but Rossi relished the agent's perceptible undermining of his own overt discourse. Something as elusive as a tonal shift solicited connivance. You and I, implied this secondary language, are birds of a feather; we live on several planes.

To Rossi, lifelong exile and funambulist, the invitation to volatility was irresistible. Since the Paris revolution brought down the regime he represented, he had been drawing closer to the Roman one. Both Minghetti and His Holiness unofficially turned to him for advice. Weeks ago he, and he alone, had been granted an advance look at the new and grudging constitution – the first ever granted here – while it was still a draft.

'Your Holiness,' he had exclaimed, 'it is not a constitution. It is a declaration of war on Your Holiness's subjects.'

Nothing mealy-mouthed about that! But the Pope published the thing anyway. A neophyte ruler – especially if more bishop than king – needed delicate handling. Had Rossi lost his touch?

As a young refugee his misfortune had had the glamour of a war wound. But wounds, over time, become disabilities, so he learned to hide his and three times made his mark in new territory. After being exiled from Bologna, where he had been one of the law school's shining lights, he had glowed a while in the firmament of the Swiss Diet, then moved to Paris where he could have had a cabinet post if he had not preferred the ambassadorship. *That* had been a coup. Alone among political exiles, he had returned on his own terms! All his roads led here – though in the end it was a near thing. Guizot, his master at the French Foreign Ministry, was now an exile himself, yet here was Rossi, home and dry, with more political nous than any man in the peninsula!

Impetuosity tempted him as it hadn't done since he risked his Chair of Jurisprudence to join Joachim Murat's daredevil bid to unite the peninsula. Thirty-four years ago. Be prudent, Rossi.

He always had been. After that one wild act he became a byword for it. His work on a constitution for the Swiss and in Guizot's government in Paris were – he now hoped – an apprenticeship for his real task: to help glue together the jigsaw parts of his own country: Italy. It would be his youthful dream realised! A prickle of anticipation played along his skin.

He must have smiled, for Dottor Vigilio took this as a cue.

'Gentlemen, I have a new supplicant . . .'

Will Minghetti think ill of me, wondered Rossi, if I encourage the agent?

But now the minister, a man unable to spend his day in cafés, took his leave.

The other two, like a couple left unchaperoned, lowered their voices. The agent's new supplicant was called Nardoni and, like all old spies, he had a file of papers to barter for protection. The agent, moving at a tangent, asked Rossi's opinion on a case in the file. 'It concerns a lady who, while married to one nobleman – let us call him Don X – had a son by Don Z. Certain parties wish to know whether the child has any standing in law.'

'Normally such offspring is assumed to be the husband's.'

'Ah, but in this case the mother chose not to foist spurious issue on him. The child was delivered in secrecy while her lover stood outside her door with a cocked pistol. This lover was a foreign gentleman who returned in time to his own country. The child was bundled out to a foundling hospital and brought up by strangers. Now, however, the legitimate male line is extinct, following the deaths of Don X and his son.'

'And to whom will the family fortune go? I presume this to be the pivotal interest here,' said Rossi.

'There is a daughter who married into a Republican family.'

'So the bastard's sponsors must be – don't tell me – the Gregorians? Well, my answer is the same: a child born in wedlock is the husband's. *Pater est quem justae nuptiae demonstrant.*'

'Indeed. But the mother has scruples. Her former confessor told her that the real sin was in importing alien blood into the family and adulterating the stock. Women who sin can be seized with an aversion for the sin's fruit. The lady's present confessor, a more humane man, hopes to persuade her that her attitude lacks charity. *She* wants to apprise the Pope of her dilemma.'

'And your friends distrust His Holiness?'

The agent turned up his hands.

'You think he is surrounded by bad advisers? Perhaps,' it struck Rossi, 'you wonder about me?'

'Excellency, you are a known moderate.'

'So you are testing me?' The case, Rossi guessed, was no doubt a fiction and so perhaps were Nardoni and his file. In seminaries such cases of conscience were regularly invented to try the resourcefulness of aspiring priests.

'If the case were to come to trial would you think the present climate favourable?'

'To Liberals or Republicans?'

The agent nodded.

'No.' Rossi rose.

'I'll walk out with you.'

Outside, the agent murmured. 'It *is* a real case. I know Your Excellency is discretion itself. It would be hard to win, would it not, if the mother were to declare the boy a bastard?'

'Would she?'

'Who knows? These are strange times. It is probably your duty, Excellency, to save us from the extremes which threaten us.'

'If I did, would they threaten *me*?'

The agent's hands sketched the gestures of a priest offering up the sacrifice of the mass. Perhaps he was offering up Rossi? Returning to the Nardoni file, he whispered: 'Any man who takes power will need information he can use for his own protection . . .'

Rossi interrupted him: 'No,' he said. 'Blackmail is what you're proposing, isn't it? So: no.' He felt elated. Challenge was like wine to him.

A letter had come from Monsignor Amandi. It was addressed to the Rector. Pale fingers folded it into a trumpet, turning the writing from Nicola who would not be shown the contents.

'You're to leave us.'

The Rector looked harassed. He lowered the paper trumpet and began to mumble. A pity to interrupt one's studies. Normally – but where now was normality? The school itself might shortly be closing down. 'Don't forget the principles we have endeavoured . . .'

It was a demobilising speech. Man and boy looked at each other with tired sympathy.

'Pray for us,' said the Rector. The light was silver on the surface of his soutane. The Jesuits wore their clothes until they were too threadbare to be given to beggars.

Tears filled Nicola's eyes. 'I'm sorry, Father . . .' It was the washing out of something he had not had time to quite feel: the quick quitting of a debt. Oh God, he thought – and the tears sprayed. God would be staying here in this target for threats and missiles. It was shameful to be so glad to go.

Before leaving, he divided his few possessions and gave away one or two of the things he liked best: a magic, propitiatory move.

His confessor embraced him. 'I have information for you.' Father Curci drew him into an empty classroom. 'I have discovered who first delivered you to your wet nurse.'

'The bishop . . .'

'It wasn't he.' The confessor's eyes were bright. 'I'm not happy about telling you. At another time I'd wait but we'll soon be packing our bags. Hotheads are pushing the Holy Father into this war with Austria and we're seen, God knows unjustly, as Austrophiles . . .'

Nicola waited.

'Before I tell you,' Father Curci looked severe, 'I want you to remember that anyone living under obedience should let himself be directed under divine providence as though he were a corpse – *perinde ac cadaver*. A corpse or a staff in an old man's hand. Remember that when you see us kicked out. You won't hear a murmur from us. Just

93

remember why when we're maligned by men like Gavazzi. It was he,' Curci paused, 'who brought you to your wet nurse.'

'The preacher? Father Gavazzi?'

'Yes.'

'Is he a bad priest?'

'Who can look into his conscience? He was a prison chaplain in Parma and seems to have been unbalanced by what he saw. Now he'll unbalance others. Letting him loose among the common people is like throwing a live brand into hay.' The confessor squeezed Nicola's hands in his own and kissed him on both cheeks.

Nicola went to take his leave of the Prefect of Studies and found his cell door open and Father Grassi standing at it. He was in mid-harangue. 'Sixty!' cried Grassi. 'Sixty bishops have declared their support fur us, yet the Holy Father will not let their letters be published!'

There was a gentle mumble from inside the cell. The Father Prefect was no doubt in favour of behaving *perinde ac cadaver*.

Grassi was impatient. The Jesuits, he reminded, had been founded to deal with this world and even Pope Clement, when on the point of suppressing them, had said they should not change. *Aut sint ut sunt aut non sint!* 'Remember,' urged Grassi, 'let them be as they are, capable of dealing with the world as it is.'

'By scheming?'

'Using our heads!'

'Profiting by an adultery?' Here the voices sank. 'My sister . . .' groaned the Father Prefect.

Grassi stepped into the cell and closed the door behind him. 'She could,' Nicola heard him say, 'be taken to law!'

After that the argument was muffled. Then Father Grassi came out and strode off, kicking his soutane as he turned the corner.

Nicola said goodbye to the Father Prefect who was tremulous with distress. 'Can you believe that our probable refuge,' he said, 'will be Protestant England?'

Martelli, who was leaving too, was waiting in the porter's lodge. They arranged to meet. Nicola was to spend some days with Don Eugenio, and Martelli would be with his cousin.

The porter had a story about how the Pope had promised to support the Jesuits but – there was no time to finish. As Nicola's carriage left, a glove waved. It looked like a broken hand.

*

News of fighting in the North now held up his plans, for Monsignor Amandi sent word that until things settled he should stay put and Don Eugenio agreed. He had just heard that the Pope had agreed to let a volunteer force from here march to the aid of Piedmont and appointed Father Gavazzi to be its Chaplain General.

'Gavazzi's leaving with them tomorrow.'

'Tomorrow?' Nicola was gripped by disappointment. Supposing the chaplain were to be killed before he could question him.

'Yes. With four of his brothers.' Don Eugenio's tone was mocking. 'Five vigorous Gavazzi off to fight the Austrians! Plus a ragtag of volunteers! A crusade, they're calling it.' He shrugged his shoulders. His Holiness had ordered this. Could we be returning to the awful era of popes and anti-popes?

Nicola explained why he wanted a word with the abate. Was there any hope of this? Don Eugenio said Gavazzi would be at the *Circolo* this evening. It might be hard though to get his attention.

'He's the hero of the hour. He gave a speech in the Colosseum which I'm told would melt stone. More to the point, it stiffened our Mammas who began offering up their sons like Roman *matronae*.'

Not even Nicola's news of Gavazzi's connection with himself could disturb Don Eugenio's phlegm.

Martelli was at the *Circolo* and pointed out celebrities. A greasy-haired, heavy man with a mustache was the famous Ciceruacchio, the people's tribune. Gavazzi was not yet here. An English clergyman, going from group to group, kept asking about the morality of Roman women and whether civil servants objected to the obligation to confess and take communion once a year.

'The *obbligo di Pasqua*,' he kept repeating. 'Will it be abolished?' His name was Archdeacon Manning and he pronounced the letter 't' as though imitating a bird.

People told him that nobody minded the requirement since a certificate of compliance could be bought for a half *scudo*. No, they did not think this hypocritical. Were English civil servants not expected to show loyalty?

But now Gavazzi was said to have arrived. Nicola's heart pounded. 'Gavazzi,' said unknown gentlemen to each other. His name was on every lip. Had he really persuaded the Holy Father to make war on Austria? Now that he was leaving would his influence wane? A schism? Might there . . . Hush.

95

Nicola returned to the hall. By the door stood the man whom he had been told was Ciceruacchio. He had his arm around a young boy.

'This is my son,' he was saying. 'The apple of my eye. But he's off to war. We're sending our best!' The boy did not seem embarrassed. 'Mmm!' said his father, kissing him and making eating noises. 'I could eat him.'

In the next room the abate Gavazzi was telling how he had waylaid the Pope at the door of St Peter's and begged a blessing for the volunteers who were in the Vatican gardens. 'He smiled graciously and came and blessed them. They were all deeply moved. Then I asked for an audience and he told me to come back this evening. I've just seen him now. He was warm and open but said we must not ask for reforms which diminish his authority since he must transmit that intact to his successors.'

The abate's listeners began exchanging anecdotes about the Pope's warm heart. Then a gentleman with a dissenting eye said, 'If he cannot diminish his authority, he cannot grant *any* reforms.'

'That's the ex-French ambassador,' whispered Martelli who had joined Nicola. 'Count Pellegrino Rossi.'

'How can I get the abate's attention?'

The abate was talking of a veiled crucifix which the Pope had given him, saying he was not to uncover it until Italy was free.

'It's not a good moment,' decided Martelli.

The ex-ambassador asked: 'Are our volunteers to cross into Austrian territory where the fighting is?'

The abate frowned. 'His Holiness is reluctant to go so far.'

'In that case, it will be hard for them to join the war.'

To Nicola's dismay, a footman now whispered something to the abate who left the room. He started after him, but had trouble moving past the animated talkers. He bumped into several, then found himself hedged behind three immovable backs.

'Excuse me,' he begged, but the backs did not budge. Beside him was a closed door. He turned the handle, slipped through and into an alcove where Gavazzi was teasing a fellow priest.

'But I *do* listen, Filippo,' he was saying. 'To prove it I'll tell you what you're about to say. You'll say: Don't rely on the good will of the Supreme Pontiff who will change his mind the minute we leave the city. Secret forces are at work. The General of our order wants me suspended. I'll end up in prison. I mustn't preach against Austria. Also, my hair is too long. I don't keep my eyes lowered and my clothes smell.

See. I remember. But what can I do? The order keeps me short of money. Preaching in out-of-the-way places, I have to lodge where I can. I can't afford sheets . . .'

'Alessandro, they're biding their . . .'

'I know, Filippo, and ruining our friendship because – yes?' The abate had seen Nicola. 'Forgive me.' He put a hand on his friend's arm. 'The youth are our special concern now. Are you planning to volunteer?' he asked Nicola.

Nicola, blushing and stuttering, managed to explain why he was here, but as he did so the priests' faces grew chilly. The one called Filippo whispered something to Gavazzi who said, 'My friend asks if you were sent by the Jesuits? He thinks you're a spy.'

Nicola started to deny this, then paused. Trying for accuracy, he repeated what Father Curci had said. The two were sizing him up. Desperate to explain his need he said, 'You asked if I would join up, but how can I until I know who I am? I might have Austrian blood. Forgive me. I know you're an important man.'

The abate asked, 'Haven't I seen you before?'

His friend said, 'He was in the piazza Venezia. I recognise him. Who knows what his masters are up to. They're as mad as wasps! And they think your influence devilish. They're all spies at the Collegio Romano.'

The abate smiled. His friend's anxiety seemed to amuse him. He turned to Nicola: 'See what mutual suspicion breeds.' His tone was mocking. '*Are* there spies in the Collegio?'

'No.' Nicola, seeing the one called Filippo frown, added quickly, 'Well, there's one. I think. A man called Nardoni.'

The faces sharpened. This was serious. Nicola went cold, then hot. What had possessed him? But there was no withdrawing now. He told what he knew. He felt mesmerised, yet untrustworthy.

'You hope,' the abate was forthright, 'to trade secrets. But the one you want to know isn't mine. I deplore this, because mysteries breed scandal. Listen.' He gripped Nicola's arm. 'These are times for looking forward, not back. Your generation will see the fate of Italy decided. That is more important than any individual story. 'All of us alive now are lucky . . .'

'My mother's name. Please. You must know that. Foundlings' fathers aren't always known, but their mothers – who gave you the task of delivering me to the wet nurse?'

'Monsignor Amandi.'

This was circular. Back to the bishop.

'And my mother?'

'The less you know . . .'

'Why? Is she married? Mad? Diseased?'

'She's a nun. In an enclosed order.'

Now the door opened. Several people came in and Nicola was pushed aside. Other people's business was, apparently, every bit as urgent as his own. Forgotten, he walked back to the first room where scraps of argument blew about his head. 'Tooto!' exclaimed the English clergyman whose eye was as wide as an owl's. 'Tootee!'

Nicola collapsed in a chair. Behind him Gavazzi's voice was raised to its rhetorical pitch. 'Christian revolution . . .' it cried.

Nicola burned with fury against everything Christian. An enclosed nun! Shame upon shame! His Maker had botched His job. He wished he could disbelieve in Him. As of course he could. He had been warned often enough how easily faith is lost and now he was drawn to that magnetic nullity. In his mind, even as he sat here, he could begin the process and, slowly, God would cease to exist for him, just as Nicola had ceased to exist for his parents. A nun! Oh Christ, who could the father be? Some convent handyman? They were usually semi-morons, chosen on that account.

The egoism of his reaction began to shame him. It was, surely, a contagion of this loud prideful place – the Englishman was still twittering and Gavazzi declaiming. Painfully, Nicola began to contrast the abate's self-concern with the kindness of the Jesuits. Guileless men in chalk-stained cassocks, they had not, it seemed to him now, produced in all the years he had known them one fourth of the rhetoric he had heard tonight.

The footman, who was carrying their lantern, said there was some disturbance near the Collegio Romano. Ah, said Don Eugenio. One of the mob's little tantrums? No, said the man, from what he'd heard it was serious this time. There might even have been a murder. The city was excitable, as was to be expected, with all the volunteers getting ready to leave for the front.

'Well,' said Don Eugenio, 'we'd best walk home another way.'

Nicola couldn't sleep and was up so early that only Don Eugenio's factotum was about. This old fellow's mind was tottery and his head permanently bent sideways. He was cleaning the hearth when Nicola came on him and had stirred up a cloud of dust. The room was cavernous. Claw-footed furniture gripped the floor and the man's shoes, which were too big for him, looked as though they too might be concealing claws. His stockings were stuffed with false calves which had swung round to the wrong part of his leg.

'You're wondering how I got my crooked neck.'

'No.'

'I was half-hanged is how.'

Nicola had heard this story several times. The reason why Cencio – that was the factotum's name – had been condemned varied but the rescue was always the same.

It had happened long ago, before the French brought in the guillotine: a novelty which would have done for him if they'd had it here then. 'You can't be half-guillotined!' Cencio's eyes popped at the thought. Then he described his great moment in the public square and how, just as the rope was tightening around his neck, he'd heard the crowd cry '*grazia, grazia*' and then '*Viva San Marco*' and thought he was dead and in heaven. Only he wasn't. He'd been saved by the Venetian Ambassador who had happened to pass at the right moment and made a sign to the hangman who, instead of climbing on Cencio's shoulders, cut the rope. Ambassadors had that privilege. But Cencio, being blindfold, understood nothing except that St Mark was being praised. So for all he knew the Venetians had taken over heaven – or hell, because that could just as well have been his destination.

'So the crowd begged him to save you.'

Cencio spat. The crowd, he said, liked a surprise. 'They'd have been as pleased to see me swing. Or topped. Did you know that the guillotine was made famous by a Jesuit? Well, it was. A man called Guillotin. They say the crowd here in Rome killed a Jesuit last night. A message came for you. You're to go round to the Collegio. They're leaving today, so you'd best hurry.'

He handed Nicola an envelope.

'Did you come to gloat?'

Nicola had been seen at the *Circolo* talking to that rabble-rouser, Gavazzi. Father Curci, dressed in layman's clothes, stood on the Collegio steps waiting for a carriage.

'It didn't take you long to turn coat!' The priest was beside himself.

He showed Nicola a letter, saying that he must recognise it, as indeed he did. It was the one Martelli had asked Gilmore to post and then, somehow, himself conveyed to the police. Father Curci, it seemed, had a penitent who worked for them and – but never mind the circumstances. Here it was. Black on white.

'But Father . . .'

'Don't call me that! This,' waving the letter, 'is clearly the source for the lunatic lies told about us last July. Who put you up to it? Martelli's cousin, I suppose. We wondered why his family left him here. Now we know. But you! My own penitent! And your lies have led to a murder! Take a look at your handiwork!'

The priest drew Nicola to where a pinkish mess was smeared onto the side of the wall.

'Those are the victim's brains!' he said. 'The work of the crowd. Your work. They smashed his head there and the Civic Guard either couldn't or wouldn't protect him. I don't understand. For six years you've been my penitent and I couldn't see this venom in you. Well, I can only suppose that God wishes me to see the vanity of human affections. I thank Him for the lesson.' Father Curci's face was alarmingly red. 'Do you hate us?'

Nicola opened then closed his mouth and fumbled for reasons which had seemed cogent once. 'We thought' – how feeble it sounded – 'that the guns had been planted here . . .' But the words lay like stones in his mouth. For Father Curci there never had nor could have been guns. Erect and steadfast, he looked, in the rampart of his borrowed greatcoat, like some figure in feudal armour who could all too easily be felled by mean and mobile men. By me, thought Nicola, and saw that the things he wanted to say could not be said. He had lost another father.

Just minutes ago, on reading Curci's note, he had felt a rush of affection for his teachers and, on learning that the worst had happened, intended offering to help in any way he could. Already others had rallied and the Father General been whisked away in an English gentleman's carriage. He was wearing a wig.

'Come quickly,' the note begged. Clearly written before Curci spoke with his informant from the police headquarters, it must have been dispatched last night. 'We leave tomorrow and must establish reliable contacts within the city. Dear son, I think of you as one of our most trustworthy. L.C. SJ.'

Greeting his confessor, Nicola started to commiserate. But the priest sprang from his embrace. 'Why did you come?' Father Curci's eyes were bloodshot. With bent head, he peered through thick brows like a beast gone to cover. Pointing at Brother Pietro's lodge, 'The corpse is in there,' he said.

As if accepting his confessor's last penance, Nicola went in and saw a body with a mashed head lying on Brother Pietro's table. There was no sign of the porter himself. Two policemen sat in his place. Looking at the dead man, he recognised him as the one who had asked him to post a letter for him last June.

'Who was he?' he asked the policemen.

But they would say only that they were waiting for a police carriage.

Did Father Curci not wonder what the man had been doing in the Collegio? Or, *perinde ac cadaver*, did he ask no questions?

And now a carriage did come. Not the police carriage but one to take Curci and several other disguised Jesuits out of the state. In their borrowed greatcoats, it struck Nicola that they looked like orphans. They waved, but not to him.

Leaving the square, Nicola bumped into someone. It was Ciccio, looking more squint-eyed and broken than ever.

'Did you tell the Jesuits? Was it you?' Nicola, remembering that Ciccio had worked in a ministry, began to shake him. But the small man evaded his grip. He didn't pretend to misunderstand.

Why would he tell them now? he asked reasonably. The Jesuits were finished. He was glad he hadn't seen the Rector that time. And as for denouncing Martelli and Nicola, why would he? They were known, he said admiringly, to be in with the new powers. They'd played their cards well. He, alas, had not.

'That's why I came. I wonder,' he asked hopefully, 'could your friend, Martelli, put in a word for me? I have,' he promised, 'something to tell which will interest him.'

Since neither had money for a café, they walked about, heading first for the meat market where a dog gnawed at some fur and another lapped at a gutter. Further on was the marble torso of Pasquino. There were no papers stuck on it today, perhaps because censorship had been relaxed.

Ciccio's tale centered on the guns which had been removed from the Collegio last June. They had reached the police during an interregnum when some old employees were still around and new ones already come, yet nobody wanted to take decisions until they saw how the political cat would jump. The upshot was that the guns had been hidden, then lost.

Ciccio, his face quivering as though it, like the carcasses in the San Eustachio market, had been flayed, explained that the ministry where he had still been employed had been in disarray. Papers were getting shuffled around and humble pen-pushers getting to know more than they should.

On they walked, winding like Ciccio's narrative, and came to the piazza Montanara, a meeting place for country folk, where scribes rented their skills to the illiterate and there was a smell of donkey droppings. Red aprons. White head-dresses. Peasant girls and agricultural implements. A barber cut swathes of lather off a customer's chin and Nicola realised that he was being offered the guns. What, he thought, could I do with guns?

'I need help,' explained Ciccio who was out of a job.

'Maybe Don Eugenio could use you?'

A thought stirred in Nicola's mind. Gavazzi needed guns. As army chaplain, he was already fund-raising to try and buy some.

Martelli, on hearing of Ciccio's offer, rushed Nicola to the Barnabite convent of San Carlo a Cattinari, where the abate was saying his last goodbyes before setting off with the troops.

'What have you to lose?' he asked, when Nicola hung back.

The abate, euphoric, with a tricolour crucifix on his chest, was packing and trying to rid himself of a hanger-on.

'Try Padre Ventura,' he was saying. 'He has His Holiness's ear. I'm leaving. I respect you, Don Mauro, which is why I won't give you false hopes.'

Martelli whispered something to him and the abate looked interested. Beckoning the man he had addressed as Don Mauro, he murmured in his ear, then turned to Nicola.

'Don Mauro,' he told him, 'is from the same part of the country as Monsignor Amandi. He will tell you, at leisure, more than I could last night. You were conceived in turbulent times and now the turbulence is back. Perhaps God has marked you out to take part in it? Your friend tells me that you have assistance for us. Good. Christ is suffering in the persons of our beleaguered brothers who are struggling against tyranny. It is our duty to come to their aid. After all, His Vicar is with us, so how can we have doubts? Don Mauro too needs help. You might recommend him to your patron. God bless you both.' The abate took both their hands in his, then turned briskly away. He had many calls on his attention.

Don Mauro, a small, vaguely clerical-looking man, smiled at Nicola. 'We have been given short shrift. I lodge at the Palazzo Spada in the apartment of an English lady called Miss Foljambe. My days are utterly idle. Come tomorrow if you like.'

As Martelli and Nicola walked through the Barnabite convent, priests gathered to stare at them. Clearly the abate's visitors were a source of scandal.

'Who is Don Mauro?'

'A defrocked priest.'

'What did you tell the abate?'

'What Ciccio told you. How to get the guns.'

Nardoni's smashed face came back to Nicola. But it was too late to worry about him. Since infancy, he had been praying at the end of every mass that God should thrust Satan back down to hell. Now the Austrians were to be thrust back to Austria. Guns would be needed.

'Shall we watch the troops leave?'

'All right.'

Martelli warned that they were a bit of a ragtag. 'But the useless ones will drop off as they march north. And they'll be getting some training.'

And they'll get our guns.

'Yes.'

After the troops had left, they stared at some gentlemen who, in honour of the martial occasion, had pinned decorations on their frock coats. Martelli, *sotto voce*, quoted the lines:

> So here's what's new in Fortune's pitch and toss
> The thief's no longer hung upon the cross!
> While Mary weeps and Jesus grieves,
> Crosses are hung on clever thieves!

They were still loose in the city when the Ave Maria bells rang and windows began glistening like mica in the darkening air. Martelli, drunk with such unwonted freedom, confided that he planned to fake his age and join the troops up north.

Seven

Old grime filtered the light and the air was the conniving colour of weak tea. Count Pellegrino Rossi sat in a spice shop patronised by returned emigrés. Earlier, finding himself heading for the Quirinal Palace, he had done an about-face and, returning to the Corso, avoided the places which ministers were likely to frequent. A man without a position could start living by proxy.

The spice shop was austere. Blue and white jars lined the walls. There were benches, three tables and a newspaper on a stick. Sunlight, like other frivolities, stayed outside. Some faces looked familiar. All looked purposeful. Like himself, these men hid their idleness. They also looked damaged and he felt ashamed of his distaste.

An ex-priest moved from group to group with a diffidence, and perhaps a hidden arrogance, learned in the seminary.

'*Monsieur l'Ambassadeur?*'

'Sit down, Father.'

'Not "Father", Excellency. I was defrocked.'

'So was I, Don Mauro. I am only an honorary Excellency now.'

'So the days of diplomacy are over?' Sliding onto a bench, the ex-priest fixed Rossi with needling eyes. 'Did you see Ferrari's piece in *La Revue Indépendante*? Someone smuggled me a copy. "Diplomacy," it says, "that empty science of interests, has been abolished. The question of liberty must now be put first."' Don Mauro's face was pale with concentrations of pink. Ill, thought Rossi, feverish. His coat covered him like an unfriendly shell. It was gaudy with bold tartan checks.

'A glass of wine?'

'No, no!' The priestly hands might have been turning it to blood. The man leaned forward. 'We're one revolution behind France. Since February. Ferrari says, "Italian reformists are merely shoring up enlightened despotism." It's too late for that. Do you agree?'

'Here in this spice shop, it sounds well enough, but a revolution would meet obstacles. Austrian bayonets perhaps.'

'Oh, indeed, the national question comes first. Mazzini says so.' The ex-priest cited his authorities as he must once have cited scripture. Rossi thought: how dare I despise him? It was the words' source he disliked. He had met Mazzini once in an exiles' *trattoria* in Ostender Street, London, and thought him woolly-minded.

Don Mauro leaned close. 'Surely France will help? Now that it's a republic?' Pleading, as though with Rossi with whose services the new republic had dispensed.

'What if the worst happens? Do you,' Rossi could not forbear mockery, 'expect Resurrection to follow the Crucifixion?'

The ex-priest flinched. 'My new faith is weaker than the old.' Exile had tuned him too finely. The count sensed a tormented effort to reach – what? Perhaps he was merely watching a dim mind struggle with its limits? 'Count,' came the appeal, 'if you saw hell all around you, would you not think *any* move to save those in it better than none?'

'Hell?' Rossi edged away from this raging nucleus. The hurts he had had the luck to escape in exile were incarnate here.

'I believe you know Monsieur Lammenais?' Don Mauro's breath was sour. 'It was he who gave me the courage to think this.'

'Monsieur Lammenais is changeable. What is he saying now?'

'That universal reason, that common to all men, cannot err. Well, I think he says that. I myself am a doer, not a thinker.'

'Can one divide the two?'

'Oh yes. The man who acts stops hesitating. Thought is hesitation.'

Rossi was struck by this. Don Mauro's story came back to him. He was one of those men who pass their ordinands' exam by learning Togni's manual off by heart, then spend their lives in rural parishes, hunting a little, growing tomatoes and playing cards . . . What went wrong?

'Monsieur Lammenais . . .'

Another unfrocked priest! Rossi had met him in Paris in General Pepe's house. Amused, he relished the memory. The General was a card. Comical. Affable. Forever quoting memoirs in which he referred to himself as a hero. Turgenev used to visit too, and Madame Sand, the novelist, and Lammenais whose ideas had the distinction of having been condemned in two encyclicals. Don Mauro would not want to know that, after perorating brilliantly on various topics, his mentor told Rossi, 'I mean what I say, but sometimes it strikes me that I may be insane.' No wonder, thought Rossi, he sought an infallible guide! First it was the Pope. Now it's universal reason.

'Why were you exiled?' The count wondered if he was breaking some rule of refugee etiquette. 'I,' he offered, 'was unwise enough to sign proclamations. Ink, as they say, can convict you.'

'Oh, Signor Conte, your story is well known.'

My story, thought Rossi, is that I wrote rhetoric for Murat, that bogus Italian who, like his master, Bonaparte, wooed and raped our peninsula, then left his rapist's seed to burgeon: the idea of nationality. I helped scatter it.

Don Mauro admitted to a crime of action. 'How could I desert my parishioners when they were preyed upon? I was their shepherd and the others were – *Centurioni*. I had, it seemed to me, no choice. My bishop saw it otherwise.' Don Mauro's smile was a wound. He had been condemned to death and ceremonially defrocked. He described the ritual: an ordination in reverse which had, he claimed, left him, even now, less than alive. 'I couldn't, you see, be executed as a priest. The bishop had to snatch the chalice from me. With the host. Then I was stripped of my vestments and given a blow on each cheek with the stole as a sign that I had betrayed the gospel. They scraped my thumbs and tonsure to remove the holy oils. Two days later, the prison was seized by rebels. I was in a numb trance, and when I came to my senses, was in Marseilles where they had fled, taking me with them. I hadn't a word of French. Signor Conte, men like me look to men like you. Hope is abroad again. The Pope's subjects are free the way deer are free in a park. Do you see how intolerable that is? A facsimile of freedom.'

'I'm not in power, Don Mauro. I'm not even a citizen.'

'You will be.'

For a moment the little man had communicated his anguished state – or a mimetic moment of it. Then Rossi recovered his sang-froid. A bit mad, he thought. No wonder. That appalling ceremony. What a loathsome regime the Church had run here. He looked sadly at the wrecked creature in the tartan shell. Don Mauro kept rubbing his hands. Like Pilate or Lady Macbeth. But he had picked up the wrong gesture. *His* hands had been scraped clean.

'Do you need money?'

Don Mauro refused. 'This city,' he said, 'extends more charity than any other. Fair is fair, the deer in the park have to be fed.' Laughing for the first time, he rose.

*

Don Eugenio took Martelli and Nicola to a puppet show to see a play about a priest from the border with the Duchy of Tuscany. 'Great smuggling country,' he told them, adding that the priest had smuggled wanted men and saved many before being caught and forced into exile. 'He's a new sort of hero. It seems that we need priestly heroes now to show that the Church has always been on the side of the downtrodden.' Don Eugenio's voice was impassive.

Jumping shadows from oil lamps and the musty warmth of the little theatre roused their spirits. Walking in, they passed a man snoring in a corner.

'That's the censor.' Don Eugenio explained that the theatre management always got him drunk.

The air was muggy and the floor crackled with the spat-out shells of sunflower seeds. All this, however, was forgotten when the performance began with a story about Charlemagne's knights. The puppets, cunningly manipulated by strings, wore perfectly articulated suits of armour. They even rode horses and wielded swords with which they triumphantly skewered infidels.

Then the new play was announced: *The True and Veritable History of Don X, the Smuggling Priest.* A puppet in clerical black bounced his horse over the 'salt road' which was the name of the tracks along which goods were carried to avoid customs duties. Others burdened by bags sneaked a zigzag course across the small stage: smugglers. People cheered them for breaking a bad law. 'We shouldn't have internal borders,' yelled a man sitting close to Nicola. 'Look at the shape of the peninsula!' He drew a boot in the air. Chop it up and how could it advance? Everyone laughed.

Meanwhile Don X's horse looked alarmed. His ears twitched and, turning his head comically, he showed the whites of his eyes.

'Look out!' warned the crowd. The customsmen were coming. *I finanzieri.* A chase. Shouts. Shots. But the puppet priest outwitted them and, in a humorous interlude, baffled the gendarmes who came to his presbytery to interrogate him. Later, he was denounced by a spy and a cage closed over him: prison. His horse wept. Then came a new, liberal pope and proclaimed an amnesty. The cage was whisked off and there was the gallant little puppet reunited with his horse. Bowing to the audience, they cried *'Viva Pio Nono'*.

'That could not have been put on last year.' Don Eugenio applauded with the tips of his fingers. 'Rightly perhaps? People take advantage of the Holy Father's good heart. I brought you here,' he told Nicola, 'because Don X is Don Mauro whom I know you are planning to see.

Everything is known in this city. Bear that in mind. He lodges with an English lady who is said to be a spy.'

Miss Foljambe tried to keep her lodger cheered up.

His blunt fingers inexpertly stroked her cat. They were black-ribbed and reminded her of freshly pulled carrots. 'I have no conversation,' he apologised.

To fill silences, she found herself saying more than she had intended, mentioning her limp and explaining – why on earth? – that she had never desired marriage.

He looked attentively at her, seeing, she supposed, a pleasing young woman with a copper-coloured plait wound around her head, a neat waist and a sensibly discreet, grey crinoline.

'Surely you could marry if you chose?'

'Because of my money?' Her harshness was for foolish ghosts. 'I do not choose. Private life can be a prison.' She did not wish to shock, but what was the point in opening your house to a man beyond the pale if you could not yourself overstep? He had heard confessions. He must surely understand more than her Roman friends who were baffled by her failure to buy herself a man. One or two had advanced the suit of a biddable nephew or cousin: good-natured youths who would cherish a wife richer than themselves without wanting to even the score. She was, she told him, clear-eyed.

'Ah,' said he, surprising her, 'that could be a mistake. People's prejudices bind them together. If you strip them away, they're confused and unhappy.'

He was teasing her. Or else lacked independence of mind, as Roman Catholics often did. She worked a half inch of her *gros point* before recollecting that he had suffered for his.

Did she not, he asked, miss having a family?

She, who had come here with her mother precisely to escape the tyranny of family, was vexed. Did bullying penitents in the confessional – an institution which it gave her goose flesh to think of – produce such indiscretion?

'I am alone,' he said, so candidly that she warmed to him again. 'The Church was my family. But I was put out of it.'

'So now you could have an ordinary one.'

'No. The family would know they were second best: worse, an impediment.'

His dilemma interested her.

'If I am reinstated,' he mused, 'my voice will have some power. This is a time when we can hope, at last, to act.'

'Against your Church?

'I don't see it as against.' He had begun to glow. She knew he was a Liberal and had an inkling that this, here in Rome, might be thought heretical. Her own church, being so regarded, was situated pointedly outside the city gates. The glow stimulated her. It was the connection she sought with men: fiery and disembodied. Adam's fingers in the Sistine Chapel were picking up just such a charge.

However, it flickered out and the cat must have felt this too, for it slid off the lodger's lap.

It had struck her that a priest might incur blame for lodging with her, and she had raised the matter with the consul before agreeing to let Don Mauro use the upstairs flat. The answer was not to worry. Trivial rules were not to the point. Radical priests would soon either triumph or lose definitively. Her own government, she had been allowed to guess, was playing these men like cards.

Politics had tantalised her ever since her tomboy phase when Papa used to praise her pluck and fascinate her with speeches pitched above her head. It had been years before she knew that he could as happily have tried out his oratory on his gun dog.

God or the Pope must have let her lodger down in some similar way. He was said to have been a man of action, though he had a tic in his chin like a bubble in gruel and didn't look you in the eye.

Disappointment – never explained – had caught up with Papa too and led to his retiring to the country, where, for a while, he amused himself by teaching her to jump perilously high fences and protecting her from Mama's remonstrances. Then, quite suddenly, he handed her over to their adversary and seemed to think of her as one too. No longer a surrogate boy, she was no good as a girl and her limp – from a fall at one of the fences – exasperated him. He kept away while she fumbled through the hoops which Mama was obliged to raise for her. A dancing mistress was heard to say that her name was apt – 'Madleg Foljambe!' the woman had quipped cruelly – and although Miss Foljambe was hurt, she did learn to dance, more or less, and also to laugh at herself.

'If you become a great man, Don Mauro,' she said, 'I may figure as a footnote to your biography. Foljambe of the footnotes: a syllable from scandal. Footnotes instead of footlights,' she annotated. But he didn't smile. Despite exile in Manchester, his English was poor.

And he was preoccupied. 'If a man had a public mission . . .'

Confessor to a confessor, she danced in her head. This was sheer stimulus – or would be if Don Mauro could bring himself to talk without mincing matters. It seemed he could not.

Patiently, she went on with her *gros point*, knotting threads and waiting for light to break. He spoke of the discredit which could be brought on the cause if its supporters were not seen to be above reproach. Liberal priests must not give scandal . . . Did he, she asked timidly, mean himself. No? Ah!

'Yet in a way I do. You see I could prevent a scandal – take it, that is, upon myself. The institution must be protected, even if it becomes a Moloch.'

'Moloch? You mean the idol to which children were sacrificed?'

That startled him. 'Children?' He looked flustered and was perhaps going to pieces – as happened with Papa who, after years of tyranny, ended up shamelessly dependent. He whined. Whined! Yet when Mama, as a young bride, had run home to her family, he hauled her back and locked her up. A court case taken by *her* father failed on the grounds, said the judge, that hard cases made poor laws and he would not condone the flouting of a husband's authority. After that, Miss Foljambe was born and trapped Mama for good.

'If you mean the institution of the family,' said she, 'I would sacrifice nothing to it. Not a thing.'

At the end, her delightful riding companion became a dribbling wreck whose disease, said the doctor, was best not named. Once, unmistakably, he attempted to get his hand under her skirt.

Her lodger, she surmised, had a mistress. Possibly bastards whom, of course, he *must* give up. Archdeacon Manning, who had been subjecting the Romish Church to scrutiny, believed that the present pope was strongly opposed to laxity. Don Mauro's cause would founder if he had such complications. Perhaps, as he had been living in exile, the complications were conveniently abroad?

Don Mauro welcomed Nicola and introduced him to a lady whose name appeared to have no vowels: Flljmb. She stared at him in a way which set his mind whirring, then gave him a glass of port. Could she be his mother – no, *she* was supposed to be a nun.

He hoped Don Mauro recalled that he was to discuss her.

'1831 . . .' Don Mauro spiralled away from the topic – though maybe not? It was the year of Nicola's conception. 'France . . .'

Tremulously, Nicola emptied his glass and wondered if his mother could be French. His throat was painfully dry.

'General Lafayette . . .'

Nicola asked nervously if he might pour himself more port. Ms Flljmb had left the room. Don Mauro shuffled foxed papers. A cat lay nose to tail on an overstuffed chair. Its stomach throbbed and it struck Nicola that the apartment was made in its image: furry with pink ruchings and padded curves.

For something to do, he picked up the beast which leaped away with plump agility then began to play with a bell connected with a bell-pull several floors below. Someone was clearly pulling it, for the bell, though stuffed with tow, began to vibrate and, as the cat extracted the stuffing, to ring. The sound seemed to Nicola to be coming from his own head.

Don Mauro, ignoring it, continued to reminisce. History poured from his mouth which sported a black tooth among yellow ones, like a paternoster among aves. Because of this, his mouth seemed to wink, but his eyes were sad.

'Hope,' he said, 'is the climate of our story. You must try and imagine it. Hope and panic. Listen to the oath taken by the Grand Elect of the Carbonari Sect. Mmmm,' he mumbled, '". . . and if I should have the misfortune to break this oath I consent to be crucified in a cave . . . stripped and crowned with thorns as was done to Christ our model and redeemer. I agree too that while I am still alive my belly shall be ripped open and my guts and heart torn out . . ." Do you think this was play-acting, youg man? It was terror. People were trying to ensure that their friends would stick by them in spite of their fear of the regime . . .'

'And my mother . . .?'

'Wait.'

Outside the window were roofs. Terracotta tiles overlapped like the scales of a fish. A pigeon preened. Don Mauro talked of villas where gentlemen conspired. He had travelled from one to another, carrying correspondence or guiding refugees.

'People despise such activities now. They say we achieved nothing. I say we were preparing what's happened since. If you want the butterfly you must first have the worm.'

Even the Duke of Modena had conspired. A world of stealth, nocturnal sessions, rumour and disguise was described by Don Mauro and half imagined by Nicola, whose head was affected by the port.

Somewhere along this narrative, revolution broke out. The Duke panicked, denounced his confederates and sent for the hangman.

'There was no telegraph then,' reminded Don Mauro, 'and rumours ran riot.' A cardinal was kidnapped. Legates fled. And in the diocese of Spoleto a motley lot of refugees converged on a Capuchin convent in the mountains. There were far too many for the convent to house, but the monks lent them their barns and outhouses and hayricks and they stayed there for some days to hide from the marauding troops. 'Among them were some nuns and a girl who was put in their care. She was a cousin of your patron, Monsignor Amandi. In the confusion someone – nobody knows who or even how many people – forced her. Nine months later you were born.'

'Didn't she name anyone?'

'No.'

'Was she a moron?'

'No. Ashamed. Stunned? Hysterical perhaps? Anyway, she seemed to forget the experience later and the nuns let it drop. It was a mad time. You could say you were born of the revolution. Father Gavazzi, who travelled around preaching, did Monsignor Amandi a favour by bringing you to the capital. Your mother became a nun. She is not accessible.' Don Mauro looked sad. 'Especially not to you. Ill-disposed people could dig up old gossip. Father Gavazzi is in the public eye and so is Monsignor Amandi. It would discredit them if it were thought that either of them was . . .'

'My father?'

'There is nothing but malice behind such talk. But the abate did not want to be seen speaking to you at too much length.'

'*Is* my mother sane?' He had to know.

'She is more than sane. She may be saintly. These things are – elusive.' Ruddiness glowed patchily on Don Mauro's face.

'A saint?'

'Some say so.'

'How horrible!' This too broke out despite himself.

'Yes.'

Nicola, who had expected to be contradicted, said primly, 'I don't think I meant that.'

But Don Mauro had the bit between his teeth. His voice shook as he cried that the story conformed to a hateful pattern. First came the fall, the breaking of a spirit, then the forgiveness which ensured submission. Sanctity as abasement. The image of the Magdalene wiping Christ's feet with her hair said it all. Woman's glory, he ranted, became a foot-rag.

Bubbles of saliva hung on his lip.

Nicola asked whether Monsignor Amandi would approve of Don Mauro's talking like this.

'Why not? I can be disowned, you see. We are between orthodoxies and it is better I speak rather than someone who could embarrass others.' A smile tripped on the assymetry of Don Mauro's teeth. Nicola guessed his nervousness to be stoked with pride.

'Was my mother some sort of . . . revolutionary?'

'No.'

'But *you* were?'

'I was a priest trying to love my neighbour. Can one be responsible for a man's soul and let his body be destroyed?'

'I suppose not.'

'Bravo. We lived under an unjust papal government. If the salt lose its savour wherewith shall it be salted? God forgive me if I'm wrong. I hope this present pope will let me be reconciled. The last one wouldn't and my bishop made an example of me.'

This load of adult grief frightened Nicola. He looked at the priest's pained mouth and felt ashamed to be young and intact.

'I'm sorry,' he said.

'You're a good lad, Nicola.'

'No.'

'No?' Don Mauro laughed. 'Ah, you've been thinking ill of me, is that it?' Shrewd-eyed and at bay.

Nicola must have blushed.

'Don't worry.' Don Mauro kissed and absolved him with a blast of appalling breath. 'I had thought,' his smile revived a lost, convivial, hard-riding, outdoor man, 'of pretending *I* was your father. It would stop mouths and prevent trouble – but I couldn't do it to you, lad. You'd have been too unhappy, eh?'

Taking in Nicola's discomfiture, he closed one piercing, bloodshot eye. 'We have to have some thought for the individual, don't you think? After all, the institution's not a Moloch!'

Gently, he squeezed his shoulder.

After Easter, which fell on 23rd April, Don Eugenio arranged for Nicola to travel north and meet Monsignor Amandi at his brother-in-law's villa near Bologna, which turned out to be an old haunt of Don Mauro's. The Villa Chiara? Home of the Conti Stanga? The old smuggler remembered it well.

Nicola, coming to say goodbye, found him suffering from eczema and hope deferred. The tic in his cheek kept burrowing deeper.

'You'll be travelling some of the same route as the troops!'

He spoke enviously. There was no question of his leaving Rome. The Pope had not agreed to see him and he must keep up the siege. He had been watching the political weather intently for, as he told Nicola, even fleas suffer in a conflagration and his hopes were tied to those of the Liberals.

The Pope too was said to be in great agony of mind. A manifesto, issued by one of his generals, containing the words 'God wills it!', had turned the deployment of Roman troops along the Austrian border into a crusade and committed God and His Vicar to making war on Catholic Austria. An unheard-of thing! To send in the troops could provoke a schism and to disown the general a mutiny. Yet how keep our men idle while fellow Italians fought? What could Pius do now? Don Mauro hung around tobacco shops and clubs, picking up rumours then brought them home to Miss Foljambe, who took a sporting interest in all this.

The English were cheering for the Liberals and Miss F hoped the dear pope would grasp the nettle and send in the troops. However, the signs pointed the other way. Mastai was thought to be suffering from a paralysis of the will due to Austrian protests.

Don Mauro's bad luck dazed him.

'I was advised,' he confided, 'yesterday to take a rest cure at a spa.' He hissed the word: an insult which could – Nicola saw – have been kindly meant.

Don Mauro's eyes called out for cover: bandages or eye patches. They had the inturned burn of a man whom life has over-tested. He said he must pen a note to Father Gavazzi which Nicola should deliver. 'He'll make Bologna his headquarters for a while. It's a good place to raise funds for the troops, so you'll find him there.' He withdrew to write his letter.

Later, he walked half way down the Corso with Nicola whose last glimpse of him was outside Merle's bookshop where he would spend the next few hours sifting rumours and peering between the uncut pages of books. He was wearing his round layman's hat.

*

114

Nicola left the city in a roomy posting coach which swayed nautically through damp streets. A watery sun emerged, and housefronts in yellows, cinnamons and maroon steamed like cooked crabs and gave off a reek of brine. An unstable image of St Peter's swung in, then out of, view, as they crossed the Ponte Molle, the bridge beyond which, it is said, the world stops for true Romans. Passengers loosened their coats and belts.

A lawyer took charge of the conversation. The Campagna, in his opinion, should be ploughed. Dug. That would release the poisonous vapours which caused malaria and agriculture could become intensive and profitable. 'Open it up!' he cried of the lands which stretched on two sides of the coach like a monotonous, russet sea. Local labour, he noted, was unobtainable and only desperate migrants from the Abruzzi were prepared to work this pestilential earth. Nicola was reminded that his wet nurse's husband had done so and died.

Looking out he saw nothing but goats, grey oxen and a crumbling aqueduct. He fell asleep, rocked by the motion of the coach, and when he awoke the distant mountains had turned blue. Men in long cloaks passed in the distance. Shepherds? Some time later he saw a line of mules tied together by their tails.

'We're a country of carnivals and footmen,' spat the lawyer, furious because someone had used the word 'picturesque'. Why, he raged, were only the ruined and rotten worthy of being put in a picture? Industry was what we needed. Factories.

When the coach pulled in at Civita Castellana, Nicola whose rump felt as if he had been sitting on walnuts was glad to stretch his legs. He found hospitality that night in a convent, and next day had the excitement of seeing the troops from the Kingdom of Naples trudge north. There had been no rain here and their boots raised white dust so that they looked like an army of pizza-makers. The coach passengers dined at Terni and spent the night at Spoleto, where Nicola again stayed in a convent but could not sleep for thinking of the refugees who had fled from here in 1831.

Waking, he tried to remember Monsignor Amandi's face and whether it was like his own. Absorbed by this, he did not become drawn into the wave of patriotism which gripped everyone else.

Next evening there was no convent to lodge him. The troops had slowed progress on the roads and the only inn was crowded. A party of foreigners – 'English milords' said the innkeeper – had taken the best rooms and the coach passengers had to do with what was left. Nicola's was hardly more than a cupboard with walls so thin that the foreigners' conversations seemed as close as his ear.

At first they were incomprehensible, then broke into meaning. A man's voice said, 'I don't want the others to understand! Tell me in Italian. Who is he?'

'Just a boy I used to know.'

The second speaker sounded familiar.

'Before you rose in the world?'

'It's still before. I intend to rise higher than your employ, Milord.'

'Invite him in for a glass of something. No? Supposing I do?'

Invite whom in? What boy? Could they mean Nicola?

'If you do, you won't see me again.'

The listener put his ear to the partition. It was the orphan! Flavio! Nicola hadn't seen him since the day the Russian Jesuit said he might know his family. After that, he had heard some talk of a fortune which the orphan might be able to claim. It hadn't sounded credible – yet here he was with rich foreigners! Could he – Nicola was envious – have *found* his father? The other voice did not sound fatherly. But then, Nicola was no judge.

'Don't you like me at all?' asked the possible father.

'Not enough to show you off.'

'You're quite horrid. Go and sleep somewhere else.'

'Where? With Milady?'

'I doubt if she'd welcome you. But please don't feel challenged.'

'So I shall go next door.'

Overwhelmed by shyness, Nicola wished there were somewhere to hide. But already the door of his cupboard was rattling. 'It's Flavio,' said Flavio's voice.

'It doesn't lock.' Nicola decided to be impassive. Flavio had a knack of making him uneasy.

Flavio stood in the crack of the door with a lighted candle. 'Hullo, Nicola.'

Nicola moved over. Flavio sat down beside him. 'You heard all that, I suppose?'

'I didn't understand much.'

'It's simple really. He who plays the piper likes me to dance to his tune. But I'll only do it for so long.'

'Do you work for him then?'

'Yes.' Flavio explained that he was like a sweet-seller at the Carnival, one of the 'ambulant' ones whose licence required them to keep on the move. 'I have to be spry.'

'I heard you'd come into a fortune?'

No, said Flavio. There would have to be a court case and this was no time for it since his backers, the Jesuits, were in exile. His mother had been found but refused to acknowledge him.

'She says I'm a bastard and have no claims. She says she'll say so in court.'

Nicola was so stunned by this story that when Flavio's fingers ran up his spine, he didn't try to remove them. Then he began to enjoy the sensation, as Flavio whispered that he had learned the art of massage from one of His Lordship's Turkish grooms. He pressed his knuckles into Nicola's neck muscles which, after several days on the road, were knotted and sore. 'It's a good feeling, isn't it? Mmm? Isn't it? Ah you're so hard here!' He had raised his voice as though talking for the benefit of the man next door. 'Jesuit boy!' Flavio pinched Nicola's neck muscles so that he groaned despite himself. Was Flavio a friend? Nicola, who had been feeling lonely, was comforted at being with someone he knew and whose fate was parallel to his own. Both had unnatural mothers. Flavio was straddling him now and saying things which did not quite make sense. 'You've never done this to yourself, have you,' he said in that voice which was undoubtedly addressed to the foreign listener.

'Don't ask why I didn't want you to meet him. He's dry-hearted!' His knuckles kept time to the words.

Abruptly, the door opened and a censorious whisper hissed: '*Vos excommunico, turpes!*' A light swung, and a hand made a thumbs-down sign. 'Into the pit of hell!' went the theatrical hiss. 'Into the third mouth of triple-jawed Satan.' As the light rose, the hiss was revealed to be coming from one of the slit-eyed, mitre-shaped hoods commonly worn by fraternities for the dead. To Nicola, the word '*turpes*', though issued in mockery, carried a real charge. He was attempting to wriggle free of Flavio's weight when the hooded figure leaped on top of them both.

Quick as a fish, Flavio slid away and pulled Nicola after him.

'Sorry, Milord, working hours are over.'

'I thought you'd be amused!'

Hood and cloak were now off and the man sitting in the midst of their shed billows was laughing. He looked not much older than they were.

'You think only you have rights to privacy.'

'My dear Flavio, half the inn must have heard your charade. Introduce me.' The Englishman extended a hand to Nicola.

Flavio, half sulkily, said that Nicola was Nicola and this was Lord Blessington. The Milord had small clever eyes, a horse-shaped head and a cloud of beery hair. A closer look showed that what Nicola had taken for youth was a replica of it. The Englishman's skin was pomaded. 'You're angry with me,' he said, smiling and clasping his hands. 'It's a bad beginning. But it was a joke. Do you know about jokes?' he asked Nicola. 'They're more necessary as one grows older. How can I make amends? Come and have a glass of cognac with me and we'll drown our differences.'

'He spies a bit,' said Flavio later. 'The English worry about France interfering on the side of the Piedmontese.'

'How do you know?'

'Because I spy too. I spy with my little eye, which is how I know that you have a letter for Father Gavazzi. Do you know what's in it? No? Shall we have a look?'

'Did you go through my things while I was at dinner?'

'Yes.'

'I should hit you,' said Nicola. 'I don't know why I don't. That was a despicable thing to do.'

Flavio took Nicola's hands in his. 'You don't because you fear we may be alike. Or else opposites? A couple, of sorts! And because you've left your tidy Collegio and don't know the wild world outside and I do. I can guide you a bit, Nicola, but not much, because we're not really alike.' He kissed Nicola on the cheek. 'I like you, but I'm not like you. And, anyway, I may be coming into your world where *you* can guide me. Friends?'

For a shy, half-angry moment, Nicola turned his back. Then he swung round and said, 'Oh, there's no point fighting with you, Flavio, so: all right. Friends.'

It was now 4 a.m. and Flavio's Milord had fallen asleep. He had a wife, Nicola gathered, a Milady, now asleep too out in the yard in her double-springed barouche, which was more comfortable than anything the inn could provide. Their arrangements seemed odd but Nicola was more interested in hearing Flavio's story and in how the Father Prefect had taken him to see the priest's own sister who, it now appeared, was Flavio's mother. The Jesuit, who had been deeply agitated, had warned Flavio that the meeting might not go off smoothly. He had then taken him to various outfitters and had him dressed like a gentleman, lest he disgust her on sight. The naive man had imagined that, given help, a maternal instinct would suddenly assert itself, and Flavio too seemed to have entertained some hope. But no such thing had happened.

'Her legitimate son is dead and she must be enraged to see that I, the unwanted one, survived him. Anyway she was as cold as stone. The Father Prefect was dumbfounded. No wonder he "left the world", as he calls it. He's not fit to cope with it.'

Flavio laughed. His small teeth were like a cat's. His lips were charmingly modelled, his nose straight, his hair feathery. He had a quick, cool eye and Nicola imagined the reluctant mother being frightened by its intelligence. She would surely have hoped to be confronted by someone less likely to judge her.

'The Father Prefect is *soft* and the shameful thing is that so was I. He made me *pray*. I'm sure God thinks the less of me!' He had been introduced to the duchess – yes, she was a duchess – by her own name which must, her brother had decided, now be his.

'Oh,' she'd said, 'so you've got the same name as we have? I believe there is a family somewhere in the south which has it too. No relation of course. Perhaps you're one of them.'

'I stood gaping,' said Flavio. 'She's a plump little woman with a mouth like mine. My mouth on a bad day! And it was closed against me. Tight and rancorous while mine was catching flies!'

Her brother had tried to talk, but she interrupted him. 'I'm sorry, Bandino,' she said, 'but you'll have to excuse me.' Then off she went and didn't come back. Later she told her brother that she would not let her husband's inheritance go to a bastard. She owed it to the dead man not to. And to his live daughter.

'Yes,' said Flavio, 'of course I want it. Can you imagine being denied by your mother? To your face? I even look like her, for God's sake. Yes, I want the inheritance because it means acknowledgment. That's not the Father Prefect's reason. He wants to keep it from her daughter, who has married a Liberal. Money is something the Jays pretend to despise. But don't be deceived. The parade of poverty, mended cassocks, etcetera, means something else. They give it up *because* they prize it. And remember that though the individual gives it up the Society keeps it. It's a small shift really to change from "me" and "mine" to "us" and "our".' He nodded at the sleeping Englishman. 'He's amiable because he's rich. If I get this money I'll be amiable myself. Just think, Nicola, you can't even take vows of poverty unless you have money to give up! It buys fine feelings. Oh yes. I want it.'

119

'Who does she say your father is, if not her husband?'

'A Russian lover of hers who went back to his country years ago. That's how the old Russian Jesuit guessed who I was. Her brother argues that she must have been sleeping with her husband too and so my paternity is to be presumed legitimate. She says her husband never came near her. Here.' Flavio handed Nicola the letter to Gavazzi. It was unsealed. 'I haven't read it. I'm not mercenary all the time. I'm practising to be a gentleman.'

They had breakfast with the Milord: beer, cheese, sweet bread and hot chocolate. The beer was for the Milord's apparently exploding head which he kept touching as though it were an imperfectly mended vase. Milady was not awake. The Englishman drank to peace. England wanted it. Palmerston did. Sensible man. Prime Minister Russell was sensible too. Queen and Prince Consort a bit Austrophile. Less said the better. Lord Minto the other way. Balanced out. Peace! Let's drink to it. *Pax*.

In the post coach Nicola read the letter to Father Gavazzi, who was said to be weaving back and forth across the country, recruiting and raising funds for the troops. He might run into him at any moment. Flavio, before bidding him goodbye, had provided an old seal with which to reclose the letter. It was obsolete and had the wrong pope's coat of arms on it but if Nicola applied it clumsily and blurrily, nobody was likely to notice this.

> Dear Alessandro,
>
> News of your triumphs heartens your friends. It is good that the Romagnols respond so generously to your sermons. I pray that you may be able to continue. Do you detect a caveat? Alas, I have bad news. It is that Padre Caccia, the General of your Order, has submitted a request to the appropriate Congregation that you should be expelled. Charges against you include heresy, refusal to stay in your cloister, insubordination, etc. You have stirred up the Gregorians. For now all this is secret and, so long as His Holiness favours the war, the Barnabites will not move against his Chaplain in Chief – but for how long will he continue to favour it?
>
> Cover your retreat, Alessandro. Avoid seeming to intrigue and remember that the bearer of this is a source of scandal. Addio,
>
> Mauro

Foligno, Gualdo, Sigillo, Cantiano, Cagli, Acqualagna, Fossombrone ... They were crossing the Apennines, past chestnut scrub and monotonous villages whose wind-shy roofs were steadied by roped stones. Conversation languished then revived to wonder if they had crossed the Rubicon which the coachman thought might be today's Uso or Fiumicino – each had claims – or a stream called the Pisciatella or 'Little Pisser'. The lawyer, briefly roused, talked of Roman history in a way which would have startled the Father Prefect.

At night, fireflies were so thick that the air seemed to condense in drops of gold. Fano, Rimini, Cesena, Faenza. Riveted walls bulged haphazardly. Bricked-up windows had been repierced and rebricked. Sometimes, in a blind arch, you could discern a stony eye, or a broken pilaster mimicked a nose or mouth.

Nicola left the coach in Bologna where he was to wait to be fetched from the Albergo San Marco. The lawyer joined him for a meal nearby: boiled pigs' trotters, capon and tongue.

The waiter had a copy of *Il Povero* and read aloud an attack on rich citizens who gave stingily to the national cause. 'That's Gavazzi's paper,' he said. 'It sows hatred.'

The lawyer demurred half-heartedly. He was dealing with a drumstick.

A customer said that one of the city's most illustrious citizens, Gioacchino Rossini, the composer, had been insulted by the mob which considered his contribution miserly. King Mob! Yet he had given two horses and 500 scudi.

'The horses were on their last legs. One died.'

There was an argument. Some said Rossini was as tight as the skin on your elbow and wouldn't give you the sweat from his balls, speaking with respect. Shuttup. There's a young boy listening and, anyway, here's Father Bassi.

A lean young priest came in. No: on second glance he might be forty. Long-haired, dressed as a Barnabite with an alert eye and a quick smile, he came up to the lawyer and grasped his hand.

'May I sit with you a moment? I'm off then. Just time for a coffee. You'll have been hearing ill of me?' The priest nodded at the copy of *Il Povero*. 'The Rossini story? He left town in dudgeon, but I'm hoping to achieve a happy ending. The ultras are quick to blame the people and say they're disorderly. And it's not true. The people are wonderful. In Senigallia, the Pope's home town, the offerings were beyond anything you could imagine. Women gave their ear-rings – I've started a fashion!

The "Bassi fashion" they're calling it. Wear one and give one to the cause. Women are among the most generous. One young girl gave her trousseau. And an old labourer took the shirt off his back. You could see him pondering what to give and feeling wretched because he had nothing. Then he thought of his shirt, which was new, and pulled it off and flung it on the pile of gifts. There was a moment of silence and for a while nobody came up with anything else.'

The lawyer ordered coffee. 'That's a happier story than the other,' he acknowledged.

'Oh there are many like it. A girl offered her long hair. Beggars gave their takings. The Cardinal Legate gave 500 *scudi*. Melted down, the gold and silver we collected over Easter brought six million. I sound dazzled by wealth, don't I?'

'You're a generous man, Ugo,' said the lawyer, 'but you're misleading a generous people. That labourer's shirt has gone to a cause which will do him no good.'

The priest shook his head, smiling. The lawyer said, 'This goggle-eyed youth whom you're magnetising with your dangerous charm is Nicola Santi. I'd warn him to beware of you, but what good would it do? This, Nicola, is Father Ugo Bassi, a military chaplain like the abate Gavazzi, who is only slightly less deluded.'

Bassi gripped his hand. 'The ultras are calling Gavazzi the Anti-Christ. I say he's Christ in the temple. He preaches dangerously against some of the higher clergy.'

'He doesn't go far enough.'

'How far would you go?'

'I,' said the lawyer, 'would get rid of the Church and of property too. Half measures are a waste of time. And false friends worry me more than enemies: the Pope, for instance.'

Bassi, when hurt, looked like a girl. His hair curled over the small, white collar of his black habit and his eyes grew sad.

'Now you're attacking me,' he told the lawyer. 'How do you think I manage to survive when I'm attacked by the *oscuranti* and then by you? Not by myself. How could I? I keep going, thanks to my faith, and so do the people. It's all we've got. Why do you want to take it from us? God sent a Liberal pope to guide and unite us. It's a miracle. It has given the people courage. I'm going to the front with the troops to help them fight, not for Piedmont, but for their own freedom and the freedom of the Church and for Pius IX.'

'And if he lets you down?'

'We'll fight anyway and pray.'

The lawyer shook his head. 'A holy innocent! Bound for the slaughter!'

Bassi grinned at Nicola, nodded at his companion and said, 'A doctrinaire!' Then he shook hands with both of them and left.

At the hotel, a carriage was waiting for Nicola, so, saying goodbye to the lawyer, he climbed in. A crowd blocked the strada Maggiore and he caught sight of Father Bassi standing on a balcony.

'Thanks to Signor Rossini,' he was shouting, 'we don't have to listen to German music. We can play our own. Shall I write and beg him to return to our city?'

'Yes,' yelled some of the crowd.

'No,' cried others. 'Let him stay away with his tart of a French wife!'

'I'll write then,' said the preacher and signalled the crowd to let Nicola's carriage through.

Eight

A guest is expected: one of our distant cousins.

Cold last night. A hand-warmer was passed around but was, as usual, ineffective and, anyway, causes chilblains from which I – milksop – suffer. My father, hoping to harden me, will not have a fire. The ancient Romans, he claims, were hardy. Else how could they have conquered Gaul, Germany, etc? Rome, he raved to Minghetti during M's last visit, may again lead the world. If France and England don't help our just cause, it is because they fear this. Our generation will see great things. 'I mean,' he corrected himself, 'yours. You must be thirty years my junior.'

That surprised me. I had thought M nearer his age. My father makes people seem old. It is as though they stayed on guard in his presence, as one does with children and volatile substances. M talked of how he and colleagues in the new ministry yearn to change *everything*, but that His Holiness resists and suspects laymen.

My father grew miffy at this. The Pope's liberalism is *his* contribution to history. 'You're getting changes now,' he says.

'Small changes and small change is all we get,' said M. Arms and money, he said, are the crying need.

Shortly after this he resigned from the cabinet and went north to join the Army. Before leaving, he recommended me to a man likely to be called to head the government: Count Pellegrino Rossi, who, it seems, needs a secretary. I haven't told my father.

The Villa Chiara, mottled in tints of peach and plum, was set, as though for its own good, among symmetries of box. Further containing it, old, over-arching trees tied it to the sky, so that this too came to seem part of a dogged regulatory plan.

Nicola's first impression was of a convulsion in the foreground.

'That,' said the coachman, 'is the Contino Prospero.'

A cassocked youth was doing somersaults on a trampolene.

'He's delicate. That's why his father got him that thing to bounce on.'

The last black somersault formed a circle and, in the quiver of noon, could have been mistaken for a bee swarm. Uncoiling, the young man came to help Nicola out of the gig.

'You're Santi? I'm Prospero Stanga, a disgraceful show-off. No modesty! I thought it best to let you know.'

In a small procession – two footmen carried Nicola's bits of baggage – they moved through spaces where cracks of light lit galaxies of dust. There was a smell of mildew and their shoes rang on tile.

'Look!'

Beyond a flight of rooms, light eddied in a mirror: a sword was being agitated by a gentleman whose paunch had burst the buttons of an ancient dress uniform. He had a peg-leg.

'Captain Melzi!' whispered Prospero. 'He fought with Murat during the Hundred Days. Thirty years ago! Imagine! He just tried to join up!'

The two laughed.

'How old are you?'

'Sixteen.'

'I'm eighteen. Old enough to fight. My father wants me to. Here's your room.'

It had a window painted in *trompe l'oeil*. The real one looked onto a prospect of distant hills.

Prospero left Nicola to wash in a tub filled from jugs carried in by the footmen. Assorted clothes lay on a chest. They had, said Prospero, been his. 'My uncle wrote to say you'd need some.'

His uncle was Monsignor Amandi which might mean, might it not, that Nicola and he were connected too? Nicola was eager for relatives.

The clothes were adult and secular and, having put some on, he stared in surprise at the grave young man in the mirror. He ran downstairs.

At the turn of a landing, something prodded him in the stomach. A voice cried, 'On guard, Prospero! You need to stay alert!' Then: 'Bugger, it's not Prospero.'

Nicola saw a blade shiver between himself and the officer with the wooden leg.

'Sorry,' mumbled the old man.

Nicola continued cautiously down.

'It's his last campaign,' Prospero explained. 'Getting me to join the Army. He may kill me to prove I'd be safer at the front.'

He had taken off his cassock, to which, he admitted, he had no right. 'I may even be breaking some law. Maybe I'll get caught by it? Like Hercules by the shirt of Nessus.' His father, Nicola's host, would be here this evening. 'Meanwhile, I'll show you round.'

They began at the stables where they cradled horses' velvety muzzles in their palms. These smelled like freshly baked bread.

'You will witness a row or two while you're here.' Prospero pressed his face into a horse's. 'They happen at dinner. I thought it best to warn you.'

Nicola, who had no idea how relatives behaved, thought a row would be instructive.

Prospero showed him a secret apartment – the door was in a fireplace – in which conspirators had met during the late pope's reign. It smelled of mice and damp.

'Organising the future,' mocked Prospero. 'Think how heady it must have been! Shall we go for a ride? The old mare won't throw you. She's as stately as a nun.'

Returning from this – Nicola was elated at having roused the mare to a ponderous gallop – they passed a shrubbery where, said Prospero, his mother had been shot.

'Your mother?'

Nicola had a moment of panic. Was he being mocked? Or somehow tested? Prospero made his horse caracole.

'She died of my father's plots.'

Could that be true?

Prospero touched Nicola's knee. 'You have to be told so you'll understand when we get carried away. You see, all through my childhood there were plots. Strangers slipping about. Mysterious comings and goings.' It was not, he said, that any of them came to much. 'What they did do was attract the attention of the *Centurioni* who, unknown to us, were patrolling our grounds. Then, one evening – it was my birthday and I had been allowed to stay up late – she and I came out here with my dog, Renzo. It was drizzling and she wore a cloak with a hood, so the *Centurioni* may have taken her for a man. Anyway, when she stepped into a clearing to whistle for Renzo, who had taken off after a rabbit, they shouted *Alt!* She ran towards me and they shot her.'

Nicola was stunned by the fragility of this briefly evoked mother.

'My father can't get over it. Which,' said Prospero, 'is why this house is such a shambles.' Aunts, he said, had offered to come and housekeepers been recommended, but the count would have no woman here who could seem to take her place. 'It goes to show I'm unfair to bear him a grudge. We upset each other horribly.'

Nicola envied them. A mother to be mourned was better than a blank: a mental quicksand which drew you in.

'Our trouble is that he wants to be an atheist.'

'Wants to be?'

'So as to be a man of the Enlightenment. But it means he cannot hope to see *her* again, so *I* am his only future.'

They were back at the stables. Prospero said, 'Her bedroom is kept as though she were still living in it. A shrine! It's as if *his* sorrow crowded mine out. Oh, I know I'm ungenerous.'

'Where did you get your cassock?'

'It belonged to a tutor I had.' Prospero unbuckled his horse's bellyband and handed Nicola the saddle. 'Can you hold this? Under the last pope,' he explained, 'it was prudent for a Liberal like my father to engage a clerical zealot to teach his son principles opposed to his own. It was a sporting compromise and gave the authorities a chance to win the child's mind – as my tutor might have if he had been astute. Instead, poor man, zeal undid him. He was a glutton, you see, and had qualms about enjoying our table and allowing his sins to blind him to ours. From sheer scruple, he threatened to report my father for reading English newspapers obtained from smugglers. He had a list of "disadvised" periodicals issued by the Office of the Cardinal Secretary of State.

'Since the smugglers had worse to hide, my father agreed to abide by the list which turned out to disadvise everything he wanted to read. All he could have were *The Freeman, The Dublin Evening Post* and *The Catholic Herald.* As it happened, he didn't have to put in orders for any of these because I got into a fist-fight with my tutor and broke his nose. Monsignor Mastai had to smooth things out with Rome.'

'And the tutor left without his cassock?'

'Yes.'

Their laughter stirred Nicola, who was often unsure what to feel.

127

Purposeful people amazed him. Prospero clearly *felt* things. Nicola would have liked to be recruited by him as Martelli had recruited him.

While further exploring the villa grounds, he brought the conversation back to Prospero's mother who had, it seemed, been Piedmontese and spoken French.

'English too. Her father was an ambassador.'

What about my mother? Nicola wondered. Why did these polyglot relatives neglect her? But as Prospero spoke, the mothers fused in his mind.

'In summer we went for walks. I had a sailboat which I would sail on our pond and she would sing *"Y avait un petit navire / Qui n'avait ja- ja- ja- / Qui n'avait ja- ja- ja / Qui n'avait ja- ja-jamais navigué / Ohé, Ohé!"'*

Nicola clapped. 'I think I prefer not understanding. The meaning – expands.'

'That's a romantical notion.'

'What's that? A new heresy?'

'Yes. Its followers look for the infinite in the finite. As you might expect, they're disappointed.'

Idleness twitched in Count Pellegrino Rossi and the city too was twitchy: inactive, yet animate like a dog growling in its sleep. To his left, in café windows, he could see his pale, circumspect face; on the right, wheel spokes spun and churned. He was back on the Corso where people in carriages smiled greetings. It was the hour of the promenade and he was only half here, for he was roughing out an essay in his head. It would take the form of an open letter to Teresa Guiccioli, Lord Byron's last love. Rossi had known Byron, translated a volume of his verse, and heard him describe the Italian struggle as 'the very poetry of politics'.

A wheel spattered dung. That, in popular superstition, meant gold: perhaps the salary he would receive from his soon-to-be-made appointment? Pensively, he scraped it off his boot. Livery-braid, brass harness-fittings and crested door panels swayed past at the pace of a river whose surface movement belies an underlying torpor.

'*Buon giorno, Eccellenza.*'

Androgynous gentlemen dressed in the bright silks peculiar to the papal household were succeeded by ladies, one of whom was reputed to have the Pope's ear. Contacts here were everything, for this was the ark: last gaudy remnant of a world swept away elsewhere in 1789.

'Come and see me, Conte!'

'With delight, Contessa.'

That was the Contessa Spaur whose upholstered carriage gave off a scent of the boudoir. The Corso, for the duration of the promenade, was one enormous salon with the advantage that those not on visiting terms could still scrutinise each other. Up and down went the two rows of carriages between the piazza Venezia and the piazza del Popolo, round and round like a carousel. After a few tours, they might enlarge their orbit to take in the Pincio gardens, where another ring of victorias, berlins, calashes and phaetons mimed an image of life as cyclic, circumscribed and fairly easily controlled. The names of passengers echoed those of nearby palaces: Bonaparte, Salviati, Torlonia, Lante, Doria, Chigi, Odescalchi, Ruspoli and Niccolini. Here in one hour the whole of good society could roll by on its afternoon airing. Here skill and merit had never been valued, which was why these affable people had nobody to defend them against the results of their improvidence.

Earlier, Rossi had sat in an apothecary's shop among men whose frock coats had stains so ramifying as to resemble the design in watered silk: meandering logs and maps of their owners' vicissitudes. They were discussing the latest revolution in Paris which looked like toppling the government which had toppled his. The topic didn't hold them though, and soon a young man was complaining about his mother-in-law's having tied a bag of badger hairs around his son's neck to scare off witches. A black-eyed youth with a three-day stubble, he kept clenching angry fists.

'While I was away she got the upper hand. I left my wife under her roof, so now, according to her, I haven't a word to say!'

'Leave it,' he was advised. 'Your own mother probably hung the same gear on you and you're none the worse for it.'

'Superstition,' shouted the father.

'Some of these old women know a thing or two.'

'Balls!'

'You don't need balls for everything!'

Laughter. The talk wrangled on, then turned to the war which could be a shambles. Father Gavazzi's sermons were lovely to listen to, but why were we fighting? For the Milanese? What did they ever do for us? They were half Austrian anyway.

'They want to get rid of the Austrians,' instructed the young man who had complained about his mother-in-law. 'The Piedmontese are helping them and the Neapolitans! And so must we.' He mentioned 'Italy' and was shouted down. What was 'Italy' anyway? And who believed the Neapolitans would ever truly fight? They'd turn tail before reaching the field of battle.

'Maybe.'

'There's no maybe to it. Did you see them go by? Crawling up the peninsula as if they were on crutches! Their king,' said a cynic, 'only sent them because he had a revolution on his hands. But revolutionaries go home. They leave the piazza and what they won gets taken back. You'll see.'

Rossi watched the apothecary weigh out a measure of powder, wrap it in a twist of paper and sell it to a small boy who had come in with a note. Then, slowly, he withdrew a barley-sugar stick from a jar. The boy's eyes were like those of a stalking cat.

Behind him came a burst of laughter: that sour, puncturing laugh of men who expect to be deceived and put their pride in knowing it. The small boy grasped the barley sugar and raced off like a marauding animal. The talkers were discussing treachery.

If Rossi went to power – the idea had become real to him and so more daunting – he would have to deal with men like these who had learned to distrust all leaders. Even the best, they claimed, were out for themselves. Ferdinand of Naples was a two-faced tyrant. Carlo Alberto of Piedmont was fighting the Austrians – but on whose behalf?

'He's trying to unify the peninsula.'

'Ever hear of the stork who united frogs in his belly?'

It struck Rossi that Pius was very like these men. He had the occasional impulse towards reform but no sustained faith in things secular. Here belief in the deep flaw of nature was bred in the bone. Voices had sunk.

'How,' whispered one, 'do Republican frogs get out of the royal belly? Through the anus. They fall into royal shit!'

More fatalistic laughter. It set Rossi's teeth on edge. Fatalism fed fanaticism and extremism excused inactivity.

'A republic,' he was surprised to hear his own voice, 'is not possible here. France, which has one on her own soil, would not tolerate one on ours. She wants stability on her southern border.'

He had not meant to speak, but now it struck him that the company had been waiting if not laying bait for such a remark.

'Excellency,' the apothecary was sycophantic, 'you mustn't take our joking seriously. We're all loyal subjects of His Holiness.'

'So you know me?'

130

'Your Excellency is a well-known patriot.'

'Might His Excellency,' said a bearded man, 'be attributing notions of his own to today's France?' The man had a squint which made it hard to look him in the eye. 'God speaks through the people,' he said sternly. 'Its will is sacred.'

Hot breath blew on Rossi's ear. 'Excellency,' begged the young father who had objected to badger hairs, 'I have a wife and child and depend on my mother-in-law who . . .'

'The point of change,' Rossi murmured quietly so as not to shame the man, 'is to do away with personal recommendations.'

'I write a good hand. They're taking on new men in the civil service . . .' The whining voice pleaded doggedly, as if Rossi had not spoken. 'I could keep Your Excellency informed. I'd be devoted . . .'

'Why aren't you with the Army?' Rossi asked aloud.

The young man looked at him with hatred.

'Why aren't all of you?' He threw the question wide.

'It's no time to join up, Excellency. We're not mad.' The squint-eyed man's face was at odds with itself.

Rossi drew on his gloves. 'You're not mad enough!'

The contempt in his voice surprised him. It was an axiom that a politician must make himself liked but here, in his own country, he was like a seducer who, on finding his feelings engaged, loses technique. Yet irritation was giving way to a fizz of hope. After all, he was getting a second chance at the poetry of politics.

From Prospero's diary:

Yesterday I spoke with my father about going to Rome to work for Count Rossi. He wept, felt old and was gloomy all day. Nonetheless, I think my going might be a relief.

This morning, early, I went for a ride alone in the mist. The sun was a smear of bruise-colours and Moro's hooves left tracks in the frost. Keeping my cheek on his neck, I let him hurtle through whippy undergrowth so as to rake my mind clear of thoughts about my mother. I have been afflicted by these and blame Nicola. He asks more questions than a confessor.

When she was alive, we used to celebrate our birthdays with fireworks, and I remember her singing songs for my father about dead, beautiful women. They were mostly French, and I have sometimes felt that they – he and she – poisoned themselves with French ideas. My father airs them still and young Nicola asks questions. Encouraging him.

Moro's coat foamed. His smells were an antidote to French poisons. Then I saw the man with the musket.

'*Alt!*' he shouted.

It was what the *Centurioni* had yelled before they shot her. I was remembering this as I calmed Moro who was ready to bolt. '*Calma!*' I kept saying: 'Easy!' I was partly saying it to myself.

Then I saw the second man and, through the trees, a shooting blind. He too had a musket.

'Signor Prospero!'

I knew him. He's called Storto and used to work for my father as an odd-job man. The other one was a customs guard.

'That was stupid!' I said. 'You frightened the horse.'

'Signor Prospero, come and see what we have here.' He pointed at the blind. I followed him in, while the other one tied up Moro. It was dark, but after a moment I made out two men lying on sacks.

'They're the ones who killed your mother,' said Storto. '*Centurioni!* Sons of whores! Their day has come.'

The men stared at us the way animals do, without really focusing. They must have been there some time because there was a smell of shit. I suppose one or both had lost control.

I said, 'Nobody knows who did that.'

'With respect, Signor Prospero, people do know. Don't you trust us?'

I didn't of course. What I was thinking was that these fellows might lynch their prisoners and implicate me and my father. They could say *I* had ordered them to do it.

'This has nothing . . .' My voice stuck and I couldn't go on. I didn't believe the men were *Centurioni*. Most of *them* fled months ago and since then a lot of private vendettas have been pursued under the cloak of politics. 'If you believe what you say,' I managed at last, 'you should take them to the police.'

Storto leered. 'You know better than that, Signor Prospero. *They* never had truck with the law. They *were* the law. Was anyone charged with the death of your mother?'

My teeth were chattering.

'You don't want to think they did it,' he marvelled. 'That these lumps of running shit could have done it.' He kept studying me, then nodded as though he had reached a decision.

So had I. It was true: I was offended on my mother's account. I did not want her memory touched by what was going on.

My tutor, Don Pietro, used to talk to me of carnal impurity and as I turned fourteen his questions grew insistent. He thought me hypocritical but avoided quite saying so. Perhaps some confessor less crude than himself had warned him against planting sin where it had not taken root. Now, for the first time, I felt the self-distaste on which he used to harp. Storto kept nagging. 'To get justice, Signor Prospero, a man still has to take things into his own hands. Only now our lot has a chance.'

He gave me his slow grin and I guessed we were thinking the same thing: my father is known to have been a conspirator. The police no doubt still have him on their lists. I wondered how long Storto and his friend had waited for me to happen by. But, to be sure, they'd know that I ride this way often.

'I'm leaving.'

'Signor Prospero, you offend us. All we want is justice.' The other man was untying the prisoners. I realised suddenly that Storto had not been an odd-job man at all but one of my father's less reputable confederates in the conspiracies which criss-crossed the country for so many years. He holds power over him now that my father supports the new regime and that the bid is for peaceful reform which extremists, naturally, do not want.

'They *are Centurioni*,' he told me. 'Murderers. You think we don't know? When they were riding high they didn't conceal themselves.'

'You're not going to butcher them?'

I think the word worked on him. He must, after all, hope to tell about this exploit one day.

'Not butcher, Signor Prospero.'

'What then?'

'The *cavaletto*.'

It seemed mild after my fears: the wooden horse. You put a man arse-up on a flogging-stool and let him have it. The *Centurioni* used it a lot. So did the papal authorities. In Hungary the Austrians stripped a noblewoman naked and 'horsed' her in front of her husband who had conspired against them. She went mad and he killed himself. But that was because they were gentlefolk and because of their ruined honour. To do it to thugs could be an insurance against worse. I decided to stay. If I left, who knew what might happen?

I am not sure I was right.

I suppose I had better record the rest. The men were stripped, tied

133

down and beaten with a stick which left weals the colour of raw meat. They screamed. The thing went on until there was blood and I kept thinking that the shouts were a queer form of triumph, as though they were proclaiming their own liveness. This was an eccentric idea. My mind was chasing whims so as to absent itself from what was going on. It couldn't though. There was no purging: just shame which touched us all. I think the kidnappers felt it too, because there was a dullness in the customsman's voice when he said, as the victims were fumbling for their britches: 'A taste of their own medicine. They gave it out often enough.'

Storto mumbled. The let-down had reached him too. I watched as the beaten men hobbled out the door, paused and then, as nobody stopped them, stumbled off at a crooked and, no doubt, painful, lurch.

I am worried, which is why I have noted this down as faithfully as I have felt able to do.

Nicola asked: 'Is your father unhappy?'

'I suppose so,' said Prospero. 'He can't catch the moon in his teeth.'

They had walked to the nearest village and were resting in its *osteria*. It was a small village whose lanes were dark. Through open doors Nicola had glimpsed caverns of poverty, from which children tumbled, looking like boar cubs striped with sun and dirt.

The proprietor asked about the count. 'A pity he's not going to Rome. Someone,' he lowered his voice, 'should see to law and order round here. There are murders all the time now and with the war it'll be worse. Soldiers on the rampage.'

'The war's north of the Po.'

'The Po's easily crossed.' The man touched his genitals. 'Someone should warn His Holiness about what's happening. Hope is a dangerous thing. Those priests who came through with the troops said things that may be all right in the city. Country folk don't understand. They gave away what they can't afford and are expecting to get it back a hundredfold.'

Later he said, 'My sons have gone north to fight. No fool like a young fool.'

'That's a reproach,' muttered Prospero. 'Why haven't I joined up?' But the host's mind was on public matters. Drawing Prospero aside, he made recommendations so urgent that Nicola thought it best to step outside.

134

As he did, a carriage drove up and splashed him with water from a deep puddle in the road.

He swore, then blushed, and a lady who had been preparing to step from the carriage blushed too and broke into apologies and reproaches to her coachman. What a way to drive! 'Here.' She took a scarf from her neck and handed it to Nicola. He must dry himself, she insisted. 'Please,' she begged, 'you must.'

She was rosy and ringleted and very determined. The coachman must dry the young gentleman, she insisted. Yes. With her scarf.

Nicola protested; she insisted; the coachman was at a loss and the three voices were mingling and responding like parts in an opera when the landlord and Prospero stepped out the door.

'. . . if His Holiness won't listen to your father,' the landlord was saying, 'if he won't listen to Count Stanga . . . Ah,' he broke off, 'you here . . . Donna Anna! Can I do anything for you?' He seemed flustered and so did the rosy lady who had lost her colour.

'No,' she said faintly. 'I was just leaving.' Turning to Nicola she snatched the scarf which he had been trying to hand her back. 'Well, if you won't . . .' she mumbled and got back into her carriage, whereupon it started up and was gone before it occurred to him to marvel at the speed with which the coachman, regaining his box, had anticipated his mistress's change of mind and mood.

Count Stanga was a delicate, fine-featured man whose fingers made a papery sound when clasped. He was excitable and in his presence Prospero was often silent, as though hoping to calm him by contagion. The count, however, was not calmed, but rattled like dry corn and had kept up a barrage of chat since Nicola's first evening, when he had been full of news about the troops. Two nephews of the Pope's had joined up, he reported, and the Archbishop of Milan was encouraging seminarians to fight.

'Seminarians!' He stared at his son. The cassock, said the stare, was no longer an excuse.

This evening, again, they met at dinner. A single candelabrum cast a focused radiance outside which the room seemed to have no walls. Back and back stretched the depths of blackness, plumbed here and there by glints of metal or glass.

The count raked a hand through hair which must once have been the same golden colour as Prospero's. It was a small hand, neat as a comb. He was depressed by Prospero's account of the *osteria* owner's worries.

'Be careful what you say in places like that,' he warned.

'I saw Storto not long ago,' said his son. 'He had a musket.'

'That's the sort of thing I'm worried about.'

'I believe smuggling is going on as much as ever.'

'Oh it's inevitable! There's talk of a league which will rid the peninsula of tariff barriers, but His Holiness gets no co-operation. Foreign governments won't give up what they have without a fight – which is why anyone with nerve should enlist.'

'I have nerve,' said Prospero. 'It takes nerve to resist you. Don't you suppose I'd *like* to please you?'

There was a pause.

'Why don't you then?'

'I saw someone shot once. You ought to understand.'

This time the pause was longer. Prospero's face recoiled into a clench.

'Yes.' His father sighed.

A large hound lying under the table – Nicola had got a shock when his foot landed on it – was now fed a tidbit and caressed. The count, Nicola saw, needed to cuddle something. Father and son had the same wide, even, alabaster smile, but in the older man's face it had an avid brilliance.

Captain Melzi – no longer in uniform – now cut into the conversation. He was worried because the Pope had not formally declared war.

'He will,' assured the count. 'He's a patriot! An Italian – and he blessed the troops.'

'If he doesn't our army is illegal and captured men will be treated like common criminals.' Melzi had had a letter from an old comrade in arms, a man his own age. 'Colonel Guidotti. He joined up and they've made him a general. Well, *he* hasn't a peg-leg.' The captain banged a spoon on his wooden limb. No other part of him, said the set of his jaw, was false.

'There was talk,' said the count, 'of Don Mauro being appointed a military chaplain.'

'Wasn't he defrocked?'

Nicola asked if this was the Don Mauro he knew. It was. Old conundrums were turned over in the light of the changed times. Years ago Don Mauro had been condemned for fighting and now here was the Archbishop of Milan encouraging seminarists to fight. Here were Fathers Bassi and Gavazzi riding with the troops.

'As chaplains. Unarmed. He was armed. He was taken with arms in his hand.'

'A fowling piece!'

'Still and all . . .'

'But if Peter looses today what Peter bound before . . .'

The two argued hammer and tongs until Captain Melzi, sodden with wine and jealousy of General Guidotti, slipped from his chair and had to be carried to his room.

Nine

'He's the apple of my father's eye!'

Prospero and Nicola had spent the morning with the dog whose clever mouth would hold a shot bird as softly as an egg.

'Fetch it!'

They threw sticks, sending the creature skidding through undergrowth. Back and forth it looped, linking them to the luminous day and to each other. Pink-flowering Judas trees stained bright air; bluebells and scabius speckled grass and, in the woods, invisible creatures crackled with surprising purposefulness. The country and its codes were now less strange to Nicola who elected to wait by a gazebo near the pond while Prospero discharged some task which should, he said, take no time at all.

Nicola, lazing on grass, gave himself up to a bemused recognition. Here, on this April morning, was that play of physical life which his education had so energetically heralded and denied. For, what had the delirium of foliate Baroque been celebrating if not these branches of copulating birds? And the Jesuit choirs? Here flew dragon-flies like slivers of stained glass and here, animating the seductive surface of things, was the urge to lose one's separateness, as the birds were doing and, no doubt, those crackling creatures in the undergrowth. Feathered glories. Gilded couplings. Glee. All, said the Church, were metaphors for union with the godhead. Carnality – the Urge – had its mundane uses, best contained. It was heresy to quite deny it – witness the Manichees. Better to marry than to burn. Mentally, Nicola was prepared, having, over the abstract years, learned all the words – but now, immersed in nature's unchaste dishevelment, only hoped to burn. He yearned to copulate with – oh, anything. Possibly the pond? Maybe he'd strip and jump into it? In Greek myth, Daphne became a tree, so might the bark of this one, under his fingerings, turn back to skin? Some goat droppings – sniffed, they were sweetish – suggested satyrs. He rolled the shiny ball of excrement between finger and thumb and rejected the impulse to eat it. Communion? Of a sort?

Again, he considered a dip in the pond and was squinting at its cross-hatched sheen, when his eye was drawn by a movement under a willow tree. A girl materialised.

'You should wear a hat.'

He thought she might be a servant sent to tell him this. She was younger than he. Maybe she was a new servant and didn't know her place? She began counting daisy petals.

'One for yes, one for no – guess what I'm wondering?'

'Whether I think you're pretty?'

'Oh!' Playfully indignant. 'Fancy yourself, don't you?'

'No, but I'd fancy you if you let me.' Responses rose as if rote-learned. Perhaps they had slid into his ear on days when city breezes blew through the corridors of the Collegio Romano? She stood so close that he smelled the rank sap of daisy stems. Was he so bold because he thought he might be dreaming? It was easy to think this in the light of her behaviour. When he reached for her hand, she said: 'Let's go into that hut.'

So he followed her into the musty gazebo, where her manner changed. 'Signor Prospero. I have a message . . .'

'I'm not Prospero.'

But was, he remembered, wearing Prospero's clothes. Anxiously, she went back to her coquettish mode, as if to snare an admission that he was, indeed, Prospero.

'I'm his guest.'

Taking this for some gentleman's joke, she looked sulky and her lip began to quiver. 'Only you, you see, can help . . .'

Now was his chance to kiss her. He knew it with a sporting instinct, but was held back by something alien to sport: sympathy.

'Only who?'

'Please.'

He let her speak, though what she said made no sense to him. It had to do with her father who was not what, from malice, people said, but was in fear for his life. Prospero's father too came into the thing and a Donna Anna who did not know the girl was here.

'Listen,' Nicola spoke sadly. 'You're telling secrets to the wrong person. I'm Prospero's cousin and I'm wearing his clothes.'

'Truly?'

'Yes.'

139

'Oh.' It was as if air had gone out of her. She wasn't angry. Thriftily, wasting no feelings, she handed him a letter. 'For him.'

Captain Melzi was out of puff. Walking with a peg-leg was no joke. The day was gorgeous, but the two boys struck him as glum. Glum as mummies. What was on their minds?

The war was on his. Would the Austrians make mincemeat of our raw troops? In Milan last month the whitecoats had been taken unawares – but then rioting civilians always had soldiers at a disadvantage. The captain's sympathies wavered as he thought of men under discipline being jeered at by hordes, and depression deepened as he thought of Guidotti. A general! At times like this *anyone* could be promoted, providing he had two good legs.

'This part of the country,' he said, 'always bred soldiers. Your mother's family,' he told Prospero, 'claims that the blood of the Malatesta runs in their veins, and *they* claimed that of Scipio Africanus.' He stopped, remembering that the count had asked him not to keep taunting Prospero. It could drive him to put on a cassock for good. Then their line would die out and the priests have the last laugh. The skirted capons would savour that! Melzi groaned, having reminded himself of an outrageous rumour that the Pope had disowned his own troops.

Leaving the captain by the pond, Nicola and Prospero strolled into the village. 'His youth dazzled him,' said Prospero. 'He's forever looking back to the Battle of Borodino. Oh, I shouldn't be so disobliging. I'm sure he proved his courage which is more than most of us can say.' He frowned.

It was hot; dogs lay under carts; the shade was minimal and the sun high in the sky. Crossing the small square, they had the glare in their eyes and almost collided with a man and woman. Nicola gripped Prospero's arm to move him aside but, as the other pair moved too, they nearly collided a second time. The man looked agitated, but the girl threw them a baleful glance and steered him past. Nobody proffered the customary greeting.

'That girl,' said Nicola, 'is – do you know who she is?'

'No.' But Prospero looked forebodingly over his shoulder. The man was one of the two who had been 'horsed'.

'She came looking for you about an hour ago,' Nicola told him. 'She left a letter.'

'Girls like that can't write letters.'

'Here it is. Maybe someone gave it to her?'

Nicola fished it from his pocket and the two stared at the neatly pasted characters cut from a newspaper. It was addressed to the Contino Prospero Stanga. There was no envelope but it had been folded and sealed with a blob of wax. Prospero opened it. 'It must be a threat.' He smoothed it and read:

Signor Contino,

It would be wise to remember that (1) those who persecute *Centurioni* seek trouble; (2) the new pope's friends need to avoid it; (3) Christ said 'Love your enemies'.

To show you understand you should provide the 'horsed' men with compensation and a safe-conduct to leave the province.

Prospero swore. 'I wonder who composed it? Not her and not her father! I'd rather *my* father didn't know about this.'

Swearing Nicola to secrecy, he told him what had happened and, after the two had pondered the matter in all its aspects, they took a boat onto the pond and spent the last of the twilight silently casting for fish. At first the water's enamelled surface showed up the faintest movement, but later they could see nothing at all.

Back at the villa the count was waiting for them in some agitation. Had they got his dog? It hadn't been seen for hours. But they said they hadn't seen it since lunch.

Early next day the dog was found with its legs stretched stiffly out and a gummy substance on its eyes. It had been poisoned. The count took the thing badly and servants magnified his grief, exclaiming and commenting in voices which at times sank into inaudibility and at others floated in through Nicola's bedroom window.

'The two Signorini took him for a walk yesterday. He could have eaten something in the woods.'

'They should have been more careful!'

'The Signor Conte is half out of his mind!'

'. . . loved him like a Christian. Could *be* a Christian next time. A nod is as good as a wink.'

'You don't . . .?'

'I do!'

At dinner the row which Prospero had prophesied finally broke. It had been on the horizon all day and when it started, Nicola tried to leave, but the count said, 'Stay.'

He spoke carefully, biting off his words as though forbidding himself to shout. This household, he said, like it or not, was involved in his affairs. The poisoning of his dog meant something and he wanted to know what. Also: he had had an anonymous letter. Well? Nicola and the captain looked at their plates while Prospero told what he knew.

'Why didn't you tell me this before?'

'I thought it was over. That no more would come of it.'

Exasperation sparked from father to son, and Nicola, eyes flicking between them, thought: it's as if one could see through to the hurt in their organs. It's as if they *shared* an organ.

Prospero looked swollen and ready to bruise. 'I was there by chance – caught by surprise.'

'Chance, my arse,' shouted his father. 'They laid a trap and you fell into it. I'm a target for both factions: the old Zelanti because they've always hated me, and the extremists of my own side because I want to give the Pope a chance! You're my Achilles heel and they know it!'

'I'm sorry I failed you, father.' Pause. 'What more can I say?'

'Oh, if your blood's milk and water, then not much!'

'Father, we're talking about a dog . . .'

The count closed then opened his eyes. 'We are *not* talking about a dog!' He lectured them furiously and Nicola, having been raised by priests, saw that, for this man, outward signs portended enormities and actuality meant little until invested with expectation. Having established the significance of the dog's death, the count, as though adjusting his vision, added that the dog as dog mattered too: 'I valued him. He was a courageous beast with red blood in his veins.'

Prospero stood up.

'Stay.'

'We may both regret it.'

'Your impulse is always flight, isn't it?'

142

Prospero had moved from the lit area. His voice trembled out of the dark. 'It's because I'm sick of . . .'

'Shut up, Prospero!' The captain was worried by that tremor.

'No. Speak. What are you sick of?'

'Words,' whispered Prospero. 'That's all your action ever amounted to. Except for my mother's death. You gave *her* life for your cause, all right, and I had to face that because I was there and you weren't. You didn't see her until they'd laid her out with flowers all over her. Narcissi. Lilac. You were away. Conspiring, I suppose? When you got back she was in her bridal dress. Did you even know that she'd been shot in the stomach and that they had to stuff her guts back in and bind her up? I saw them do that on my tenth birthday. I wouldn't leave. They couldn't make me. So I saw it.'

'Stop, now!' The captain tried to push Prospero out of the door, but Prospero clung to the jamb.

'We've never talked, have we?' His voice was implacable. Energy had shifted to the shadows.

The count was crying.

'That's enough.' Melzi, unsteady on his good leg, wrestled with Prospero who held to the door post, letting himself be spun this way and that. In the end the captain limped back to the table.

The count stared at the candelabra. His tears fractured the light like prisms.

'I'll tell you my reasoning,' said Prospero. 'Rightly or wrongly, I guessed that Storto, to compromise you, must have picked men whom the other side would recognise as their own and that if I tried to release them, he would shoot them. That would be his back-up strategy. I, which means you, would get the blame.'

The count's head was in his hands. 'I see,' he acquiesced. 'Yes.'

There was a pause. Then the father, prompted by some sudden buzz in his brain, broke into a tantrum. 'I didn't die for our cause,' he raged, 'but I lived for it! We conspired – what else could we do? What other means were there? Melzi here went to war – but how often did you fight, Melzi, for our cause? Eh? How often did you get the chance? Mostly you were being lied to. Used. First by Napoleon who promised us freedom if we would fight for him, then by the English who promised it if we fought against him! "Warriors of Italy," said Lord Bentinck, "we don't ask you to come to us; we ask you to defend your own rights and freedoms. Call us and we'll fly to your aid." Honeyed words. Then they

143

sold us to the Austrians. No wonder we turned to conspiracy. Now new generations revile us. My own son . . .'

'I don't . . .'

'You just did!' The count was on his feet and pacing.

Up and down he walked, in and out of the light, while Nicola picked furtively at his congealing meal and smuggled morsels into his mouth, ashamed to satisfy his belly when the count's need was of the heart.

It was awkward. Yet should he not stay in case things got out of control? And if he stayed, should he not behave as if it were normal for his hosts to be pacing like jaguars through the embattled dark?

'My Elena,' said the father, 'your mother, didn't suffer. The doctor gave me his word. Was he lying? I'll never know for sure. You've poisoned the past. Bravo! It's not an easy thing to do.'

Prospero protested. His father rebutted his protests and Prospero rushed off into the night. His father ran after him. Doors opened. The candle flames fell flat, then wobbled back to life. After some minutes, the captain stole quietly out.

He returned with a finger on his lips. 'It's all right,' he told Nicola. 'They're sobbing in each other's arms. Will you have another portion of this while it's half-way edible?'

Next morning, Nicola was staring idly out the breakfast-room window when he saw the girl – yesterday's girl – approach the back of the villa in an unstraightforward way. Skirting the path, she dodged through raspberry canes, then into the stables. A little later, he saw her retreat equally furtively. Mentioning this to Captain Melzi, who now joined him, elicited no interest.

'Maybe she's a friend of one of the grooms?' suggested Melzi.

Just then the count rode out of the stables and into the woods. He had not returned when Prospero and Nicola went for their usual ride.

'My uncle's expected in the next day or so,' said Prospero. 'Monsignor Amandi. Race you!'

The two took off at a gallop. Nicola's horsemanship had improved, for they rode out almost daily to explore the countryside which was in full metamorphosis. Vines, which had been as bare as basketwork, now had a dancing softness, and the fish-bone poplar trees were feathered with green. Today they were fairly far afield when one of the horses caught its foot in a rabbit hole and lamed itself. Prospero, anxious to spare it the walk home, began casting around for somewhere to leave it.

144

This was how he came to remember a villa belonging to a distant cousin which should be somewhere near here. A man, who came by driving two oxen, confirmed this. The Villa Tartaruga? Just pass that hill. So off they went and had soon turned in a driveway leading to a flight of granite steps. Nicola, leaving Prospero to hold the horses, ran up these and pulled the bell. Yesterday's girl opened the door and behind her was the count. He and Nicola stared at each other. Nicola said, 'We had an accident.'

'Prospero?'

'Yes, but he's all right. He's here.'

The count mumbled something and descended the steps to look at the lamed horse. Then he and Prospero took it round to the back.

Nicola turned to the girl. For moments his voice failed him, then it volleyed out questions. Who was she? Did she live here? She worked here, she told him. Her name was Maria. And the letter? Who had . . .? She shrank. Please, she begged, he mustn't mention it. Not here. It was nothing to do with here. She seemed frightened and he saw that, in his excitement, he had been hectoring her.

'Maria,' called a woman's voice, and a manservant appeared to say that the *padrona* wanted her.

He asked if he could do anything for Nicola, who said he'd join his friends at the stables. Glancing back as he descended the steps, he felt himself observed from a window and recognised the lady whose carriage had splashed him outside the *osteria*. She had a child in her arms.

'Well!' Prospero had driven silently for some minutes. The gig the count had provided was making slower progress than the horses they had left behind. It was poorly sprung too. 'I suppose we draw our own conclusions.' His face was sombre and his mouth a knot. 'My father's free to do what he likes. As secretively as he likes.'

The count had explained that their cousin was busy with a sick child and they should leave without bothering her. The groom would bring the horses home when the lamed one was better. Meanwhile borrow the gig. He gave orders with aplomb and the groom took them without surprise.

'That's my father's love-nest. What else? The child must be his.'

Nicola could think of nothing to say.

'Odd that he hasn't married her yet. How could he though,' Prospero gave a barking laugh, 'while the shrine of my mother's bedroom

145

continues to be garnished with fresh flowers? It would be a sort of ghostly bigamy. I'm sure he's mortified to be caught out.'

'Perhaps he's relieved?' Prospero, it struck Nicola, must have been an unforgiving little boy and his father's efforts to propitiate him – the 'shrine' – had turned into a trap.

'It seems I've a brother born on the wrong side of the blanket – oh forgive me, Nicola, I didn't . . . I don't think that way. Truly!'

'Then you won't discourage your father from marrying?' It was no business of Nicola's, but he was refusing to let the slight pass. Also: the woman in the window had moved him. He had a soft spot for mothers.

At dinner, trouble boiled up again and, this time, was harder to track. The captain was taken by surprise, but Nicola, being privy to the afternoon's doings, saw how a disagreement over the merits of a dish of artichokes could lead to rages and pacings which quite eclipsed those of the previous night. The words 'bigot', 'tight-rump' and 'hypocrite' were flung about and, at last, after Captain Melzi had cajoled the pair into returning to their seats, a stiff-jawed silence led to Prospero's flinging down an orange he had been dissecting and the words: 'I'm off.'

'Why,' asked his father, 'don't you bugger off altogether?'

'You mean leave the villa? Very well! I shall!'

'Good!'

It was like the ritual of the flower-filled shrine. How change course now? Nicola saw that, without help, neither man could. 'No,' he cried, trying to supply some. 'Listen! Please!' And urged that nothing real divided them at all. But they paid no mind and his words sounded so inconsistent that he wondered if they had emerged from his lips. 'Captain, you tell them!' he begged.

But Melzi had given up.

Nicola caught Prospero's elbow and was shaken off. Unused to families, he was appalled by what was happening. His tears made a blur in whose rainbow hub gleamed a fruit-knife. 'Listen! Well, if you won't . . .' And he plunged the blade through his hand into the table underneath. 'Now,' he yelled as they stared at the impaled hand in a harmony of shock, 'will you listen?'

'My poor son,' said the confessor whom Nicola had been advised to tell about his wound, lest dangerous rumours get about. 'Libertine lures

146

have found you insufficiently wary! Did you truly do this to yourself? Debauchery, young man, destroys feeling. I have known many young men and none, I promise you, gave himself up to unsanctified passion without losing the ability to love. Vice dries the heart! Sinners cut themselves off from love! Even in this life, my son, they are cut off. I sit here, day after day, breathing in the contagion of sad and terrible lives.'

Nicola wept. It seemed to him that the contagion was reaching him, through the brass grating, on the priest's metallic breath.

'Those are good tears,' approved the confessor. 'Beware of those who tell you nature is good or human affections reliable! See where that sophism leads. It has led to the abuse of your body. It leads to the abuse of the body politic.'

Only now, as luck would have it, did news reach the villa of a papal allocution published on 29th April. In it Pope Pius disclaimed all intention of making war on Austria. He could not, he declared, prevent his subjects volunteering to fight but he, as Christ's Vicar, must embrace 'all . . . nations and peoples with an equal . . . paternal love'. This bid to conciliate both sides had instead enraged them. His ministers resigned and the Civic Guard were hard put to prevent a revolution. Count Stanga, who had invested so much hope in his old friend, heard the news in silence, then shut himself in his room.

Nicola hoped to see the girl again. At first he expected to run into her by chance then, learning that her father had been smuggled to some place unknown, he proposed to Prospero that they return to the Villa Tartaruga to fetch home the horses. But it appeared that the lamed one was still lame and, after that, he did not dare bring the matter up.

Monsignor Amandi, courteous but decisive, arrived with a secretary and a valet but stayed only two nights, for he was *en route* to Rome where he had to report to the Holy Father on a confidential mission. Finding Nicola with his arm in a sling and the villa simmering, he promptly recommended that Prospero and Nicola should leave as soon as could be arranged, one for Rome, the other for Bologna, where he was to have a place in the Curia.

Amandi spoke with authority and his host deferred to him. Church-

147

men in a church-run state must, for the time being anyway, know best. Come the revolution, joked the count, and we'll see who'll be protecting whom! *He* was in better spirits and had been heard cajoling Prospero in the small hours of the night when Nicola punctured his hand. It was Melzi who, on getting up to see if the patient had a fever, passed outside the count's door and heard whispers seeping from under it.

'*Prosperino mio*,' he heard him coax, 'how could I ever want to replace . . .' Who? What? Prospero's voice didn't carry and Melzi could only say that a reconciliation had been effected.

Melzi had heard a story from soldiers in Bologna on one of his news-gathering trips. He believed it to be the truth behind the Jesuits' departure from Rome.

A mild man when sober, he had drunk more than usual and was visibly incensed by the sight of a cassock. Amandi affected not to notice this.

The story was that the Jesuits, knowing that they might be expelled, conceived the notion of digging up the remains of the man who had fought to save them, seventy-five years ago, at the time of their last banishment. Their hope was that these had been miraculously preserved. Opinion, said the captain, was divided as to whether they truly hoped for a miracle or planned to fake one. Either way, the enterprise was delicate since it could damage their cause if it were seen to fail and the remains – like their reputation! – prove rotten. Yet they feared to proceed with stealth lest they be taken for grave-robbers and arrested by the anti-Jesuit Civic Guard. Accordingly, they begged Mastai to send witnesses which he did. He sent them, said the captain, because he was as anxious as they to know the message from the grave. So, accompanied by the Pope's own envoys, a party set forth by dead of night but had no sooner opened the tomb than they were interrupted by revellers returning from one of the patriotic banquets which had become so popular in recent months. Drunk on wine and rhetoric, these fellows paused to sing songs in the vicinity of the working party which, fearing to be discovered at a task whose symbolism was as unfavourable to it as were the odds if it came to a fight, closed the tomb, blew out their candles, hid their tools and dispersed, the papal witnesses returning to the Quirinal, the Jesuits to the Collegio Romano. Here, another surprise awaited them, for Nardoni's lynched corpse had just been flung on the steps. He was dressed as a Jesuit and it seemed likely that it had been left there with the intention of stirring up a scandal in the morning when it came to be discovered. Why, people would want to know, had this police spy – notorious and hated – been hidden in the Collegio? Why was he dressed as a Jesuit? What had he gone out to do? The grave-diggers did not know, but, fearing the worst and, in the interests of peace, the good of the Society and *ad maiorem dei gloriam*, they wrapped the corpse in a blanket, put it in a carriage and took it back to the unsealed tomb where, since there was now nobody about, they were able to conceal it. This was intended as a provisional measure. Where else could they hide it? The open tomb offered providential concealment. Again they went home.

Meanwhile, at the Quirinal, Mastai, who had been eager for news, was disappointed when his emissaries returned without any.

'You mean,' he marvelled, 'that you opened the grave then failed to even look? You ran off just because a few harmless *popolani* came by! You must not be so suspicious of our good people,' he scolded. 'How can they love and trust you if you don't do the same for them? Go back at once,' he ordered, 'and examine the dead Jesuit's remains. If necessary, ask one or two of our good *popolani* for help.'

He had no sympathy with his emissaries' alarm or fatigue. A little suffering could only benefit their immortal souls. He was teaching them charity and faith. So back they went in the dim light of dawn, skulking through back streets – for by now rumours were about: deformed, magnified and frightening, of the mob's activities earlier that night. Once again they pried open the tomb, sweating and breaking their finger nails as they did so, for they had seen no willing *popolani* and wouldn't have dared ask for help if they had. Then – but, said Melzi, there's no need to say what they saw: a dead man dressed as a Jesuit and smelling – for the Jesuits had, for their own comfort, scattered this earlier – of attar of roses! Unfamiliar with the spy and by now too tired to think straight, they believed that this must be the miraculously preserved seventy-five-year-old body of the Jesuit saint. Back they raced to Mastai who, beside himself with joy – since any sign from heaven was a sign to him! – sent a detachment of papal guards to bring back the sacred remains. Then, in the Quirinal, by the light of the dawn and in the presence of several senior prelates who had been roused from their beds, he recognised Nardoni.

Here, said Captain Melzi, seemliness must draw a veil. We may imagine the fury and loss of face. But better not describe it. 'Naturally,' he added, 'the episode has been suppressed. It is a non-event. The Jesuits were promptly banished and the papal guards sworn to secrecy.

149

Perhaps not even Monsignor Amandi will hear echoes of it? After all, it reflects well on nobody.'

'But it's not true!' Nicola was upset by the cartoonish evoking of his worst nightmare. He still dreamed of Nardoni. 'It can't be! I saw Nardoni's corpse myself in the Collegio the morning after he was killed. Civic Guards were watching over it.'

'It's not meant to be true,' intervened Monsignor Amandi equably. 'It is an emblematic tale! We shall hear more before things settle.' He smiled at the captain.

Later, looking at Nicola's bandaged hand, he remarked that his young protégé might not have the character for a clerical career. Why had he been so distressed by Melzi's story? Was there a reason? Amandi listened while Nicola spoke of Nardoni, then asked whether he had ever heard of the bee which chanced to sting a bull just as the butcher was delivering the death blow? 'What a dangerous sting I have!' thought the bee and flew off full of pride and misapprehension. A number of people, said Amandi, had known of Nardoni's presence in the Collegio. And the spy had become imprudent. It was likely that some of those whom he had been trying to blackmail had enticed him out and let his death look like a lynching. 'You,' he told Nicola, 'are like the bee who stung the bull. You say you informed the police? But the police knew about Nardoni all along. He was a policeman.'

Amandi wore his violet stockings with dash and had the assurance of one who not only knew the world, but saw through it. Rashness, he told Nicola and Prospero, was worse than sin for it robbed virtue of its wisdom and could precipitate the unforeseen. Each of them needed a mentor. Prospero, happily, had found one for himself. 'You too,' Amandi told Nicola, 'need a period of apprenticeship. I shall ask a very astute prelate to take you under his wing. Cardinal Count Carlo Oppizzoni is eighty years old and needs someone to do just about everything for him: cut up his meat, be his memory and write his letters. You must be a staff in his hand.'

'*Perinde ac cadaver.*'

'Yes. Don't be offended if your functions are servile. Think of this as an honour. Oppizzoni, who has both pluck and wit, has held high office and seen the inside of gaol. In his youth, he was appointed to the diocese of Bologna by Napoleon to spite the then pope; yet he was true to his cloth rather than to his patron, and when the Emperor divorced Josephine to marry a Habsburg princess, denounced the bigamy. For that he lost his diocese and the right to wear red. He became one of the "black cardinals" who suffered exile and, later, gaol. He has seen a lot of history and is as wary as a fox. Watch how he handles things. You can be a son to him.'

'I was told,' Nicola hoped to take the bishop by surprise, 'that my true father could be Father Gavazzi.'

Amandi raised an eyebrow. 'By him? I thought not. You heard Captain Melzi's legend. You will hear more and may figure in some. Learn not to care. I am offering you a spiritual father in Oppizzoni. Gavazzi would be a less useful choice.' Amandi smiled. 'Neither am I proposing myself. Cousinship will suit us better.'

Before leaving, Nicola received a letter from the front. It was from Martelli, who was disillusioned by the treatment which the Roman volunteers were getting from their Peidmontese allies. 'They despise us,' he complained, and wrote rancorously of old flintlock muskets which jammed and of being issued with the wrong ammunition.

'What could they expect?' lamented Melzi when Nicola told him this. 'Disowned by their own prince, the Pope, they're orphans. Naturally, Piedmont doesn't want them to do well on the battlefield. It's looking to its own ambitions, which are to eat this peninsula as one eats an artichoke: slowly and relentlessly, leaf by leaf.'

Not wanting Melzi to think he was retaliating for his slander of the Jesuits, Nicola did not pass on Martelli's account of seeing civilian prisoners hacked to pieces by rioting volunteers. 'The prisoners,' wrote Martelli, 'were said to be spies and the men were maddened by the conditions in which we've been living, but, all the same, the officers' incompetence is frightening. Only Father Bassi, the chaplain, was able to calm the rioters. He snatched a bayonet from a man who had impaled one of the prisoners' fingers on it and looked angry enough to hit him. In the end he restrained himself, and, by simply speaking to the fellow, reduced him to tears. This made the officers' failure look worse.'

Bologna, 1848

Cardinal Oppizzoni's face had the fine fragility of age and he disliked wasting time. His first act, after welcoming Nicola, was to send him to be rigged out in a costume which must be neither secular nor downright

151

priestly. He was to be lodged at the archiepiscopal palace and to receive a small salary. For the first time in his life he would have money in his pocket.

'Your cousin,' said the cardinal, 'recommends that you and I try and trust each other more than is usual for men in our circumstances.' His Eminence turned his bony head sideways and scrutinised Nicola with what must have been his better eye. It was yellowish but piercingly alert. '*Temporale*,' he went on, 'used to mean two distinct things: a storm and the temporal power of the Pope. Of late, the distinction has been lost, and, just now, one is breaking over my head. This is why I want you to take over a file which we have opened on the military chaplains, Bassi and Gavazzi, whose activities in this diocese have created havoc. I am being pressed for a decision which would oblige me either to condemn His Holiness's policies of last month or the quite different ones which he has seen fit to embrace since the Allocution of 29 April. I am temporising but time will catch up with me and, when it does, I shall expect you to provide me with a clear and up-to-date account of current opinion in the diocese. My clergy is too divided for me to give this task to any of them. Who is your confessor?'

Nicola told him. The cardinal looked sad. 'I see that in him your cousin has provided you with a guide to the spiritual sphere and in me one to things temporal. I wish I could suppose it to be the other way around. Keep the file locked up. My priests keep appealing over my head to Rome, so mum's the word when you go to confession. I place myself in your filial hands.'

Nicola withdrew.

The file contained:

Newspaper accounts of the military chaplains' recruiting and fund-raising activities since their arrival here on Easter Sunday, 23rd April.

Letters from admirers contrasting their energy with the indolence of the diocesan clergy.

Letters from the clergy protesting about the two firebrands. Copies of these had, said their writers, been forwarded to Rome. Just what, they demanded, did the cardinal plan to do?

Queries as to how to deal with the pair. Should they or should they not be allowed to preach in local churches? Given lodging?

Accounts of the festive popular welcome extended to the preachers. Flags, garlands, poems, parades, recruitment ceremonies, etc., etc., were described with exuberant enthusiasm in the patriotic newspapers.

Nicola divided the file into piles marked 'Pro' and 'Con'.

Cuttings from the *Gazzetta di Bologna* claimed that Gavazzi's sermons had a conceptual energy unknown since Savonarola, and that his patriotism was a challenge to other priests to say where they stood with regard to the sacred cause which the Pope himself had blessed. To oppose it, opined the *Gazzetta*, was to oppose *him*. Four days later, noted a marginal comment, Pius said he could not fight Austria. So was the clipping now 'pro' or 'con'?

Nicola started a third pile which he labelled, after some thought, 'Dubious'.

Several vehement notes to the cardinal deplored Gavazzi's harping on cases of clerical corruption and his unseemly appeal to Bolognese women to give to his fund as a penance for having bastardised Italian blood by taking Austrian lovers. Surely, more decorum could have been looked for in a priest?

The margin-writer – Oppizzoni? – noted that the chaplains had presented no papers to the Curia, claimed to be answerable only to the Pope and were protected by the people: an alliance dangerous to challenge, as was clear from a list of clerical contributions made – before the Pope's change of heart – to Gavazzi's fund, which he was calling 'the National Bank'. The following items figured on the list:

Cardinal Archbishop Carlo Oppizzoni: two horses with their tackle and 200 scudi; Cardinal Amat (the Legate): 500 *scudi*; the Vicar General: 50 *scudi*; members of the Curia including bell-ringer, choir boys and sweeper: 85 *scudi*; etc.

News of the Pope's decision to back out of the war had led to such civil disorder and fear lest the city of Bologna secede from the state that the Legate had had to beg Father Bassi to speak to the people and calm their passions. He had done so but in such a way as to lay up trouble for the future, since his message was that the Pope must have fallen victim to Jesuit trickery.

After that, he and Gavazzi left for the front.

The cardinal's troubles, however, did not end and, as Nicola read on, it became obvious that he been presented with a viperous tangle which could not be reduced to the balanced symmetry which Oppizzoni seemed to require.

He took all his meals tête-à-tête with the old cardinal, who preferred not to be seen in public slopping food on himself or spilling wine on days when his palsy was bad.

'*Mens sana in corpore sana!*' Oppizzoni would groan in self-mockery as

Nicola mopped peas or polenta from his napkinned chest. 'Would I even know if I were losing my mind? Would they?'

'They', the scandalised Nicola came to see, was Rome.

'Thank you, *figliuolo*. Pour yourself a glass of something. We need cheering, eh? You think Rome trusts me?' And the old eagle's eye gazed milkily yet sharply into Nicola's. 'They trust me to cover for them if there's a débâcle! It's an old trick. Blame it all on a sick old man. Sick here!' Tapping his temple. 'You're cover too,' he managed to say, while Nicola spooned semolina into his mouth.

So was he a sly or a sacrificial lamb? Or both?

'Keep that file up-to-date', he mumbled between mouthfuls. 'You've no idea how useful such things are when it comes to proving that inaction was the only possible policy.'

The file did lend itself to such an argument, but indignation was mounting in the material arriving on Nicola's desk. Recent complaints were mostly at Oppizzoni's failure to defend his priests from the attacks made on their morals by the two Barnabites.

'Your clergy,' ran a typical one, 'is ever more scandalised that Yr Eminence, as Shepherd of this Flock, has not driven off the wolves which have been devouring it. Has Yr Eminence become a silent watchdog in Israel? Alas, what damage is being wreaked while frenzied and rabid wolves, bears and hyenas in clerical garb are free to batten on the Ministers of the Sanctuary!' There were several pages and the signature was 'the clergy of Bologna'.

An equally enraged protest signed by 'the laity' had been written in duplicate, one copy being sent to the Pope begging him to refute the pestiferous doctrines of the Masons, Bassi and Gavazzi.

Hot on its heels came instructions from His Holiness to the cardinal to hold a three-day public ceremony of repentance for the scandals provoked by the chaplains who – leaflets, pamphlets, broadsheets and even magazines printed by them came daily from the front – were still claiming to be *his* spokesmen. So was Pius performing private acts of repentance? Decorum forbade the cardinal to ask. His answer was short and dry – '*secco, secco*'. Order, like spilled milk, could not always be restored and having expressed filial submission, he regretted that the prescribed ceremony, if held, must occasion even greater scandals, since the chaplains' supporters were liable, if provoked, to do violence to the conservative clergy. Could Rome itself not recall the firebrands?

This request elicited three letters, dated the same day, from, respectively, the offices of the Cardinal Secretary of State, the Congregation of Bishops and Regular Clergy, and the Ministry of Police, variously informing the cardinal that: (1) the Barnabites were being arrested; (2) he should arrest them himself; and (3) Gavazzi, being now in Austrian territory, could not be arrested. This last item was from the police who, surmised a bit of pencilled marginalia, had no doubt tipped Gavazzi off.

Rome, to judge by its communications with the cardinal, was in a state of paralysis and terror and, apparently being administered, said another marginal gloss, like a huckster's booth. Nicola read these comments with interest, wondered if they were intended for his eyes, but did not mention them in his discussions with the cardinal, who had, perhaps, forgotten having made them, if indeed he had.

The Curia of Bologna was not in a much better state, as was clear from several draught copies of a pastoral letter which the senior clergy desired to have addressed to them 'to show that we ever are and will be at one with the adorable Prince Pius IX'.

The draughts contradicted each other, for the priests were unable to reconcile faith and freedom. True freedom, they finally concluded, consisted in obedience to authority. Unfortunately, the position of the supreme authority – Pius – had grown hard to pin down.

A last item: a confidential report to the cardinal stated that a memo had been secretly submitted by the General of the Barnabites, requesting the expulsion of Bassi and Gavazzi from that order. The cardinal's informant believed that a rescript granting this request had been issued by the appropriate congregation but could not be acted on for fear of antagonising the populace. Once it was, the two would come under Oppizzoni's jurisdiction as ordinary of their diocese of origin and, if he tried to discipline them, the people's odium would all be for him. Letters from the cardinal requesting official information on the matter had received no reply.

Ten

The patriots' war was going badly and the Pope held to blame. Priests drew black looks and Nicola fancied people stiffened at his approach. Did they think of him as the cardinal's eyes and ears? It astonished him that a sinister colour could be put on his mild menial duties – unless, to be sure, His Eminence had intended that they should? Perhaps less innocent organs needed attention distracted from their activities?

The notion mortified him and, once or twice, he stared down a starer, half ready to end with a duel on his hands. Duelling, though illegal, did occur. Nobody challenged him though – perhaps because he was protected by the cardinal's cape? Piqued, he stared even more boldly at those he suspected of suspecting him. Some must be the 'laiety of this diocese' who had sent cowardly protests to Rome. Others had welcomed the troops with garlands. So why were they not at the front?

His black suit embarrassed him. Shut up all day with His Eminence, he rarely met fellow employees and feared that, for them too, he was Oppizzoni's tout.

Seeking relief from solitude in the throng shuttling under the city's flights of stone arcades, he breathed in convivial air. Open cafés exuded stews of smell and noise: frightening, yet exciting emanations of the citizenry whose plottings were known to him from Oppizzoni's files. Here, as in an open menagerie, he could come cautiously close and even, as a visitor might riskily stroke a pretty feline, exchange pleasantries. Mostly, he was passive, letting secret susurrations blend with banter in his ear, and smells of vanilla, vinegar, chocolate, sweat, shit, musk, coffee and tobacco struggle in his nose. Scent-soaked handkerchiefs and whiffs of incense put up weak defences against fermentings of urine. Delicate diction was a protective filigree, like the iron window

156

grids raised all along these charming streets, against irruptions of impatience, scepticism and despair.

Once he thought he saw Maria, the girl from the gazebo, but lost her in the jostle. It was the afternoon promenade. Count Stanga, he knew, had sent her family somewhere to lie low – very likely here. If so, they would have trouble finding work. Talk in the curial offices was all about how the hemp trade was at a standstill, thousands living off charity and the charity likely to be cut off.

'Men have bodies as well as souls,' was what the cardinal said when he needed help to adjust his cassock and climb onto his commode. 'How,' he asked on other occasions, 'can we ask *them* to abide by the gospel if we don't love and serve them as ourselves?'

We did, he explained, try. Protestant England, for all her proud commerce, did not give her poor a fraction of the charity ours received. But our means were limited. Our weakness was that, for want of a thriving economy, we couldn't afford a proper army, so had, when faced with civil disorder, to turn to the Catholic Powers whose cure was worse than the disease. When the French came, they ruined our aristocracy by abolishing entails while Austria rode roughshod over our people, then beggared us with bills. Gone were the days when Pope Julius II, entering this town in armour, had quelled rivalries and claimed it for God.

Oppizzoni grew glum. In his fifty years as archbishop, papal claims had become a ramshackle ritual which must, though, be kept up. We had to do this, he told Nicola, for the sake of the Faith and the millions who believed in it – few of whom lived here. We here were in a trap, for this state, like the Christmas crib, must continue to convey its message even if, groaned Oppizzoni, in moments of choler or despair, 'I sometimes think my role in the crib is that of the ass!'

Again he thought he saw her, but wasn't sure. Her sort of prettiness was common in these northern Legations. It was that pale, chicken-bone beauty so delicately painted by Duccio and Fra Filippo Lippi which, when less than perfect, lets veins show through and reddens round the eyes. Sorting her out from poor copies, he saw that her ivory smoothness was rare.

This time she was with another girl who must have said something knowing, for the gazebo girl blushed and he saw that he was not to reveal that they had met. Later, though, the friend proved a help for he ran into her alone – she turned out to work at a tobacconist's – and, striking up an acquaintance, was able when next he met the two, to offer them a refreshment. He learned that Maria – the friend was Gianna – was now a seamstress.

'I see you frequent the daughters of the people,' said a young man called Rangone who worked at the archiepiscopal palace. 'Ancillary loves! Is that it?'

Rangone was the son of a *marchese* from Imola. 'You should know,' he teased, 'that girls like that have brothers and the brothers have daggers which they would have no qualms about sticking into our intemperate flesh. A neat return for what we hope to do to their sisters.'

Nicola said he didn't hope to do anything. Rangone said, 'I have my own lodgings with my own key. I could lend it to you for a few hours. No obligation. You'd be safer there.'

'But I'm not thinking of making love to her.'

'Well, *stuprum* is what our employers' minds will turn to if you're seen offering girls ices. Not to mention brothers!'

Sure enough, when Nicola found Maria in the cigar shop and spoke to her, a glowering young man pulled her into the street.

Gianna looked out to where this protector was pinching Maria's arm. That, she said, was her brother. 'You innocent boys are the worst. You'll do her no good and get her into trouble too!'

What did that mean? He asked Rangone, who said, 'You're ruining her market value.' Rangone spoke bitterly, having, he claimed, suffered over a woman in Imola. He was convinced that elsewhere – in Milan for instance – there was less hypocrisy. 'We are the most materialistic people in Europe. Honour here is what shows: a tangible thing. And you avenge it tangibly by sticking a knife in someone's stomach. Pff! French bravos wield their knife differently. They go for the heart, which is stylish – and easier to miss. Here men skewer the belly because it's where they suffer and the reason they sell their sisters. If your friend's brother could set her up with a fat prelate, don't think he wouldn't!' Rangone spoke from experience. In Imola he had fallen foul of a Monsignore who had an arrangement with the wife of a clerk. 'Very convenient. The husband was at work all day, so the Monsignore – no need to draw you a picture. Then she fell in love with me – and guess who was jealous? Not the husband. So the Monsignore went to see my father, complained of my immorality and issued threats – and here I am, exiled.'

'Are you in love with her?'

Rangone wasn't sure. She was corrupt – but he couldn't forget her. On reaching the lodgings which he had offered to lend, he paused in front of a pier glass. 'Do I look weak?' He jutted his chin. Who had been unworthy of a great love? Himself? The woman?

'If she was corrupt . . .' Nicola consoled.

'Oh, but so was Manon. Do you know the story? She was rotten, yet her lover followed her when she was deported. That's love,' said Rangone eagerly. 'Besides, there's something moving about female corruption. Because of what she couldn't give me, she gave me . . . other things. She was totally – can you imagine that? – compliant. She told me I owned her soul and that she would accept any brutalities. In the end ours became a spiritual sort of love.' Rangone turned away shyly. 'I think she would have killed herself if I'd asked.'

'Weren't you play-acting a bit?'

'Maybe. She went on her knees to me once.' He spoke with a mixture of embarrassment and pride.

Rangone's talk struck Nicola as extravagant – but others might think the same of his desire to have a harmless friendship with Maria.

'Will you really lend me your key?'

Rangone smiled.

Nicola bristled. 'I only want to talk!' he insisted. 'If you don't believe me I won't trouble you.'

'I do. I do. I'll have a copy made. But don't let the neighbours guess. I might be charged with pimping!'

Arranging to meet Maria at Rangone's was easy. Nicola was at last doing the expected thing. He had cakes delivered and watched with pleasure as she ate them. He avoided touching her but felt infinitely elated and playful. She could neither stay long nor come every day. But he liked the challenge of smuggling ice-cream up the stairs, slyly, so as not to alert watching neighbours, and fast, so that the treat should not melt.

In the hot summer, every window was a watching post. Women sat there and sewed. Men sat there and smoked. Conversations wove back and forth and who went in what door and for what purpose was of acknowledged interest. Maria pretended to be going to a haberdasher who had a shop at the back of the courtyard for thread and other sundries. She came and went by herself and he waited a good half-hour after she had left before venturing out.

'What can you find to talk to her about?' marvelled Rangone. 'Girls like that aren't for talking to. Besides, talk's dangerous. A coachman who works for an uncle of mine was gaoled in Rome for talking to a girl. He had to marry her before they'd let him out and the ceremony took place with him on one side of the bars and her on another. Admittedly, that was under Pope Leo XII who was a mad martinet. The coachman now says he was let out of one gaol and put into a worse one: matrimony. But to go back to talking, I can't imagine it. What do you talk about?'

Nicola couldn't say. All he remembered was how she once got pistachio ice-cream on her nose or her fright when she thought she might be seen by a friend of her brother's. He was tempted to tease her but didn't. Remembering Rangone's account of his poor tormented mistress, he restrained himself.

She, however, teased *him* and even adopted a habitual little smile as though she was finding him comical. He wondered if she discussed him with Gianna? Or her sisters? She was one of seven. Her mother was a laundress and her brother was employed on one of the public works which had been invented to keep the idle from starving, building a road around the city. In the room, alone with her, he enjoyed a domestic privacy which he had never known.

From delicacy, he did not offer her money. She, however, brought the matter up. She had had, she said, to ask Gianna to deliver her sewing each time she came here. 'We should give her a present.' What sort of present? Oh, she'd find something if Nicola gave her the money. Mortified, he gave her what he had on him which must, he guessed, be more than she earned herself in a month. Even he was not so simple as to think it was for Gianna.

He had not kissed her and, now that money had passed between them, felt unable to try. He might seem to be calling in a debt.

Then, one day when there was a last spoonful of ice-cream on his plate she scooped it into her mouth, clapped wet lips to his, trickled the melting stuff onto his tongue then, drawing it back, sucked at the tongue so fiercely that he thought she would pull it out by the root.

Laughing, she took off out the door and down the stairs and when he went, incautiously, to the window, did not look up but skipped down the street, twirling and flouncing her skirts with what he recognised as erotic mockery. His tongue hurt.

It was now August.

Walking back to work, he hugged the shade, grateful for the stone canopy of the *portici*. Suddenly hot with lust, he blazed, as a fire banked overnight will do when its crust is broken in the morning by the chambermaid's poker. Rangone was right. Talk with a girl like that was only a kindling, to linger over it unmanly! His aching tongue licked vestiges of ice-cream from his lips.

He quickened his step and wondered why he had been so slow to see what was clear to Maria and Rangone and even to Pope Leo XII. In his mind's eye, he saw the shine on her inner lip. He was practically at the archbishop's palace when he noticed knots of people urgently talking. What was happening? The Austrians, he was told, had crossed the Po and were marching through the Pope's lands, mopping up remnants of our defeated army. They were already in Ferrara and looked like coming here. Atrocities had been committed and they had burned a village to the ground.

Some citizens were incredulous. Why would Catholic Austria make war on the Pope?

'Because he made war on them!'

'But he didn't!'

'Tell that to Marshal Welden!'

Nicola went into the palace where the same speculation was going on. A copy of a proclamation, issued by Welden at his headquarters in Bondeno, had been received and a clerk read it aloud. 'The Holy Father, your lord,' he mumbled.

Someone shouted, 'Speak up.'

'. . . declared that he did not want war. Yet papal troops and his Swiss mercenaries fought our men at Treviso and Vicenza and, on being defeated, undertook not to take up arms against the Empire for three months. Woe to any who break this vow. I refer especially to those bands of so-called "crusaders" who defy their government and deceive the population with lies and sophistries aimed at fomenting hatred against Austria *which has always been friendly* . . .'

The clerk's drone kept being interrupted. The room was filling with people from other offices, all with rumours to report. The Germans had occupied several communes. No, they were still in Ferrara. The postal service had broken down.

'Where the voice of reason fails,' read the clerk mildly, 'I will make myself heard with cannon . . .'

This drew comments about German arrogance. The cannon was their true voice! Barbarians!

This reaction surprised Nicola who knew from the anonymous letters how lukewarm the diocesan clergy had been about the war.

'My sole intention,' droned the reader, paying no heed to the interruptions, 'is to protect peaceful inhabitants and preserve the lawful rule of a government which is being subverted by a faction.

'Woe to those who fail to heed my voice. Consider the smoking ruins of Sermide. That village was destroyed because its inhabitants opened fire on my men. Given at my headquarters in Bondeno, 3 August 1848. Marshal Welden.'

That evening the cardinal had no stomach for food and ate rice without condiments and drank watered wine. Even the archiepiscopal kitchens were feeling the effects of the war. Nicola tied a napkin around Oppizzoni's neck and placed another on his lap.

'Sit down. Sit down. Eat your own dinner. A good digestion is a blessing. What are you having?' Oppizzoni sniffed. 'Do they cook your food properly? Complain if they don't. Tell me what they're saying in the offices. That we'll all be burned in our beds?'

Nicola said they were wondering whether His Holiness had protested at the Austrian invasion.

'Too soon to know,' said Oppizzoni. 'Anyway, protests never stopped soldiers. I'm glad not to be in charge of things temporal this time. I was Legate *a latere* in 1831 when the Austrians came to restore order and stayed on. Commerce came to a halt. We were clean out of funds and Rome kept asking me for money. That's what it always wants of Bologna. *Bologna la Grassa*, Fat City, that's our reputation, but it's a long time since it was true. In the end I sent back the request, saying I assumed it had been sent to me by mistake. You can't get blood from a stone. The Austrians will have a try, though. Welden has sent on his list of requirements. I have it here. In any commune where his troops stay they are to receive four ounces of rice, eight of beef, one and three quarter pounds of bread and to be provided with coal, wine and three Ferrara ounces of acquavite per man per day. Officers either to have two good meals each per day or forty-eight *baiocchi*. You'd be astonished at how much of a churchman's life goes into dealing with figures. Hay, straw and oats for their horses. Money is the root of most of our troubles. Always was. Luther would *never* have started his schism-shop if Rome hadn't been squeezing the Germans for tithes. People don't like paying out temporal coin for the spiritual and now that the Germans want ours we don't like paying up either.

'However,' here the cardinal looked Nicola hard in the eye, 'I must paternally advise you, young man, to have nothing whatever to do with the hotheads who will presently turn up on the piazza, brandishing rusty fowling pieces, and hoping to stop the imperial forces by luck and a miracle. I want your promise.'

Nicola gave it.

'If you were to be caught with arms in your hand,' said the cardinal, 'I would try to save you, and Marshal Welden would refuse my request for my own good, just as his troops are laying waste His Holiness's dominions for his. You would be shot. I would look weak. The Marshal would be seen to lack respect for ecclesiastical authority, and who but the enemies of order would be the gainers?'

Nicola's mind was less on fowling pieces than on his plan to make love to Maria. His imagination was hot with it. It was as though time had begun running out. It had certainly speeded up. Perhaps the city's excitement was stoking his? By next day – 4th August – people were becoming exalted. Strangers talked in cafés, speculating and raging at the treachery of the troops for whom we had, after all, put our hands deep into our pockets.

'The Germans,' a customer was declaring in the Caffè degli Studenti, where Nicola paused for a lemon juice and water, 'are heading this way in hot pursuit of the volunteers. *They* drew them on us and now, it seems, won't defend us. So for what was all the money collected?'

'Maybe our government doesn't want us defended?' The author of this cynical suggestion looked nervous, but found backers. Incaution was the order of the day.

Another proclamation had now gone up. It was signed by the pro-Legate and stated that, since the best military experts believed the city could not be defended, the Army was leaving and everyone should keep calm.

That afternoon Nicola waited in vain for Maria. Perhaps her family would not let her out? When he went down to the street, he felt feverish. So, it seemed, did everyone else. Wild notions were being tossed about. Could ordinary people hold out now that the Army refused to do so? If they did, might Bologna, like the village of Sermide, be burnt to the ground? Surrounded by hills, it was an easy target for howitzers and cannon. But café strategists had grown reckless. Hope had gone to their heads.

After dining once more with the cardinal, Nicola came out to merge his restlessness in the general seething.

The latest proclamation, pasted on a pillar in piazza San Petronio, was an appeal from Bianchetti the pro-Legate. Someone held up a lantern and the words shifted in its flicker:

'People of Bologna, this comes to you from a man whose hair has grown white in public service . . . from an Italian who has faced danger and exile for Italy . . . Suicide is fanaticism . . . Unwinnable struggles are for savage peoples . . . To risk a town whose site makes it impossible to defend is not heroism but folly . . .' Shadows from the lantern fell on raised faces, making them scowl like anxious gargoyles.

Nicola had arranged to meet Rangone. Normally the streets would have been cleared by now and police patrols on the lookout for nocturnal vagabonds, but tonight the police were closing an eye. Martial music thrummed from a window. Anarchy trickled through warm air.

'I'm going to make love to Maria,' Nicola informed his friend. 'I think she's perplexed by my lack of ardour. When it's so hard to be alone with a man, you expect him to seize his chance.'

'That,' said Rangone, 'is because, despite what our pro-Legate thinks, we are a savage people. In France . . .' He dreamed of it. Women there, he had been told, being freer, were more complex. What could that mean? It was like trying to imagine a new colour.

'Would you fight?' Nicola's mind shifted.

But Rangone said there were no guns and the only trained men left were police and customsmen.

Next morning came news that the Pope *had* protested at the violation of his territories. A *Motu Proprio*, published in Rome on 2nd August, declared the Austrian invasion 'a mere act of *force majeure* which must in no way be read as affecting the full and sovereign rights of the Holy See over the province'. Surely, argued those who wanted to fight, this was a licence to do so?

A deputation delivered a formal protest to Welden's headquarters; the city bells were rung and anyone who could get his hands on a gun which worked armed himself.

Next: another proclamation by the pro-Legate called for prudence. The mood in the streets vacillated and some barricades which had gone up were taken down. Nicola was kept busy all day doing paperwork for the cardinal.

On the morning of the 7th, the Austrians were at the city gates demanding to take over five of them. A deputation went out to haggle over terms: three gates only to be turned over and no soldiers to come into the city. By afternoon, however, Galliera Street was swarming with white-coats.

'Bit of a smell here!' Rangone drew Nicola out of a café as a group of Austrians walked in.

Again Maria didn't come.

By next morning there had been trouble. An Austrian officer and several soldiers had been wounded in a scuffle and the Marshal was demanding hostages. The pro-Legate offered himself. Shops closed. Barricades went up again and the volunteer-hostage was unable to get through. Again the bells rang. People gathered on roofs and balconies. A proclamation by the pro-Legate, so fresh that it smelled of paste, apologised for his inability to deliver himself to the Austrians. The city held its breath.

Nicola was near Rangone's lodging. He did not expect Maria today but had, like a homing creature, headed in his usual direction. Then he saw her. His heart's thud was echoed by a dull boom: cannon. He caught up with her.

'Maria! Let's get off the street.'

Even if Rangone was home he would surely offer them refuge. He wasn't home. From an undiagnosable direction came sounds of artillery fire and an insistent rattling of shot. More booming. It was like beams beating sullenly on hollow wood. Then silence.

'They're firing on the city!'

Nicola drew her from the window. 'Where were you all week?'

'I couldn't get out. I've just taken my mother's laundry round to her customers. She'll think I'm sheltering in one of their houses.' She laughed.

They kissed. 'Why are you laughing?'

'Excitement. Nervousness. Do you think they'll burn the city?'

'No. I don't know. We can't do anything about it. Kiss me.'

'Listen.'

'Don't listen. We're safe here.'

'Unless they burn us out.'

Their love-making was sudden and simple and Maria did not pretend to be a virgin. This was a relief. All the other times they had met here it had been to eat and now they could have been eating each other, as they exchanged sups of stale water from a jug which Rangone had left by the bed. The air was hot and they moved like creatures on a spit, exploring and sucking reassurance from each other with hard mouths.

Outside, noises boomed, stopped, then took up again. Twice he went to the window but could see nothing except a few neighbours as uninformed as himself. So back he came to where Maria lay half-wrapped in a petticoat which she had declined to remove.

'Look.' She showed him bluish love-bites and he was astonished to have marked her after all.

'Don't do it on my neck!'

The third time he went to the window two bodies were being carried past.

'What's happening?' he called down to the men bearing them and learned that the Austrians had two cannon and a howitzer, inside the walls, on the high ground of the Montagnola and that, despite the hail of projectiles – fire balls and bullets – a group of young fellows had managed to press in and were actually on the point of capturing the cannon. The men being carried past were badly hurt. There had been deaths and some houses had caught fire.

'Shall we go down?' he asked her.

'Why?'

It was true they had no weapons – but he wondered how many of those fighting could be armed at all.

'Stay with me. Anyway, what good could you do? You wouldn't even get through the barricades.' She held him. 'See, you're ready again! You won't always be able to do this, you know.' Smiling in a sisterly, matter-of-fact way.

She's used to this, he thought. And she's used to men past their prime. His mind vacillated, flickering out, as his energies focused on the rhythms of rutting. After all, what right had he to be jealous? But he was.

'Give me a thousand kisses, then a hundred more!' she encouraged.

Who had recited that to her? Some prelate?

'Might you,' he asked with late caution, 'have a baby?'

She said she didn't think so and he didn't ask how she knew. Making love to her again, he thought of the next line of the poem, 'When once our brief light fails . . .' There was the cannon again. '*Nox est perpetua una dormienda.*' *Nox, nox, nox*! Then the cannon stopped. Maybe the Bolognese had captured it! This was the first time she had not been afraid to be out so long. Could that be because her father and brother had joined the Austrians, as all the old *Centurioni* and their hangers-on were said to be doing? Gone off to their camp, leaving her free and unsupervised?

Their joint stickiness was beginning to disgust Nicola.

'Won't your mother be worrying? Things seem to have calmed down.'

166

They got dressed, which was just as well, for Rangone's key turned in the lock as they were smoothing down his mangled sheets.

'So you're here?' he greeted them. 'Heard the news?'

The Austrians were retreating. Impossible! No, true! He had heard it from an eye-witness. They'd only just got their cannon away from the Montagnola and the last of the fighting was going on now down by the Galliera Gate – rearguard action. 'They've definitely taken a licking!' The Carabineers had fought side by side with the people. It was wonderful. Heroic! Worthy, enthused Rangone, of the city in its prime.

Maria didn't believe the Austrian Army could have been been beaten by a mob. Her mouth made a moue at the word and Nicola felt angry with her stupidity in not recognising that who had licked the Imperial Army was the *Populus Boniensis* and no mob.

'It started,' Rangone said, 'when the soldiers shot into the crowd which was taunting them and killed a fruit-seller near the San Felice Gate. The people went berserk. They'd got arms earlier from the Civic Guard, then found a deposit of Swiss munitions. Now they're building more barricades in case the Croats come back.'

'As they will,' said Maria. 'The Austrians are our saviours.'

Who was she parroting now? Poor thing, she had not grasped yet that it was time to turn coat and be a patriot! Rangone, amused, began to tease her while he and Nicola walked her home. Two escorts were less compromising than one and offered better protection. From Rangone's banter, Nicola saw what he thought of her.

The air was thick with smoke and charred particles. A few captured Austrians were herded past in dirty coats. Nicola wondered whether the Imperial Army would make a return attack. Rangone thought not. A quick incursion was one thing. A war in the Pope's territory would be harder for Vienna to disown.

'They may just withdraw.'

Maria couldn't believe this and the two young men's conviction made her redden with annoyance. Nicola, remembering that she was being loyal to her family, relented and took her hand.

Rangone wondered whether people had captured many weapons.

'Well,' she said, 'there are arms in secret storehouses.'

The young men went quiet, Rangone asked, 'Where?'

She looked sly. Did she know? No, only that people hid them. Oh? Gaining courage, she said: 'It was in the Austrian warning that people mustn't have arms. So, they'll hide them, won't they?'

Nicola saw that she did know something. Wasn't her father a . . . 'If you know,' he said severely, 'you should say. If only for your father's sake!' He was provoked by her air of quailing deceit. Were the arms, he asked, on the Stanga estate? She shook her head. 'In a convent, then? A Jesuit house? A church?' He tried to remember where she had said her brother had worked before being put to dig at the public works. Hadn't he been a sawyer? 'The saw mills?' It was like playing hunt-the-slipper. He watched her face and saw that he was warm, hot, possibly burning.

So was she whose blush blazed angrily at him. 'I don't know.'

But she did and now so did he.

Cardinal Count Carlo Oppizzoni was eating his usual meal of plain boiled rice. He owed it to his flock to stay healthy, especially since his co-shepherd, Cardinal Amat, the Legate in charge of its temporal welfare, had not done so and was now recovering from unspecified ills at a spa. At Bagni di Lucca, was it? Or Porretto? Some spa. It was remarkable how often the health of senior prelates broke down at the selfsame moment as that of the body politic. That, said His Eminence, was now volatile, not to say feverish. Victory had gone to the heads of the people and, more dangerously, left weapons in their hands. 'My own idea is that Father Gavazzi should be invited here to persuade them to turn them in. Don't they call him "the people's priest"? Well, let's see the priestly side of him!'

'Your Eminence is surely not expecting a revolution?'

'No,' said the cardinal. 'Even Marshal Welden — we've heard from him — says the "mob" was stirred up by the Pope's *Motu Proprio*. He's right. What fired them was nothing more newfangled than allegiance to their own ruler. Good old municipal pride. I feel it myself.' Amazement thickened in the canny webs of his face. 'Welden, in revenge, is letting us stew in our own juice. So, Gavazzi is our man.'

'Was Your Eminence not meant to arrest him? There were letters from Rome . . .'

'Contradictory,' whispered the cardinal. 'But you'd better let me have that dossier. Could be awkward if anyone got hold of it.'

Nicola did not expect to see Maria while the city was out of control and the streets in a fever. Passing Rangone's door, however, he had an impulse to see the room which now felt more like home than any he'd

168

had. It was an hour when Rangone – who, unlike himself, kept regular hours – should be at work. So he used his key and walked in.

The vestibule was dark and, as he paused to adjust his eyes, he heard a band playing some streets away. Pleased, his blood leaped to the military flourish and to something closer which was keeping time to its tantara. This fusing music could be the city's heartbeat.

Rangone's voice was keeping tune too. Rangone was in step and always would be, thought Nicola, whose mind lagged behind what the rest of him already knew. Tum tarara! The brass underscored the repetitiveness of experience. These were the volunteers marching back. The cardinal had been worrying about them all week! He had been warned to expect as many as 4,000, all armed and unruly after their failures at the front. Turbulent.

'. . . Nicola . . .' That was Maria!

She was not calling but talking about him. The bed was moving in time to the band which was drawing close.

'He . . . won't . . . know!' panted Rangone.

'He's a . . . nice boy!'

'Of course he is! And what harm are we doing him? Eh? Tell me. Hmm?'

'Don't . . . Oh!' Maria gave a little yelp.

'No harm!' The band had moved past and the words were now clearer. 'I'm keeping you warm for him. I'm not one to keep things for myself. Warming you up. Teaching you . . . new tricks.'

'What new tricks? Think I didn't know that one?'

'Think I don't know any others?'

'Let's see then.'

Moving more quietly than when he came in, Nicola let himself out the door.

'When we truly love,' Nicola's confessor told him, 'we want to save the soul of the one we love. Not the earthly envelope.'

Why, he wondered, did confessors all talk to him of love? Was it because he revealed some excess of eagerness in their sly, tenebrous play-box where he lurked as tensely as he had sometimes done in cupboards and cubby-holes when playing hide and seek? A hope or need?

*

169

He visited the Villa Chiara which seemed to have shrunk. Count and captain looked wistful and smelled of dog. They had a new one now and were busy training it – perhaps from lack of anything else to be busy with? Their inaction, which he had not noticed before, was palpable and it was as if they could not quite find ways to fill their days. They were excited, though, by the news of Bologna and grateful for his visit. His status had changed. He could feel this as his story dilated in their minds. It blossomed there, its colours brightening as they exclaimed and slapped the table. He told them of the white-coats he had seen herded along and how wretched they had looked. He had heard later that seventy had been taken prisoner and had seen the ruins of a burned-out house where they had put their dead before turning it into a pyre.

'People say there were one hundred and fifty corpses.'

They called the footman to fill his glass. This was a rite of passage. *He* was telling *them*.

In turn they spoke of how Prospero's prospective employer, Count Rossi, had been offered the highest position open to a layman in this realm. One created by the new reforms.

'He's a moderate,' said Stanga. 'Prospero would never work for what he'd call an *esaltato*, meaning a man like me!' His chin bobbed in amused resignation. 'Well. He's seeing life. Visiting drawing rooms. Maybe he'll fall in love?' This was the count's hope, just as his fear was Prospero's becoming a priest.

'We think there may be something in the air,' said Melzi.

Nicola smiled to think of them scanning Prospero's letters for reticences. But the word 'love' felt like heat on a nerve.

When the count took his new dog for a run, Melzi confided, 'He's stopped seeing his cousin. That's for Prospero's sake. She wants him to marry her, but he's reluctant to bring in another heir. Meanwhile, he's lonely. Prospero,' the captain murmured, 'should be more attentive. Write. Visit. You should let him know.'

Later, it was the count's turn to confide. Poor Melzi had been devastated by the news of Guidotti's death. A bad business. And he reproached himself even now for having envied his old friend's promotion. What had happened was that the general, though devoted to the idea of Italy, failed to hold the line at Piave and was blamed by his superiors. Crazed by the disgrace, he brooded for some days then, putting on his dress uniform and medals, made a mad sally out under enemy fire. Pride? Suicide?

Whatever it was, out he went and Bassi, the chaplain, had to coax him to take shelter by insisting that, if he would not, Bassi would stay with him, at the risk of his own life. To be rid of him, Guidotti returned to safety, then rushed back towards the bullets. Back after him went Bassi and so on, back and forth, ridiculously, until the general was dead and the chaplain had three wounds.

'The worst of it is,' said the count, 'that Melzi has a visceral hatred for priests. And now here is our old hero making a bollocks of things and the priest a hero. Prospero would laugh.'

Nicola turned to the matter which had brought him here: the guns. Glibly, he told how the name of the old *Centurione*, which he remembered from here, had turned up on one of the lists at the Curia. 'I guessed this must be his son. He was employed by one of the charities we've set up. Digging . . .' The pay was poor, twenty *baiocchi* a day, so Nicola had gone to see the family, knowing they must be in want. He had discovered that the guns were hidden at a saw-mill and, in the present climate, dangerous.

'I didn't tell the cardinal because it would be difficult for him. Compromising . . .'

'How,' asked Stanga, now restored and businesslike, 'did the man come to tell you about this?'

'Fright,' said Nicola. 'The Austrians, you see, threaten to shoot people who hide arms, so when I mentioned your name, he told me . . .'

'We'll have them moved and rehidden,' decided the count, 'where neither side can get them. Luckily, I still have connections. Peace is what this pope needs. We'll take them into protective custody.' He was rapturous at having something significant to do.

Nicola saw Maria at the Montagnola, which had become a place of pilgrimage. Idlers re-enacted the battle, reliving the highlights of 8th August. She was listening to one of these myth-makers and he, remembering how she and he had spent that afternoon, grew absorbed in a myth of his own. Yearning back to before their Fall, he began dreaming of an Eden – then remembered that even that day the Fall had begun, perhaps more through his fault than hers. He had felt – what? Unelated. Depressed. Had she guessed?

There she was. He could have touched her. She hadn't seen him. Light, falling through the weave of her hat, threw golden flakes on her skin, and her tongue, edging forward, lolled on her lower lip. A strand of hair fell across her eyes and, taking off her hat, she tossed it back with a movement which brought her body so cosily into play that he again felt the fever which she could rouse but not satisfy, and turned, unhappily, away.

The city was divided between warring factions and so was some elusive part of himself over which he lacked control.

God was at His game of suspending help so that men might help themselves and the diocese, though perhaps not in the forefront of the divine mind, was being tried. In the end, the cardinal had left the Gavazzi–Bassi dossier with Nicola, for it had to be kept up and His Eminence's eyesight prevented his doing this himself.

One of its thornier items was a run of letters from Venice, where the volunteers were fighting the Austrians and their chaplain, Bassi, had, with unpriestly verve, referred to the city's pro-Austrian patriarch as a lickspittle. Since Bassi enjoyed his commanding officer's protection, the patriarch had applied for help to Oppizzoni.

Meanwhile, letters from Rome announced that, since the chaplains had been expelled from their order, they were now under His Eminence's jurisdiction.

'Oh, no they're not!' cried Oppizzoni. 'Until they're informed of it, the expulsion has no legal effect, and *I* shall not inform them. For now, we must stay on the good side of Father Gavazzi who has agreed to persuade the populace to give up their arms. Write,' he instructed, 'copies of letters telling the Venetian Patriarch and the Roman Congregation what they want to hear. Then file them. We shall claim the originals were duly sent and lost. Everyone knows the post is disrupted.'

Nicola went to hear Gavazzi urge the Bolognese to give up their arms and noted that the better class of citizen seemed greatly soothed by this appeal.

'They're clutching at straws,' said Rangone who was there too. 'Can anyone *believe* that those who have arms will give them up?'

'I'm not imaginative,' said Nicola. 'What people do often surprises me.'

Rangone gave him a look. 'What's the matter?'

'You can surely guess.'

'No. I'm not imaginative either. Tell me.'

The scene was tedious. Nicola walked back to his office. Lies, he thought furiously, prevailed everywhere. Even in his own head. Even in his passion for Maria. From the beginning, she had been frank enough. It was he who had chosen to deceive himself. It was not concern for her soul which kept him awake at night and made him gnaw his knuckles and see her name in the syllables his pen was tracing on curial stationery. Maybe the notion of soul was simply a word for emotional intensity: something like the steam which rises from an over-heated body then condenses in clammy drops? He could well believe that, swinging from a fierce idealism to distrust of the spirit.

Trying to stun himself with work, he spent the afternoon roughing out replies to the letters in the file. The one from the Barnabite General was sour. Why, it permitted itself to wonder, had His Eminence not acknowledged earlier ones? Might the General humbly beg His Eminence to do him the favour now of letting him know through one of his secretaries that he had received the present communication? Maria, thought Nicola angrily, Maria! Wishing to express his deepest sentiments of veneration, the Barnabite General kissed the cardinal's sacred purple. Ridiculous monkey! Nicola, hearing himself exclaim aloud, was unsure to whom his annoyance was addressed.

The chaplains impressed him. They risked their flesh for disincarnate passions, whereas he was even more shamefully carnal than Rangone, who seemed able to nibble at pleasure then move lightly on. Nicola, a would-be cannibal, wanted to devour and annihilate Maria.

The thick, creamy paper was her skin. He wrote on it: 'I acknowledge receipt of two rescripts from the Sacred Congregation of Bishops and Regulars concerning the Secularisation of the two religious, Fathers Gavazzi and Bassi.'

A letter from Bassi to his Barnabite superiors had been forwarded as no longer concerning them. 'By God's grace,' claimed the chaplain, 'I have till now lived a blameless life here in Venice. Neither taverns nor cafés have had a glimpse of me . . .'

Nicola filed this with the chaplain's attack on the Venetian patriarch, who had claimed that all established authority, including Austria's, must be taken to represent God. Such a doctrine, argued the priest, gave credence to Montesquieu's claim that Catholicism suited tyrants and Protestantism suited republics. This could lose us the allegiance of all high-hearted and generous young men. But . . . Nicola was pondering the word high-hearted and whether it applied to himself, when there was a knock.

'Wait.' He locked up his file then opened his door to find Rangone outside it.

'I realise you must have guessed.'

'I didn't. I heard. I came to your rooms when you and she were there.'

Rangone turned away. 'Hell!'

'It has been, rather.'

'Is it any good my apologising?' Rangone looked him fitfully in the eye. 'I'd offer to keep away from her, but I imagine you think her tarnished or something. Different? I could, if you didn't think this worm-base of me, prove to you that it's not so.'

Nicola felt tired.

'Sit down,' he invited and slumped morosely in a wooden chair.

'I wish I could undo it. It was self-indulgent and not really much fun.'

'It sounded like fun.'

'Shit!'

'Oddly, I get the impression that you want something from me. Absolution?'

'Have I lost your friendship?'

'Were we friends?'

'You're sour. You don't mean that.'

'You want us to shake hands? Or go drinking? A conciliatory ceremony? You probably had them in your family as a child? I never had a family and don't know how to play.'

'Is there something I can do?'

'A penance?'

'If you like.'

'Give her money. As much as you can afford. You're far richer than I or I wouldn't ask. It's for her family. They're poor.'

'It's not very moral,' said Rangone. 'Encouraging her to sell herself. All right, all right!' He fluttered appeasing hands. 'I'll do it. I'm only wondering if you know . . .'

'. . . that she had other lovers. That's what you're going to say, isn't it? I see it in your eye. But why should it be more moral for her *not* to get money for her family?'

'Oh, her family . . ..'

'I know about them.'

'Do you want me to stop seeing her?'

'No. Don't drop her! That would be cruel.'

'I don't think she expects much from me.'

'But she may from *me* – and you'll have to make it up to her.'

174

Rangone laughed. 'This has been like going to confession to a quite immoral priest.'

'Oh, there are different sorts of priests and moralities now,' said Nicola, thinking of the dossier.

'None I think who would say "Go and sin some more".'

'I just don't want her to be lonely.'

'Like yourself? Why don't we go out to dinner or something? There are more fish in the sea, you know. I could get you another girl. That was more what I expected to do.'

But Nicola said he had to dine with the cardinal.

Eleven

The war was now a side-show, for only the Republic of Venice was holding out. A ritual. A morality play. Nicola, unscrolling it in his mind, imagined Father Bassi, to whom Garibaldi had given a horse, riding unarmed in the front line. A man of forty-seven. A poet whose hair curled over his collar. Some of his verse turned up in the dossier. Discovering that he could have made a soldier had banished priestly humility. Intercepted letters from him showed a closed world expanding and the mind's walls blown down.

Nicola, like a spectator at a play, would have liked to warn him that he was riding for a fall. He couldn't, of course. It would make trouble for the cardinal. But neither could he quite bring himself to disapprove of Bassi whose excitement was infectious and whose failings brought him close – for instance, he craved praise. Writing to a friend, he exulted in his physical courage – a surprise? – and complained at not being mentioned in dispatches. More selflessly, he pleaded with the military authorities to improve the men's conditions. Poor lodging and sanitation demoralised them, he argued, and, with practical charity, hammered at the indifference or inefficiency of GHQ.

Sanitation! Nicola used the word to punish a riot of rhetoric in his mind. It also led him to ask the cardinal whether Maria's father could have a job sweeping the cathedral. The present sweeper was old and in need of a helper.

'But dear boy,' cried His Eminence, 'that position is one whose bestowal requires at least as much politicking as the appointment of a bishop! Who is this candidate of yours? Can he handle a brush? It's no sinecure, you know. People spit and litter and, though I'll spare your blushes, do worse in the cathedral. Would he be prepared to do a little spying?'

'In the cathedral?'

'Indeed! You'd be astonished what goes on there, especially now that there is all but a schism in the Church. I speak freely because it would be tedious to have to watch my tongue with you. I leave it to your sense of honour to let me know if I should.'

The cardinal, who had from the first enjoyed Nicola's eagerness, noted a wistful quiver to it now and diagnosed religious doubt or some such teething trouble due to youth and a generous spirit. *Not my business, though* Oppizzoni comfortably. *Let his confessor take care of it.* He relished that quiver though. And because he did, Maria's father became the cathedral's second sweeper: *lo scopatore sostituito.*

'Gavazzi,' noted the cardinal, 'is being accused of pocketing funds raised for the Army. I fancy his trouble is poor bookkeeping. I don't suppose, do you, that he can be good at sums? Here he's been teaching us charity and scolding shopkeepers who sack their assistants in thin times! Now, he must refute charges made, no doubt, by those same shop-keepers. He's learning that it's easier to preach than do.'

It was September and Rome had a new ministry whose mainstay was Count Pellegrino Rossi.

'Perhaps he is tired of life?' said Oppizzoni, whose own experiences coloured his outlook.

'Perhaps,' said a priest known for his patriotism, 'things look more hopeful to those in the know.'

'*We* know enough,' said the cardinal with asperity. 'We pay enough spies, God knows, to know. You can take it from me that the national question will be his downfall. Patriots including, I think, Your Reverence, are pressing for the war to go on and never asking from whence the money is to come. Rossi's friends won't forgive him if he doesn't fight, and if he fights and loses, neither will they forgive that.'

Shyly, Nicola disclosed that a friend of his was now the count's personal secretary.

'Does he write to you?'

'Not much,' Nicola admitted. This disappointed him but the cardinal praised discretion in the employees of great men.

'If you do hear from him,' he added however, 'let me know.'

177

Pink clouds, sphery as cherub's limbs, were heralding a storm. It was hot and close and Count Rossi, finding the Caffè Venezia crowded, was pleased to be hailed by someone with a spare place at his table. This was Don Bibi Abbondanza, a priest whose violet legs twinkled in motion like those of a marsh bird. Just now, he was at rest and his belly, bright in the swathe of its cummerbund, had a reassuring stability. People liked Don Bibi.

'*L'homme du juste milieu!*' Don Bibi pulled out a chair for Rossi. 'A dangerous thing to be. Have you ever witnessed a bullfight? The matador has nothing at his back while the men who stir up the bull stay near the fence so that they may vault over it.'

'Yet men like me are accused of sitting on fences.'

Don Bibi bent towards him. 'The man in the middle,' he instructed, 'annoys everyone. He seeks to reconcile but it is not in our nature to be reconciled. We are fruits of the Fall! Ours is a nature designed to be godlike then spoilt by Lucifer, the first revolutionary. We're a mix, a mess, and have an itch in our arse which keeps us on the move. *You* shuttled between countries. Your agility was your defence. Beware of settling.'

'Here?'

'For the world. It's a cave of shadows. A Limbo and a vestibule. I remind myself of this daily,' said the fat man. 'If I didn't I'd go mad at its stupidity. I'd lay about me with an axe! Ours is a wise religion. I derive infinite comfort from it.'

'You're speaking to a politician, Don Bibi. We have to deal with what you call shadows.'

'I', said the priest, spooning into his ice-cream, 'have only one message which I repeat. Remember Monseigneur Affre, the Archbishop of Paris, was killed, you'll recall, in the riots of last June. People are calling him saintly because he went out to mediate and was killed by a stray bullet. I say a man who can't defend himself can't defend his institution.'

After a while the count left for Lepri's restaurant. He decided that Don Bibi was simply advising him to throw in his lot with the Curia. The question was would it do as much for him?

Don Bibi's last remark had been, 'Beware of tolerance, Count!'

He meant tolerance of revolutionaries, but one must presume both sides were plotting. Arms – whose? – had been discovered in the palazzo Sciarra. Embittered volunteers were rampaging through the northern

Legations; the war was lost; the state coffers were empty and the Pope, having warred a bit and reformed a bit and chopped and changed his policies, was turning to Rossi to save him. How work with such a man?

Rossi reflected that his was not a new dilemma. Perhaps he should study Castiglione's advice to courtiers on how to navigate the shallows around an unreliable prince?

And how deal with the mob? Firework shows were one method. Watching one last Easter, he had been struck to see a protest organised by democrats dribble away when the great Catherine wheel surged over St Peter's followed by a huge VIVA PIO NONO! Waste, at a time of war and hunger, did not trouble the crowd. Seeing them applaud, he knew them for what they were: an ancient and unreliable rabble. They, no doubt, thought of him as chillily Swiss.

Outside the restaurant, the streets were poorly lit. It was, however, only a step to where footmen with lighted torches stood outside the palace where his friend, the Comtesse de Menou, was holding a reception. This connection was a weakness to which some might have warmed: a sign of humanity in the cold Rossi. But they would not have the chance. A Protestant wife was compromising enough without letting the town know he had a mistress.

The startling radiance of light and colour might have charmed him less if he had come by carriage. After the dark streets, the effect was entrancing. Prudently cool, he did not linger with his friend. Not greeting her with the intimacy he craved caused an ache which spread desolately along his nerves, then gave way to a sensation of pleasure. This sensuous metamorphosis always caught him by surprise. It was a paradox of the body which puzzled him as much as he puzzled others. Ravished for moments by narcotic bliss, he felt unable to respond to those around him with more than a gelid bow. He was considered haughty and remote.

Dutiful, he joined some ladies who were being lively with a trio of prelates. Death was their topic. A French prelate listed the heroines of Italian literature, marvelling at their poor health. Were real women here as prone, he asked, to die young as Clorinda, Laura and Beatrice? He dared hardly address those present lest they go into a decline and oblige him to write propitiating elegies to their ghosts. It was a safe parody of courtship and the Italian clerics smiled at his dexterity.

A pert, ringleted French lady intercepted Rossi. Was it true that the French Government had opposed his becoming the Pope's minister and that he had dictated conditions to His Holiness?

The prelates melted away.

'If I were younger,' said Rossi to the bubbling lady, 'I would hope you had frightened them off so as to be alone with me.' He felt like an old horse taken out to canter over low obstacles. Still bubbling, she offered her fortune-teller's advice.

'Your fortune-teller is probably a spy.'

'They say that here of every second person.'

'It is true of every second person.'

'Then which of us two is one?'

'Surely the one asking questions!'

'Well, to disarm suspicion I'll tell some gossip about a person with influence in High Places, a rival to your learned self.'

'A lady, naturally?'

'A nun.' The ringlets shook. 'They say she prophesies. In exchange, will you tell me some stale old gossip? Is it true the Countess Spaur used to have some influence?'

'Oh, I imagine she still has. She has for a long time been a friend in what you call High Places. Shall we say HP? We should have a code. Masons have a glossary of words which mean one thing to the initiate and another to the generality. "Money" for instance means "weapons", "charity" freedom and "secrecy" revolution!'

'Gossip has it you were a mason yourself.'

'Gossip is wrong. If I had been I would not have been accepted as ambassador here nor now as minister. My enemies would have ferreted it out. As it is, they merely spread it about.'

'How interesting to be a man! Here, as they were saying when you came in, there are only two roles for a woman: to die and become a Beatrice or to give birth and be a Mamma.'

'Or a nun.'

She made a face.

'Or, like Lord Byron's friend, Teresa Guiccioli, dilute your respectability. Become either more holy or less respectable,' he teased. 'That's all I can suggest.'

'Yours is a dangerous influence. I shall pray for the Pope.'

She left him, laughing, and now, at last, he talked to his hostess, a lady who had come to Rome for his sake and gave receptions like this to help his career.

'I have a bad feeling,' she said. 'Details are coming out about the troubles faced by the last ministry. Whoever takes over risks being a scapegoat. For the Pope, reform is bitter physic. He knows he needs it yet cannot swallow it.'

'You've been listening to gossip.'

'Of course. What would you have me do? Read the papers which contain nothing but accounts of who kissed his slipper? Gossip comes hot from my footmen, who use the same sources as the police – other footmen.'

'Do they spy on as well as for us?'

'If they do they must be bored.'

Resentful! His discretion mortified her. But what could he do?

'My dear, I'm obliged to ask you to rise to new heights of discretion.'

She was ahead of him. 'Whom do you want me to seduce?' Brisk. Game?

Plodding, yet tempted to pretend it was a joke, he suggested she feign interest in an agreeable young man. 'If your footmen think he has been made happy, it will distract their attention from me.'

'You haven't much shame.'

'We agreed to have none.'

'And is this . . . puppet to be privy to our secret?'

'No. He's nineteen and, I'm told, amiable. I haven't met him yet but Minghetti vouches for him and his father used to be a friend of the Pope's. Officially, he is to be my secretary. The idea only just came to me of using him as a *chandelier* – you remember Musset's play? Cover! A fig leaf.'

'In the play the lady and the *chandelier* fall in love. Will you risk that?'

'What choice have I?'

'You could give up your ambitions.'

'If you ask me to, I will.'

'I am asking. Will you?'

She doesn't mean it, he thought. The hope of power is what draws her to me. Without it, what am I? An old man with a face like a paper bag. But might she enjoy the power of refusing power? Maybe she too gets that thrill which I find in tormenting myself?

'If you ask, I cannot refuse you.'

But what about my sons and Charlotte? he thought. I need a position. Paris is closed to me. All my protectors have fled. My teaching posts are forfeit. Switzerland would be difficult. I am sixty-one and too well known. And – I have no money. Not enough. Aloud, he said, 'All right! I'll give it up.'

'Will you hate me?'

'How can I say?'

Eye stared at eye. They knew each other too well. This was the *braccio di ferro* where each tried to force down the other's arm. There was no gender here but a clash of wills and a testing.

181

'So. Put me out of pain.'

'You're in pain?' She smiled.

'Well?'

'I want you to take power.'

It was almost a let-down. He had been so taut. Fluids in his body made themselves felt as they boiled or curdled or flowed back to where they should have been. He might have been about to have an attack.

'You mustn't do this to me again.'

Her hand brushed his sleeve, delicately, imperceptibly. A feather touch. The footmen would have nothing to report. 'No. It was because of what you just asked.'

'I am still asking it.' It was his turn to be hard.

'I understand.'

'His name is Prospero Stanga. I shall bring him tomorrow.'

'Very well.'

They walked in different directions. He talked to various people. The originality of this drawing room was that it was one of the few open to people of different persuasions. Prelates met Liberals. Democrats met great noblemen. The stiff conservatives were curious and came. Political men came for Rossi.

The French prelate approached him and nodded to where, in a corner, Rossi recognised the ex-priest who some months before had told him of his unfrocking.

'A sad case,' said the prelate. 'Perhaps you could invoke lenience on his behalf?'

'You're asking the wrong man. My argument is that the Pope should leave temporal matters to the laity. How then can I intervene in religious ones?'

'But if he is sympathetic to reforms, surely he will be sympathetic to priests like Don Mauro? Don't you agree that we must go forward or back? That there is no half way?'

'No,' said Rossi. 'I don't. That's a religious way of thinking. Feminine and visionary. I have a theory as to why most visions are of the Virgin and seen by girls. It's because men respect hierarchy and are ready to work their way up. Girls hope to rise in one leap. If they are religious, they see the Virgin. If not, they try to marry a powerful man. The Virgin is the prime interceder and bypasses all rules by being conceived immaculate then whisked up to heaven in the teeth of bureaucracies and the laws of gravity. Something similar, to be sure, can happen to popes.'

The French prelate laughed. 'My mother,' he said, 'has two sons. My brother is an ambassador and able to receive her in some state. She prefers, however, to stay with me. She says I am like the daughter she never had. Other priests' mothers say the same.'

'I am not,' Rossi objected, 'casting a slur on femininity. Women – but what can be said on the topic is well known.'

Across the room, Madame de Menou was teasing a cardinal.

'What do you think your mother meant?'

'Perhaps that clerics make better friends than other people. A priest I know says he is in love with friendship: *amoureux de l'amitié.* That savagery which I notice in heterosexual love – a bit tigerish, don't you think? – is absent.'

Tigerish, thought the count. Is she? Why am I throwing this youth in her way? A breath of jealousy caught in his throat.

Leaving the drawing room, he retired to a small study to wait for the guests to leave. Half dozing, he sipped Marsala. How old was she now? Twenty-nine. They had known each other for ten years. She – her name was Dominique – played her game with skill. She was childless. That fund of attention which women give their families now held the Curia in its sights, the Republicans, the Prince of Canino's clique, and the Pope.

On the wall hung a portrait of her painted some years ago. She wore a ball dress, was downier than now and flirted, questingly, with the world: russet hair, feline eyes, sloping shoulders, silky skin. Optimistic, her upper lip rose slightly to reveal small, even teeth. He suspected her of underrating a factor which, talking to her, he called 'Fortuna' and talking to Pius, 'God'. In his mind he thought of it as impish: a disruptive daemon which defies good planning. Despite a lifetime's rational behaviour, it stimulated him in ways he would not even try to explain to her. Instead, he would follow all her wise advice then, like a Theseus whose Ariadne has furnished him with too short a threat, would proceed fearfully but determinedly alone.

Monsignor Amandi, back from investigating visionaries, found some of their threats realised. The honeymoon between Pope and *popolo* was at an end, though Pius could not see this. Friends grimaced behind their hands. He still walked among the rabble on foot! And was impervious to advice.

Metternich, Pius liked to remind would-be advisers, had had to flee. Months ago now. Off he'd had to lollop with his tail between his legs to London. So had Guizot and Louis Philippe. And here was he whom

183

they had presumed to advise, four, five and six months later with his good people still cheering him. Ha! No thanks to himself, to be sure! As he said so, he would tilt an ecstatic face heavenward in a way maddening to ministers, since it was how he brushed their opinions aside. How could facts and figures compete with the *doctrina infusa* floating down to him like gold beams in a sacred painting?

Cardinal Gizzi, his first Secretary of State, had resigned after twelve months. He had been succeeded by Pius's cousin, Gabriele Ferretti, who later fled in the night. The present Cardinal Secretary, Soglia, couldn't wait to resign.

'I've been hoping,' Soglia confided to Amandi, 'that *you* might relieve me. I could go then with a good conscience.'

Amandi was named Consultor of the Holy Office.

'It could,' hoped Soglia, 'be a precursory token?'

Amandi, though often invited to dine in the Quirinal Gardens, doubted that Mastai would turn to him. Perhaps he was reluctant to trust himself to a man who had influenced him in the past? The great complaint about Pius was his lack of constancy.

'He doesn't just lack it,' Soglia confided, 'he dislikes it. He feels that, as the spirit bloweth where it listeth, we should all bend like reeds. Just now he wants me to resist Pellegrino Rossi's attempts to deal with foreign affairs. He hates a layman to have power – but why then ask one to govern? I ask only to go back to my diocese in Osimo,' said the cardinal on a warm evening in the Quirinal Gardens when the trees were hung with lanterns and the footmen's livery glowed like fruit. 'Osimo!' He sighed and squashed a mosquito on his red silk thigh.

Nobody cared to stay in Rome in October, when infections were rife, though less so on the Quirinal Hill than in the Vatican, where the *mal aria* was at its worst.

The count, whose inner self ached, received young Stanga with courtesy. The boy was handsome, just as Minghetti had said he would be. The young, he told himself, are another species. Their skin covers them differently.

Prospero, seated on a divan, gave a lively account of events in Bologna, was deferent and drank a jug of barleywater without observing his host's distress. Meanwhile, to Rossi's distracted eye, he looked, at moments, like a satyr. Through layers of summer clothing, the host could, or thought he could, see the stirrings of rampant flesh.

Not for a moment, though, did His Excellency's thoughts betray themselves. Old habits stood to him and he smiled his affable smile. 'Later on, we'll pay a visit to a friend of mine,' he told the boy whose skin, on closer inspection, was not so perfect. 'Madame de Menou is French but knows this city and can introduce you to its ways. Go with her to the Corso tomorrow and learn the names and political persuasions of the people she will point out. You mustn't be embarrassed to ask quite simple things. You'll be of no use to me until you've learned your way round.'

'He was open and easy with me,' Prospero told Nicola later. 'He had a reputation for haughtiness, but I never saw that. He was kindness itself and so was Madame de Menou.'

'He thinks of me as a mother,' Dominique told the count. 'I'm not saying it to reassure you. The poor boy's shocked by the city whose perfidy I at once described. He's devoted to you already and full of righteous indignation. Your squire! He sees us a couple and thinks we're the same age.'

'Does he attract you?'

'Now you're trying to make something happen which would do nobody any good.'

'It might bring you some enjoyment.'

'To you, I'm young. To him, old. Which do you suppose I like?'

'You might enjoy changing his opinion.'

'I might if I had nothing else on my mind. As it is, I have just learned that plans to murder you are being toasted at the Osteria del Forno in Orvieto wine.'

'Your footmen may invent such things to earn your gratitude.'

'Do you think they invented this?' She handed him a letter in a manifestly disguised hand.

He read:

Filthy Jacobine,
    Your lover is no fit minister for this state. How can a mongrel turncoat who, not content with taking a Protestant wife, deceives her with a French atheist, be loyal to God's Kingdom?
    You will perish in the city you pollute and so will he. Be warned,
                                                        A loyal Catholic

Rossi folded the paper. That's how they think, he told himself. That's the good old Roman gutter. Venomous scorpions are coming out of the woodwork.

'You're right,' he told her. 'What you must do is engage some ex-soldiers as footmen and take them wherever you go. Meanwhile, show yourself in public with the boy. I shall see less of you. Let's try not to torment each other.'

She embraced him. 'What about your safety?'

'I promise to be careful,' he told her – though how avoid a dagger? The spies' dossiers he had been reading emphasised the difficulties. Their contributors were all terrified.

To the boy he admitted that the state of the state was worse than he had supposed. 'I'm going to have no time for private life, yet everything in this city is done by contacts and, though this may surprise you, more influence moves up than down. Small men – clerks, stewards and accountants – think for the rest. They know everyone's business, while the great landowners don't even know their own, so what's said in the counting house and sacristy will be thought tomorrow in the papal court. Frequent them for me, Stanga. Keep your ears open. Drop a wise word when you can.'

The city was lurid with rumour.

In the evenings when Madame de Menou's guests left, Rossi and the boy lingered over a last glass of port to compare what they had heard. Prospero's naïvety rid the other two of their fears as it set them laughing at his.

'Forgive me,' he said one evening, 'but I can't see why you invite men like the Principe di Canino to your house. That fat little beast is scattering money in all directions in the hope of having you killed and himself named leader of a radical Italy. The police and dragoons have pocketed bags of his gold.'

'Oh,' said Rossi, 'it can't be easy to be a minor Bonaparte. I'm told he's a good naturalist. That's probably his true vocation. The rest is theatre. Pretence. The real danger is small men.'

'Well, he pays *them*,' said Prospero. 'There's a cabinet-makers' shop in the Monti district where people go to plot after dark. Galletti, the ex-minister of Police, drops by, but the moving spirit is the prince. He invites the ringleaders back to his palace. They're so indiscreet that I could get invited myself.'

'Theatre!' Rossi nodded. 'They need a public.' Sometimes he felt the city shake like canvas as he walked through it.

Madame de Menou had heard of other conspirators meeting in the piazza del Popolo and – but Rossi distrusted spies' reports. 'When they say "conspire",' he argued, 'they may mean "talk". Remember that there is no tradition of free speech here.'

More dangerous were the veterans from the volunteer corps. These were now half-disbanded, and the men, embittered by defeat, felt betrayed and, speaking in confidence, had been. By Pius.

'You' said Dominique, 'are the target for the resentment he arouses. You,' she said mischievously, 'are his *chandelier*!'

Prospero, taking the city's pulse, found it feverish. October had emptied the great palaces. All that was left were disgruntled civil servants kept to prepare Rossi's reforms. He was working round the clock himself, but they were used to their October vacation and in their small way added to the disaffection. Things could take on a momentum . . . Seeing Madame de Menou blench, Rossi made signs to the boy. Hush. Prospero stopped. She turned and caught the count signalling. They laughed. Their sessions, counterparts of those in the palace of the Principe di Canino, had the thrill of a cabal.

Prospero was impressionable and Rossi reflected that young minds did tend to thresh about like Laocoön's sea serpent. To be accurate, though, the one grappling with ancient coils was himself.

What grew increasingly useful were the boy's accounts of the city's byways which, venturing where the other two could not, he diligently explored. Up and down grimy stairways Rossi followed him in his mind, corkscrewing through palaces where dried turds – feline and human – hollow beetle-shells and less diagnosable droppings crackled into dust, and stone steps were so worn as to seem to the deluded eye to undulate like festoons. Here clung ancient odours of the dried cod left to soak for the twenty-four hours preceding every day of abstinence. Laundry dripped in inner courtyards. Women sang. Artisans conspired and Jesuits lurked. Prospero had found one who, loath to leave with his fellows, had locked himself in a room where he was recording the evil being done during the Society's exile. He had his eye on Rossi. Retribution would catch up with him, he assured, and prayed for this daily when celebrating mass on a chiffonier.

The count's unpopularity with the Society had started when he helped suppress their schools in France but now a new crime was being laid at his door. This was the Church Property Mortgage, a measure which had been introduced before he came to power and for which he was not in the least responsible. He was blamed for it, though, by priests who saw it as the greatest blow levelled at religion since the fall of Jerusalem. What had happened was that last spring there had been a run on the

Banca Romana which the state – being in debt to it – had allowed to function without a reserve. The bank ran out of money. Foreign loans were unobtainable and the Pope, in desperation, authorised the floating of a loan for two million *scudi*, using Church property as security. The first payment was now due and the mortgaged property in danger of being sold. To prevent this, Mastai begged the clergy for a contribution of 200,000 *scudi* and they, reluctantly, agreed to make the treasury a gift of four million, payable over a fifteen-year period, so as to free their assets of all liability: an astute move.

'If they hadn't paid off the mortgage now,' said Rossi, 'a more radical government could confiscate their property later. I praised their shrewdness in my address of thanks.'

'It might have been more tactful to praise their generosity.'

'Oh, they won't forgive me anyway. Especially since I have set up a commission to reform the tax system and abolish exemptions. You can't imagine the fury. I'm reforming the law courts too and the Army and police. More fury!'

'The police? You're provoking the police?'

'Not provoking. Reforming. People *want* reform. Everyone says so. They want industry, railways and telegraph lines and the advantages of modern living, but they still want tax exemptions. Well, they can't have them.'

His eyes swivelled, reviewing projects in his mind. He was tired. Hadn't been sleeping. Hadn't made love to her in – how long? Sixty-one years old! Racing the clock.

'What are they saying in the drawing rooms?' he asked her.

'It's all stale. Most people are away.' She no longer spoke to him of conspiracies.

'Bologna,' he said, 'is in a frenzy. The "victory" went to people's heads.' His eye glittered with irony. He liked to deflate a myth. Myths did damage and he stepped on them, as he might on a puff-ball or a kelp-bladder. Pff! Out oozed the airy lies. 'Intelligence sources show that Austrian orders were not to occupy the city lest the Anglo-French mediation over the armistice be affected. Even before the skirmish their troops had been told to retreat. Yet, now, a legend has been born. The brave populace wins through. David defeats Goliath. Republicans are puffing the people up and the idle poor are not only holding onto their guns but demanding payment for "keeping watch" over the city. How is your father?' he asked Prospero. 'Villas are being burgled and worse.'

Prospero thought his father could look out for himself.

The count said he had ordered the arrest of the demagogues, Garibaldi and Gavazzi, who were fomenting trouble up there.

Later, while driving on the Pincian Hill, Madame de Menou lamented to Prospero that the count, being the only man of calibre in the government, had to think of *everything*. 'If the conspiracies don't kill him, over-work will. He's sixty-one.'

That was ten years older than Prospero's own father. Until now he had not thought of his patrons as having ages at all. Astounded, he stole glances at her as she rustled from her carriage and again as she raised the parasol which threw scalloped shadows on her neck. Young enough to be Rossi's daughter – or granddaughter!

'In a way,' she said, 'he's creating a constitution.' She shook her head over the oddity. In a true parliamentary system no one man would have had such a burden. An absolute monarch perhaps – but *he* would be properly protected.

In mid-October a baker, who had somehow found himself in the confidence of desperate men, came to Rossi to reveal an antiquated sort of plot. Carabineers and dragoons were to march to the Quirinal and demand that the Pope renounce his temporal power. All cardinals and princes would be seized and a republic declared. The plan was demented. Perhaps it was a mere provocation?

Yet the baker gave details which inspired confidence and, though the designated date passed without trouble, Rossi, writing in the *Gazzetta di Roma*, menaced those who might be 'tempted to carry out certain projects'. Was he foolish to dare them?

'Let's go to Frascati,' proposed Madame de Menou. 'We'll drink that lovely wine. It doesn't travel at all,' she told Prospero. 'If you drink it here it's not the same.'

Could the baker have been settling a private score? Or was there a plot within the plot? Prospero knew from his father that in secret societies there was often an inner core whose plans differed from those discussed with the rank and file.

'He's had another anonymous letter,' said Madame de Menou. 'Something unpleasant. He won't show it.'

Again they were in her carriage. The hood was down. They saw veterans wearing a characteristic oilskin known as a *panuntella*. That meant 'oiled bread' and seemed to horrify her. It was as if they were sandwiches looking for meat. Some lacked shoes. By now those who really wanted to fight had re-enlisted and gone north.

Her sunshade would not stay open. Taking it from her, he tested the device on its shaft. Pink and silky, it expanded like a sea urchin, and light, falling through, coloured the cloth of his trousered thighs. She leaned a little way towards him so that the silk shaded them both. Then the toylike thing snapped shut. 'I'm foolishly superstitious today. Is it broken?' Her scent hypnotised him. The silk and the kid of her glove seemed as live as grass. The carriage was a moving boudoir and people in other ones stared. A lady raised her lorgnette. Shyly, he moved away from her; then, aware that this manoeuvre too would have been noted, pretended to be intent on the wayward movements of the parasol.

He thought: she doesn't understand the small-mindedness of this city. There's the Duchessa di Rignano observing us now. And Prince Volkonsky. Fumbling at the sunshade, he became aware that his embarrassment amused her.

The letter which Rossi had received ran as follows:

> So, count, we find
> You're the horned kind!
> Your luck won't hold,
> Cuckold!
> So now
> Bow
> Out to youth,
> As, in truth,
> Age must.
> You'll soon be dust.
> Trust,
>
> *Vox populi*

Rossi felt as though he had been dipped in a privy. To be sure, *vox populi* was only mouthing the lines he had fed it, but its readiness to do so upset him. He did not show Dominique the jingle, for what pained him in it was a measure of pity. It could have been more abusive. Such things usually were. He found himself adding to it:

190

Don't you see
That he could be
Your son's son!
You're sixty-one!

Truth wrote as woundingly as *vox populi* – and indeed, maybe *vox populi* was a friend.

He left for Frascati, refusing to let the other two come. He feared they too might have received jingles and be hiding them. Collusive pity could play Cupid, but he would not think about this. The Chamber was to reconvene on 15th November.

In Frascati, he drove about in a hired carriage, showing himself everywhere in the company of his wife, who had come from Switzerland to help him play the judicious and solid citizen – he had, to be sure, become one – of this theocratic state. In tall hat, frock coat, lawn shirt and discreet waistcoat, he manifested propriety. This was the State of the Church and he was its Minister. The visible manifested the invisible and he, who hoped to reconcile the Rights of Man – some of them, anyway – with the Commands of God, had better be winning in his ways.

Before leaving Rome he had gone to see the Pope and found him evasive. Possibly he was planning to replace him as minister. With whom? There was nobody even half as capable. But Mastai lacked realism. He had betrayed his last government, had betrayed his soldiers in mid-war, and might well betray Rossi.

Mastai's lower lip had protruded damply and he had made puns. They were his passion and, thought the minister, suited the doubleness of the priestly ruler's vision. Did he hope to turn this state back into the police state he had taken over two years ago? Interestingly, he was believed to have the evil eye. People, meeting him on his walks, sank on one knee, doffed their hats and, in the shelter of the hat's crown, made the horned sign with index and little finger. If able to do so with discretion, men touched their privates and women their keys. There was, thought Rossi, a logic to God's vicar having demonic properties. Christianity had, after all, inherited the city from paganism and small gods been subsumed. Why should not one be in attendance on Mastai?

Rossi spent his week in Frascati visiting acquaintances – all capable of writing anonymous jingles. Innumerable nephews were recommended to him for employment. On asking what the man had done so far, he was always told:

'Nothing, but if he were less indolent, he could surely do anything at all.'

Often the man was thirty or thirty-five. 'Ah,' quipped Rossi, 'the state has a great reserve of indolent men!'

'Well,' the supplicant's friend would argue, 'why not? The *prelates* who run it receive no practical training.'

'But we all know,' Rossi would reply, 'that a prelate is good for anything. More is expected of a layman.'

His irony was too mild for them. Roman aristocrats – possibly the idlest in Europe – had not exerted their wits in a long time and were uncomfortable when a fellow wouldn't come out with what he thought. Till now, they had had no role in government and their lands were farmed by agents who had begun to form the nucleus of a new class. Cardinal Antonelli, one of the cleverer prelates, had sprung from it and Pius who seemed to trust him might trust Rossi too if only he could believe him capable of holding the state together. Faith was what was needed. Confidence. To secure it, Rossi was pinning his hopes to the programme outlined in a speech he planned to deliver to the Chamber tomorrow and to the Pope this afternoon.

At the thought, he felt his hand make the horned sign.

After seeing Pius – he was thinking this on the drive back to Rome – he would make love to Dominique and exorcise the phantoms which had come between them. He was bringing her a basket of Muscat grapes not unlike the colour of her flesh.

Order in Bologna had broken down.

'It's not even political now,' lamented the cardinal. The latest death was that of a night watchman in a sawmill. 'They tell me he was a harmless poor fellow and the father of two. He was knocked on the head!'

Nicola asked the name of the sawmill and, on hearing that it was the one he had mentioned to Captain Melzi and Count Stanga, went cold. Was he to blame for another death?

Garibaldi, complained Oppizzoni, was back in town. 'Staying at the Pensione Svizzera. Rome wants him arrested. Him and Father Gavazzi!' He groaned at the folly. 'We'd have a revolution in the piazza. I've managed to persuade General Zucchi to take Gavazzi only.' There was a pause. 'I want you,' he said quietly, 'to warn him to slip away. He's in the Barnabite convent. I'll give you a letter for the Father Provincial to get you in. Then you must alert the abate. They'll aim to trick him, so he must trust nobody. On no account compromise me.'

Nicola hurried to the convent – only to find a police carriage already at the door. Two policemen and an official-looking gentleman were talking to the porter.

'I need to see the Father Provincial.' Nicola waved his letter.

'It's a bad moment.' The porter slid his eyes from the gentleman to Nicola. 'Nobody is to go in or out.'

'I'm on the cardinal's business. It's urgent.'

The porter was in a quandary and Nicola about to resolve it for him by skipping past, when Father Gavazzi arrived in a state of high excitement.

'You wanted to see me?' he asked the important-looking gentleman.

'We have a message from His Holiness. He wants to consult with you and we are to convey you to Rome. There is a letter at the government palace.'

Gavazzi looked at the police carriage.

'For security,' said the gentleman, 'in these troubled times.'

Nicola now greeted Gavazzi. But the abate's attention was all for the bearers of the papal message. One of the men turned to open the carriage door and Nicola, who had been making warning signs, was caught out and had to pretend to have been stung by a bee. Shyly, rubbing the fictitious sting, he hummed the *Dies irae*. Gavazzi, however, wasn't listening. Irritably, he waved away Nicola and his bee and begged the police to tell him more about the Holy Father's summons. Did it mean that Pius had had a change of heart? Was he eager for a first-hand report on the fighting?

As a last resort, Nicola began to stroke the police horses and launched into a sort of clowning parody which had been popular at the Collegio: 'Beware,' he warned them. 'Put not your trust in masters, for they are fickle and you, dearly beloved dobbins, could easily end in the knackers' yard. Even the noblest humans lack your Hippic candour and if you could but see into their secret minds, you would make a run for it now!' Here he had to stop for a policeman laid a hand on his arm, while Gavazzi raised his in a hushing gesture. Holding himself erect, the abate was marvelling, 'So His Holiness wishes to see me?'

'Yes,' said the policemen.

'Ah!' breathed the abate. 'I've prayed long and hard for a chance to speak to him face to face and God has answered my prayers. Thank

God! Thank God and may He bless the Angel Pope!' His vindicated smile was painful to see.

Four days later the *Gazzetta di Bologna* carried the following item:

Deplorable incident at Viterbo. Yesterday brought yet another example of the breakdown affecting the fabric of our society when a group of ex-volunteers obliged policemen to release a man whom they were taking through Viterbo in custody. Recognising the prisoner as their former army chaplain, the abate Alessandro Gavazzi, they bore him in triumph to the town's Liberal Club where he delivered a fiery speech. His police escort – some of whom were former soldiers – are suspected of having connived in this lawlessness.

Twelve

This morning Madame de Menou's footman had found several slips of paper stuck in her front door. All said the same thing: the Civic Guard could not be trusted. Tomorrow, when the Chamber reconvened Count Rossi must surround himself with carabineers.

'He won't bring them inside,' she told Prospero. 'It would offend the Democrats.'

All day, she had been receiving visits from politicians. 'They can't stop what they began!' Twisting a wisp of handkerchief, she managed to smile and Prospero was reminded of the mother who had died at about her age. He recalled sitting somewhere, swinging short legs, while a maid unhooked her gown. A doomed sweetness from that time coloured this.

'Read me the bits you've cut from the papers.'

'They're rubbish. Rhetoric!'

'Read them.'

'"Our minister",' he read, '"is employing tactics learned in France, but they will fail on the Tiber's banks as surely as they did by the Seine." That's from *Epoca*.'

A *ponentino* with a sea-tang rose as the sun sank and rippled the cuttings.

Someone had sent a copy of a cartoon which was to appear in tomorrow's edition of *Don Pirlone*. It portrayed a quixotic Rossi leaning on a pike. A chit detailed his salary. His neck was bare, but the rest of him was ironclad and surrounded by poppies. Prospero held it up. 'What do poppies mean?'

'Sleep?' She rose. 'Dream? He's late.' She moved to the window. 'Or that reformers are dreamers? I suppose some are. In real life things age and rot. Reforms try to turn that around. Naturally, they would . . .'

'. . . appeal to a man of sixty-one?' The count had possibly been in the doorway for some time. 'Sorry, children, I told Pietro not to announce me. He's bringing up some grapes. I brought these myself.' They were roses. 'A pastoral impulse.' He kissed Madame de Menou. 'I can see you're worrying. Everyone is. Even the Pope whom I've just seen. Just remember I'm the cat with nine lives and so have an unwieldy past. Think of the obligations! They kept me late. Ah, you have the papers. May I?' He began to scan them.

Madame de Menou – Prospero saw – could see no way to make good her gaffe. The count talked of security arrangements. Five hundred carabineers were to come into the city and he had to see Colonel Calderari again . . . Then he must polish his speech. 'His Holiness, whimsically, complained only of its style! Too many biblical quotations. Does he feel I'm the devil citing scripture?'

Again he kissed her, begged Prospero to look after her – and left. They would not meet again until after tomorrow's ceremony.

Madame de Menou put her face in her hands. 'He's hurt! That cartoon is right to dress him in iron. He's hard and sensitive! An impossible mixture.' She would not, she decided, go anywhere this evening. Prospero, though, *must* go into the city and see what echoes he might pick up. 'Look after him, Prospero.'

'He told me to look after you.'

'Please.'

So he left, at first walking at random, then pausing in a café where, on taking off his coat, he found Rossi's speech in a pocket. He must have picked it up with the newspaper cuttings. Sitting down, he skimmed the headings: confidence . . . hope . . . deficit of one million to be anticipated . . . trade, the sea . . . Romans were paid an average of three scudi per head, the French nine, the English ten. If production could be increased, then . . . Meanwhile the clergy's gift must tide us over . . . For moments, the optimism astonished him. Then he felt its contagion.

As he was leaving, Don Vigilio – he had met him with Rossi – waylaid him. The agent's wrinkles had a prestidigitator's deftness. Up they went, then down. It was as though he had switched masks. Ordering the arrest of popular men like Gavazzi was, he murmured, rash. His Excellency should . . .

Outside again, Prospero made for Rossi's *palazzo* and delivered the copy of the speech. Then he looked into a wine shop where legionaries in *panuntelle* shouted and sang. His mind snatched at meanings. The pressure of Madame de Menou's handclasp lingered on his skin.

Elsewhere there was talk of a doctor whose demonstrations in the Teatro Capranica showed – what? 'Get it in the neck . . .' he heard. His mind was aswim. Might the mummery turn real?

A man offered him a woman. Safe. Clean. The fellow had a revolutionary's beard and long hair. No, said Prospero.

'The carotid artery . . .' These must be medical students.

'She only does it sometimes,' argued the pimp. 'She's my sister.' He told of exile and ill use. Prospero bought him a *foglietta* of wine and heard an apologia for pimping delivered in a preacher's vocabulary. 'Your health, sir.' The pimp smoked and his words scurried between rapid puffs.

Prospero bought another *foglietta*.

Pimping was a social service, said the returned exile. Had the gentleman ever asked himself what men did who couldn't find solace for their needs? Had he wondered to what they might be driven? On what weak flesh they wreaked their brutality?

The medical students were discussing knives.

'I wouldn't sully my lips telling you,' said the pimp and spat for emphasis. 'Nature foiled turns savage.'

Parish priests, he claimed, trained people to denounce their neighbours. If a man was seen going to a woman's house, the PP had the police around to arrest her for *stuprum* before he could lace up his shoes. She'd as like as not get a whipping or a five-year sentence and even the man could be locked up.

How then, asked Prospero, did the pimp practise his trade?

'We have our ways!' Encouraged, he gave his name. Renzo. 'She's only twenty-three.' He stood up and Prospero was aware of opportunity fizzing like a chemical held to the nose.

'I'll come with you.'

'You'll like her,' said Renzo. 'Bring wine. Not for yourself! Wine's no help for a man going to a woman, but it softens her. Hard for soft is the bargain, eh?'

As they went out, someone said, 'Tomorrow!'

Prospero had caught the city's fever. A greed for freedom stung the air. Down the via Ripetta they walked, and over Ponte Sisto, into lanes where darkness was as thick as fur.

'Better spring a leak.' Renzo unbuttoned. 'We drank a lot.'

'How about your neighbours and the police?' It was occurring to Prospero that he could be robbed. The optimism of drink began to wane.

'They rarely bother gentlemen,' said Renzo. 'Besides, if anyone spots you, they'll think you're me. I'll wait for you to come back out. They mustn't see two of us at once.'

So up a reeking, pitch-black stairway Prospero groped, key in hand, and, only as he fumbled for a door, did he remember that Renzo hadn't told him the girl's name. Was this the door? Somewhere a dog yapped. What if . . .

It opened. A woman said, 'Renzo!' She held a lamp. 'Is he in trouble?'

'No.'

She let him in. She did not look like anyone's idea of a whore. A picture of St Catherine and some dried olive twigs hung on a wall. Ridiculously, he said, 'I'll go and send Renzo up.' She had a gold chain around her neck, and somewhere under her thick cotton nightdress would be a holy medal. She saw the wine.

'Ah!' She sharpened with understanding. 'So he's below?'

'St Catherine,' prayed Prospero, 'make it as if I never came!'

'I'll get glasses.'

She was back before he could bolt, having loosened her hair. It was probably her best feature: electric, frothy and thick as a bush. She poured wine and he thought of her in gaol in fear of a whipping, a Magdalen. She drew him to her and he felt softness through the shawl. Her breasts slid, reminding him of those games where you grope for prizes in a barrel of bran.

'Come.'

In her bedroom was yet another holy picture: a polychrome Christ whose hand fondled a bleeding heart and whose lips smiled rosily. Prospero, too befuddled to manage buttons, was stripped of his frock coat and learned that his companion's name was Cesca. She murmured invigorating praise, assuring him that Renzo never brought her anything but the best. This reversed things, turning them about as if she were Messaline, the lubricious Empress, and he a man procured for her night's pleasure. Weren't Messaline's lovers drowned at dawn? In the Tiber? Disregarding omens, he remembered that he was to give hard for soft and found himself doing so, as she groped for her own bran-tub prize, then fell asleep and dreamed that Count Rossi was looking sadly at him from the bleeding, gilt-framed image of the Sacred Heart.

He was awoken by a row.

'I froze stiff in that doorway.' That was Renzo. 'You should have sent him down long ago.'

His sister said the customer had been half cut and to send him out in that state would have been asking for trouble.

Well, we had trouble now, said Renzo. There he was slug-naked and the city full of police. How get him out? What if he was seen?

'Say he was taken ill and you brought him home from charity.'

'Ach!' was Renzo's response, followed by the sound of a spit.

The two withdrew and Prospero made a move to get up, but was overcome by dizziness and fell back into his stupor which felt like the bottom of a deep, shuddering well. Could Renzo, he wondered half lucidly, have put something in his wine?

When next he awoke, light was cutting his eyeballs and a policeman saying he'd have to take him to the Vicariato, which was the court where morals charges were heard. The pimp and whore were there already. Prospero tried out the story about being taken ill but was advised to save his breath. Renzo had a record as long as your arm and the girl had been in and out of stir. However, said the policeman, we were never keen to embarrass the sons of good families. Prospero, his wits returning, said his papers were at his lodgings and thumbed an empty wallet. The policeman had a twitchy, insinuating moustache. What time was it? Prospero, who should by now have been at the Cancelleria, began to tread a tremulous line between using and protecting Rossi's name. In the end, he went home in a police carriage then, having bribed the policeman to release him, bribed him again to drive him to the Palazzo della Cancelleria. The streets around it, however, were so crowded that it proved quicker to get out and make his way on foot.

The square seethed. There must be 3,000 people here. Prospero craned his neck and contemplated anarchy. Damaged faces stared and gummy mouths revealed dark twists of gullet. These were the plebs! They had no mind of their own. Like the riderless horses which were raced down the Corso in carnival time, they took off when released, pooled panicked energy, then must somehow be halted and brought under control. The horses were stopped by a great curtain stretched for that purpose across the Corso. Was there a way of halting these?

He couldn't advance. Bodies were packed so tight that if anyone were to faint – as some surely must – they would be trampled. Closer to the palazzo steps, the crowd looked different. It seemed to consist of legionaries, men back from the front with cold, savage eyes. Oddly, there were no regular troops in sight. No police either and not many Civic Guards.

An elbow caught him in the chest. A youth in an oilskin was skewering his way through. 'Here's Beppino!' he shouted. His face blazed.

The boy was dizzy with joy at seeing so many men from the legion which he had thought disbanded for good. Eagerly, he was shouting greetings even before he was able to get within earshot: celebratory yells and battle cries and his own name or, anyway, the one some might know him by. He felt drunk from relief at finding them all together again.

'Beppino's coming,' he began announcing himself, when he was not half way across the square, for though he couldn't see their faces, the sight of those massed *panuntelle* warmed his heart. 'Wait for Beppino, fellows! Don't start without me!'

Beppino was how the military authority knew him, but he had been christened Mario because of having been born on one of the Virgin's feast days and, perhaps for the same reason, was apprenticed to a legless cripple who made a living carving crucifixes. The man had taught him to paint the blood on the five wounds of Jesus, but, more importantly, Beppino had had to pull him around on a tray with wheels and perform a number of intimate services which turned his stomach. He had been thinking for a long time of running away, so when Father Gavazzi came to his town to recruit volunteers, he lied about his age and joined up. He was fourteen but said he was older and that his name was Beppino, short for Giuseppe, like General Garibaldi. He loved the Army. He had loved the war. Even retreats and bad food were a lark when you were with friends and could moan about it together. What shocked him was being disbanded. Told it was over. Where could he go now? Not back to the cripple – and his parents wouldn't want him. They'd had six more kids after him.

He'd been begging. That was what he'd been reduced to. Then he'd run into a fellow who said things might be starting again and there was some action planned for today. What sort of action?

'Just you be there,' said his mate. 'All our lot will be.'

He couldn't see anyone he knew though. Not a soul though he was close enough to see faces. Never mind. They were legionaries and so was he.

'We've been betrayed,' his mate had said. 'And we're not going to let the traitors get away with it!'

That was the stuff. We were still we! That was what Beppino liked to hear. And of course we'd been betrayed. Right from the start, men had said it, when the ammunition didn't come or there was nothing to eat.

200

Well, it stood to reason, didn't it? That was why we'd been defeated and why we must stick together. Maybe, here in Rome, we would have a chance to pay out some of the bigwigs who'd been behind it all. The deputies. The politicians. There had been talk about doing that around many a camp fire and on many a sodden march. You talked, but never thought it would happen. Yet here Beppino was, in the heart of Rome, squirming his way up the Chancellery steps. Panting, he turned to look down on the square which was jam-packed with people who must have come to petition the deputies for something or other. Climbing higher, he kept hoping to recognise companions from his too short war. A shambles was what the end of it had been. Girls jeered at our 'oily bread' oilskins and the Pope had found nothing better to say than that, though he'd never meant us to cross the Po, we should, once we did, have fought better. Well, whose fault was it if we hadn't? Who'd mucked us?

In the courtyard a carriage horse lowered then jerked up its head and whinnied. The boy quivered. For moments the vibrating black lips seemed to be insulting him. Steady on, Beppino!

A bearded fellow asked, 'Weren't you at Vicenza?'

'Yes.'

'Come,' said the man and winked.

Beppino followed him to where a crowd of veterans were waving drawn swords and shouting. Meanwhile, a man in a dark suit got out of a carriage and began to climb the stairs. A voice yelled from above, 'Is it him?'

The bearded felloow cupped his hands and called up, 'No.'

'*Carogna*!' yelled the voice. 'The bugger mustn't be coming. He's too afraid.'

The politican walked carefully, not hurrying but looking deliberately from side to side. For a moment his gaze locked with Beppino's and Beppino thought, He's putting on a brave face. He felt elated to be part of the gang threatening this man with the gold watch chain and top hat. Belatedly, the Civic Guards started clearing a way for him.

'Who is he?' he asked the bearded man.

'Nobody we need worry about. We're waiting for the top man.'

Beppino felt it would be stupid to ask who that was. He hadn't been following what was happening and since being discharged had been drifting miserably. He had no money to sit in wine shops or pick up the news. The officers had told him to go home. But it stood to reason: the top man was the one to blame. 'How will we know him?' he asked.

But the other man had gone stiff. 'Here we are,' he whispered to himself with a small private grin.

Another carriage had drawn up. A servant opened its door and lowered the step and another soberly dressed gentleman got out. His smile was thin-lipped and haughty. He began to climb the stairs.

There was a hush as though the crowd had drawn breath. Then with a rush of sound, voices swelled and echoed.

'It's him! Kill him! *Ammazzalo!*'

A sibilant hiss rose. The Civic Guards who were trying to hold back the crowd were shoved forward and Beppino, pushed from behind, surged ahead with the rest.

'Get him!' he roared, then his breath failed with surprise for he had not meant to yell. Yet excitement pounded through him. Pressed back, then forward, he was almost lifted off his feet. Again he shouted, this time with more conviction, and his blood charged through his veins as though he was part of a great train and being whirled along by its sparking, blazing engine.

The haughty man walked up the first steps and Beppino saw that, unlike the one before, he was ignoring the crowd. People were still hissing and whistling but it was only when someone hit the man on his right side that he turned slightly towards his assailant and exposed the left side of his neck. As he did, another veteran stabbed him there.

'Nice work!' said the bearded man.

'Who was it?'

'Don't ask.'

'The victim though?'

'Pellegrino Rossi.'

Suddenly now there was so much movement that Beppino could see nothing. Several men shouldered past him and out of a door leading to the via dei Leutari. Then, for a moment, there was space around the fallen politician. There was blood on the ground.

'Shove forward,' said the bearded man. 'Cover their retreat.'

'What happened?'

'He was stabbed in the carotid artery. That's fatal.'

Alas, Rome has become a forest of howling beasts, overflowing with men from every nation who are either apostates, heretics or teachers of communism or socialism, driven by the most terrible hatred of Catholic truth, and seeking . . . by might and main to . . . disseminate pestiferous errors of every sort.

Dispatch to Paris newspaper, The Dawn of Freedom, from its Rome correspondent:

My readers should know that Rome is not the 'forest of howling beasts' described by Pope Pius from his haven in Gaeta whither he fled four months ago.

While accounts of his flight differ, all agree that it was effected in the coach of the Bavarian Ambassador with the help of our own, who had had a private audience with him just before. Indeed it was under cover of this that Pius slipped into his disguise and out of the Quirinal, while His Excellency kept reading aloud, so that listeners might think the two still in conversation. By the time the deception was discovered, Pius was being conveyed across the border to the Kingdom of Naples. France is thus partly to blame if Rome, abandoned by its prince, has had to govern itself. Indeed the city's representatives have since made a number of bids to be reconciled with him, but all have been haughtily repulsed. This is the background to their decision to proclaim a Republic and to his denunciation of them as 'howling beasts'. My readers should remember it when listening to the rumours current in our sacristies. They should know too that Rome is functioning under its new leaders. Life goes on. Cafés are full. Your correspondent sits in one as he writes. Though the servant class is suffering because many employers have left, the general populace is in good heart. There is not a howling beast in sight.

Gaeta

'Have you seen this impudence?' Father Grassi showed Amandi the piece of low journalism designed to win French support for the so-called Roman Republic.

They had met by chance. The Jesuit was here to report to his General about their scattered fellows. He looked bedraggled and sick and Amandi found it hard to argue with him. Indeed, it was no time to argue with anyone, for ranks, very naturally, had closed.

What had happened after poor Rossi's murder was that dragoons and Carabineers had fraternised with the mob which then marched up the Quirinal Hill to ask Mastai to appoint a ministry of their choice. On his refusal, they attacked his Swiss Guard. Shots were fired and when his secretary, Monsignor Palma, put his head out the window, it was blown off.

Under protest Pius then granted the ministry and, a week later, fled to this small port in the Kingdom of Naples whose monarch – nicknamed 'Bomba' when he got mercenaries to bombard his own people – was such an unsavoury host that it was assumed Mastai would move on. The Catholic Powers vied in offering hospitality but he, perhaps because of the invidiousness of choosing between them, ended by staying where he was. An exiled court was then set up as prelates rushed to join him, either because he needed their services or because they feared to become targets for the turbulence in Rome.

Monsignor Amandi had had no such fear and, when great cardinals were disguising themselves as – seeing no irony! – shepherds and sneaking from the city, had gone quietly about his business as he would still be doing if Pius had not summoned him.

Conciliatingly, he told Grassi of his regret at having been unable to save the wretched Nardoni on whose account they had last met. The Jesuit shrugged.

'I didn't have the influence you supposed . . .'

'Oh, bishop, given that which has happened since . . .'

'Yes.'

They were in a cramped, stale-smelling room filled with Grassi's baggage. Space and privacy were scarce in Gaeta, so Amandi had let himself be inveigled here to talk. The Jesuits were still wary – Pius disliked their General – yet their modesty was charged with paradox. They, after all, had been proven right. General Roothan's flight had prefigured the Pope's. He was a John the Baptist who would have made straight the paths – would do so even now if he but knew which path Mastai planned to take. Amandi guessed that Grassi thought *he* knew. He didn't – and doubted that Pius did. He suspected him of waiting for a sign.

'Don't advise me,' had been Mastai's first words to Amandi when they met. 'I'm getting Liberal advice from Rosmini and the opposite from Antonelli and what I need from you is to know the mind of God. Tell me about the children of La Salette.' The wisdom issuing from the mouths of babes was what he craved and, if Amandi did not quite provide it, he did confine their conversations to things spiritual, with the result that the two were never closer.

'Rosmini . . .' The name could have been choking Grassi for whom priests who advised compromise with the Roman Republic were quite simply traitors. Rosmini, an advocate of reform, who had first come here as Piedmont's official representative, did advise this and had seemed at times to have Pius's ear. It was repeatedly rumoured that he was to be the next Cardinal Secretary – but then this was rumoured of Amandi too. Both had been promised red hats. Meanwhile, Cardinal Antonelli, who already had one, held the office pro tem.

Grassi put a hand over his eyes and when he removed it, Amandi saw that the whites were yellow and the skin around them raw. He was waiting. For what? Abruptly, despite himself, Amandi was seized by hilarity. Here was another one who hoped for a sign! Rosmini too had come to him for enlightenment. I should, thought the bishop, set up as a seer!

From the diary of Raffaello Lambruschini:

It was in Gaeta that Amandi became a cardinal and that it got about that he would soon be Cardinal Secretary of State. Accordingly, he was courted and consulted, for vital decisions were being made and he, as an ex-diplomat, understood the wider web of interests and was acquainted with many who now converged on the exiled court, where emissaries were packed as tight as herrings and matters of high import discussed in cubicles and back rooms.

Four days after the Pope's flight, France had dispatched 3,500 men in three steam frigates, allegedly to ensure His Holiness' safety, but, in reality, to prevent Austria doing so first. Piedmont too was opposed to Austrian troops being invited into the state: a prospect so alarming to Liberals that several warned against it with an intemperance which harmed not only their cause but the hopes of their candidate, Father Rosmini, whose advice, though he had affected to be enraptured by it,

Mastai never actually took. Baffled, Rosmini turned for guidance to Amandi. What, he asked, should he think or do? Although he himself had not sought this, His Holiness had plainly said that he wanted to make him a cardinal and maybe Cardinal Secretary and so, having been lent 10,000 *scudi* for this purpose by Pius himself, he had bought robes, two carriages, four horses and an appropriate amount of plate. Now, quite suddenly, Mastai was grown evasive. It looked as though Rosmini was not to be a cardinal at all and people had begun to criticise his extravagance. Bewildered, he assured Amandi that the carriages had not been expensive. They had belonged to dead cardinals. He was being maligned. As for his advice – which was to negotiate with the more moderate men in Rome – it had been a dead letter since January, when the Pope broke with those now trying to govern that city and fulminated an excommunication against all who collaborated with them. Rosmini was mystified. Had Pius gone completely over to the reactionaries? Did anyone know?

Amandi felt unable to enlighten Rosmini, a man so fallen from favour that his books were now being examined for heresy by the Congregation of the Index. This information was confidential and Rosmini, if told, could not be trusted to conceal his source.

'Don't fret,' said Mastai when asked to be candid with Rosmini. 'He's a dear fellow! *Una carissima persona!* Unworldly. Maybe even a saint. But I am obliged to yield a little to the other side. Let's talk of something more uplifting.'

Bologna, 1849

Things were thorny for priests under a government disowned by the Pope. Cardinal Oppizzoni proceeded like a man picking his way through a blackberry bush.

When the dissidents in Rome convoked a Constituent Assembly and called for state elections, a papal *Monitorio* declared all who cast their votes excommunicate.

'That's Bomba's doing!' opined the Pope's old supporters, then, refusing to believe Pius had written the discreditable *Monitorio*, burned all copies they could lay their hands on and broke up the type in printers' shops.

'Even if he wrote it, we're not bound by it. The Pope-in-Gaeta is not the Pope-in-Rome,' declared self-appointed tribunes, including the troublesome Father Bassi who was back in town dressed, said Oppizzoni, 'like a buffoon!' He was referring to the chaplain's army uniform. The tricolour cross on Bassi's chest especially scandalised the cardinal, who forbade him to say mass anywhere in the diocese unless he presented himself in proper attire. It was hard to discipline him further for, since being wounded at the front, he was idolized by the troops. Police reports that he had been seen drinking with officers at the Caffè dei Servi and the Leon d'Oro were tamely confided to the file which the Curia was keeping like a rod in pickle.

One of the chaplain's more provoking habits was that of conscripting God and Pius to his cause. 'Holy Father,' he begged in an Open Letter, 'by the love I bear you, I conjure you not to heed those now around you. Instead, give us our nation and our independence. Return to Rome, oh Saviour of Italy! Do not linger in the cage of Gaeta . . .' Copies of this were on sale for fifteen *baiocchi* apiece. Proceeds to go to the poor.

'He's right!' Rangone spoke fearlessly, being off to Imola, where the jealous *monsignore* had been obliged to sing small. Priests no longer dared antagonise the laity, and quarrels over mistresses were taboo. 'Why should we be excommunicated?' he demanded. 'If we vote, we exercise our rights as citizens. We don't touch the Pope's spiritual power at all.'

'So now you're a theologian?'

'Why should I have to be?'

'Why should any of us?' asked a customer of the Caffè degli Studenti where this conversation took place. 'Theology's what led to the Army being left in the lurch. If the Pope can't make war, he should give up his crown. Why should we be unable to defend ourselves just because he happens to be our prince?'

'Priests,' said another, 'may be eunuchs for the Kingdom of Heaven's sake. The rest of us would like to keep our balls.'

Talk like this was copiously reported to the Curia and worried the cardinal.

'That wretched *Gazzetta di Bologna* has stirred everyone up. It printed the Monitorio which I certainly never gave out. I hid all my copies.'

'They got it from the Tuscan papers,' said Monsignor Giuseppe Passaponti, his Vicar General. 'And now our parish priests are in need of Your Eminence's paternal advice. They keep asking what to tell their flocks.'

'Don't answer.'

'With respect, Eminence, the twenty thousand men in this diocese who cast their votes need to know whether or not they're excommunicated. Many are priests. Some are parish priests.'

'There's worse!' A frail old cleric rustled like parchment in a breeze. 'News of Your Eminence's failure to publish the *Monitorio* has appeared in a Roman handbill. I have it here. It prays that Your Eminence's patriotism may enlighten the Pope.'

'Let me see!' The cardinal snatched the handbill. 'Where are my glasses? Here,' he told Nicola, 'you read it! Oh God,' he prayed or swore, 'what did we ever do to You to be so afflicted?'

Nicola read that Oppizzoni had been advised by theologians not to publish the excommunication which would thus remain a dead letter. The cardinal cracked his knuckles. The Vicar General seemed to suffer a spasm. Imaginary theologians were giving their *nihil obstat* to the revolution.

'We must,' said Passaponti, 'issue a denial.'

The stricken cardinal waved a limp flipper-like hand. 'Very well.' Christ-the-fish! thought Nicola sympathetically, remembering the symbol in the Roman catacombs.

'There's more!' The old curial priest probed with a scandalised finger. 'Foreign newspapers are saying that Your Eminence and Your Eminence's household voted for the Constitution.'

'Deny it.'

'And what about the twenty thousand penitents?'

The cardinal was exhausted. 'What are other dioceses doing?'

'Other dioceses have had smashed windows, arson, physical assaults and priests pelted with rotten vegetables.'

The cardinal's eyelids descended. 'Mmm!' he murmured to his private darkness and was, apparently, vouchsafed enlightenment, for the lizardy skin flicked up. 'I have it! We'll do what the handbill says! We'll solicit the advice of theologians. It will gain us time. Perhaps we might indicate that a merciful interpretation might be . . . No?' A steely flicker from Monsignor Passaponti's glasses reminded Oppizzoni that he stood convicted of laxity by Liberal handbills.

After that, news had come from Rome that a republic had been declared, the Pope dethroned and the new government was to be a democracy.

'Mad!' was the opinion in all but the most advanced circles. Liberalism was the very most that could be hoped for. Democracy was a frill. It was a red rag to papal bulls and could only divide patriots. The hotheads

208

were weaving a noose for everybody's neck. However, they had the troops so, for now, it was necessary to celebrate. Cannons sounded. Bells were rung, houses illuminated and a masked ball – tickets one scudo – held to raise money to help the Venetians who were still holding out against Austria.

Out in the square, papal coats of arms, torn from the fronts of public buildings, were being burned. Monsignor Passaponti, looking out of the window of Nicola's office – he had come by with some papers – remarked that what we now had in the city's heart were Satan's own insignia. Flames! He sniffed fastidiously and flicked away some ash which had floated in.

Street lighting had been promised, the price of salt reduced and the milling tax abolished. On the other hand, the Catholic Powers were said to be making ready to come and restore the Pope.

One radiant Sunday, Rangone came to say goodbye and Nicola and he took a last walk in the hills. Below them, Bologna was as neat as a cake within its ruff of walls.

'Have you been seeing Maria?'

No, said Rangone. Her brother had become awkward. 'I did what you asked, though. I gave her money. She claimed to be pregnant, so I would have had to anyway. To avoid a scandal. But as sure as guns neither you nor I were the first. I swear that girl's passage could accommodate my fist. She was probably corrupted by her brother or father. It's quite common.'

Nicola started to rage at him, then apologised. He too, after all, had hoped to be rid of Maria and knew his anger for a disguised spurt of shame. What right had he to have idealised her, then been disappointed? Now, again, his mind was filling with her name. Maybe *that* was what had confused him from the start? Maria! Tower of Ivory! City of Gold! Help us! But it was she who needed help.

Next day he went to the cathedral and spoke to the assistant sweeper of his job, his rheumatism and the price of tobacco, before slipping in a casual query: how was his daughter these days? The one who used to work for Donna Anna? Married perhaps? He spoke lightly, but the sweeper's face became as red as steak. Knots tightened in his neck and his body was suddenly clumsy with pain. It was kind of the *signore* to ask, he managed to mutter. Then he burst out: daughters! Blood ties! What were they but millstones to drown a man! The noises wheezing up his throat were perhaps attempts to deal with some natural obstruction.

Maria's friend, Gianna, was no longer at the tobacco shop. She had married a greengrocer and Nicola found her selling lettuces and looking swollen and pink. She greeted him with good humour. Yes, she was expecting a child and, to be sure, happy. Her husband was good to her. Here he was, tying up bundles of pot herbs. She described Nicola as a customer from her days at the tobacconist's. There were congratulations and the husband said nobody could say he was slow at the job! Then, after some whispering, she asked Nicola into the back room and gave him a glass of barley-water.

Maria, she said, had had to leave. She'd gone to Rome. To San Rocco. 'It's where women go, you know, in her condition.'

He knew. All Rome did. San Rocco was the lying-in hospital for secret pregnancies. Women there were allowed to keep their faces veiled, and it was said that to no one, not even to a husband or father, would the authorities divulge their names.

The babies were usually put on the revolving wheel at the door of the Santo Spirito Hospital. Tata, his wet-nurse, had sometimes taken babies from there, though she preferred not to as the money was bad and sometimes not paid at all.

'When was she due?' he asked.

Gianna thought May.

Nicola's confessor, having voted in the elections, was being sent to do penance in a monastery.

'I'm not complaining,' he said. 'Just letting you know why you won't see me for a while. Do you want to step out of this box and have a coffee with me? Let's talk for once like normal men.'

Nicola wanted to talk about Maria, but the confessor said they could do that in a café if they kept their voices down. On the way, he remarked that a number of priests, aghast at events in Rome and Gaeta, were thinking of leaving the Church. His name was Father Tasso and, seen in the open, he was in his early thirties. All bone. Intent and intense with a high forehead and receding hair.

'I won't do that,' he said as he sat down. 'I'll stay inside and make it uncomfortable for the authorities.'

Nicola told him that the authorities were uncomfortable already. He ordered a milk with honey and talked about Maria. Father Tasso admitted that she could have been corrupted by her own relatives, even if it was self-serving of Rangone to say so. Surprising numbers of children in this parish were the offspring of their official sisters. Mothers registered the births as their own to avoid scandal. Midwives connived. The family was the single most efficient unit in this state. 'Efficient at keeping up appearances, and thus an image of the state itself – which is driven to Holy Hypocrisy because it represents heaven! Bear with me,' said the priest; 'sometimes I fear I'm losing my reason!'

Nicola thought this possible. There was a tremor in Tasso's voice as he talked of sin and how we were all responsible for it. Not just the sinner. Perhaps the sinner least of all?

Nicola asked if he meant we should have more charitable institutions. Like San Rocco? But Tasso said, no, what we needed was employment. Industry. 'That,' he confided, 'is why I voted for the constitution. Mazzini can't do worse than we did.'

'What should *I* do about Maria?'

'What are you prepared to do?'

Nicola wasn't sure. Better do nothing then, said the priest. 'If you took her out of San Rocco and made her your mistress, then got tired of her, you know what would happen.'

Nicola said he might help the child. Stop it being put on the wheel. The priest looked doubtful.

'It might have been me.'

'Or Christ.'

Nicola said he would go to Rome. His confessor disadvised this. However, the idea of Rome enthralled him and he remarked that if Nicola did go – against his advice – he might see historic changes. Besides, he wasn't Nicola's spiritual adviser any more or anyone's. 'Pius IX delivered a forked message and I'm at a loss.'

'What about obedience?'

'To whom? Pius the Liberal or Pius the Conservative?'

Piedmont now denounced the armistice with Austria and was defeated by her at Novara. This alarmed the French.

Don Vigilio brought Cardinal Amandi copies of secret dispatches sent by their Ambassador to his superiors in Paris. The originals had been in cypher, but here they were *en clair*.

'We have copies of their seals too.' He spoke with professional pride. 'So we can reseal the letters.'

211

'Regretfully,' wrote the ambassador, 'hopes of effecting a reconciliation between the Pope and his people are quite illusory. They do not want the priests' government back and he will hold out no hope of introducing liberal institutions. The clique around him is Austrian to the core!'

'I am not Cardinal Secretary of State. Have you shown these to Antonelli?'

The agent winked. 'The wind is on the turn. France may end up by siding with the men now in charge in Rome.'

Amandi read his mind: if that happened, men like himself and Rosmini would be in the saddle and Antonelli – who was compromising himself with Austria – out.

'I told the Pope,' wrote the ambassador, 'that our Republic would come up against grave difficulties if asked to go to Rome to destroy a sister-republic.'

There was also a copy of a note sent by the French Embassy in Gaeta to the one in Rome:

'Speaking in strict confidence, our mission is to convince the Roman Republic that we, as Republicans, are on their side, while letting the papal court in Gaeta suppose that, as Catholics, we are on theirs. We may thus hope to prevent Austria from taking Rome before we do.'

'In which case,' said Don Vigilio, 'conciliatory policies would be imposed!' Turning up his hands to show acceptance of the divine will, he bowed and withdrew.

Bologna, April 1849

Nicola's new confessor disagreed with the old one. Of course Nicola must go and save that innocent girl! Did he realise how dangerously he had been living? He lectured him at length.

'Go to Republican Rome?'

'And would you leave the girl alone in that rabid forest?'

Don Carlo was a frowning inquisitor of a man with a head like the eagle on the Austrian bearings which managed to look two ways at once. Lean in his cassock as a charred string bean, he had a blaze of white, wispy hair which flared in a halo from his shrivelled skull. He had imposed himself on Nicola, saying he was taking over Father Tasso's penitents and implying that they must be tainted and in need of being spiritually gingered up.

Cardinal Oppizzoni, who seemed in need of this himself, said Nicola might go to Rome. 'Was your conscience so very troubled?' he asked, and Nicola guessed that he should not have spoken frankly to the new confessor. Oppizzoni did not say so, but neither did he say – as he had of Tasso – that Don Carlo could be trusted not to abuse the confessional.

Gaeta, April 1849

Amandi, who was being sent to yet another mountain village to see yet another female visionary, guessed that he was being got off the scene.

'God's voice,' hoped Pius, 'may be speaking through her.'

But with the chorus of reaction now baying with full throat, it seemed unlikely that any messages, divine or otherwise, would get through. Conservatives were zestfully hunting down proponents of the tolerance which had led to Rome's falling into radical hands and Rosmini was their prime quarry. His books were being combed for heresy and this would almost certainly be found, perhaps after he too was off the scene.

Mastai was being pressed to make a decision but could not, his friend knew, bring himself to make one while Rosmini and Amandi himself were nearby. He liked them better than Antonelli, who was not his kind of man – yet, for him, this discredited them because it was by yielding to human preferences that he had brought things to their present pass. He knew himself to be too easily moved.

He was shrewd too though and, if the sceptical Amandi was again being plunged like a demon in the holy water font, might not the papal aim be two-fold? Might he be counting on Amandi to ensure that the new visionary was not a tool forged by the forces of reaction – Antonelli and the Jesuits – to manipulate Pius himself?

We are being played off against each other, Amandi decided, and left Gaeta just as the Catholic Powers – animated by equally divergent aims – prepared to send in their troops.

Monsignor Bedini was to be the new Legate to the northern Legations just as soon as the Austrians recaptured them for the Pope. This was a reward from Cardinal Antonelli, on whose behalf Bedini had secretly gone to France to stir up Catholic opinion in favour of His Eminence's policies.

Cardinal Amandi's behaviour gave Bedini pause. Was he playing a deep game? Why was he haring off after demented shepherdesses? Was his disinterest in politics a screen – and if so for what? Gossip – Gaeta was a gossip-shop – had it that he had some unassessable hold on the Pope. Might he, Bedini, be backing the wrong horse?

Reports from Bologna said that Amandi's main connection there was a youth as green as duckweed who was in the employ of that old fox, Oppizzoni. The usual speculations had been made that the boy could be a catamite, a spy, or the son of the Pope's reputedly wanton sister, Isabella. Of Isabella and – whom? Rumours could make your head spin.

Bedini instructed his informant, Don Carlo, to offer the boy a suit of clothes, but neither to reveal Bedini's expectations of being the next Legate nor premature sympathy for Austria. When Don Carlo found that his penitent wanted to go to Rome, Bedini was cock-a-hoop. Encourage him, he advised. He'll lead us to his master. Encourage Oppizzoni to let him go. There was, wrote Don Carlo, some story about a girl. A pretext? *Optime*! Clearly, the boy was going there to make contact with Amandi. What else?

The tailor measured Nicola for the promised suit but said it could not be made ready in time if the young gentleman was leaving. Nicola, who had been puzzled by the gift, said never mind. He must leave now if he was to catch up with Maria before she was confined.

'He must think he's clever,' said Don Carlo irritably.

'We'll start building the suit anyway,' promised the tailor. 'You can come for your next fitting when you return.'

Thirteen

On 30 April, a French attack on Rome was repulsed. In the aftermath the city grew eloquent. Even the slow, swag-necked oxen began looking like emblems. Even the mimosa blossom which hardened like gun shot. Romans knew about gesture. Putting defiance into their nonchalant habits, they prolonged siestas until late breezes had turned laundry into pennants and curtains into parodies of gun smoke. Ordinary living became a thumbing of the Roman nose at the French camp. Spies would make known the city's self-possession – and its contempt for fellow-republicans fighting on the wrong side. So thought the citizens who had learned showmanship from the Church, and were stimulated by their new role. Danger spiced what was already a near-sexual glee.

'Italians don't fight,' was what the French commander had said. Then his men had been driven back!

The Roman Republic had life in it yet and, in the pollen-laden waft – of lime, acacia, horses, hay – customers at open-air cafés lingered to argue the toss. The intentions of the sister-republic were unclear. Protective or punitive? Rome was on the qui vive. The horses, so sweetly redolent of spring grass, had been commandeered and gravel strewn on the cobbles lest the cavalry skid.

Nicola had come straight to the Foundling Home where girls sat squinting over a froth of needlework. There were maybe a hundred, all with deferent eyes, and, though one might have looked for gloom, expectancy rippled when the door opened. Any break was welcome in their numb routine. These, said Don Mauro, were the 'spinsters'. Left as infants on the Foundlings' wheel, they would work here until they died, unless picked out at one of the processions when they were paraded for inspection by men who needed wives. Country lads were glad to get them – and glad of their small dowries.

Don Mauro, looking blithe and rosy, had the run of Rome's charitable institutions. Since the Pope's *Monitorio*, there had been a shortage of priests, so he had been filling in for absentees and saying mass all over town.

Mass? Had he been restored to the priesthood then? How could he have been? Nicola guessed that, in a flight of wishful thinking, he had re-ordained himself, then compounded his fault by collaborating with the Republic. If so, penalties would be implacable, but the little cleric seemed oblivious of this. He was rigged out in stole and cassock, having just heard the spinsters' confessions, when he stepped into the hall to find Nicola badgering the doorkeeper about recently abandoned infants.

'They have tags around their necks,' the doorkeeper had been saying. 'With a mark. You must describe the mark.'

But Nicola didn't know whether Maria had even had a child, much less whether she had put a tag on it or left it here.

'Over eight hundred a year are left,' scolded the doorkeeper.

Don Mauro took Nicola to see the wheel on which a woman out in the street could leave her bundled infant, then ring a bell and run off without being seen. A nurse, inside the building, would then turn it so that the baby passed inside the wall. The space was designed for newborn infants but, in bad times, two- and even three-year-olds had been known to squeeze through. Times now, Don Mauro admitted, were bad. He too, it struck Nicola, was trying to smuggle himself inside an institution: the Church.

He showed Nicola around with proprietorial pride. 'We,' he said, referring to the Church, but also to the Republic. A reconciliation had taken place in his heart and he forgot that it did not prevail. Yet he saw himself as practical. 'I went to see Mazzini,' he disclosed. 'The Republicans are not priest-haters. That's a lie.' And he wagged a monitory finger. 'People gave me petitions to submit. They had high hopes. But, we have less money than the Pope. This war is an expense and we can't borrow because international bankers won't lend. Cardinal Antonelli made the diplomatic corps in Gaeta agree to warn them not to!'

As he and Nicola left the building, pale arms waved from a window. The *zitelle* were enjoying a break. If the Republic survived, something would be done for the poor creatures, assured Don Mauro. 'By the way,' he remembered, 'I met a friend of yours among the wounded. A man called Martelli. He's at the Trinità dei Pellegrini. Father Gavazzi's in charge there. He's having trouble with his order. The secular authorities obliged them to house him and do his laundry – can you believe that they were refusing? Now he says they piss in his soup. There was bad blood over the setting up of military hospitals. Convents had to be requisitioned. It was during the siege.'

Cassock hitched up, Don Mauro skipped over ruins left by the French bombardment. Clutching Nicola's elbow, he asked: 'Have you seen Prospero Stanga? His father complains that he doesn't write.'

The French encampment outside the walls was close enough to wave at. *Vive la fraternité!* jeered ironic citizens. The French Republic was just fourteen months old. Surely its soldiers must dislike this assignment? Washing lines outside their tents looked harmlessly domestic. A number of Rome democrats had spent their exile in France.

It was harder to forgive the Neapolitans. Those Austrian puppets – Bomba was allied with Austria – were to blame for the Pope's harshness to his own city. Even now, Garibaldi's troops were fighting off their incursions to the south and jeering verses were being bandied about:

> Pulcinella, discontent
> At serving in the regiment,
> Sends his Mama this lament:
> 'Bad conditions, lousy pay,
> So in the pinch I ran away.
> Now I'm caught I rue the day!
> Mama darling, Mama *bella*,
> Pray to God for Pulcinella!

Pulcinella, the Neapolitan puppet – a relative of the English braggart, Punch – would not soon set eyes on Rome; nor would any other puppets of Austria unless they chanced to see it on a map!

Meanwhile, there was a ceasefire and the empty days were suddenly intolerable. Young men and those who were not so young felt an urge to be doing something significant.

Nicola and Prospero were self-absorbed, but then this was one of those times when the self absorbs the world. Dressed in tight-waisted jackets and soft hats, they took garrulous walks or went to play bowls, but were apt to pause in mid-play, holding the wooden globes forgotten in their fingers. Each carried a silver-topped cane which Prospero had bought in a mixed lot from a junkman.

'Looted property?' he guessed. 'I'll give them back if I discover whose they were.'

He hinted at private misadventures but, when pressed to confide, was apt to turn the talk to public ones. News from Bologna was bad. Austrian troops had it surrounded and Prospero, who got long letters from his father, discounted the old man's optimism.

'Count Rossi,' he told Nicola, 'had proof that the Bolognese resistance of last August was not the miracle it seemed. The Austrians had orders to retreat before the fight began.'

He hated heroics. It was as though his father's animating spark risked setting the world on fire. Scepticism had not saved Rossi but was at least adult, and it pleased Prospero that the French, on their march here, had found their route lined with large notices bearing exerpts from their own constitution: 'France respects foreign nationalities . . . She does not . . . take arms against the freedom of other peoples.' Etc. Lies deserved to be shown up!

His mouth squirmed. 'They didn't expect to have to fight at all. Read this.' He handed Nicola a copy of *La Solidarité Républicaine*, printed in Paris some days before.

Nicola read:

INTERVIEW RECORDED OUTSIDE ROME WITH RELEASED FRENCH PRISONER

The man, who asks to remain anonymous, said: 'Our Roman captors were amazed at fellow-Republicans coming to fight a people who are seeking nothing but freedom. Our ministers in Paris are in the hands of the clerical faction. They told us a pack of lies and that we would be liberating Rome from criminals. Well, we saw no criminals, only decent folk who cheered when we were released. There were tricolours at every window, ours and theirs. We're back in camp now and afraid we'll be sent out again to fight our brothers!

Prospero took back the paper. 'They *will* be,' he said. 'Whoever killed Count Rossi threw away the last chance of a compromise. The diplomatists are wasting their time.'

Nicola found his friend's cold-eyed disillusion impressive. Might their generation achieve wisdom without the drudgery of ageing? At the same time, he felt rather attracted by the ideals of *La Solidarité Républicaine* which must be the same ones as animated Father Bassi who was here with the troops winning new praise for his bravery. Nicola, glancing shyly at other young men in the ornate, churchy café, wondered which way they inclined.

Prospero's eye followed his. 'They're spending their paper money,' he observed. 'The Republic simply *printed* money!' After his apprenticeship with Rossi this shocked him.

'Which side are you on, Prospero?'

Prospero didn't believe in sides. People deluded themselves – and so had he. Abruptly confidences began to flow. They concerned Madame de Menou with whom all was now over.

'But,' Nicola put his question with the care of a man handling a divining rod, 'you're still in love with her?'

'Perhaps.' Prospero looked gloomy. Love was, apparently, as unwelcome in its recurrences as a case of malaria. It had started, he explained, on the day of Count Rossi's death when he went to her palace in shame, wondering how to tell her that he had not been with the count when he died. True, he had seen him later but, by then, Rossi's son had taken charge and Prospero found that he had no claim. Belatedly, it struck him as odd that he should have lived for months in daily intimacy with his employer without meeting a single member of his family.

'I then realised how distinct he kept the two sides of his life. I belonged to Dominique's and so became an intruder once the legitimate family appeared. And he can never have expected much of me. He had real secretaries at the ministry and I – was his boudoir lapdog.' Prospero could have been about to lose control.

Giving him time to recover, Nicola talked about himself. He had come to Rome in search of Maria but found no trace of her.

Prospero, however, was intent on his own troubles. He had been caught between fears: that he was presuming by blaming himself and that he was truly to blame.

'For his death? How?'

'I spent a lot of time with him. So did she. We might have contributed to the way he felt.'

'But it wasn't a suicide!'

'Wasn't it? He didn't take precautions. Not really. He was on the point of victory in the Chamber. He knew this and knew that it increased his danger. He'd had warnings. It was like Caesar.'

'So what could you have done?'

Prospero's skin burned. 'He may,' he burst out, 'have thought I was sleeping with Dominique.'

'Were you?'

'No. But if he thought so, it could have been the last straw.'

After the murder, he had gone to see her, hoping to be reassured. But she was feverish, having heard that the assassin had been smuggled away by a rabble which was now parading around the city shouting, 'Blessed be the hand that slew the traitor!' They had chanted this outside the windows of Rossi's house and the Civic Guard had not chased them away.

'They didn't come here!'

'Forgive me,' said Prospero. 'I . . . need to ask . . . It's that he may have thought you and I . . .' He couldn't get it out.

Her finger on his lips surprised him. 'Hush!'

'Dominique!'

Again the finger pressed his lips. She drew him into her bedroom. 'It's all right,' she whispered. 'I think he expected this. He thought of you as our lightning deflector. Instead you attracted it. We stood too close.'

'Did you believe her?' Nicola marvelled.

'I wasn't sure. He was such a politic man. It was a strange moment. The assassins were being feasted and toasted in the city. We could hear it going on. Rowdiness. Torchlight processions. Threats. I ended up thinking that making love to her was somehow being done in his memory. At least we loved him.'

'Did you go to the funeral?'

'Yes. It was quick and furtive. There was a danger lest the assassins create a scandal there too and by then his family had fled to Civitavecchia. It was in the Church of San Lorenzo in Damaso. She didn't come.'

Their love-making, said Prospero, had saved his sanity. Cut off from the city, which was going through its own fever, they stayed inside for ten days. Servants brought food. They had no shame. In between making love, they talked of Rossi. 'I imagined that I was him. Or that he was in me and we were both making love to her. "This," she told me, "is the only eternity there is! Take it now, now, now!" She meant it. It's only looking back that I see that for her it wasn't just bed talk.'

'That woman's a pagan!' Nicola marvelled.

'Yes. Another time she said: "He was too wise for jealousy. He knew what mattered most for him. It wasn't this."'

She was, said Prospero, an intoxicating creature. Golden-fleshed. Her

220

limbs moved like shoals of fish. Opalescent light fell through rippling curtains, splashing her as though she were in a forest – or were a forest. They ate Rossi's grapes, the ones he had brought from Frascati, sliding them from mouth to mouth and letting the juice dribble so that they could lick it off and learn the contours of each other's flesh. She knew more about the arts of the bedroom than the poor professional who had initiated him. This, despite what people said, was a lady's game. You needed hot water, leisure and fresh sheets regularly supplied by servants. Apart from his dash to Rossi's funeral, he stayed locked in with her, sweating out his lust fever. Silly, in his exhilaration, he told her how cannibals had given St Thomas Aquinas food for thought. The Divine Doctor had worried about how, for the body's resurrection, eater and eaten could be restored to carnal integrity.

Furious at the thought of Rossi seeking her at the throne of judgment, he nailed her to stake his claim. She was *his*!

'Yes,' she had tried to console him, 'but there's only now. This life isn't a vestibule! The old Romans knew. *Carpe diem*!'

He wouldn't have it. She was amused. His vigour too amused her. Only a nineteen-year-old, she informed him, could have kept up this rhythm. And how often did a woman like her find herself in bed with one? She had been Rossi's mistress since she herself was nineteen and had been married two years before that.

'You are my youth,' she told Prospero. 'I haven't had it until now. My husband too was older.'

'Where is he? Dead too?'

'As good as dead. Locked up. Mad.'

That sent a chill through Prospero.

'Can't you get an annulment?'

'It's difficult.'

'Could you?'

'I came here for that. But one needs influence.' She and Rossi had been waiting for a judicious moment. 'Now I'll never get it.'

'Mad?'

'Raving.'

Prospero feared he too could be infected. 'I resent your having a soul,' he heard himself say, 'because I can't possess it.'

She laughed and her laugh shocked him. 'You do possess it,' she said and that shocked him more.

He went back to his rooms to collect some clothes and found a letter from his father. While he had been in bed with Dominique, there had been time for news of Rossi's death to reach Bologna and for his father's letter about this to reach Rome. It said Prospero must return to the villa.

'I couldn't,' he told Nicola. 'I had no avowable reason to stay in Rome, but I couldn't leave. I raced back to her and stayed for several more weeks. Again we hardly went out. The city was dangerous. Factions were taking over. The Pope was in Gaeta. From there he appointed a *Commissione Governativa* which the Romans ignored. Then they appointed a *Giunta di Stato* which called for a Constituent Assembly. It was like those games children play, forming and reforming groups. *Giunta di Stato, Giunta di Stato!* You could pat ball to the sound. I hardly paid more attention to the papers the servants brought in than to the rhymes the doorkeeper's son was chanting out in the courtyard. Authority seemed meaningless. At the same time, I became possessed by a desire to distinguish myself from the ant-like crowd. It seemed to me that only by reaching some peak of passion could I do that. She encouraged me. I'm telling you this so as to show *myself* how corrupted by passion I had become. One can more easily be sincere with someone else than with oneself.'

'With her?'

'Yes, but she encouraged my folly. She was keeping me. Oh, with great delicacy. She pretended that I was protecting her and so must share her purse. She claimed to owe me money – used all sorts of subterfuges to save my vanity and perhaps none of this would have mattered if I hadn't needed her so much. She affected me like a fever. I mean this. I couldn't see well. My mind too was blurred and I was all the time possessed either by satisfaction or need, always either drained or on the boil. The two alternated. I felt hot. My skin tingled. Meanwhile I dreamed about Rossi, my adoptive father, and couldn't answer my real father's letters. I felt an urge to do some violent thing: castrate myself, kill her, take ship for Africa. Absurd, childish impulses.'

'Why,' Nicola asked indignantly, 'say one is not sincere with oneself? Or are you insincere *now*? You're turning her into a succubus!' He hated to see the story dwindle into a parable and felt that, given Prospero's wonderful good luck, *he* would have risen better to its challenge.

'I only mean that one has an ideal self and likes to pretend one is living up to it. Looking back, I can see how egotistic I was. Think of *her*, bereaved, generous, trying to make me happy and being blamed for it. She couldn't placate me because it was my passion I hated: not the sin, but the loss of control. That and the fact that Rossi had used me for cover – if he had. But then if he hadn't, what I was doing was even more reprehensible.'

In the end – here Prospero's voice sank until it was almost inaudible – deliverance came from a third party. Don Vigilio, seeing him as a likely customer, told him that he had proof that his mistress was sending letters to her family in France, begging them to get rid of her husband. 'It seems that they might have been prepared to do it. He showed me a letter.'

Prospero stood up. 'Shall we take a turn in the city?'

Nicola followed him. Outside the café, people were talking agitatedly. News had come from Bologna.

'It's fallen.' A man leaned from a carriage window. 'I've come from there. The Austrians sent the keys of the city to the Pope.'

Someone began to curse and Prospero took Nicola's arm and drew him down one of the streets leading to the river and the Ripetta harbour. 'It's better this way,' he said. 'Some sort of calm will be restored. Your cardinal will be pleased.'

'Your father certainly won't.' Nicola thought of Don Mauro and Father Tasso. Even Rossi. 'People,' he told Prospero, 'had great hopes of this Republic. Surely,' he hoped, 'this city won't fall?'

'It will.'

'You sound pleased.'

'Maybe I'm pleased to have proof that she was wrong with her *carpe diem*. This *is* a Vale of Tears. Ours *are* the right metaphors. Look at the facts. France isn't fighting for us and the rest of Catholic Europe is on the Pope's side: Spain, Bavaria, Austria, Naples. They all believe we're rabid beasts.'

'*You* think you're a rabid beast!'

'Was, was! Now I'm repentant, as they'll all be soon. This is how he planned for it to turn out.'

'Count Rossi?'

'No, not him. The Pope,' whispered Prospero, 'lost his nerve towards the end. He wanted to undo his reforms, but didn't dare. He feared bringing a hornets' nest about his head like the one he brought when he reversed his policy on the war. So – this is a guess – he began to hope that something appalling would happen: something so catastrophic that he could call in the Catholic Powers to restore him on the old terms. And it's happening! France alone is trying to keep the terms from being the old ones. She wants him to preserve some reforms and make some concessions to Liberal ideals – but her government is divided and she

223

won't prevail. The Pope will get his way. Rossi is more useful to him dead than alive. Pius can point to his death and say "See where reforms lead!"'

Nicola was appalled. 'Prospero, what are you telling me?'

'Nothing. I'm giving you a chance not to hear. This is dangerous and useless information. It's like knowing that the king in the old story had ass's ears. Remember the barber who discovers the secret and can't keep it to himself? It rots inside him. It chokes and suffocates him, but he has been threatened with death if he passes it on, so what he does is go into the country and lie on the ground and whisper: "King Midas has long ass's ears." Later, willows grow on that ground and whisper the secret to the wind so that the barber is in trouble. I'm the barber,' said Prospero. 'You're the ground. If you breathe a word the wind will catch it.'

'Tell me how you broke with the French lady.'

Prospero thought back to the afternoon when the spy-broker had come to see him. Don Vigilio's back was hooped; his bones looked too big for his skin and his facial wrinkles were dirty as though drawn with soft charcoal. There was a smudgy spill from the funnels of his eyes. 'Sorry,' he would always say deprecatingly in the days when he used to come up to Count Rossi's table in a café. 'Forgive me, gentlemen, but . . .' By then he would have insinuated himself into their company.

'He's a jackal,' Rossi used to joke, 'and I'm his lion. He thinks he will pick up scraps from my kill.'

Rossi had been wrong. He was no lion and his killers, the men who crowded round him on the parliament stairs, weren't lions either, but cat's paws – and who knew what king of the Roman jungle had sent them out? Republicans? Jesuits? The remark made by Pope Pius when he heard of his minister's death had left some people pensive: 'Well, who knows where he would have led us!'

Don Vigilio had approached Prospero without preliminaries.

'Madame de Menou has been writing letters.'

They were in the Caffè Ruspoli and the broker sat down unbidden. He held a folder. 'They have fallen into alien hands.'

She was being spied on. Unsurprisingly, her letters were being opened for political reasons, but what Don Vigilio had found was not political. 'Her husband,' he confided, 'is under the care of relatives who seem to be under her influence. She is a persuasive lady and has suggested that they "put him out of his pain". It would appear that she has reasons for wishing to be nubile. There is a possibility of marriage – not a legal one,

224

to be sure.' The broker's breathy voice could have been coming from inside Prospero's head. 'A widow,' he instructed, 'may not marry the lover with whom she had relations during her defunct husband's lifetime. Canon law forbids it. The impediment is intended as a safeguard to the husband's life. Perhaps you should let the lady know?'

He left.

Prospero, who had not had the presence of mind to say a word, saw a letter in Dominique's handwriting half unfolded on the table among the yellow crumbs of Madeira cake.

'His impudence,' he told Nicola, 'stunned me. I suppose he was working for someone who wanted Dominique to leave Rome. That could have been anyone from the Pope to the Republicans. Or wanted hush money from her? Nothing was spelled out. Though, to be sure, he implied that we – she and I – were contemplating murder.'

'You were going to tell me what her letter said?'

'It did talk of putting him out of pain. But that's ambiguous, isn't it? She said it referred to the opium he needs for his agitation and neuralgia. There had been difficulty importing it. Customs trouble. The letter was about that. So she said. I don't know,' said Prospero. 'We had an appalling scene.' He shuddered and walked away from Nicola.

Boats creaked. They paused at the Ripetta harbour where there was a groan of wood and ropes yielding, then being jerked back by the suck of the tide. Masts tilted. Water splashed on stone. There was an odour of mud and, from the meadows across the river, of freshly mown grass. Rome was an oddly pastoral town, thought Nicola, comparing it in his mind to Bologna which, he remembered mournfully, had now fallen to the Austrians. Unlike Prospero, he resented this bitterly and was feeling less at one with his friend.

Walking through fecal smells in the lanes behind the via Ripetta, Prospero went on with his story which, it turned out, was not a love story after all. Dusk brimmed in alleys, while in *piazzette* and *larghetti* the airy silhouettes of free-standing statues caught a last luminosity from the sky. Madame de Menou, shocked by his lack of trust, had left for Paris.

'I was frantic. I needed her as her poor, mad husband needed his opium – but I hated my own need too much to follow her. Besides, she had left no address.'

'Then why didn't you go back to Bologna?'

Prospero merely shook his head.

Sitting on a fountain edge, they trailed their fingers in suspect water. A group of young men passed, arms linked, singing a martial song.

Reminded again of Bologna, Nicola felt a spasm of melancholy. Ought he to be fighting? Like Father Bassi? A vein of pessimism ran through him, planted by his teachers. Prospero had it too but for other reasons. His father had used up the dash and hope that should have been his. Passing the Pantheon, they crossed in front of the amber-fronted Minerva Church and turned towards the Collegio Romano, which was now being run by secular priests.

'I've decided to take orders,' said Prospero.

'You're mad!' shouted Nicola, suddenly rowdy with shock. He was upset by this turn. 'Why?' he harried. 'Are you running for cover?' This was meant to provoke Prospero, but he merely looked melancholy. 'What about what you said about the Pope and Count Rossi's death?' Nicola challenged. 'What about Madame de Menou? How,' he urged, 'give up something so powerful? So rare?'

'But I,' Prospero told him, 'see those stories as reasons for giving up the world. It's disorderly, and I'm disorderly myself. I'm too much like my father – a maimed romantic. Dominique frightened me. Maybe I *am* running for cover, but I don't see that as disgraceful. Do you?'

Rome, 3 June 1849

Emile Aubry, Rome correspondent for *La Solidarité Républicaine*, was unable to keep up with events. On 29th May – he had been officially assured – the French envoy, Ferdinand de Lesseps, had signed a treaty with the Roman Republic on behalf of France. By its terms the city gates were to be opened in return for a pledge that France would respect the Republic's rights. However, no sooner had the ink dried on Aubry's report than news came that Lesseps had been recalled to Paris and the treaty repudiated. Why? Embassy officials were not prepared to say.

One might as well read tea leaves as official communiqués, decided Aubry, whose clever eyes were set in a face like a good-looking whippet's. He wore a snuff-coloured greatcoat, a shot-silk waistcoat slightly frayed, and spent his time in the Caffè degli Artisti, calling for ink and writing his articles there and then on a smeary tabletop. He doubted if they would be published. Paris was fabricating new truths.

Professional pride, however, impelled him to note down the facts – ? – supplied by touts. Commodities were scarce in Rome just now, so they were pleased to sell him all the information on which they could lay their hands. Foreign money was a powerful inducement and, as his readiness to pay for *notizie* became known, he was besieged by servants eager to sell their masters' bedroom-, alcove- and even pantry-secrets. Haphazardly, he recorded irrelevancies, feeling like a junk-dealer who hopes to find a diamond in the dross. If even a fraction of what he was hearing was true, he could set up as a blackmailer. Great ladies, it appeared, were receiving comfort from their coachmen while their husbands, in Gaeta, gave theirs to the Pope. Requisitioned convents had revealed scabrous secrets, and as for what had been found on the premises of the Holy Office, all his informant would say was that the sight of its cellars had turned the Republican inspectors' hair white! Horrors! *Cose dell'altro mondo*! Worth more than a few *scudi*, eh?

'Worth not one *baiocco*! We scribblers invent our own lies.'

Subtler spies tried to provide support for the changing conduct of France. Licentious living, they reported, had flourished under the Republic. The new class – lawyers, bankers, doctors and the like – had no morals. Church bells had been melted to make cannons and nuns violated . . . Bored with these banalities, the journalist made his way to the hospitals where – according to his informants – common prostitutes, enrolled as nurses, were polluting the hallowed halls where nuns had prayed – or, alternatively, caroused. Here the Princess Trivulzio di Belgioioso was in command but gave him short shrift. This lady had presided over an emigrés' salon in Paris which he had visited once or twice but, though he sent his card with compliments about the good work she was doing, she refused to see him. She could not, ran her message, be friends with the French while they tried to destroy in Rome the freedom they had extolled at her table in Paris.

A priest called Gavazzi told him that there was shortage of essential supplies and asked whether fresh attacks were expected. This hospital was dangerously exposed.

Aubry didn't know. The city was full of rumours and all he could do was try to check them, which was what he was doing now. Was it true, for instance, that nurses had been enrolled without too nice a concern for their background? The priest said tightly that, though Christ had not rejected the ministrations of Mary Magdalene, he did not think the women here were anything less than respectable. Would it not be more useful for the journalist to write of our lack of bandages and tourniquets? Perhaps someone would find us some.

On his way out, Aubry nearly tripped over a young, noisily sobbing girl who had, she confessed, just been dismissed by the Princess for indecent behaviour with a patient. He offered to drive her in his carriage and when the girl said she had nowhere to be driven to, suggested that, while giving thought to the matter, they lunch together in an *osteria*. 'We may have an inspiration and you can tell me about your indecency. Mmm?'

More tears and indeed snuffles and in the end he had to supply a handkerchief.

'It wasn't me,' she kept protesting. 'It was him! The dying man! His hand kept reaching between my legs. I couldn't wrestle with him, could I? Not without breaking open his wounds. But he did this himself and while he was doing it the Princess came in and said I was a disgrace to the Republic. She said a foreign newspaperman was prying into our affairs at this very moment and there was I giving him ammunition. She sacked me on the spot! Out! The foreigner must have really upset her because she's never been like that. Then, while I was trying to explain about the patient, he died and . . .'

The waterworks were now working overtime, so Aubry beckoned to the coachman and half helped, half bundled, the girl into his carriage. Her name, he learned, was Maria and she was from Bologna.

'Take us somewhere jolly,' he told the driver.

'*Oui, Monsieur.*' The man was rousing his nag with a lickerish flick of his whip when a noise like great wooden clappers burst over them. '*Madonna santa!* They're bombarding us. Get in, get in, sir. We'd best make off. The hospital is in the line of fire.'

'So the treaty *was* disavowed!' exclaimed the journalist.

'French bastards!' yelled the coachman, forgetting his fare's nationality. 'They've attacked without warning!'

As the shelling grew heavier, buildings burst open like pods. News of the fighting was brought by those who ventured out to watch it, by chaplains like Ugo Bassi, who raced between the front and the hospitals, and by the wounded who were so many that these hospitals overflowed.

A protest sent to the French commander, General Oudinot, by his compatriot, Aubry, received no response – until news came that Aubry's paper had been closed down. A wind of reaction was sweeping France whose Prince-President, Louis Napoleon Bonaparte, was courting the Catholic vote and whose Catholics had been thrown into a spiteful frenzy by tales of Garibaldi's men breaking into Roman convents and eating omelettes made with consecrated hosts. These fables, originating in Gaeta, looked like leading to the reduction of Rome to rubble. Aubry knew the man who printed them and was not surprised that he conceived of sacrilege in culinary terms. Louis Veuillot, France's leading Catholic journalist, was often to be seen dining in the company of prelates who had to sit well out from the table to accommodate their bellies and looked as if the only martyrdom awaiting them would come from their livers. They were now in Gaeta, whence they were clearly sending tall tales to Veuillot.

Meanwhile, if French cannon did not bring down the Roman Republic, the financial crisis would. Aubry calculated that the reduction in customs duties and the price of salt plus the abolition of the corn-grinding tax had drained the Treasury. Money was worth less every day. Shopkeepers were refusing paper currency and everyone hoarded coins. The cost of grain had doubled since February and olive oil gone up by one third. The money-changers in the temple had been defeated not by their defiance of the laws of religion but by those of their own medium.

Ironically, he himself was one of the few to whom this ill wind was bringing good. French currency had shot up in value and he could afford to stay here in idleness.

'So,' he told the little Bolognese girl, 'let us live and love.' She had a nice little body. Retiring with her to the bedroom, it struck him that love *alla Bolognese*, a local term for sodomy, was an apt metaphor for what was happening to this state.

A loud booming kept coming from the French camp.

'They're getting closer together,' said Maria.

'Every two minutes. Never fear. I'm sheltering you with my body which is what we French are supposed to be doing for His Holiness's subjects. I'm your bit of the French Army. You're my bit of the Roman *popolo*.'

The booming grew louder until it sounded like giant croquet mallets hitting hollow balls. 'Be brave,' he encouraged her, 'and I'll take you to Spillman's restaurant. It's time,' teasing her, 'the *popolo* had a taste of the good life.' The teasing was really aimed at himself who had expected to see this happen after last year's French revolutions. Instead, in January, troops quartered in Paris had obliged a National Assembly with a Republican majority to vote its own demise. The Prince-President would soon have done for the very term 'republic' both here and in France.

'We're both being buggered by history,' he told Maria who was adjusting her hair.

'I've no clothes fit for a restaurant.'

'I'll buy you something elegant. Why shouldn't you have it? The Army will soon be here dressing up its trollops.'

'Is that what I am?'

He tried to comfort her. But she had gone cold. 'My father was a *Centurione*. People called them "the Pope's brigands"!'

'Why are you telling me?'

A shrug. 'Everything amuses you. Doesn't this?'

'I've upset you! I didn't mean to.'

But she accused him of thinking that she was the gutter and that he had to lower himself to be with her. She didn't want to be joined in her gutter. She paused and understanding dawned. He had, he told her, been looking forward to buying her gifts. But she said she wanted currency. Francs.

'Very well.' He gave her the sum she wanted although this spoiled his pleasure. It made him feel he was paying for what he would have preferred to think he had had for free.

Later, in the restaurant, he quailed a little when a compatriot of his came and sat briefly at their table. But Maria, dressed in the finery which he had made it a point of honour to buy her anyway, was affable and quite amusing about how Aubry had tried to persuade her to buy a cardinal's hat which an old clothes vendor had been trying to get rid of for a few *baiocchi*. Looted property, to be sure, said she, lowering her voice. 'Best not to be caught with it when things change. For now, though, it's the colour of revolution and I could decorate it with a tricolour.' She mimed herself doffing the imaginary hat.

The other man laughed and Aubry began to feel possessive. The gap between private pleasure and the appearance one presented in public stimulated tenderness – and, really, he noted with surprise, she was looking very nice. Maybe he should take her to a few drawing rooms?

Contrasts were vital. Think of sour toffee apples or pears with cheese! Many of his republican comrades would disapprove. Austere men and all of a piece, they had been easily deceived by the two-faced conservatives – which proved, did it not, the drawbacks to austerity?

Taking leave of his friend, he and Maria moved to a café where, in the glow of an onion-shaped lamp, he saw her face grow agitated. A young man approached. Introducing himself – his name was Santi – he begged leave to exchange addresses with Maria, whom he clearly knew, saying that he needed to talk to her. Aubry acquiesced but she refused, saying they had no reason to meet. The young man, labouring under some press of feeling, said he needed to ask her something in confidence. Ask it now, said she. He hinted that it was private. She refused to take the hint. 'Speak,' she challenged, and Aubry laid bets with himself as to the source of all this. It was not far to seek. Santi – brother? lover? – was worried about a baby. She denied such a creature existed. He mentioned a mutual friend who had told him . . .

'Lies!' said Maria.

A silence ensued. To break it, Aubry offered the lover-or-brother a brandy. The two together interested him more than Maria alone. The boy restored context to her. He accepted and sat down. Aubry told her she was lucky to have friends concerned for her welfare and detected panic in her eye. Was he, she must wonder, going to hand her over? Changing the subject, he asked about the latest news and learned that 221-pound shells were falling on the hospital at the Trinità di San Pellegrino.

'That's where we met,' he reminded Maria, who looked sulkily away.

Patients were being moved from there to the Pope's palace on the Quirinal, said Santi. Some saw this as a sacrilege! 'As if we hadn't been commanded to help the sick!'

A believer? Aubry's sympathies flickered. In France he would have taken the young man for a hypocrite. But to come to Rome was to move back in time. Here was a boy whose mental world must be close to that of Pascal. As if this compounded his youth, Aubrey felt protective towards him.

Maria was questioning him irritably. 'So you talked to Gianna?'

'Yes. Because of what Rangone told me.'

'Rangone!' She was suddenly in a fury. A Merimée heroine, thought Aubry with delight. A Carmen! Exasperated, she leaned across the table and hissed: 'It died. All right? If you must know, I hid it in the latrine in Casa Salvione in the via dei Burrò. It was as good as dead. I lived on a farm. I've seen lambs and calves. It had no life in it.' Her voice had grown as hoarse as an old woman's. 'You wanted to know,' she repeated furiously. 'Both of you! Well, now you do!'

The young man looked stunned.

'It wasn't yours,' she told him. 'I went to Rangone, but he sent me away.'

The young man drew breath. Aubry put a hand on his wrist. 'Don't talk to her of religion,' he advised. 'Not now.'

To change the subject – give her a chance, he signalled, to simmer down – he asked if Santi knew why Father Bassi was so popular. 'The

231

people have their own saints,' he observed. 'And their own orthodoxies. I've seen the words "Down with atheistic religion" on the walls of Rome. At first, I thought they'd been put there by priests who saw that Republicanism was a sort of religion and were attacking it. Then I learned that it was the Republicans referring to the priests.'

Santi, still stunned, answered dully. He said he thought that Father Bassi was sincere but did not understand politics.

'You astound me. I thought he was your great political *padre*. He succours men in the front line, riding a white horse and carrying the crucifix. He's a legend. Our men – the French – captured him during the last siege and he so impressed them that they used him as a go-between, then let him go.'

Santi shook his head. 'I mean he doesn't understand the politics of the *Church*! He has enraged the whole hierarchy. I know this because I work for the Cardinal Archbishop of Bologna.'

Aubry was fascinated. 'Tell me more.'

But Santi shook his head. He couldn't think just now. Sorry. Aubry was asking whether they might meet again when Maria cut in suddenly. 'What I said before . . .'

'Yes?' For a moment the men had forgotten her.

'I don't know why I said it. No, I do. It's because it *could* have happened. For months I dreamed of its happening, but it didn't. It didn't!' She was sobbing, washing away what she had said. 'I went to see Rangone,' she confessed, 'in Imola and stayed there until his father cut up rough. Then I came here.'

Santi asked: 'So what did happen here, Maria?'

'I wasn't pregnant at all. It was a mistake. Women make mistakes. Ask any midwife.' She was shaken by sobs and hiccups and rage at the abstract indifference of men.

That night Nicola spent several wakeful hours being tantalised by the thought of her. She had looked beautiful in her fine clothes, and his two confessors' warnings pursued him. How would she end? And what of the story about the baby in the latrine?

Next day he called on the journalist. There was no sign of Maria so, after walking to the city walls with Aubry to see the fortifications, he came disconsolately home. But home was merely a cell which had been put at his disposal in a monastery and, though the purpose of its scanty furnishings was to encourage meditation, his was the wrong sort. It was as if the Frenchman's easy capture of Maria had released him from scruples and he begun to dream of her with a flaunting, greedy and angry love.

He returned to see the Frenchman who raised an amused eyebrow and said, 'She's not special. You should try another girl.'

Nicola burned with embarrassment and Aubry said he knew what it was to be Nicola's age, adding, 'You mustn't think she cares for me. I'm a purse and a place to stay. She'll move on when she finds something better. Meanwhile, I teach her what I can, which isn't a great deal. She will never be any of the things I imagine you fancy her to be – an imperilled soul, a passionate woman, or a possible friend. She is a little peasant who doesn't want to spend the rest of her life as a servant. She has had a whiff of the good life, senses the coming of the French Army and hopes to make hay while the sun shines. It won't shine very long for her because she is not very clever.'

Nicola wanted to hate him. It would have been an outlet for his humiliation. But he knew the Frenchman was only pointing out what he needed to know.

They were sitting in Aubry's outer room. A little later, the journalist excused himself and went through into what must be his bedroom. Nicola could not resist straining his ears.

'. . . doesn't come for me,' he heard. 'Why don't you come out for a few minutes? The poor fellow would be so pleased.'

Then he heard Maria's sulky voice and when the door opened caught a breath of body smells mixed with scent. He left as soon as he decently could.

Fourteen

After sustaining a month's siege, Garibaldi retreated from Rome

The French were entering the city. Wave after wave – there were said to be 20,000 – poured up the Corso on horseback and foot, carrying their arrogant flags. Nicola stood in a sullen crowd. When a horse raised its tail and did what the French call 'dropping incense', that too looked arrogant.

A priest pushed to the edge of the footpath and began to applaud. Voices hissed: 'Don't clap, traitor!' But he paid no attention. He was a tubby little priest and beside himself with glee. Defying the warnings, he raised his clapping hands and shouted, *'Vive le Pape! Evviva il Papa Re!'* His face shone. Someone caught his arm; he staggered, slumped against Nicola's legs, then rolled into the gutter. Blood oozed from the back of the cassock. A man whispered to Nicola. 'Best remove him fast.'

A third man lent a hand and the three carried the body into the nearest house where it was laid on a bed. The dead man was heavy and there was still a trace of elation on his broad, simple face. A woman said she would inform the parish priest, and sent them quickly away. Better if they weren't around to be called as witnesses. They separated without telling each other their names.

Cardinal Amandi was expected soon, so Nicola decided to wait, pay his respects, then leave for Bologna. Meanwhile, he went looking for Don Mauro.

A French soldier, on duty at the hospital, refused him entry, so he hung about until a nurse came, then learned that priests, now in charge, were sacking nurses and accusing the Republicans of having stolen things. 'They're drawing up inventories of things nobody ever saw,' whispered the girl. 'They're threatening to charge the Principessa and

Father Gavazzi. Don Mauro has been told not to come back. They say he's not a priest at all. Could that be true?'

Nicola said he didn't know and went on looking for him.

He found him in the *Circolo*, sitting with a dispirited Martelli, who was insisting that Don Mauro must get out of the state fast and would need false papers. Don Mauro did not protest. Reality had descended on him and with it shock at his own imprudence. He had administered the sacraments while defrocked. 'My case,' he tried to justify himself, 'was going forward and Father Rosmini said I could count on a favourable outcome. At the time he was tipped to be Cardinal Secretary of State. How could I not trust him? Then, later, there was so few priests here and so much need if people were not to turn from religion . . .' His voice trailed off. 'My intentions were pure.' But the word from men close to the Curia was categoric: Don Mauro had better leave while he could.

'You should have gone before the French came,' said Martelli. 'They're sour now. Several were murdered on their first night.'

Martial law had been proclaimed, with a curfew at nine o clock.

Outside, the three ran into Gilmore, whom neither Martelli nor Nicola had seen since school. Despite his protests, they took him in near custody to lunch. He was on an errand for his rector and looked dazed, having been immured in the Irish College for months. Under the Republic, this, being under the protection of the British crown, had offered asylum to a number of conservative prelates. Gilmore looked as though he expected to see a citizenry with horns and hooves. He was clutching a small case which caught Martelli's eye. What was in it, he asked, but Gilmore clutched it more tightly and wouldn't say. Martelli made his nose quiver, which was an old trick of his and made them laugh. The conversation then turned to the menu, the recent lack of food and how, thanks to the French, supplies were now arriving.

Suddenly, while Gilmore was busy with his soup, Martelli snatched and opened his case. 'English passports!' he cried with delight. 'Your prayers have been answered, Don Mauro. Your name is O'Ferrall and if there's trouble, just grease the customsman's palm. As for you,' he told Gilmore, whose elbows were being held, one by Nicola and one by Don Mauro, 'you can say you were attacked by wild Republicans who threatened to cut your throat. If you like, I'll make a little slash in it for plausibility's sake.'

Nicola asked for whom the passport had been intended and was told it was for a double agent named Don Vigilio who had reasons to avoid the French. By now Gilmore was almost in tears and Nicola persuaded Martelli to give back the other passports, arguing that the Irish rector, if sufficiently provoked, might give a list of the names on them to the customs. He might do this anyway, so Don Mauro had better leave at once. The priest kept shaking his head. This had all happened to him before. It was destiny. He'd have to head for Marseilles. There would be plenty of others in the same boat, they told him. Hurry. Meanwhile, Gilmore mustn't be let out of sight until Don Mauro set off. Nicola, unable to dissociate himself from Martelli's violence, held Gilmore firmly by one elbow until Don Mauro's possessions were packed and they had seen him onto a diligence. Mustering his spirits, the exile thanked his rescuers and said he'd pray for them – unless they thought his prayers were no good? What an idea! they yelled. Who said God was a reactionary? That's heresy, Don Mauro! Laughing and waving, the three – even Gilmore joined in – made a great hubbub.

'I hope you won't be in too much hot water,' said Nicola as they returned the Irish boy's briefcase.

Gilmore said he wouldn't ever want to refuse help to a man in need. It was a tentative peace-making – like the one the city must soon make with its pope.

Walking off on his own, Nicola marvelled at the silence. After weeks of bombardment, the sound of a cobbler's hammer or the clatter of a window startled by their ordinariness – though the ordinary was not yet to be trusted. Confident rats quivered grassily among the ruins. You had to be alert for unstable masonry and the ground was strewn with debris. When it rained, pulverized plaster made a great boil of paste and bubbled as though a new, unimaginable creation were about to emerge from the chaos left by the old one. The 'Rome of the people' had lasted only a few months.

From the diary of Raffaello Lambruschini:

The banishment of Rosmini, the Liberals' spokesman in Gaeta, showed the rest of us the uselessness of putting our heads on the same block. While we hoped to prevail, it had been our duty to give our prince candid advice, and I had done this in a series of articles in the Tuscan paper, *La Patria*. As late as May, I still hoped to wean Mastai from the cabal which had gained ascendancy over his conscience. Then I stopped signing my articles, but continued to put the case that it would be folly to provoke the people by answering licence with repression and so perpetuating the vicious circle in which we had for so long been caught. 'If any hand can break this circle,' I wrote, 'it is that of Pius IX.'

Rereading this appeal, I see that I had lost faith in him yet longed to recover it. Half Italy was in the same plight for he had extended our moral scope – then reduced it; a grim, Procrustean trick. No need to record what he did do next: restored the Tribunal of the Inquisition, flogging in the prisons, etc., etc. Once it was clear that the French would hand Rome over to him, he lost all interest in reconciliation.

Unlike myself, Rosmini failed to foresee all this and was shocked to be greeted with the words '*Caro Abate*, we are no longer constitutional.' This was on the 9th June and two days later the police ordered him out of Gaeta. Incredulous, he asked to hear his sentence from the Pope's lips, but could not get an audience. No one knew his face. Doormen were stricken by oblivion and men with whom he had spent convivial evenings stared through him. It was, the poor saintly man said later, a deeply unsettling experience.

At last he shamed Cardinal Antonelli into taking him to Pius who was caught off guard. He said that, yes, Rosmini must leave and that his books were being examined for heresy by the Congregation of the Index. He was hazy about why, but promised to pray that God, who had granted Rosmini so many gifts, would grant him that of seeing how his writings displeased Him. 'Submit to this Holy See and you will surely be enlightened,' advised Pius.

Rosmini was bewildered. What enlightenment could God give him which Pius could not? His books had not yet been condemned, so who knew that they displeased Him? Had Mastai implied that Rosmini's gifts – intelligence, for instance – were a liability?

'Do not,' I wrote to Amandi, 'intercede for him.' Prudence, I warned, must be our watchword, for our day would come and, when it did, we would need men of integrity who had Mastai's trust.

During the siege, Miss Maria Foljambe – whose first name rhymed, as she liked to explain, with pariah – had taken to feeding the wild cats which lived in the Forum and around the Pantheon. At first she brought food in bags, then marshalled a servant with a cart. This activity was looked on askance, for since she was only twenty-six, her lapse into oddity was premature and, to the minds of her compatriots, deplorable since some ridicule devolved on them. She was well connected, which made things worse. The sight of her, her cart, her liveried servant, and the disease-ridden hordes which she had chosen to adopt was unpleasantly suggestive. Protestants were not allowed to have their church within the city walls lest it contaminate those within. Now, as if to prove that such contamination was indeed to be feared, here was this cat lady who was also a genuine English gentlewoman and distantly related to a peer.

Her servant defended the cat food with a cricket bat and had been seen waving it at children.

'Children are fed by the charities,' argued Miss Foljambe. 'Nobody feeds the cats.'

One thought of Egypt. Cat deities. The creatures looked like emanations of the stone. Ancient. Savage. Wild. They seized the nasty stuff and leaped to the top of a broken pillar or some equally defensible high ground to tear at the heart or whatever other organs she had brought. There was a latent insult here, for she had found herself a flock or horde and the terms were grown explosive, having been much in official use, as the Pope, Supreme Shepherd, fulminated his anathema on his flock-turned-horde.

At mass, when heads were bowed for the consecration, Nicola, feeling a hand in his pocket, thought it had been picked. Instead, a note had been slipped into it. Someone had scribbled: 'Intercepted by our agents working for mail-coach; pass on to person concerned.' He opened it and read:

Excellency,

As Yr Excellency feared, Santi has been frequenting suspect persons, among them one whose scribblings in the French press could have done untold harm to our Sacred Cause. Happily, thanks to Providence and Yr Excellency's endeavours, his impudent opinions are no longer printed. Why, then, is he still in Rome where he and S share a mistress? One must wonder whether all three belong to a network dedicated to promoting the interests of a sect which all but wrecked this Realm! Of the three, she is the easiest to arrest and interrogate. Since Austrian forces would be the best agency for this, a letter should be sent telling of her father's illness and summoning her back to Bologna where these forces are now in charge.

While awaiting Yr Excellency's instructions, I humbly kiss Yr Excellency's hand.

The signature was illegible. Horrified, Nicola rushed to Aubry's lodging, only to find that he had left. And the girl? She, said the doorman, had taken up with a Garibaldino and retreated with them. She was a camp follower, said the man, looking at Nicola with pity. Returning in gloom to his cell, Nicola found a note from Cardinal Amandi who was in Rome and wanted to see him this evening.

'It suits the Church's enemies,' said Amandi, 'for religion to seem incompatible with freedom, and we have fallen into their trap. If those few priests whom the people trust are shot without our lifting a finger to protect them, we shall have fallen into another.'

'Few?' The languid syllable came from the lips of a layman who had been reticently introduced as His Excellency. 'Are *few* priests trusted?' His Excellency had an Austrian accent and a mocking tone.

They were dining in a room which had been whitewashed to cover slogans with which its recent Republican occupants had defaced its walls. Lettering leaked through the paint and Nicola thought he could make out the words: 'Down' – or dawn? – '. . . religion'.

Amandi had come from Gaeta with a party of prelates; a trickling prelude to the return of the exiled court.

'Trust,' he said, 'needs to be restored.'

'As' – the Austrian sipped his wine – 'spilt milk to a jug?'

The cardinal ignored this. Could not Nicola, he urged, take a message to Cardinal Oppizzoni? *Sub rosa. Viva voce.* Fast. Since the roads between here and Bologna were infested by every sort of enemy, he must carry no paper but memorise the following: General Grozkowski, the Austrian governor of occupied Bologna, would be replaced by a more humane officer if Oppizzoni fulfilled a certain requirement. This would save lives. 'If Your Excellency agrees.'

His Excellency jibbed. Our men, he said, as devoted sons of the Holy Father, were hurt in their filial feelings. Our flag had been insulted. 'Grozkowski's a soldier. What can you expect?'

His own affectation of civilian nonchalance was belied by his bearing. Stiffening at the word 'flag', his lean frame achieved heraldic abstraction. Excesses, he admitted, were being committed. Shootings. Court martials. Lack of court martials. Well; war was war! Still, though the

239

Imperial High Command was under no obligation to do so, some of us – here His Excellency's stance softened – felt that to appoint a more lenient governor could heal wounds. We must not, be it understood, seem weak. There must be a quid pro quo. Being the policeman of Catholic Europe was proving thankless and what faith could one have in a population which had resisted our efforts to liberate it? Not to speak of what had gone on under the Republic. 'I believe that in the hinterland Republicans crowned a man with thorns.'

The cardinal said, no, those had been papal supporters and the victim a Republican. Yes, he was sure. Smiling: 'The Republican imagination is less traditional.'

The Austrian produced a copy of an apology sent by Cardinal Oppizzoni to Gaeta and read mockingly: '"While upheavals were afflicting this unhappy province, the sharpest thorn in our heart was our inability to deliver the gullible from the snares of those whose impudence was compounded by their being in Holy Orders ..."' Speeding his delivery, he began to skip: '"They corrupted consciences ... zzzz ... brought legitimate authority into disrepute ... In the words of St Jude ..."' He flicked the paper with his nail. 'The cardinal's excuse for his culpable tolerance is that he was biding his time. He writes: "*Sapiens, tacebit usque ad tempus!*" Our belief is that *even now* the true purpose of this furtive apology is to save the black sheep in his flock. Am I right?' he asked Nicola who – *sapiens tacebit* – said he didn't know. 'I am,' said his Excellency. 'He hopes to save the black sheep and the corrupt shepherds.'

'Opinion in Gaeta,' said Amandi, 'is that the punishment of priests pertains to the spiritual authority. But Grozkowski ...'

The Austrian told Nicola, 'Learn this: the cardinal must make his apology public. He must publish this letter in the *Gazzetta di Bologna* and condemn the priests who used the gospel to preach socialism and revolution. Only then will Grozkowski be replaced.'

When the Austrian left, the cardinal gave Nicola passports and a dispatch with a papal seal. These would get him past any French or Austrians troops he might encounter. The roads were filled with them, for the hunt for escaping Garibaldini was widespread. The dispatch merely named Nicola as an accredited envoy. The message would be in his head.

'The truth is,' confided the cardinal, 'that opinion in Gaeta is less sympathetic to this move than I wanted our Austrian friend to guess. My influence is on the wane and I think it fair to tell you that if you are planning an ecclesiastical career you may find our connection more of a hindrance than a help. If you want to refuse this errand, do.'

Nicola said he wanted to do it. The cardinal looked older, yet the gap between them had diminished. It was as if Nicola's acceptance had given him something like a battlefield commission.

'This is the Ark,' said Amandi. 'But who knows whether we have weathered our last Flood.' He had seen His Holiness before leaving Gaeta and predicted: 'He will put off his return here to avoid the French. They want him to grant reforms or at least to promise not to repeal those he granted last year. He hates saying "No" to people's faces.' Amandi, now in his forties, had deep-set eyes and the leashed, stealthy energy of his caste. Nicola, he said, would find a coach and horses ready in the morning. 'You'll have to sleep while you travel. I've kept you awake.'

The groom, an ex-soldier, would be armed.

Next day Nicola did indeed sleep through much of his journey, only waking when the coach drew up in dim, fly-blown places to change horses. Soon they had left the French troops behind and entered Austrian-controlled territory. Nicola, getting out to spare the horses as they toiled up a slope, was joined by the groom, Enzo, who had heard reports of Austrian atrocities. Villas had been broken into, mirrors shot at and wine cellars looted. Did the villas belong to Liberals? Enzo closed an eye. The white-coats didn't look too carefully into that.

Meanwhile their coach had been stopped. An officer with an oak-leaf badge leaned so close that Nicola caught the smell of his waxed moustache. On seeing the papal seal, he saluted with what could have been irony for he spat as the coach moved off.

One of Enzo's stories was about a young girl, a glove-maker who had been denounced to the Austrians for saying she hoped her town would not fall back into the bigots' claws. Well, what the soldiers had done was strip and whip her. A girl! Just think of it! Eyes fixed on a birch tree which had caught the sun, Enzo wondered what it must have done to her feelings about *men*. Could she ever now make someone a proper wife? They passed trees wreathed lacily in Old Man's Beard and heard owls hooting and saw a hare. But Enzo's mind stayed unwaveringly on glove-making and slim fingers easing supple fabrics over their own pallor. After he and Nicola had gone back to their places, he must have nodded off, for Nicola heard him wake up and yell 'God-damn Croats!'

They were stopped again by Austrians looking for Garibaldini and advised to take a side route. There was an ambush ahead with orders to shoot anything that moved. The coachman nodded and took off at as fast a pace as was safe on a side road. 'Poor bleeding misfortunates!' he said of the Garibaldini, as they drew up in the yard of an inn.

This was the usual mouldering warren but the innkeeper said they couldn't stay. It had been requisitioned by a joint unit of pontifical and Austrian troops. Enzo threatened him with trouble. The young gentleman, he said, indicating Nicola, was journeying on the Pope's business. He had urgent dispatches. See. And was in the service of Cardinal Oppizzoni. Know who he was? Well then. The innkeeper swore and gave in and Enzo went into the kitchen to order dinner. Nicola was stung by the way he had taken charge. Had Amandi told him to? Was he a sort of nurse? These doubts were only increased by Enzo's return with an inn servant and their dinner.

'Best grab what we can,' he advised Nicola and the coachman. 'When the soldiers come they'll eat like locusts.'

And indeed the three had hardly finished their boiled fowl when hooves clattered outside. A detachment of papal troops were yelling for the landlord. They had a prisoner who needed locking up. Was there a room with a key?

'Who's the prisoner?' Enzo asked a soldier.

'A girl. A Garibaldino camp follower. They shot the men with her. They were . . . trying to escape.' The soldier's cockiness faltered and it was clear the Garibaldini had been gunned down in cold blood. As for the girl, he said, the Austrian officer seemed to have his own plans for her. 'He's gone after some fugitives, but he'll be back.' The man added, as though arguing with himself, 'Well, anyway, she's a whore.'

Nicola didn't have to see her. The rush of his pulse told him: it was Maria. When she was bundled through the room it was no surprise. She was dishevelled, but it was her limpness which struck him, in the presence of those stiff, armed men. She drooped, boneless as a shot bird or an empty glove. She was prey: wide-eyed, confused and horrifyingly vulnerable. *Miserere!* he prayed and, after she had been locked up, wondered briefly if he had imagined her. She hadn't noticed him.

Then a fear-numbing urgency boiled in him and his brain felt clear as glass. Desperation? Never mind. Take advantage of it, he told himself. Act! He ordered grappa, to the surprise of the other two, then asked Enzo: 'Do you think we could rescue her?'

'Us, Excellency?' The title showed Enzo's shock.

Nicola told the papal soldier to take him to his senior officer and, picking up the bottle, followed him to where the officer was eating boiled capon. He was chubby-faced and perhaps twenty-four: young, if you weren't yourself seventeen with peach fuzz on your cheek. Was there a humorous twitch to his lip? He accepted a glass of grappa.

'Captain,' sitting opposite him, Nicola spread his knees in an attempt to enlarge his presence, 'may I speak candidly?'

There *was* a twitch. Nicola ignored it. Gravely, he knitted up a story backed by a display of his passports and dispatches. The captain, a man used to responsibility, must understand his reticence about the true identity of the girl he had come to arrest. Yes, the one here in this inn. Seeing the other man sharpen, Nicola said, 'You sprung our trap,' explaining that the girl was to have been arrested further along the route 'by our agents'. The Church wanted her in its own custody and not the Army's – much less that of the Austrians.

'You won't be surprised to know that the interests of the Austrian High Command and our own' – with a bow to the officer's papal uniform – 'are not always the same and that there are matters which we keep from them.' The girl, he improvised, was an associate of the Principessa di Belgioioso and of Father Gavazzi, 'whose ordinary, Cardinal Oppizzoni, is my superior'.

The captain said his sergeant came from Bologna.

'Then,' said Nicola coolly, 'he may know me by sight. To return to the girl, the interest of the Holy Office,' he slid a glance at the officer to see if this absurdity was being accepted, 'is in tracing responsibilities which,' he smiled blandly, 'I may not discuss. Our allies are inclined to be precipitous . . .' Like a novice player of a new game, he was trying out turns of thought which he had encountered recently – some as recently as last night. But he was aware that his rigmarole contained contradictions. Would the other man notice?

Apparently not. The young captain – their ages were beginning to feel closer – downed another grappa and said the trouble was that the Austrian officer outranked him. To overrule him, he would need authorisation. Besides . . .

Nicola, fearing lest the man's wits might be stirred by speech, interrupted with indignation on behalf of Our Holy Father on whom two overbearing allies were attempting to impose their will. A hotchpotch of feeling steamed as he refilled the captain's glass.

'What do you want of me?'

'Let me take her in my coach. Now, before your Austrian colleague returns.'

243

'I'll need something in writing.'

The balloon of Nicola's imagination began to dip. 'Brigands,' he pleaded, 'stole my writing case.'

The captain, however, had caught fire. 'You may use mine. Have you a seal?'

A seal? Nicola's hand clapped to his chest and felt the small bump of the one which Flavio had given him. It had the wrong pope's arms on it, was indeed a seal from before not one but two Roman Republics, but, if he smudged the wax, would anyone notice this?

The officer meanwhile confided his dislike of the Austrians. His had been a disappointing war and having to work with the Croats was the last straw. Butchers was what they were. Here, abate, can you use this?

It was a leather writing case with silver ink bottles, paper and wax. 'Order me to hand the prisoner over to you,' said the captain, 'and I'll handle the Croat. But hurry. If they come back before you get her away, they'll enjoy refusing you.'

Nicola wrote the letter, signed it in Cardinal Oppizzoni's name, sealed it with Flavio's seal and within half an hour was in the coach with Maria, bowling out of the yard, while Enzo, on the coachman's box, kept his gun at the ready.

Maria sat stunned and listless.

At first Nicola was pleased that she had not spoiled his story by greeting him too familiarly. Then, as the coach jingled over dusky roads and she still sat as unmoving as Niobe, elation fell away. As it did, he began to wonder whether his cleverness was not beside the point. Almost angrily, he tried to rally her, but persuasion had never worked with Maria. She had, he knew, seen her lover killed. Yet – jealousy nipped at his sympathy – for how long could she have known this lover? A week? Less? Until two weeks ago she had been with the Frenchman and the memory of what *he* had said of her buzzed like some foul fly at the edge of Nicola's mind. He refused to acknowledge it. Death had consecrated her most recent lubricity.

'Do you want to tell me how it was?'

Numb headshake.

'I'm taking you to the border with Tuscany. There's a priest there who'll smuggle you across. A friend of Garibaldi's.' Nicola remembered this from the dossier on suspect clerics which he had kept for Cardinal Oppizzoni. 'Are you,' he asked the numb silence, 'hungry?'

More silence. She drooped and it was an anguished rapture to have her here safe from everyone except his own soured desire. His was a bruised love and he tried to make it generous, telling himself that he wanted nothing from her – only to make her happy. But that hope, in the immediate circumstances, was childish. She made him seem perennially backward in experience, feeling the wrong things and unable to catch up.

Modigliana was a small town heaped in a valley like eggs in a basket. It was also off his route which meant that he was not proceeding to Bologna as fast as promised. One mission of mercy was interfering with another.

Don Giovanni Verità, a convivial countryman who, like Father Bassi, committed the solecism of wearing trousers instead of a cassock and a round, instead of a three-cornered, hat, groaned at news of the Austrian ambush, rallied, gabbled a prayer, then told them that Garibaldi had been here and was almost certainly now in safety. Rumours were coming thick and fast and the latest was that Garibaldi's wife, Anna, was wounded or ill and that Father Ugo Bassi, who had been with the couple, had left them, set off alone with one companion and been taken prisoner. This news revived Nicola's sense of urgency and he asked whether they could get a change of horses and press on for Bologna tonight. But the priest, the coachman and even Enzo opposed the idea. Driving after dark was illegal and, besides, the roads were infested by dangerous men. They must spend the night where they were.

'But you go out at night?' Nicola reminded the priest.

Ah, said the reverend smuggler, that was different. He knew the country around here as well as any goat. Even so, he would not brave the dark tonight. Tomorrow, he would take the girl over the border and see her into safe hands.

He spent the rest of the evening telling smuggling stories.

Early next morning, Nicola and his two companions drove off into a lemon-bright dawn. An image of Don Giovanni Verità, waving his round hat, danced behind them at the door of the presbytery which, when the cloths came off the cages in its small corridor, vibrated with a private dawn chorus. The priest had explained that though, as a smuggler, hunting was his great cover, he loved birds and spent winter evenings making these light, roomy cages from reeds and willow twigs.

245

'He's like the Pope,' said the irreverent Enzo. 'He loves his subjects so much that he keeps them caged in.'

Nicola had not tried to say goodbye to Maria who was asleep.

Outside Fognano one of the horses cast a shoe and they had to look for a farrier. While the man heated the metal to a red-hot transparency, a procession of schoolgirls in white pinafores dawdled past. Two nuns walked with them and their black habits against the white had a bleak, prophetic harshness.

'That'sh Shishter Paola,' said the smith, speaking through a mouthful of nails. 'Clever woman! Ushed to be the Pope'sh penitent. She cured my back.'

The slim nun waved at the smith who waved back, then went on hammering. 'Look out for Garibaldini,' he warned as he pocketed his fee.

Again the roads were hilly and Nicola imagined Don Giovanni Verità negotiating one with Maria riding pillion behind him. He wondered if he would see her again. As the coach was moving at a snail's pace, he decided to dismount and relieve himself.

'I'll catch up with you,' he told the coachman, then, a minute or so later, hearing Enzo's whistle somewhere above his head, guessed that, if he were to climb straight through the woodland, instead of following the road's bend, he would come out ahead of the coach. Accordingly, he struck up the hill.

Suddenly he was thrown to the ground. The sun, blazing through a ring of heads in silhouette, fell into his eyes. The sole of a boot loomed. He heard a shot.

'Idiot,' said a voice from one of the silhouetted heads. 'What's he trying to do? Attract the Austrian High Command?'

More men, dressed half in military, half in civilian, clothes now pushed Enzo and the coachman through the bushes. Garibaldini!

'Why did you shoot?' asked the one who had spoken before.

'Had to,' said one of the newcomers. 'He,' indicating Enzo, 'had a gun.'

Nicola, addressed a dazzle of sky. 'Please,' he gasped, 'I'm being sent to get better treatment for the captured men. It's more urgent now because the Austrians have got Father Bassi.'

'Lies. General Garibaldi's party got over the border.'

'They got separated.'

The boot rose again and pressed down on Nicola's chin. 'Tricky little abate!' The boot's owner's voice lilted and the boot pressed. 'A bit young for an abate, aren't you? But when did priests play by the rules? We don't care for Father Bassi, see?' The boot rose and Nicola squirmed away his face. 'You let a few priests stay with us so that if we win you'll be able to say you were really on our side. Decoys is what they are. Bassi too. The priest at Modigliana is another.'

'Stop tormenting him.'

'Why? Like pretty priests, do you? Got plans for him, eh?'

There was the sound of a scuffle and Nicola found that he had been released. Dust however had got into his throat and a cough jolted him so that he missed seeing the fight. When he recovered, Enzo had been stripped and tied to a tree. Someone unbuttoned Nicola's jacket. 'Sorry, abate, we need your clothes.' Then he too was tied up and some red shirts left beside him. 'In case you're cold,' mocked a voice.

'Leave the dispatches. What use are they to you? Mine is a mission of mercy,' he argued.

'So is ours. Mercy for ourselves! Save your own skin is the first rule of war. Here, though, keep your dispatches.' And they were tossed on the ground beside him.

By the time Enzo had wriggled free of his bonds and released the other two, it was again dusk and, under its cover, having decided against wearing the dangerous red shirts, they got into their carriage which their captors had preferred not to take and drove back to Modigliana in their underclothes, reaching it just as the priest returned from delivering Maria across the border. She was safe, he assured, though still mute. Not a word to be got from her. Don't worry. Young women recover. Come and I'll get you some food.

So they spent another night, drinking the priest's sharpish wine while he confided that he had argued hammer and tongs with Father Bassi because he, Don Giovanni Verità, had never had any hope of this pope or any pope and did not think the Church should rule the secular roost. His was a family of smugglers whose smuggling was a moral act. It was a defiance of borders which should not exist and a remedy for the wounds which criss-crossed Italy. A lot of priests smuggled, he said, and conspired. Always had. Yes, he had heard of Don Mauro. He'd been unlucky. Let's drink to him, poor man! In exile again, was he? Well, this life was an exile too and while we were in it, shouldn't we defy oppression even when, here he lowered his voice, it came from our own Church? Which in these parts it often did. See what had just happened!

247

How the Pope had called in the Austrians to brutalise his people into submission! You couldn't close your eyes. You had to follow your own lights. If you didn't, how could you pray or ask God to help you? Smuggling was a short cut, a stop-gap while waiting for a new dispensation which wasn't going to come tomorrow. It was safer to take the law into your own hands than to trust popes or kings.

'This pope,' he said, 'is not a lot better than the infamous Duke of Modena who intrigued with nationalists and then betrayed them. That was what started the troubles of 1831, which in turn shocked Mastai-Ferretti into thinking he was a Liberal. Spiritually speaking, he's the progeny of the duke who murdered his confederate. How many of *his* followers will end up dead?'

This cast a gloom over the company which began arguing as to whether treachery was endemic to Italy. Enzo declared it to be a matter of poor timing at a time of change. The traitor was the man who got out of step with it.

The priest's view was that traitors were men dazzled with hope, like poor Bassi who thought you could bring God's kingdom to earth but was now – the news had been confirmed – in the hands of authorities which would judge him by mean and rigid laws. 'I admire his heart but not his head,' said Don Giovanni. 'If you serve two masters, as I know well, you've got to keep your wits about you and be as tricky as a fox.' By two masters, he explained, he meant God and the Pope.

All four men were by now drunk on wine and on the strain of keeping up with reality, so they said good night, lay down where they could and blew out their candles.

'I must get to Bologna!' Nicola, who had had a nightmare, sat bolt upright in a sweat of desperation.

'Hush!' said Enzo with whom he was sharing a bed.

Nicola's nightmares were filled with knife-blades which, when he finally woke up, turned out to be the cracks in a shutter. Again the priest's birds filled the air with their sweet captive chorus and the travellers left at dawn. All three wore such oddments as their host had managed to lay hands on without arousing suspicion or alerting anyone to their presence.

Cardinal Oppizzoni threw his arms around Nicola's neck and wept a little. Yes, he confirmed, Father Ugo Bassi was indeed in Austrian hands and about to be brought here to Bologna. General Grozkowski was unlikely to handle him gently. The general was stiff-necked and the cardinal was on bad terms with him. All communications now passed through the hands of Monsignor Bedini, His Holiness's *Commissario Straordinario*, an Austrophile who, between ourselves, was less helpful than he might have been. The cardinal had been nettled by the General's refusal to let him hold the Corpus Christi procession. A slight. A deliberate annoyance. Never in the fifty years that he had been at the head of this diocese had the procession not been held. As he had told Monsignor Bedini who had failed to support him – but he was losing track. What was this message from Gaeta then?

Nicola told him.

The cardinal looked sombre. So they wanted him to condemn Fathers Gavazzi and Bassi in the public newspaper, did they? By name? But, *figlio mio*, that would be tantamount to throwing them to the wolves. The Austrians would take it as a repudiation of their ecclesiastical status, a withdrawal of the protection of the Church. Surely, surely this would be unwise? The two could then be treated as common criminals.

Nicola explained the bargain. The cardinal was to publish his repudiation of Republican priests and the Austrians would replace Grozkowski. Father Bassi would then receive a more lenient sentence. 'If *you* condemn him, *they* won't.'

'But can I rely on this promise?'

'Cardinal Amandi says the Pope agreed to the plan.'

'He said that? Clearly?'

'Yes.'

Oppizzoni put his head in his hands. 'The Austrians hate us now. They even hate His Holiness. They can't be trusted.'

He sent Nicola for a copy of the letter they wanted published. He hadn't written it – or rather, he had, but under duress, to satisfy the reactionary clergy of this diocese. 'I'm too old for such gambles. If only we had the electric telegraph here we could ask His Holiness for clarification.' Changing tack, he noted querulously that he couldn't publish the letter even if he wanted to. The Austrians wouldn't let him. He had to submit every word he wanted published to their lapdog and lickspittle, Bedini, who had to submit it to *them* for their sanction and imprimatur. 'Can you imagine the humiliation! They won't forgive us for supporting the war against them. Poor Bassi will pay the price.'

*

249

Having lost a suit of clothes to the Garibaldini, Nicola remembered the one promised by an anonymous donor and went to see the tailor, only to learn that the order had been cancelled weeks ago which was when Amandi lost the fame of being a Future Secretary of State. 'From now on,' he had warned Nicola, 'our connection may be more of a hindrance than a help.' Well, thought the young man with regret and amusement, it had already cost him a suit.

On 6th August, Oppizzoni's *Notificazione* appeared in the *Gazzetta di Bologna*. It was a copy of his letter to Gaeta, explaining his failure to condemn unruly priests at a time when, since the Republic was in power, the condemnation could have had no practical effect. Nicola was struck by the implication that this effect now could and should ensue.

Heading for the episcopal palace, he was held up by a press of people watching captured Republican soldiers being marched through the streets. They looked alike, as though defeat had soldered them into a homogenous mass.

'They've come from Rimini,' said someone; 'they were captured at San Marino. The poor bastards don't look as though they can remember a square meal. I heard there were eight hundred of them.'

'If there are they'll have to be released. The Croats won't want to feed all those mouths.'

'It's the shepherds not the sheep that should be punished,' said a man. 'Let them catch the priests!'

Nicola found the cardinal squinting with an anxious eye at a copy of the *Gazzetta di Bologna* and his own *Notificazione*. 'It's terrible!' he said. 'I never wrote it. Don Vincenzo Todeschi did. He's an auditor of the Ecclesiastic Tribunal and knows how to blacken a man. There's a bit about a *bordello sacrilego*. Oh Madonna! He must have stuck that in after I'd passed his copy and now it's in the paper. And the bit about talking of God in taverns is as venomous as it is vague. What will people take it to mean?'

The cardinal began wondering whether he could offset the bad impression of the *Notificazione* by protesting at Bassi's arrest. There were opposing considerations: first, this had already been tried to no effect when Bassi was first arrested. Why think the Austrians would have softened? Courting a rebuff did nothing for ecclesiastical authority.

Second: Grozkowski was in Mantua today; and, third: it was Monsignor Bedini's province. 'But he's a lickspittle,' said the cardinal.

It was lunchtime and through open windows drifted smells of lunches being prepared in nearby palaces. Life was going on, onions being fried, and sweetbreads and leg of lamb served up with rosemary.

'Let's visit the cathedral,' said Oppizzoni and Nicola lent him his arm to cross the piazza where vendors were putting away their wares. Ex-votos, small silver and tin facsimiles of limbs and inner organs blazed in the sunlight: lungs, hearts, arms and legs. Heat fell through coloured awnings and caught the old cardinal on the back of his neck as he removed his hat to enter the cathedral. His padded hand clutched and unclutched Nicola's wrist.

'Let us pray for him,' he whispered and lowered his unreliable old frame onto a kneeler.

Nicola wondered whether Bassi was in a military gaol and whether he would be handed over to the Church which had its own places of confinement. Would he have done better to flee like Don Mauro to heathen England? Life without belief must be random and sad.

Oppizzoni, still clinging to Nicola, stumbled as they tried to genuflect in unison on the way out. Crossing the square, they were met by two priests who had brought a large cotton sunshade for the cardinal and an item of news. By order of General Radetzky in Milan, General Grozkowski was to surrender his governorship and move forthwith to Venice where the war was still going on.

'God be praised!' Oppizzoni gave Nicola's hand a secretive squeeze.

The general's replacement said the priests, according to a source inside the military governor's office in Villa Spada, was to be General Count Strassoldo, who was to take over the day after tomorrow. 'He's said,' they exulted, 'to be as mild as milk!'

Next morning there was fresh news from the Villa Spada where Ugo Bassi was now being held. It was that his sister, Carlotta, whose husband owned a busy hotel in the middle of town – yes: the one in the via Vetturini! Well, this sister had driven over to the villa yesterday afternoon to see her brother and, though the officer in charge had refused permission at first, he had softened later, moved by either her tears or the knowledge that Grozkowski's time was short.

A fraternal pity for the unfortunate Bassi now seized the fickle priests of Bologna, and in the episcopal palace anxious prognoses ran around offices and from desk to desk. Almost everyone had a detail to add to accounts of what Bassi and his sister had said to each other, for Austrian soldiers had been present and had talked later in the presence of waiters, melon-vendors and grooms. These people's linguistic skills, however, were haphazard and reports varied as to whether the officer in charge had been courteous and compassionate or had had the brother and sister torn from each other's breasts.

Painstakingly, a nucleus of probable fact was assembled: Bassi had said that he had not received a trial but stood falsely accused of having been caught with weapons; his fellow prisoner, Captain Livraghi, also faced a false charge. He was considered a deserter by the Austrians because he had once fought under their flag. The priests took less interest in his case.

On the evening of the 7th, General Grozkowski returned from Mantua and next day took formal leave of the city's notables. By then Strassoldo had arrived and an interregnum prevailed. In the hot white stillness of the August day, Nicola was glad to have a message to deliver to Monsignor Bedini at the legative villa at San Michele in Bosco where he could catch a breath of air. During the slow, uphill drive, his coachman spotted General Grozkowski's carriage on the road ahead of them and when they arrived at the villa the general and Monsignor Bedini were closeted in a farewell meeting. No sense waiting, the major domo told Nicola. He might as well leave his letter. So Nicola left, his heart lightened by the success of his mission for Monsignor Amandi, now that Grozkowski was as good as gone. The breeze was refreshing and the carriage horses seemed to trot at an expanded, high-stepping gait.

As soon as he entered the city, he knew something was wrong. By now it was that tranquil, digestive hour of the afternoon when the heave and sigh of deep breathing should have been all-pervasive; a lazy ticking over of the city's pulse. Instead, there was a tight silence as though breath were being held. Shutters and blinds were shut but awry as though to accommodate a discreet and vigilant watch. Knots of people dissolved as he passed. In a sliver of shadow Father Tasso – back from his spiritual exercises – waved his hat and mouthed with shocking indiscretion: 'They shot Ugo Bassi!'

'What? Shush. Wait.'

'Murdered him.' Tasso climbed into Nicola's carriage. 'Didn't you hear the firing squad? Yes. Bassi.' The priest repeated his information with a cold restraint as though to show that a new way of dealing with things must be learned. 'They can't have held a trial. If they did it was illegal, for the Church wasn't informed – was it?' The priest had a moment's panic, then: 'No,' he reassured himself, 'it couldn't have been.'

'But General Grozkowski is no longer governor. He was at the legatine villa just now taking leave of Monsignor Bedini.'

'Well, Father Bassi was shot at noon. In the Cimitero della Certosa. Shot and shovelled into the ground. I want you to take me to the cardinal. That general must be excommunicated. Protests must be sent to Gaeta.' Tasso dredged up words he had never thought to apply to his own town or time. Barbarism, *sacrilege*! Did Nicola realise . . .

But Nicola was further along the road to disillusion than Tasso. Seeping into him was the knowledge that someone had used him to trick Oppizzoni. Who? Amandi? The Austrian? Or – who?

'Bassi,' whispered Tasso, weeping. '*Il povero Ugo!*'

'Come into my office,' offered Nicola when they reached the archbishop's palace. 'This is the cardinal's nap-time. We'll have to wait.'

In the palace, indignation was being ground out between locked teeth. The priests' wrath was turning towards the door behind which the old cardinal lay under the four faded cloth pineapples which topped the posters of his curtained bed. He had not yet learned the news.

The *Notificazione*, which until now had bothered none of them, had begun to look sinister. Was a purge of priests to be carried out by the secular arm for the hierarchy and at its nod?

A thin priest, called Padre Farini, polished his eyeglasses with a striped handkerchief. Perhaps he felt his vision needed adjusting? He was one of the two who had exulted at General Grozkowski's removal.

'*Sapiens tacebit usque ad tempus!*' he quoted meaningfully. 'The wise man waits for the right time – time for *what*?'

Nobody answered. Time worried them. Had they paid insufficient attention to it? Failed to see that eternity was made up of an infinity of tricky bits of it? Bassi, said Tasso, had been a saint and a martyr.

'And a scapegoat,' said Farini shrewdly. 'Catholic Austria could not kill all its prisoners, nor take revenge on the Pope who blessed their arms. A military chaplain is the perfect stand-in for both.'

'It's a sacrilege,' said Tasso, 'he wasn't defrocked.'

Padre Farini held up the *Gazzetta di Bologna*. 'Not quite.'

'You mean . . .'

'Read it. How can there be a protest on behalf of a priest who is said by his own bishop to have been untrue to his cloth?'

'He's not named.'
Farini laughed.

'Don't weep for Bassi,' said the cardinal. 'I'm sure he died gloriously. Men like that do.' He let a hand rest on Nicola's shoulder. 'They blame me, don't they? Don't take it hard. Just tell yourself that I have been fifty years at the head of this diocese and that the most useful thing I can do for it now is to magnetise blame. That's politics, *fili mi*! Your confessor despises it, as did Ugo Bassi, who used to ride his white horse up and down the front line and write poems which I thought it wise to read. They're irreproachable,' said the cardinal, 'and not much good. His poem was his life. He had a muse: a married lady, I believe. But his love was disembodied, which is the worst sort since it can never be dealt with and saps the soul. He wasn't quite adult, which means he was one of the little children whom Christ calls to Himself. And I'm the Judas who'll be to blame for his death. Judas or Caiaphas? Both perhaps. But Judas first, for he – you should know – is the secret patron of all active prelates since he was the man of whom Christ said that the thing had to be done but woe to him who did it. Poor Judas! I often think of him managing the disciples' money and losing track of the long view. Serving the Church Militant has its risks. They're angry aren't they?' He nodded towards the outer offices. 'They want me to *do* something. Me, not Monsignor Bedini whose province it is, because they've no hopes of him. Me!'

'They want the general excommunicated!'

'No less!' Oppizzoni laughed. 'Ah well, they'll end up no doubt on Christ's right hand. With Ugo Bassi.'

'But Eminenza . . .'

'Yes?'

'Surely whoever is to blame should be . . .'

'Whoever is to blame?' Oppizzoni held Nicola's gaze so firmly that Nicola dropped his own. 'Even me? Or you? Who,' said the cardinal coolly, 'did not come here as fast as you might have done. Don't explain,' he interrupted. 'Explain to your confessor. Reports were sent to me about your journey, but I didn't read them. I have to keep my mind clear of small things. For you, however, this may be a big thing, so you'd better tell Father Tasso why you spent two nights in Modigliana, which is not on the main road. If you had not done so and had got here earlier, the general's last day would have been the 6th not the 8th. Everything

254

might have been different. Don't cry. You must learn not to give way, or you will never be the foxy defender of the faith that Cardinal Amandi hopes. He sent you to me to learn to be that. From the first I took this as a rather painful judgment of myself – but also as a gift, since a young innocent is a delight to have around. Now I must destroy your innocence; it is refreshing in the young, but dangerous in older men and if let loose like Bassi's wreaks havoc. No. I'm not being hard-hearted. I shall say masses for him. Publicly, however, don't expect me to join in the Bassi-cult which I have no doubt will soon start up.'

'Eminenza, do you really think I'm . . .?'

'To blame? My poor Nicola, we're all to blame for Christ's suffering. Our sins drive in the nails. And,' added the cardinal, 'so does our stupidity.'

Fifteen

Father Tasso had spent the night trying to comfort Father Bassi's '*confortatore*', Don Gaetano Baccolini, a bookish man who had had the misfortune to be assigned the task of administering the last rites to the condemned priest. It had been his bad luck to be to hand when his pastor, who was getting ready to celebrate a sung mass for the soul of a parishioner, received a message from the police. Two priests were wanted at Villa Spada.

Tasso's skirts cut the air like blades. 'Think of it!' he invited Nicola whom he had again dragged from the confessional. 'Baccolini had been working on a series of sermons. Apart from dashing into church to say mass, he hadn't left his room for days and hadn't heard of Father Bassi's arrest.'

Nicola and Father Tasso were climbing the Montagnola to get some air. Reaching the summit, they stared down to where the Austrians had been defeated a year ago. Bassi had been shot on the anniversary of the battle. A tasty revenge!

Nicola listened with resignation. He had come to confession full of his own scruples, only to find that his confessor couldn't concentrate on them. He refused to say whether Nicola should or should not have left Maria to be raped.

Baccolini and another unpractised priest had been taken to prepare 'two delinquents' to face the firing squad. This was bad enough. Worse followed when, after cooling their heels for an hour in the great saloon of the Villa Spada, they learned that the delinquents were Father Bassi and Captain Livraghi who had just been informed of their sentence. The four were then brought together, whereupon Bassi had to protect the '*confortatori*' from Livraghi who was ready to throttle the 'Austrian priests'. Bassi, convincing him that he was dying as surely for freedom

256

as if he had fallen in battle, managed to calm him as he had calmed the dying on battlefields in Lombardy, the Veneto and Rome. He even comforted the men sent to comfort him.

Baccolini, said Tasso, had dwelled painfully on his own inadequacy. Over and over. Weeping, saying his *mea culpa*, drinking port. By the evening's end, Tasso had the account by heart and repeated it now, then broke off to wonder where Bassi had got his courage. Was it the priest in him or the soldier who had dealt so decorously with death? Without him, Livraghi would have died cursing, for the official '*confortatori*' had, by their own admission, been as useless as a brace of ganders.

Bologna knew of the execution right away. The closed police carriage was seen driving to Villa Spada and, later, people recognised the beat of loose-skinned drums as the condemned men were taken to the cemetery. Then they heard the shots.

Over night the people's hero became their saint, and Austrian grenadiers, posted by the ditch where his body was interred, were kept busy chasing away women who came with tricolours and wreaths. Bitter graffiti appeared on walls whose owners had to remove them on pain of a fifty scudi fine for a first offence and twice that thereafter plus a spell in gaol.

A smoky contagion compounded of patriotism and piety prickled the air. It was hot, even for August. There were rumours that cholera had broken out and that the authorities had discredited themselves with God. Caiaphas and Pontius Pilate were mentioned. A legend was taking shape and the authorities hastened to abort it.

'The Zelanti want Baccolini to say that at the end Bassi repudiated his political faith.'

'Which Zelanti?'

Tasso didn't know. Bedini? The cardinal? Who knew which of those two was the puppet and which pulled the strings?

Nicola spoke up for Oppizzoni who was no zelante, but Tasso said, 'Don't tell me he's not an old fox!'

'He says he's a fox for God.'

'*Barca!*'

Twinned by its image, a toy sailboat skimmed the pond while a child of maybe six struggled to get around and meet it on the other side. '*Barca!*' the child shrieked again then, finding he had lost a shoe, flopped down on sodden ground, dug it from the mud and began laboriously putting it on. Hair fell across his eyes. This must be Prospero's step-brother. When he stood up, the seat of his britches had a muddy patch.

'So,' Prospero had been asked in the inn where he changed coaches, 'you missed your father's wedding?' Inquisitive eyes slid sideways. 'Likely he didn't think you could get away. Not with what's going on in Rome!' Then the gossips asked about *that*. Discreetly though. Weighing their words, for Bologna was under martial law. 'How's Rome?' they asked.

But Prospero's news was stale.

'If he'd been expecting you, the Signor Conte would surely have delayed the wedding.' He read their thoughts: the count's fancy woman was now his wife. How was the son taking that? 'It was a quiet wedding,' they told him.

Well, so it should be! A widower-bridegroom, even of the count's station, could be subjected to the charivari: a serenade of saucepans. His impulsive father was as vulnerable as the toy boat which was now listing to one side. Ten to one, he was agonising about what to say to Prospero who, in turn, had been worrying about putting *him* at ease. Needing time to prepare a spontaneous face, he had had the coachman put him down some way from the villa. Walking through familiar vegetation, he was nipped by the immediacy of known sounds and smells, every one of which reminded him of his mother. Mushrooming with her, black-berrying, heaping up mounds of leaves into which he could then thrillingly dive. Sailing the toy boat.

When he reached the pond and saw it, a phantom on silken waters, a jostle of feelings choked him. But, meanwhile, here was the small usurper in difficulties. Prospero had been observing him from behind a tree. Up and down the shore stumbled the short, stubby legs, for the craft was marooned in mid-pond. There were weeds there, Prospero remembered, and the only way to reach it now was by rowboat.

'You'll have to be your brother's keeper,' Nicola had joked when they met this morning on Prospero's way through Bologna. 'And your father's!' Nicola had been sent by Cardinal Oppizzoni to warn Prospero that his father was making last-ditch efforts to win the Pope back to Liberalism. 'It's too late for that,' he warned. 'He's drawing attention to himself and that, in the present climate, is unwise. Especially, if he's up to anything else.'

'Nicola, my father supports – no, idolizes, the Pope.'

'Yes, but the pope of today is not the pope of last year!' Nicola reminded him that old portraits of Pio Nono were being collected and destroyed, the ones where he said 'God bless Italy' and blessed the troops. 'He doesn't want embarrassing reminders. Your father could become one.'

Prospero wasn't sure whether to dismiss this as sacristy gossip. Besides: his thoughts about his father tended to be laced with irony. This helped dissipate the enfevered murk which was the count's climate. As a cuttlefish sprays ink, so the old conspirator had always darkened the atmosphere around himself and Prospero's adolescence seemed to him now to have been a long, frustrated fumble towards the light.

Seeing his stepbrother ankle-deep in the water, he remembered that the ground here shelved and, emerging from behind his tree, introduced himself and said that the thing to do now was to take a rowboat. When they were settled in it, he asked the child's name.

'Cesco.'

'And how do you come to be alone?' Prospero was poling them towards the middle.

'Daniele was with me. The soldiers took him.'

Prospero knew Daniele, his father's gamekeeper.

'I hid,' said Cesco. 'I'm good at hiding. Like you.'

Where was his mother, asked Prospero. At the house, said Cesco.

'Well, there's your yacht, free.'

Launched on the syrupy surface, a wake fanned behind it, as neat as a printer's caret. Prospero swung the boat around, and it was then that they heard pistol shots.

'Bang!' cried the child. 'Bang! Bang! Bang!'

So, in the end, there was no ceremony to Prospero's meeting with his stepmother. The noise which brought Cesco and himself running to the villa had given their father a seizure and he was stretched on a couch when they edged open the door. Someone had ridden off for the doctor and a woman who must be the new contessa was holding the invalid's hand. Seeing Prospero, she gravely and just perceptibly tilted her head towards Cesco who was straining to be let run to her. Take him away, said the head-tilt. Prospero, who knew what it was to be confronted by a felled parent, did.

'Is Papa dead? Did the soldiers shoot him?'

'No, but we mustn't disturb him.'

'They didn't shoot him?'

'No.'

'Who did they shoot?'

'They shot in the air. It's a thing soldiers sometimes do.'

'Could they hit God?'

'No, he hasn't got a body.'

'They could shoot birds. Daniele shoots ducks. I help him pull off the feathers.'

'Well today they were only trying out their guns.'

'Did the noise make Papa ill like it does Cook?'

'Yes.'

'I think I'll go and see her. She may be ill too.'

'That's a good idea. If she's well, ask her to give you supper.'

'It's too early.'

'Ask for a *merenda* then. Don't bother Papa. He needs to rest.'

'Why do you call him Papa?'

'He's my Papa too.'

'Yours? Your Papa?'

'Yes.'

'Really?'

'Yes.'

'Oh.'

The square, freckled face considered Prospero, who guessed that the thought towards which Cesco was groping was, 'So I've got to share'. He guessed it because he had been thinking it himself.

Cesco put a thumb in his mouth, then said, 'Is my Mamma yours too?'

'No. I had a different Mamma.'

'Where is she?'

'I'll tell you another time. Now you'd better see Cook.'

Cesco left.

*

In the courtyard, soldiers were looking hangdog and their white coats were dirty, no doubt from looking up chimneys and through hay lofts. Their officer apologised for what had happened. It had not been one of his men who fired the pistol but a local man who had enticed them here with assurances that the count was hiding Garibaldini. The fellow, said the Austrian, had now been sent packing and would not have been listened to in the first place had there not been previous reports of odd activity in the Stanga grounds. Queer lights and movements had been seen after dark.

'We had to investigate.'

Prospero said he hoped his father might now be left alone, adding that the count was a friend of the Pope's. At this, the officer saluted and marched away his men. Friendship with this pope was not, in Austrian eyes, much of a recommendation. As they left, the soldiers made way for a carriage belonging to the doctor, a nimble old man, who jumped out without waiting for the step.

'Where is he?'

Prospero accompanied him to the drawing room, then waited with his stepmother who admitted that she had perhaps been over-zealous in sending for the doctor – but women were expected to fuss, were they not? 'Do you hate having a stepmother?'

'It's too late for you to do the bad things stepmothers are accused of doing.'

'Yes. You're too grown up.'

He reflected that his father had kept her hidden for years on his account and that living in furtive solitude could not have been easy. She talked of his father's health, guessing now that the seizure had been no more than a little palpitation. Prospero wondered whether his father had reason to be worried by the soldiers' visit and whether she knew.

She wore a peony-shaped crinoline and her face was frilled with laugh lines. Running his eye down her friendly figure, he saw that she was pregnant. Seeing him see this, she blushed.

'I'm delighted for you both.' Looking shyly away, his mind swerved towards Dominique who must be about his stepmother's age.

Just then the doctor came to report on his patient. Dottor Pasolini had, like the count, been an ardent *Carbonaro*. 'He's all right,' he told them. 'He had a fright for sound reasons. Not medical, but something should be done about them.' Then he asked Prospero to come with him as far as the gate, so the two walked in single file, between the ruts, while the carriage ambled behind.

261

'She's a good thing,' said the doctor. 'Jokes about old men's wedding songs turning to dirges don't apply. I suppose you knew they'd been together for years?'

'Well, the boy must be six.'

'They were together long before the boy. Your mother agreed to it. Oh yes. Your parents' wasn't a love match. It was a pooling of resources for political reasons. Don't look shocked. Your father's passion was all for our struggle – or so he thought until he met Anna. Your mother had money which he needed for a cause in which they both believed. She, as a woman, couldn't act on her own account. It was a fair bargain.'

'Until he betrayed it!'

'Until history betrayed them both. Conspiracy fell out of fashion. The *Centurioni* who killed her were chasing shadows. An appalling thing. Your father couldn't get over it. That's why he took so long to marry Anna. I thought you might not know.'

'I didn't.'

'Well, now you do and had better ensure that Anna too knows what she needs to. She was always kept in the dark about his conspiracies. It was part of the bargain with your mother. That was *her* province. It's too late now for secrets, but *he* can't see that, so it's up to you.' The doctor smiled and, as Prospero felt unable to say anything, they walked silently as far as the gate where they embraced. Then the doctor drove away.

Prospero did not go back the way he had come, but, returning to the pond, took the boat out to the middle and sat staring into its shadowed waters. He didn't think of what he had just been told, but the liquid darkness soaked soothingly into his mind. After a while, he rowed back, moored the boat and returned to the villa, approaching it through the kitchen garden where the air was heavy with smells of wind-fallen plums and evening-scented stock; a mix which seemed to typify the domestic life which would now go on here without him. Oh, he would visit. He would bring gifts for the new baby and for Cesco who, no doubt, would one day farm the place. Why not? Prospero had never been interested in it. His was the melancholy of the dog in the manger.

The thought made him laugh. After all, this was a good moment; the one when the intrusive dog, with a last yawn of regret, bounds forth to freedom – and useful activity. The laugh became a shout. His sense of purpose was honed. Rejecting his father's way of life, he would be true to his father's more worthy ideals. The old *Carbonari* had struggled gallantly for an embattled cause, but the flame animating them had been stolen fire. They, like all heretics, were impatient. They wanted heaven *here*.

Striding through fireflies, he resolved to attend at once to tidying things up. Anna must be told about the villa's secrets, whatever they now were. Absorbed in this thought, he almost tripped over something which smelled gamily of mortality: a sack of dead rabbits. Pushing it away, he cleaned his hands in grass then, looking up, saw a man standing on a low wall. It was Storto, the fellow who had forced him to watch the beating of the *Centurione*.

The poacher's pose was one of cartoonish attentiveness, and the only movement about him came from a small bag. Apparently forgotten in his clenched hand, this heaved and jiggled. A ferret?

'Storto!' Prospero pulled his coat and the man looked blindly around, then wheeled his gaze back to whatever he was watching. 'Are those your rabbits?'

'Signor Prospero! It's the Madonna.' His voice was aghast.

Prospero climbed up beside him. Ahead, clearly visible against a background of outbuildings, sailed a luminous figure. Larger than life, it had a white garment with bits of red and blue, black hair, touches of gold at the throat and shoulders and some sort of dark shape above its pale face.

'Holy Mary . . .' gabbled Storto, spiritually turning his coat – for had he not been a free-thinking conspirator? 'Pray for us sinners,' he begged, and tightened his clasped fingers so that his stifling ferret went mad inside its sack.

'It's not the Madonna,' judged Prospero. 'Not in a black hat!'

'Halo.'

'Not black.'

'. . . hour of our death, Amen. Who then? The devil?'

Prospero screwed up his eyes. The image was too soft-edged for a transparency and anyway there were no windows facing this way. 'It's rum,' he admitted, then: 'It's Napoleon.'

'Napoleon, Signor Prospero?'

'From a magic lantern,' Prospero realised. 'Poor Captain Melzi's lantern! Someone's throwing images on the barn wall!'

The captain had died, possibly of a broken heart, but more likely of a ruined liver, for he had taken increasingly to drink when the war, the world and his friend and rival Guidotti disappointed him. One of his hobbies had been making slides of the heroes of his youth and prime.

Storto, however, had never heard of a magic lantern. '*Viva Napoleone!*' he cried, to conciliate the old invader. 'Why's he haunting us then?'

'Listen, Storto, you keep your mouth shut about this. The Austrians were here earlier and they wouldn't like it.'

'He gave them many a licking!'

'Exactly. Listen now. Remember that *Centurione* you thrashed?'

'He's gone. The whole family is. There'll be no trouble from them, Signor Prospero.'

'Maybe not from *him*, but his friends are back in power. And if you say one word to a living soul about what we've just seen, I'll tell what you did to him. Not to mention the rabbits.'

'What rabbits?'

Prospero indicated the sack. Storto said he hadn't seen it until this minute. And the ferret? Where? In the bag in his hand.

Storto gave in. 'All right.' He climbed down from the wall.

But Prospero hadn't finished. Grasping him by his distorted shoulder, he said, 'What's more, I want you to tell me everything my father's been up to in the last year.' He shook him gently. 'I'm *much* more dangerous than that image up there.'

The count relished the story of Storto's seeing the Madonna in poor Melzi's last remaining slide with which Daniele had been amusing little Cesco. 'Ha!' he roared, 'that restores me!' And he raised his glass. His veneration for the Pope had turned to vinegar. 'Our lantern doth magnify Old Boney whom the zealots see as Antichrist I. Antichrist II is Garibaldi! I drink to them both,' said he, although he had been told by Dottor Pasolini not to drink at all. Wayward and unbiddable, he insisted while his wife remonstrated and she, when he wasn't looking, emptied his glass into a potted plant.

Storto, said the count, wasn't all that far out in confusing the Madonna with Napoleon. Both had brought down Republics, if one was to believe Papa Mastai, who was ascribing his restoration to her rather than to his allies. The count stared in puzzlement at his empty glass, then signalled to the footman: more wine. He banged the table so that wax flew from the candelabra.

'I remember him when he was bishop here. Good-hearted but emotional. You can't rely on emotion. It's womanish!' He slapped his wife's marauding wrist. She had been after his glass.

She smiled. 'Women . . .' He launched into a disquisition and she let the smile fade, placidly, not minding in the least.

Prospero noticed the wobble in his father's wrist and the shine of his scalp through the chicken fluff of his hair. Hers, he thought, is an impossible situation: responsibility without power, the very one in which *he* would like to put the Church!

The count was persuaded to go to bed early and his wife led him off, smiling a promise over her shoulder. She would be back to talk to Prospero who had told her that he had something to discuss. Storto had informed him that his father had been spending time in his old secret hiding place and might have something there. Guns? He wasn't sure. The count didn't trust him now.

Left alone, Prospero paged through an old book of fairy tales. Once his, it had been taken over by Cesco and the black and white illustrations had been vividly coloured in.

'Look at the *Orco*,' Cesco had invited earlier, showing a purple ogre with teeth like scythes. 'It gives me dreams that make me get up and look for Mamma and disturb everyone.'

'Do they get angry?'

'Yes, but in my dream I can't help it. I think it's real.'

Prospero thought the whole villa might be mired in the same dilemma.

'I'm not asking you to be disloyal,' he told his stepmother when she came back. 'It's just that he's getting . . .' He stopped, since harping on his father's age must offend her. 'He's always been,' he corrected this, 'rash. I used,' he heard himself blurt, 'to blame him for my mother's death!'

He had shocked them both.

'I'm sorry.' His mouth felt stale from eating ancient wedding cake. They had saved a dusty piece for him which he had pretended to enjoy.

Into his bruised mind came echoes of the doctor's words and his revised version of Prospero's childhood myth. Prospero's own memories were of his mother as smilingly cool and of his father as besotted with her. How fit this into the new frame? Meanwhile, whatever his step-mother's emotion, he was drowning in his. Pique? Jealousy? As the magic-lantern image had done at first, it evaded defining. Perhaps it was suspicion? The canon cited by Don Vigilio, which forbade those who took a lover during a spouse's lifetime to marry them if the spouse died, cast its shadow into the mix. A lawyer's ruse to prevent uxoricide, it had no relevance here. His father, a gentle, irresolute man, must

265

have married Prospero's mother on some absurd understanding that theirs was to be a purely political partnership, then fallen in love with her *after* becoming entangled with Anna who, even now, seemed to know little of his political interests. She must be told of them, decided Prospero, and soon had her so alarmed that he began to feel remorse.

'You see why I had to speak out?' He wanted an admission of his own rightness. 'His laughing at the magic-lantern story,' he scolded, 'is worrying.' And he told how the Austrian officer had mentioned people reporting strange goings-on at the villa.

'I see.' Her soft frilly face puckered anxiously.

'I'm sorry.' He had an urge to take her protectively in his arms.

'No. You were right to tell me. Well, if there's something in that secret apartment, we'd better see what it is.' She stood up.

This startled him. 'Now?'

'I couldn't sleep without knowing.'

So he had to accompany her. The apartment, he explained, as they made their way there, had two entrances – one through the chimney in his father's bedroom, the other from behind a piece of statuary in the front of the house. Somehow, he had now plunged them into the very sort of situation which he most abhorred: histrionic, furtive and probably unnecessary.

Moonlight was milky on the gravel and, further off, on potted lemon trees. By contrast the old hideaway smelled of enclosure and rancid hopes.

'Mildew!' diagnosed Anna with housewifely distaste. '*Muffa!*'

'There's a lamp!' Guiding himself by a shaft of moonlight, he got it alight.

'This place is horrible.'

He had always thought it silly. Now, however, taking its danger seriously, he tapped walls, searched cupboards and even prised up floorboards to find nothing more sinister than bales of pamphlets tied with string and copies of the now banned portrait of Pio Nono blessing the troops. '*Viva l'Italia*' ran the legend, with the memorial date, 10 February 1848. Just nineteen months ago. Shiny with varnish, the prints gleamed, as Prospero's light-bearing hand shifted, and the Pope blessed them both.

'It's like keeping old love letters!' whispered Anna. As though reprimanding her frivolity, a sound came from her husband's room and the two froze. A draught rippled a curtain, bringing home to them the dangers of what they were doing. There were no guns. What there was

was the danger of a confrontation which could engender misunderstandings and sour the marriage for which she had waited so patiently and long.

'Come *on!*' She drew him outside, then ran with him across the front lawn and into the safety of the hall where, relieved and laughing, they hugged so spontaneously that Prospero was afflicted by a sensation which he recognised as pure carnality; cocksure and misplaced, like a bit of monstrous marine life taken by error in a trawl.

Seeing him shy from her, she tried to soothe him, saying, 'Prospero, don't worry! It's perfectly normal and understandable.' For she guessed his trouble and saw no reason to pretend otherwise. Then, to calm the poor muddled chap, she said something about Madame de Menou, the lady to whom he had made skittish references earlier because, as he had explained, half- but only half-jokingly, he wanted his stepmother's advice, having no other female relative to whom he could turn. This, however, only compounded his disarray, making him shy even more and stiffen alarmingly as though with an onset of rigor. Poor, motherless, difficult boy, thought Anna and to show that he was truly part of his father's new family and not an outcast, threw her arms around him and gave him a friendly kiss.

At breakfast, Cesco announced that he had had a dream last night, but that though he had called, nobody had come. 'The *Orco* was in my room, so I got up to look for my Mamma but she wasn't in her room so I went downstairs.'

'You dreamed that part,' said his mother comfortably. 'We'd have seen you if you'd come.'

'No,' argued the child. 'You didn't see me, but I saw you. I was on the landing looking down and you were kissing Prospero. Are you his Mamma too then? He said my Papa was his but you weren't. But you were kissing him. Does that mean you are? Is she?' he asked his father. 'Is my Mamma his Mamma too?' He kept asking his question and, as he got no response to it – a rare event – became obstreperous, banged his spoon, and had to be sent away from the table, leaving the three adults to avoid each other's eye.

'I'm the wrong sort of Frenchman,' was Aubry's answer when asked to intervene with the Occupying Authority.

After the siege, Maria had disappeared, then reappeared as the mistress of a French officer and he, not wishing to spoil her chances, did not make himself known. Bowing to her once at the theatre, he was impressed by the social grace with which she acknowledged him. Perhaps, after all, the little peasant might become a *grande horizontale*?

French solidarity with Roman Republicans had evaporated and would, anyway, have had little effect, since efforts to persuade the Curia to preserve a semblance of civic freedoms came up against a phrase to make diplomatists grind their teeth. '*Non possumus*,' smiled the clerics. 'We can't do it. The Temporal Power cannot be diminished. This is a sacred principle and numbers voting for or against it are immaterial.'

In Paris, though, the Church used votes and numbers for all they were worth. French peasants, shepherded to the polls by their priests, produced a parliamentary majority which pressed the Prince-president to yield on all points to the Pope. In Rome, the Church had sacred principles, in Paris none. Aubry was disgusted. So: 'I'm the wrong sort of Frenchman,' was his reply to all requests for introductions or the exercise of occult influence.

'I think you're the right sort for me,' retorted Dr Moreau, an army doctor who wanted to do some research. He had worked at La Salpêtrière and was interested in cerebral diseases and in the recent rash of visionaries claiming to have experienced ecstatic states. How closely did the Church look into these? Could he meet the cardinal in charge of investigations? The doctor had heard that Aubry had an entrée? And indeed, an evening was arranged, for prelates, eager to temper the harshness of their *non possumus*, were glad to do favours for French archeologists, academicians and – why not? – scientists. Besides, Aubry let Amandi know that he was a friend of Santi's. So the doctor was invited to dine.

Amandi asked about experiments in the hospitals of La Salpêtrière and Bicêtre, and learned that clinicians now submitted to statistical evidence what had previously been decided by 'common sense', a criterion, said Moreau, more rigid than you might think.

'The new method,' he told the cardinal, 'allows us to reject nothing out of hand, neither the possibility of lunar influence on epilepsy, nor a divine one on visionary states.'

The doctor was lively-minded and Amandi, who had been missing the free play of talk – surely it was part of that sweetness of life which Talleyrand located in a lost *ancien régime?* – found himself looking with fresh sympathy on the ecstatics on his list. Had he, in assuming they were manipulated, escaped the bias of piety only to succumb to that of common sense? Most visionaries, assured the doctor, were sincere. Cheered, the cardinal sent to his cellar for a Barsac in which to drink to life's complexities. It was gone, said the major-domo. Drunk by Republicans. All they had left was a syrupy Aleatico. Bring it up, sighed the cardinal, hoping good fellowship might work a Cana-miracle.

Dr Moreau's speciality was epilepsy. Exalted ideas, he said, could be characteristic of sufferers and the malady caused by fright. Seeing Amandi's interest sharpen, he talked of the *furor epilepticus* and the belief – deprecated by him, but held by some of his colleagues – that wasting one's seed could be a prime cause. To be sure, a connection with sexuality had long been suspected. 'Venus,' he quoted, '*in hoc morbus ut pestis fugienda.*' But frank debauchery was thought less perilous than solitary excess. He cited Tissot and Schroeder van der Kolk and disclosed that some doctors favoured castration.

'Men of science, Eminence, can be as dogmatic as inquisitors. I foresee the day when my colleagues' reign will make people regret the gentler sway of yours.'

Politely, Moreau admired the cardinal's apartment which was being redecorated to efface Republican devastations. A bust of St Francis – a conciliatory choice – was to replace that of Beccaria. It was not, said the cardinal, that he did not admire the great advocate of legislative reform, but one must neither confuse the loyal nor give one's fellows a stick with which to beat one.

Talking of which, said the doctor, the *furor epilepticus* interested lawyers, since men had been known to commit murder under its influence and neither know nor remember what they had done.

'So they could do anything at all and be oblivious of it?'

'Yes.'

It was now that a suspicion on the edge of the cardinal's mind swam into focus: this conversation was leading somewhere. As visionaries see a blaze of light then, at its hub, a face, he too saw the particular emerge from the general. Elusive, then recognisable, like a head on a coin, was not the profile that of someone he knew? Exalted? Suffering memory-losses and great rages? Formerly epileptic and now, under the influence of fright, grown strangely unpredictable? Who but the man who sent troops to war, then said he couldn't make war; who granted a constitution, then told a flabbergasted adviser, 'We are no longer constitutional'?

Were the particulars known to the French doctor? Or had this diagnosis assembled in Amandi's mind only?

The cardinal filled his guest's glass and talked of other things: archeology, the opera, a diligence which had fallen into a ditch killing its two passengers, the new church bells being cast to replace those melted down by the Republic . . . Underneath, his mind ran like a mill-race. What mattered was not whether this man had or had not deliberately led him to a conclusion, but whether the conclusion was correct. If it was, we had an unbalanced pope.

Nicola Santi had had a letter from Prospero Stanga, who was now in Rome at the Collegio dei Nobili Ecclesiastici, a place where a gentleman could study in decorous surroundings and keep his own servant. Why should access to the priesthood be made uncomfortable for those used to polite living? asked Prospero. Only fanatics or starvelings would then apply, and the Church needed balanced men. Might Nicola join him? If he was planning to enter the prelacy, why not go all the way and become a priest? Remember Pascal's wager? If you accepted his reasoning as to the wisdom of wagering on the existence of a hereafter, why not wager all you had?

Besides, it would be glorious if they were to study together. Skirting the delicate issue of whether Nicola was well enough born to be accepted – he wasn't – he hinted that the patronage of two cardinals could surely get around this. Then he described his apartment: walnut bookcase, Turkey rug, and other pleasant appurtenances. Candidly, he had resolved to forswear the extremes of asceticism with their attendant pitfall, pride.

The letter's recipient – miffed by the reference to his lineage – felt that, as far as pride went, Prospero was like a man who stinks so badly that he can't smell.

The next argument was more engaging. Now, urged Prospero, when the Church's prestige was damaged, was the time for the generous-hearted to join it. If its truths were truths, should they not be most ardently defended when most challenged? Concessions must not be made, for the faith was an old plant entwined in a complex civilisation – 'Ours! Nicola, ours!' – and to straighten or prune or tamper with it to please Liberals and suchlike could destroy it.

'We need our prejudices,' argued Prospero. 'Beware of letting self-criticism stifle the exaltation which is our strength. Analysis should be used sparingly. Beware of the lucidity which does not lead to the Light! Join me,' begged the letter, and Nicola was moved by the appeal.

That same day he had a visit from Father Tasso who was visibly going to the dogs. It was hard not to think this for he was grimy and smelled gamey, and the whites of his eyes looked like tea-stained china. He was still carping about the 'false Church' which must be renewed and purified and had brought Nicola a chromotype of Father Bassi got up to look like Christ.

Bassi, said Nicola, had not been selfless enough to be Christlike, for – the letters were in our file – he had written to the Republican Government demanding recognition for his bravery.

He was sorry to see how crestfallen this made Tasso and reflected that he had done just what Prospero deplored – attacked piety with the cold tool of accuracy. But then, Tasso's was now a counter-religion, so might Prospero approve?

From the diary of Raffaello
Lambruschini:

Amandi decided, after some thought, that Dr Moreau's diagnosis was incomplete, since it failed to consider that epilepsy might be God's way of tempering a chosen soul.

His Eminence wrote to me about this in terms which made me wonder whether his commerce with mystics might not be affecting him who, as I recall, maundered on about how a grain of folly might be needed to keep a man on the move in convulsive times. He was himself dancing like a cat on a stove. It was a dance of loyalty, a courtier's dance, and it distressed me, who could not see why he should *want* to be Cardinal Secretary. For, said I to myself, depend upon it, Raffaello, that is what this is about. I knew the moment was gone. But he could not see this, being too strung up after playing Patient Griselda for so long, and biding his time, holding his tongue and letting himself be dispatched regularly into mountain hamlets stinking of cabbage to interview inbred cretins.

Now at last, on the eve of the Pope's return to Rome, a decision had to be made as to who would be permanent Secretary of State and Amandi nourished hopes, since the Liberal Rosmini had been eliminated and Antonelli, who had the acting appointment, had edged towards the high ground of conservatism.

Mastai, however, had come to hate statecraft and was loath to burden his friend with it. He saw it as a rather base activity and may even have found it appropriate that his Pro-Secretary of State – like his headsman – was neither a priest nor a gentleman.

Amandi, though, was only too eager to get his hands dirty with what he saw as an urgent challenge, for he ardently believed – I have his letters – that not only did the Church need defending as never before, but that never before had humanity so needed the Church. Only an inner peace could procure peace in the land. Only a heartfelt acceptance of law and order would make freedom possible. Some authority *must* be recognised and whose would even the proud-hearted accept if not God's?

Gaeta, March 1850

'I suppose by now,' said Pius, 'you are my oldest friend?'

Marine reflections shimmered on the ceiling: blue, orange and gold. They were in the royal palace to which the King of Naples had brought boxes of plate, linen and other consoling luxuries on that desperate day, sixteen months ago, when Mastai arrived as a fugitive from his own people.

The fright, thought Amandi, had shaken him badly. A man his age – nearly sixty – could have died of it. Think of him slipping through back lanes with his heart in his mouth to an assignation with the Countess Spaur, now the wife of the Bavarian Ambassador but formerly – when married to an English antiquarian called Dodwell – a lady whose name gossip had coupled with his own. His old patroness, Donna Clara Colonna, was said to have resented the countess's easy access to His Holiness who, having first changed the palace rules for *her* sake, had then extended the new facilities to la Spaur. Anteroom gossip. Yes. But must he not have suffered from the irony as he fled like a malefactor in her unlit carriage? At the border she had passed him off as an upper servant. To a man attuned to signs, this must have read as a divine reprimand. The 'Servant of the servants of God' had been plunged into a simulacrum of a bedroom farce!

All Rome, Amandi told him, was praying for his return.

Pius shrugged. 'He' – lately an unexplained 'he' meant Antonelli – 'doesn't want me back yet. Order,' sadly, 'has to be restored first. With unimpeded vigour.'

'Whose order?'

Dispiritedly, Mastai ignored the pun. Optimism, he declared, was dangerous. Presumption and despair were two sides of the same coin. 'I have come to see that it is cruel to expect too much from people. It exposes them to temptation. *I* did that.' He was thinking of the mob, but of others too. 'The Jews!' He shook his head, broodingly, for he had been told a story about a young student who had made friends with one at the University of Florence. The Jew had a pleasing appearance and played the violin and when the Christian invited him home, one of his sisters fell in love with him. It was an indocile passion. Naturally, the Jew was then forbidden the house, but the harm had been done. 'I was wrong,' said Mastai, 'to relax the laws confining them to the ghetto, and Duke Leopold of Tuscany is wrong to allow them into the universities. They are a source of contamination, you see. It is like releasing a cholera virus. I have written to warn the Grand Duke.'

'What happened to the girl?'

'They have to keep her locked up. And, as we cannot do that to our whole population, it is clearly better to confine *them*!'

It would have been unwise to argue. Instead Amandi broached a matter which could no longer be put off.

'Holiness, do you remember my cousin's boy, Nicola Santi? If he's to be a prelate, there will have to be a capital sum pledged to guarantee him the mandatory stipend of 1,500 *scudi* a year. I,' said His Eminence, 'haven't got it.'

Mastai looked roguish. 'Ah, a personal request!' His voice was all relief. 'You are so modest. Is that all I can do for you?'

Amandi was shocked. 'This, Holiness, is not for myself!'

'No, no!' Mastai's quick courtesy conveyed a contrary belief. He smiled and his plump face creased like cake dough. Could he have forgotten the boy's connection to himself? Amandi began resolutely to plumb the depths of the papal amnesia. From loyalty, he had not brought up Nicola's name in many years but – with Dr Moreau's words ringing in his head – surely he should now?

'You remember my cousin, Holiness? Sister Paola of Fognano?'

'My old penitent! Give her my blessing if you see her.'

This was no help. 'You remember the talk' – he was courting a

273

contradiction – 'that one of the Bonapartes might have fathered her child whose name,' he said with emphasis, 'is Nicola Santi.'

'People,' Pius looked at the light playing on the ceiling, 'are always asking me to recall old connections. One does not wish to appear proud, but it is sometimes best to cut particular ties. The nuns at Fognano have a new confessor.'

'Her uncle was also suspected.' Amandi rambled with intent while trying to recall what the doctor had said about such phenomena as *déjà vu, jamais vu*, old experiences vividly relived and others blotted out. How totally could one lose a memory and was it a weakness or a strength? Taking his courage in both hands, he asked, 'Do you remember your flight to the mountains in 1831?'

'Ah!' Mastai's eye gleamed like that of a robin which has seen a worm. 'I see what you are working round to!'

The cardinal felt a chill. Had he gone too far?

'Yes. You think I am exploiting a connection with the Prince-President, Louis Napoleon. Going back,' he smiled, 'to 1831. Old friendships, to be sure, are often too precious to be besmirched with claims. My pride is of small account, but I must free myself from links with individuals. I am the Universal Father.'

Amandi bowed. The Pope was foxy rather than mad. Good.

'If Louis Napoleon sends us his men to defend us from Garibaldi, should I scruple to accept? My view is that the hand wielding the sword need not be clean. A saviour is a saviour and many crusaders were brutes.'

There was a silence.

'You may have the capital sum,' said Mastai kindly. 'I had feared you were going to ask me for the post of Cardinal Secretary of State and that I would have to refuse. It would be your undoing. We need a man bred to higgling and haggling to handle that! Remember the juggler in the story who juggled for the love of God? Well, men of merchant stock can do the like with statecraft. Not you. You have the wrong instincts. Too gentlemanly. Look how you tried to argue me out of exploiting my credit with Louis Napoleon!'

*From the diary of Raffaello
Lambruschini*:

That was in March. Next day Mastai-Ferretti and Antonelli performed a ceremony which both thought unobserved. But nothing, as they should have known, goes unobserved in our palaces, which are full of hollow places and listening posts, often known only to the generations of servants who initiate each other into the secrets of their caste. This ceremony echoed the one whereby each new Doge of Venice used to conciliate the sea by flinging a ring into its depths. Mastai, in much the same spirit, presented Cardinal Antonelli with a very fine emerald ring. 'An ocean of an emerald' was how one secret observer described it and, later, all who saw it on the cardinal's finger agreed, adding only that this compressed ocean glowed as if it contained a sunken sun. Mastai, while presenting it, vowed never to be separated from Antonelli and confirmed his tenure in the office of Cardinal Secretary of State.

With hindsight, one sees that what was being conferred was one of the two papal keys, the one to things temporal, and that the cardinal, in accepting it, took up a challenge to struggle, intrigue and perhaps sacrifice his soul for the sake of this attribute of the papacy which he secretly knew to be doomed. His was not an ignoble act.

So Amandi's hopes were dashed, but his downfall was unlike Rosmini's for, whereas the abate had found himself invisible, Amandi was treated with regard since it was expected that he would exercise an informal – and so perhaps more powerful – influence. Worldly wisdom deceives itself with old paradigms. It now looked back to the last reign when the Pope's barber had been the man to know. Though Gaetanino was no longer shaving Pope Gregory when his ascendancy was at its peak, this did not stop people picturing an intimacy of cool fragrances, hot towels and susurrations of advice hissed at close range into a foam-flecked papal ear.

Mastai, however, had quite another idea of his role. Wishing to preserve parity with kings, he was surrounding himself with high-born prelates and, on the eve of his return to Rome, began choosing new private chamberlains – in practice his secretariat – all four of whom would be noble, and one, Xavier de Mérode, the son of a man who had been in the running to be King of Belgium. Spiritual nobility would be manifested by its temporal equivalent. Respect for hierarchy led to respect for heaven. He was half way to believing that the ills of our time were due to the breakdown in the chain of command, whereby God-anointed kings had formerly passed divine authority to their peerage, and through them to lesser men, so that even the petty nobility to which he and Amandi belonged had been invested with a measure of it. Power was conferred from above, not below. In short, he was sick of the mob.

Speculation about the new appointments may have prompted the action now taken by a schemer who, fearing the ascendancy of men like Amandi, sent Mastai an anonymous letter. It alleged that His Eminence had consulted a French quack about His Holiness's mental instability and that this quack would bruit abroad the indiscretions which the cardinal had traded for his unrepeatable advice which the letter proceeded, nonetheless, to repeat, to wit that, in the quack's opinion, epileptics should be castrated to prevent – pardon the grossness, Holiness – their wasting themselves in solitary practices. The anonymous delator finished with a flourish so compunctious and verbose as to leave no doubt of his being a man who had had, at least, a notary's education.

Reports of Mastai's reaction varied. Described, echoed, then flatly denied, the scene ballooned into legend, bobbed across the mental landscapes of titillated clerics, then was recognised as the transcription of an account of an epilepsy attack from one of the very books which the quack had quoted and, on that basis, regarded by some as spurious, by others as all the more likely to be true.

Was Amandi really struck in the face by the papal slipper? Old curial myth mingled with Moreau's lore. A learned Jesuit recalled that 'it' was probably the oldest recorded brain disorder, having been mentioned as early as 2080 BC in the Hammurabi laws. The Jesuits were still smarting at having been expelled from Rome and let down by Mastai. He hadn't defended them in their need, so why should they defend him?

But had he got 'it' at all or ever had it? What were the proofs? His reluctance to be recruited for the Russian front and the testimony of venal witnesses, servants or corner-coves, who swore they had seen him fall down in a frothing fit, but were the sort who would sell their souls or balls for a scudo. The Mastai family had surely bribed them to say that so as to keep him out of the Army. Stop. Not so fast! There was also the testimony of the Scolopian Fathers. Mastai-Ferretti had been a boarder in their school in Volterra until he was sent home on account of having fits. Father Inghirami, the headmaster, remembered the case.

Malicious fingers turned the pages of the *Corpus Iuris Canonici* which stated, black on white, that a candidate so afflicted might not be a priest,

276

but that – see Grat. dist. xxxiii, c.2, c.3 and c.5 – he might if cured. So had he been cured? And relapsed? This was treasonous talk. Republicans could turn it to account. Maybe they'd started it? But then what did happen? Did anyone really know? They didn't. Amandi was back in Rome and the Pope was still in Gaeta and when, at last, in April 1850, the Pope came back to Rome, Amandi seemed to have business in places like Bologna and even Paris. Confidential missions? Or was he keeping out of the way? Who knew. Speculation could be dangerous. Touch your balls.

Sixteen

Father Tasso was leaving to live in Austrian territory where an unjust government could, being secular, be opposed without sin.

Nicola said: 'There's shit daubed on the archbishop's palace.'

'Because the reprisals against "tainted officials" were a flagrant injustice! *They*'re no more tainted than the Pope! But, as people can't take their shit to Rome, the archbishop gets it. Do you want my copy of *Le Pape?*'

This was goodbye. Nicola had called in on his way to the cathedral where he was to help the cardinal vest for high mass. The vestments handled like armour for they were stiff with gold thread and had taken nuns in enclosed orders years of eye-straining work.

'Do you want this wine?' Tasso was clearing his room.

'He wants *practical* work!' the cardinal had observed with amusement. 'Imagine. I have served my time in the world and know when a man has an aptitude for it. Father Tasso does not! I shall advise his new bishop to let him teach in a seminary: a bigger box than his confessional but still a box. He should not be given his head.' His Eminence was remembering Bassi who should not have been given his either and had, in the end, lost it.

Tasso too remembered Bassi and dreamed, shyly, of carrying on his torch. Strangely enough, Nicola saw, he did have a sort of inner light but, somehow, it was ridiculous. You thought of a turnip lantern. He neglected himself – which could be why he smelled. Someone should tell him.

'Will you take the wine. No? Is it so bad? Should I offer it to someone else? I have no palate.'

Nicola said, 'Throw it out.' He feared it might be his duty to mention the smell too, but felt unequal to this. Anyway the confessor was now talking of his visits to the Albergo San Marco to hear the confession of

Ugo Bassi's mother. 'She thinks he's alive and imprisoned in an Austrian fortress. They've organised a conspiracy of pity at the hotel.'

'What happens when she goes out?'

'She's bedridden. She keeps giving me letters to General Strassoldo, begging him to let her see her son. I tear them up. But now she is threatening to drag herself from her sickbed to go to Strassoldo herself. Here are some books to remember me by.'

Nicola took them, embraced Tasso, despite his reek, and left for the cathedral.

Mass was at eleven and the air already hot. Candles consumed it. Fans moved it, but there was no freshness to be had, and there were the usual cases of ladies swooning and having to be carried out. The choir was in full fig and soaring voices spun bonds of unity. At the ceremony's end, communicants, weak from fasting so late, were lining up to approach the altar, when someone whispered, 'That's Ugo Bassi's mother, Donna Felicità! There, see, coming down the nave. That's his sister and her husband supporting her. She's mortally ill. I'm surprised they let her out.'

'People are making way for her.'

Straight to the altar rails went the invalid, flanked by her minders who must be hoping to prevent her getting into a conversation with anyone who would tell her the unthinkable truth. They had – Tasso had said – spun her such a consoling fable about the privileged conditions her Ugo was enjoying in prison that an irruption of reality was likely to be fatal. Perhaps – people guessed as they watched – these fictions had been less than convincing. Perhaps contradictions had slipped in? At all events, the old lady was restless and when she saw the communion wafer proffered by Oppizzoni, put out her hand, blocked its approach and begged, '*Eminenza*, won't you help me to see my Ugo before I die?'

Oppizzoni didn't recognise her, so she had to explain that she was the mother of Ugo Bassi. 'They won't let me visit him!'

The cardinal could make nothing of this request to visit a dead man. His hand still held the wafer when she grasped his wrist, and, inadvertently knocking down the paten which a sub-deacon was holding under it for just such an eventuality, shook the wafer to the ground where the flustered Oppizzoni stood on it.

In no time, his enemies were spreading the scandal: a priest had trampled the sacred host! He had stepped on the body of Christ! That

279

this was an accident was no defence, since what were accidents but signs and what could this one mean but that the lambs of God were in the hands of evil shepherds?

Messages accompanied by black crosses appeared on the houses of Zelanti who had to spend money having them removed – which was no great harm at a time when so many were indigent and work scarce.

Tasso and Nicola now left for seminaries. The priest was to teach in one in Mantua and Santi to study in, of all places, Paris, which would, advised a letter from Cardinal Amandi, be a testing ground for the bad times ahead. The clerical career, warned His Eminence, would soon cease to be comfortable in this peninsula, as it had long ceased to be in France. 'Think of yourself,' he advised, 'as training to work in a mission country.'

So Nicola prepared by spending four years in an isolation akin to that of an African missionary or a man in gaol. These were years lived outside of time, for seminarians, being expected to fix their minds on the City of God, were denied news of the cities of men. Rumours did, to be sure, filter in when Louis Napoleon's *coup d'état* changed his mandate from President to Emperor and plunged their own city of Paris into a bleeding turmoil. That, however, was a brief temporal parenthesis in what Nicola would later remember as a ritualised eternity mimed in an odour of boiled greens and damp – he missed the Roman sun – soot, smoke, polish, lye, paraffin and incense, among youths who would have been incredulous if he had told them – which he did not – some of the things he had witnessed in the diocese of Bologna. His classmates were embattled, pious, all of a piece, and took to their regimented lives with a single-minded ambition: they hoped for parishes. Some were boisterous and their wrists erupted like malignant growths from the containment of inadequate sleeves. All feared the Republicans who could be heard building barricades to defend the state against Louis Napoleon's *coup* of December 1851, only to be mown down two days later by his troops. Throughout the massacre, the seminary stayed closed, but sounds of fighting were sometimes just outside its walls.

There was no pretence of impartiality when news came of the legitimate government's fall and the transportation of 10,000 prisoners to Algeria. For the seminarists, a republic, legitimately elected or not, was a threat to their careers and evil, and if any French Catholics thought otherwise the news did not reach them.

Not much did. Unlike their fellows in Rome who could live with relatives while attending classes or, like Prospero, have apartments in a comfortable college, these French youths were austerely isolated from the world and so was Nicola, although two visits from Cardinal Amandi in four years gave him prestige. He had no others but received letters from Prospero from which censored bits had been removed with a nail scissors. All but four hours of the day were spent on religious services and the image of Roman life which his fellow seminarists treasured astonished him.

He got no letters from Father Tasso, but when he left the seminary, two intercepted notes were released to him. By then, Tasso had been hanged by the Austrians, after being defrocked by Bishop Giovanni Corti of Mantua, a Liberal whose heart, he told friends later, had been broken by having to do it. It had not, the bishop confided, been the order from Rome which sapped his resistance – he might even have defied that – but the threat from Vienna that several more priests would be executed if he failed to comply. In desperation, Monsignor Corti implored the Pope by letter and Marshall Radetzky, whom he went to see in person, to intervene with the Austrian Emperor. It was all to no avail and, meanwhile, Tasso had been in gaol six months with fetters on his feet and so had the other endangered priests. Their crime was that they had conspired against Austria by clandestinely raising money for Mazzini's movement. Father Tasso had kept a scrupulous register of contributers and this was their undoing, for, though the register was in cypher, the cypher was revealed and this led to further arrests. A rumour got about that the priest himself had broken under torture and given it away. He denied this, but the charge lingered and poisoned his last days, just as Monsignor Corti's days were poisoned by the bitter letter which Tasso sent him from his death cell. Times had changed since Ugo Bassi died with such serenity. Nobody, as Amandi pointed out to Nicola when relating all this, could count hereafter on having an undivided conscience.

On leaving the seminary Nicola, who had been away from the world, had to catch up with its news. But not from too close! Priests in Rome, whither he returned after his ordination, were warned against trimming between the secular and religious spheres, and asked to show their allegiance by their dress. The cassock was now favoured, the old rig of knee breeches, redingote and tricorne hat merely tolerated, and civil servants were expected to shave off facial hair.

Tit for tat: in Piedmont the special courts for the clergy had been abolished and the Archbishop of Turin fined 500 lire for denouncing the new law. In Rimini, a statue of the Virgin was seen to throw up its eyes.

Gaslight and the electric telegraph had been installed. Change was speeding up, but Roman ministries watched it closely and edicts kept track of the smallest matters. Viz:

> Circular from the Ministry of the Interior No. 53128.
>
> On the approach of Carnival Week, it has been decided that the usual entertainments shall be authorised: i.e. races, balls and routs. Fancy dress may be worn, but none shall dress as a nun or priest or wear any military uniform, badge, colour or costume offensive to public decency. Masks are forbidden as are facial disguises such as false beards, dyes, etc . . .
>
> Your Illustrious Lordship is authorised to sanction the appropriate number of tombolas on the understanding that two tenths of the cash received shall be paid to the public purse . . .
>
> Rome, 3 January 1852. Signed: Vice Chamberlain of the H. R. Church, Minister of the Interior, Domenico Savelli.

From the diary of Raffaello Lambruschini:

These were the years which allowed Cardinal Antonelli to consolidate the ravaged fortunes of the state and extinguish the public debt. He was an energetic minister whose skilled management of the day-to-day affairs left others free to aim for spiritual glory. He seemed to accept this bargain easily.

EDICT:

> Giacomo Cardinal Antonelli of the H.R.C.
> Deacon of Santa Agata alla Suburra, etc.
> . . . this year again it will be necessary to demand sacrifices of the State's subjects. Consequently:
> The tax increase on the dativa reale will be maintained.
> The price of salt is to revert to that of July 1847.

The Comuni are to pay 250,000 scudi . . .

Imported groceries will be taxed even in towns enjoying exemptions. These include sugar, coffee, cinnamon, cloves, nutmeg, tea, cocoa, pepper.

From the Secretary of State, 8 August 1854, G. Cardinal Antonelli.

From the diary of Raffaello Lambruschini:

Though nobody knew what had passed between Cardinal Amandi and the Pope, people guessed at a mutual discomfort being given time to heal. Hence, concluded observers at the papal court, the missions which so often took Amandi away from it. Hence too, perhaps oddly, his respect for Cardinal Antonelli. Amandi acknowledged that he could not have worked for Mastai with the abnegation displayed by the Cardinal Secretary – who, to be sure, was profiting by his status as a layman and growing richer by the hour. He and his brothers were doing very well indeed from the planned state railways while less well-placed investors lost their shirts.

Amandi intended no irony. The Temporal Power was Antonelli's domain. He was doing well for it and if he also did well by it, the price was small. Better a man who could help the Treasury and himself than one who could do neither. Who would want to employ a cook who didn't eat?

What did shock Amandi was what Mastai himself was doing. Quietly, he was changing the nature of the papacy. Authority was being centralised, bishops in other lands Romanised and their national Conferences eliminated. Bit by bit, thread by thread, Mastai drew power into his own hands and in December 1854 sprang a surprise on the Catholic world. He defined a dogma, single-handedly and without the collaboration of a Church Council. This was the Immaculate Conception of the Virgin Mary, and his aim could only be to test the acquiescence of Catholic opinion. To be sure, he had taken soundings in advance, but he had also forbidden public discussion on the matter! Then, one fine day, 'off his own bat', he elevated the doctrine to a dogma. He was extending his powers, taking, as the peasants put it, a step just a bit longer than his leg. Yet he got away with it and the reason – did he guess this? – was the enormity of the scandal there would have been if he were to be brought to book for it, plus pity. Times were hard and theologians loath to challenge a beleaguered pontiff with unsteady nerves. It was only four years since Mastai's return from the exile while had caused his character to set in a new mould. He had grown crafty and was still stubborn, impulsive, charming, and often sick. He had exceeded his powers and, by so doing, created a precedent.

The dogma's message pleased his new allies. If only one human creature had ever escaped nature's flaw, then hopes of progress were illusory and strong rulers needed to save humanity from itself. Catholic princes took the point. Queen Isabella sent a gift of a tiara, "Bomba" of Naples let off artillery salvoes and the episcopacy, on whose prerogatives Masti had encroached, failed to protest.

Amandi blamed himself. It had been he who, when Pius was a Liberal, had suggested that he go over the heads of his bishops and pay court to the lower clergy. Indeed, Amandi had started the process during his trip to La Salette when he engaged Father Dubus as his man in the Diocese of Grenoble. Father Dubus was not his man now. He was Pius's man and so were growing numbers of his fellows who had a craving for an authority which would defend them from their bishops. Amandi, for the second time in his dealings with Mastai, had started something he couldn't stop.

He began to have dreams in which the Pope's evil eye subjugated him. These began after the accident – later to be called the 'miracle' – at Sant'Agnese Outside the Walls. Here, in April 1855, the floor of an upstairs room gave way under Pius and a number of his cardinals. Amandi had been standing diagonally across from him, next to Cardinal Wiseman of England, when he saw the pontiff's gaze fix in a dull, trance-like stare on their corner of the room. He was wondering whether Mastai might be feeling indisposed when, with a slow splintering of woodwork, the floor began to tilt and sink like a tipped raft so that the entire company were soon slithering at a stately gait down its slope. The low point was where Amandi and Wiseman had been standing, and the Englishman must have scrambled aside, for Amandi found himself alone in the path of a cupboard whose doors flew open as it fell, encapsulating him with the neatness of an upturned boat. His cassock, with its pelerine and double sleeves, was pinned under the sides, so that he could neither move his hands nor attract the attention of rescuers, while his shouts were drowned by the noise which, for all he knew, could be signalling the death of half the Curia.

As it happened, almost nobody was hurt in the freak event, but later, in the cardinal's dreams, the anguished experience grew horrific and, in their darkness, Mastai's staring eyes multiplied, swarmed like luminous fish and gleamed with menace.

Amandi grew claustrophobic. This happened slowly for, at first, fear stayed trapped in nightmare. Then, one day, at a ceremony in the catacombs, losing his Roman indifference to dust and skeletons, he became unable to breathe and had to leave. After that, he could not go into a confessional and, not being what the Romans called a 'confession priest', that is, obliged to attend to pastoral duties, did so rarely and then only in order to train himself to overcome this weakness.

The collapse of the basilica floor under the Curia's feet was a dangerous metaphor which had to be wrenched from the use to which the ill-disposed could have turned it, and Amandi could only applaud Mastai's shrewd insistence that what had happened be seen as a miracle for which hymns of praise must be sung and thanksgiving ceremonies devised. Had not the papal court been saved? It had! So this was a sign of divine favour. Monies were straightaway found to repair the damage and a mural commissioned to commemorate the happy event.

Bologna, 1857

'A *baiocco*, your Reverence?' A beggar, wearing a beggar's badge, was demanding his due.

But Nicola had been distracted: 'Diodato!'

Lingering on after he became a duke, Flavio's old foundling's name was both congratulatory and a joke. Diodato: God's gift! It was an apt commentary on the fact that his mother had tried to give him back to God. For Donna Geltrude, having for years concealed her maternity, had continued to deny it until faced with witnesses in court. Even then, she denied that her husband was Flavio's father, which looked like leaving him no father at all – no human one anyway, for, as Roman wits observed, laying him as an infant at the door of the Holy Ghost Foundling Home must, if seen as an attempt at affiliation, make him a half-brother of Jesus Christ.

Blasphemy goes down well in holy cities, and Flavio's law suit had rivalled the lottery in popular appeal. The case had been heard before the Sacra Rota and, even as elsewhere in the world the wheel of fortune was spinning as never before, the Eternal City remained agog at the findings of the Tribunal of the Holy Wheel.

Those were the years when France became an Empire, the English built a Crystal Palace and held their Great Exhibition, and, up and down the west coast of North America, the Gold Rush spread hopes so dizzy that whole crews jumped ship and left the hulks to rot in the San Francisco docks. Railway track was being laid all over the Western world; experts on apparitions pondered the Spectre of Communism and the Virgin at La Salette; and still Roman attention was trained on the bedroom activities of the Duchessa Cesarini in the year before Flavio's birth – or rather on her alleged lack of such activities.

Naturally, the proceedings were secret and, naturally, they leaked out.

For months, processions of friends and servants bore solemn witness to the duchess's claim that she and her late husband had not, at that time or for a year previous to it, had had any sort of marital relations. Even the late duke's mistresses were called to testify. He had had two at once: sisters who were pleased to recall enjoying an attention so constant as to leave him neither strength nor leisure to have serviced a wife as well. Then Donna Geltrude admitted to having herself had a lover: a Russian gentleman, now long back among the watery flatlands of his distant estates, where he no doubt shot teal and reminisced to neighbours about the time when he had kept watch with cocked pistols in the anteroom to the one where she was giving birth to Flavio.

This caused a sensation. Who, after this, could deny that Romans had temperament and needed the firm hand of the Church? These were the years when tedious old laws repealed by the Republic were being reinstated, and the duchess's case was grist to the clerical mill. Rarely can the downfall of an illustrious personage have pointed so many timely morals, from the demon dangers of lust to the connection between spiritual and carnal depravity.

Father Gavazzi had been Donna Geltrude's confessor and she, affected by the contagion of his opinions, had begun frequenting Republicans, with the result that her only daughter had married one. Indeed, it was to preserve the family fortune for this daughter that she was so brazenly confronting the tribunals of the Sacra Rota and public opinion.

Conversely, it was to wrest this same fortune from Republican clutches that the Jesuits, among them the duchess's own brother, had taken the case to court.

A strange case! For why did Donna Geltrude go to the risk and trouble of repudiating Flavio? Normally, married women foisted spurious issue on their husbands without more ado. Simply palmed them off. It was the easiest thing in the world. From time out of mind, ladies had adulterated their blood with that of their lackeys and gentlemen theirs with that of chambermaids. In the process, scandal was avoided and tired stock renewed. Feudal living afforded innumerable chances for blood-mixing and there were cases – who knew how many? – where the baby in the lackeys' quarters and that in the ducal nursery were half siblings. Such arrangements, like gossip itself, provided relief from a tight, strangling system and had been available to the duchess. Why had she not availed herself of them? After all – and this made the question harder to answer – the adulterating in her case was not with plebeian blood at all. Her Russian lover was a man of impeccable descent.

He, while this speculation was going on, was sent a writ by the court demanding to know whether he acknowledged having been her lover during the time indicated. Excitement simmered. Would he understand what was wanted? A Russian? So far away, living no doubt on one of those unimaginable estates where serfdom persisted and Tsar Nicholas ruled with an iron hand! He had travelled of course. He was a Westernised gentleman and must have assumed that he should answer with gentlemanly discretion, for back came his answer that indeed he had been a friend of the *nobildonna* Geltrude – to whom he took the opportunity of conveying his devoted homage – but his relations with her had not overstepped the bounds of propriety. He added, for good measure, that when he knew her, she had been on excellent terms with her husband!

This, if believed, would have left Flavio with no father but the aforementioned Holy Ghost. It was a defeat for Donna Geltrude who was, however, a woman of resource. She summoned her confessor – not Father Gavazzi who at this point, anyway, was in England apostatising – but an old friar to whom she had confided her dilemma, during the crucial year, all that time ago. He was a barefoot Carmelite from the convent of Santa Maria della Scala, too weak to appear in person but who revealed, in a notarised statement, the confession that she had made to him at the time of Flavio's birth. It confirmed what she had told the court: Flavio was a bastard and not her husband's son.

Public opinion was outraged. The Russian lover had shown more discretion than the Roman friar! Confessions should not be revealed, and certainly not at the convenience of penitents! After all, if they were, penitents could tell a confessor whatever suited them, then call him into court to testify! No! Eh no! Donna Geltrude, her friar, and her friends became dangerously unpopular and were for a while afraid to walk the streets. Flavio was taken to the public's heart and the prelates of the Sacra Rota fell back on the safe old rule of jurisprudence whereby the father is the man indicated by the legal marriage bond: *pater est quem iustae nuptiae demostrant*. Flavio was thus declared to be the legitimate son of the late duke and eligible to inherit from his deceased elder brother whose will in favour of their sister was set aside.

All that had been five years ago. And now here was Flavio again. Passing through Bologna on a wet November afternoon, Nicola had been bolting across the street to shelter from a downpour and from melancholy memories of the years when he had worked here for the late Cardinal Oppizzoni. Clouds scudded. Grey light made stone pillars and vertical rain seem to exchange substances and he had an impression of something similar happening to the polarities of his mind. He was now a Monsignore with purple stockings, piping, cummerbund and buttons, and corseted by as many certainties as he could wrap around himself – but also gnawed at by doubts.

'That's to be expected,' Amandi had told him, but Nicola, looking around him at the comfortable drawing-room *abati* who populated Rome, did not believe this.

To combat those who, in London, Zurich, Paris, etc., were mapping the predicted course of the Spectre of Communism, he had been assigned Amandi's old task of doing the same with the prognoses of those who reported sightings of the Virgin. At first he had eagerly accepted this assignment, being exalted by the prospect of working with the innocent and unspoiled who, at the very least, took their religion passionately. By now, however, the tedious sameness of the rural pythonesses had begun to depress him. The idea of a comparative study of their insights and foresights had been abandoned. There was nothing to study or compare.

The sight of Flavio was just what he needed: a truer and more stimulating apparition! Flavio burst out of a café as Nicola passed, flung his arms around him, thumped him on the back, shouted, kissed him, exclaimed at his purple trimmings and drew him into the warm fug of a semi-private alcove spicy with vanilla, coffee, hot chocolate and cinnamon. After the grey exterior, the plush and glitter dazzled.

'. . . circus,' he heard Flavio say and thought the word a metaphor. But no: Flavio was here as a patron of the Circo Ciniselli whose chief attraction, here in this very alcove, smiling and extending her gloved hand was the equestrienne, Miss Ella, whose fame had reached even

288

Nicola's provincial ears. From close to, she was a muscular, blonde girl clad in a riding habit.

'You must see her perform!' Flavio insisted. 'If you think *I'm* an apparition, Miss Ella will ravish you! She's a phenomenon! A dancer as graceful as la Taglioni except that she does it all on horseback at the risk of breaking her delicate swan's neck! She's performing this evening at the Teatro del Corso. You can sit in my box, back in the shadows so as to hide your purple and scandalise nobody. She's the only member of the fair sex whom I wholeheartedly admire,' said Flavio kissing Miss Ella's hand. She was, he added, an American from Louisiana.

Flavio, though now a duke, could have been the circus performer. His pale innominables were as taut as skin. His waistcoat was watered silk. His watch fob glistened. He was a gilded creature: a living challenge to the grey, stony, papal town.

'What happened to your mother?'

Oh, said Flavio, no doubt she flourished like the green bay tree. He hadn't seen her since the trial, nor Rome either. 'I had to flit! The Jesuits expected me to join or at least divide my fortune with them. They might not have sponsored my case otherwise. Mobilised their connections. Pushed it through. I had to conciliate them – or so my Jesuit uncle explained. Poor man, he was torn, being himself unworldly. The Society, on the other hand . . . Damn! Sorry. Shsh!'

Flavio moved swiftly into the café corridor just next to the alcove where they were sitting. 'If anyone wants trouble,' Nicola heard him say, 'I'm their man. Swords, pistols or a punctured nose!' For moments he could be heard patrolling the corridor, then he came back. 'Gone!' He flung out his hands. 'Evaporated!'

Miss Ella smiled.

'That imbecile,' said Flavio, sitting down. 'Did you see him? He walked past three times. Three! He's mad for Miss Ella. Infatuated. Well, why not, you may say? But this idiot has been threatening to blow his brains out during the performance! He sits in the front row night after night. If he did – not that he will! – imagine the effect on the horses! More champagne? What were we talking about? Me, I expect. Let's change the subject. Miss Ella knows all my stories.'

Miss Ella's Sphinx-smile had not relaxed. Maybe she knew no Italian? Or was half a horse? Yes, thought Nicola uncharitably – he had had one of those inexplicable physical revulsions on touching her gloved skin – a female centaur, a demi-mare!

But he agreed to come to this evening's performance. Meeting Flavio again was to be made the most of and at least, in the theatre, *she* would be some way away. People talked of first love but, from what Nicola had learned in the confessional, the aftermath of *that* was often oblivion or loathing. First friendship, on the other hand, was surely more lasting. Flavio had first shaken Nicola into consciousness – as Martelli too had done in a more obvious way. Hard to say how, in Flavio's case – perhaps just by giving off that extra charge of the life force which one picked up from healthy young animals. And he had been shocking! Shock, when one was young, freed the spirit. It made one question things – though who could say, thought Nicola gloomily, whether that was such a bounty after all?

'You're not listening.' Flavio was unaware of competing with his past self for Nicola's attention. Best because past? No: because *first*! Vivid, prism-images dissolved in Nicola's head as the last of the champagne was doing in his glass. 'Wool-gatherer!'

'Sorry. What was it?'

'Really, Nicola, if you were anyone else, I'd say you'd fallen in love with Miss Ella.'

The idol smiled on and shortly afterwards they got into a silk-upholstered carriage and dropped her off at the theatre where she had, it seemed, to limber up and prepare for the performance. The other two drove to the Albergo Brun where Flavio changed into evening clothes and talked about money.

'My uncle despises it,' he said. 'Well, we know that he gave up a position in society to join the Church and a position as cardinal to join the Society. Yet the irony is that he has had to be more worldly since than he need ever have been in a secular sphere. Since he brought the Jesuits a fortune, he was given the task of persuading me to do the same – and, alas for the Js, nobody was less fit to do it. First he took the longest time conveying the fact that the good fathers expected some quid pro quo from me, some undertaking that they as well as I would profit from the law suit they were helping me win. What about my becoming one of them? Had I no inclination? Well, I saw that I had better show willing so, to cut a long story short, I entered their seminary and a miserable time I had. Poor as I was, I was used to my freedoms and when they handed me a whip to use on myself on Fridays – in memory of the Passion – and a barbed-wire ring to clamp round my thigh every morning between rising and the breakfast bell, I took it first for a joke and then for a vice. They're touchy about being called worldly, so now all the old, forgotten savage rules are being revived. You don't look your

superior in the eye but lower your head and keep "custody of your eyes",
etc. Meanwhile, need I say, the political members of the Society are
intriguing as never before to get back into the Pope's good graces. My
uncle is an innocent. I used to divert myself – one has to survive
somehow – by asking him whether, as the family and the Church are
equally worthy institutions, it can be right to take money from one to
give to the other. In his case and mine there was a clash of loyalties.
What about our nephews? As one who had not had the benefit of family
rearing, I was, I told him, asking in all innocence what I owed my new
family. He was genuinely upset.' Flavio laughed and pirouetted in front
of a pier glass. 'Do you like my duds?'

'Do you know that the first thing you said to me was, "I like your
livery"?'

'And now I don't. Despite your smart purple!'

'We're not all the same, Flavio!'

'Oh I do know that. There's you and my uncle and maybe three or
four honest clerics to ransom the rest.'

'Far more. Have you heard of Ugo Bassi? And Tasso?'

'Dead, aren't they?'

'Tell me the rest of your story or I'll start feeling I have to save your
soul.'

'Don't you want to save it?'

'Yes, but I suspect I'll have to be sly. How did your uncle save you?'

'First he got removed from my case. Father Grassi – do you know
him? – decided he was too soft and I a hard nut to crack. So they locked
me up and put me on short commons to break my spirit and I, if I
wanted my fortune, couldn't run off. Wearing me down was their best
option because they couldn't rush me into final vows the way other
orders do. It's against their rule. So they went at it hammer and tongs:
starvation, religion, soft talk alternating with harshness and no mention
of my case ever. They claimed to be interested exclusively in my soul.
You're right, Nicola, I'm a veteran at escaping spiritual snares!'

'How do you know they weren't sincere?'

'I couldn't afford to see things their way. After ten months of their
treatment, I pretended to be a convert. I looked it too: emaciated,
hollow-eyed, etc. Perhaps I had been half won over? I *was* praying, but
to a sort of counter-God of my own.'

'That was God!'

'Mine!'

'Everyone's. The same. The one!'

'My captured image of Him. Private! Personal! He helped me too. My uncle turned up again – they'd sent him to Naples, but he came back and demanded to see me and was shocked at how I looked. He insisted on my being brought to the country and fed properly. He told me how the law suit was going. By now he was furious with Father Grassi. He said the case had been taken to right a wrong, that profit was a worldly concept and that he didn't care whether the Society agreed with him or not because it and the Church were becoming images of the thing they fought: materialism, and that he was going to put in a petition to be secularised. Well, then they really grew worried because they feared losing us both, so Father Grassi was overruled – my uncle had gone over his head to the General – and I was released.'

'In the end, then, you got what you wanted from everyone: from the Jesuits and from the Sacra Rota.'

'Oh it was too late to stop that. My mother's impudence had cooked her goose and there was no reversing things. Yes, I won.'

'And your uncle?'

'He's still a Jesuit. He and I have a truce. He says I never grew up, but can't be blamed because I had to live like an adult when I was small. Also that I'm vulgar but that vulgarity is a worldly notion. Do *you* mind my vulgarity, Nicola?'

'I've always liked it. It's robust!'

'Then you'll like Miss Ella. Let's go over to the theatre.'

Outside, in weak gaslight, flights of porticoes gleamed like stalactites. Bologna's gas, said Flavio, was of poor quality, being obtained by burning horses' carcasses. Nicola laughed disbelievingly, but Flavio swore that it was true. And why not? Why shouldn't the remains of hacks and nags be turned – like the souls in Dante – into light? Briefly and wretchedly – but still it was a glittering end! This reminded him of the lights of Paris, where he planned to stay until he had learned how to make money make more money. This was why he had had no scruple about keeping his fortune from the grasp of both his half-sister and the Society of Jesus, since he, unlike them, would make it multiply. 'Don't laugh. One day I shall come back and teach you. I'll bring you profitable lore. I've already started acquiring it.'

'In the circus?'

No, said Flavio. The circus was a sideline.

Walking into the theatre, Nicola drew a cloak over his clerical costume and was quickly installed in a shadowy corner of a box. Priests were forbidden to attend the theatre, but a blind eye was turned if a man was discreet.

Flavio left him alone while he went backstage to encourage Miss Ella – and to remind the doorkeepers that her excitable admirer was to be refused admission.

Meanwhile the music struck up and two clowns came forward to warm up the public. The show was, thought Nicola, innocent and wise: a handmaid to religion rather than, as was sometimes thought, an enemy. The circus swank showed up the vanity of vanities and the clown, arse up in sawdust, mocked the haughtiness which kept Roman landlords from learning how to read a balance sheet. He felt clairvoyant. Something was about to happen.

Flavio came back and sat in the front of the box nodding and bowing at people in other boxes while, down below, clowns with floury faces and great wounded smiles seemed vicariously to suffer the sorrows of the world.

'*Bravi! Bravissimi!*'

Spangled limbs whirled and acrobats took their bow. The crowd roared and vendors profited by the pause to hawk fizzy drinks. These were new here and said to have anti-hypochondriac properties. '*Seltz! Seidlitz!*' cried the hawkers.

'She's next!' whispered Flavio. 'Sit forward.'

Nicola did and could now see the stalls where enthusiasts were shouting for Miss Ella. 'Meezella!' they pronounced, domesticating the sound so that it had an almost meaningful ring – and indeed it did mean something. *Misella* – from the Latin, *miserella* – was a disused old word for a female leper, and though the claque would not be thinking of it, the forgotten meaning gave an enfevered edge to their cry. 'Meezella! Meezella!' It was to see her that they had paid their money, returning in many cases, said Flavio, several nights in a row. She was the draw. Without her, the circus could not have appeared in a theatre like this.

'Here she comes!'

Among Miss Ella's public, Nicola idly noted a man with a bright beard, something now rare, since civil servants who made up a large part of the population were forbidden to sport one.

'Watch!' whispered Flavio.

She was quite unlike the girl Nicola had met in the café. As though released from a chrysalis, she had shed gravity and seemed transfigured as she smiled her glazed smile – justified, he now saw, by the inner

293

concentration it must take to risk life and limb before this public which screamed, as though driven by cannibal appetites, until quelled by the ringmaster, a cartoonish gentleman in lavender gloves. *Silenzio!* Silence for Miss Ella and her horse, Starlight. 'What you are about to see . . .' And he named the crowned heads who had admired the spectacle. Then the horse piaffed and executed various caracoles and curvets, after which the dancer rose to her feet on its back and began her dance. Taut as a bird in flight, she stood on one silken leg and extended the other, landed on Starlight's back, repeated the movement in reverse, landed again astride the gently moving mount, then, leaning so far back that her throat was parallel with the ceiling, raised her marvellous legs like stamens and for moments was standing on her head as the horse proceeded around the ring at its docile, steady pace. Entranced, the audience held its breath and the moments were both painful and thrilling. A current bound them in a communion as close as the one between the dancer and her mount. Feeling Flavio's hand in his, Nicola gripped it in recognition of the marvel. Then it was over and Miss Ella smiled for the first time with an easy, open smile.

'*Bis! Bis! Bis!*'

'*Brava! Bravissima! Bis.*'

The imperious demand for an encore would not let up. The ringmaster flourished a hand towards the dancer. It was up to her.

'*Bis!*' bullied the customers.

'She's tired,' whispered Flavio anxiously. And indeed her taut, professional smile was back. Down in the front stalls, the bearded man fumbled, perhaps for a bouquet. Several had already appeared but were being withheld in the hope that she would perform again. She seemed to hesitate, patting and placating her horse, then, as if on impulse, urged it forward and began a briefer version of her routine, ending with her legs scissoring air like some cryptic hieroglyph. Suddenly she was down under the horse's hooves, in a commotion of bent limbs, while members of the audience restrained the bearded man and someone snatched the pistol which had gone off, scaring Miss Ella's mount so that it swerved and dropped her. Already the ringmaster had pulled the frightened animal clear of where she lay on the sawdust. Ladies screamed. Gentlemen tried to block their view.

'Come with me.' Flavio tugged at Nicola's elbow.

Nicola found himself raced through agitated spectators, then past circus people in various stages of undress – a clown's nose hung oddly around his neck – to where a small procession was carrying the dancer on a stretcher. Flavio and he followed this to her dressing room where Flavio insisted on being left alone with her while Nicola and the rest waited at the door. After some minutes, he emerged.

'I don't want anyone touching her until her own doctor comes,' he ordered. 'Damn him! He's supposed to be here.' The man, he was told, was being searched for through the city's cafés. He drank, Flavio explained, and had in fact been debarred on that account or on some similar count from practising in his own country. 'But he's devoted to Miss Ella. She may be concussed.'

He sent everyone away and asked Nicola to guard the door. Please. This was a vital favour. Nobody but Flavio himself or the Irish doctor – his name was O'Higgins – must be let in. He thought he knew where O'Higgins might be and was going to look for him. Please, he pressed his friend's hand, and left before Nicola could mention the trouble in which this could get *him* if his superiors were to hear that he had been seen lurking outside a circus dressing room, trying to hide his purple socks behind a clothes hamper and clutching his cloak to his chin.

When Flavio came back alone, Nicola made these points with vigour, and insisted on being let into the room. Standing in the corridor was courting trouble and he feared to run into gawkers if he tried to go out alone.

Inside, Miss Ella had begun to groan. Her spangled costume was constricting her, but couldn't be removed without turning her over and Flavio's attempts to do this hurt. She would have to be cut free. Shouldn't they call one of the circus women for this, asked Nicola. But Flavio, tight-lipped, said 'No' and began to nick at the garments with a scissors. 'Ella,' he kept whispering. 'We'll get you more morphine in a moment. Hold on. Hold on.' He looked demented, could not be argued with, yet was deft, perhaps, remembered Nicola, because he had been a leather worker. It was a slow business, though, and, after twice jabbing the flesh with his scissors, Flavio asked Nicola to get his finger under the stuff and hold it while he cut.

Miss Ella was now as still as a funerary statue: one of those crusaders' wives carved in modestly compact folds and flutings ready for centuries of inactivity.

Nick, nick went the scissors, cutting the cloth pod so that it peeled away in a flurry of sequins, underneath which was a layer of padding which fell to reveal male genitalia.

Flavio covered them with a protective hand. 'This is under the seal,' he told his friend. 'Only you, I and the doctor know.'

Then he began to weep.

A crinolined female dwarf, shaped like a pyramid, was in ambush as Nicola left. 'Father, did you give her the last rites?'

'No.' He explained that he was not here as a priest. The eyes of two acrobats, an animal-trainer and the dwarf were on his violet stockings. Death-and-mourning colour, they registered. What but bad luck could his visit bode? They made gestures to ward it off and cursed the jackass with the pistol. Their season was ruined. An acrobat hissed that the public was stupid! Without his spangles, he looked like a coal-heaver! He spat. Then swore. Nicola fled.

Two days later, looking feverish, Flavio called on him with news that the doctor feared the dancer might have irremediably injured her back. 'Her' he said with a faint emphasis. They were thinking of taking her to a local thaumaturgist, a nun who was alleged to work miracles. What could they lose? Doctor, dancer and lover had been in confabulation for twenty-four hours in the small room, which smelled of pomade and urine, while outside the theatre the single word 'Closed' spelled ruin for the Circus.

Flavio said it was intolerable that someone like that could be crippled.

'I won't apologise for the deceit. You'd hardly want me to give scandal? My mother did enough of that. "Scion of great family practises vice of Sodom" is a scandal-sheet title before which I rather quail. They haven't burned anyone for the offence lately, but why gamble?' Miss Ella's real name, he added, was Olmaz Kingsley and she had been born in Louisiana twenty-two years ago. Convenience aside, female horseback riders were more popular with the public.

'Did you seduce Miss Ella?'

'She seduced me. Look, Don Nicola, I'm not pure. Is that so bad? I'm doubtless seeing the mote in others' eyes, but, as I see it, prideful purity is the plague of our times. It leads to bloodshed. *I* don't kill anyone. And don't talk of souls because they can be shriven, for instance by you. Do you know why I don't flounce out of this glittery, tottery, hypocritical old Church? It's because I like being in it. I was brought up as Nobody's Child and now enjoy being one of this state's ducal ornaments and am even ready to work for the privilege, which few are. I want it to go on, not to collapse. The Church is supposed to have many mansions – so why not a niche for me? At the moment you're all busy cordoning off half the rooms and I do see why. You're under fire, etcetera. But you shouldn't reject friends. I'll make a bargain with you if you like. I'll promise not to hurt anyone too much and in a year or so I'll be back to do you some practical good.'

'Simony! You want to buy a licence to sin.'

'Not at all, I'm showing *esprit de corps* by not leading a mutiny within St Peter's barque. If it weren't for loyalty I might. There's no reason for the Church to condemn my love for Miss Ella. Don't talk to me of "nature" because you don't hold with it. It's fallen. That's your doctrine.'

'We must redeem it!'

'Bollocks! Keeping up appearances is the vital tribute and I'm making it. Don't let's quarrel. I have to go back to her. She can't be left alone and the doctor isn't as gentle as I am. We have to help her to relieve herself. She can't move, you see. I'm her slop-emptier. Does that surprise you? I'm attached to her as I am to this doddery old state. Both she and it are rare phenomena and if it can't perform its vital functions we'll have to help it. Empty its slops. I must go.'

Nicola didn't see him for a while after that. Six months later, though, he saw a poster for the Circo Cinisello featuring 'the miraculous Miss Ella', and guessed that either the doctor or the thaumaturge had cured her back.

Seventeen

About then he chanced to meet the lady who had done her best to bastardise Flavio.

The link was Miss Foljambe, who hailed him on one of her sorties with what must be yet another resigned young footman trundling a cartful of offal. The two were sheltering from a nipping wind between the columns of the tiny Temple of Vesta. Reminding Nicola of how, some years before, he had sent her Don Mauro's address, she confessed that, from time to time, she sent the exile news that the Pope's regime was on its last legs. It seemed, said she impishly, the kind thing to do. Now it was *her* turn to put Father Nicola in the way of doing a good deed. Would he call on her? There was a poor soul staying with her who needed consolation. 'I think you know her son, Flavio. Wake up!' shouted Miss Foljambe, but was only chiding her footman for failing to defend the offal from brigand cats. A near-earless tom, looking more simian than feline, had started a fight. 'Come this afternoon,' she cried while turning to deal with this.

On leaving her, Nicola's thoughts turned to poor Don Mauro. Shortly after his ordination, he had heard that the ex-priest was in Paris, and, on looking him up, found him suffering from phthisis and living with a woman of whom he was ashamed. Though known locally as Monsieur Maur, and, presumably, resigned to lay status, he had been upset when Nicola walked in, dressed as the priest he now was. The Maur/Mauro ménage lived higgledy-piggledy in one room; privacy was impossible and Maur had insisted on getting out of bed.

'Wait in the café,' he told Nicola and began to shout at his companion, who had objected that he was too sick to move. Nicola, retreating from their conflict, reflected that if Don Mauro had had a beautiful mistress, the game might have seemed worth the candle; conversely, austerity would have had claims to respect. Failures of both flesh and spirit were hard to redeem. Almost at once, though, while entering the acrid fug of the smoky café, he remembered that Maur/Mauro was a victim of failures not his own.

It was March and cold and when the exile arrived swaddled in a dingy scarf, discomfort grew. Nicola had hoped to be invited to witness peace restored in a tidy room. Instead, there was a prolonged palaver about credit with the café owner who, in the end, grudgingly, supplied two glasses of absinthe. No, no, said Mauro, Nicola must not pay. Very well. Pride was pride. He did not insist.

Looming between sunken cheeks, the sick man's nose quivered tetchily. He was avid for news of home but turned out to know more than Nicola did. Had Nicola heard of the by-law forbidding cafés in Bologna to close their curtains? He tittered over that bit of petty repression, wondering what official snitchers hoped to see, then, as though challenged by candour, began to talk of his companion. A good woman, he stated a touch belligerently, but, well ... Discomfited, he changed the subject.

Did Nicola know who was to be buried tomorrow here in Paris? The ex-Abbé de Lammenais! A brilliant spirit! 'Remember what he said about Liberalism? "Do you fear it? Then baptise it!"' Don Mauro repeated this several times, slapping the table and looking pugnaciously around. Nicola wondered whether he was running a fever. 'He believed in the people,' wheezed Don Mauro. '"Freedom and love," he said, "will save the world."' Whispering, Don Mauro's voice carried further than if he had spoken aloud, and its laboured suspiration gave it a ghostly authority. 'He was the prophet of our time,' breathed the sick, imperious voice. 'He said the popes would lose their temporal power. Democracy will triumph, so the Church *must* come to terms with it. Just remember that, Father Nicola! Remember those words!'

Nicola caught the eye of a girl who kept wiping the counter and watching him with curiosity. What, she must be wondering, was a young priest doing with Monsieur Maur? Looking with her eye at his companion's stubbly face and room-dried linen, he guessed that he must be seen in the neighbourhood as a card.

'He was a friend of Mazzini's!' said Monsieur Maur. 'His funeral is tomorrow. Elise wouldn't let me go alone. Now I can tell her I'm going with you.' He could not, he explained, upset her too much. She worried lest he be taken ill. There was a rigmarole about why she couldn't come herself. 'Fate sent you!' he concluded.

'I'm not sure I can.' Nicola, fresh from the seminary, did not want a scandal preceding him to Rome, where his career had already been mapped out. How say this, though, to the ruined priest who was now excited about tomorrow? The girl at the counter was listening to every word. Curiosity? If this had been Rome, Nicola would have guessed her to be a spy – then he saw that she was making eyes at him. He blushed. In the seminary he had forgotten about girls.

'Wear secular clothes,' commanded his friend. 'He was condemned by two popes, don't forget. And though he had a fashionable following in his day, you won't see any duchesses tomorrow. But the people will come and won't tolerate priests. It's to be a pauper's funeral. That's what he wanted.'

Nicola's efforts to beg off failed. They caused Don Mauro to choke in a coughing fit, then when he suggested bringing some wine upstairs to the woman, Elise – she might be an ally – Don Mauro said no. She was a lace-maker and gone to deliver her work.

'I'm ill!' He gripped Nicola by the elbows. 'You can't refuse me!' There were red, fever spots in his cheeks. 'Yes or no?'

So, Nicola had to say 'yes'.

Next morning, his carriage made slow progress, due to the number of streets being dug up to facilitate the improvements ordained by M. Haussman, the new Prefect of the Seine.

'You're late,' accused Maur. 'And you can't wear that cassock.'

The patron of the café was somehow browbeaten into lending lay clothes and at last a disguised Nicola, smelling faintly of old beer, was on his way to the funeral of one renegade priest in the company of another. He had paid off the carriage. They were to wait here for the hearse to pass, then fall in behind it. He prayed ardently that there would not be trouble.

Then it arrived, a poor-looking contraption. A police officer called: 'Constable, remove that man.' And a priest was hustled off.

The procession walked down the middle of the street. Men wearing aprons and smocks came out of shops and manufactories along the route and stood with bare heads as it passed.

Don Mauro said: 'He didn't believe in hell.'

Outside the graveyard, another crowd was waiting and when the two mingled, disorder broke out. The police seemed to be clubbing people at random and word was passed down the line that very few mourners would be let into the graveyard.

'There's the poet Béranger!' someone shouted.

Nicola craned his neck and glimpsed an old man leaning on the arm of a companion. 'Do you want to take my arm?' he asked Don Mauro who was galvanised with excitement.

'Can you imagine a better funeral for a revolutionary,' he said, then reddened. Had he been thinking of his own?

A quick-eyed fellow in a cloth cap caught his wrist. 'Come on,' he said in Italian, 'we'll squeeze in with the bigwigs.'

Quickly, he drew them past a police barrier in the wake of Béranger. Just behind them two or three gentlemen who had had the same idea were driven back and one shouted that he would sue the police. He had received a blow of a baton across his wrists as he tried to push back the barrier.

'Bolognese, aren't you?' said the spry Italian and shook hands. 'My name's Viterbo.'

Nicola gave his name and, when Viterbo called him 'Signor Santi', felt ashamed of his disguise.

There were two squadrons of police armed with sabres on the left and right of the hemicycle. The coffin was lowered on ropes into a trench already filled with a row of coffins, and there were no speeches. As the grave-diggers shovelled in the earth an official told them, 'Leave space for a child in case we get one.' The filling in and levelling off was finished in silence.

'Are we to put a cross?'

'No.'

A grave-digger tied a bit of paper with the name Lammenais on a stick and planted it in the fresh earth.

Viterbo caught up with the other two outside the graveyard. He had been nosing about and learned that the coffin had cost eight francs and the hearse-driver been surprised to see a silver plate of false teeth in the corpse's mouth – a queer thing for a pauper.

Turning into a small *tabac*, he and Don Mauro made the speeches which the dead man had forbidden at his graveside. They were garrulous and expectant as though the denuded funeral had left them dangling. Don Mauro was soon flushed with drink and kept saying that they must rid their minds of that 'last orthodoxy, the notion of a good death'. When Nicola said he had to leave, Viterbo asked, 'Does your old woman keep you on leading strings? We can't,' he urged, 'let the poor corpse rot without drinking to his safe passage to the next world. He went without the help of the black beetles!'

'What have you against priests?'

'Joker!' Viterbo elbowed Nicola in his borrowed waistcoat.

He promised to take care of Maur and a last glimpse showed the invalid to be in congenial company. By now other mourners were around the pair and an aviary of hands making signals so graphic that, even from afar, Nicola could read a convivial cynicism in the shaking of steepled fingers and in the irreverent sign of the fig.

When Nicola gave her a small gift of money, Maur's woman revealed that her companion was ill in ways hard to understand. It was mental. 'Monsieur,' she called Nicola, although he had resumed his cassock, which showed she had no grounding in the religion lying at the root of her friend's trouble. He, she disclosed, was in a sick panic lest, despite Monsieur Lammenais, there be a hell and Pius IX have the key to it. 'Why,' she sighed, 'is the Pope so cruel?' Maur, who would not bow the knee to the papal turncoat, was torn between this world and the next. He had nightmares. 'He wouldn't want you to know.'

Nicola could only pray, blasphemously, that his friend would continue to find solace in making the defiant sign of the fig.

Before leaving Paris, he took his remorse to a teacher at the seminary, a French Legitimist with a linenfold face, who warned that the World, the Flesh and the Devil had new disguises, namely Freedom and Love. Always remember, warned this Gothic figure, that indocile priests could cause a schism! Some were actually advocating the surrender of the Temporal Power and wanted His Holiness to be a purely spiritual leader! The priest spoke with pity for these soft-heads who wanted Pope Pius to divest himself. Was he to be a mere Italian bishop? Without land or independence! How then could he deal with Catholics living in other states? How pretend to be impartial? See where the false light leads! The Frenchman's mouth compressed itself into a crack so taut that the top of his head looked in danger of falling off.

In Rome, Nicola found the same row raging, for Republicans had informed the people that the Gift of Constantine – which their priests had always told them was the basis for the existence of the Pope's state – was a fable. This knowledge, though not new, was dangerous to disseminate at a time when Garibaldini were once more plotting to seize the Pope's territory.

Besides, said Prospero, the *habit* of scepticism was bad for the simple. Legends were cohesive. 'Tailors say you should think nine times before cutting your cloth and I say the same about throwing out a good legend. The one about the Emperor Constantine is very good. He,' reminded Prospero, 'was converted from paganism when he saw the cross shine in the sky with the words "In this sign shalt thou conquer!" He then did conquer his enemies and in gratitude gave the Church its own lands. We need a new vision like that.'

Prospero smiled. They were in his apartment – not the one in the Collegio dei Nobili Ecclesiastici; he now had his own. 'May I offer you something?' He stepped towards the bell pull. 'No?' His cassock suited him for he had a waist like a girl's. He was making headway in the Church. Already, he had taken his degree *in utroque iure*, had practised at the bar for two years and was launched on the ceremony of entering the prelacy, a leisurely affair which he described lightly, while admitting that it had been an ordeal, since he had had to submit himself to the separate scrutiny of the seven voting prelates of the Signatura Iustitiae, at each of whose lodgings he had been required to call. He had worn black. Only when His Holiness granted him a position would he put on a purple mantelet which – he could not resist showing it – he had already purchased.

'*In hoc signo vinces!*' quipped Nicola, fingering the cloth.

Prospero's opinions were consistent. 'We need less scepticism,' he had told Nicola recently, 'and more visions.'

This was an allusion to the visionary Caterina da Sezze, whose fortunes had prospered since Cardinal Amandi first investigated her case. Now famous and fashionable, she travelled regularly between her village and the papal court where she enjoyed the hospitality of the Pope's steward, to whose children she was godmother and where her readiness to tell fortunes earned her a flow of cash which was managed by an entourage of three priests and a friar. Cardinal Amandi believed her to be an impostor, and had given Nicola the task of finding proof.

'Don't talk about it,' His Eminence had advised and Nicola hadn't. Yet his friend had said 'We need more visions!' Chance?

'Everything about this case is delicate!' Caterina, said the cardinal, had a great sway over His Holiness whom she kept exhorting to defend the Temporal Power. This message, supposedly relayed from heaven, was suspiciously timely.

If hers was an imposture, her attendant priests must be collaborating in it. Others too perhaps? The scale of the potential scandal was daunting. Souls could be troubled. 'We must pray,' said Amandi and, having done so, decided that Nicola should seek the truth in Caterina's village.

It had taken him a while. Local reticence had had to be circumvented. Her village, a huddle of mucky lanes, owed it to her if it was on distinguished persons' maps. For a foreigner – and anyone from over ten miles away was that – to ask probing questions could raise hackles. So, instead, he let it be known that he was writing a pious booklet about her and hoped to gather the sort of detail which, if one waited for her sanctity to be declared, would be surely lost. Her first tooth? Her early charity? Anything, he assured, was welcome.

'I'm like a squirrel,' he told the parish priest, recalling his schoolboy nickname. 'I gather my hoard in the fruitful season.'

The priest, a poor devil in a patched cassock and shoes so scuffed they seemed to have sprouted scales, was overjoyed to have a Roman priest stay in his comfortless presbytery whose mattresses were stuffed with corncobs. They went shooting together, warmed themselves with plum brandy and played passionate games of draughts. Slowly, from scraps and hints dropped over weeks, a picture took shape. Caterina, far from being simple and humble, had had some education. Her priestly bodyguard kept her isolated. No, the parish priest had not recently heard her confession. She had her retinue for that. Nor could he remember much about the innocent days before she saw the apparitions which had been so frequently described. It was only after the three priests took her in hand that she had developed her fluency at relaying what her voices said. How had the three priests first heard of her? They had come to preach a mission and it was during this that she had first seen the Virgin. Now you could only approach her through them.

The priest, being human, felt pique. There was talk, he let slip, about her domestic arrangements. Mind, he told Nicola, he had reproved the gossips. But it had stuck in his head. He shook this self-reprovingly. Then, surprisingly, for the hour was late for a man who had to save charcoal and count candles, asked Nicola to hear his confession. Yes, here and now. He needed to deliver himself of the buzz in his mind.

Plopping on his knees, he told under the seal of secrecy the story being whispered from village to village in that desolate, superstitious, brigand-ridden region. It was that the saint was no saint but the concubine of three cassocked devils who gave her powers to tell fortunes, predict the weather and perform small, surprising acts which gained her sway over people's minds including, Lord save us, that of the Pope, to whom she gave bad advice so that he would end up losing the Gift of Constantine.

'How,' marvelled the priest, 'did people in this village hear of that? I myself had forgotten what it was and had to look it up!' Uneasiness widened his ingenuous eyes and his upper lip quivered. But his information was hard to dismiss. It came from the woman who laundered Caterina's sheets. 'She says Caterina has a lover!'

When Nicola left the village, the *parrocco* was like a man bereaved. He would miss their games of draughts and Nicola's company on long hikes and lonely evenings. He had no hope of ever again finding so engaging a companion.

'It's a Godforsaken place,' he joked bravely, as they embraced. 'That's one reason why I don't believe in Caterina's visions. Why would God cease to forsake us?' Then he pressed a bottle of home-made brandy on his departing guest and, for dipping in it, some local biscuits hard enough to break a tooth.

Nicola who, for professional reasons, had set out to win the man's heart, felt a mixture of elation and remorse.

In Rome, he told Amandi under the seal what he had learned under the seal and they agreed that they lacked evidence. Perhaps a reliable witness had better be slipped into the papal steward's household. This move, though made with caution, must have come to the attention of Father Grassi, S.J., for he paid a call on Nicola and, coming quickly to the nub of his concern, asked why he had chosen to enter the Church.

Grassi's face was purposeful. There was a jut to his jaw and his eyes were like gun bores. Did Nicola, he asked, want to destroy or to restore our power? This was the only question now. And closely connected to it was whether French Catholics could make their Emperor keep his troops here to protect us from Garibaldi. We must not make it hard for them. Miracles were salutary and necessary.

'But not tricks?'

No, no, said the Jesuit irritably. Of course not! But to the eye of the sceptic truths could *look* like tricks. Sceptics had a way of getting hold of the wrong end of things and taking the part for the whole. Remember the story of the three blind men and the elephant. Each thought he had the whole truth, but one felt only the trunk and another the tail. Anyway, there were myths on both sides. Take the rubbish being talked about the death of Father Bassi! Bassi died howling! Shaking like an aspen tree!

'I spoke to Father Tasso at the time,' said Nicola coldly, 'and he said otherwise. He had spoken to the *confortatore*!'

'Tasso was a mythomaniac. I,' said Grassi, 'spoke to Monsignor Bedini who talked to the Austrian firing squad.'

The two men were themselves shaking like aspens. Then Grassi changed tactics. He had not, he said, Nicola's art of winning people. 'I am not seductive,' he said. 'It's a gift which carries responsibilities. You'd better be sure you're right.'

Nicola was now sure that Grassi knew of his visit to Caterina's village. The source must be her priestly acolytes – who else visited the place? – which in turn proved their connivance with the Society of Jesus.

Grassi said sadly, 'I have succeeded only in making you suspect me. Yet, as priests, our aims must be the same: to preserve the faith. Just remember that the cult of "truth" can be a fetish! One may be holding the elephant's tail!'

Nicola was troubled, and might have been influenced by the Jesuit's appeal, if Amandi's spy had not discovered that Caterina was pregnant, which put an end to his role in the affair. Events took their course and in February 1857 the Holy office condemned her to prison 'for deliberately inventing apparitions of the Most Blessed Virgin and Jesus Christ, for laying fraudulent claims to prophetic gifts and for immorality'. Her friar and priests got three years' penal servitude apiece, but the Jesuits got off scot-free, although they had probably engineered the whole thing.

Donna Geltrude, a faded beauty, was bloomless but elegant, with eyes like cobwebbed pansies.

Nicola was grateful for the ritual of tea which allowed him to get his bearings while sampling thin sandwiches and remembering Flavio's account of his single meeting with his mother. He imagined her, who was still fine in a sketchy way, proffering the tips of her fingers for a kiss, then simply walking away. She had an insubstantial look, as though ready at any moment to do just such a disappearing act – and must have become skilled at performing it. She had been living in retirement, she told him, in her villa near Imola and also in Paris. It was there that she had heard that Flavio was planning to marry a circus performer.

'Miss Ella? I suspect,' Nicola told her, 'you have been misinformed.'

'Ah?' Her teacup rose, then paused. 'You have heard of her?'

'Flavio and I are old friends.'

'I suppose your own mother was so close that you cannot conceive of a mother like me?'

Nicola explained that, on the contrary, he, like Flavio, had been brought up in institutions.

Air evaded Donna Geltrude who began to cough. Getting it back with difficulty, she managed to say, 'I have no feelings now. Only maladies. Tell me, Father Santi, have you any idea what Flavio feels about me? Please be candid.'

'If he feels anything,' said Nicola, 'it is anger.'

'I see!' More catching for air. 'Is that what may make him marry a circus rider? Revenge? A shaming of our name which I tried to deny him? I have been wondering whether if he knew why – there is a why – he would feel less bitter?'

Miss Foljambe now offered to withdraw but her friend said she was welcome to hear what she had to say. People, Donna Geltrude knew, thought her a monster, but their imaginings were more monstrous than the truth which, for good or ill, she wanted to tell to Father Santi, who could decide whether to pass it on to Flavio.

Her story started in the century's second decade when she, as a child, was spending much of her time mooning in her parents' garden in Rome, which was so overgrown that the air looked like pond water and the mossed statues were as plump as kitchen maids. Her family belonged to that Roman aristocracy which someone had compared to lizards living in the dried-out carapace of an ancestral crocodile. And indeed her earliest memories were of complaint. Times had, it appeared, been palmier once, and the brocade draperies in a better state. Now her relatives lived by improvisation and spent their best energies addressing formal supplications to each other for such favours as tax-exemptions, state pensions and ceremonial sinecures. Recurringly, they marvelled at the good fortune of their only resourceful acquaintance, the Marchese de' Lepri who, being unable to pay his cook, had granted him permission to open a restaurant in his palace courtyard, which was now the most profitable eating place in Rome. The unpredictability of that delighted them. It was like winning at the lottery and spurred them to ponder lucky combinations of numbers in the hope of a like windfall coming to themselves.

Such hopes had nothing to do with greed. Cutting a fine figure was a duty imposed by their caste and by the papal court which required that outward signs of divine favour be kept up. Ceremonies were lessons for the illiterate and playing one's inherited role in the pedagogic pageant was a defence against social upheaval.

Requirements were a matter of custom, not choice. Prelates of a given rank must, for instance, have three footmen when they drove out on certain feast days, so the less affluent would hire some loiterer to squeeze into their livery and make up the number. This, observed Donna Geltrude, was of course still true of cardinals. Then, it had also affected the lay aristocracy. She remembered only too well the cost of such masquerades and the skimping which went on in secret. The French occupation had imposed taxes and abolished entails, thereby reducing some of the greatest families to penury; and when Pius VII returned from exile to an empty treasury, it was again the aristocracy who paid the price. He simply refused to honour the banknotes issued years earlier to depositors of gold and silver specie, thus pauperising many more families and dissipating enthusiasm for his restoration.

'How could we feel loyalty to the papacy after that?' demanded Donna Geltrude, who had, Nicola remembered, Republican leanings.

Cynicism had been the order of the day and she and her brothers grew used to thinking that they had been born into a ruined world. She had three brothers. The eldest was to become the Father Prefect whom Father Santi knew from the Collegio Romano, and the next and nearest to her age was her brother Cesare, with whom she enjoyed an intimacy so close that there was no need for speech between them. The eldest brother was too pious to play with them and the youngest too young. So, they were thrown together.

'He had asthma!' Donna Geltrude laughed, choked a bit, then laughed again. 'As I do now!'

When she was fourteen, Pope Leo XII was raised to the tiara and set about moralising the city. No need to remind her listeners of what was notorious. Sunday card-playing could get a peasant ten strokes of the whip and, as there were myriads of such laws which nobody observed, nobody had any morality at all. The law was an ass and everyone knew it. If a peasant could get ten lashes for playing cards during mass, what punishment was left for a real crime? This, anyway, was what Cesare said and Geltrude believed him, for he was three years older than she and took the lead in all their games. The one he proposed shortly after Pope Leo's accession did not surprise her at all. At first it seemed childish – a relapse into nursery play – and by the time she saw that there was more to it, they were lovers.

The word, said she, might seem shocking, but the reality brought no more guilt than going for a ride on their ponies. Public impropriety was what the pontifical police were after and Cesare and she were privacy itself. They were always either in their parents' *palazzo* in Rome or in the country on their own land. They had governesses and a chaplain to chaperone them, but these were lazy and when the children ran away from them, held their tongues so as not to be blamed. The chaplain was their confessor too and naturally Cesare and she did not embarrass him by confessing their sin of the flesh. Besides, repeated Donna Geltrude, she had never thought of what they did in those terms. After all, so much of life was private – wasn't it? – out of consideration for other people. One did not parade one's intimate functions. One kept up a front.

'Am I taking too long?' Donna Geltrude sighed and speeded up. She had finally confessed all, she said, when she was pregnant with Flavio, and been advised to repudiate the fruit of her sin. This was much later though and, by then, her luck had long run out.

What happened was that one hot September morning, when Cesare and she were supposed to be studying with the chaplain, they persuaded him to let them go cool their feet in a stream which ran about a hundred yards from the villa garden. It was no distance to let them stray and he, favouring his arthritic legs, sat on a bench to wait and fell asleep. Meanwhile, their father and his steward came by with guns in search of the wild fowl which they liked to eat, after these had been spit-roasted between sage leaves, bacon and oiled bread. The foliage by the stream was so dense that they might have shot the lovers had they not been alerted by the vigorous rippling of a clump of reeds. Suspecting a poacher, their father crept forward stealthily and pounced.

'He was,' said Donna Geltrude, 'a man of iron restraint. He said nothing, gave nothing away. He simply prodded Cesare's naked backside with his boot, waited to catch his eye, then withdrew silently and led the steward off in another direction. He even said something to the chaplain, as he passed him, about the dangers of sitting in the sun. Next morning he left the villa without saying a word and, returning ten days later, announced to Cesare that, asthma or no asthma, he was to join the Austrian Army as a private and serve under an officer who would ensure that his spell in the regiment either killed him or turned him into a man.' The officer was a notorious martinet and Cesare could look forward to getting the sort of discipline which he, his father, had culpably failed to provide.

'To me,' said Donna Geltrude, 'all he said was that I was to be locked up until he could find me a husband, which he did within a month. The duke was thirty years older than I, and knew at once that I was no virgin. He had, he told me, deflowered so many that I could not have hoped to deceive him, but in deference to their memory he would not complain. He had, however, married so as to have children and wanted these to be his own, so he was taking his sister out of her convent to keep an eye on me day and night. This horrified me. I had met the sister at our wedding and she was a spiteful poor creature with a squint who could not forgive the world for its prejudice against the squint-eyed. I told him that if he would leave her in her convent, I would undertake neither to foist a bastard on him nor to take a lover without letting him know. I think he was amused. In the light of all the married and unmarried women he had slept with, he could not hope to find more virtue than the sort I was promising. After all, a city without brothels and full of celibate prelates can be forced by popes like Leo XII to keep up appearances but never to change its ways. "Very well," he said, "if you give me your word of honour." So I gave it to him and did my best to keep it.'

Donna Geltrude sighed. She must be coming to the worst part of her story. She had, she said, two children by her husband and then Cesare came back. He had spent three years in the disciplinary regiment being subjected to the regime of kill-or-cure, but the outcome had been neither. He had run away, been caught and punished horribly, and now his face looked flayed. It was desiccated, lean, superficially humorous and deeply, intimately sad. He had lost a front tooth. Although he never spoke of his time with the Austrians, he began to conspire with their enemies – those were the years when the activities of *Carbonari* and Masons were at their peak – and was imprudent and, no doubt, ineffective. After the papal police had raided a meeting and arrested him and proven to him that half his group were spies, he threw up politics and astounded his family by becoming a priest.

'"Well," he said to me when I wondered at this, "all the preferment in this town is for priests, so why shouldn't I have some of it? I presume that as our father generously raised your dowry to make up for your damaged state, he will equally generously endow me with the property qualification needed to attain the *Prelatura*!" Then,' said Donna Gel-trude, 'he caught me by the throat – we were in my father's *palazzo* – and asked, "Do you prefer your old dried-up debauchee of a husband to me?" And when I resisted him, he raped me. He was very strong now and brutal and he kept his thumb on my windpipe until I thought I would choke. My asthma dates from then.'

She did not consider that the rape broke her promise to her husband, but she now kept out of Cesare's way. He seemed to her demented. His character had changed and he had developed a hatred against her whom he thought of as having betrayed him. He told her that while he was living through hell in an Austrian military gaol, he had imagined her pining and waiting for him and had been in despair when he heard of her marriage. She had broken their pact and when she said there had been no pact, he was outraged. They had *understood* each other as children, he said, and repeated this over and over as though nobody had understood him since.

'My husband had a villa in the Legations, and it was while I was there one autumn with my children that Cesare turned up again. He simply arrived one wet evening in a dripping carriage like a black bird of prey. He was by now a priest but had not acquired the violet stockings he craved, for my father was refusing to put up the money. They disliked each other and had had one of their worst rows – which boded ill for me. My husband was in Rome pursuing an amorous interest of his own. We had already begun to live apart and I was reluctant to have my servants throw Cesare out. He counted, to be sure, on my eagerness to keep up appearances – was it not, after all, what had led me to betray him? I would give into it again, he reckoned, and now it would serve his purpose.

'"Surely you can't want to force my affections?" I asked. "Why do you want to spoil the past and my feelings for you?"'

'"You spoiled mine!"'

'He threatened to tell my husband about his rape of three years before which he would not, of course, describe as a rape. Then he raped me again – and again. He stayed for a month, wreaking his rage and lust on me at irregular intervals. I became numb. No, it was worse. It was as though he had sucked me into his nightmare and as though I had lost my will. I began to see that this could go on for the rest of our lives because I was also losing my ability to distinguish disgust from pleasure and, in between, I hated myself and him. I didn't go to confession. How could I? I didn't know a trustworthy priest – and didn't see how one could have helped me if I had. I saw only one decorous way out – and, remember, I was brought up to put decorum before everything – so I adopted it. I began to poison him with *acqua di Tofano di Perugia*, slow-working arsenic, which I gave him in regular doses in his food. I saw a symmetry there. He was poisoning my mind and senses and I was poisoning his. As he grew weaker, I recovered. My numbness faded. I began to hate him increasingly and in the end I refused myself to him and he was too weak to force me. I went on giving him the poison. It is, of course, a common one, used frequently by jealous wives, and is said to be impossible to detect. Certainly, nobody saw anything strange about Cesare's death and I think my parents were relieved. Looking back, I see now that, even during our childhood, he was slightly mad. I think my father must have seen that the day he found us among the river reeds. It explains why he chose to give me a good dowry, even though his own finances were not flourishing, and found me a considerate husband. It would have been cheaper and easier to shut me up in a convent – but he chose not to.'

Donna Geltrude paused. 'I should hate to think that Cesare's heritage is poisoning Flavio's life too – but how do I know whether telling him all this would merely embitter him more? I don't know him. I couldn't let myself. I was trying to honour my promise to my husband not to let his name and possessions pass to a bastard, and Flavio, as you must have guessed, is Cesare's son. You,' she told Nicola, 'must decide whether or not to tell him.'

Defensively, she added, 'I did pay a lump sum to a family which engaged to bring him up in modest comfort. Such arrangements are common, but this one went awry. A middleman pocketed the money.' She wheezed and sighed. 'How could I have explained this when we met? Just when I was preparing to deny his legitimacy?'

Her remorse, Nicola saw, was all for the living. A practical woman. Some might shudder at the *acqua di Tofano*, but Miss Foljambe apparently did not. She had her arms around her friend's shoulders and was suggesting brandy, but Donna Geltrude wanted to keep her mind clear. There was more to tell.

It was during Cesare's funeral – which she did not attend; it was not the custom – that she learned she was pregnant and had better take steps to conceal the incestuous source of her condition.

'I had to protect the reputation of my own blood kin.'

Miss Foljambe nodded. To be sure. She had, said Donna Geltrude, gone hotfoot to Rome where she tried and failed to rouse her husband's interest. Her friend's smile was a *miserere*. How glad she was she had stayed a spinster! Donna Geltrude, a more active one, had spun a web of deception. Desperate for a putative sire, she now encouraged the attentions of a handsome but-not-very-sharp Russian and, to her husband's undoubted relief, since his own affections were engaged with the sisters who would one day testify at the Sacra Rota trial, flaunted herself with this new lover.

'An old shift!' she admitted.

The custom of having a *cavalier sirvente*, though not as common as formerly, had not died out and, anyway, great ladies enjoyed freedoms denied ordinary folk. Besides, the rigid reign of Leo XII had finished and a reaction set in. Rome had defeated him. Morals were relaxing and cafés serving ices and taverns wine, as merrily as if he had never forbidden such possible occasions of sin.

The gallant Russian, supposing the child to be his, helped her give birth in secrecy, sent his manservant to leave it temporarily at the Foundling Hospital, then sent him back to arrange to have it boarded out with a respectable family. It was this man who pocketed the sum entrusted to him, unknown either to his employer who was soon on his way back to Russia or to Donna Geltrude who, supposing the child to have been provided for, put it out of her head. Nobody would ever have been the wiser had it not been for the 'Russian' Jesuit who had been her Russian lover's confidant and guessed that Flavio – who resembled her – was Donna Geltrude's son.

The Jesuits had then converged like eels or gulls on the inheritance – which in the end they didn't get. 'I wasn't surprised when Flavio outfoxed them! He's Cesare's son!' She stopped, then visibly bracing herself, said: 'They immediately began spreading the word that my daughter and I were Republicans, which was the worst thing you could say about anyone that year. Remember, it was just after the fall of the Roman Republic. And it was a lie. My daughter and her husband have always been moderates.'

'But you were Father Gavazzi's penitent?'

'Ah,' said the duchess, 'there was a man without guile! He wanted me to say who the father was! Imagine. I couldn't – if only because my mother was still alive. And what did honesty do for *him*? He had to leave his country and his Church!'

This was prickly territory and Nicola chose not to venture onto it for it was his duty – her story had convinced him – to save Donna Geltrude's soul. The question was how? Tact was called for and kid gloves. She was embittered, having suffered at the hands of the *Sacra Rota*, and it was likely that he was the first priest to whom she had spoken in years. Awed by the challenge, he murmured, 'I can give you some comfort. Flavio won't marry the circus rider. I can't tell you how I know this. But you may rely on it.'

'You're a man of secrets!' approved Donna Geltrude. 'So keep mine too – except from Flavio.' Catching his wrist, she drew him so close that he was shocked by the cutting gleam of her eye. There was a secondary ambient one from a diamond choker designed to conceal the ruins of her neck. 'I would like to think of him as like you, because,' she said, 'you are an agreeable man. Sensitive. I imagine orphans often are. After all, they have to seduce the world, don't they? Nothing's given to them!' Her laugh startled him. Before he could muster a reply, she was telling Miss Foljambe that she would have that brandy, after all.

Afterwards he knew he had failed Donna Geltrude. The word 'sensitive' had stopped him in his tracks. And her laugh! Unnerved, he had not dared offer the spiritual consolation which she was likely to rebuff for, surely, she must have grown sceptical of clerics' appeals and, like a flayed creature, impossible to touch. Yet how leave her to a cynicism which must lead to her damnation? Must it? Would God condemn her for what had come about as a direct result of living in His state?

At several points, Nicola had been ready to intervene in her narrative with uplifting words – which died on his lips. It didn't lend itself. They would have sounded like cant. Anxiously, he unscrolled her history in his mind: Pius VII had ruined her family by failing to honour his debts; Leo XII discredited morality by demanding the impossible; the require-ment that her ruined family manifest eternal values by keeping up a decorous front had contributed to her brother's cynicism. Inexorably, conditions prevailing in this state had trapped her – and Flavio. So how blame either of them for sins or cynicism? As for the cynicism of the *Sacra Rota* – but here he stopped himself. Blame was soaring dangerously high. Checking wild thoughts, he leaped out of bed – which was where the thoughts, profiting from his disarmed and drousy state, had found him – and flinging himself onto the floor, made a heartfelt act of contrition. He saw now that he had opened himself to mental temptation and that the contagion came from her, an unbridled creature who should have aroused horror rather than pity. For was her suffering not her own fault? The result less of misfortune than of resisting it, and of following her own lights instead of yielding with a good grace? For what had she gained? Nothing. If, as other women did, she had passed Flavio off as her husband's son, things would have been at the beginning as they now were at the end – and without troubling people's faith. But no: she, come hell or high water, had had to keep her promise to her husband – and to her own self-pride. Hers was the disruptive modern spirit incarnate: a force as dangerous as a cholera virus because it was powered by such obstinacy that it would burn itself up rather than give in. Lucid, insubordinate, contagious and wrong! See the outcome! She was a revolutionary of the bedroom! Nicola, still on his knees, acknowledged to himself that he had briefly surrendered to a half-filial attraction to Donna Geltrude. Because of that cold, suffering flame in her and because she was a lost mother like his own, he, whose thoughts should have been on winning souls for Mother Church, had instead let them nuzzle around this ruined flesh. Despite her tart style and fissured face, he had felt his own flesh stir as he wondered what it would be like to be Flavio, and about incest and the young Cesare and how she must have looked when aged fourteen. Before trying to save her soul, he had, he saw, better look to his own. Turning for aid to the Virgin, he recited a rosary before returning to his bed.

Only when he had did he remember that if Donna Geltrude had not poisoned her brother a more unmanageable situation would have developed. By then, however, he was too tired to tackle the moral tangle. Authority, he thought sleepily, should have been invoked. Who had said that mankind was too wicked to live in freedom? Christ, was it? He fell asleep.

'To be sure,' said Miss Foljambe, the next time Nicola came to tea, 'everyone should have some religion. But I can't see that it matters which.' Over the years she had grown so English that now she could have been acting the part – which perhaps she was? Amateur theatricals were a favourite pastime with foreign residents, who had perhaps forgotten other ways of being themselves. 'It's like praying in different languages,' she elaborated, 'which is why I can't see why the dear pope minds people bringing in bibles. It is so tedious when they're seized, and makes a poor impression on first-time travellers.'

Her nose had acquired an increasingly rosy flush and he would not have been surprised to find she rouged it. Looking comic set her apart which was, he sensed, where she wished to be. Miss Foljambe, for whatever reason, did not like to quite belong and, after years spent here, was in danger of doing so. Nicola, who relished belonging, recognised the opposite quirk. At first, therefore, he took her reference to Bible-smuggling – a favourite sport with English ladies – as a random part of her 'act'. But it turned out that smuggling was what she wanted to discuss.

Confiding in him – she had once admitted – was her way of trying out the confessional: an institution which repelled and fascinated her. Admiring church art was no longer enough, and she made sly excursions into other aspects of Catholic life against which her own pastor, a perspicacious gentleman, had warned her. Being High Church himself, he saw the lure. But Miss Foljambe reassured him. Her principles would never allow her to come to terms with the Catholic Church. The priests she knew were all dissidents of one sort or another. 'I told him,' she told Nicola, 'that I am more of a threat to your faith than you to mine! So you stand warned!'

Nicola said he didn't think of himself as a dissident.

'But you're tolerant, which is why I trust you. Perhaps you know that I am acquainted with some of the leading Democrats here?'

'Please don't tell me anything I should feel bound to report to the authorities.'

But what she had to tell was that she had already been *caught* by the authorities who had then, astoundingly, looked the other way. More tea? A scone? Did he, she asked, know a priest called Grassi? Well, said Miss Foljambe, she had recently made his acquaintance at the frontier where a number of carriages were held up and passengers cooling their heels. She, who had been on her way to England, was carrying a parcel for Democratic friends. They had asked her to do this because it was easier for foreigners to take things out. It was money and when the customs impounded it she had been terribly upset. Frankly, the officials looked villainous and she had feared lest her friends not see their money again.

'Well, there were some Jesuit priests in the carriage behind mine, so I threw myself on their mercy. One was this Father Grassi who could not have been more gracious. He intervened, got my money back for me and kindly advised me against carrying specie on trips like this. There were brigands on these roads. He had a distinctly ironic look to his eye as he suggested that we travel on in convoy as far as Leghorn where I was to take the steam packet.

'But do you know the odd and embarrassing thing? It was that, later, when I looked at the package, its outer covering had been ripped off revealing the name of the addressee in England. My friends had been deplorably imprudent and there for all to see was the Holborn address of the Democrat and refugee Colonel Pieri who, as you know, was an associate of Signor Mazzini's at the time of the Roman Republic. The customsmen must have seen it and so must Father Grassi. So why did they return it to me?'

Nicola could only speculate. 'Perhaps they already have him under surveillance in England?' he wondered. But it was an unsatisfactory explanation.

Eighteen

Nicola was back in France, that forcing house for visions where, though the glimpsed Virgin was, reportedly, still as pretty as stained glass, her messages were fierce. Odium between cleric and anti-cleric had been smouldering for some years and in May the Pope, travelling to the shrine at Loreto, had brought along his own altar wine and hosts for fear of poison.

It was no time for priests to fall out, so when Nicola and Father Grassi came face to face outside the Church of St Medard, their skirmish was almost cordial and Nicola accepted the offer of a coffee at the nearby Jesuit house in the rue des Postes. 'Though how appropriate,' Grassi sniped, 'to find you where a notice once hung, saying, "By the king's orders let God perform no miracles in this place!" You were contemplating the acts of your predecessor!'

Nicola – he had just read this in a leaflet issued by the parish – retorted that the miracles at St Medard had been performed by Jansenists and that they had been no friends of the Society of Jesus.

Grassi was prepared to take the long view. 'They reproached us with laxity, but now, we are the ones fighting that. Which is why I do not,' he reassured Nicola, 'hold the Caterina da Sezze business against you! Let's go and have that coffee. Did you know that coffee-drinking was once thought to be the height of laxity?'

Outside the Jesuit house, a man stepped forward and Nicola recognised the printer, whom he had seen at the Abbé de Lammenais' funeral four years before. Viterbo. He whispered to Father Grassi: 'Can I have a word?'

'Later,' said Grassi.

Viterbo went rigid. This was not the cheery man whom Nicola remembered. 'I can't . . .' he stuttered. 'Not . . .'

'Oh, very well, come and have a coffee with myself and Father Santi.' Grassi sounded amused, as though he were indulging a whim.

The three moved down a corridor, their heels clicking on a hard floor, then came to rest in a parlour where Grassi tugged at a bell rope. 'Coffee,' he ordered the lay brother who appeared almost at once. 'For three.'

But the man had a message which he murmured into Grassi's ear.

Grassi told his guests to drink their coffee when it came. He'd be back when he could.

Left alone, Viterbo began to laugh. 'Jesuit obedience! He'll be eating his liver out at leaving us together. I've been reading about them. I'm like a naturalist confronted with a new species.' He waited, then asked, 'Forgive me, but you are the man I met at Lammenais' funeral? Were you a priest then?'

'I was.'

Viterbo spread his hands and looked at them. They were trembling slightly.

'We're wondering about each other,' said Nicola.

'Oh I,' Viterbo waved his hand in an indeterminate way, 'am adrift in wonder these days. May I ask why you were there?'

'For Don Mauro's sake.'

Viterbo nodded. 'Poor Mauro!'

'He's not dead, is he?'

'No, no! Just unhappy – like others.' Another leery pause. 'I'm a Jew.' Viterbo spoke as though some inner resistance had given away. Not a religious one! But I support those who promise equal rights to people of all faiths. *Any* Jew must. Even a rationalist.'

'I understand.'

'Well, can you understand this? What if I told you that I had agreed to spy on my comrades? For Father Grassi?'

'Why . . .' marvelled Nicola. 'Ah,' he saw with sorrow, 'you think we're birds of a feather?'

The printer's cheek twitched.

'Are you,' it occurred to Nicola to ask, 'hoping to drive some sort of bargain with me?' He was sorry to bully the man, but Grassi would be back at any moment and he couldn't have *him* hearing of his having gone to Lammenais' funeral in lay dress.

'Please,' the printer's hands captured and held each other, 'don't take offence. I think of you as a man who sees the cruelty of these mangling divisions. Have you heard of the Mortara case? Well, my sister is the Signora Mortara.'

Nicola was shaken. 'The mother? So your nephew . . .?'

The story had been all over the papers for weeks. Catholics were appalled, Jews furious, and anti-clericals having a field day.

'I'm sorry.' Nicola did not dare say more.

The Mortara child had been kidnapped. By the Church. Secretly baptized, six years earlier, by a Catholic nursemaid – no doubt a common enough occurrence – he was, when this became known, taken into protective custody, lest his Jewish parents prevent him practising the religion which must now be his. God's gift could not be repudiated. The abduction took place in Bologna whose Cardinal Archbishop, Monsignor Viale Prelà, chose to abide by the letter of an antiquated canon law. This was the man who, as nuncio to Vienna, in 1848, had sent dispatch after urgent dispatch warning Papa Mastai not to support Italian nationalism. Mastai had ignored them, and shame over that error may have prevented his tempering the cardinal's zealotry.

'He's seven years old!'

What could Nicola say?

'Disappeared without trace!' mourned the printer. 'There have been protests in the London and Paris papers – but what good do they do? I'm dealing now with Father Grassi, and that's like digging a hole in water. *He* got in touch with *me*, but behaves as though it were the other way round. I don't understand. Do you?'

Nicola didn't. The case was odd. Put at its lowest, the thing was impolitic. It was discrediting the Church with moderate opinion and driving it into the embrace of extremists. Could *that* have been some-one's intention?

Coffee was brought in and Viterbo, downing it, stared morosely at his cup, as though reading the future in its dregs.

A memory nagged at Nicola. It went back to last Easter when he had helped out with confessions to get experience of pastoral work – but it evaded him.

Vivid and assymetrical, the printer's profile sawed the air and Nicola imagined the child whose equally vivid features must have won the nursemaid's heart. Strictly speaking, she had been breaking the law by working for Jews. No doubt she grew fond of the child, worried lest, being unbaptized, he be ineligible for heaven, and, when he caught some childhood malady, took the law into her own hands. Baptizing him, she

320

became a secret godmother and, six years later, foolishly boasted about this.

Now the scene from last Easter swam into Nicola's memory. It had been the end of Lent and confessionals were assailed by penitents come to get their certificates of compliance. In corners and side chapels, whispers moved stale air, candles flickered and a sepia light held everything in condensed solution. Statues, cowled in purple cloth, signified that Christ was crucified but not yet risen. It was a time of heightened feelings when Nicola heard weeping on the other side of the grille. A maid servant whose husband had died some years before was reliving her woes in the only place she could. She worked for Jews, she told him.

'She did it when Edgar was one,' Viterbo told him, 'but only told about it last month. Six years later. Why?'

'Had she had a row with your sister?'

The printer didn't know.

Nicola was trying to conjure up that wraith in the darkness. But all he could recall was a congested eagerness to break out of isolation. It was as if the woman had lost the knack. Where the girl in the Mortara case spoke too much, this one gagged. Did anyone maltreat her, he had asked. No. She foundered. Shy. Breathy. Unable to find words – but what was troubling her was perhaps less a matter of words than a need to linger here in the small, secret box. Equally needy, the Mortara maid might have blabbed her story simply to have her own people acknowledge her.

Little Edgardo, he told Viterbo, might have turned on his nursemaid. One could imagine that. A seven-year-old parrots what adults say and could, unknowingly, have hurt her.

His penitent had finally got out a question. Her employers, she said, made her light all their lamps on certain days, holy days, she thought. 'Not ours, though. Theirs.' They said that on these days it was a sin for them to touch a lamp or do any sort of work. 'They call me their lamp-lighter.' Then: 'Is it a sin for me?' she asked. Invisible in her dark compartment, she breathed heavily and he guessed that her concern for lamps was a code. It meant, 'I am one of you, still, am I not?'

He told her she might light the lamps, but knew that this did not address her real trouble since, in her employers' house, this freedom marked her isolation. The Jews were clannish, gathering snugly because of their exclusion from the larger clan outside. A Christian servant did not quite fit in either.

'The authorities won't even say where he is.' Viterbo's train of thought was stalled. 'What can I do?' What he had done so far was to mobilise the French press. As a printer he had contacts and journalists had seized on the story. Why, they demanded, should France, Motherland of the Rights of Man, keep a garrison in Rome to preserve a regime which trampled on the most basic human right of all: that of families to stay together? The case was wrecking the French Catholic party and radicals hoped that the Emperor would now seize his chance to abandon Pius.

Too late, Viterbo realised that in the process his nephew's interests could suffer. Father Grassi had remarked that if the family was counting on bringing down the papal regime so as to get back little Edgar, theirs might be a long wait. Would it not be wiser to come to an understanding? Viterbo's smile was wry. 'His words were: "You don't catch flies with vinegar!"'

'What does he want of you?'

'I'm to stand by. Wait.'

'Does he promise to get the child back?'

'Nothing so clear. He hints and jokes – if they are jokes! The claim "Give me a child at the age of seven and he's mine for life" does not strike our family as funny. Edgardo *is* seven. Then he seems to back off, saying that it's not the Jesuits who have him at all but the Holy Office. Do you think,' asked Viterbo, 'he can help us? We don't even know that.'

'Oh, I think he is quite powerful.' Nicola spoke reluctantly, not wanting to help Grassi make use of Viterbo.

Bologna, 1857

It was December. In chestnut-vendors' braziers, the charcoal glow was like a vestige of sunset. Optimistic and diminuendo, the hawkers' cry faded behind Nicola and Prospero as they drove to a rural *osteria*.

'*Castagni! Bell'e caldi!*'

Martelli, arriving from abroad, had arranged this dinner, catching the two friends on the wing. We'll go somewhere quiet, he had urged. But the evening started badly. It was Advent, a season full of days when there were penalties for eating meat. Oddly, nobody seemed to have warned Martelli about this yesterday when he ordered a donkey stew, a dish about which he claimed to have dreamed in England where he had had a surfeit of bland food.

The host was visibly shaken to see two priests arrive in a house bubbling with forbidden smells and, unmoved by Martelli's blandishments, did not crack a smile. 'You'll no doubt,' he hoped, 'have dispensations!' As far as he was concerned, he told them, roll on the day when gentlemen could eat as they chose but, for now, he must ask them to do so in an inner room. With or without a dispensation, public consumption of *grasso* on days of *magro* was against the law. So the three let themselves be boxed into a space the size of a hen coop and Martelli started firing off jokes, as though offering his guests encapsulated bits of a life which they, as clerics, must surely miss. Nicola supposed he felt a need to bridge the abyss – judging by his frantic geniality, it must seem great – separating ordinary folk from those who served the regime.

Prospero said, 'Our host fears a trap. He could deal with you and your meat or with us and our Roman collars. The combination perplexes him.' Prospero, now an Apostolic Delegate, was travelling and could have claimed licence to eat donkey stew. Instead, he chose fish. Nicola, mindful of the abyss and the need to bridge it, agreed to sample the reddish, fibrous stuff which the waiter brought in to help his customers make up their minds.

'It's a communion and reunion!' Martelli chewed with pleasure. 'Christ rode into Jerusalem on a donkey – so why not make a communion out of eating donkey! Sorry, gentlemen, sorry. I didn't mean that *you* eat Christ – though, to be sure, you do! Oh, dear, I'm a little light-headed. I'd better order wine so you can catch up. Red makes blood, they say. Would you like red? Or champagne? I brought some. Let's have some fizz!'

And on he rattled in the hope of melting Prospero, who had stiffened as though in a private frost.

'Here's to friendship.' Martelli raised his glass. 'Nicola and I mingled our blood once, which was thought shocking at the Collegio Romano. So, to fraternity!'

But Prospero said the word was so contaminated by 'Liberty' and 'Equality' that he agreed with whoever had said that if he had had a brother he would call him 'cousin'.

Martelli laughed. 'You'd be following in your father's footsteps! Didn't the *Carbonari* call each other cousins? I paid him a visit on my way here, by the way. He sends his greetings.'

He waved his napkin as his *stufato di asino* arrived in a fume of fragrance. Too many topics, he said, were booby-trapped. Fraternity! The dinner menu! It was a sign of the times. People were sick of petty restraints. Small things rankled, he told them and sniffed his stew. 'Pinpricks!' He ground pepper into it. 'I've had my ear to the ground, and all I hear are rumblings of irritation. Can you credit that the archbishop here has had several young women shut up in the Good Shepherd Home for Fallen Women? Young women who, if anything, had risen rather than fallen. They were the concubines of solid citizens!'

The other two said nothing and for a while Martelli was busy with his stew. Then he returned to the attack. One girl, it seemed, had had her hair shorn and her protector had said that, if anyone else had touched a hair of her head, he would have cut their balls off, but how do that to the archbishop?

'He was trembling like a whippet!'

'The peasants,' Prospero said severely, 'say a woman's pubic hair can pull more weight than a team of oxen. Indifference to sin is the sin of our time.'

Martelli tiptoed to the door and stuck out his head. Drawing it in again, he said, 'Do you know why I ordered stew? It was to give us a chance to talk confidentially. I'm glad you know the force of a pubic hair.'

Nicola saw Prospero colour. Martelli, though, seemed to mean this as a compliment. It was important, he said, to remember things like that. Ordinary things. Many no longer did – emigrés who spent their days in the backrooms of cafés in London and Zurich arguing with Irishmen and Hungarians and the victims of Tsar Nicholas. 'They discuss something called "man", which is unlike any human who ever lived. They've lost touch with how things are.'

'Do they matter?'

'Yes, because they are spurred on by *agents provocateurs*, false friends who – I must tell you, Monsignori – are sometimes friends of yours.' He told his guests that he was here because he hoped they would help dismantle a plot in which both sides had a hand, revolutionaries as well as priests.

'Priests!'

'Exactly.' Pleased to have roused their interest, he ordered more champagne.

'You've started something,' said the waiter. 'A crowd in the big room wants *stufato di asino*. They smelled it and the *padrone* is on pins and needles because they won't take no for an answer. They've had a glass or two, so he doesn't know whether to be more afraid of them or the police. If it were up to me,' said the man, 'I'd throw it in the pigswill.

324

But . . .' Touching his elbow, he winked and grinned. His employer, tight as the skin on a bent elbow, hoped to save the stew for tomorrow.

He left and Martelli resumed his story, which concerned Felice Orsini, a man who, at the time of the Roman Republic, had had the thankless job of disciplining his own side. Well, Republican refugees, with nothing to chew but the cud of old resentments, had since given him the cold shoulder. In power the spoils of office kept men together, but exiles fell out. Orsini, brooding and chafing, could be provoked into imprudent action by, Martelli lowered his voice more, '*your* friends.'

Nicola guessed: 'The Jesuits!' Martelli said 'maybe'. Something was brewing and the Pope's supporters were capable of engineering an attack on Pius himself. They needed a counter-scandal to swing attention from the Mortara case and stop Napoleon removing his garrison. Not long ago a man had tried to knife Cardinal Antonelli – so why not the Pope? 'They say the cardinal paid the man to stage the attempt so as to blacken the nationalists.'

'But the cardinal had him executed!'

'Of course.'

Prospero didn't believe any of this. He said the imagination at work here was coloured by reading the ancients: Suetonius, Procopius. Maybe even *The Arabian Nights*! Men who read didn't act. Martelli disagreed and said moderate men must stop the lunatics, or anarchy would ensue. Prospero was on his way to Paris and London. *He* could discreetly warn the police there. If there was no plot, where was the harm? If there was, think of the damage prevented! But Prospero, sipping brandy, had a sceptical smile.

'You don't trust me,' lamented Martelli, 'because I'm an Italian nationalist. But let me tell you something. Sooner or later we'll get our nation. That's my belief. Or we won't. That's yours. Either way, we'll have to live together in this peninsula and *that* will be easier if wild men are prevented from embittering matters. Your father agrees.'

But Prospero wouldn't listen to Martelli's appeal which, for all he knew, hid a trap. Mention of his father made him more adamant. No. Well, at the least, begged Martelli, would he warn the nuncio in Paris? 'As you may imagine,' he said reasonably, '*I* can't do it. I wouldn't be believed.'

Prospero was pondering this modest request – Nicola had already agreed to pass Martelli's suspicions on to the police in Rome – when the conversation was interrupted by a commotion in the main restaurant.

There were shouts and the sound of falling chairs and a hubbub so loud that Martelli went to investigate.

No sooner was he well gone than two men in plain clothes entered the cubby-hole, closed the door behind them and told the priests that their orders were to convey them out of this place with maximum discretion so as to avoid a scandal. Stanga began arguing that if it was because of the donkey stew, he had a dispensation . . . But their rescuers deprecated the very idea. Please, Monsignore, don't embarrass us who are obliged to invoke your indulgence for the special circumstances which . . . And so forth. Vague phrases edged smokily towards an undefined threat, while the two were eased from the room, down a back stairway and into a waiting carriage. One of the gentlemen in plain clothes – clearly, they now saw, a cleric and a policeman – explained, between further apologies, that everyone else in the inn had been taken into custody and that if the two of them had either been arrested or seen not to be arrested, this could have given rise to sonnets and epigrams which would have been at best indecorous and at worst subversive of good order and respect for our holy regime.

Nicola asked about Martelli.

'He's an agent,' said the policeman. 'Here to stir up trouble. We've had him under surveillance, and the meat-eating gave us a chance to arrest him without scandal. He will be taken to the border and released.'

What about the other men arrested? The policeman shrugged. Small fry. The law would take its course – which meant that the landlord would be fined and the sinners – depending on rank – given a few days in gaol. Those who had jobs might lose them.

'Indifference to sin,' he said, nodding his head wisely, 'is the sin of our time.'

Nicola looked to see how Prospero liked hearing his own words on the policeman's lips, but his friend's face gave nothing away.

Two days later a note from Martelli begged him to persuade Prospero to look into the matter they had discussed and to alert the nuncio. The Paris Opera House, said the note, was full of Italians. It mentioned the name of a doorkeeper there who would be helpful. Nicola passed this on without comment for he knew that his advice would carry little weight. Prospero was stubborn.

It seemed to Prospero that his soutane drew frosty looks. Cautiously, he watched the gaudy Parisians. Their zest abashed him and so did their sharp, chattering voices. They reminded him of birds with their beaky mouths from which sounds burst like bullets. A century's scepticism had sent them into spasm. The women, to be sure, were built on more fluent lines – but then women, even here, could probably not afford to show much character.

The day before he was to leave for London, he received a note from Madame de Menou, from whom he had not heard in nine years. It was a *petit bleu* and contained only her address and the hour at which she would be at home this afternoon. *There* was a woman of character with whom he had shown a lack of it! He no longer believed her to have been a potential poisoner and marvelled that he ever had. His imagination had been inflammatory – like his father's. Confessors had since warned against this and, for years now, he had kept it under so tight a rein that friends would have ben surprised to know he had any at all.

Clinging to dullness like a sick man to his pills, he was glad to have steered clear of the arena of private feeling – just as he was glad he had evaded Martelli's efforts to draw him into his *imbrogli*. Prospero needed to live under orders and away from emotional anarchy such as, no doubt, pullulated here in Paris. Impulse! *Vo-lup-té!* Horses' hooves hammered out the syllables in sensual French. The city struck him as smeared with it. Chestnut buds had a sticky shine. Pigeons looked like bits of erupting pavement. Human juices – he witnessed a whore committing fellatio – were insufficiently contained.

Yes, his escape had been providential. Poor Dominique! How old had she been? Thirty-one? He wondered if the mad husband was still alive. Heading for her house, he thought of their meeting as one where she would grant him absolution.

It was more uncomfortable than that, for it soon became clear that she was expecting something from him. Letting silences settle, she grew ironic as he rattled on about this and that. Small talk. Politics. As if in pity, she rang for tea. Armed with a cup, he looked and saw that even in the filtered light she was no longer young. Her husband had died. Yes, poor man, she said, to prevent him doing away with himself, he had been put in a strait waistcoat. Backing away from the past and – he now began to fear – present implications of that, Prospero asked about the Peace Conference which had been held here in Paris to wind up the

327

Crimean War. This caught her interest, as during it she had, she told him, met Cavour. Was Prospero still a patriot, even though . . .

'Though I'm a priest?' Nearly all Italian patriots now were anti-clericals. But she must know this.

'Ah,' she nodded, 'the great impediment!' Half laughing.

He didn't follow.

'Gaston,' she named her husband suddenly, 'was like a clever dog. He could smell things out. He knew, for instance, that *he* was an impediment to me. When I came back from Rome he tried to kill himself. Then he calmed down until last year when he tried again.'

Her failure to protect herself left Prospero unprotected too. Like a mouse in a clock, a bit of emotional anarchy slid into his mind. In the dimming room, flashes of her old beauty gleamed but were clearly as little to be relied on as a wig in a wind. She must, he calculated, be forty.

She told him that she hated God.

'Before,' she said, 'I didn't believe in Him. Hearing you were going to be a priest gave me back my faith. Hating is, I'm sure, regarded as better than not believing, am I right?'

He saw he was being baited – or courted. Outside the window – he had retreated to it – the streets looked like a haven.

Love, she was saying, was a persuasive fever. 'I have lived for nine years with a madman who was perhaps no madder than I. Poor Rossi too was a victim of madness. I mean that of his killers. He himself was dangerously sane – too sane to predict what the mad might do.' She paused. 'I reminisce too much. I became trapped in a past which I mistook for the future. I thought, you see, that you would come back. Well, now I shall be cured of thinking that. I can see that you are embarrassed. Never mind, Monsignore. I know this visit is painful for you. Suffer it as a kindness to me. A sort of surgery is being performed as you stand there looking wistfully at the street.'

Prospero, finding tears in his eyes, turned to display them. They were his defence – and less dangerous than words. He could feel her avidity and knew it must not be encouraged.

However, her face quickened. Was he crying, she asked, for the past or for now? 'I have no shame,' she warned. 'Shame is trumpery when set against a chance of happiness. I thought once we could marry. Then, when I heard you had been ordained, I thought I could be your concubine. Lots of priests have arrangements like that. You don't want me though, do you?'

'No, Dominique.'

Somehow – shame blotted out the moment – he was released into the last of the Paris afternoon. He felt that it should have been midnight for he had surely spent hours in that drawing room. Yet it was not even dark. Mist haloes furred the gas lamps, trapping rather than shedding light. It was the hour after the Angelus, the Ave Maria, which in Rome was reckoned as the start of a new day. Here in Paris the evening commerce was starting up. Streetwalkers looked hopefully at him as he plunged uncertainly about and drew his cloak tight to hide his purple. Twice he turned to go back – then didn't because what would have been the point? He seemed unable to focus properly and such was the ferment of his nervous distress that he imagined himself starting to scream or run or plunge into the river. Instead, he walked along a dank pavement, slipping on rotted leaves and wondering how much of the misty magnitude of things was due to his erratic vision. Then he hailed a cab and, for want of a better idea, gave the address of the Théâtre de l'Opéra, rue le Pelletier. It was – he forgot why – in his pocket with the name of a Roman doorman who, presumably, would help him find a good seat.

There were, though, no tickets to be had, for tonight was a gala occasion. The Emperor was expected. Hadn't he known, exclaimed an official with brisk, French surprise. Prospero asked for the doorman, guessing that, unless he had lost his Roman ways, he would have a few places to trade for bribes. The man, he was told, would soon come on duty and indeed, within minutes, 'Monsieur Angelo' had arrived in a glow of brass buttons and eau-de-vie. He greeted Prospero in bad French and Roman dialect, assuring him that he was always delighted to help a distinguished compatriot. Delighted and honoured, he repeated, while waving away, yet managing to pocket, a gratuity. Yours to command, Excellency. Prospero said he was not an Excellency and Monsieur Angelo winked and bowed and beckoned.

Guessing that he was being taken by some back way to a seat, Prospero followed him up stairs and down corridors to a room where he was told to wait while his guide disappeared amid promises of a speedy return.

'*Un momentino, Eccellenza*! *Un piccolo attimo*!' Smiling like some Mephistopheles understudy at a rehearsal.

The door closed, then opened again to admit not the brass-buttoned Angelo but another operatic figure dressed in stage attire. This was a ruddy-faced girl of sixteen who dropped him a parody curtsy. 'I'm

Jeanne!' Smiling radiantly from a mouthful of alluringly crooked teeth. 'Excellency – I mean Monsieur.' Clearly, Angelo had given her speedy instructions.

There was, Prospero now noted, a couch. Where were they, he asked. Whose room was this? Oh, she said, it was one we used. Who was 'we'? Us. The girls in the chorus. Monsieur Angelo knows our timetable.

'And promised you a little present.'

'*Bien sûr!*'

'I see! Well ... will you sing me one of your songs?' He was wondering whether a little sin might not keep off worse. Clearly, Jeanne, a plucked rose, would suffer little in the process.

'What would Monsieur like?'

But she didn't know the songs he named. Meanwhile, his hand was somehow lured inside her bodice, to feel the caky resilience of goose-flesh, and he grew a little sad to find how simple things could be and what an infinity of tender consolation lay in cuddling this adaptable creature who could be a gipsy – she was dressed as one – or nymph or peasant as the evening's bill required.

He was, it seemed though, too slow in his dalliance.

'Better look slippy,' she warned, 'if you want to take your seat by the time the curtain goes up.'

Then she drew the pins from her topknot and shook out her hair, releasing a smell which he found moving and reminiscent, somehow, of childhood kitchens. It was a little fatty, a bit like the coat of a dog, and the mood was comfortably domestic as she suddenly swept it up again and twisted it in a knot. This was a teasing move. Hurry, it implied, or I'll shut up shop. Next she asked him to help her stick back her hairpins. There was no mirror.

'There!' she directed. 'No. More to the left – Jesus! What was that?'

He had imagined it might be to do with the opera – a thunder sheet perhaps? But: no, she told him. *No!*

There was another explosion. Then another and another and sounds of shattering glass.

'Let's go!'

This, he saw, was the real Jeanne who had shed her stagy manner and bundled him out the door in seconds. Down the wooden stairs they raced, but were stopped at the corner leading to the rue le Pelletier. Mounted soldiers had closed off the entrance. Horses reared. Carriages were backed up. Someone shouted that the lights in front of the Opera

House had been shattered. People hung out of carriage windows arguing.

'They've killed the Emperor!'

'Who?'

'English bombers!'

A *sergeant de ville* shouted, 'Everyone off the streets!' The wounded were to be taken to an apothecary's shop. 'Clear the way,' he yelled.

'Come on!' Jeanne drew her customer into a café just as the shutters came down.

Here too the news was garbled. Customers drank spirits to restore themselves and someone came in with a report that the latest detonation had been nothing but a pistol shot, as a horse was put out of pain. So how many injuries were there? Nobody knew. There was so much fraternising of every sort that Prospero was unworried about being seen with Jeanne.

Now the shutters were opened again and a man came in who claimed he had seen everything. An eyewitness! So, *was* the Emperor hurt? No, said the man, he had escaped miraculously. A bit of debris had made a hole in his hat. The Empress had a scratch in her face. That was all. The bombs, thrown under the carriage, had exploded sideways so it was the escort which took the brunt.

Jeanne wanted to see if she could get in the stage door. Prospero followed her doubtfully and again they were stopped. Two policemen were on duty and with them was Monsieur Angelo who drew Prospero aside. 'It was Italians,' he whispered. 'Not English. I just heard from the police. A man's been arrested. He's been babbling, giving names and they're all Italians. About a dozen people were killed.' Monsieur Angelo shook his head. He was white as paper. There would be trouble now for the rest of us – not for gentlemen like your Excellency, but for ordinary Italians. 'How,' he remembered his professional duties, 'did your Excellency like Jeanne? You should come back when things are quieter. She's a nice girl. Ah, and here she is. Everything all right, Jeanne?'

'Yes.' Pertly, 'All present and accounted for!'

She was her old self, Prospero saw. Her professional self. And with the perception came a nausea which he recognised as guilt, though about what or whom he no longer knew. It was a private, personal, secular guilt and possessed him like a fever – he was shivering – and, to propitiate it, he slipped money to Jeanne and some to Angelo who took it without protest. The performance would go on, he told his client. The imperial couple had to show they weren't intimidated. But His

Excellency must go round to the front. No need to hurry. The curtain would be late rising.

Back in the street, opera-goers' carriages now edged forward in response to a signal from the *sergeant de ville*. Pale faces gleamed behind glass. Here, boxed in a convoy, was *le tout Paris*, the fine flower of the Second Empire which, for all it knew, was being borne to its own funeral. The last revolution in these streets had been exactly ten years ago. While thinking this, Prospero felt two arms flung about his neck. It was Jeanne who, finding he had given more than she expected, had run out to thank him. 'You're a generous little padre,' she cried, excited into indiscretion. 'Come and see me again!' And exuberantly kissed him on the mouth.

Over her shoulder, while still imprisoned by her hug, he found himself within inches of a carriage windowpane through which the alarmed, beautiful, astounded eyes of Dominique de Menou stared at him in shock.

DESPERADOES STRIKE AT CROWNED HEADS. After an early appearance among the telegraphic dispatches, this item was to move to the front page of the *Giornale di Roma*, where it soon squeezed out THE RELIEF OF LUCKNOW, a topic which had enjoyed pride of place for weeks because, being of no interest to anyone, it gave no trouble to the censors. By contrast, the new story's implications were entirely favourable to the Pope's regime and the *Giornale*, making the most of this rare circumstance, was soon able to announce that the miscreants had brought their murderous hand grenades to Paris from London, and a little later, that the would-be regicides were in custody thanks to the panic of an accomplice, Davide Viterbo, who, losing his head at the scene of the crime, had blurted out the ringleaders' names. These were Pieri and Orsini.

Triumphing, *Il Giornale* printed exerpts from the French and English press.

'Some of the refugees,' marvelled the naïve *Times* of London, 'were of the better sort with plenty of money in their pockets.' And indeed 9,000 francs in English gold and banknotes had been found at their lodgings along with a stock of weapons.

In Paris, *Le Constitutionnel* concluded that the crime was the work of a subtle brotherhood of fanatics which had its headquarters in London. There followed a war of words between the two papers – gleefully reprinted by *Il Giornale* – about England's refusal to abridge the liberty of those seeking asylum on her shores.

It was delicious for the Roman press to see the Pope's enemies fall out and Piedmontese conspirators alienate at one swoop the French Emperor and English opinion.

'Can they be so stupid?' Nicola Santi asked Cardinal Amandi. 'Might they have been manipulated by the other side?'

'What side?'

'Ours.'

'Beware, *figlio mio*,' said Amandi, 'of growing too cycnical.'

'In that case, could we not,' asked Nicola, 'try to do something for the unfortunate Mortara family?' Then he described how Viterbo, in a desperate attempt to help his nephew, had been almost certainly persuaded to infiltrate and betray the bombers. But Amandi reasoned that if he was an infiltrator his masters would look after him.

'And the little boy?'

'I'm afraid there's nothing to be done about him. The decision, from what I hear, has been taken by the Holy Father personally. He has made an offer of the child to God: a soul for religion. How ask him to take him back?'

'It's giving rise to gossip, though. Quite unedifying.'

Amandi shrugged. Everything did that.

Had he heard the story, asked Nicola, of how when His Holiness was a young layman he had a Jewish mistress and got her pregnant? Then she married a Jew who brought up the child as his so that it was left without baptism. Gossips said the Mortara child was payment: a soul for a soul.

Amandi wondered whether Nicola had heard stories about himself. Brusquely, changing the topic, he said:

'I've mislaid my spectacles. What else is in the paper?'

Nicola turned from the front page – showily adorned with the Mastai-Ferretti coat of arms – to the second where the cardinal watched him skip an advertisement for a cure for chilblains and the schedule of foreign-language sermons at San Andrea della Valle: Polish, French . . . 'Does Your Eminence want to hear about the glorious French campaign in Algeria? No? What about the list of foreign visitors to the city?'

Amandi chose that, which was how they learned that Duke Cesarini, Flavio, had at last returned to Rome.

Prospero was staying with the nuncio whose balconies overlooked a garden where branches were as black as iron and tree roots arched with a knuckled clench. Lingering here, he thought several times of visiting Madame de Menou, but did not. Neither did he go back to the Opera, for what had happened with Jeanne had revealed a way of being which he was convinced could only be open to men who lived on the surface of themselves. Passion bore witness to human scope but tepid comfort with the likes of Jeanne denied the spirit.

He turned his back on it.

Once he had, however, the tabooed memory acquired dignity. Jeanne renounced grew more worthy and it was in a mood of stimulated gloom that he at last made his way to the rue le Pelletier – only to find that she had left for the country, 'To see her mother,' said Angelo with an air of improvisation. He, though, had other resources. If His Excellency would leave it to him, he . . . No? *Bene*! *Bene*! Angelo did not insist. In a week or so then. If His Excellency had taken a fancy to little Jeanne, *pazienza*! Never deny the heart was Angelo's motto.

When Prospero returned to the house, the nuncio, Monsignor Filippo Sacconi, was talking to an unwholesome and worried-looking fellow whom he addressed as Viterbo.

'You remember the Orsini case,' said Monsignor Sacconi to his guest. 'Listen to this.'

Viterbo produced some crumpled papers which he smoothed out on the nuncio's desk. They were rough drafts, he explained, of a letter to the Emperor which purported to come from the condemned cell of the would-be-assassin, Felice Orsini, but had, in fact, been written by journalists. Penny-a-liners. Men he knew.

'It's an appeal,' explained Monsignor Sacconi, 'to be magnanimous and help Italy gain its independence. Apparently it's to appear in the press on the day of Orsini's execution: a voice from the grave. The trick is likely to strike people's imaginations. It's a bold, not to say impudent, stroke which could do us damage. Viterbo here got wind of it some time back, since when I have been trying to have the thing censored but keep coming up against resistance. Someone highly placed seems to want it to go through. This is why I have asked Signor Viterbo to come round here again. 'Do you know who commissioned it?' he asked Viterbo.

The man shrugged and the shrug turned into a shudder. He could have had palsy. 'Excellency,' he pleaded, 'I can't concentrate on anything until I get news of my nephew. I've been going from one Church authority to another looking for help.' His voice shook. 'May I sit down? I'm all in. I don't sleep. Not a wink. You understand I've come to you and am selling out my principles in the hope of a trade, some assurance. But I've been disappointed. People have begun to suspect me. I – it was I, you know, who gave the alarm at the rue le Pelletier. That was at Father Grassi's instigation. It was a risk. I pretended to lose my head, but not everyone believes it. Especially as the police released me too soon. There are spies among your servants. I don't want to be seen coming here, especially if it's all for nothing. I've been threatened. See.' He handed the nuncio a letter. It reminded Prospero of the ones Pellegrino Rossi used to receive. This time though, instead of individual letters or words, a whole chunk of print had been cut out and mounted. He read it with a vague sense of recognition. But of course. It was the *Carbonaros*' oath. 'And if I betray this,' he read, 'may I be cut open from neck to toe and all my blood . . .'

'Were you a *Carbonaro?*' he asked the man.

'No. But they're trying to frighten me. At first it was to stop me testifying, but my testimony wasn't needed. They found enough to convict Orsini at his lodgings. Maybe they even know I've been seeing you. I don't know . . .' He stood up, then sat down again. His mind seemed to whirr like an unhinged mechanism. He was half stunned by panic. 'Meanwhile, Excellencies, my nephew . . .'

'It's the Mortara case,' explained the nuncio to Prospero. Then to Viterbo: 'I can't promise anything. I haven't the power.'

'If we even knew where he was. His mother is half demented. Can you imagine? Seven years old . . .'

'He's well cared for,' said the nuncio. 'What difference could it make where he is unless you're thinking of kidnapping him back!'

Viterbo did not deny that he had thought of this. 'We may make representations to the Emperor.'

'It would only anger the Pope.'

'What have I to lose? Or gain by helping you?'

'You're an exile. You could be granted an amnesty. A passport. You'd be safer back in Bologna than here. All the dangerous men are in exile. Things are quiet in Bologna. They're preparing for carnival and, to show how tranquil the Government is, masks are to be allowed this year.' Talking of masks, said Monsignor Sacconi, he was counting on

335

Viterbo's unmasking the false Orsini and finding out who was behind the appeal to the Emperor. He knew too much not to know that. Why was he holding out?

The Jew stared at his hands. 'I don't know where treachery is any more.'

It was a bit late to worry about that, said Monsignor Sacconi crisply. 'You need our protection. You've already betrayed Orsini. So.' He tilted his chin encouragingly.

Viterbo's face suffered a spasm. 'Well,' he said, wrenched by a shift of mood, 'it looks as if he'll have the last laugh because this letter will do what his bombs could not. It's to be used to mobilise sympathy here in France for a war against Austria.' Viterbo cocked his jaw. 'They say Louis Napoleon is ready to help the Piedmontese take Lombardy and Venetia. After that, can it be long before they take the Pope's state too? That's what's being said in Italian circles here.'

'Rumour?'

'Everything starts as rumour, Excellencies.'

'So who paid for the letter to the Emperor then?'

'My best information,' said Viterbo, 'is that it was written to the Emperor's own specifications.'

Nineteen

That July, Napoleon and Cavour met secretly at a spa and agreed that if Austria could be provoked into declaring war, they would unite to expel her from the Italian peninsula. Piedmont would then take Lombardy and Venetia.

Paris, September 1858

'The constable, Excellency, was shitting his drawers!'

Monsignor Sacconi, the papal nuncio, was discouraged by the sight of the hot face mouthing at him. His guest was a journalist whom he had hoped to sound about a sensitive matter, but Louis Veuillot would clearly choke if he couldn't first get his anecdote off his chest. Letting him finish, His Excellency gazed through high windows to where trees appeared to float in autumn mist. An early frost had yellowed the leaves and drained them of substance so that they glowed like monstrances and hung in ungrounded majesty, dazzling and irritating his eye. Facts were what he had been seeking since Viterbo's disclosures nine months ago.

The summer had been trying. In June, an informer had picked up a hint that something was brewing between the Emperor and the Piedmontese. That was all. The informer then disappeared and His Majesty, as though to tease the nuncio, began chasing around France like a ringing fox. In July he was at a spa in the Vosges, in August in Brittany and now he and his family were in Biarritz. It was hard to know what was afoot, though Sacconi's hopes rose when a man of his managed to suborn the personal maid of H.M.'s favourite, the Comtesse de Castiglione. That, however, came to nothing when the girl was caught spying by fellow-servants, whom one must suppose to be counter-spies. It was all likely to bode ill for the Church which was not popular. The

337

Mortara case was still explosive and for months the nuncio had been walking on eggs.

A remark about this had started his guest on his rigmarole. Perceiving that he was expected to sing for his supper, Veuillot had picked the wrong tune. What His Excellency wanted to know was this: would our Imperial protector let us down? So far, the connection had worked out well: shamefully so, to the minds of yesterday's friends. Royalists, supposing God to be of their own persuasion, spoke of bishops 'blessing a brothel' – by which they meant Imperial France. They could neither see that our chief concern must be the maintenance of the French garrison in Rome nor that we were beholden to Louis Napoleon – 'the new St Louis' – for fighting a war in the Crimea to protect our interests in Palestine. How expect us to drop such an ally? The fear was that *he* might drop *us*.

'Marriages of convenience,' mused the nuncio, 'are prone to adulteries.'

His guest looked surprised.

'The age of faith,' Veuillot's voice drummed in the nuncio's ear, 'is still intact in mountain provinces. Lourdes survives on agriculture and a few rundown hotels which cater to travellers on their way to the spa at Cauterets. Naturally, it yearns to be a spa itself, and the hope is that this new spring . . .'

'Ah,' said the nuncio. 'There's a spring, is there? A spring and a young girl. French visions are all the same.'

'No, no, Excellency!' Stocky and pock-marked, Veuillot had small, restless eyes which made the nuncio think of a creature about to break cover – a boar perhaps? He had strong shoulders and a bristle of fierce hair. 'This one,' he triumphed, 'is different because the civil authorities are playing into our hands!'

Must I humour him? wondered Sacconi. God give me patience, I suppose I must.

The faithful, said the journalist, were forbidden to go to the grotto! The police built a fence, then prosecuted some local women for putting it about that the Emperor had countermanded the order. 'You don't handle people like that. It was asking for trouble.'

Triumphing! Rubbing his hands. Gulping down the nuncio's excellent claret as though it was *pinot*, he confided humorously, 'This is when *I* started to plot. *Une petite intrigue!*'

Veuillot's mouth was as tight as a scar. A cooper's son, recalled Sacconi. If there were scribblers like this in Rome, nobody knew them.

Here in France, though, he was our foremost champion. His bigotry appealed to country priests, though many bishops found it embarrassing and, some years ago, forty-six of them had published a reprimand in an attempt to moderate it. Imagine their shock when a papal encyclical took Veuillot's side – thus bolstering Rome's power and weakening theirs! Mastai's madness had method.

'As I told you, the police prosecuted women for saying that the Emperor had countermanded the grotto's closure. Well, I resolved to make their allegation come true.'

The nuncio was growing interested in spite of himself. 'What about the local bishop? What role did he play?'

'He was playing possum until I woke him up.'

'So you caused a miracle?'

Veuillot tittered. 'Excellency! I think I can claim to have performed one at Lourdes.' His story buzzed with relish, and His Excellency, worried by the imprudence of this rogue fighter, listened.

Veuillot had first gone to Lourdes after reading of the acquittal of the women accused of spreading rumours. As a journalist, his curiosity was piqued. Pausing in the local café, he picked up what gossip he could, then set off in search of three bishops: Auch, Montpellier and Soissons. In short, he organised a conspiracy. The nuncio digested this. Impudent. Directed against the Bishop of Tarbes, the local man who, the nuncio knew, had been judiciously dragging his feet – a sound policy but unsustainable in the face of Veuillot's manoeuvrings. The conspiracy was two-pronged, for Veuillot then inveigled Madame l'Amirale Bruat, the confidante of the pious Empress Eugenie, to join him in forcing the police to let them enter the grotto. – 'At the thought of refusing such fine folk from the court, the constable, Excellency, was shitting his drawers!' – He then followed this up with a five-column article in his paper, *l'Univers*, while the Archbishop of Auch went to see the Emperor at Biarritz and Madame l'Amirale Bruat spoke to the Empress. In short . . .

'The grotto is to be opened?'

Veuillot grinned vengefully. 'And some careers ruined, I hope. Those of the Mayor, the Prefect and one or two others.'

This chilled Monsignor Sacconi. 'You know for a fact that the Emperor is disposed to override the normal procedures?'

'Yes, Excellency.'

Why? wondered the nuncio. Had His Imperial Majesty got a bad conscience? Was he throwing us a sop while preparing to stab us in the back? That would be like him! Or giving us rope?

Meanwhile, this fireball of a journalist was dangerous. Had he finished with the case? Veuillot said he had. But weren't there other visionaries in Lourdes? More girls at the age of puberty?

'Too many,' judged Veuillot. 'Only the first one should be promoted. The others may be hysterics. Besides, the police managed to prove that what *they* took for the Virgin was a stalactite.'

He talked on, but the nuncio had stopped listening. He pitied the Bishop of Tarbes. If the Prefect, Mayor and Inspector of Police really did suffer as a result of all this, Church–State relations would be prickly for some time in the Hautes Pyrénées.

1859–1860

The bargain struck between Sacconi and Viterbo brought neither man luck. Viterbo, fearing a dagger in the ribs from his old confederates, accepted the offer of a passport and returned to Bologna, where, being suspected by both factions, he could get no employment, and had to live off the brother-in-law whose son he had failed to rescue.

Things did not go well for Monsignor Sacconi either, for, by the end of 1858, he was finding it impossible to penetrate the intentions of the French Government. 'We would,' he wrote sorrowfully to Cardinal Antonelli, 'need an army of spies, for lack of which I am become a haruspex and student of straws in the wind.'

Some of these were alarming. The papal state was suddenly infested with returned exiles. Droves of them, arriving from Paris on the pretext of sharing their relatives' New Year's Eve lentils and boiled sausage, must surely be up to something. Piedmont was mobilising and, in an address to its parliament, the King spoke of 'the cry of pain reaching us from so many parts of Italy'. At a January reception in Paris, the Emperor greeted the Austrian Ambassador with a hint that their countries might soon be at war. Cavour was known to be in secret contact with Louis Napoleon's mistress or physician or both and, at the Scala in Milan, when the chorus of Bellini's *Norma* invoked war, the audience sang along under the noses of the Austrian High Command, which was attending the performance. The provocations were impossible to ignore.

Deeply apprehensive, the nuncio obtained an audience with Louis

Napoleon who assured him that there was no need for anxiety. 'Let the Pope know,' said he, 'that he has nothing to fear.'

He had, though, and so had Austria, and in April the blow fell. Piedmont, by goading Austria into a declaration of war, was able to activate its defensive alliance with France, whereupon insurrections broke out all over northern Italy. Agents had been busy and a noose began to tighten around the papal state.

Battles at Magenta and Solferino went against the Austrians.

It looked as though the pope-king's days were numbered when, confounding all expectations, the Emperor's purpose seemed to falter. In July, he proposed an armistice, then made peace with Austria on condition that she hand over Lombardy. Nationalists were stunned and papal choirs prepared their Te Deums in gratitude for the state's salvation.

Events, however, had taken on their own momentum. The withdrawal of Austrian garrisons from the Pope's northern territories had left agitators free to orchestrate plebiscites which resulted in a vote for annexation by Piedmont.

Monsignor Sacconi watched with the divided eye of a man obliged, as a diplomat, to play his part, yet who found welling within him a dark pessimism over the futility of human effort. Facts, by the time he discovered them, had usually ceased to be facts, for the plan elaborated by Cavour and Louis-Napoleon was quickly superseded. Unexpected factors took over – horror of carnage, fear of the Prussians, the plots of wilder and lesser men. Was God's finger on the chessboard? If so, He was in a punishing mood. Autonomously, it seemed, aims shifted and expanded. Tuscan moderates, fearing their own Left, requested annexation by Piedmont. Parma and Emilia wanted the same. Then, in May of 1860 Garibaldi sailed to Sicily with his red shirts and, later, ignoring the armistice, began marching towards Rome from the south. Under cover of heading him off, Cavour's troops promptly invaded from the north. Rome was caught in a pincer grip and now the Emperor made only token efforts to restrain his ally. 'Those who go with ideas whose time has come,' he liked to say, 'prosper. Those who resist them perish.' Clearly the idea of a united Italy struck him as more timely than the temporal power of the Pope.

For once, the Left agreed with him. Garibaldi was an optimists' hero, a living myth. His opponents magnetised anger and, in Paris, a live rat was thrown through Monsignor Sacconi's drawing-room windows and he was villainously caricatured in certain sectors of the press. These, however, were but pinpricks in comparison with the agony of mind he suffered while Rome urged him to discover whether or not its French garrison had orders to defend the Pope's state, city or, failing all else, person. Napoleon had saved the Pope's regime in 1849. Would he abandon it now?

For God's sake, exhorted a stream of telegrams from Cardinal Antonelli's office, find out! Enlighten us! Give us some idea what to expect! Where should we send our own small volunteer force? North? South? What *are* the Emperor's intentions?

Neither by guile nor prayer could the nuncio discover these. Nobody in Paris seemed to be in control. Everywhere he met faces so blank as to seem featureless: white, hallucinative blurs. Nobody at the Ministry of Foreign Affairs knew a thing and, unbelievably, the Emperor had gone on a Mediterranean cruise and could not be reached. On a *cruise?* Yes, Excellency. My God, thought Sacconi, Pontius Pilate never thought of this! For how long? Heads shook and faces appeared to be dissolving like damp soap. Sorry, Excellency. We have no information. Well, what about Monsieur de Thouvenel, the Foreign Minister? *Mille regrets*, Excellence! He did not come into the office today and is not at home either. We don't . . . Tomorrow perhaps? But tomorrow the news was that Monsieur de Thouvenel too had gone on holiday, nobody knew where. A free-thinker's smirk, fleeting and perhaps hallucinatory, seemed to the nuncio to slide from face to face. 'We are not dealing with the matter, Excellency. This office has received no instructions.'

In Rome the French Ambassador had received none either, so Cardinal Antonelli continued to bombard the harried nuncio with panicked appeals. Had Louis Napoleon a secret agreement with the Piedmontese? If so what were its terms? Had he arranged all this with Cavour? Answer. Now. Urgently. *In nomine Dei.*

Sacconi, coming up against walls where once there had been doors, was reminded of Viterbo, the Jew, who had also been isolated and snubbed. He was reminded of him again when he received reports from men sent to listen in the exiles' cafés where the printer had once been at home, for one of the rumours picked up was that Viterbo's efforts on his nephew's behalf had contributed to the shift of French policy. Appallingly, God, or some such ineluctable force as the dawning of an idea in the Emperor's mind, was bent on trying men's spirits. The Pope risked being cast down from his seat because those of low degree could now influence public opinion – a force with which, as the nuncio kept warning his masters in Rome, one must now count.

'The two things Louis Napoleon holds against Pio Nono,' a man in the know told him, 'are his refusal to crown him emperor and the Mortara case. The second is more determining because it made French Catholics unpopular and allowed him to defy them.'

By the time the nuncio discovered the bargain struck between Cavour and the Emperor, it had been outflanked. Piedmont had secured four-fifths of the Pope's territories and, as a broker's fee, given Nice and Savoy to France. Plebiscites had ratified this: *vox populi vox dei*. 'Italy', as Piedmont was now calling itself, needed God and had pressganged Him. Pius, on the grounds that the plebiscites were rigged, excommunicated all who took part in them and ordered that a Brief proclaiming this be displayed on the doors of all basilicas. He wanted it known that, whatever about the Emperor, God did not defect.

In the end, the moral shadow of the anathema was to touch Sacconi too, and Cardinal Antonelli would attract still bitterer blame. Whose fault was it but theirs if the gallant little international force which had volunteered to fight for the Pope was slaughtered at Castelfidardo? Treachery and misinformation, said the mourners, had delivered it to its enemies. Nobody wanted to blame the dead young men, so live older ones were blamed instead: Sacconi, Antonelli, the French Ambassador and General Goyon of the French garrison, who had led the volunteers to think he would come to their aid.

Louis Napoleon, returning from his cruise, found his victims quarrelling among themselves. The French volunteers had been mostly monarchists, so their defeat was a bonus. Moving with an idea whose time had come had proven every bit as profitable as he had hoped, and in March 1861 the kingdom of Italy was proclaimed with Victor Emmanuel as king.

Rome, 1861

'We must be passive,' Cardinal Amandi told Nicola. He spoke dully, for his heart was giving him trouble. Waking in the night, he could hear it boom with the rashness of a flimsy gong. 'We must be seen to be fleeced lambs. Only if shamed will the Catholic Powers intervene to restore what is ours.'

This was now policy. The Powers were to be God's instrument and Rome must wait for them to hear His call. Meanwhile – this was the

343

message with which Nicola was being briefed – France must not be alienated, nor her visionaries let say one word which could inflame an already dolorous situation. Traitor or not, the Emperor was needed!

'I've communicated this to the bishops of Grenoble and Tarbes,' said Amandi. 'If they won't listen I can do no more. My recommendation is that they muzzle those young women.' He spoke gently in his mild, heart-sufferer's voice.

'Local piety ...' Nicola did not bother to finish. It was an old difficulty.

The cardinal laid a testing hand on his heart. 'I've lost my taste for irony', he sighed, 'but failure to recognise it is a weakness, and *the* irony of our time is that loyalty and piety can be vexatious.'

He was thinking of the 'Zouaves', which was the new name for the papal volunteers. These pious adventurers had come to restore the Pope's ravished lands and Romans marvelled idly at their optimism. But the Zouaves were simple souls from places like Ireland and Poland. Hard-drinking and outlandish, they annoyed citizens by singing loud, tuneless, prayerful songs late into the night. Monseigneur de Mérode loved them. But then, he too was a half mythic creature from another age.

And the dreaming Pope had appointed him Pro-Minister of Arms!

'He,' said Amandi, 'does more damage than Garibaldi. His Franco-Belgian contingent is the worst liability of all.'

These – their officers were monarchists to a man – itched to score off the Emperor by undoing the wrong he had done. But there weren't anything like enough Zouaves and only a mad mystic like Mérode would see them as anything but a disruptive sideshow.

Amandi, having sacrificed his own ambitions to Antonelli and supported his polices, was indignant at Mérode's attempts to foil them.

'Is there anything,' Nicola wondered, 'to the story that Mérode hopes to be Cardinal Secretary himself?'

The cardinal took a pinch of snuff. 'There is. But I wouldn't bet on his chances. His Holiness will see sense. Not that Mérode isn't a good man. On the contrary. I stayed with him once and was never more edified or worse fed. He lives like an anchorite and adores practical jokes – even plays them on officers of the imperial garrison! I'm afraid that what's left of this realm is in the hands of a saint and an adolescent.'

'A saint, Eminence? You can't mean the Pope? After his behaviour to you?'

Amandi's heart condition had been brought on by a series of painful scenes with Mastai, whose tantrums had become alarming. Losing his lands had possibly revived his epilepsy. The worst had been when Amandi tried to invervene on behalf of the Mortara boy.

'Shsh!' said Amandi.

This evening Nicola was to take a message to Mérode's friends. It was unofficial but he was to let them know that it came from the Holy Office. The Orleanist faction – Mérode's – was *not* to exploit this girl, Bernadette – what was her name? asked the cardinal.

'Soubirous, Eminence.'

'That's right. She is not to be turned into a Joan of Arc calling for their pretender to be crowned. Let them know we know that the Legitimists tried that with the La Salette girl, and we're warning both groups not to start with Soubirous. She's being carefully watched, you might add. Apart from that, enjoy your evening. You'll eat well anyway. Foreigners keep better tables than our own thrifty aristocracy which,' lamented Amandi, 'imitate the least admirable aspects of the clergy's conduct. All they learned from us is how to make a show and pass the plate.'

'Flavio!'

The duke was being escorted to a distant place at table whence, at intervals during the meal, Nicola was able to catch the swivel of his smile.

'You know him, do you?' A nearby gentleman was wistful. 'If we touch him, do you think some of his good luck will rub off? They say he trebled the fortune he was granted by the *Sacra Rota*.'

'Later,' said Flavio's dumbshow to Nicola. 'We'll talk.'

'Mind you,' the wistful gentleman lowered his voice, 'his luck implies that the *Sacra Rota* erred. *Our* class has used ours up. It's an argument for bastardy. New blood calls to new money!' Don Marcellino laughed without resentment and greeted his food festively. 'Ortolans!' he exclaimed. 'The French do one proud.'

The evening was indeed splendid, for the Orleanist Crusaders – that was their other name for themselves – had rented the *piano nobile* of a palace belonging to one of those Roman princes who had learned their style from the Church. Footmen moved liturgically, and candles blazed like the high altar at Easter.

'Rome,' noted Don Marcellino, 'is already occupied by foreigners. *We* can no longer live like this.' He waved at the room.

Afloat in glitter, it was porous with false perspectives. Surfaces dissolved. Silks rippled. Solidity invited distrust, and the whole was conducive to a belief in the spirit whose creation it was. To be sure, enemies might read it differently! Nicola imagined them arriving to draw up inventories and attach price-tags. It could happen any day. Aware of a constriction in his chest, he let the lady on his left persuade him that Italy, a cobbled-up absurdity, could not hold together another month.

'After all,' she exclaimed, 'the provinces can't even understand each other! Did you know that when the Piedmontese landed in Sicily, the Sicilians thought they were French?'

From down the table, a burst of laughter greeted a sally by Monseigneur de Mérode who was no doubt peddling a like optimism. In a lull, his voice rose with that messroom joviality which shocked the Curia. An English guest had asked about the castrati he had heard sing in the Sistine Chapel.

'There are only four left now,' said Mérode, 'and my musical friends assure me that only the one called Mustafa is worth hearing. I'm told that, not long since, a compatriot of yours, milord, lured him to his lodgings and bribed him to sing. Poor Mustafa was in hot water. They're sacred singers and not for hire.'

'But how exactly – I mean what do you do to . . . create them?' The Englishman was a wispy youth.

'*Mon cher*!' Mérode's laugh was genial. 'That has nothing to do with the Pope's administration. It's a by-product of what your countrymen call private enterprise! Our peasants, you see, raise pigs and also children. Sometimes they leave them together with unfortunate results. Pigs are greedy. *Très vorace*! Are you familiar with the animal? When they bite off vital bits of the children, our choirmasters make use of the victims. From,' Mérode smiled, 'charity'.

'Is it true,' whispered the lady on Nicola's left, 'that Antonelli and Mérode are at daggers drawn?'

'Gossip suggests so.'

'Come, Monsignore!' encouraged Don Marcellino. 'We can be frank among ourselves. The foreigners have ears only for the mitred colonel!' Nodding at Mérode whose voice thrummed rowdily:

'We are more humane than your English dean who suggested that the poor eat their children.'

'But *was* it the cardinal,' the lady wondered, 'who enticed Monseigneur's Crusaders into a trap?'

346

'That was . . .' The young milord's French was deserting him. 'A joke!'

'They say the French Ambassador swore to the cardinal that General Goyon would be bringing 10,000 French troops as reinforcements! So the cardinal passed this on to the Crusaders.'

'A *joke?*' Mérode affected an appalled amazement.

Nicola warmed to him, then remembered that he shouldn't.

'Irony, you know.' The Englishman stammered. 'M-m-meant to be taken the other way round.'

'You mean,' Mérode sounded solicitous, 'that they should *stop* eating their children?'

'Then no reinforcements came.'

'If it was a trap, who,' asked Don Marcellino, 'set it? Napoleon to discredit the Orleanists? Or Antonelli to discredit Mérode? Do we *know* that the French Ambassador made such a promise?'

'Mérode thought so.' The lady's whisper hissed like silk. 'I heard that he accused him to his face of being the faithful lackey of a lying master *and* that the Crusaders' General seized Antonelli by the throat and called *him* a traitor!'

Don Marcellino looked right and left. 'Also,' he lowered his voice, 'that His Holiness's indignation triggered a,' he mouthed silently: 'fit. The battles fought in Rome were as fierce as the one at Castelfidardo!'

'Where,' intoned the lady, 'the flower of Royalist France was cut down! Have you seen the names of the fallen? It's like a list of those attending a levee of Louis XIV!' She closed her eyes, perhaps to savour a vision of the Sun King receiving his shirt from some gentleman whose name knelled for the death of a descendant at Castelfidardo. 'Old France,' she opened them, 'has paid its tribute . . . I think something's happening.' Breaking off, her voice grew brisk. 'A young woman appears to have been taken ill!'

Don Marcellino craned his neck. 'She's with *your* friend,' he told Nicola, who recognised the source of interest as Miss Ella, whose flow of muscle struck him, even at this distance, as scandalous. Rising from the table, she was pulling at her apparently suffocating bodice as though to open it. Remembering what it did and did not contain, he froze. Gentlemen in her vicinity were flapping napkins. She undid a button. Someone called for air.

'Too tightly laced!' judged Don Marcellino. 'Ladies . . .'

Conjuring away scandal, Nicola prayed. 'Let her not faint!' It was mischievous of Flavio to have brought her to a place like this. Brought *him* – as if, wary of mind-readers, he corrected himself: *her*! 'Oh God! I,' he admitted to God, 'should have made them break off the connection long ago. If You spare us a scandal, I'll do it.' And apparently his prayer was answered, for the second bodice button remained unopened and Miss Ella accepted a glass of water. Nicola, to discourage his neighbour's twitter of curiosity, returned to their former topic. 'The list of Frenchmen who died at Castelfidardo,' he told her brutally, 'is short. Austria sent ten times more men than France, and even Ireland sent twice as many!'

The diners now left the table. Flavio walked Nicola to a quiet corner. He was so vivid with good fellowship that it was hard to start reproaching him. But Nicola did.

'How *could* you have brought her here?'

Flavio put a finger to his lips. 'It's all right. I've introduced her as an heiress from Louisiana. See? She's collecting admirers.'

And indeed there was a knot of men around her. Foremost in the knot was the wispy milord.

'I saw your mother. I wrote to you about that. She was afraid you might marry Miss Ella. I suppose that was nonsense.'

Flavio drew him deeper into their alcove. 'Not quite.' It was, he said, an obsession with his companion who, indeed, had been threatening him with a scandal because he would not agree to it.

'What kind of scandal?'

Flavio, looking hangdog, admitted that this varied. Just now, for instance, she might as easily have stripped off her clothes as told her true life story or a false horripilant one. 'She's capable of anything,' he said with admiration. '*I* tell her she's a demigoddess and being a duchess would be a come-down.'

'Is that what you told her this time?'

'No. I held my tongue.' Ruefully: 'To say anything could touch her off. I have plans which a scandal could spoil.'

Gambling, Nicola saw, was the pulse of life to his friend – friend?

'Listen. I know I can't marry Miss Ella if only because you might denounce us . . .'

'*Would* denounce you. I'd have no choice.'

Flavio kept his voice soft. Marriage, he supposed Nicola was going to say, was sacred – but what about the marriage of his own legal parents? How many like that were there in this sacred city? Were *they* not travesties? 'Moreover, Monsignore, you have no right to presume that my relations with Miss Ella are carnal. Supposing I say I want my friend

348

to have a claim to my name and fortune? That I want a blessing on a business arrangement! What would be so unusual about that? The Pope regularly blesses the city's nags and waggons!'

But Flavio's reproaches turned out to be half-hearted – a tribute to a half-shelved indignation. Because the whole thing was probably over anyway. Miss Ella was leaving with her circus on a tour of the Ottoman Empire. 'It may last a year. She'll be dazzling pashas and may settle for one. I'm not irreplaceable. Tonight's little show was – oh, her way of keeping reality mobile and me on the qui vive.'

Nicola was greatly relieved. 'So will she go?'

'Unless I give in.' Flavio drooped. 'How could I give in? Marry her? *Could* I, Monsignore?'

'No.'

'Well, there you are then. She won't stay on any other terms. She and I are both stubborn as mules – and as deprived of posterity. My sister's brood will recover the fortune I took from her. I suppose you'll feel I deserve this?'

Nicola was spared having to reply, by the arrival of their host with a loquacious lady in tow. She, a marquise and a cousin of Monseigneur de Mérode, began to blast the Bonapartes and, more particularly, Plon-Plon, the Emperor's dissolute cousin, whose marriage to poor little Princess Clothilde of Piedmont had sealed last year's thieves' bargain with France.

'King Victor Emmanuel has let everyone down! The Bonapartes have always aimed to marry blue blood and the House of Savoy is one of the oldest in Europe! How *could* he consent to the alliance?'

Old herself, she was a fossil layered in deposts of amber, jet and jade. Her hair, on its scaffolding of combs, could have come from some reliquary and, like relics, her purpose was to put backbone into the faithful.

'Poor little princess. Fifteen years old and offered up like Iphigenia.'

'For wind, marquise?'

'Hot air! Cynics say her father accepted the *mésalliance* for the alliance. A calumny! It was his ministers who made him do it. Minestrone-makers, I call them. That's what ministers are; half-cooks, half-liars! Clerical ones are no better.' Her words rang fearlessly. 'Can you credit this? A priest told His Majesty to his face that it might be a good thing if he were to lose his throne, since a Republic would be so repugnant to the Catholic Power that they might then intervene!'

The old lady looked as though she had cocked a snook at Nicola and, for a moment, there was a glimpse of a flirtatious girl. A spurt of coyness. It was as though, roused by the turn of events, she had been summoning old strategies. In the alliance between throne and altar, the latter was not pulling its weight and this aged tease was here to ginger up the men of God. Some, 'offspring of factors and stewards' – a clear reference to Antonelli – were not to be trusted. 'Blood tells!' She looked at Nicola as though wondering about his. 'Such people have their fortunes to make, whereas we can give our energies to serving our God and our king.'

It was the aristocratic argument in its mouldy nutshell.

'Take Antonelli's brother, the banker,' she invited. 'There's a corrupt...'

Nicola moved off. The Cardinal Secretary might have observers here. Seeing his host momentarily alone, he crossed the room and delivered his message. The host nodded and, for a few minutes, they spoke of neutral matters. Looking back, Nicola saw with surprise that Flavio had managed to reduce the old marquise to attentive silence. When he was next alone, Nicola rejoined him.

'Were you intriguing?'

'Promising to sell her shares.' Flavio grinned. 'Money interests everyone, Monsignore! *She* was ready to think of it as an outward sign of inward grace – as, indeed, people have since they first minted coins with crosses. Do you know that a good fifth of public money here goes into private pockets? That shows that there's no contempt for it at the papal court – only failure to understand how it works!' Flavio's eyes were shining.

'You turn it,' Nicola saw, 'into a sport.'

'Oh, once you risk anything, it becomes a sport. My boyhood was all risk and I miss that – as I'll miss Miss Ella who is risk incarnate. Can you blame me, Monsignore?'

'Yes!' Because you worship the creature rather than the Creator and because it's our mortality which you love. Our flaw, our chancy uncertainties. You revel in our fallen state!'

'How well you understand!' Laughing. Stepping behind Nicola, Flavio whispered warmly in his ear, '*Retro Satana!*' Then: 'Remember that story you told me once about the white stones? When you were a boy? You were investing promises. Competing with reality. You were already a financier, Monsignore!'

Nicola pivoted. 'Are you here to tempt us into dangerous venturings?'

He *was* tempted. Flavio hadn't even said what he was offering, but Nicola could sense the lure of it.

'Money isn't like St Peter's rock, Monsignore. It has to move.' Flavio began to talk of a man who was sweeping old Europe off its feet by teaching aristocrats to raise mortgages on their land and invest the proceeds. So far, the profits were dazzling and this new Midas was the darling of the most impenetrable drawing rooms in Brussels and Paris. More remarkably, he was a Catholic and eager to put his genius at the disposal of the Holy Father.

'You're an emissary from the Golden Calf?'

'In this season of *vaches maigres*, shouldn't you burn a little incense to it?'

The financial wizard's name was Langrand-Dumonceau and he liked horses with stars on their foreheads and collaborators with titles. 'He, like your Crusaders, wants to serve the curia, but offers money rather than blood.'

'A gambler?'

'The Icarus of gamblers. Gambling is *the* greatest adventure as we saw when one of the leading financiers in France came a cropper. Jules Mirès, the railway king, was decorated by the Emperor last September and arrested in February. That quickened our pulses. The sight of worldly glory in quick transit shakes people up. It was Rome's delays, as it happens, which brought him down. He speculated on your railways which then did not get built.'

'Those railways may ruin more than Mirès. Our Treasury is still paying the bills for their construction, though the lands they run through have been lost.'

But Flavio knew this. He knew too that the Pope was floating a loan which was to be managed by the Rothschilds. A pity! Langrand should have been the one. Why must finance always be in the hands of Protestants and Jews? Flavio knew. It was because Catholics kept their money in tobacco jars, or locked in land. But Langrand was at last getting them to invest. 'You should cut your ties with the feudal mummies.' Flavio nodded at the Orleanist guests. 'And then you'll need new allies. Listen.' Nicola did, doubtfully, half resisting, half enjoying this new circus act of Flavio's, who teased and gleamed and dangled silver dreams of railway tracks flung across Ottoman lands and Mexico and, indeed, here. 'We ...' said Flavio, and the mercurial pronoun expanded to embrace the Church Militant.

Prudent, but disliking his own prudence, Nicola wondered whether

351

he was not keeping his imagination in the equivalent of a tobacco jar. Had his work with the visionaries – whom he had *had* to doubt – made him old before his time? Or should Flavio, a more dangerous visionary, be doubted too?

He was talking about how people must be given confidence to lend and how a papal blessing could help mobilise the savings of Catholic shopkeepers, priests and peasants all over Europe. If these were put to work, think of the good it could do. Think of the employment it could give. This had already begun to happen, but if the Church joined forces with the financier the mutual benefit would be enormous. No, no, don't talk of usury or gambling! Or, rather, do! For religion was itself a gamble! Remember Pascal's wager! Well, capitalism too relied on faith.

'And,' Flavio's eyes danced, 'Langrand will give you terms you would get from no infidel banker!' Squeezing Nicola's arm, he said, 'We must arrange how to have you moved to a useful position in the Treasury. The Church has invisible assets – no, I mean the sort negotiable in this world! For instance, this idea of a blessing for Langrand could earn you solid returns. A title or even a medal would cost nothing and secure his devotion.'

As the two went in search of Miss Ella, Nicola felt so atingle that the sight of velvety ladies bent over cards or lazily swaying fans brought him into a new harmony with the agreeably orchestrated scene. Before, he had been watching from outside. Now, he was drawn in.

The harmony was shattered when they found the Englishman with Miss Ella. It was easy to guess what had happened, for Miss Ella's amused smile told them that the boy knew who she was. How much could he know? That she was a circus-rider? This, though it had been indiscreet of Flavio to have passed such a person off as a lady, was no crime. At any moment, to be sure, she might, wilfully, reveal more.

Whinnying with pleasure, the English youth threw back his long equine head. '*Magnifique* Miss Ella!' he cried in school-room French and added that he had gone on three separate nights to watch her perform in Marseilles. Then he invited her to supper and she, asparkle with malice, said, 'Yes'.

Flavio grabbed his friend's arm. 'Wait,' he whispered, 'in the small library.'

So off went Nicola to a room which was clearly not much in use for there were jackdaw feathers in the grate. Here, he began to wonder whether this new turn meant that Flavio would not, now, be able to restore the solvency which the state had achieved on the eve of the

Italian invasion – and then, of course, lost. Measuring his disappointment, he saw that he had begun counting on it. Fool, he chided himself. How count on Flavio who was so unreliable? Or was faith called for? God often did use odd instruments to effect His Will – and manifest His glory. This train of thought was bolstered by what happened when Flavio came in with the now half-cowed English youth, bowed Nicola into an imposing, throne-like chair, and started addressing him as 'Excellency' – a title to which he had no right – with a deference which turned his purple sash and stockings into deceptive props.

Clearly this was aimed at intimidating the young milord who kept nuzzling the air and protesting incomprehensibly about his leg.

'You're pulling it, aren't you?' he pleaded. 'There must be a mistake. *Une erreur!*' The nuzzling, it grew clear, was a wobble and the milord possibly about to weep.

But Flavio assured him that there was no error. The milord had been under observation since leaving England. 'You look surprised? Did your tutors not warn you of the likelihood? Ah well, perhaps they're agents themselves. Your coachman certainly is. Oh indeed. Servants are skilled at collecting evidence of the debauchery of well-born Protestants. We store it, you see. Market forces, my lord. We buy it cheap when young men like you first travel. Later, if you become a public figure – why not, a man of your birth! – why then it could be too expensive to collect. For now, to be sure, we have no desire to create trouble. But sodomy is not a sin His Holiness's government can condone. If it were to become known, we would have to prosecute.'

And so on. The boy went white, bristled, stormed, denied and asked to speak to his host, but, on being told that, if he did so, Mérode, as Minister for Arms, would feel obliged to make the charge official, the young milord gave up the idea. He was very young.

'You're blackmailing me!' he protested.

'Exactly!' said Flavio. 'Did your mother never warn you about papist plots? Always believe your mother, milord.'

Nicola, feeling he had been used enough, moved towards the door.

'His Excellency,' he heard Flavio explain, 'prefers not to take official cognizance of this . . .'

Back in the mirrored hall, churchmen were moving like dark planets around important suns: Mérode, General de la Moricière, ladies in pale spreading dresses and one or two cardinals who were about to leave now that dancing was to begin. Miss Ella too was holding court.

'It's done,' said Flavio, reappearing. 'He's gone to his lodgings under escort and will leave the state tomorrow. He's too frightened to talk to his consul.'

'How did you know he was a sodomite?'

Flavio turned up his palms in the card-sharpers' gesture. 'I gambled.'

'And his coachman? You've lost him his job.'

'I'll take him on. I'm sorry about the deception. I know you didn't like it.'

Walking home, Nicola felt the dim, fungusy streets mime the spiral of his feelings as he circled walled gardens redolent of stagnant water and throbbing with a stridor of crickets. These recalled the fable of the grasshopper and the ant. Rome was full of the one and needed the other – but which was Flavio?

Twenty

There was a moon, and by its glimmer Nicola saw a startled Martelli wake up on a divan. He had had to wait, he explained, because he was leaving in the morning for Turin. Had Nicola got the letter?

'Your man let me in. I sent him to bed.'

Nicola gave him an envelope and his friend slid it into the lining of his boot, then, with the aid of a glue bottle, stuck a leather flap over the insertion. Nicola watched the deft movements with pleasure. 'I'm keeping this as well hidden from my friends as yours,' said Martelli. 'Our National Committee would be gobbling with rage if they knew Turin was in touch with priests. Half of them are mad Masons!' He laughed. 'I sound like *La Civiltà Cattolica*! I fell asleep over its account of factious men, which means you and me, Monsignore. Spleen animates our old teachers. They're beside themselves at the divisions in their ranks.'

Initiatives were indeed erupting in odd places, and men pledged to be staffs in the hand of the ageing Pope had, instead, begun to twitch like broomsticks. Foremost among these was Padre Passaglia. Once Professor of Dogmatics at the Romano and Rome's leading theologian, he had, last year, approached the Pope with a bold proposal. This was that Mastai resign himself to his losses and come to an understanding with the Italian state. There was no theological barrier to such a pact, assured Passaglia, provided it guaranteed the Holy See spiritual independence. For the sake of Catholics whose consciences were on the rack, why not start secret talks, using Passaglia himself as go-between? Turn the other cheek, Holiness, he urged. And Mastai, hearing it put like that, agreed to give the idea a chance.

Unfortunately, the theologian muffed his mission. To the scandal of the Curia, he was seen in Cavour's palace in Turin, and, on being taken for a renegade, for practical purposes, became one. Useless now as an envoy, he could not return to Rome where his presence would embarrass

355

the Pope. At best, as Martelli pointed out, he could become a decoy and distract attention from ourselves who, unknown to him, were taking over his plan. 'Misled by pride, he's still buzzing about.'

Nicola did not like the dig at Passaglia's pride, since for priests to renounce that *now* must look like a betrayal of their kind. He was about to protest but found it hard to stand on dignity with Martelli of whom he was immensely fond.

Raising his boot, Martelli asked, 'What do you suppose is in this? I know it's confidential, but we may surely speculate. I say it's about scudi and that Antonelli wants compensation for the annexed lands. The trouble is that Italian coffers are empty too. The war cleaned us out. So with what are we to pay?'

'Could a great international Catholic financier help?'

'Does such an animal exist?'

'I'm told he does. Why don't your people look into it?'

Martelli nodded. 'He could raise cash for both our masters. Compensation could be paid and the seizure of papal lands condoned.'

'It could lead to peace.'

'And our keeping the dialogue open will have been worthwhile.'

'A lot of people would be against such a peace.' Nicola was restraining his own optimism: 'Garibaldini, the Jesuits, Mérode . . . Why are you for it, Martelli?'

'Logic. Italy is Catholic, so a *modus vivendi* has to be found. Why are you?'

Nicola wondered whether to say that he, like the ex-Professor of Dogmatics, hoped the papacy would grow more spiritual once it no longer needed such worldly pomps as land and possessions. This did seem in keeping with the gospel's message – unless he had got hold of the wrong end of the stick? Padre Passaglia's thought processes were notoriously elusive and, exalting though it might be to think of the Pope renouncing riches, if he needed cash to bring this about, might he not have to welcome in by one door the vain pomps ushered out by the other? Even at the height of his prestige, Passaglia had been thought fond of unsound German ideas which could lead him too far – and perhaps had? They had certainly led him away from Rome.

So Nicola's answer was evasive. 'I'd like all my friends to be able to sit down at one table.'

Martelli clapped him on the shoulder. 'Put down some young wine and let's hope it's drinkable when the day comes. I won't have breakfast with you. I have to find a barber before I leave.'

Nicola walked out with him, then stood a while in the courtyard which gleamed in the moonlight and smelled, since it was Thursday, of the dried cod which had been left there to soak. 'A fish out of water!' he heard himself say and realised that he had been thinking of Passaglia. For where could the eminent theologian now go but out of the Church?

Upstairs, feeling too stirred-up to sleep, he opened Martelli's copy of the *Civiltà Cattolica* and read the piece on Liberal sympathisers. The noblemen among them, said the Jesuit writer, could only be nincompoops. As for Liberals of the middling sort, these were either 'men of letters whose smattering of knowledge has addled their wits, doctors mad to exchange the task of prescribing enemas for the nobler one of running a province or estate managers who fancy that dealing with herders and horse-manure has fitted them for government, plus a mob of idlers who, lacking the means to feed either themselves or their vices, welcome change of any sort. To these join a throng of unruly schoolboys and you'll have the roll call of factious Rome.'

Nicola wondered how then to account for himself.

A peace formula had been worked out. Still secret, it was the fruit of the patient ingenuity of Cardinal Antonelli and Prime Minister Cavour, and its terms were as follows: the Pope would regain sovereignty over his old territories but delegate civil powers to the king who thus became the Vicar's vicar. Anti-Church laws were to be repealed and indemnities paid. The genial simplicity of this and the speed with which it had been agreed surely proved that heaven was helping men of good will to help themselves. Gold had been sent by Cavour to ease the way with minor officials, and agreements reached about compensation to Cardinal Antonelli's family for the losses it must incur, once such monopolies as the bank and railways passed from its control.

Meanwhile, the war party, knowing nothing of all this, was putting its trust in the Zouaves and had kitted them out with with new uniforms consisting of baggy trousers, red cummerbunds and braid frogs, which gave them the look of fanciful figures devised to give interest to paintings of the Colosseum or to advertisements by traders in Turkey rugs.

Those who knew that they need not, after all, depend on these swashbucklers, were able now to see them with a less exasperated eye. It was as though the city were playing charades, for the new plans had emptied the present of reality. Foreign voices, floating from the barracks on warm evenings, added to the feeling of carnival. Songs invoking a sanguinary, but now – God grant! – obsolete, future filled the initiate with a relieved and tremulous joy:

> Oh we'll hang Garibaldi on a high short rope,
> Hang Garibaldi for crimes against the Pope!

Luckily, ordinary Romans, many of whom had an intense admiration for Garibaldi, knew no English and listened as they might have done to zoo creatures when the foreign riffraff took to roaring in Polish or Breton or other barbaric tongues. The French volunteers were better born and their refrain had a ring of the nursery:

> *C'est le bataillon morbleu*
> *Des diables du Bon Dieu!*

Some were as young as sixteen and Pius adored their company. Last spring, his health had been bad and bets laid that he wouldn't last the summer. Cavour was thought to be counting on the Church electing a more accommodating pontiff next time. It stood to reason. If the new peace plan was to work.

Instead, in June, confounding all expectancy, he died himself: a bolt from the blue, for he was only fifty-two.

The hand of God? Or the devil?

'Is there a chance,' Nicola asked Cardinal Amandi, 'that His Holiness will carry on with the peace plan anyway?'

But Amandi had already pleaded for this and got short shrift. 'I kept saying, "*Santità*, can we not repropose the formula? Simply submit it to the new ministry in Turin?" But no. Cavour made a bad death. Ergo everything to do with him is contaminated. He who touches pitch, etc.'

Already the network of communications had been dismantled. Mastai was uncompromising. Contacts must cease. Amandi had been retired from his curial functions; Nicola was to be moved to the Ministry of Finance – Flavio's hand was possibly to be seen here – , and Martelli forbidden to put foot in the shrunken papal state.

Cavour, on his deathbed, had tricked the Church, so neither he nor his works could be trusted. Not even Talleyrand had done anything like this. On the contrary. On *his* deathbed, twenty-three years before, the great tergiversator had made his peace, as always, with the incoming regime which this time was God's. He was, after all, a man of the old stamp. Cavour's free-thinking was more modern and disconcerted Mastai. There was something underhand about his death.

News of it had reached Rome in a telegram from the nuncio, Don Gaetano Tortone, to the effect that the deceased had duly received the last sacraments. This was edifying and the Pope thanked God. Cardinal Antonelli then urged Don Gaetano to make sure that Count Cavour had repented of his crimes against the Holy See. The nuncio discovered that he had not. How, asked the cardinal, could a man under ban of excommunication, have received the sacraments? Back came the reply: Padre Giacomo, a friend of the count's, had taken it upon himself to administer them and was now nowhere to be found.

The scandal was soon plastered across the pages of the Liberal press while, throughout the Catholic world, bishops wondered whether to sanction requiems for the dead prime minister and nuncios' telegrams sought advice from Rome. At last Padre Giacomo reappeared and was summoned to an audience with the Pope, who had persuaded himself that the priest must have been hiding, not from him but from the Liberals, and that it was from fear of their reprisals that he was denying the only possible truth, namely that the dying man had indeed disavowed his godless policies.

But the priest dispelled this illusion. Cavour, fearing to be refused burial in sacred ground, as had happened to a colleague some years before, had laid his plans in advance. Padre Giacomo had promised to shrive him when the time came and had kept his word. That was the long and short of it.

A sacrilegious deathbed confession! Pius couldn't get over it. Had the count no fear of God? Had the priest no fear of *him*? No. Both, it appeared, were at ease with their consciences. Padre Giacomo claimed not to have known that he should ask for a retraction – and, to be sure, many priests were imperfectly acquainted with canon law. But Pius guessed that this ignorance was wilful and, behind the blank face, divined a political thought, namely, that the count had been excommunicated for reasons which were no concern of religion. Temporal reasons! Politics.

Pius was outraged to find the logic of the peace-talks intruding into a spiritual matter. Clearly, the count's motives had not been religious at all. At the very moment when he was about to meet his Maker, Camillo Cavour had been less concerned with God's kingdom than with the one he had made himself. His confession had been designed to validate in the minds of his people his objective of 'a free Church in a free State'.

Coolly and with malice aforethought, he had secularised the sacrament for his own ends.

The old pontiff was stunned.

When Amandi came to plead in favour of continuing the peace-talks, he found him suffering something close to a seizure. The Pope's plump face could, in a swell of indignation, seem as fragile as a paper bag caught up by alien winds. Such winds, Pius now saw, were blowing within the Church itself. For minutes he could hardly speak and his speech, when he did recover it, mumbled in shock at Padre Giacomo's insolence.

Retailing the thing to Amandi, Pius held himself in like a coiled spring, fearfully, husbanding his forces as he now must. For here was how Jansenism trickled into the Church. Protestantism. Indifferentism ... All heresies were linked and he, he whispered, must, somehow, smite them all. Scales had fallen from his eyes. He had been too tolerant before.

Amandi sighed. 'There's no talking to him,' he told Nicola. This being so, he was not sorry to be going to the provinces. He had been given Imola, a diocese in the Kingdom of Italy, and was to live among the Pope's enemies. Well, at least, he was unlikely to be debarred from taking up his duties, as more conservative bishops had been, now that their flocks, as some bitter wit had put it, 'were no longer sheep'.

'What will happen to Padre Giacomo?'

'Suspended. He's a casualty of war. We can't help him. What we can do is take up negotiations again, this time unknown either to Mastai or Antonelli. We can prepare the way for an understanding as soon as the opportunity arises. I can't do it alone.'

Nicola reminded him that *he* was to join the Treasury.

'An excellent place,' said the cardinal delightedly. 'The duke and his emissaries will be coming and going. He's eager to raise a loan for us, isn't he? Well ...' Amandi smiled. 'What better cover could you have?' Then, checking himself: 'Say straight out if you'd rather not help. I shall understand.'

Nicola did not believe he would. People had grown passionate about their strategies and he, who had joined the Church in search of certainty and fellowship, felt continually and painfully torn.

'You should know,' said Amandi, 'that Pius dislikes me now. His last words were: "No doubt you'll do things differently, Eminence, if ever you're in my shoes. For now, though, they're to be done my way!" So if you help me you may be risking your career.'

'I'll help,' said Nicola.

From the diary of Raffaello Lambruschini:

The shrunken state tottered on as best it could. Cardinal Antonelli compared it to a dwarf's body trying to sustain a giant's head, and indeed Rome's needs had swollen, for its ministries were as active as ever and salaries still being paid to hordes of civil servants who had fled from the lost provinces and converged on the capital. What with refugees and plotters and foreign defenders, the city was crammed and the most illustrious asylum-seeker, the deposed King of Naples, was all three in one, like an unholy Trinity. He had come with his court, as if to reclaim the old debt incurred by Papa Mastai when he found shelter with the King's father, Bomba. And he was plotting. Spending a fortune on it. Men in his pay went out regularly to stir up trouble in his and the Pope's lost dominions. But most of these agents were bandits and did the loyalist cause more harm then good.

Meanwhile, counter-plotters wanted Rome for Victor Emmanuel, to whom an address on the occasion of his coronation as Italy's first king was stealthily circulating. It begged: 'Sire, if a nation has a right to choose its capital . . . Rome cannnot be denied to Italy. Rome awaits you, sire; she opens her arms to you and calls for your flag, the flag of Italy, to fly over the Campidoglio.'

Father Passaglia had written it. Through living in Turin, he had lost touch with Rome – but had the illustrious philosopher ever known ordinary folk anywhere? – and supposed citizens would sign it. Few did. On the other hand, the papal police could not get their hands on a copy. Neither signing nor squealing, the *populus romanus* was lying low.

Cardinal Amandi had driven north to his diocese, in a convoy of drabbed-down carriages from which the red bits had been painted out and the panel crests removed.

Back in Rome, Nicola tidied His Eminence's affairs and received visits on his behalf. One was from a man whose finger-nails were as black as his cassock. *Il Canonico* Reali was in mourning for many things – including perhaps his sanity.

'It's over!' These were his first words on being introduced into the drawing room. '*Non possumus* is the watchword from now on. We – that's to say Pius – can't and won't budge! No argument. *Finis!*'

He was dripping sweat. 'What's that opera of Signor Verdi's?' he asked. '*Un Ballo in Maschera*! That's what we're all in. Dancing to *his* tune.' The canon's mouth slid sideways and one saw that this *tic douloureux* was the ghost of a habitual smile. He was – no, *had* been, and the correction set off the rictus once again – a canon of the order of the *Canonici Lateranensi* but had been expelled, and news of this had been prematurely published in the *Gazzetta Officiale*, which was a violation of the rights of canons!

'Hihih!' The ex-canon's mirthless whinny skirled and he wiped foam from the corners of his lips. He had heard that the thing had been done at the Pope's personal behest!

'Forgive me. I should have introduced myself: Don Eusebio Reali at your service. Forgive my emotion. I've had a shock. May I sit down? If you'll bear with me, I'll disarm your distrust. You see before you a loyal Catholic. Sincere, obedient, I submit my judgment to that of the Head of our Church. With the docility and humility of a son! Yes. I assure you that I do, when it is his judgment, Monsignore! His! But how can I believe it to be that when he speaks in the accents of that foul rag? You know the one I mean? Of course you do! For twelve years the compilers of the *Civiltà Cattolica* have been exploiting the majesty of the Supreme Pastor for the benefit of their own clique. I show this in my book which is now to be put on the Index. I've been warned in confidence by a clerk. Only the lowly know things in today's Rome. One has to crawl on one's belly to lick up news. Keep one's ear to the ground. Nuzzle in muck! And the muck is rising, Monsignore! It's rising! Adam was made from clay. And when Christ's Vicar turns religious questions into personal ones, he ceases to be the Vicar and reverts to being the man of mud!'

The canon apologised, sweated, coughed and accepted a glass of water. No, thank you. Nothing more. Sorry, Monsignore. He knew what a wretched figure he was cutting – but who was to blame? His persecutors. The Jesuit clique. Cardinal Amandi would vouch for him. Reali would have come to *him* if he had been here. As it was, knowing Monsignore's friendship for His Eminence, he had taken the liberty of throwing himself on his mercy.

He produced a document issued by the Congregation of Bishops and Regulars stating that as he, Eusebio Reali, had returned to his vomit, the Pope felt obliged to isolate the mangy sheep – *ovem morbidam* – from his fellows.

The words 'vomit' and 'mangy' incensed the ex-canon who explained that his 'vomit' was Liberalism and the return to it the publication of his book, *Freedom of Conscience with Regard to the Temporal Power of the Pope*. Now that one Congregation had stripped him of immunity and privileges, another, that of the Index, was about to condemn his 'vomit'.

Reali bent towards Nicola so that his breath revealed the labouring anguish of his insides.

'The truth is, Monsignore, that the Ultras don't trust the Pope and are trying to get him to alienate Liberal opinion. Then he will have nowhere to turn but to them!' To Nicola's relief, he leaned away and confided that Padre Passaglia's work on the same topic was under the same threat. Indeed – Reali had this from an impeccable source – it was to be condemned as anonymous so as to deny its author the right to self-defence conceded by *Sollicita ac* of Pope Benedict XIV's Bull, *Provida*. Why? Simply and solely because, as all Rome knew, no theologian could get the better of Passaglia, so none dare face him! Reali laughed bitterly. See what we had come to! Again he leaned forward.

Cardinal d'Andrea was Cardinal Prefect of the Congregation and Monsignor Stanga a consultor. Would Monsignor Nicola solicit their good offices? Put in a good word?

Nicola's first thought was, This man has been sent to trap me into an indiscretion! Then he felt ungenerous. Then, once more suspicious. He said he would need to think about this. Reali, looking knowing, said he understood.

Leaving, he paused in the doorway. 'People will ask whether it is wrong to try to reform our house when it's under attack. But, if we don't, is it worth saving?' He wiped his face with a red check handkerchief which seemed to have been wrung out and re-used. Then his fist closed tremulously on the cloth which, for a moment, had the look of something live. When he had gone, a whiff lingered as if he had been dossing down in insalubrious places.

Distaste drove Nicola to help Reali. Also pity, since the ex-canon would probably antagonise most of those to whom he made his appeal. Could Passaglia too be like this? Rabid and a little mad? It seemed unthinkable – yet, the theologian, who had begun as a conciliator, was now a propagandist for our enemies. Why? Could it be that men without roots become magnetised by whatever factional flotsam came their way? The thought was alarming and meant that, nowadays, the risk on leaving the fold was not of being eaten by wolves but of becoming one.

Cardinal d'Andrea proved receptive to Nicola's appeal. He was an impetuous man and, on this account, thought dangerous to know, for he talked too openly, being a relic from the days when great aristocrats had been a law unto themselves. Also, as a southerner, he lacked that sly, affable, two-faced Roman caution.

Son of a marquis who had been Finance Minister to the Royal House of Naples, His Eminence had the genial vivacity of a man who, after being educated in France, had received the red hat at forty – eight years ago now. He assured Nicola that he would do anything he could to remove the blinkers from the droves of clerical mules and donkeys surrounding the Holy Father. Men who stood on their own two feet were a rarity and needed protecting. He was ready to resign from the *Congregatio Indicis* rather than condemn Passaglia. Reali too, though a less likeable figure, deserved support.

'We are not monks,' said His Eminence, 'so preaching monastic humility at us is hypocritical. If the Curia wants power, which it does, then it must try to understand it. Ergo, it must tolerate some freedom of debate. I don't say Reali is right, only that he should be *heard*. He's not turning the other cheek – but then the Holy Father doesn't set us an example of humble pacifism, does he?'

The cardinal said all this in loud, easy tones, taking no notice of his own footmen who stood, as if carved, here and there in the suite of saloons through which he chose to reaccompany Nicola. 'I'm told H.H. has had a vision of St Philomena. That may explain why the Holy Spirit is failing to make itself heard! Too much traffic in the holy head, eh?

I'm glad,' he said with amiable condescension, 'that you came to see me.'

Prospero was less glad. His smile was forbearing. Nothing I say can be new to you, reproached the smile, and it is tedious of you to make me say it. At the same time, it delivered a quite opposite message, which one would miss if one were to close one's eyes. The glow of Prospero's charm led people to ascribe to him a cordiality which was in fact in *them*. It was their response to his good looks. He began to lecture Nicola about corporate loyalty to the Temporal Power.

'But if it's nearly gone, surely one must deal with reality?'

'One must deal with principle. I cannot be a party to an act alienating something for which I am answerable to another.'

'Do you mean God?' Nicola grew exasperated. 'Don't you see that you've made something mystic out of property? The Temporal Power is becoming the Eighth Sacrament!' He shouldn't have said it. Unlike Cardinal d'Andrea, Prospero was affected by words. Once said, they became hard, irreducible things and got between you and him for whom the word really was made flesh – or something which chafed the flesh, like a burr! He went cold now and bitter, so that Nicola was provoked to say worse and ended by shouting that, though Christ, by dying for us all, had made us spiritual equals, Pius was behaving towards men like Passaglia, with a feudal arrogance. 'That's the outcome of the Temporal Power!'

'You're shouting. You could be heard.'

'Yes. I'm sorry,' said Nicola, but knew that this would not mollify Prospero. 'It's not Passaglia's fault that I shouted,' he pleaded. 'All he wants is freedom to speak his mind.'

'But see how pernicious freedom is!' triumphed Prospero. 'The faithful have a right to be protected against errors which could make them lose their souls. *You* need protecting from them. Don't mock!' he raged, for Nicola was laughing. But it was only because his friend looked heroic when he grew heated and this amused him. Here was Prospero, a prig and a pillar of righteousness, benefiting from the chance fact that legions of painted – then widely copied – St Sebastians and Stephens and Aloysius Gonzagas and Christs had been endowed with his particular cast of North Italian features, pallor and fair hair. These, as a result, evoked aesthetic suffering, and it was likely that the faithful, who all over the world were now being urged to contribute to St Peter's Pence and succour the 'martyred pope', pictured him as looking like Prospero.

Whereas, in reality, thought Nicola, martyrdom must often have reduced people to the sweaty ignominy of the ex-canon Reali on whose behalf he now made a last appeal.

'All I ask is for your Congregation to hold its hand a while.'

'I'm only a consultant.'

'The Cardinal Prefect is sympathetic.'

Prospero's jaw tightened and Nicola remembered, too late, that d'Andrea, being bound by an oath of secrecy, should not have told him this. He began trying to repair any damage he might have done, and when Prospero interrupted him, forced himself to listen submissively while his friend excoriated and blamed the wrong cardinal. Amandi, for some reason, drew his wrath. Did Nicola know that he, because of his culpable laxness, had been Cavour's choice as the next pope? 'It's no recommendation! And I say that, even though he's a cousin of mine!'

This, opined Prospero, was a time when personal ties should be set aside. 'Even if he were your father . . .' he told Nicola, who saw that he was being told that, in Prospero's opinion, Amandi *was*. Although the notion was not new, it upset him in ways he hadn't time to disentangle for – the St Sebastian now was himself – a multiplicity of arrowy reproaches were contained in it, among them the charge that he was loyal to a man rather than to the Church and hoping to benefit from Amandi's possibly being the next pope. This, said Prospero, was being predicted in the more knowing sacristies of the city. Such talk was close to criminal. Consider the implications for the present pontiff's safety! And Prospero recalled how two cardinals tipped for the succession – the conservative, Della Genga, and the Liberal, Santucci, had died suddenly, one from apoplexy and the other from a heart attack. He interpreted this to mean that someone was clearing the way for a still more Liberal candidate which – given that both had in fact met their end after, and possibly as a result of, fierce scoldings by the choleric Mastai – made no sense to Nicola. However, he did not argue. Instead, for the sake of Passaglia, d'Andrea and Reali, he kept his temper, let the exchange simmer down and, not wishing to leave on a sour note, asked after Prospero's father.

'How is he?'

'As irresponsible as ever,' he was told. 'Pleased with the new regime. So is my brother. I doubt though that they'll like the new royal taxes. They're much heavier than the papal ones.'

*

Nicola's forbearance turned out to have done little good for, though Cardinal d'Andrea resigned in protest from the Congregation of the Index, Passaglia's and Reali's books were then condemned and when Passaglia, who had returned to Rome in the – vain – hope of being allowed to defend himself, refused to submit to the decree, Mastai called him 'an impious traitor'. Friends advised the ex-Jesuit to flee before an order for his arrest could be issued. Miss Foljambe, with whom he had been staying, got him a herdsman's clothes and members of the National Committee smuggled him out in the early hours of the morning. Accounts of this event varied, the more lurid claiming that he was wheeled out in a barrow under cover of a malodorous load of cat meat.

Unable to side wholeheartedly with either the Curia or the nationalists, Nicola envied those who could. Old clerical Rome now seemed the weaker party, so how betray it? He felt an anguished pity for his fellows, knowing that sooner or later, if there was no conciliation, there must be another siege. Walking in the city, he sometimes found himself touching the rough stone of an old palace and thinking how easily it could be reduced to rubble.

1862

Truth's True Friend, a paper which advised Roman families of the better sort to take out three subscriptions – one each for drawing room, kitchen and stables – had begun challenging its readers to think for themselves: a novel notion but necessary, now that the tides of modern mendacity were upon us. It was their duty, said the paper, to learn to distinguish truth from sophisms. For example, Rome was the Capital of Christendom, a proud title. Did they want to trade it for that of a trumpery kingdom like Italy? They should also reflect on the fact that the Catholic world embraced 200 million souls who expected its head to be an independent sovereign.

'So we're to be sacrificed to the 200 million, is that it?' asked a gentleman in the Caffè Nuovo, at a time when it was full of customers come in to escape the bone-chilling tramontana which had been raking the Corso all day. Consuming warm alcohol in the hope of thawing themselves out, they must have grown befuddled for, afterwards, none of them could recall who it was who said that the best use for the current copy of the *Friend*, the one containing the Pope's latest speech, was to use it to clean his bum. Perhaps more than one person said so? A police spy reported as much, but the men he named had witnesses to prove that they had been elsewhere that afternoon and the gentleman who lowered his trousers to suit his actions to his words was apparently a stranger and quite unknown.

Bystanders admitted that they had seen him bare his bum. Indeed, they told the police, they had been so mesmerised by the impropriety of it there in the middle of a decent café that they had failed to notice the face going with it. That would not have been visible at the crucial moment and, later, in the disturbance, both disappeared.

Anyway, a face, *Signor Direttore*, is a normal thing in a café. What struck us all was the bum. What was it like? Oh, no distinguishing marks! Quite ordinary. Neither fat nor thin. Speaking with respect, it was a bum like yours or mine.

The manager had not witnessed the incident and, though interrogated at length, was unable to shed light on the matter. He was fined and given a warning.

Nicola, who was shortly to be posted to the Treasury, listened, like everyone else, to the rumours which are the small change of history. The city, though livelier, had altered little since his boyhood. It was now gaslit and crowded, being filled with French officers with bright epaulets and spurs, befrogged Zouaves and Neapolitans from the exiled Bourbon court. In essence, though, it was as he had always known it: lazy, grimy and as vibrant with rumour as a great boarding-school. It was also riddled with spies. The French military police were watching the pro-Austrian faction, and the papal police the pro-Italian one – which had now split – and both, as happens with fishermen, found a lot of useless game in their nets.

'You,' Prospero warned Nicola when they met at a ceremony at the Minerva Church, 'figure in one of the recent police bulletins about the day's events. These are submitted to Cardinal Antonelli, but also to Monsignor de Mérode who has won the loyalty of the Director General of Police. I expect you to keep your own counsel about my mentioning this.'

'Why do I figure there?'

'Because of the duke.'

'Flavio?'

'Yes. They're watching him.'

Prospero said no more. He was close to Mérode, with whom he had once nursed cholera victims during an epidemic, and was informed about a great range of matters including the burning topic of the day, which was Mérode's rivalry with Antonelli, whose office the Arms Minister coveted with an openness which aroused – well, truthfully, what it aroused was hope. The Cardinal Secretary had been in power for a dozen years. Promotion at the bottom of a hierarchy can depend on shift at the top, so the prospect of a change heartened those whose careers might otherwise remain stuck.

For the moment, the Arms Minister's army was tiny but, in his mind, theirs was a mystic mission and a challenge to God to help them help His cause. To keep their battle-will alive, Mérode wanted a larger share of the state's military budget but, as most of this had been allocated to the garrison provided by the French Emperor, the hard-pressed, papal Finance Council refused to disburse.

Mérode's response was to run up bills and by this means he had managed to build his men a barracks, a hospital and schools for their children. His colleagues fumed, but a man ready to bully God and Mammon – incarnate in the Finance Council – is hard to gainsay. As he saw it, a holy war was in progress so, like an officer in the field, he commandeered.

In the process, illustrious feathers were ruffled and the murmur grew that his hostility towards the French garrison, which was defending this state, disqualified him from ever governing it. He failed to sense this and soon observers were relishing the spectacle of a man frantically scaling the heights of an ambition from whence he must, at any moment, fall. His ladder was not grounded in firm reality. He was reaching madly for the moon and became widely known as 'the lunatic'.

Opinion, however, was not steadfast. Waverers were heard to say that one man's lunatic was another's saint. Moreover, Mérode was congenial to the Pope, so in the end a party of key prelates, including Monsignor Matteucci, the Director General of the Police, threw in their lot with him.

This fresh factionalism was soon spreading an unease which was compounded by the roughness of Mérode's manners. He had learned them as a captain in the French campaign in North Africa – where he should perhaps have stayed. If he had, his prowess among the untrammelled adventurings of a colonial war might have led to a crop of statues of le Colonel or even – why not? – le Général Mérode gracing French municipal parks.

Instead, he had come here to engage in what he conceived of as a nobler struggle and had enticed his old commanding officer to follow him. General de la Moricière, the hero and 'captor of Abed el-Kader', was now training Zouaves and struggling with skinflint papal bureaucrats. If only for *his* sake, Mérode felt it incumbent on him to do as Romans did, namely intrigue.

That anyway was the gossip which reached Nicola while he awaited his posting to the Treasury – a ministry directly under the control of Mérode's rival, Cardinal Antonelli.

The gossip was fuelled by reports of the practical jokes, some tasteless and one featuring rats, which the Minister had played on officers of the Imperial garrison. Such pranks were not peculiar to him. Others, it transpired, could put them to more sinister use.

In February 1862, several European monarchs and other prominent persons received through the post packets of lewd photographs of the ex-Queen of Naples who was living with her deposed husband in Rome. Since the papal police knew the ex-king to be trying to destabilise the regime which had ousted him, their suspicions fell on men who supported it and on whom they already had an eye. Sure enough, it soon came out that the so-called Action Committe had commissioned a certain Signor Diotallevi to fabricate the images by attaching a likeness of the queen's head to that of a nude body belonging, they guessed, either to a woman of ill fame or to the photographer's own wife.

The incident caught the imagination of the city's preachers. Father Grassi was particularly struck by the role played by science, which rationalists often aimed to substitute for faith as a path to truth. Science, they claimed, could not lie! And yet – Grassi's eyebrows knitted passionately as he leaned from his pulpit – without Monsieur Daguerre's photographic process, could this slanderous chimera have had the impact that it had?

'Who have we here?' he demanded. '*Chi? Chi?*' And his voice shrilled like an owl's. 'We have a Chimera!' Modern thought was just such a fire-breathing monster as the Chimera with her lion's head, goatish body and serpent's tail! 'Alas, dearly beloved!' he mourned, 'for what have we exchanged our precious birthright of faith?' Over and over, during a series of Lenten sermons, he brought his congregation to tears by describing how the young queen's beauty and innocence had been demeaned by the instruments of modernity. The camera was Lucifer's gift.

Cardinal Amandi too had been sent the photographs, and Nicola came on them while sorting a bundle of his post. The lard-pale body disturbed him. Its lewd poses were ridiculous and compared, say, with Miss Ella's, upsettingly clumsy. Its nakedness – he had so rarely seen nakedness – seemed unnatural, a violation and, like the flayed carcasses at San Eustachio, evoked butchery. The navel was like the gouged eye of a peeled potato. What was shown here was a misused lump of matter which haunted his mind. There was a familiarity to it too and though, at first, he thought this traceable to some painting of a martyrdom, discomfort led in the end to a personal memory, Maria.

Did this body resemble hers? He could not have said. It was older – but then so would hers be now. He burned the photographs, but a memory of them oozed back and stole the substance of everything white, so that milk, mashed parsnips, paper, pasta, clouds and linen altar-cloths took on a protean tendency to form themselves into contorted hunks of thigh or buttock. Anxiously, he consulted his confessor, who asked if he was relishing this and, when told that, on the contrary, it was a torment, said that there was no sin here. Maybe not, said Nicola, but there was anguish.

'It's a cross, then,' said the confessor comfortably. 'Bear it.'

Bearing it, Nicola walked through churches, looking at marble and canvas flesh, in the hope of matching up the limbs which had begun to haunt him, and so leaving them behind with those which grateful supplicants donated in the form of silver simulacra of hearts, livers, lungs, legs and other parts which specialised saints had cured of their disorders.

Could Maria be the photographer's wife? Signora Diotallevi? Or the loose woman whom the Diotallevi couple swore had come for one sitting and then disappeared into the city's underworld? Nicola decided against trying to find out.

Once he had so decided, the pale image ceased pursuing him, or did so only intermittently, as it must be doing with half the men in Rome while the judicial inquiry continued to dig up facts. Costanza Diotallevi had a past. As the mistress of an aide-de-camp to General Goyon, Commander of the French garrison, she had spied both for the French and for the Action Committee and now, to obtain a pardon, was ready to reveal what she knew about both.

When it became known that a deal had been struck and that she was working for Monsignor de Mérode, a shudder of anxiety rippled through the town. *He* was thought to be short on scruple and *she* was unlikely to stick to the truth.

Meanwhile, at the Secretariat of State, Cardinal Antonelli plodded manfully on with his labours, ignoring his rival's manoeuvres and, presumably, biding his time. Security, diplomacy, finance and foreign affairs engaged his energies. Son and grandson of men who had amassed a fortune through their own industry, the cardinal had an impressive appetite for work and figures. Eschewing balls and *conversazioni*, he rarely took a holiday but, unlike the slovenly Mérode, was known for the elegance of his dress and carriages. He had alluring dark eyes and, in the privacy of his own palace, permitted himself to soothe and refresh them by revelling in choice collections of antiques, flowers and precious stones. Here too he received visits from great ladies who were enthralled by the ambiguity of his status – the cardinal was a layman – and whose appeal for him was, assured his friends, of the same chaste, aesthetic order as that of his hot-house flowers. Perhaps. Perhaps not. The Italian press laid bastards at his door, but Romans found as much piquancy in the perception that his role in his twelve-year association with Mastai was that of a woman. Pius, who was wilful, took decisions and Antonelli, who was ingenious, had often to repair the damage incurred. Like the good wife in old manuals of husbandry, he managed the economy as well as could be done without reforming it, which meant that the cleverer of the two men was condemned to continual improvisation.

Nicola's appointment had come through and he was now at the Treasury, where he spent his first weeks learning the ropes under the benevolent direction of a hierarchy at whose apex was Monsignor Ferrari, the Finance Minister, with whom he had few dealings at first. Then, one morning, he was told to go to Ferrari's office.

When he came in, the Treasurer rose, walked around his desk, removed his spectacles and stared at him. Monsignor Ferrari had a reputation for caution. When he put back the spectacles, his eyes seemed to press against the glass like blunt-nosed fish.

'His Eminence wants to see you?'

'Cardinal Antonelli?'

Ferrari's chin sank so that Nicola could see nothing of him but an entanglement of eyebrows. 'I must warn you that you have been named in the Democratic press.' The Treasurer's mouth shot forward, then closed like that of a draw-string purse. Centripetal wrinkles met in a knot. He handed Nicola a copy of a paper called *Roma O Morte*, in which a letter to the editor had been circled in ink. It was, said Ferrari, a clandestine publication.

Nicola took it and the word 'clandestine' triggered a fear that his more tormenting fancies had somehow oozed from his head. He almost expected to see the name 'Maria' in the swimming print.

'Read it.'

He made an effort and the print steadied. Signed 'Indignant patriot from Subiaco', the letter informed the editor that Marco Minghetti, a minister in the Turin Cabinet, was secretly corresponding with priests in Rome. 'Indignant patriot' warned the minister that he would no more be a match now for priestly perfidy than he had been in 1848, when, as one of the first lay politicians to try working with Pio Nono, he had been bamboozled, double-crossed and led by the nose. The letter named Monsignor Nicola Santi as one of the priests. Ah, thought Nicola, and his heart lurched a second time. Politics! He longed to be clear of them.

Monsignor Ferrari took back the paper, put it in a drawer and turned the key. 'His Eminence fears that forces hostile to himself could be planning to make something of this. Since you are now a dependant of his, it could be a repetition of the Fausti case.'

Nicola felt a chill.

Fausti, a childhood friend of Cardinal Antonelli's and a member of his household, was serving a twenty-year sentence on an implausible charge, and many believed his innocence to be the reason for his conviction. He had always been a fanatical supporter of the papacy, yet when Costanza Diotallevi accused him of plotting against it, he was arrested and Monsignori Pila and Matteucci – respectively Minister for Justice and Director of Police – rigged a trial designed to strike terror into the cardinal's camp by displaying their own power and the erosion of his. Their tactic had worked too, for His Eminence made no move to save his friend.

The Treasurer's knuckles were the colour of milk. La Diotallevi's proofs had been arrogantly flimsy. To be sure, her accusations were backed up by compromising papers found in envelopes addressed to Signor Fausti. But this proved nothing, since plotters regularly put respected names on their missives in case their courier was stopped by the police. Normally, the outer wrapping was discarded before reaching their addressee. The fact that this had not been done in Fausti's case was proof of the intention to discredit him. Indeed, the police had probably concocted the letters in the first place.

'They're vermin!' whispered Ferrari. Emotion – a novelty? – and

373

solidarity with Fausti were carrying him away. Mérode had perhaps overreached himself, for how, *now*, could the most ardent papist feel safe? And why, feeling unsafe, should he be loyal? 'I'm assuming there's no truth in this story either.' Monsignor Ferrari indicated the closed drawer. 'Go and see the cardinal.'

Nicola lingered. 'Surely Monsignor de Mérode himself would not collaborate on such a scheme?'

Ferrari shrugged. 'He needn't know! Pila and Matteucci . . .'

'I see.'

'Besides' – Ferrari's breath was so close that Nicola was breathing it in – 'soldiers, being absolutists, can lack scruple. His Eminence, thank God, deals in the relative. My experience,' Ferrari, breathing hotly, conveyed wisdom in the ardent manner of the Holy Spirit, 'is that, compared with our colleagues in – to take an example – the Holy Office, we in the Treasury are honesty itself. Keeping accounts is a salutary exercise. Why do you think Justice carries a scale?'

Cardinal Antonelli's apartment in the Vatican was above the Pope's, and Pius was known to amuse himself by invoking 'the one above', to the bewilderment of hearers who could not tell whether he meant God or Antonelli. '*He* decides,' Pius would add, compounding their confusion and, if his visitors were supporters of Monsignor de Mérode, pique. He did this with a jocular slyness aimed at shuffling off responsibility for unpopular measures, and had been so successful that the image of an unworldly pope being misled by a wicked Antonelli had wide currency.

'Don't believe it!' Amandi had often told Nicola. 'Taking the blame is one of Antonelli's duties.'

This, he had argued, was why he and Nicola should take some of the burden off the Cardinal Secretary by secretly resuming the correspondence which had been let lapse after Cavour's death.

Nicola, who had expected to be kept waiting, was instead introduced so quickly into Antonelli's presence that he had no time to settle his countenance. The apartment was simple – four rooms – because the cardinal had his own palace elsewhere, but no doubt also because a fine simplicity spoke in his favour.

'Monsignor Santi.'

His Eminence's tone gave nothing away and Nicola, kneeling to kiss the proffered ring, was unable to check his superior's face for ambushed bad feeling. Raising his head, he met a large-eyed, level gaze. Before the ring-kissing, the cardinal had been tending a potted orchid. Returning to it with a graceful movement, he invited his guest to consider the flower.

'Frail!' he pronounced. 'Exquisite but frail! I raise them in my own palace and sometimes bring one here to keep me company, but they don't survive well. Sit down, Monsignore.' The cardinal sat. 'Is what that rag says true?' Then, as Nicola hesitated: 'We can't wait for Cardinal Amandi's *nihil obstat* to your avowals. We must trust each other. Shall I take silence for consent?'

He knows, thought Nicola. He must. Amandi had guessed that Antonelli would want a channel kept open for eventual use or denial, according to how things would turn out. Indeed, how could their activities have escaped detection by the spy-network which, having once extended over the whole state, must now be as tight-meshed as a shrunken sock?

'I think Your Eminence already knows. I forwarded letters. I doubt if there was much in them. We were a means waiting to be used; a bridge. I believe our contacts in Turin felt the same way.'

'A floating bridge? Disconnected at both ends?' The cardinal held Nicola's gaze for a moment, then appeared to make up his mind. 'Very well,' he said briskly. 'But now it must be sunk. Scuttled. Understood? We shall deny it ever existed and so, I imagine, will Turin. *Roma O Morte*, luckily, enjoys little credibility and, the better to give its story the lie, your move to the Treasury must be seen as a promotion. Officially, you will be second-in-command to Monsignor Ferrari. In reality, your responsibility will be limited and you are to take no secret initiatives. Can I trust you?'

'Absolutely, Eminence.'

Nicola felt remiss, forgiven, deeply grateful and somehow possessed by the cardinal whose physical presence was powerful and impressive. Dressed as a cleric – and very elegantly so: his cape and soutane were beautifully tailored – he had an extra animal charge, due either to the rampancy of unconsecrated flesh or the natural cast of his features which were bulky, a little African, but even and strong.

To finish with the scandal, said the cardinal, it was true that, from time to time, we were obliged to make use of secret channels of communication with Italy – if only to discuss such matters as vacant dioceses. Every third one in the kingdom was vacant. Flocks could not be left without pastors. We *had* to negotiate. At the same time, we must not give our French defender any pretext for abandoning us. 'Rome,' said the cardinal, 'is like a raped woman. She must not be seen to have any understanding with the rapist. It follows that a go-between who is unmasked must either be denied – like Padre Passaglia – or, as is possible in your case, whitewashed. *You* are lucky and so owe us extra loyalty!' The cardinal looked keenly at Nicola. 'Yes? Yes. So now you will be working for a near-landless Church whose lifeblood is real money. You and Monsignor Ferrari must try and get your hands on some. I say 'real' because your task will be to assess very coolly the promises of this Belgian financier, for whom your friend, Duke Cesarini, is working.' Antonelli's eye was vigilant and disabused. 'You should know that we normally prefer *not* to deal with Catholic saviours whose enthusiasm can be detrimental to their business sense. Monsieur Langrand-Dumonceau is far from being the first to propose his services. The reason why we may be obliged to turn to him is that the Rothschilds, with whom we have dealt satisfactorily until now, have begun making unacceptable political demands. Are you a practical man, Monsignor Santi?'

'I seem not to be.'

'Self-abasement,' said the cardinal a touch brusquely, 'is not useful in human relations. Keep it for those you have with God. You made a mistake – you or Minghetti. That means that one of you has a false friend or confessor. Beware of both from now on.'

And, said His Eminence, bear in mind that this state's current annual deficit was about thirty million francs and the national debt alarming. The Treasury was planning to float a new fifty-million-franc loan like the one the Rothschilds had floated for us in 1860. '*They* sold thirty-six million bonds at par and fourteen million at 77.5. We shall expect our Catholic financier to do at least as well. What you must ensure is that he helps us rather than himself, and God rather than Mammon. Be assured that he will express great piety, which the Rothschilds, thank God, spared us, while thinking of his profit. Be alert. Be suspicious. Remember that we are short of time and that if he can buy us some, anything may happen. The kingdom of Italy may collapse and God put an end to our trials.'

Nicola left the room in a state of exalted and exhilarating loyalty which, it seemed to him now, was something he had always wanted to feel. And as Amandi too admired Antonelli, there was no conflict.

Twenty-one

Gossip continued to chase after reality. A staple topic was the band of mercenaries whom the ex-King of Naples did or did not pay to burn and pillage his lost lands. They wore old French uniforms so as to discourage regular troops from shooting them, and many people claimed to know the address in Rome where the uniforms were kept. Other staples were the imminent conversion to Catholicism of various members of the British royal family and their offer of Malta as an asylum to the Pope, the Mérode/Antonelli row and, more topically, one between the French Ambassador and an English agent over the Malta offer which must therefore have really been made and, perhaps, provisionally accepted by the Pope, whose epilepsy, by the way, was leading him a dance.

At a reception in the Belgian Embassy, Nicola was approached by Father Grassi who made a remark which, though it sounded at first like the other pious fancies floating about their ears, later struck him as odd. Something to do with how the pronouncements of the little thaumaturge at Lourdes had been put to use. Did Nicola remember what the Madonna had said to her? She had said, 'I am the Immaculate Conception!' Four years earlier, noted the Jesuit, His Holiness had defined that doctrine by himself which, according to many experts, he had had no right to do. It was, they claimed, a usurpation of his bishops' powers. And note who his adviser had been: Padre Passaglia! Grassi's black eyes gleamed and he began, quite shockingly, to laugh. 'But who could complain once he had the support of the Madonna! Eh, Monsignore?'

Nicola could not tell who was the butt of this merriment. Himself? The Madonna? Could Grassi be losing his mind? He said dampeningly, 'I can't believe you are criticising the Holy Father.'

'Would you be troubled?' Grassi drew closer. 'People's minds are on the succession. His health is so poor.'

'Father Grassi,' Nicola spoke carefully, 'I hope you will forgive my

377

supposing that you are trying to trap me into an indiscretion. The only alternative is to suppose you disloyal – which, obviously, I resist. In the light of your known devotion to the Holy See . . .' Irritably he mumbled on, unsure how much of this was a charade. A group close by was discussing the expedition to Mexico. Markets and raw materials would be opened up, said an enthusiast. A Catholic empire would . . . But he lost the rest.

Grassi nodded, as though congratulating Nicola on his perspicacity. He wore a small, approving smile.

'Anyway.' Nicola felt offended. 'I heard His Holiness's health was better.' Testily, he snatched a water ice from a passing tray. He needed to cool down.

'It's precarious!' The Jesuit whispered, 'The Emperor has been taking soundings. He,' Grassi paused, 'wants a conciliator and many people's minds turn to Cardinal Amandi.'

'Who is out of favour.'

'What would you expect?'

'. . . to stop,' cried the Catholic imperialist, 'the expansion of the United States!'

'I would expect *you* to back a conservative,' said Nicola.

'Cardinal della Genga? But he died and the Church needs unity. If I am driven to making an alliance with you, Monsignore, what will you have against me? That I am a turncoat? That is another word for "convert"!' Smiling that ambiguous, encouraging smile, he whispered: 'I have a warning for you. Your connections – the duke and his business friends – are dangerous. Beware, Monsignore. A scandal could damage all our plans.'

'The Belgian Midas is courting us.' Monsignor Ferrari handed Nicola a parchment scroll. It was long, sealed, ribboned and headed ADDRESS TO THE HOLY FATHER. 'Skip the flourishes,' directed the Treasurer. 'It is astonishing how laymen like to preach.'

Nicola skipped with difficulty, for the text was a web of wordiness. '"If humbly prostrate at Your Holiness's feet . . . we submit to Your attention our project for the establishment of a UNIVERSAL CATHOLIC FINANCIAL POWER, it is not because we suppose that, without it, the Church or the Holy See would perish . . ."'

'Skip! Skip!' Ferrari cracked his knuckles. 'Some tame *abbé* wrote it. Can you find anything into which we can get our teeth?'

' "... we conceived the idea of a UNIVERSAL CATHOLIC FUND and of a CATHOLIC FINANCIAL POWER: (*ideam UNIVERSALIS CATHOLICI FUNDI et PECUNIARIAE POTENTIAE CATHOLICAE conceperimus ...*)" '

'Blessed if I can,' said Monsignor Ferrari.

' "One need but look at the state of finance in our time to see the heavy monopoly (*premens dominium*) exercised ... by Jews and Protestants, both adversaries of the Church.

' "Even Catholics invest with them! And recent examples show how ready such bankers are to use investors' money to help governments hostile to the Church: such as that of Italy.

' "The World is divided between Protestant and Jewish financiers ... and Catholic wealth and the forces of conservatism ..." '

'Preach, preach!' said the irascible Ferrari. 'Do they think we need telling?'

' "The first ... induce Catholic princes to assign key posts to ... enemies of all religion, so as to turn humanity towards temporal delights and to keep it under their financial yoke ... Catholics, investing with infidels, nourish in their bosoms ... to free them from bondage ... a CENTRAL UNIVERSAL CATHOLIC FUND must be set up ... if the Holy See, by giving its apostolic blessing to the project, would recommend it to Catholic rulers and priests ... we have found a man who is truly Catholic, zealous and devoted to the Holy See ... Monsieur André Langrand-Dumonceau ..."

'There's nothing about money for us,' said Nicola.

'That's what I thought,' said Ferrari. 'It is a request disguised as an offer.'

Passing a photographer's window, Nicola's attention was solicited by ogling models wearing the costume of the Roman Campagna. Stuck in cheap frames, the photographs were souvenirs for an undiscerning clientele: for French soldiers perhaps or foreign governesses. He dismissed them, then saw, in after-image, that one ogle was, after all, for him. The eyes were Maria's. And so was the rest: a ruined mnemonic. He turned. It was indeed she – which meant that so, from the neck down, had that other scandalous photograph been, since, clearly, she was a model and here was the missing face, faded like an old flag, but smiling gallantly, although its mouth was in the harsh custody of two wrinkles.

He pushed open the photographer's door. A bell jangled and a youth in an apron, answering from the gloom, gave an address which dispelled all doubts. La Diotallevi, said he, had provided those photographs and would know the models.

So off went Nicola to lay a ghost and perhaps find luck for the papal loan: a mixture of motives which drew him like a rope.

La Diotallevi and he assessed each other in her small hallway, for he had found her cloaked and bonneted and unsure whether she could spare him a minute. Relenting, she said he might walk with her to the ferry, so they took a narrow path along the river, but were held back by a cart lumbering ahead of them, which, being laden with stones, swayed slowly from side to side.

Nicola showed her the photograph he had bought and explained that he did not want to meet the model but only to have the address of her parish priest. The reasons concerned an old debt.

'Ah!' smiled la Diotallevi, perhaps remembering old adventurings of her own. A teasing gleam came to her eye and she laughed girlishly and quickened her step – but just then the carter in front of them came to a dead stop because of some difficulty with his horse.

Impatiently, she asked, 'Shall we try and get by?' Not waiting for an answer, she skipped up the grassy slope and passed the cart, which suddenly – had she startled the cart-horse? – swerved, tipped over and, borne down by its load, hurtled into the river. Trapped in its harness, the animal gave a bone-chilling, equine scream. The carter too let out a howl, then everything sank under the swell of racing yellow waters. It was astounding: a moment of suspended time. Then Nicola was down the slope. Slithering and scrambling, he hung onto some willow saplings with one hand, while edging out in the water to where the carter was thrashing and gulping, and, by extending a stick to him, slowly eased him back to safety. Hauling laboriously, while skinning the hand which still grasped the willow, he got him up the bank. Then, for moments, they both lay there, gasping with delayed terror.

'I confess . . .'

It was some time later and Nicola and la Diotallevi, drawn close by shock, had warmed and soothed themselves with hot cinnamon wine.

'. . . to Blessed Mary . . .' Her voice produced the blunted words with a renovating vigour. '. . . that I have sinned grievously.'

She had. To start with, she admitted to having made a number of false confessions. This, she swore, was a true one.

Nicola, whose wrung-out cassock was hung somewhere to dry, sat wrapped in a blanket, wondering if he was being unwise. She had insisted on her dire and present need of spiritual succour and he was unsure whether this was what she did want. Possibly, he had to allow, after the brush with sudden danger, she had felt a need to get close to the only man to hand and taken this way of doing so. If so, God's strategy might have her in its grip. No doubt her ears, like his, were throbbing with the cries of the rescued man who had gibbered and mourned his dead horse and seemed to be in such despair that he had had to be spoken to firmly and given money and ordered to go and change his clothes. Else, as he kept threatening, he might have jumped back into the river.

It was then that *she* had taken charge, insisting that the dripping Nicola come back to her house. They were bound now by their adventure, while the ruption of mortality, even if only that of a horse, had apparently moved her to confess. It was now or never, she said and, on hearing of her past sacrilegious confessions, he was bound to believe her. She had, she pointed out, had little choice about these since what she had to confess was a history of denouncing the innocent and colluding to destroy them. Colluding with whom? She named Monsignori Matteucci and Pila. How, she asked reasonably, could she have safely made a confession implicating *them*? Her faith in the secrecy of the sacrament was nil.

'I trust you,' she said, whereupon he distrusted her.

Amazed at his imprudence, he imagined the papal police bursting in to find him dressed only in a blanket with a known harlot on her knees before him. What if there were spies behind the foliate candelabrum or the Chinese screen? He feared a flash of light and being fulminated by Monsignori Pila and Matteucci. Reassuring himself, he recalled that the circumstances leading to this had been fortuitous. The photograph, the carter's accident. No, no, if there was a design here it must, as she seemed to think, be God's. Ashamed, he saw that her motives were purer than his own.

'Why,' he asked ploddingly, 'confess at all if you couldn't do so truthfully?'

Surprised, she reminded him that, to stay on the government payroll, she must obtain an annual certificate proving that she had done so. She had, for the same reason, made a sacrilegious communion every year as well. Did he absolve her?

Only, said he, if she promised to put right the wrongs she had done. There were men in gaol – Fausti for one – because of her. How absolve her while they continued to suffer? Yet he knew that asking her to take back her lies was unrealistic. She had handed him a dilemma and he was stumped by it. Slowly, an idea dawned. Did she think, he asked, that Monseigneur de Mérode knew of the crimes perpetrated by his henchmen? If not, she should confess all this to him who would, on finding the sins on his own conscience, be obliged to deal with them – which he had the power to do.

She began to moan and protest.

'But as a priest,' Nicola assured her, 'he's bound to forget, on emerging from the confessional, what he learned within it. You don't trust him?'

No, she trusted nobody, except, it seemed, Nicola himself, because of his selfless bravery just now in helping the carter who could, she pointed out, have dragged him under.

'My heart was in my mouth!' she said. 'Seeing you on that slippery slope with nothing but a few willow twigs between you and – can you swim?'

He could not but hadn't, he realised, been afraid at all. Too excited. But he was frightened now, feeling caught, like herself, in a web of dubiety. If *he* were to tell Mérode, he would still have to name her and . . . No, she implored. Mérode could have her re-arrested. He could revive the old charges of spying and falsifying the Queen of Naples' photograph and . . .

'But would he?'

Mérode, objected Nicola, was a gentleman and . . . But la Diotallevi knew too much about gentlemen to be impressed. Knew them up close, Monsignore. And as for moral codes, she knew how notions like the greater good, a just war, the interests of the Church, etc., etc., could be invoked to justify *anything*. 'Anything at all, Monsignore!' She had seen it happen. Over and again! She knew.

Humiliated, Nicola asked, what if she were to write out several copies of her confession, sign and give them to him for use if anything happened to her? It would be a protection and . . .

'And my salary? I have to live. He'd cut it off.'

'I could ensure that you received one from the Treasury instead.'

She said she'd think about it and he gave her provisional absolution. Then he accepted some more hot cinnamon wine with a slice of lemon and a spoonful of sugar, and they sat quietly for a little, chatting as if they had known each other always. She had spirit. He liked her and would have liked – oddly – to be friends with her, but that, to be sure, was out of the question.

1863

'This is where the *barberi* are caught.'

'Barbarians?'

Nicola laughed. 'No, no, Barbary horses. They race here in carnival week. Without riders.'

Langrand-Dumonceau's agents marvelled, and he explained that the animals were urged on by spiked metal balls which hung from their backs to prick and madden them so that they rushed down the city's main street, known on that account as the Corso, to where a canvas was stretched to stop them. Was it true, asked the Belgian, that, formerly, leaders of the city's Jewish community had run this race on foot? His smile acknowledged an omen in men of God engaging in a temporal struggle and perhaps imperilling their health.

Nicola wondered if they were abreast of the latest rumours. An incision made in the Pope's leg to help the discharge of matter had begun to close and this, said his doctors, could cause his erysipelas to attack his vital organs. At Easter, he had collapsed while giving his solemn blessing *urbi et orbe* and, as the National Party was thought to have plans to take over the city the minute he died, the Curia was laying their own for a break with custom whereby a Conclave, held *cadavere presente*, could elect a successor before the pubic knew of his death.

Such talk could worry investors who must, therefore, be steered away from the whispering galleries where guesses were rife and names of *papabili* bandied like those of horses. On the Conciliatory side, d'Andrea and Amandi were heavily tipped and d'Andrea had confided to friends that this made him fear for his life. Most people, however, put this down to His Eminence's Neapolitan flair for drama.

'Talking of barbarians,' said the Belgian's companion, a quick little lawyer from Pest, 'our hope is that Rome will treat modern powers of finance and industry as they did the fourth-century invaders, namely baptize them!'

This meant that they wanted some sort of accolade for Langrand-Dumonceau – medal, blessing, title. Nicola smiled and kept quiet. He had grown good at this over the last months, during which he must have met a dozen agents sent from the financier's centres of activity in Brussels, Paris, Vienna and Pest. Some were figureheads, like today's Belgian, whose name rang like a motto and whose face had the shape of an escutcheon. The real business was left to men like the lawyer who buzzed with purpose and had, over lunch, described Hungarian flatlands which Langrand was buying up to resell in small profitable lots. Almost lyrically, he had evoked pale waterlogged demesnes which could be regenerated by land-hungry men who had never, until now, owned property. Was this, he exulted, not a reconciliation between the spirit of the times and that of the gospels? Church lands in Hungary could benefit from a similar scheme if only the local clergy could be made to see that wealth locked in land gave no return. If it were mortgaged and the bonds sold by Langrand's enterprises . . .

The Belgian, affable in a haze of cigar smoke, talked of Langrand's being such a good family man, devoted to his boys and to his fat little wife, Rosalie, who looked like a pile of buns! But what vision, Monsignore! What energy!

'Our companies,' murmured the lawyer, 'know how to recompense those who help us in our mission.'

Nicola pretended not to hear.

'You could do worse than let us raise money on Roman property.' The lawyer puffed his lips as though ready to kiss something. 'Prayerbook and pocketbook!' He wanted to marry them. 'Morals and money!' It *must* circulate, he said. Practising what he preached, he had donated 20,000 francs of his companies' money to St Peter's Pence – now the mainstay of our economy – and to several churches which the Pope was having restored. Pius was fond of saying that the generosity of the faithful was a silver lining to current clouds, but the Belgians' gifts only sharpened the doubts of Ferrari and Antonelli, whose notion of a silver lining was a knife between the ribs.

Turning back down the Corso, they passed San Carlo's Church where a handbill had been pinned to the door. Nicola read: LETTER FROM EMIGRANT PATRIOTS TO THE PEOPLE OF ROME. Profiting from the agents' momentary interest in a beggar, he stepped closer and ran his eye down the smaller print. 'Rome . . . owes it to herself to crown the Italian Revolution by a spontaneous insurrec . . .' Here a breeze curled the paper, concealing a paragraph. Further down, he made out the words, 'a new conciliatory pope . . .'

Flushing – some unsavoury-looking characters were amused at his interest – he moved off and caught up with the lawyer who returned to an argument started earlier when they had witnessed accredited beggars receiving their daily allowance. Giving them money, he repeated, was not the thing. One must make it possible for them to earn.

Nicola's mind slid away. Amandi's appointment to Pius's old diocese had been presented as a chance for the cardinal to recover his health. But now that the invalid was Mastai, the thing took on other aspects: plotting in the provinces; exile in the hostile kingdom! That could be how the excitable old pontiff would see it.

To whom was loyalty now owed? Clearly, not to a man but to the institution. Jokes were circulating about God's summoning Pius to himself and his refusal to obey.

But Nicola should be attending to his birds of passage. They had reached the Caffè Ruspoli, so, proposing a refreshment, he waved them in. 'Ruspoli,' remembered the lawyer. There had been a prince of that name recently in Pest. Sent to stir up revolution!

People turned to listen and Nicola warned the Hungarian to lower his voice. But he had gone ahead and didn't hear. 'I met Kossuth too,' he called over his shoulder. 'Louis Kossuth, the Hungarian revolutionary. He's our Mazzini. A man of '48.'

Nicola, almost knocking down the Belgian, pushed forward, through a thicket of chairs, and hissed, 'You mustn't talk about men like that.'

'Oh, I assure you,' cried the insensitive lawyer, 'my interest was mere curiosity. One meets such men as one might go to the zoo.'

The waiter, sticking to them like a limpet, must surely be a spy? No, he was only making sure that they got a good table. Am I mad, wondered Nicola, to think that being seen with men who have met Ruspoli and Kossuth could discredit me? After all, I'm here at the behest of Ferrari and Antonelli! But could they save me – or would I sink them? Maybe that's the plan? These fellows – Belgian envoys after all – could have been put up to this by Monsignor de Mérode! Across from him, the mirrored face of la Diotallevi smiled recognition. He thought, that's it! She's following me! For him! The confession was a . . . No. Why no?

'Are you all right, Monsignor Santi?' asked the waiter.

How, thought Nicola, does he know my name? Suspicion whirled in his head as he stared coldly through la Diotallevi who was greeting him indiscreetly, nodding and waving. Frowning, he turned away.

'A glass of water?' The waiter proffered it.

It tasted odd. Did it? Under Nicola's clothes, his sweat had gone cold. Pulling himself together, he remembered that the waiter had worked here for years, knew him as a customer and had even talked to him about his hobby, which was keeping pigeons.

'I'm all right,' he told him. 'Just a moment's dizziness.' Having ordered lemon sherbet for them all, he looked about for la Diotallevi to make up for his boorish discourtesy. She had left.

There was no plot. Spooning into sweet, granular globes of frozen citrus juice, he stared beneath the tables at the reassuring ordinariness of cassocked, hoop-skirted and trousered knees supported by brightly coloured ankles and heard, yet again, the gospel according to Langrand: all evils came from failure to free capital from entails and mortmain. How reassuring monotony was! Their minds moved like clock hands.

Thirteen per cent of our Belgian shareholders, they told him, were priests. Too many legacies to the Church were being challenged in our courts, so now we advise the pious to sell their property and use the proceeds to buy our bonds, which yield four and a half per cent during their lifetime and can be handed to their priest on their deathbed. Greedy and godless next-of-kin are foiled!

'I see,' said Nicola, who didn't quite.

'The merchants are back in the temple but as saviours.'

And now it came to him that these could be the agents not only of Langrand-Dumonceau but also of an older and more dangerous agency which was about its old business of kidnapping souls. He was sorry he had snubbed la Diotallevi, who had given him her trust.

He had left the businessmen back at their hotel and was on his way to the ministry when he felt a pull at his elbow.

'Monsignor Santi.'

It was Viterbo, whose tone was challenging as if daring Nicola to take offence. He looked unhealthy. Eye-bags, soft and grey as small, dead field-mice, bulged beneath his eyes.

He was, he said, here with his sister who had come to see her son. The Mortara boy. They let her see him now. They were so sure of him! Viterbo grinned with a wheedling aggression, as if eager for Nicola to confirm his worst expectations. His character, thought Nicola sadly, had been damaged. The likeable man he remembered from Lammenais' funeral was as thoroughly buried as the heretic priest! Persecution did not improve people. Was it true, the printer asked, that the Rothschilds were not, after all, to float the new loan?

'They tried to use their influence on our behalf. Naturally, it was a blow when we heard that they may be replaced by this Jew-baiting Belgian, who . . .'

'Nothing's decided,' Nicola told him.

Viterbo had put on weight, but it was slack and hung about him like pockets of chaff. 'Will you see my sister?' The question came out like a bullet. 'You won't have to go to the Ghetto. That rag-and-bone market distresses her. In Bologna our people live with dignity now. We can meet at the Englishwoman's. Miss Foljambe's. Is that discreet enough?'

His rudeness was like a smell – pervasive, elusive and impossible to remark on. Perhaps it was a form of pride? Or perhaps he was unaware of it.

Nicola agreed to come and later in the afternoon made his way to the Palazzo Spada, where Miss Foljambe was holding a gathering.

The first voice he heard was Cardinal d'Andrea's. Booming with convivial indignation, it was audible across the courtyard. 'Eight thousand, nine hundred and forty-three priests,' His Eminence was saying, 'signed the address to the Pope last year, begging him to reconcile our people's two heartfelt cries: "Long live the Pope!" and "Long live Rome, capital of the new Kingdom!" *That* was despite fear of excommunication. How many, Monsignore,' he called to Nicola as he came in, 'would have signed if they had been free?'

'My own signature,' Nicola told him, 'is the only one for which I can answer. But as I was too prudent to sign, Your Eminence must allow me to be too prudent to regret that now. Besides, many signatures were withdrawn. Only the very brave remained.'

'You disapprove of bravery, Monsignore?'

'I disapprove of being excommunicated.'

The cardinal drew him into a corner. 'You may be right!' he said. 'Letting ourselves be driven out would suit *him* too well. To tell the truth, I may have been unwise. Since resigning from the *Congregatio Indicis*, I'm a pariah. One feels the tide go out around one. I'm not even sure I'm physically safe. I haven't been well, and one always wonders . . . How is Cardinal Amandi?'

Nicola, wary of the implied linkage between the two cardinals' health, said the air of Imola was doing Amandi good.

387

D'Andrea's profile shifted, chopping the air like a predatory bird's. 'I,' he whispered, 'have been receiving queries from certain quarters. I imagine he too . . .?'

'I don't know, Your Eminence. I'm here, you know . . .'

'And he's in Imola where, as you say, the air is healthier! I did think of going to Naples for a while. I have family there. But as a cardinal in Curia, I am expected to be here. Naples is now seen as enemy territory, so *he* would take it badly. To tell the truth, I asked for permission and it hasn't come. Appalling, isn't it, that the Servant of God indulges in petty spite? I mustn't hold you. We mustn't seem to conspire! You must greet your hostess.'

She seemed hardly to have changed since Nicola had met her first. Eager, shiny-eyed, with a flush on her cheek-bones and a quick smile from teeth as small as milk teeth, or a young girl's first string of pearls. With her was a woman whom he recognised by her colouring as Viterbo's sister.

They were introduced and Miss Foljambe packed them off to a small drawing room where they would, she promised, be undisturbed.

'Thank you for coming,' said the dark-haired woman who kept her hands so still that he wondered if their impulse was to break into mutinous gestures. Her husband was a lace-merchant, but she was wearing no lace. Austere then, but not, he knew, resigned.

For the last three years she had been a subject of the new Italian government which, thanks to her persistence, had appealed for her son's release. So had half the monarchs of Europe, but Pius was impervious. He had turned the case into a symbol. The boy's conversion was to be like the first swallow in spring – a harbinger and promise. Besides, he liked the child who had settled in well with his new teachers. *This* was what upset the mother most.

Hands still in each other's custody, she talked of how Edgardo's affections had been stolen. She could not blame *him*. His qualities had been used against her. 'He was always so alert, you see, and loved learning new things, so, of course – what's that?'

Something was happening in the corridor. Voices were raised.

'Pay no attention,' advised Nicola. 'It's just a bit of high spirits.' He guessed that d'Andrea had been provoking someone.

'It's strange.' The Signora was remembering the evening, five years ago, when they first came for Edgardo. 'It was a June evening, still bright, yet late enough so that we didn't open the door at once, but asked who was there. The answer was "police". I keep hearing that word

388

that started it all.' She gave a small, shy laugh. 'I thought I heard it now.' The laugh meant, 'Tell me I'm being foolish.'

But Nicola too had heard it. He thought, If they find us here alone together, what can I say?

'Have you permission to be in Rome?'

Yes, she said. She had papers.

Nicola was filled with shame. He was going to have to ask her to lie. 'If they interrogate us, could you bear,' he asked her, 'to say you were asking me about the Catholic faith? It won't help Edgardo if they think we were plotting.'

'But I was not intending to plot with you, Monsignore.' Sitting up very straight. 'What would have been the use? And I did intend asking you about Edgardo's present beliefs. I want to know how real they are to him. What do you mean by "interrogate us"? Is this house under suspicion then?'

Nicola put a finger to his lips. For several minutes, they stayed quiet; then they heard the outer door close. Then the drawing-room door opened. It was Viterbo. His sister, he warned, had better wait a while before leaving. The police were still outside, though Miss Foljambe had sent a complaint to her consul. He broke off. Did they not *know* what had happened? Well, the police had appeared, demanded to be let in and gone straight to a bedroom where they found Miss Foljambe's English maid making love to a man in a cassock whom nobody knew. It was all too pat to be genuine. The girl must have been bribed to let herself be caught. The police story was that neighbours had denounced her for enticing seminarians here. They wanted to discredit Miss Foljambe and perhaps expel her from Rome. Her political friends were in bad odour. However, the thing had backfired.

'The officers waited outside while subordinates made the arrest. When they came in, they were shocked to find so many people here – including, of course, the cardinal.'

'His carriage is in the courtyard.'

'Ah, but they came in the back way and only saw him when they had made their arrest. They were quite put out of countenance and scuttled off without taking people's names.'

Nicola and Viterbo and his sister drank tea with Miss Foljambe while she awaited word from her consul, to whom she had sent an indignant account of the outrage. She was eager to protest with maximum publicity in the English and Italian press and was with difficulty dissuaded. Mud sticks, Nicola and Viterbo reminded her. A bargain with the police would be her wisest course. No denunciations on either side. *Pax*!

Meanwhile, Nicola remembered, he still didn't know how he could be of service to the Signora Mortara.

She said she wanted help from someone who could safely approach Edgardo. A person who would be neither supervised nor spied on but could talk to the boy and learn what was in his heart.

'Does he miss us still? Or would he rather we didn't come at all? Does he blame us for not having been able to defend him? He has been five years in Rome!' On her last visit, she thought she had detected a shrinking when she touched him. 'Maybe,' she tightened her lips, 'we should leave him alone?'

'But,' her brother was indignant, 'the Pope is about to lose his last bit of territory. They're thrashing around. Even what happened here this evening confirms it! All you need do is wait.'

'No,' said the Signora in her painfully controlled voice. 'He's twelve now. If they've won his heart, we could only break it. They've had him for half his rational life. It would be cruel to keep tugging at his loyalties. Remember the baby whom two mothers claimed and brought to King Solomon for a judgment? The king said it was to be cut in half and the false mother agreed, but the true one said she'd rather give it up!' She began to cry.

Nicola promised to see the boy, then report back to her.

Waiting for him at home was a letter from Flavio, asking for a title for Langrand-Dumonceau. 'I mentioned this to His Holiness last time I was in Rome,' wrote Flavio, 'and *he* said that nobility was a gift from God. Why then, I asked, should it not be one from God's Vicar? He laughed and seemed well disposed. He likes the nobility and says Jesus Christ did too. "He," he told me, "chose to be born noble, of the House of David! The gospel gives his genealogical tree." The nobility, he says, are the best support any throne can have. Thrones supported by the plebs are never stable! Remind him of all this when asking for a title for L-D. Stress that we need it to help us collect pennies for heaven from the faithful. I'm talking about your loan!

'*My* task is to persuade L-D to launch it which is the last thing on his mind. Floating one for the Vatican just now won't be easy. He'll need inducements. I suspect the Rothschilds were happy to be dropped! The official reason – that they were demanding the return of the Mortara boy – doesn't ring true.'

Edgardo Mortara had been moved to the College of St Peter in Chains where Nicola went to see him.

On his arrival, a priest took him round the church and, in the course of an exploratory chat, intimated that the boy should not be upset. 'Better not mention the parents. Their visits distress him.'

'You mean he's distressed when they leave?'

'Not at all, it upsets him to meet them. We have to insist.'

They paused before Michelangelo's Moses – a frowning, muscular old man with horns. The marble, especially in the parts close enough to be touched, was faintly discoloured and as smooth as a sucked sweet. It was to have been part of a funerary monument planned for himself by Pope Julius II.

'Julius II!' The young, fresh-faced priest shrugged at the ironies. All the great warrior-pope's conquests – Bologna, Urbino, Piacenza, Reggio, Parma – had now been ravished from the papacy.

'Why the horns?' Nicola wondered what the once-Jewish child made of the old prophet's being presented with demonic attributes.

'A mistranslation of Exodus. It seems that what was meant were rays of light.'

Nicola headed for the door and the sunlight. 'Who shall I say I am?'

'He wants to take orders. You could have come to ensure that no pressure is brought on him, a routine check of his vocation.'

Above them stretched the Esquiline Hill, planted with fruit trees and vines. Military and bare in their wintery alignment, they recalled the chains of St Peter to which the church was dedicated.

The child, a self-possessed twelve-year-old, was, Nicola reminded himself, having the best education the state could supply and had received several visits from the Pope who made him a personal allowance. He was used to being shown off, had been paraded through the Ghetto, and was reputed to answer questions like a little Solomon. Sitting next to him on a garden bench, Nicola asked why he wanted to be a priest. Had someone suggested it? He was young to decide.

The boy considered. The most striking thing about him was that, as with his mother, his hands and every muscle were perfectly still. His mother's and uncle's eyes looked oddly old in his chubby face. 'The Holy Father,' he said, 'took the tonsure at my age.'

'Did he tell you that?'

'No. I found out.'

Nicola decided to dampen this exaltation. 'Sometimes,' he said, 'boys take it so as to qualify for benefices to which their families have a claim. I believe that that was the case with him.'

'But what I feel is that I must lay claim to a religious heritage which is not mine at all, but was given me as a grace. I can't take it for granted as others might.' Having scored this point, he produced a surprisingly boyish grin.

Coached? Genuine? How could one *know*?

'And family life? You'll have to renounce it.'

'I have renounced it.'

'Why?'

'We live briefly in this life and in eternity for ever. How choose the first?'

'But why should loving your parents be a choice against eternity?'

'Because they want me to apostasise. I am a Catholic now.'

'Don't you care for them?'

'Oh, I pray all the time for their conversion. But if they don't convert, they will not be sinning against the light which never reached them. It reached me. How could I live with them as a Catholic?'

'Are you not repeating words which you've learned off?'

The boy looked puzzled and Nicola asked, 'Can you remember ordinariness? Playing with your brothers? Sleeping together at night, while the lonely and unattached wander outside in the dark? There must be things you miss? Secrets? Jokes?' He himself had often imagined families like this.

The boy's head was turned away. 'Why are you saying all this, Monsignore?' he asked.

Nicola remembered his role as a vocation-tester. 'I have to make sure,' he claimed, 'that you don't make an intemperate decision. Maybe we should send you back to your family for a while. You may have forgotten about everyday things. Lives are made up of them, especially,' it struck him forcibly, 'as you grow older. An impulsive choice can be as disappointing as reaching for the sunlit bits of a stained-glass window.'

The boy said nothing. Nicola drew breath. 'Can you remember,' he

392

asked – amd immediately felt foolish – 'the taste of artichokes *alla giudea*? Jewish cooking?'

'What do you want of me, Monsignore?'

'To be less sure. Humbler perhaps? Doubtful?' He was, he supposed, describing himself.

'To lose my faith?'

'To make surer that you have it.'

The boy raised his chin. 'It's not something you can ever be sure of,' he said slowly. 'You have to keep earning it.' He smiled. 'That's what I want to do.' The smile was spreading, luminous, convinced.

Nicola was stricken. 'Ah,' he said enviously and with wonder, 'you do have it!' Then, on impulse: 'Pray for me, Edgardo.'

There was both a radiance and a reliable ordinariness to the boy, standing in unruffled certitude among beds of pruned boxwood and dormant, winter plants. Not, the Monsignore reminded himself, that anything at all was reliable! In the long run, ordinariness, like radiance, withered into dust.

As though pondering this very thought, Edgardo-Pio said, 'I have to have faith, Monsignore. You see, I cost everyone such a lot. The Holy Father says that when he comes. "Oh," he says, "if you only knew how much you have cost me!" This is because my family turned the French Emperor against him because of me. But my soul is in his keeping and, though the great of the earth try to snatch it, he cannot let them. I told him that if I cost so much, then maybe he *should*, but he said "No, *non possumus*!" The choice, you see, isn't his. It is not permitted to bargain over even one soul. Both of us have to have faith.' The boy's finely modelled, fruit-like lips split apart, and he gave the Monsignore his mesmerised and mesmeric smile.

'Well?' The priest who had been waiting in the *Collegio* vestibule was ready for a pious chat. 'What did you think?'

'I'm impressed,' Nicola felt it fair to say and did not add that he was horrified as well. The Pope's spiritual arithmetic appalled him and he kept thinking of the Signora Mortara's story about King Solomon and the disputed baby. 'Is it true that he has taken Pio as his middle name?'

'Edgardo Pio. Yes. He plans to take Pius Mary as his name in religion when he enters the novitiate.' The priest looked disappointed when Nicola said he had to leave at once. 'I'll walk with you as far as the Campo Vaccino,' he offered and, swinging along in step with his companion, noted that this case was a perfect example of the naturalist prejudices now dominating popular thought. Even Catholics seemed to care less for Christ in whom we were all members by baptism than for the claims of the natural family. 'The Holy Father had to make a stand,' opined the priest, half tripping in his efforts to keep up with Nicola's stride. 'Naturalism is as dangerous a heresy as individualism.'

At the Campo Vaccino, Nicola managed to hail a hackney carriage and left the gregarious priest looking forlorn. He had an appointment with Viterbo in a quiet alley where the printer was waiting in a second curtained carriage. Nicola had his draw up alongside so that Viterbo could step unseen from one to the other.

'Don't bother telling me,' was his greeting. 'I've guessed your news. He's happy with his privileges. I'll tell my sister.'

'I thought *you* were arguing against resignation.'

'Yes, but not because I have illusions about Edgardo–Pio. He follows power. *My* hopes were in the Baron de Rothschild. Is there no chance that you could advise the Treasury to deal with him?'

Nicola said that he was less influential than Viterbo seemed to think, but he saw that the printer disbelieved him.

April 1864

Dilecto Filio, Nobili Viro, Andreae Langrand Dumonceau,
Bruxellas in Belgio.
Pius P.P. IX
Dilecte Fili, Nobilis Vir, salutem et Apostolicam Benedictionem . . .
Intelleximus quoque Te ac Tuos Socios . . .

'Translate it! Translate it!' The Belgian was laughing at his own excitement. Grey-eyed, with a cocked nose, a solid body and curly mutton-chop whiskers, André Langrand-Dumonceau had the likeable, plebeian good looks which befitted a self-made man. He really was self-made, he told Flavio and Nicola, for his grandfather had been a foundling, a *filius exposititius*, as was noted on his baptismal certificate, the family's first document in Latin which this one went a long way to avenge. 'Translate it,' he repeated.

Nicola obliged. '"To our dear son . . ."'

'No, the bit about our companies.'

'"We learn that you and other Catholics of the Kingdom of Belgium have founded loan banks so as to foster agriculture, industry and trade . . . and to save Catholic families from the rapacious hands of usurers by . . ." Do you want to hear it all?'

'The last bit.'

Nicola read him the papal exhortation to despise the lure of riches and persist in his obedience and devotion to the Pope's Person and the Holy See, in anticipation whereof, Pius, lovingly and wholeheartedly, conferred on Langrand and his associates his Apostolic Benediction. *Datum Romae apud S. Petrum die 21 aprilis Anno 1864. Pius P.P. IX.*

The document was Nicola's triumph. Prodded by Flavio, he had worked to obtain it in the teeth of the do-nothing policies of Monsignor Ferrari and the cardinal. It was, Flavio had urged, essential if Langrand was to manage the papal loan – a thankless task since the faithful, who were already contributing to St Peter's Pence, would jib at an investment promising neither the spiritual return of outright charity nor likelihood of profit.

'The Vatican,' he said brutally, 'does not look like a safe bet. If Langrand's agents are to sell the bonds, they will need suppport from bishops and priests to persuade the pious to buy.'

And in the end, Langrand, while refusing to put up any money of his own – he said the statutes of his companies forbade it – had agreed to handle the loan. Then Monsignor Ferrari asked for an advance. One and a half million francs per month for six months. The financier didn't think he could raise it, but Flavio hoped the Apostolic Blessing would do the trick.

'I took him to the mountain and showed him empires waiting to be won – convent and diocesan funds, parish priests' and pious peasants' savings. All these, I assured him, will now flow into his companies.'

He then pressed into service a young man called Moeller who had fought at Castelfidardo, and the two worked on the financier, describing the perils threatening the greatest historic institution of the West, and the loyalty and courage of those struggling to save it. Most were noblemen, said Moeller. Why, at Castelfidardo, his own commanding officer, the Baron de la Charrette, had been a cousin of the Comte de Chambord, pretender to the throne of France. The very survival of Old Europe hung, said Flavio, in the balance, and Moeller dwelled on the gaiety of the mess and the gallantry of the young men even now pouring in from all over Catholic Europe to defend the besieged city. The scions of all the great noble houses would, he assured, be there. And Langrand, whose own boards of directors bristled with coats of arms, became in spirit a recruit. A buccaneer in business, he was enough of a gambler to be romantic, and it was during a dinner genial with military exaltation and the glow of fine Burgundy that Flavio raised the idea of a title. Arise Sir Langrand. A battlefield commission.

So, as an advance on this promise, Langrand received his Apostolic Blessing though, for a while, there had been trouble with Monsignor Ferrari, who wasn't sure he wanted to deal with the Belgian at all. But Flavio spent money like water, bribing his way through the Curia, paying newspapers to promote the alliance, then, as the Belgian hesitated over the advance, dangling the title.

'Between ourselves,' he confided to Nicola on their way to Brussels with the papal Brief of blessing, 'he himself is having to borrow money from the Jews, Bischoffsheim and Hirsch.'

At this, Nicola felt a chill of doubt. But Flavio pooh-poohed it. The money-shortage was, he assured, temporary and due to the American war. If anyone could survive these bad times, it was Langrand – and anyway we couldn't change horses in mid-stream. Baptizing capital was our best and only hope.

Twenty-two

'This time it's not my fault.'

Nicola nodded. He and Flavio – who was then in Pest – had arranged a visit to the rusticated Amandi. Instead, at the last minute, he had been deflected by telegram to Cesena, near the Adriatic coast, and thence to this convent garden. Tablets luridly depicting Christ's passion were nailed to trees and, ranging in their shade, was an unrecognisable Flavio. He looked as though some large animal had chewed, then spewed him out.

'Miss Ella's back.'

For over a year now the epicene and her circus had been touring in Ottoman lands and Flavio had not seemed to miss her. The marriage gambit, he claimed, had been no more than that. A move in a game. Nicola must not judge Miss Ella by other people. Reality bored her and that included the *stuprum* which so haunted the clerical mind. Wanting to be a duchess was a joke such as children enjoy when rifling someone's wardrobe.

Nicola reserved judgment. Whatever about sin – a matter, claimed Flavio, for *his* conscience only – a scandal could cause havoc in a papal court where the balance of power now hung by a thread. He had, therefore, been at pains to persuade his friend to end his entanglement, and at last Flavio wrote to tell Miss Ella that she must neither return nor try to see him.

'She's here! Threatening suicide. She means it too. Risk thrills her. Besides, it would delight her to drag us both – you too, Monsignore – down with her.'

It seemed that there was a nun here who had cured her back that time she had fallen from her horse: Sister Paola, a respected thaumaturge. It was on her account that Miss Ella had chosen this meeting-place and it was Sister Paola who had sent for Flavio. However, now that he was here and cooling his heels, neither nun nor protégée would see him.

397

Three times he had been refused entry by the portress who told him he had been given a bad character. Portrayed as a heartless seducer, it behooved him to marry Miss Ella, and the whole convent was praying that he would.

'That's why I need you here. To speak for me. For them she's a ruined maiden.'

'But, Flavio, I can't tell them the truth! I suppose I condoned it. What did I condone? Sodomy? Certainly deception.'

We must, said his friend, trust each other. Be my advocate. Tell the nuns she's demented. Bully them. The portress tells me that this Sister Paola enjoys prestige because of having cured Miss Ella's back. The word miracle is whispered, and there's talk of her trying for a second by softening my stony heart. Apparently, though, that's to be done at a distance, for, as you see, I'm being kept out here like Henry IV at Canossa. I'm lucky there's no snow.'

So Nicola told him to go to an inn at Cesena. He would see the nun.

Some time later, he was in the convent parlour when the abbess rushed in with news that Miss Ella had slipped off to take part in a balloon flight. The abbess, breathing hard, had clearly come with un-nunlike haste. The beads at her waist clicked and swayed and she lacked composure. Two noted French balloonists, said she, were to participate in a local charity-raising event. Feats would be performed. What nobody had known was that Miss Ella had made arrangements to sit astride a horse suspended from the basket of their balloon. A sort of trial by ordeal. She might leap off and kill herself. Given her state of mind.

'Sister Paola had been trying to pour balm, but the unfortunate young woman . . .'

Nicola contemplated enlightening the abbess.

'. . . driven, it seems, to despair . . .'

He let her talk. Then, 'Does your convent claim that this Sister Paola performs . . . miracles?'

The abbess froze. Backing from the romance which had clearly bemused her community, she remembered caution. 'No, Monsignore. Nobody *claims* anything. Sister Paola, it is true, is a holy . . .'

'Holy? *Santa*? Saintly perhaps?'

'Well, that was a way of speaking, but . . .'

'Not a claim?' He smiled that indulgent smile which shows those who have overstepped the bounds of orthodoxy that they need rescuing.

The abbess, however, had recovered her poise. The concern now was practical and in practical matters, he saw, she would bow to no inquisitor.

398

The balloon flight might take off any minute from a park in Cesena. She had, she told him, sent to warn the duke and to dissuade the balloonists from allowing Miss Ella to go up.

Why, he asked, had the convent failed, up to now, in its custodial role? Pressing the point, he asked whether the unbalanced young person had not been stirred up here rather than calmed down. She answered, with spirit, that this was no time for debate, and, walking to the window, asked whether he would not himself drive to Cesena. He was spared having to consider this when a carriage appeared in a cloud of dust, out of which, like a demon in a morality play, stepped a priest. This, said the abbess, was the convent chaplain, Padre Gamba.

He had news. The balloon flight had duly taken off; Miss Ella and her horse were suspended dangerously beneath it and the wind was blowing the wrong way.

'Wrong?'

'Seawards,' said the chaplain, 'so it should be visible from here. Come.' He led Nicola and the abbess to a place from whence they did, presently, spy a brightly striped globe – yellow and blue – whisking through puffball clouds. Hanging from its basket, was a horse and – but before they could see who, if anyone, was astride it, the whole thing was blotted out by the sun's dazzle.

The wind had changed unexpectedly and now, said the chaplain, the balloonists risked being driven out over the sea to a certain death. All we could do was pray. The duke, he reported of Flavio, had gone to the coast.

Hours later there was still no news. Lunch had been served and after that Nicola and the chaplain had worn themselves out with prayer and speculation. Nicola's prayers were that scandal be averted, though it was hard to see how, since a dead Miss Ella must be a source of it and a live one of mischief – unless, to be sure, she were to disappear totally at sea. But he could not very well pray for such an outcome, however convenient.

In the afternoon, the nuns took their recreation on a sweep of gravel outside their front door. Drawn up in two facing rows, so that one of the two was always moving backwards, they walked one way and then the other, to-ing and fro-ing, ebbing and returning with the rhythm of a double-bladed scythe.

Nicola, watching from a window, asked Father Gamba to point out the thaumaturge but was told that she was in retreat. After some minutes, the abbess detached herself from the scything lines and joined the two priests. Still no news, she sighed, and when the Monsignore marvelled at the convent's kindness to Miss Ella, who was to his certain knowledge not a Catholic at all, said, reprovingly, that the equestrienne's was a deeply religious nature. And then, so it seemed to him, she gave him an ironic look.

Had Sister Paola nursed Miss Ella, he asked, seized by a tremulous suspicion. Could these nuns *know*? But it appeared that Sister Paola had merely laid her hands on the injured rider.

'And then we, who had seen her walk crookedly and in pain, had the joy of seeing her perform acrobatics on her wonderful white horse: a pure prayer, Monsignore, a glorious *Magnificat*! As Father Gamba told us later, circus riders come up hard against the limits of their human skills and, like soldiers, learn to fling themselves into the merciful arms of God. Father Gamba,' said the abbess, 'was a military chaplain.'

Seeing the nuns and their chaplain so in thrall to Miss Ella, Nicola did not argue. Knowing him to be from the Treasury – this had been established earlier – he supposed they must think of him as blinkered by accountancy and blind to the realms of mystic risk which they had come to see in acrobatic terms. This was, to be sure, understandable. Imagining the drab, serge-swaddled women raising deprived eyes to the rider's sequinned glories, he was moved by the incongruity of their joy. Tower of Ivory, he thought, Gates of Pearl! Hope of the Shipwrecked! Would they now picture the Madonna doing the splits on a white horse? How enlightened of their bishop, he remarked, to have sanctioned the display!

But the abbess, suddenly chary, twisted her bride-of-Christ's wedding ring and avoided his eye. The See, she confessed, had been vacant at the time and the Vicar-General overworked. 'So we,' she admitted, 'followed our own discretion.'

'The better part of valour!' Nicola, scoring a much-needed point, assured her of his.

'She's such a humble person!' She was talking, he realised with a start, of Miss Ella. 'She came here this time in a great crisis of self-distrust. I would call it a *religious crisis*! She begged Sister Paola for a more difficult miracle than mending her broken back and, when asked what it was, said "Make a true woman of me!" Can you imagine greater humility?' asked the abbess.

Nicola drew breath and thought I'll tell her. I must! The breath

400

escaped and he drew another. Then the chaplain said, 'Here's a carriage.' He had been standing at the window. 'It's the duke's.'

The three rushed downstairs.

Flavio was distraught. The balloon had indeed been swept out to sea. He wailed, 'They should have landed! *Oddio*! Why didn't they? I waved from the beach, but they paid no attention. People have gone out in boats. Could they rescue them if they fell into the water? It seems unlikely. I hope you're all praying!'

He sounded frantic. Oh God, prayed Nicola with embarrassment – recent dealings with *Him* were all tinged with that – don't let him let the cat out of the bag. You, Yourself, he argued mentally, said it was better for a man to be drowned with a millstone tied around his neck than to bring scandal! But thoughts of drowning had a discomforting immediacy to them and he had to stop himself wishing a murderous wish or praying a blasphemous prayer.

Meanwhile, the abbess, looking gratified, told the duke that the convent was indeed praying for his intention. She waved a hand to where the two rows of nuns, rosaries in hand, moved back and forth like the pendulum of a clock. A voice rose thinly, listing the Five Sorrowful Mysteries. The abbess looked at Flavio, as though hoping that he would now at last promise to marry the desperate Miss Ella. False worldly distinctions, she must be thinking, were all that prevented this. Human respect! Arrogance of lineage! Sternly, she looked him in the eye.

Nicola marvelled that good people – the abbess was undoubtedly good – should be left by God in such ignorance of the way things were that their best efforts were misdirected. Perhaps God was flummoxed by today's world?

He frowned at Flavio who might be tempted to try trading false promises for a true miracle. Just now, Nicola guessed, he had the Prime Mover in his sights and, no doubt confused by his own shifts, failed to see that he was being punished by Mobility's own avatar: the wind. Pinching his elbow, Nicola whispered: 'Don't even think of it!' His eye caught the abbess's. She looked amazed.

Flavio's eyes bulged painfully. They were netted in red veins, for he had spent hours on a windy hilltop scrutinising the sky and had, he said, ended up seeing globes everywhere. At last, blind from scanning clouds, he had given up. If only, he exclaimed, there were something one could *do*!

'Oh Christ! Oh shit! Sorry! Sorry, sorry! Better stay quiet!'

But moments later, he was raging again. Fancy her having the gall to

401

come asking for a miracle! he exclaimed. Mind you, it was in character! She would see nothing wrong with a whole convent being turned upside down on her behalf. Arsyversy! It was the circus-player in her. Not just a convent either! Half Cesena had taken to horse and carriage and gone to look out over the coast. Maybe they too expected a miracle? Or a disaster? It would, he cried bitterly, no doubt, be all the same to them!

Rushing to the window, he thrust a spit-moistened finger into the wind then pulled his arm in with a movement which menaced the sky. He was like a rabid beast which bites itself.

The chaplain reproved him. The people of this parish were, he said, God-fearing and devoted to Sister Paola. 'They're undoubtedly praying that she'll be able to persuade heaven to send us a miracle!'

'We must each do what we can.' The abbess looked at Flavio as though to mesmerise him. 'It was His will that brought you here!'

Flanking him, like good and bad angels, Nicola and she stood ready with contradictory advice.

'*Oremus!*' The chaplain, a well-intentioned umpire, fell on his knees.

Under his lead, the abbess ground out a decade of the rosary, interceding with the Virgin in the interests, thought Nicola, of a marriage not much odder, after all, than that of celibates like himself whose female soul was bride to the divine groom! Going down on one knee to murmur responses, he thought: our imagery is mad! Divinely mad? I am under strain.

Standing up left them all at a loss until the abbess proposed a refreshment, which was accepted with gratitude. Afterwards, Flavio drew Nicola out onto the balcony on the pretext of again testing the wind. He said, 'I'll have to say something. They won't leave me alone until I do.' And he tied a silk scarf to the iron balcony. The wind blew it eastwards.

'Tell them,' advised Nicola, 'you'll do anything short of sin.'

Flavio did this and Nicola kept his eyes on the rippling cloth while listening to his own ventriloquised casuistry.

Thanking God for what she took to be a promise, if not indeed a miracle, the abbess hurried off to inform Sister Paola. The chaplain went too.

'What you should know,' Flavio told Nicola, once they were alone, 'is that we are in no position to alienate nuns or their chaplains.'

The loan, he confessed, was going badly. Bonds were not being bought. Clerical support was tepid and it looked as though the Catholic financier would do less well for the Vatican than Rothschild had done in the past. Moreover – here the duke's voice sank to a whisper – our reputations were under fire. It appeared that Langrand's agents in Hungary had tricked Catholic peasants into signing papers they could neither read nor understand. In return for small land parcels – probably too small to provide a living – these illiterates had bound themselves to make payments which would enslave them for life. 'They're the new serfs,' he admitted, 'and will surely end up having to surrender the land.'

Nicola was horrified. 'Have we compromised the Vatican? Did the Papal Blessing influence these victims? We must dissociate ourselves at once!'

'*Piano*, Monsignore!' Flavio shook his head. 'That would depress the bonds further and then Catholics whom we have persuaded to buy would be out of pocket or even ruined. Nuns. Poor priests. Other peasants. Not to speak of His Holiness himself!'

'But these wretched Hungarians!'

We must, said Flavio, find a way to remedy that. Langrand might not know what his agents had been doing. Once told, he would surely make reparations. 'Trust me,' said the duke and Nicola wondered whether he should.

But then, how trustworthy was he himself? He had, it now came out, been sadly imprudent. Flavio had more bad news.

'La Diotallevi . . .' He raised a quizzical eyebrow.

'What?'

'Told the Mérode faction that you instructed her to denounce them, so they want to bring you down – and "you" may mean us!' Flavio looked like a man forbearing to throw the first stone.

'What I told her . . .' Nicola stopped. There was no defence. He who intrigues to no purpose is doubly to blame. Institutional pride – mistaken for selflessness – had been the beam in his eye.

In a bafflement of remorse – must he now engage in further remedial politicking? – he was gazing out to where the scarf was still streaming eastwards when he saw something amazing. The balloon was coming back! Rosy in the sunset's glow, and travelling westward like a second sun, it reached the pitch of its trajectory just as the first, more constant orb sank. Just then, like an eyelid raised for a celestial wink, a cloudlet lifted off it. The Monsignore, feeling absolved and reprimanded – a familiar blend – told himself that visions came from yearning and certitude: two forces which could in incandescent moments unite to constrain the universe. They could also, apparently, accommodate deception.

What surprised him was that his own diffident nature should witness the nun's miracle. His mind refused it, finding it unjust and keenly troublesome, yet here it was! The balloon was sailing into the very teeth of the wind which was still blowing Flavio's scarf the other way!

'God!' he cried. 'It is a reproof to reason!' And indeed logic must have lulled, for he felt a leap and lightening of the heart.

Later, he would be shocked at his egotism in supposing God's signal to be directed particularly at himself. Later still, he saw that it had brought distinct messages to those who beheld it. God was thrifty in His ways.

The French balloonist slapped himself, then opened and closed his fists and, flexing a leg, indulged in a little *gymnastique*. He had gone through this routine several times since landing. One must, he explained, keep the blood circulating. It was remarkable how little most people knew about the body, not to speak of the world. They lacked *instruction*! Especially here.

'Not that I'm being critical, Monsignore! Our own rural population is no better. Some Breton peasants burned a balloon on me once when I landed in their field of artichokes. I was lucky not to be burned myself as some sort of devil. I suppose I looked like one, slithering from the basket on my belly! I'd twisted my ankle, you see. You'd be surprised at the lack of progress in our hinterland. So you lived in Paris for a while, Monsignore? Ah now, that's a different kettle of fish! Another universe, you might say! There were balloons there in the days of Louis XV! You wouldn't find Parisians imagining that rising up to catch a contrary wind was a miracle!'

'Did you expect all along to do that?' asked Nicola.

'Of course! We watched the clouds! Science is a matter of observation, Monsignore. We knew that when we wanted to we could throw out ballast, rise, catch the east wind and turn around. No need of divine intervention! No need of saintly nuns!'

Nicola invited the two balloonists to join him in a hot drink. Punch? Cinnamon wine? They were just driving into Cesena.

They accepted. They were Monsieur et Madame Poitevin, internationally known balloonists, at your service, Monsignore. Mind, the flight had not been without its hazards. They were suffering from exposure on account of the height to which they had been obliged to rise and, due to navigational difficulties, things had taken longer than foreseen. But they were in high spirits. Laughing with ebullience and relief.

It was no surprise, they noted, that Miss Ella should be wedded to the idea of a miracle. Circus folk were superstitious – unlike balloonists, who were scientific. That was why ballooning was largely a French pursuit! It was a logical business. Take today's adventure with the wind. Of course the horse had suffered, poor beast! The Poitevins hadn't wanted to take him and hadn't predicted the long flight when they did. But Miss Ella had held out. Hippophiles could be temperamental. Monsieur Poitevin had noticed this. Horses themselves were stubborn and impulsive and, over time, an exchange of character could occur between rider and mount. Not that she had used her own mount on the flight. No, no. This was some poor nag who would, doubtless, now end as dog-meat. And it went without saying that she had not spent the flight on the wretched creature's back. As soon as we were well out of sight of the crowd, she had skipped up the ladder and into the basket. A true professional. One did not perform for seals and sea gulls!

'Very good of you, Monsignore, to take us back in your carriage! Being stranded is one of the hazards of our sport.'

Spending time in the convent, though they didn't say so, would clearly not have been congenial. Hot punch in the best Cesena could supply in the way of lodgings was more like it. And a fire and a rest. Then back they would go to Bologna. They had a show to prepare. Come and see it, Monsignore. Better, let us take you up and show you what it's like. Unfortunately, one cannot steer a balloon, or we would take you to Bologna in ours!

'But you did steer it!'

'Ah, but that was approximate. As you saw, we landed in a field. Very good of you to come and get us.'

'How is Miss Ella?' Nicola had hardly seen her before she was taken off in Flavio's carriage.

They told him that she was suffering from cold. She had insisted on wearing her circus rig! Wanted to do acrobatics in the air! Well, I ask you! Madame Poitevin cranked her forehead. Luckily we had some blankets. 'Oh dear! I was about to say she was a bit *montata*! *Exaltée*! Well, she does have her head in the clouds! She may be ill for a while.'

So it was not a miracle! Nicola's relief gave way to a mild disappointment which reproached him, for he must – he saw – have inflicted worse

405

when exposing the thaumaturges who had transfigured the reality of small stinking villages.

Miracles brought scope and significance to trapped lives. Did it matter whether they were true? The question frightened him. Shelving it as tricky – for what was true? – he prevailed on Flavio to keep quiet about a story which did not reflect well on their personae as solid businessmen and pillars of the Papal Loan. There was an instability about the episode which would not reassure possible purchasers of bonds. And Miss Ella must now be got rid of.

'So,' said Flavio, 'we're back where we started!'

'Where else would we be?'

Perhaps Flavio was more worried than he let on about business confidence – an equivalent, as Nicola now knew, of the Faith. At any rate, he gave in and some days later Miss Ella came to see Nicola in his hotel in Cesena. Her carriage was outside, loaded with trunks. A second one, drawn up behind it, was heavily curtained, but he saw the curtains twitch as though someone were nervously pulling them to.

She was leaving, she told him, thanks to him, who had ruined what had been a pure friendship. As it happened, she was not sorry to go and it was in no spirit of disappointment that she was confronting him. No, merely of justice. He deserved punishment, and so she had written a letter to Monsignor Pila, the Justice Minister – she smirked – denouncing Flavio and himself for taking bribes from Langrand-Dumonceau.

'Naturally, I would not be telling you this if I were not leaving straight away for Louisiana with a friend.' She curtsied, pirouetted, then ran down to her two carriages which, moments later, rattled impudently down the street and out of Cesena.

Nicola wondered whether it was by chance or design that she had hit on the most dangerous person to whom to denounce him? He had thought her childish, but children can manipulate malice with a cool finesse. Though unable to gauge the randomness of her bull's-eye, he was sufficiently dismayed by it – since Monsignor Pila would surely seize any pretext to ruin him – to head for Bologna whither Flavio had fled from Miss Ella. He had hoped to consult him but found that there could be no question of that, for Flavio was mournful and *furioso* in the way Orlando must have been when his brain joined those of other lunatics in the valleys of the moon. He had been drinking absinthe for days and, startled by his friend's arrival, fell and hit his head on a brazier, so that Nicola, to prevent any further éclat, had to nurse him with the help of a valet, but without that of a doctor, after Flavio tried to assault one they did bring in. He charged the bewildered man with conniving with lecherous priests. After that, it was several days before Nicola dared leave him alone.

When it finally seemed safe to do so, he went out for air and, feeling in need of a change of scene, called on Monsieur and Madame Poitevin and reminded them of the offer to take him up in a balloon. The couple were delighted. Tomorrow then.

Oh, by the way, said they, they had seen Miss Ella. Yes, she was bound for Livorno where she planned to take ship for North America. The Poitevins nodded pinkly and their cheeks bobbed like apples in water. She had introduced them to her new friend, the convent chaplain who, in the course of trying to convert her, had himself been converted. Padre Gamba planned to join some Protestant sect in North America which, he hoped, would have him as a priest. Madame Poitevin presumed the two would marry – what other advantage had the Protestant priesthood over our own, she asked teasingly, but the Monsignore was not up to engaging in the sort of banter which such queries aim to elicit from a prelate. He was thinking that Flavio's remarks about lecherous priests now made sense! Poor gull, he thought of Padre Gamba! He was crossing an ocean in pursuit of a false religion and an impossible love!

It was a week for confrontations.

La Diotallevi was in the hall when he returned to his hotel. Hiding her light – she had a scandalous visibility to her – under a shawl, she was lurking with her back to the door. *Sotto voce*, she murmured that they must talk. She had come from Rome to do so.

They agreed to make their separate ways to the cathedral which was one of the few places where they could be seen together without scandal, and there, standing in the middle of the nave, so as to give no cover to eavesdroppers, he learned what had happened with Monsignor de Mérode, to whom she had not, she swore, denounced him. Instead, her efforts to have a confidential conversation with the Arms Minister had attracted the attention of his henchmen, Pila and Matteucci, who insisted on knowing why she wanted it. She, since she had to tell them something, said she had scruples over what they had made her do. The pair promptly took fright and locked her up for a few nights to teach her to keep her mouth shut. This, however, proved their undoing, for Mérode heard about it and summoned her, whereupon she told him that she had committed perjury in his interests and that her testimony against, for instance, Signor Fausti, had been entirely false.

'You were quite right, Monsignore,' she told Nicola. 'He was stunned. Disbelieving at first, then indignant. His first impulse was rage. He's a choleric man and I thought he might hit me. He who touches pitch, said he, meaning that I was pitch, must expect to be defiled. Then he said pitch couldn't help being what it was and that I was less to blame than he. "Well, you came here to confess my sins to me," said he sarcastically. "Not your own! So I'm the one in need of absolution!" Then out he stormed, ranting something about the waters of tribulation.'

She was now terrified lest he wreak his fury on Pila and Matteucci who had endangered his soul – Monsignor de Mérode was genuinely devout – and tarnished his honour. Because, if he didn't utterly destroy them, they would then wreak theirs on her.

'I've come to you, Monsignore, for my sake, but also for yours.' The word scruples had, she explained, alerted the two as to the likelihood that she had been to confession to some enemy of theirs. They had made inquiries. Her maid, a simple creature, had been interrogated by the morals police and had told them that a Monsignor Santi had come to the house one day in a wet cassock and had had to remove it and . . . La Diotallevi stopped. 'Need I say more, Monsignore? Forewarned is forearmed. I came to tip you off. I'm doing my best for you.'

And he, ran the implication, should do the same for her. For now she intended lying low here in Bologna, where, as it happened, she had friends. He too, she warned, should take measures to protect himself. To be sure, Monsignor de Mérode might effectively clip the wings of his underlings. But best be on the *qui vive*.

That night Nicola did not sleep at all. Flavio was now better, but news like this might send him back to the absinthe bottle. So, left to wrestle with his demons alone, Nicola read his breviary and tossed and turned and lit a candle and read some more and blew it out again maybe six or seven times over. What had he done wrong? He had associated with people – Flavio and Cardinal Amandi – who had enemies and so drawn these on himself. But that answer didn't reach his deeper anxiety. The question gnawing at him was why such naked evil should be rampant among us and ready to pounce on our smallest mistake. Surely, it hadn't always been like this?

The Pope had addressed himself to this very matter last December in an encyclical to which he had appended a list of the errors of our time. The *Syllabus Errorum* censured pantheism, naturalism, nationalism, indifferentism, socialism, communism, freemasonry and a host of other contemporary views, including the proposition that 'the Roman Pontiff can and ought to reconcile himself to, and agree with, progress, liberalism and contemporary civilisation'. The conservative clergy hoped this censure would save us from the flood of errors. They saw the Church as a house whose foundations could be sapped unless dykes were built around it. Others, like Amandi, thought of it as a barque which could ride the flood. *They* believed that changing thought reflected a changing world and that if we engaged in a dialogue with it we could pick out the good and reject the bad. Quarrels between partisans of these differing strategies were by now sourer than the one with the Italians.

Perhaps it was partly due to light-headedness after his sleepless night, but Nicola's jaunt in the Poitevins' balloon brought a joy such as he remembered only from dreams, and he felt his anxieties melt as the couple took him soaring through sunshot clouds and circular rainbows and over a Bologna which looked as one might imagine it being seen by God. Neat within its pretty walls, it gleamed, after a baptism of rain, like an illuminated miniature of one of the towns of old Christendom, garlanded in Faith's dicta and vivid with gold leaf. A God looking down at this might suppose it to be easier than it was for His servants to take the long view. Faith, He would imagine, could sustain them.

And in this instance, He would, as it turned out, be right, for there was no move from the Mérodiani, who had other fish to fry. In less than a twinkling – as seen from Eternity – an amazing thing was to happen. On an October day in 1865, Monsignor de Mérode would be sacked quite suddenly and obliged to remove himself bag and baggage from the Arms Ministry on the piazza della Pilotta. He had, said the usual gossips, been caught stealing funds. No. His subordinates had! Well, anyway, they must have done something reprehensible. No smoke without fire and the Mérodiani, a Curia-within-the-Curia, had been insufferably overweening. Having the Police and the Justice Ministry within their ranks, they had thought themselves untouchable. Well, they'd learned otherwise. Gaining in colour, the news spread through Rome.

Nicola heard it with a grateful relief. In its way, it was a miracle as unlooked for as the balloon's return, but his notion of the miraculous was increasingly leery. He was not willing to waste faith on untenable outposts of his creed. Perhaps he had simply grown up? He preferred to think of the once conniving sky as empty. No God looked down with a balloonist's eye or replaced whatever kind, tutelary face had bent over us in the cradle. Faith was vulnerable and Nicola's instinctive way of protecting it was to refine it to something interior and abstract which offered less of a target to disillusion.

To his surprise, the abbess agreed. He went to see her in trepidation, fearing that she would want to publicise Sister Paola's miracle by printing up cards and calendars and maybe even finding some spring whose waters could be bottled. But no. None of that was on her mind. Sister Paola, she said, would not want it either. Though she knew nothing about winds blowing differently on different levels, the abbess had, it appeared, enough experience of truth's shifts to choose caution over enthusiasm. And sure enough, when news came of the wretched chaplain's having absconded with the *miraculée*, this caution proved wise. Perhaps she had intuited something? The convent was, it seemed, a web of intuition and Sister Paola, though still in retreat, sent Nicola a message.

'To me? What had you told her of me?'

'Nothing,' said the abbess, 'though Miss Ella will have described you to her as the devil's advocate, if not the devil himself. Sister Paola, however, is not easily taken in and has startling perceptions, so listen. She says you need not worry about Miss Ella's venom but must forgive her because she is unhappy and her revenge will fail. Don't ask me what she means. It may become clear to yourself. We find that detachment from personal appetites hones the perceptions. Sister Paola, for instance, is an excellent dowser. She found a well here with a hazel rod. We're not calling that a miracle, as you may imagine. We'd be laughed out of the province, where quite a few people can dowse and tell cards and set bones and prophesy with or without almanacs. That's why we don't believe in making claims. After all, as you, his advocate, must know, Monsignore, more magic comes from the devil than from God. God is remote but the devil is close and uses cures and tricks to make people trust him. Her other message to you is that you and she will meet soon.'

And, sure enough, the revenge failed, for Monsignori Pila and

Matteucci soon lost their places, being cast down from their seats by Cardinal Antonelli who, while refraining from gloating or triumphing over Monsignor de Mérode, of whom he spoke everywhere with generous courtesy, ruthlessly crushed former minions of his own who had gone to work for the former Arms Minister and made sure that they would never again get their treacherous hands on the levers of power. Pila and Matteucci, who had cooked up false charges against his friend, Fausti, could, like the fraudulent in Dante's hell, expect the worst penalties.

In time, details came out about Mérode's fall. He had not, as vulgar gossips claimed, misappropriated funds. However, he had been high-handed and drawn out monies for his men without bothering to discover whether the Treasury could afford them. Then he had turned the Council of Ministers into a bear-garden, insulted people and even been disrespectful to the Pope. This misconduct had, Nicola noticed with interest, increased markedly after the Diotallevi told Mérode of his responsibility for injustices and fraud. Perhaps, in an expiatory spirit, he had drawn punishment down on his own head?

The Pope's mode of dealing with him was swift. Mérode was dismissed 'for health reasons' and given a hundred *scudi* a month while awaiting a new appointment. But, some days later, as scandalous calumnies were being bandied about, Pius asked the sacked minister to walk down the Corso with him so as to show that he, Pius, did not believe them. It was Mérode himself who reported his retort on being told that this was the reason for their walk: 'But Your Holiness,' said he, 'is seen every day in the company of every sort of rogue!' He was as arrogant as ever and refused to accept an archbishopric *in partibus*, saying, 'I didn't become a priest for such gewgaws.'

Flavio admired him. 'He's been driven mad,' he claimed, 'like some hero in a Greek tragedy. Like Orestes! Trying to get anything done in Rome could do that. Think of his situation. He brought his old commanding officer, General de la Moricière, here to try and create an army in the teeth of a hostile bureaucracy, lack of money, subterfuges, affable lies, etcetera, etcetera. Mérode felt both impotent and respon-sible. I'm surprised he didn't kill anyone! Someone will yet!'

But by the time Flavio said this the Papal Loan was an acknowledged fiasco and he, understandably, was sour.

Twenty-three

It was the eve of Cesco's twenty-first birthday and Prospero and Nicola were house guests. Neighbours dropped by and dogs and children were under foot. Smiling with indiscriminate goodwill, the count kept saying, 'I remember . . .'

'What, father?' Prospero found the old man aged.

'How *he* came here!' Airy syllables were released like soap bubbles: '*Il Pa-pa*!' The old man's memories were irridescent, for Dottor Pasolini's medications kept him in a state of bliss. 'Cesco does too, don't you, Cesco?'

Cesco and a girl were leafing through an album bright with verses copied in the colours of the *Carbonari*: flame-red, coal-black and smoky-blue. Blue was for hope. Marking his place, Cesco's finger nestled among riffled pages. 'The Pope's visit,' he mocked, 'is our great pride. One day we'll erect a plaque!'

The girl laughed. She was so young that she had only just put up her hair. Martelli, her uncle, was now a deputy in the Italian parliament.

'A breeder,' thought Prospero, noticing her hips. He felt the unease which was one reason why he rarely came. Another was work. As a consultor for the Congregation of the Index, he had accepted a press of it and brought some with him in a locked leather box.

'Monsignore!' Daniele offered sweet wine.

Prospero smiled at Daniele who had once, eight years ago, put him out of the house or anyway refused him admittance. 'You mustn't come in,' he had told Prospero, who had just arrived from Rome. 'It would revive things! I'm afraid he's demented.'

This was six months after Anna's death, and Prospero had had no answer to his letters. After the funeral his father had been too ill to see him. Daniele turned up his palms helplessly.

'What about the boy?'

'*I* look after him.'

But the place smelled. The dog's ear was frilled with ticks and Daniele's eyes looked as though images of domestic degeneracy were imprinted on them. Did the doctor come? Prospero had asked. Yes, he was told, regularly. So, still covered with travelling dust, he got back into his carriage and drove off. Later, at his insistence, the doctor arranged for Cesco to be sent to the Scolopian Fathers' boarding school.

Meanwhile, Prospero made his way by taking a degree *in utroque jure* and working in a number of capacities – voting prelate, ponent, regent, auditor for various tribunals – and did not try to see his father who had a bee in his bonnet and blamed him for Anna's death in childbirth.

Then, one day in 1857, Monsignor de Mérode told him that the Pope wanted Prospero with him on a tour of the Romagna. It was, though nobody knew this, to be the last of such touring, for two years later the province would be annexed by Piedmont.

'He wants to see your father.'

In May the Pope set off, and, in June, Prospero joined the papal party at the Legatine Villa outside Bologna from whence side trips would be made, among them one to the Villa Chiara. Greying wisteria blooms drooped on every wall.

'My father will torment His Holiness with requests for reforms.'

'They'll be refused,' said Mérode. 'At most he may lift the state of siege – and maybe not that. This is a disloyal province. Skinflint and unruly! They say this visit is beggaring them. I say think of the loaves and fishes.' Mérode's long arms waved. He had a windmill's silhouette: quixotic and thin in his shaft of black cassock. He had one bad eye.

Prospero asked whether, on its way here, the papal party had stayed in the Pope's family home in Senigallia. Yes, said the chamberlain, and described the house as a large four-storey box full of apartments for hangers-on and poor relations. 'Tribal and down-at-heel, with coats of arms stuck all over it. The Mastai-Ferretti turn out to be quite small fry. It seems that a not-so-remote ancestor made his living selling combs. Locals were quick to tell such things.'

'Did he know?'

'We protect him some of the time.' Mérode grinned. His rough tongue was notorious.

The coming meeting filled Prospero with apprehension. Though his actions had been those of a dutiful son, his father's suspicion of him had grounds. Prospero had not wished him well in his marriage.

*

413

'We shall intercede for each other,' His Holiness had told him when planning the visit. Doubtless, he aimed to catch his old political mentor on the wrong foot. The peace-making between the Stanga father and son could be a useful red herring. Pius had a flair for such wiles and liked to inspire diffidence before dispelling it.

For example, at the start of this audience, he had seemed so immersed in a book that Prospero, having made the three ritual genuflections and kissed the ring abstractedly presented to him, had to remain on his knees for over a minute, until Pius, as though only now realising who was here, snapped the book to, waved away ceremony, and ruffled his kneeling visitor's hair.

It was Mérode who had – impishly – reminded Mastai of Prospero's existence. Though not yet Arms Minister, the chamberlain's presence in the papal household was like a gundog's in a roomful of cats. His father had been in the running to be Belgium's king; his motto was 'honour, not honours'; and, though devoted to this 'pope-king' whose ancestor had peddled combs, he reserved his respect for the Pope.

On the appointed day, Prospero reached his father's villa in a separate carriage from the Pope and waited while the old men reviewed the incompatibility of their hopes. They were of an age: sixty-five, but relegation to provincial idleness had eroded Count Stanga's vigour, whereas Pius, though often ailing and despaired of, had the stamina of power. When Prospero joined them, the Pope displayed his charm. He throve on conviviality and it was known that his ministers had often to retract concessions made in its glow. Now, however, it was he who extracted one from the Stangas. Father and son embraced and the embrace received a papal blessing. He, alas, could not reciprocate, said Mastai, handing back the list of requests which the count had drawn up. Being answerable to God, he was not free to say 'yes'. Then he beamed the full force of his personality on them. How describe this? Manliness plus godliness? Belief in his mandate? Yes, both of these plus a rush of energy which Prospero, later, would not be able to explain. He heard the Pope's words as clues through which a fuller meaning seemed spasmodically to flash. A radiance transfigured them, as flames will a dish of – say – *flambé* kidneys which seconds later will be no more than singed meat. In the same way the Pope's words could, in retrospect, seem flat. But then, was a pained flatness perhaps Mastai's message?

'The world, old friend,' he lamented, 'is not so much divided between conservatives and the other sort as between men who do and do not believe what they say.'

Following him down dim corridors, they saw light catch the nap of his soutane and halo his silhouette. The count, as they emerged, held his rejected petition with a tender triumph, and it was clear to Prospero that he believed he had received satisfaction. Tomorrow, he would have trouble explaining this to lucid friends.

Outside, a convoy of carriages awaited and the household was on its knees on the gravel as the white sleeve semaphored a blessing. Then the convoy shook itself into motion and departed with snorts, equine tremors and a whirr of reedy wheels.

Prospero and his father walked back indoors.

'I challenged him,' said the count whom age was thinning like an old broom. '"Trust your people, Holiness," I said, "take a risk!" Maybe he'll think about it.' For a moment his eyes brightened. But then he startled Prospero by asking: 'Do I know you? Forgive me. My mind slips. It's why I prefer not to meet many people any more. It can be embarrassing.'

Now, seven more years had passed. '*Il Pa-pa!*' The count, repeating his trick, released imaginary soap bubbles from playful lips.

More than bubbles had collapsed since that visit of 1857, and a prime casualty had been peace at the papal court, where some put their trust in the French Emperor's garrison, and others could not see why Louis Napoleon sent men to fight Liberalism in Mexico while, here in Rome, he let it threaten the head of Christendom.

Even at the Villa Chiara such matters had their impact, having caused Prospero and Cardinal Amandi to quarrel. This was why His Eminence would not be attending Cesco's party. The disappointed family held Prospero to blame, and discomfort lent momentum to a skirmish over the guest list.

On arriving, he had asked, 'Aren't you inviting the parish priest?' But several guests, including the girl whom Cesco was to marry, belonged to families with whom the *parocco* would not wish to break bread. A number of convents had been expropriated. Deputies who had voted for the measures were excommunicated; the girl's uncle was one of these and the *parocco* had denounced him from the pulpit. Well . . .

Prospero let the matter drop. However, just before the birthday, a guest fell ill, leaving the party at thirteen, an unlucky number. There had been thirteen diners at the Last Supper. Thirteen at table heralded a death, and with the reputation the villa already had ... Prospero, reluctantly, picked up the allusion. Deaths came in threes and a girl thinking of marrying Cesco might fear to be the third Contessa Stanga to die young.

'I'll stay in my room.'

'No, not you!'

Prospero was an ornament to the family. So was Nicola. Guests would be impressed by their purple and would have been more so by the cardinal's red *zucchetto*. Being to blame for its absence, Prospero felt unable to protest when his relatives combined disrespect for the cloth with a profane pride in it. When asked: 'Is it too late to invite the *parocco*?', he meekly agreed to present the last-minute invitation.

But the *parocco* was less susceptible to Roman charm than might have been hoped. Just last week, he complained, Liberals had thrown a maggoty, dead dog into his well and he had suffered other *disgusti* which made it seem wiser to stand on principle. He spoke under correction, being a mere rural priest.

Prospero asked, 'Should we not leave the door open for the lost sheep?'

The *parocco* said that, around here, Monsignore, what came in through open doors were wolves. 'It's money they're after,' he said. 'That's why they closed the covents and sold up what was in them. Money to pay the soldiers who expropriate us. That's what it comes down to. Robbery! I had two sisters in a convent that's been sold. Now they're like lost souls!'

Prospero, imagining his sisters and the trouble he was having with them, felt ashamed of his errand.

'Don't come,' he blurted.

The *parocco* looked down at his hands. 'I know how to hold my tongue,' he said with dignity. 'I took the liberty of telling Your Excellency how things are here. But I wouldn't do so at Your Excellency's father's table.'

'Please call me Monsignore. I'm not an Excellency.'

'Do you think I should come, Monsignore?'

By now Prospero had doubts. Was the priest sure it was *Liberals* who threw the dog in his well? What about brigands? But the priest said, 'Brigands don't waste time like that. They chop your fingers off if you denounce them. Else they leave you alone.'

'Well, you'll be welcome if you'd care to honour us. But I must be

416

frank with you. A man whom you denounced will be there. I won't persuade you to come against your own judgment.'

'May I think about it?' asked the priest. 'Say my mass tomorrow morning, then decide?'

Prospero agreed, accepted a cup of something which tasted of poverty – 'coffee' made from roasted barley? – and walked back to the villa.

'Is he coming?' asked Cesco.

Prospero had to say he didn't know.

'*Merda*,' cried Cesco rowdily. 'Someone else has dropped out now, so if he *does* come we'll be thirteen! You couldn't discourage him, I suppose?' Wheedling charmingly, Cesco looked, Prospero feared, very like himself.

'No.'

'Well, if he'd just *say* now, we could still ask the Orsini to bring their tutor. Tomorrow may be too late.'

Keeping his temper, Prospero said that could not be helped.

At dinner there was a tiff about salt. There was too much in the soup, said Cesco. Could not the cook use less? 'After all,' he told his father, 'I can't take it out, but you could put more in!'

But his father said that the cook had been following Prospero's mother's recipe.

Cesco poured wine into his bowl. 'Well, Papa, when I get married you'll have to put up with *my* wife's recipes! Tit for tat!'

'Ha! So will you!'

The two laughed and Prospero saw that what upset them was the strain of his presence. Whenever he came here, he grew stiff and became a strain to himself.

Retiring early, he locked his door before taking out the keys to a box he had brought with him. He opened it, selected a pamphlet from the stack inside and settled down to read. Outside his window, crickets kept up their churr which, he had been told, was made by a rubbing of the limbs. Their monotony irritated him. It was like that of the hack writers whose products he must assess so as to decide whether to recommend fulminating an anathema against them. A distasteful duty. Akin to sewage control. Last March he had seen foreigners look amused by the book-burning taking place on the steps of San Carlo al Corso as part of the Lenten ceremonies. Braziers had been erected and the burning was done by priests and gendarmes: an unfortunate conjunction. Seeing it with strangers' eyes, he had wished that the books had simply been ignored. There would be a risk, of course. He did see this. Sighing, he read:

> Who is Pius IX? A younger son, Giovanni Maria took the tonsure early with an eye to a benefice to which his family had a claim. Tonsured laymen could enjoy the financial advantages pertaining to such livings, while leaving the actual work to poor clerics who received a pittance for their pains.
>
> He was a poor scholar and his schooling was cut short by epilepsy when doctors advised he rest his brain. Taking them at their word, he gave himself up to the pleasures of provincial life, and was soon a consummate local lion, adept at billiards, fencing, hunting and smoking, and even trying his hand at the flute, the violincello and light verse. A would-be dandy, he had the sartorial tastes of a barber's apprentice and devised for himself a semi-military rig designed to attract the fair sex. This consisted of a grey cutaway-coat with black frogs, a red peaked cap, striped trousers, a high collar, a floating cravat and spurs. He was rarely without a flower in his buttonhole and a cigar in his mouth. Thus equipped he began with plebeian conquests but soon aspired to aristocratic game. His milk sister, la Morandi, was one of his loves and rumours hint at biblical intimacies with a blood sister, Maria-Isabella. His luck ran out when he fell in love with Princess Elena Albani, whose disdain drove him to leave for Rome where his uncle, Monsignor Paolo Mastai, was well placed to help with his career. Here he eked out a small allowance by genteel card-sharping. The old Princess Chigi was one of his victims and her grandson's recent appointment as nuncio in Paris is said to be Mastai's way of repaying what he took from her. He also frequented the Colonna, Doria and Pianciani palaces, and Count Luigi Pianciani has revealed how contacts made there were to help him climb the ecclesiastical ladder. Chief among these was Donna Clara Colonna who was later to pay the expenses of his elevation to the cardinalate, laying out, according to some estimates, over thirty thousand francs. Nor did the young man neglect the ordinary women of the Trastevere, whose Sabine blood has left them with an inborn readiness to be ravished . . .

Prospero's eyes began to close so that he could not tell whether he was reading or dreaming when he came on the venerable canard told about almost every pope, that he was a *papa universalis* who fathered bastards in the flesh and humanity in the spirit. Forcing himself to wake up, he put the pamphlet back in its box and turned the three keys in their locks.

*

Next morning, he breakfasted in the unquiet company of Cesco who roved about, eating bread smeared with honey, from which now and again, always at the last possible moment, he caught an escaping dangle with a quick flick of his tongue.

'That boy's restless,' Dottor Pasolini had said when Prospero paid a call on him the day before yesterday. 'He's seeing too much of agitators and Democrats.'

'*You* say that!'

'Oh, I'm a quiet man now,' said the doctor. 'The new authorities aren't perfect. I should know. But they should be given a chance.'

He had fallen foul of them, but bore no rancour. It had been something, Prospero thought, to do with medical hygiene.

As they talked, Prospero inhaled the fustiness cocooning the old bachelor's quarters. Dogs' coats contributed to it and so did a tang of gunpowder and memories of fruit. It was a complex, masculine smell quite unlike the one in his own rooms in Rome. Pasolini offered brandy from a bottle frosted with lichen which, when scraped with a fingernail, released a chill, subaqueous gleam. Earlier in the day, he had ridden his horse across a stream, which was why his boots and britches were steaming by the fire and he himself in need of a restorative glass.

'You'll join me, Monsignore? I suppose I call you that now?'

Prospero, forestalling the old Mason's irony, explained that his was a purely titular rank since his diocese – Philippi – fell outside the control of the Holy See. Like other Roman administrators, he had been awarded a bishopric *in partibus infidelium* – though, indeed, distinctions between real and titular had faded since Italian bishops were so often prevented from taking up their duties.

'Some would say, Doctor, that *this* is infidel country.'

The doctor mused. 'Infidel? But to what can people be said to be unfaithful at a time of change? For you it's simple, but I, you see, consider that we had a right to seek unity and that we now owe loyalty to the king who achieved it. Some, however, want further changes.'

Prospero laughed. The doctor shook his head. 'I know, I know! When we squabble, you feel triumphant. But that doesn't prove you're right.' Pouring himself and Prospero a little more plum brandy – it was fiery stuff – he said, 'Speaking in confidence, some are up to their old games. Not here. Close to Rome on our side of the border they've hidden guns. A certain prefect found out and telegraphed his superiors for orders, and do you know the answer he got?' Like paper exposed to heat, the doctor's face shrivelled darkly.

'They told him to help the gun-runners!'

'*Bravo*, Monsignore! You understand the world!' The doctor lowered his voice. 'Turin is giving the Democrats rope. To crack down on them would divide our ranks. Besides, they can be used. Last spring, if the Pope had died and an uprising taken place in Rome, our troops would have gone in to put it down and, naturally, once in, they would have stayed.'

Prospero was not surprised. Conspirators, Mérode had told him, were spending a fortune trying to corrupt the Army. And certain cardinals were being vetted and courted. The Italians wanted to see the tiara pass into pliant hands.

It was then that Prospero had confronted Amandi with a straight question: was he intriguing? Amandi had furiously denied the charge and they had not spoken since.

'Omens . . .' Cesco was saying.

His brother didn't listen. His mind was in the doctor's brownish room where muzzles rested on padded paws and golden eyes flicked. He thought of the dogs as weaving the old man into the landscape from whose mesh they would retrieve any game he might shoot and to which they surely returned with each blink of those mild, vigilant eyes. Sometimes, a limb twitched or a canine groan seemed to sense and vent their master's feelings – for the old conspirator was a prey to melancholy. Political triumph was as ashes in his mouth – and how could Prospero not rejoice? His joy, though, was tempered. He longed to taste those ashes himself!

As he and Cesco finished breakfast, they were joined by Nicola and talk about being thirteen at table was revived. Cesco was impatient for the *parocco*'s answer, but Prospero refused to harry the priest. Instead, he shifted the topic to some silver which his brother had bought. It had belonged to Il Passatore, a brigand who had got his name from his secondary activity of smuggling – 'passing' – men across borders in the days before unity. When he was killed, the police sold off unclaimed objects from his ill-gotten haul. Cesco displayed tableware from which unknown monograms had been erased, then recalled legends about the outlaw whose defiance of papal troops had given him an ambiguous appeal. Withdrawing after each outrage to the reedy thickets in the marsh, he and his band were credited with acts whose immodecacy roused awe. They had enjoyed hospitality in safe houses all over the

420

province where, it was claimed, they had dined with their women on the finest fare brought by accomplices from who knew where? The kitchens of great palaces perhaps? Conceivably the Legate's own? Menus of these banquets had been celebrated in broadsheets which were brought by the hungry and angry as finite substitutes for prayer. Food was what the popular imagination relished: cakes, roasts, jellies, sweetbreads and kidneys swimming in gravy. Dreams about these fed the fantasy better than any Eucharist. Spleen pâté flavoured with anchovies and capers, thrush pie, roasted eel and those fanciful roasts consisting, say, of larks inside pigeons inside guinea-hens inside geese: an ascending image of hierarchy whose ultimate human eater enjoys the supremacy of a lion. Sometimes, it was alleged, the bandits had distributed basketsfull to the needy, and the surplus from their banquets had fed a village. People hung chromolithographs of Il Passatore on their walls alongside those of Garibaldi and Bassi, 'the honest priest'. Of the three, the bandit was the most congenial. A creature of the night, he focused old fancies about witchlike figures who defied the laws of probability and avenged the grim lives of the downtrodden. When your oppressor was a priest, you could, said Cesco, be driven to paganism, since religion ceased to console.

'He gave them something solid to dream about.'

Prospero let this pass. He held his peace until Cesco said, 'They say he was the Pope's bastard.'

'Who?'

'Il Passatore. He looked a bit like Papa Mastai and . . .'

Prospero was outraged. 'The *Italians*,' he hissed, for his voice was failing him, 'are brigands and their defence is to call their victim the father of a brigand! Venal hacks lie and idiots listen!' The other two looked shocked. 'It could,' he whispered hoarsely, 'be lethal!'

'Lethal?' Nicola, cutting himself a slice of bread, was taken aback.

'Just think about it!' ordered Prospero. 'We know the plans of the Pope's enemies! They were in the *Opinione* of last April for all to see. Counting on his death, they kill his reputation as a prelude perhaps to worse! Like it or not, though, his health has recovered.'

Nicola, his knife poised in wonder, asked, 'Why wouldn't I like it?'

Prospero left the room. He might have left the villa if this had not meant leaving the *parocco* to dine alone with Cesco and his priest-baiting friends. Nicola too needed protection, though for the opposite reason: he could fall under their influence, being in some ways a nincompoop!

421

His orphan-state had, in Prospero's opinion, left him without instinct. A fallen nestling, reared by hand, cannot be safely returned to the wild.

Back in his room, he confronted his locked box. It was, he thought, like Pandora's, then caught himself. No. Things were not *like* any more. Things *were*. This was infidel country! The metaphors had grown real. Words poisoned. Words killed. And nobody had the right to be innocent.

Rearranging his pamphlets, he fancied that his fingers tingled at the contact. The French ones were the most dangerous, since they misled the Emperor's electorate in the hope that it would oblige him to cease protecting the Pope.

Outside the window, a horseman in dusty black was jogging up the drive. The *parocco*! Eager to reach him before Cesco did, Prospero locked his box and ran down. His father, however, had got there first. The count, whose days were spent vaguely pottering, welcomed any diversion.

'I'll call Daniele,' he was telling the visitor. 'He'll take your horse. Brisk day isn't it? Who did you say you were?'

The parish priest said he was the parish priest.

'No,' said the count. 'He doesn't come here. He's a bigot and I'm told a bit of a rustic who's not really up to a parish like this. We used to have the Pope here once. He was our bishop. This is my son, Monsignor Stanga. Prospero, this gentleman is looking for the parish priest. I've been telling him that he won't find him here, but it's come back to me that there was talk of inviting him so we wouldn't be thirteen at table. Do you know about that?'

Prospero managed to get rid of his father and tried to apologise for him, but the priest was not in the mood for soothing.

'I have been thinking,' said the priest, 'of Christ's command to pray for those who persecute and calumniate us. A man can become obsessed by petty things. What, after all, is a dead dog stinking up one's well when compared with His Passion? Or petty insults? I will dine with you.'

Clearly, he was indifferent to the whys and wherefores of the invitation he was accepting in such a sacrificial spirit. Its Prime Mover did not, he had decided, dwell in the villa.

When he left, Prospero returned to his room, where he spent the next hour reading a summary of an English pamphlet printed on cheap paper which blurred the ink. It had been published in Holborn, London, and was entitled: *Revelations by Alessandro Gavazzi, ex-Friar of the Barnabite Order concerning the True and Veritable Origins, Life and Deeds of Pope Pius*

IX, based on the Author's own Privileged Knowledge, together with Documents obtained during the Roman Republic from the Archives of the Apostolic Chancery and Other Sources:

In this brochure, the writer who, after being a priest of the Catholic faith, became a missionary for the Protestant one, brings to light an episode in the life of the Roman Pontiff to which few are privy.

Lest any wonder why the author waited until now to reveal what is narrated below, it was from reluctance to divulge privileged information. Such scruples, however, have been swept away by the publication of the *Syllabus of Errors* wherein Mastai throws down the gauntlet to the modern world.

In 1831, patriots in the Papal States were encouraged by the French Revolution of the previous July and a body of them began to march on Rome, heading first for Spoleto, where Mastai-Ferretti was archbishop. Misinformed about their strength and fearing for his life, he fled to the hills where he took refuge in a Capuchin convent. What happened there has not until now been told.

It was March. The nights were cold and to this convent had come scores of other refugees. Driving their animals before them, they converged on the convent which was soon so packed that latecomers had to sleep in barns and haylofts.

Your author was there too and dined with the archbishop, who was in a feverish state and strolled out after the meal, saying that he wanted to clear his head.

Prospero pushed the thing away, drew it back and sighed. Gavazzi had made a name for himself in England and America, where his preacher's talents gave force to his renegade's rage. The story – Prospero ran a practised eye down the pages – combined stock elements with some odd enough to suggest that this episode had not been invented from whole cloth. Gavazzi described a group of women who had found accommodation in a wash-house, their efforts to make themselves comfortable, his own good offices, and the indiscretions of a young nun who had befriended a girl with whom, alleged the ex-*abate*, Mastai now made love in a shooting blind. She told him the girl's story: a sad one of incest or near-incest with a clerical uncle living in the mountains some way from here. The nun was from these mountains herself, which was why the girl had confided in her. She understood the shifts to which people could be driven by isolation. Now, the girl had wandered off and Gavazzi helped look for her. However, it was a bright night. People had lit bonfires and it seemed unlikely that she could fail to find her way back.

423

A more pressing danger was that rebels might come here in search of food. Accordingly, he and one or two others resolved to keep watch. They posted themselves some way from the convent and it was during this vigil that he portrayed himself as indulging in musings which prepared his later apostasy. A crisis of conscience. A description of a faith's first, premonitory stagger. He was a young man then and affected, as much as anyone, by the uncertainty of the moment – as much, he implied, as Mastai himself.

It was possible, remember, that the march on Rome might succeed in separating the sceptre from the tiara. A pope had just died and the voices of the old popes had diminished authority. As the abbé Lammenais wrote of a papal encyclical, 'its lines are like the swaddlings of a mummy: it speaks to a world which no longer exists; its voice is akin to those dim sounds which echo in the sacred tombs of the priests at Memphis'. Why should choices made in the past bind the present? How could men who could not foresee it legislate for a changing future? These were the questions agitating me on that clouded night.

Meanwhile, here I was, a sentinel on the watch lest the volunteers of a new order come to rob us. Rob? Requisition? Emancipate? Free? It would be another decade before I could resolve those doubts. Luckily, nobody came except my replacement who relieved me just after dawn. I chatted with him a while, then returned slowly to the convent, for I was in no hurry to get back to those sad huddles of people whose bonfires would have gone out, whose babies would be crying, and whose doubts and fears would force me to seem more authoritarian and sure than I felt. As a priest, I represented the regime and wished I didn't.

Prospero resisted an impulse to tear the thing up. Its slyness infuriated him. Also its apparent sincerity. Undoubtedly, it would be read and would do harm! The story was like an opera libretto. Abstracted in his troubled thoughts, the ex-abate now stumbled on the shooting blind where the archbisop and the girl had spent the night. Instinctively, he hid behind a rock – for, said he, a poor preacher does not willingly antagonise an archbishop – and saw first one, then the other, emerge. Later, the women in the wash-house told him that the girl had returned safe and sound. She had been overtaken by darkness and, fearing to lose her footing and fall into a ravine, preferred to wait for daylight before returning. She had, said her friend the nun, spent the night in a shooting blind. A sensible girl, the abate observed. Yes, said the nun, she's resourceful enough.

424

Months later, finding himself near the nuns' convent, he called on the young pretty one and was received in the parlour.

> I have forgotten her name and perhaps had already forgotten it then. A sworn celibate has to be an athlete of oblivion and I was as quick to detect the onset of temptation as a shepherd to sniff snow on the wind. When I did, I turned tail. How do otherwise? I was already locked in a struggle with one fever: the doubt which was, eighteen years later and after many vicissitudes, to bring me here to England. But that is another story.
>
> I asked about the girl and the nun avoided my eye. She too had lost her candour and was now as glumly forbidding as any Mistress of Novices could have wished. The girl, she lowered her voice, was to have a baby in a few weeks. And then? She shrugged. I left and, although I met many such cases . . .

Here Prospero's pencil wrote in a furious comment: 'Many? Author tries to portray old Papal States as sink of immorality, whereas they were, notoriously, as chaste and decent as old patriarchal Rome!'

> . . . this one stuck in my mind: the sad pretty girl and the sad pretty nun. By coincidence . . .

'*Ha*!' wrote Prospero's sceptical pencil.

> . . . while preaching near Bologna, I stayed at the villa of Count Stanga . . .

Abashed, the pencil slipped from his hand.

> . . . an ardent Liberal who had contacts with my order. We, the Barnabites, partly because of our old rivalry with the Jesuits, were inclined to Liberalism and, because of our access to the pulpit and the confessional, were able to subtly spread news and ideas. Also, because of our itinerant life as mission preachers, we often smuggled letters for our friends. It may seem an odd activity for members of the regular clergy, but ours was a state where the very authorities which we were obliged to venerate as our spiritual superiors were often corrupt and oppressive as temporal lords.
>
> Countess Stanga's maiden name, being the same as the girl's, brought her story to mind and when I told it, she recalled having had cousins, now dead of cholera, who must have been the girl's parents and said another relative, Monsignor Amandi, might know more. She put us in touch. I again told the story. The Monsignore promised to investigate and, some weeks later, asked me to do him a favour. He wanted the child delivered to a wet nurse and, desiring to put as few people in the secret as could be

managed, turned to me who was already cognizant of it and whose movements, since I was a travelling preacher, would not attract attention. I agreed. He provided a carriage and a female servant for the journey and I duly delivered the infant who received the name . . .

This time Prospero did not resist his impulse, but burned the pamphlet in his charcoal hand-warmer, scorching his sleeve in the process. It was filth. One did not fulminate anathemas at filth. Pouring water from a ewer, he washed his hands which were black with the pamphlet's ink and a residue of ash.

Cesco's birthday dinner was not a success. The count had taken too much laudanum. There were thirteen diners and news of Cesco's engagement unleashed some unseemly ribaldry. Prospero, distrusting his emotions, sat at the other end of the table from Nicola, the doctor and the *parocco*, and so was unable to monitor their conversation, although the words he did catch revealed its topic to be dogs.

The count's hand seemed to lose co-ordination and he kept feeding himself with an imaginary spoon. '*Qui n'avait ja-, ja-, ja . . .*' he sang under his breath.

In a freak lull, the doctor's whisper flew up the table confiding that, while doing his rounds, he often persuaded people to ignore Rome's orders and come to terms with the new regime. 'I tell them to vote!' *Had* he said this? Nicola and the *parocco* looked insufficiently shocked and Prospero was prevented from hearing more by Martelli's chatter.

'Charity . . .' argued Martelli.

Prospero blotted him out. He would not bandy words with a man who sat in a parliament dedicated to the seizure of Rome.

'. . . *jamais navigué!*'

'What breed?' the doctor asked the priest.

'Oh, it had been dead for weeks and was unrecognisable. Big though. It could have been a gundog.'

Prospero strained his ears and, as a moment of silence greeted the dishing up of a mound of rice garnished with truffles, heard Nicola promise the priest to preach in his church next Sunday. About conciliation. Peace. The virtue of meekness! The two might have been reciting the Sermon on the Mount.

'I'll come,' said the doctor. 'I haven't darkened a church door for years, but I'll come for that!'

426

Prospero bit his tongue painfully. Nicola was unreliable, unsafe on the question of the Temporal Power, and likely to confuse the simple.

Martelli wanted to hear about Prospero's quarrel with Cardinal Amandi. Had it been about the *Syllabus of Errors*? He began to quote from this with angry amusement. Was this why His Eminence wasn't here?

'We should love our enemies,' came from down the table.

'But not the Pope's!' Prospero shouted.

Martelli pointed out that he, though the *parocco* had denounced him, was sitting down to dinner with him because on joyful occasions like this old quarrels should be forgotten. Then he stood up to toast the engaged couple and, swaying on his feet, told a story which stunned his niece and made her mother blush. It was about a quick-witted young mother walking through a market with her small son. 'Let me kiss that child,' cries an impudent admirer, 'in memory of the place out of which it came.' 'Why,' says the mother, 'don't you kiss my husband's cock? It was there more recently!' Martelli was drunk. Prospero pulled his coat-tails and got him to sit down. Then, to help the company recover, he teased the *parocco* about his offer to let Nicola preach in his church. He himself, said he, had hoped to preach a sermon there. Nicola promptly withdrew and the *parocco* said he would be honoured to have a preacher of Monsignor Stanga's distinction.

Martelli, however, had begun to brood. Talking of denunciations, he said suddenly, Monsignor Santi had been denounced in the Democrats' paper, *Roma O Morte*, by someone who signed his letter 'Indignant from Subiaco'. 'Am I right, Monsignor Santi,' he called, 'in thinking that you never did discover who "indignant" was? Well, I can tell you, and I've seen the proof! It was Monsignor Stanga. He had a go-between, of course, a man with one foot in the Democrat camp!'

'What proof?' asked Prospero coolly, guessing that there was none.

'Poor Captain Melzi,' said the count, 'was a man with one foot.'

The doctor looked shaken and so did Nicola.

'*Ohé, ohé*,' sang the count sadly.

'Is it true or isn't it?' challenged Martelli.

It was. Alerted by Mérode to Amandi's fraternising with the enemy, Prospero had taken the law into his own hands and, to minimise scandal, named Nicola rather than the cardinal. The two had needed a warning. Appeasers were the enemy's Trojan horse, as he intended saying in the sermon he would preach next Sunday. Our cause was greater than the requirements of our own moral comfort. He was not ashamed. No. But

427

neither did he relish the damage which could be done by Martelli's revelation. Many could be troubled in their faith. Candour was a luxury he must forgo. So: 'No,' he said to Martelli's question. 'It is not.' As he had guessed, the deputy was unable to prove his allegation and, just then, a diversion providentially dispersed embarrassment, as the count, about whom everyone had forgotten, fell face first into his plate of *riso ai tartufi bianchi*.

Twenty-four

Flavio slid a marrow-spoon into a bone and greedily swivelled it. Like the glint on old coins, his grin was patinous. 'This time it will be different. Count Langrand-Dumonceau . . .'

'*Count!*' To Nicola, it was now almost a bad word.

'*Noblesse oblige!* He and I plan to make good the losses which, by the way, were far from being our fault. Factors beyond our . . .'

'You've told me! The American war! Tight money!'

'Tight Catholics! But don't let's argue.' A hand landed on Nicola's sleeve. He was being softened up.

It was 1866 and the Loan, an acknowledged fiasco, had failed to generate half the hoped-for amount. Bonds, moreover, were trading at 75 per cent which meant that the good Catholics who had been badgered into buying them were out of pocket. Meanwhile, Langrand-Dumonceau was the recipient of a papal title. Nicola, who had helped get it, found it galling to have traded sacred things for money – the sin of simony – only to be bilked. What, argued Flavio, was sacred about a papal title? Whoremasters had had it! Murderers! Look, he blandished, we mustn't quarrel. The count had a new plan. Grander in scope than the Loan – but we'll talk after dinner. 'Have a savoury. Meanwhile, did you hear about the young sprigs of good family who were reported to the Pope for misbehaving in this very restaurant? They'd toasted the King of Italy. Well, Pius's response was, "It's for their papas to deal with, not for *il papa!*" The waiter heard it from Monsignor Talbot, the *cameriere segreto*. What a cosy town this is! And what a wise pope!'

'I suppose you're hoping I'll sell whatever Langrand's new idea is to the Treasury?'

Flavio leaned forward. 'Can you imagine the Treasury resisting fourteen hundred million francs?' He gleamed. 'That should balance H.H.'s mind and budget.' He raised his glass. 'Peace? It should,' he added comfortably, 'stop him firing off anathemas at the king who takes them to heart, poor man. I'm told he stays scrupulously away from the communion table.' The duke tittered.

Nicola thought, He's Hermes: a reincarnation of the old god of gossip – and theft. But Flavio, as though denying this, reminded him that he and Langrand had lost money on the Loan which colleagues had now dubbed 'the hole'. Promotion costs, agents' fees and advances had taken a toll. Delicately, he did not say 'bribes'.

'We too have losses to recoup, which is why you may rely on our new proposal.' This, however, seemed hard to describe, for he circled it, lingering on the needs of the papal and Italian treasuries. Desperate remedies were needed.

'Desperate? Do you mean criminal?'

'Don't think of it like that!'

'Of what?' asked Nicola. 'You haven't said.'

'The sale of the Church's real estate in Italy.' This, like it or not, said Flavio, was about to be enforced by the Italian parliament, so we must try to minimise the loss. *And* we must rid our minds of old comparisons. This was no time for references to the Roman soldiers dicing for Christ's robe. 'Don't look like that, Monsignore. There's no time! The Italian government may fall, so if we don't deal while we can with Catholic ministers, we may have to deal with anti-Catholic ones.'

Through Nicola's mind floated the words '. . . let this chalice pass'. How had he come to be the man in the breach? His superiors would leave the first, tricky assessment to him whom, later, they could, of course, deny. Flavio watched.

'This is no time for hand-wringing. We must persuade His Holiness to let us save what may be saved. Good can come out of it. You'll have liquid money! Let's talk like businessmen.'

'Don't you mean thieves?'

The duke recommended realism. As the property was on Italian soil, we could not prevent its being seized. And this time it would not be a few rundown convents. It could be the lot. Yet, a deal could be struck. The Church could exact compensation in return for letting the Italians claim that their action was legal.

'You want me excommunicated!'

Flavio begged his friend to consider this: the next pope was likely to be a conciliator, but *if* the property was gone when he came to power, no amount of conciliating could save it! *Now* was the time for that. Think of the future, he urged. It's only good sense.

Was it? How trust one's own good sense if that of our leading theologian had led him astray? Padre Passaglia had now been excommunicated. Debates were going on too as to whether Italy's entire army was under ban of excommunication. A definite anathema hung over its ministers.

'Describe your scheme.'

The duke did. Put brutally, the Italians wanted the Church's assets sold at once. This was crucial, for the sale ended their inalienability: *la manomorta*. Langrand's plan, saving what might be saved, was for two thirds of the proceeds to go to the Church and a third to the state. 'Count Langrand's enterprises will get a percentage – the share of a mouse. Remember the mouse which released a lion from a trap? We are your mouse. We'll buy your property outright, then resell it slowly so as not to depress the market. In the interests of winning the Italians' consent, we'll do the same for them. Over ten years you should realise fourteen hundred million. They will get six hundred million.'

'Two thirds of our own property strikes you as a lion's share?'

'We are talking of a trapped lion.'

That night Nicola lay awake and sweated as though already fanned by the winds of hell. It was a strangely warm spring and each time he drifted into sleep *la manomorta* turned up in nightmare disguise. Mingling with it was the image of himself as a stick in an old man's hand. Dead hand? Live? In one dream the stick twisted from the clenched hand and began to beat it – then the dreaming Nicola tried to fill the hand with coins. I am not, he thought sadly, a spiritual man. I haven't the passive faith of those who think God will somehow save us at the last. Someone must act. And if the Pope ... He did not pursue the discomforting thought. Yet the very stones of the city were resonant with whispers about popes who, being mad or wrongheaded, had had to be quietly disobeyed.

Over the next weeks, a freak heat encroached, siestas lengthened, and Romans in darkened rooms smoked to keep off the mosquitoes whose persistency paralleled that of Flavio, who ambushed prelates in the hot dusk of their offices, catching them in unbuttoned disarray, under peeling stucco in cafés and saloons, or on their slow, contemplative walks. Sometimes their clerical collars lay abandoned on chairs, revealing insides as brown as those of unscrubbed teapots.

'Lambs do not parley with the wolf,' was their stock reply to his pleas. Italy was the wolf. To acknowledge her existence was to collaborate in

431

her crime. Refusal to do so allowed prelates to think themselves resolute. So, no, they told the exasperated Flavio. *Non possumus!* Tirelessly, however, he kept working on key men from the Apostolic Chamber and lesser ones from anywhere at all who might, somehow, some day, turn out to be useful.

Regularly, in the evenings, he and Nicola met for a little restorative malice. Perhaps that bitter edge to Roman wit had always been compensatory? If so, it had now reached the highest echelons, being latent in the recent promotion of St Catherine to the ranks of the city's patron saints. Notoriously, she, in her day, had urged the popes to leave Avignon and break their connection with France. The choice was a sly insult to the French garrison, whose withdrawal would soon end another such connection. Good riddance, signalled the new patroness. *Bon débarras!*

As if they'd notice!

Flavio compared the curialists to small boys making rude signs under the lids of their desks.

Nicola suggested that Flavio himself bore Rome a grudge over the matter of Miss Ella. If so, could Rome trust him?

The duke's face reddened like blown coal, but he said, 'I've only myself to blame. We made jokes,' he stared into memory, 'which turned out not to be jokes, about her becoming a woman. How could I have known? Some quack she met on her Ottoman tour persuaded her that it could be done. Arabian Nights fancies! Jiggery-pokery! She was gullible like all gamblers and I'd upset her by proposing that we adopt a child. Anyway, she applied to Sister Paola, who was stunned. Yes, Monsignore. Nobody was quite frank with you. The nun saw her stripped and knew her for a 'twixter. But she kept her mouth shut, even with the abbess. She's a wise woman and saw that Miss Ella was not one to recognise the limits of possibility. I can imagine appalling scenes before you and I turned up, especially as it's not clear whether Ella made application to the good sister in her capacity as thaumaturge or amateur surgeon – she does things like lancing boils. Delicacy may be eliminated from reconstructions of the occasion. Hysterics undoubtedly included. Suicide threats led to their calling in the chaplain. The rest you know.'

Now that the story had been broached, it came up again. Flavio did not seem to harbour jealousy, but, instead, worried in a brotherly way about Miss Ella. 'How are they living?' he wondered. 'I sent them money, but it came back.'

Nicola, remembering Miss Ella's accusation, asked: '*Did* you bribe people here?'

'Do you really want to know?'

'No,' he decided, nervously.

One evening he found himself telling of his single afternoon of love with Maria, all those years ago, and of how he had fancied she might have had and left a child on the Foundlings' wheel. His confession was intended to show himself as human and humane, and, when he saw that this was why he was making it, he grew ashamed.

It fascinated his friend, who marvelled at Nicola's failure to establish the truth. A child, if there was one, would now be seventeen!

Once again they were enjoying a walk through a night dense with the energy of crickets. A plash of fountains showed that the city still had juice. That scrap of emotional detritus, the false image of the naked Queen of Naples, surfaced in Nicola's mind and shone like moonlight on mother of pearl. As it happened, the moon *was* shining and so was a bonfire on the steps of San Carlo al Corso.

'Ah, the book-burning!' cried the duke, and for moments they watched the oddly festive scene. Children were jumping in the firelight. Priests presided, and stacks of condemned or confiscated books were proving hard to burn. A policeman fluttered pages with a stick and a flame flared. In the gleam, Nicola discerned a known face: Father Grassi's. He had not seen him since the Jesuit had confided his readiness to back a conciliator for pope. Amandi? D'Andrea? Both men's stock had now slipped and Nicola doubted if Grassi would wish to be reminded. Keeping to the shadows, he murmured that he was going home.

'I'll walk along with you.' The duke was still thinking of the child. 'I'll hire someone to see if it exists,' he decided. 'If it does I'll adopt it. I can feel Fate taking a hand. It will be a seal on our friendship.'

Nicola, unable to admit, or indeed understand, his own revulsion, resolved to give Flavio no more information and, suddenly eager to shed his company, said he must get home. The duke, however, trotted beside him so that at moments Nicola was almost running from him. Somehow, plunging forward without thinking, they had climbed up to the Capitol and were looking down on the Forum. Here too a flicker of bonfires signalled book-burning. Tall, free-standing pillars rose against the reddish glow. Abruptly, he faced his companion.

'I don't want you to. I'll . . .'

'You'll stop me?' Flavio's grin caught the gleam of the inquisitors' fire. 'How? By denouncing me for sodomy? What proof could you

433

supply?' It had been a mistake to cross him. 'Unless,' he jeered angrily, 'you were to say that you and I had carnal relations which, in both our minds, I suspect we did.'

'Stop it, Flavio.' Nicola should have said more or less, but couldn't, because the smouldering in his friend's eye distressed him. Flavio was more worrying than Liberals who, after all, were predictable, whereas he was anarchic, magnetic and unsafe, so Nicola contented himself with offering his hand.

The duke batted it away. 'You wouldn't trust me with a child! You're as small-minded as the rest of your crew!' And down he strode, into the Campo Vaccino, past a dying bonfire turned to curling ashes which children had stirred so that they flew, glided, then alighted like malevolent birds. Silhouetted against the sky, the horns of an ox recalled Goya's painting of the black mass.

Flavio, thought Nicola, was mischief incarnate. And so, for all he knew, was Count Langrand-Dumonceau. Yet, over the next weeks, he patched up the quarrel and continued to work on their behalf since, in the cold light of day, theirs seemed to be the only lifeline anyone was throwing to the Church.

Indeed things had rarely looked worse, for Italy, by allying herself with Prussia in a quick summer war against Austria, now got hold of Venetia. After this, her most pressing concern could only be to annex the last piece of the state she had been assembling, as children assemble a jig-sawed image: Rome. On the day news came of Venetia's fall into Italian clutches, employees at the Treasury watched Cardinal Antonelli strike his forehead with both palms and cry aloud in shock. Meanwhile, as the French garrison prepared to leave them in the lurch, Roman householders grew sick with apprehension, and the only good outcome was that despair was making the Treasury more receptive to Count Langrand's agents. They, however, had grown impatient and, to Nicola's alarm, turned out to have made fraudulent claims in the Belgian press.

Monsignor Santi to Duke Cesarini:

Rome, January 1867

My dear duke,

Are you in Pesth? I write because of certain articles appearing in the Belgian press, claiming that the 'Roman clergy' is ready to accept the

434

agreement signed by L-D and the Italian Minister for Finance (Scialoia). Cardinal Antonelli has been obliged to deny the story and this does L-D's cause no good, especially as there seems to be evidence that the journalists were in his pay and spread misinformation in order to improve his companies' showing on the Paris stock exchange. I hope you can reassure me about this.

I walked through the piazza Pia when the French were selling off their possessions. The whole ghetto had turned out to do business and the garrison's dismantling was a foretaste of what may be ahead for us all.

Yours, etc.

February 1867

One damp day, when street cobbles were as radiant as prisms, Nicola received a visit. It was from Viterbo, who was in high feather, plumper than in the past, and pleased to report that he owned a business in Bologna, where his people were enjoying freedoms which would soon reach their co-religionaries in Rome.

'Soon?'

The printer smiled, extinguished his smile then, as if remembering that there was no longer any need to do this, let it blossom with luxurious ease across his face. The Temporal Power, he told Nicola amiably, has as little substance to it now as some old corpse in the catacombs which a breath could disperse. Pff! He blew illustratively, and again his smile unfurled. Nicola was going to say something sharp when Viterbo sighed. 'Too late for my nephew.'

Edgardo Mortara was now a priest. But his uncle hadn't come about that. No. He had brought a warning. Contrary to appearances, Count Langrand-Dumonceau's affairs were in a bad way. 'The truth is he's up the spout.' If the Vatican had an agreement with him, now was the time to back out. He added, 'I hear he's to have an audience with the Pope. Today, is it? You're surprised at my knowing? How do you think our community survives, Monsignore? We have to know things. And what we know about him is that he is paying high interest on secret loans.'

'You can't be serious?'

But Viterbo was. 'He's a flimflam artist!' He shrugged, adding that the financier's new companies had been founded to pay the old ones' debts, his profits were fictitious and the dividends he was paying were eroding what capital he had left. 1866 had been a bad year for everyone.

Last May had seen a run on the Bank of England and several companies had since closed their doors. 'Langrand's creditors, including the Prince von Thurn and Taxis who may yet sue him for fifteen million, are waiting to see whether he will make enough to pay them from the sale of the Church lands. It's his last throw and his profit on it is to be ten per cent. Now do you believe me?'

Nicola was still half-incredulous – for how believe the count could have been doing something as crude as the three-card trick which was to be seen on any market day on the piazza Montanara? Viterbo, however, swore that Langrand had indeed been moving assets from one company to another, as surreptiously as a trickster moved his card. And maybe those assets had now vanished? Langrand's company directors had, with the prodigality of desperation, distributed substantial bribes to newspapermen and officials in Vienna, Brussels, Pesth, Florence and here. Did the printer's sly politeness imply a belief that Nicola's palm too had been greased? The bribes were a bid to net contracts so as to fill coffers which must, if they were to be netted, seem already full.

'They've secretly raised loans with Jewish financiers. That,' said Viterbo, 'is how I know.'

The irony was blatant: the man who was to have rescued capitalism from Protestants and Jews had turned to them for help. An amused – and perhaps pitying – malice shone in Viterbo's eye.

'And Flavio?'

'Gentlemen like the duke sit on boards and lend them prestige, but the less they understand the better pleased is their paymaster.'

On Viterbo's departure, Nicola rushed to the Treasury where the news from the Vatican was that Count Langrand-Dumonceau, having finished his audience with His Holiness, had gone upstairs to Cardinal Antonelli's apartment. Nicola was seized with panic and rushed out again. Papa Mastai was notorious for letting charm run away with him and the foxy count, whose own charm was legendary, might have created an irresistible atmosphere. He imagined the two men locked in a magnetic contest so compelling that one or other must succumb. There could be no seduction without some yielding of the self – and the moment of yielding was one of danger. Outside the ministry, a man was loitering purposefully and Nicola recognised a Belgian journalist who had come to Rome in Langrand's train. Was he on the count's payroll? Did *he* suppose Nicola was?

'Monsignore!' The journalist's name was Brasseur. 'A good day for our cause, I think.'

'Why? Have you heard something?'

'That was what I had intended asking your lordship.'

'All I've heard is alarming news from Brussels about the count's affairs.' Nicola let this sink in. The two men eyed each other.

'Monsieur le Comte is often slandered.'

Nicola thought: what if Viterbo were an agent for the Rothschilds who might be after the agency themselves?

'Monsignore, I'd lay money that our affairs are in better train than you think.'

'Ours?'

Brasseur nodded. So he did think Nicola was on the payroll! Nicola, worrying, must have looked a little frantic for the journalist, clearly a man of quick sympathies, had in no time taken charge, shepherded him to the nearest café and provided a cup of comforting chocolate topped with winking foam.

Affairs like this, he sagely explained, demanded faith. 'Our motto, Monsignore, is the opposite of Rome's. *It* starts by saying *non possumus* and we, on the contrary, say *possumus*: we can do it, we'll find a way! We will too! You'll see. His Holiness will wait to be sure that the Italians accept our deal and then, *ad removendam maiorem calamitatem*, so will he. It's the choice of the lesser of two evils. It never fails.'

Brasseur now began to rally the monsignore by telling jokes. He had refined the art of friendship until he could slip into the role of friend as fast as an actor into that of Pantaloon.

By the time Nicola had finished his chocolate, colleagues from the Treasury had come by with the latest bulletin: no concessions had been made. They condoled with him whom they expected to find cast down by this and were perplexed by his relief. Then he and Brasseur sat on and argued as amiably and easily as if they had been in school together, which they might as well have been, since the journalist had been taught by Jesuits in Belgium. These, he explained, had only differed from the Roman ones in that they had been more severe. They had to be. In countries where the Church was embattled, they had to turn out men staunch for the faith. Warriors! Men of purpose! Even, said the journalist, men who knew how to be ruthless in a good cause!

'You in Rome, Monsignore, have no idea how it is for us. That's why you don't give your wholehearted backing to the count when he tries to defend you against your enemies. He's a crusader too!'

In the course of their talk, Nicola pumped his companion about Langrand's solvency and received such assurances about Turkish railway

437

contracts in the offing and fat profits to be expected from the resale of Hungarian estates that he began to discount Viterbo's gossip. Brasseur was untroubled by the reports of Mastai's and Antonelli's reluctance to accept Langrand's plan.

'That's the thesis,' he said with confidence. 'Later we'll get the hypothesis. That's how it always is in Rome. Principle yields to practice.'

After dinner – they'd repaired to Lepri's – and more wine, and talk and friendship, Nicola's confidence in the Langrand enterprises was almost totally restored. In return, the journalist confided that he remembered his days in boarding school at Brugelette as the happiest of his life. People might deride such sentiments, but, Monsignore, where but in such enclaves as those guarded by the rectitude and affection of the Jesuits did a man ever see the Christian virtues in action?

'I mean humility, obedience, love, meekness and inwardness – am I right, Monsignore? These are our defining virtues? Which, alas, we too rarely practise? These *are* they?'

Nicola agreed that they were.

The journalist nodded. Rome too, he said, was a sacred enclave.

The following week was one of shame and devastation.

An article appeared in a Belgian newspaper in which 'the knowledge-able Monsignor Santi' was quoted as having revealed that the Langrand plan had the secret approval of the Roman Court which was only denying it for political reasons. 'Oh, it's the usual story', was the statement attributed to the sly monsignore; 'we have seen the thesis and must await the hypothesis.' Asked to explain these recondite terms he chose to illustrate rather than define. 'When a Roman prince says he disapproves of usury, we have the thesis. When he marries a banker's daughter, we have the hypothesis.' Nicola's delivery was described as 'silky'.

An indignant denial from his pen would – he was sorrowfully advised – undoubtedly make matters worse. He had been branded a hypocrite and his protests must now arouse hilarity or scorn. Let others take over, advised his superiors who accepted his explanations with a pained forbearance.

The *Giornale di Roma* promptly denied that the plan had the Pope's approval and so did the *Civiltà Cattolica*. And this, though some prelates continued to favour the scheme, made Nicola's position at the Treasury untenable.

Meanwhile there was trouble in Florence too, where the Italian parliament – recently moved there from Turin – was equally averse to its government's agreement with Langrand. Its anti-clerical majority now presented a bill forbidding the Church to own any real property in Italy at all. This, the harshest measure yet, was said to have made the Pope weep.

In the light of all this, Nicola's indiscretion was bitterly deplored and he was obliged to leave the Treasury. Nobody, in his hearing, pronounced the word bribe, but he saw with savage mortification that his choice lay between being taken for an intriguer or an innocent – to put it mildly – who should never have been let loose! Rome now became hateful to him and his self-esteem did not improve when he read that Langrand's shares had soared sharply after the publication of the mendacious article. A man as inept as he at wordly intrigue should, he told himself furiously, become a monk. As it was, he skulked in his apartment, saw nobody, inflicted various penances on himself, and only when advised by his confessor that the greatest penance would be to show himself, reluctantly emerged to join the leisurely, gossipy, hateful and reproachful social round of semi-idle Roman prelates.

He was all the more moved to receive a warm note from Prospero commiserating on his troubles at the hands of 'that pest of our times, journalism'. He wrote back gratefully and, within days, received an intimation that the post of coadjutor to Cardinal Amandi was his for the asking. His Eminence's health – often a euphemism for 'opinions' – was giving cause for concern and it was thought that his diocesan duties were proving onerous. The prospect of a pastoral retreat was balm to Nicola. Moreover, if poor Amandi was being forced to accept a coadjutor, it was surely better for this to be a friend. Accordingly, having intimated a readiness to accept, he was summoned for a chat with a representative of the Congregation of Bishops who warned that the task might be thorny. Amandi's diocese had not recovered from its vacancy during the sullen years when the Pope's realm and that of Italy had been unable to bring themselves to communicate. As a result, many dioceses were in a deplorable state. Children had remained unbaptized or were given defiant names like 'Atheist'. Priests kept concubines. Churches were in disrepair. In Amandi's particular case . . . The prelate paused. Had Monsignore Santi heard? No? Well . . . With distaste he revealed a scandal. A nursing convent containing less than the statutory six nuns was to have been closed down in accordance with the Italian law of last July. On this occasion, however, an odd thing had occurred. Locals had seized it, declaring that they did not want the nuns dispersed, since they

439

did more good than anyone else, and that the people had not voted to escape the tyranny of a Pope-King only to be saddled with that of a King-Pope.

The prelate from the Congregation raised a monitory palm. 'Don't take this for loyalty to us, Monsignore! It is, alas, an example of the sort of folk-religion which escapes our control. There have been clashes with the police which we, to be sure, are accused of having fomented and a rumour has gained ground that one nun is an abortionist. Her name,' the prelate looked at his notes, 'is Sister Paola'.

When Nicola asked what was the attitude of the cardinal, the prelate looked forbearingly at the ceiling.

Cardinal Amandi's appearance was a shock. When Nicola arrived, he was staring at a blank wall and, when asked how he was, merely waved a limp hand. His Vicar-General, a friendly, shrewd-eyed man, whispered that, to avoid scandal, he had been doing his best to keep people away. 'He speaks only to his cat.'

Nicola remembered the creature: a white pedigree Persian with paw pads the colour of camellias and enormous amber eyes. It had been a gift from an Eastern patriarch and the cardinal's cassock was often veined with its long hairs.

'He says,' murmured the Vicar General behind his hand, 'that it, like himself, shows its wisdom by hiding under his hat!' He pointed to a chair on which the cardinal's biretta lay rakishly aslant. Beneath it, a frilly, frivolous tail emerged with the impropriety of an ostrich plume. 'Also,' the Vicar General sounded weary, 'that many red hats cover less brains! All this started after he returned from a visit to Lourdes and received a letter from the Holy Father.'

Nicola sighed. 'A reprimand?' he guessed. 'For trying to restrain the visionary?'

The other man nodded. 'His Holiness told him to stop meddling. That's why he's refusing to do anything about our latest trouble.'

'Get me a spoon,' Amandi directed and pointed to a silver one lying on a side table. Nicola handed it to him and the cardinal began to wave it about as though conducting an imaginary orchestra. The Vicar General closed exasperated eyes.

And now the cat, attracted by the patch of reflected sunlight which the spoon was bouncing on the floor, jumped down and began to chase it. The cardinal had a practised hand. A puppeteer without glove or strings, he made the creature curl and uncurl, then leap, spin and roll on its spine, as the light haloing its head enticed it this way and that.

'You,' the cardinal told it, 'chase what has no substance. You try to eat the light, don't you? Don't you?' And indeed the cat was making efforts to bite the sparkle and trap it with its claws. 'Your name,' Amandi told it, 'is Light-eater! *Mangia-luce!* You're not the only one in the realm who tries to swallow the light. Who thinks it can be taken inside themselves. And that,' facing Nicola eye to eye for the first time, 'is more dangerous than swallowing one's rage!' He pointed at the animal which was now sitting back on its haunches. 'He's shrewd, a little fat, and apt to chase figments. White-robed too. Of whom does he remind you?'

'Eminence!' reproached the Vicar-General.

The cardinal tittered. 'You're shocked! That means you understand me! Unlike poor *Mangialuce!*' The cat had now jumped on his lap and was raising its head for caresses. 'He lives,' said the cardinal pleasantly, 'in a world of reflections. It's his form of worship. *Lumen de lumine.* Yet bring him the Holy Ghost in the form of a dove and what would he do? Take communion. Some of our rituals have so lost meaning that a cat could understand them better than we do! Please take note that I do not fall into the heresy of saying that the mysteries of our religion are mere metaphors.' His voice had slipped into a singsong, like those of children repeating a lesson learned by rote. 'All I do say is that repeated prohibitions to think will not defeat modern science nor put out its light. It can neither be eaten nor caught in the claws.'

'Surely. Eminence . . .'

'Surely no one's trying? Don't delude yourself, Monsignore! Do you know where the Roman Lighteater is planning to lead us next? He's summoning a Council to dogmatise the *Syllabus Errorum* and have himself declared infallible! Don't ask what little bird told me! It wasn't the dove of peace!'

The Vicar-General drew Nicola from the room while the cardinal was still laughing. Behind them he began to intone propositions from the *Syllabus*. 'And if anyone shall say,' he droned, 'that the Church is not a true, perfect and fully free society . . .'

'I'm glad it was you they sent.'

'. . . or that it is the prerogative of the Civil Power to define its rights . . .'

'A stranger could be scandalised!'

'Let him be anathema!' roared the cardinal.

441

'You must be tired.' The Vicar-General tried to ignore the voice which had grown mischeviously loud as they moved off.

'*Reprobamus, proscribimus et damnamus!*'

The cardinal did not appear at lunch, which was a barometer of his spirits, since he usually plied a good knife and fork and would, in his right mind, have sacked the cook.

Nicola asked about the convent which peasants were trying to keep open. The Vicar-General sighed and rolled his eyes.

'And the nun?'

'She'll have to be dealt with.'

Before dealing, however, with Sister Paola, it was necessary to deal with her protectors who had mounted a picket outside her convent and were refusing to let anyone in or out. They included professional agitators who had been paid to foment trouble during the years when it was Rome's policy to make its lost provinces ungovernable. This had now lapsed. There was no pay for enforcing it and the disbanded men had nothing better to do than offer their talents to the locals. Thus what might have been a brief brawl had become a three-way deadlock, for the police were outmanned and Garibaldini, infuriated by this, were threatening to burn down the convent.

'It's just talk for now,' said Dottor Pasolini who was still hale and hearty, despite or because of the riding he did in all weathers. He had no time for the hotheads, the most excitable of whom was a smith, nicknamed Vulcan because of his trade and his jealousy of his young wife. This was the woman whom Sister Paola was alleged to have aborted. 'It's nonsense,' said the doctor. 'She developed a false pregnancy which disappeared. That's the long and short of it. Vulcan, however, a mulish fellow in more ways than one, can't accept this. He wants children, you see, and gets bees in his bonnet. The most recent is about a young red-headed curate whom he thinks was sweet on his wife.'

'And this, presumably, is why he blames Sister Paola?'

The doctor shrugged. Who could say? 'There was talk before this of girls coming to her for help of that sort. True? Half true? She has been a magnet for attention ever since it was put about that she changed the course of the wind to save some balloonists. Attention can be dangerous. And a generation has grown up which has never known the arts of peace!'

The doctor himself planned to practise these by going to the capital ... no, no, not Rome! Florence! He had friends in the government there. This incident, he would tell them, was a straw in the wind: a burning straw. Their new law on convents was too extreme.

Nicola's next move was to pay a visit to the red-haired priest who, though on his guard at first, unbent when he saw that the Coadjutor was keeping an open mind. He admitted that he had perhaps been imprudent in his dealings with the blacksmith's wife, who had come to him because of her barrenness and her fear that this might be a punishment for her husband's free-thinking. Perhaps, he admitted, he had encouraged this fear. He was a morose, tormented man. How, he asked the Coadjutor abruptly, can we know it isn't true?

'Because God doesn't take sides!'

The priest was shocked. Did Rome not represent God? Yes, said Nicola warily, but perhaps a less fierce God than the one served by the red-headed priest who, for his soul's peace – here he found the same phrases in his mouth as had been said to him when the Treasury was showing him the door – might be wise to move to another parish. The man looked resentful, seeing this as a judgment against him.

In May came the doctor's bulletin from Florence. It roused the cardinal from his apathy and revived his Coadjutor's hopes, for, confounding all likelihood, Langrand-Dumonceau had pulled off a coup! He had persuaded the Italians to strike out the worst part of their own draconian law. A contract, signed by their new Minister for Finance, ignored the clause declaring Church property forfeit, and agreed that, if the count would undertake its liquidation and pay the Italian government six hundred million francs over the next four years, the Church could keep the fourteen hundred million likely to be realised by the sale of the rest.

'Think,' Langrand had murmured into the ministerial ear, 'of the stimulus to the economy! You can develop their lands and they will need to invest their cash!'

Surely, argued the doctor's letter, this concession made it possible for the Pope to do business?

His next words fairly leaped off the page: a goodwill clause was to be incorporated whereby, in the interests of showing how a free Church could function in a free state, Sister Paola's little hospital could stay open as 'an example of the Church at its best'.

'That,' Amandi squinted through the gold wire spectacles which had a tendency to slide down his nose, 'will stick in the papal gullet! I advise you to see that it is dropped before the contract goes to Rome.'

Nicola did not argue since, as he reminded the cardinal, he was no longer involved in the negotiations and would have no say.

'The rest of it may get papal approval,' judged the cardinal. 'Happily, for His Holiness, nobody at a time like this is likely to tell him that such approval will be at odds with the opinions of his predecessor, Clement V, who pronounced it a heresy to defend the taking of interest! Mastai and all who negotiate on his behalf with your Belgian will be liable to penalties laid down by the papal law against heresy: Clementin i.5, De Usuris, title 5, as I recall. What percentage does our papal count take?'

'Ten.'

'Sixty million francs from the Italians! A hundred and forty million from us! Pope Clement must be spinning in his grave! It was simpler when the usurer was Monsieur de Rothschild! One should always do business with infidels, since one is not answerable for their souls.' The cardinal had a fake mouse made of a bit of ermine trim which he now dangled for his cat. 'Spinning!' he repeated and spun his false mouse.

Friends in the Treasury kept Nicola informed. After all, if the count's scheme triumphed, this, they reminded him, would be partly due to him. He was unsure whether to rejoice or quail. Yet what matter, he told himself, whether or not the financier was on the point of collapse? His ten per cent would save him so that he could save the Church. The miracle was a modern echo of St Peter's walking on the waves.

Which penalties had Pope Clement had in mind? Burning? Nicola remembered Roman buildings blazing in the siege of '49 and a recurrence looked likelier now than at any time since. The French had left. Their tricolour no longer flew over Castel Sant'Angelo and it was feared that the volunteers replacing them would be no match for Garibaldi, whose renewed rabble-rousing Nicola had himself glimpsed from a train window on his way here. The general had been wearing his old agitator's red shirt and, although his harangue was inaudible, one knew the words to which it would boil down: *Roma o morte!*

So maybe we'll all burn, Nicola thought, one way or another.

*

That June, Mastai invited the bishops of Christendom to join him in celebrating the eighteen-hundredth anniversary of the martyrdom of Saints Peter and Paul in the reign of that notorious Rome-burner, Nero. Fireworks and illuminations defied fears of a repeat performance and the King of Italy – 'of Piedmont Sardinia' said Pius pointedly – was yet again ritually excommunicated together with his accomplices. Did this include all his soldiers and officials, along with the butchers, barbers and other tradesmen who kept them supplied? Two curial congregations were spinning out their debate on this question and waiting, said cynics, to see how the political cat would jump.

Pius told his assembled bishops that a power emanating from St Peter's tomb must kindle and fan their ardour until they flamed like the lit tapers which they held in their hands. Had not the Holy Spirit descended on the apostles in the form of tongues of fire?

Nicola, looking around, saw tears in many episcopal eyes. All were foreigners' eyes, to be sure. Flames were refracted in them so that the bishops' faces seemed to be combustive.

'I've just heard,' Amandi whispered in his ear, 'that he was planning to have his personal infallibility declared by acclamation here and now! It was to have been sprung on us, but Orléans and Mainz got wind of the plan and put a stop to it. The General Council will be his next chance.'

It had been confirmed that this was to be held in two years' time.

'If Garibaldi doesn't get here first.'

'*He* hopes his ghostly powers will stop Garibaldi! Indeed, Garibaldi is a boon to him: an excuse to increase his own authority. The Jesuits,' Amandi lowered his voice even further, 'are encouraging priests to take an oath to fight for the dogma "even unto bloodshed!" *Usque effusionem sanguinis*. It seems that two bishops already have. Manning of Westminster is one. Converts – he was a Protestant archdeacon – like that sort of thing. Having turned coat once, they feel a need to put themselves under restraint.'

'I wonder whose blood Manning plans to shed? Ours or his?'

'Do you notice who hasn't come?'

'Your fellow dauphin, d'Andrea!'

'Don't mention us in the same breath. They say he's to be decardinalised! Mastai's spleen bloats like a tick! All poor d'Andrea did was to leave Rome without formal permission and meet some leading Italians. Then, when stripped of his powers, he protested, as why shouldn't he? What grounds are those for depriving him of his powers?'

445

Nicola whispered warningly, 'He conspired with Italians who deprived Mastai of his! Tit for tat!'

Nicola left Rome before Amandi did. On his last day, the cardinal introduced him to Archbishop Darboy of Paris, a man whose independent spirit had cost him the red hat which usually went with his position.

'I don't need a hat!' Darboy, a lean, fine-featured, chestnut-haired man in his fifties, spoke with robust humour. 'I don't suffer from colds. The Emperor was more upset than I because he'd asked that I should have it, thus ensuring that I would not. He is oddly blind to the pleasure Pius takes in biting the hand which protects him.'

On the topic of the Council, the Archbishop said he would welcome the prospect if he thought it would erase the stamp of an intolerant age which the last one – Trent – had impressed on Catholicism. Unfortunately, its more likely purpose would be to spread Rome's power into every see and parish. He himself had clashed with Mastai over his intrusiveness, and the French clergy as a whole was smarting at the revocation of their right to worship according to their own rites. 'He hates any show of independence.'

'He was meddlesome even as a bishop,' said Amandi. 'Monsignor Ficanaso was his nickname then. Bishop Nosy!'

'It is more dangerous in France,' said Darboy. 'We keep telling our opponents on the Left that if they will grant us the right to teach our children in our own way, we will respect their right to think in theirs. Yet how can they believe us when our leader issues a document like the *Syllabus of Errors?*' Today, he lamented, a Catholic bishop's dilemma was that he must seem like a yea-sayer to this haughty pope or the enemy of a besieged Church. 'Yea-sayer, not to say idolator!' Yesterday, he had heard hymns in which the word *Deus* had been replaced by Pius and, on voicing shock, learned that here in Rome the practice was widespread.

Cheering up, as he took his leave, he remarked that the Council would, after all, provide a forum and, who knew, might favour those who hoped to open the Church to new freedoms. 'After all, man proposes and God disposes and,' lowering his voice in a parody of fear, 'Pio/Dio is still only a man!'

As an afterthought, he produced a French newspaper. 'Here's a blow struck for freedom and struck, my reverend friends, in your own diocese! I'll leave it with you. Sorry if it disturbs your digestion.' He left.

Amandi shook his head. 'Brace yourself, *fili mi*, the French love to disturb. It's their national vice.' He unfolded the paper in which an article had been ringed in red ink. Entitled A VISIT TO THE POPE'S OLD STATES, it was an interview by a French journalist with Sister Paola:

The nun had to speak to us across a barricade, for the plain people of her village have locked her up so as to lose her neither to the new authorities nor the old. They think of her as one of themselves, and indeed when we saw her she was wearing clogs. She refused to talk about politics. 'For most people,' she told us, 'politics are like cholera. You pray they won't touch you and make the sign against the evil eye if they do.'

She wouldn't talk either about the miracles with which she is credited nor of the crimes laid at her door. We asked if she knew of the whispered charges: performing abortions and making women barren. Using philters as old as paganism to remedy the sins of young girls. Could she guess where people got such ideas? No answer, so we tried another tack. Had she heard, we asked, of the coming Council in Rome? It was to be held in a few years' time. Another blank look.

We, we explained, were wondering whether religion too sometimes seems like cholera to people through whose villages armies have marched so often in its name. Several visionaries, we told her, have prophesied that the coming Council will declare the Pope infallible so as to finish with strife and bring peace to parishes like hers. Does she, a holy woman, have anything to say about this?

But Sister Paola remained irredeemably taciturn.

Did she believe the Pope to be infallible? We knew he had been her confessor for several years. All she would say to this was that it was beyond her competence and, when pressed, added that the Pope was a good man but that the opinion of her uncle, who had also been a good man, was that if any mortal man were to be infallible, human endeavour would come to a halt. Trial and error were the way to improvement, this uncle used to say, and why change anything if we know we're right now?

This brought us to the topic of ballooning and the story of how, three years ago, she saved one which was being blown out to sea. Eyewitnesses swore that as soon as she had prayed for the balloonists' safety the wind shifted and blew them back to shore. Sister Paola laughed at this. The wind, she told us, was blowing in two different directions and when the navigator wanted to rise and catch a contrary wind he threw out ballast.

'Do you think the state should do the same? Throw out ballast and change direction?'

No answer.

'Should the Church?'

At this, Sister Paola must have given a signal to her protectors for they

447

hustled us away. Far be it from us to claim that this unassuming woman is a pythoness. Still, it is heartening that the Church and the Kingdom of Italy which have so long been at odds have been able to agree on one small matter: the sparing of her small hospital which is to be let stay open as a symbol and, it is hoped, harbinger of their eventual entente. As we go to press, an agreement has been signed by the Italian Minister for Finance and Count André Langrand-Dumonceau who is thought to represent the Court of Rome.

Amandi folded the paper. 'There will be trouble over this.'

Twenty-five

'By Bacchus!' Prospero, avoiding blasphemy, swore by pagan gods. *Dio Bacco*, Nicola was aggravating their afflictions.

The two were in the episcopal palace. From its walls gazed popes painted to look uniformly benevolent and stern.

'I,' Nicola reminded, 'have been looking into sanctity and the lack of it for years! Remember the children of La Salette? As the Cardinal's assistant – and assistants, let us be frank, do the work – I put together files on them.'

'So there are files?' Prospero was interested. 'And you are saying that this nun is a saint?'

'Not at all. My approach is negative. Just as medical men concern themselves with boils, tumours and the like, I . . .' And Nicola explained that, being inured to spiritual afflictions, it lightened his heart, for once, to find none.

'Can you be sure this lightness is not a more . . . human feeling?'

'She's over fifty, Monsignore!'

'Quite, but has His Eminence never . . .?'

'Talked of her? Of course he has. When the Italians ruled that only "useful" convents might stay open, it was he who let hers start a small hospital. Very modest. The stories about abortions don't ring true. Surely, a scandal can be avoided?'

Too late, said Prospero. Indeed, that was why he was here. The Holy Father was heartsick. Did Nicola think it had pleased him to read in the French gutter press of an agreement purportedly signed in his name by this Belgian trickster? 'He has disowned it.'

Nicola couldn't credit this. 'It saved the bulk of our assets!'

'It condoned the seizure of the rest. *And* he wants the convent closed down. He'll accept no favours from Florence!'

'But . . .' This was baffling. 'The people love Sister Paola!'

'Oh . . . love!' Irritably, tapping a windowpane, Prospero disclosed that the Italians were already dealing with, among others, Baron James Rothschild of Paris. Jackals would not be lacking to pick our bones. Perhaps we should rejoice? This way, even if the new agreements took *all* our property, we would not be party to them. 'How can we join the Roman soldiers dicing for Christ's robe?' His tapping fingernails did, though, sound like dice.

Nicola, too stunned to listen, caught a reference to bishops who lacked loyalty. Cardinal d'Andrea was mentioned: a controversial case. Prospero said, 'I want the dossier on the children of La Salette.'

His skin looked papery and his nose pinched, as though chary of breathing in too much air. Nicola, with a rush of sympathy, mourned the Prospero of years ago. As the dossier, though, was Amandi's and contained God knew what, he said he couldn't lay hand on it. He was angry with Rome for sending a friend to work on his feelings. So, asked Prospero, who *had* the file?'

'I'm not sure.'

'You must know! His Holiness will want it. Who has it, Monsignore?'

'Cardinal d'Andrea.' It was an inspired lie. 'He was Prefect of the *Congregatio Indicis* when some books came out on the case. As you know, there were controversies . . .'

'And he *kept* the file?'

Nicola nodded. D'Andrea, now a refugee in Naples, was the one prelate from whom Rome could not easily recover it.

'Would you get it for us? Go to Naples?

'Why should I?'

Prospero's dry-pod face cracked a smile. 'This,' he coaxed, 'is in the strictest confidence. The secret of La Salette was that the Pope should be declared infallible. Individually, by himself and apart from the episcopacy.'

'That wasn't in the dossier!'

'No. It's the secret which the Virgin gave to the boy, Maximin, and which he later revealed to the Holy Father in a confidential letter. We need to see the dossier in case there are contradictory elements there. As the secret was communicated to the child in 1846, the year of Mastai's elevation, its publication cannot fail to touch hearts. The Council, you see, will aim to dogmatise the doctrine so that there may be no more strife and the Church strengthened.' Prospero's eyes shone. 'Think,' he urged, 'of the comfort it will bring to millions.'

Nicola thought of Amandi and Darboy. 'Sudden and secret moves,' he warned, 'harden opposition. However, I'll strike a bargain with you: if you get a pardon for d'Andrea, I'll ask him for the dossier. I'll want a promise from the Pope himself.'

Cardinal Amandi wrote advising d'Andrea to make his submission, but feared, privately, that the humiliation could kill him. D'Andrea was an aristocrat, a man of another age. To have to grovel – and, bargan or no bargain, Mastai would make him do that – could destroy him. Amandi sighed. The Church, once a collegial corporation, was now an autocracy. The new instruments of communication – rail and telegraph – long seen as threats to the central power, would instead reinforce it and the *chemin d'enfer* be a *chemin de Rome*. The Council would put its stamp on that!

'This time,' he prophesied, 'you may depend upon it, the secular powers won't intervene as they tried to do at Trent. Instead, they'll sit back and watch us give the world a spectacle of archaic folly. Infidels and Protestants will split their sides and atheists wish they had a god to thank.'

Nicola, taking the train for Naples, joined the 'crows and ravens', which was how the Italians decribed the clerics dispersing, after their gathering in Rome. D'Andrea, once the drollest of prelates, received him dully. Disappointment had shrivelled him. His movements were wooden, his shoulders pale with dandruff, and he had the friable look of a pillar of salt. He was out of the running for the succession, and even here must be feeling the cold since the Italians, who had made him so welcome three years ago, knew that a cardinal likely to be 'decardinalised' was of no political use. Minor maladies seemed to beset him and there was a raw, albino look to the skin around his eyes.

'Mastai's ruthlessness,' he exclaimed dispiritedly, 'makes up for his lack of brains. Did you know I'd been suspended *in spiritualibus et temporalibus?*'

Yes, said Nicola, and warned that, although the Pope had promised to restore d'Andrea's functions once he had publicly repented, the cardinal had better not delay. Now, when Garibaldi might strike Rome at any time, lingering in the company of Italian prefects and generals could be seen as treachery.

451

'The generals *I* meet,' the cardinal pointed out, 'are the men who will restrain Garibaldi!'

But both knew that such distinctions were beyond Mastai.

Journeying back to Imola, Nicola pondered the lie he had told about d'Andrea's having the dossier, while knowing it to be among his own papers. Justified lies were now common in Rome, and his own scruples were due to a personal habit of truthfulness which he attributed to the scarcity of facts in his early life.

A foundling without a true family name, he had hated knowing that he was a false word made flesh and yearned for facts to be unshakeable. No doubt many of the Pope's subjects had since come to feel the same way.

Disoriented, as familiar reality absconded, they longed for reassurance. And now this was to be given them with the new – or, according to its promoters, old – dogma which would freeze truth so that it could never again mutate or alter or develop into something capable of flinging men at each other's throats or into an anguish of doubt.

Was this water in the desert or a mirage?

As the train chugged, and smoke shivered like ostrich plumes, he concluded with some sorrow that what men like him might once have received gratefully now brought no balm, since the grid which Pius proposed putting over their perceptions could only prevent them keeping up with the shifts of an unstoppable world. Lies, if only because the liars knew them for what they were, were less deceptive than the truths of men like Mastai.

'Poor beast!' *he* had said of Cardinal d'Andrea when Nicola obtained an audience before leaving for Naples. 'For his and my souls' sake I had to chasten him. Cardinals are a pope's creatures, so we are answerable for them to God! What choice have I? Authority carries responsibilities and freedom is a danger to most men.'

Then he beamed his celebrated smile on Nicola who, feeling his lips curve in assent, was surprised to sense a small contradictory hardening, a knot of disagreement form deep inside him, which had since spread through his limbs and brain, until he recognised an inner arming against the treacheries of his response to power.

At five one morning, Nicola was awoken and told that a band of policemen had caught the nuns' guardians by surprise – or perhaps the guardians had grown tired of the farce and connived? Anyway, the nuns had been taken in a police carriage to a fortress some miles away. He left instructions with the Vicar-General to telegraph Rome, asking whether they could not be accommodated in some convent there. Then he drove to the fortress where a polite young officer explained that the convent had been set on fire and the police had been obliged to rescue the inmates. They were asleep now, having been given morphine. Several had burns, but none was serously injured. They would, promised the officer, be safe under his protection and made as comfortable as possible.

As it happened, Nicola had no choice but to accept this offer of hospitality, for Rome's answer to his telegram was a refusal to have the nuns in a city already overcrowded with refugees. Italian law allowed ex-nuns to finish their days in their former convent and, if their community was too small, to join another one. This option, said the message, must not be accepted in this case. The controversial community must be dispersed. Where to? wondered Nicola. But a request for further guidance received none.

On St John's Eve there was a firework display visible from the episcopal palace. The Prefect and other Italian officials were presiding on a platform in the piazza, and Nicola and a party of clerics discreetly watching through an open window, when news came that Sister Paola was ill and a priest needed to hear her confession. Nicola said he would go himself.

Taking a young priest with him for company, he drove into a night which was rosily aglow, not only because St John's is the shortest night of the year but because the sky had been dyed by rockets and Roman candles in the red and green colours of patriotism. As the king's initials blazed, the younger man recalled that not long ago all sky-writing had been religious.

'They're taking over the heavens!'

At the fortress a party was in progress and it was clear that the women invited were of the light and cheerful sort. A tittering group passed the priests on the stairs and a girl paused to ask about Sister Paola. 'She's a saint!' said the girl to Nicola and pressed money into his hand to say a mass for a secret intention.

'Come on, Gatta,' called a companion and the woman ran off.

Who knew, murmured the young priest, what *her* secret intention might be? His severe young face deprecated invoking divine aid for such a pig in a poke. This reminded the Coadjutor of the scandal attaching to Sister Paola and he told the young man to wait while he saw her alone.

'She's had a shock,' said the captain who had guided them.

Nuns were praying outside Sister Paola's door. One waylaid Nicola to explain that, earlier, a rocket had fallen in the sick woman's window. He went in. Florets of steely light were spraying the ceiling and, through the window, came a cacophony of sounds from different parts of the fortress. Cheers cut across the boot-beat of a military song – the rank-and-file at play – while, intermittently audible behind the stubborn orisons of nuns, spiralled the hankering, decorous strains of a waltz. Sister Paola's face was hot.

'War ...' she murmured. 'It began with one.' Her delirium was labyrinthine. He explained about St John's Eve but saw that she had taken off on some spiral of her own. 'I let him,' she said, 'attribute paternity to the dead.'

'The Fifth Sorrowful Mystery!' intoned a nun and he went to shoo them away. Returning, he told her to say an act of contrition and that they could dispense with the confession of her sins.

'My mind,' said she with sudden lucidity, 'is as clear as a bell. I want a message sent to His Holiness.' He had written, she said, asking whether she had received any revelation concerning his personal infallibility, and when she said 'no', written back saying that what inspiration she did receive might be from the devil.

'Now, I want him to know this. He became my spiritual father in lieu of what he should have been. He told me to put human affections aside. He made me become a nun and cannot now, in all justice, refuse to let me and my sisters finish our lives as a spiritual family. It is too late for us to return to the world. Tell him we want to go to Rome.'

The Coadjutor looks startled, thought Sister Paola. God, she prayed, do You want me to keep my lips sealed until I go to my grave? So the voices which elected to speak for You always said.

I always wanted my uncle to make love to me. Why not? He had done everything else for me, having brought me up from when I was one year old and my parents died of cholera. He surrounded me with himself and, being a priest, led me to You. Living in a mountain

454

presbytery was as lonely as living on a ship. He learned to knit so as to teach me.

Then, when I was thirteen, I saw him make love to his housekeeper. He meant me to see. He was a man who played three musical instruments and knew four languages and she – well, she was the ground in which he chose to bury his talents. A plump peasant past her prime! She had wens and warts. Sleeping with her must have been like entering the grave.

I came to see that he had done it so as not to sleep with me. Incest would have frightened him. Why? It's in the Bible! Taboos meant nothing to me. He saw this and reproached himself, since it was he who had made me the way I was. In his fright he turned to her and let her turn me out.

I suppose pride rules me, acknowledged Sister Paola. I know it made the angels fall – but may it not have been what saved the good angels too? I try to imagine how You think. Mastai believes You speak to me and that I, perversely, fail to pass on messages. He wants proof that You and I have forgiven him. He is nervous.

I have since tried to help women like the housekeeper – stunted creatures, as hemmed in by their lives as their own farm animals. Living among them, I tried to help them and their daughters. Unaided by You – who leave me to my own resources – I try to invent a celestial arithmetic and give back here what I owed there. The women treat me with deference. They know that I won't denounce them when they come in panic, haemorrhaging between their legs and losing black blood clots the size of my fist. Shame makes them delay. I only see them when they are already rigid with cramps and fearful of having perforated the uterus by trying to stick knitting needles into its eye, with the help of a bit of mirror held between their thighs. Death and infertility are distant fears. The law and their menfolk are closer. Some are unmarried. Others have too many children already, or else their husbands are in the Army and the pregnancy came at the wrong time. When they meet me later, they look away.

I don't often think about the child. I gave it to You without learning its sex. Boy? Girl? Amandi knows. Would he tell if it had died? I think he would ask me to pray for its soul so, as he hasn't, it hasn't. 'Make a crib in your heart for the Baby Jesus,' wrote Mastai. That meant: forget your own baby. It will be better off without you. Boy? Girl? I would have understood a girl better. When girls came to me for help, I used to think: she would be their age now. Now she would be thirty-six and a mother if they found her a dowry, which they would have done. That would be part of *their* celestial arithmetic. Mastai took my uncle's place.

'Am I going to die?' She must have spoken aloud for the Coadjutor answered that an act of contrition never came amiss.

'Tell me a sin from your past life,' he asked, when she finished the prayer.

'I hounded my uncle's housekeeper. I disgraced her in the parish and made her life such a misery that she had to go into a convent and die in solitude. Now,' said Sister Paola with a small laugh, 'I have lost *our* convent and our group of sisters will be dispersed so that I too shall die in solitude. Am I served right?'

Nicola prayed murmurously, but could not imagine this sweet-faced woman hounding anyone. The occasion was odd, for it was neither night nor day and the solstice was vibrant with pagan memories. Our own rites were an exorcism of these, just as the Italian fireworks were of ours. But, over time, the exorcism had become contaminated and one sensed a truce between formerly hostile ghosts. Sister Paola's fancies had company. Holding her hand to show her she was not dying in solitude, he added his prayers to the forces firing through the blazing air. 'Absolve, we beseech Thee, O Lord, the soul of this Thy servant . . .'

Waltz music whirled and a pyrotechnic finale filled the sky with a great cross of Savoy. At one time, Sister Paola had felt that something was due to her for the waltzes she had not waltzed and for the conjugal comforts she might have known with some good-natured dowry-hunter. Her uncle's legacy would have sufficed for that, but Mastai had not agreed.

'*Subvenite, Angeli Domini* . . .'

She no longer blamed him. A knowledge of his mind and an ability to tune into it, even at a distance, had seeped through the confessional-grating in the years when he had her conscience in his care. He had supposed the only transaction between them to be the exchange of his wisdom for her submission. But submission had taught her the contours of his thought and made her so receptive to it that, although she did not hear the Madonna's voice as he had hoped, messages did come to her from him. She knew and was pestered by his fears and fevers, which were lately reaching a pitch.

Turning to the Madonna, and finding that his old success with feminine sensibilities would not help, he had looked for intercessors with the intercessor and had had hopes of Sister Paola. She knew, because in unguarded moments she felt him willing her to assist him. His appeals tired her and she wanted him to desist. She guessed that his

456

mounting terror was unacknowledged. Leaking into her dreams, she felt him channel towards her a dark, fearful part of himself which he dared not recognise and which his plan to have himself declared infallible aimed to assuage.

Cardinal Amandi, who was still in Rome, wrote his Coadjutor affable notes. He was a master of meandering prose in whose coils a signal could escape the censor's eye. Unfortunately, it also escaped Nicola's, who was blessed if he saw anything sly in His Eminence's bland account of afternoons spent in the company of Her Britannic Majesty's unaccredited agent, Odo Russell, a gentleman, whose tall white hat, gold spectacles and genial smile were regular features at Roman receptions.

Was the absence of a signal itself a signal? Maybe the cardinal meant to show the censor that he was innocently engaged in the social round? Joining in this had become a token of loyalty when the Nationalists boycotted carnival and the Pope's party riposted by dancing itself dizzy to the detriment of its dowagers' hip-bones and hopes of longevity. 'Ha!' ruminated His Eminence.

Nicola was reminded of his search for significance in poor Sister Paola's ramblings. 'Monsignore,' was how she addressed him, but he could tell that she had taken him for quite another Monsignore. 'You could have caught chickenpox,' she chided, and the word throbbed with inscrutable import. 'Don't fret over the convent's closure,' she urged another time, contradicting her own complaints on this very topic. 'They were sour places, really. We used to put on a pious charade for your visits! Everyone did. The whole province did it for your last one when citizens were forbidden to breath the word "reform"! The only ones to disobey were old friends of yours whom you took for isolated fanatics! Didn't you?' she challenged, and Nicola, to calm her, said 'Yes.'

'They knew!' she told him. 'They were devastated. One of them told me he wept as your carriage was driving off and all he could see of you was the white flutter of your hand. He compared it to a wounded dove. You were blessing the troops. Austrians! The occupying army which everyone hated. You blessed *them* and never noticed that the real people hadn't come!'

For a moment Nicola felt as if he had been eavesdropping – but, after all, this was under the seal of confession and he would blot out all he'd heard. Or try to.

*

457

'*Il caro* Russell,' wrote the cardinal, 'adores amateur theatricals. He and some English friends are rehearsing scenes from a play about a man feigning madness so as to disarm the suspicions of a king who fears for his succession. Some, closer to us' – a reference to d'Andrea? – 'may not have to feign.'

Prospero wrote too, praising Bishop Dupanloup of Orléans who had challenged the Italian Government to ensure that violent hands were not laid on His Holiness. Garibaldi had now been confined to the island of Caprera – a clear response to the bishop. A pity, wrote Prospero meaningfully, that not all churchmen were as loyal!

Nicola turned with relief from these letters to Sister Paola who, suspended between life and death, was in ardent communion with a pastoral dream of her own youth. He found it soothing to visit it with her and now regularly did. Her fancies about an idyll with Louis Napoleon's dead elder brother back in '31 were curiously vivid, and it struck him that nuns' daydreams were like the pits in which mountain villagers stored snow until its price rose in the summer. Like the snow, her stories were compact and ageless, though a new light could transform one, like sunshine fracturing on ice. He rejected such distortions, particularly the delirium relating to her late confessor. The scraps about her girlhood were what appealed to him, and he held in suspense a surmise which it was perhaps wiser not to verify for now.

Meanwhile, Prospero kept him abreast of Roman rumours. Hissed under the coffered ceilings of saloons and sacristies, the latest claimed that the Bishop of Tarbes, when asked why he had not made more of the miracles of Lourdes, put the blame on Cardinal Amandi, whose judicial approach, wrote Prospero, 'freezes His Holiness's soul!' Soul-freezing too were the cardinal's reservations about the pious practice of sending H.H.'s toe-and-tonsure-clippings to those who contributed generously to St Peter's Pence. 'Contempt for simple faith,' wrote Prospero, 'is no longer acceptable.'

A more painful controversy smouldered over a Spanish inquisitor whom Mastai had canonised last June. A German theologian had revealed that the new saint, Peter d'Arbuez of Aragon, had, by the time he died, caused some four to six thousand heretics to be burned alive. Döllinger – the German – thought this incompatible with sanctity. Prospero disagreed. Canonising d'Arbuez was, he conceded, perhaps impolitic. It revived old animosities, especially as the man who finally murdered and so made a martyr of him was a Jew. 'Yet might it not be that choosing this unlikeable martyr to a cause – the Church's survival –

458

which may soon require new ones is a useful reminder of what may now have to be sacrificed? Tolerance? Squeamishness?' Amandi was suspected of having used Odo Russell's diplomatic bag to correspond with the mischievous Döllinger and draw his attention to d'Arbuez. Prospero did not believe this, but warned, 'If people's suspicions fall on him, who is to blame?'

The next news to reach Rome had the effect of an artillery enfilade. Garibaldi had 'escaped' from his island – the authorities must have closed an eye – had reached Florence and from there, a living ikon in his red shirt, slipped south with the avowed intention of unseating the Pope, whom supporters were already calling the 'martyr' and 'the Word of God made flesh to dwell amongst us'. Passions peaked like winter tides.

Rumours kept alarm upon the boil. Garibaldi was acting on his own, since the king, browbeaten by Louis Napoleon, had disowned him. Thank God for that. Yet might the Emperor, who was known to support the 'principle of nationalities', again change sides? He might. At this very moment Italian envoys in Paris were begging him not to send troops to our defence. That whore the Countess Castiglione was adding her blandishments. Grandest of *grandes horizontales*, she was said to be the mainspring of Italian strategy, though it was also said that she had been supplanted by some other whore, who was unlikely to be a good Catholic, and, either way, it all went to prove the old adage about how a pubic hair could pull more weight than a team of oxen. Yet the Pope was said to be calm, praying, no doubt, but also remembering that Louis Napoleon still needed that pivotal Catholic vote in the upcoming French plebiscite.

Then came news of a victory! Near Mentana the French, armed with some new marvellous sort of gun, had defeated the Garibaldini! Thank God! Thank the new *chassepots* and the French Catholic voters who had forced Louis Napoleon to send troops!

Soberer voices murmured that France was fickle. After the plebiscite, the Emperor would need us less. If he fell, his successors wouldn't need us at all. This could be the last time France would defend us. But the Garibaldini would still be here.

Amandi learned from Russell that Mr Gladstone and Lord Clarendon, who were visiting Rome, had urged Pius to make peace with the King of

Italy. After all, they said, what other hope had he? His hope, Pius told them, lay not in armies but in Providence.

'Providence,' retorted his Protestant lordship, 'has certainly performed miracles of late, but they have all been in favour of Italy.'

It was at this unpromising moment that Cardinal d'Andrea at last brought himself to swallow his pride and make his submission. He left Naples for Rome where a few loyal friends, including Amandi who had stayed in the city for that purpose, went to greet him at the Albergo Cesari and were shocked by what they saw. He was fifty-four and looked seventy-four. There seemed, wrote Amandi with frightened pity, to be no spirit left in him. No self. 'One thinks of Lucifer after his fall! He, who had been the brightest of the angels, fell into numbing dark. This is scarcely a man, much less a priest or prince. His mind cannot sustain the shame. He will sign anything. Distinctions elude him. His body sways as though his bones had melted, and we would scarcely have marvelled if he had turned to dust before our eyes.'

The recantation, drawn up by d'Andrea's most implacable opponents in the Sacred College, declared, '(1) I beg forgiveness for my disobedience in going to Naples in defiance of the Holy Father's prohibition; (2) I deplore the scandal given to the faithful by my attitude towards the Sacred Person of His Holiness and to the Sacred Congregations in my articles in the *Esaminatore* of Florence whose heretical and schismatic doctrines I now reprove; (3) . . .' Amandi could not bear to copy the rest. The man had been left with neither dignity nor belief. He was in hell and the restoration of his offices and revenues was a sour mockery. Like decking a corpse in the livery of grandeur, it emphasised not only the death of his spirit but the mortality of his flesh – for he was visibly dying on his feet.

'He had an audience with H.H.,' wrote Amandi in a letter which he would not entrust to the postal service, 'who must have been punishing by proxy all the enemies he could not reach.'

Pius had been flanked by Antonelli and Patrizi when the suppliant stumbled into the room. Corpse-pale, he zigzagged towards the steps of the throne, then fell to his knees and began to sob. The Pope remained stony-faced while the sick man tried to pull himself together, made his request for pardon, crawled forward to kiss the papal slipper then, somehow, got himself out of the room.

'I have to say,' wrote Amandi, 'that d'Andrea's own version of the

460

thing is different. He claims that Pius commiserated with him over his appearance and advised him to nurse his health and visit some spa. However, he is in such a state of craven self-delusion that it is hard to believe a word he says.'

It was clear that Amandi, who had for so long been twinned with d'Andrea in people's minds, was shaken.

There was a last glimpse of the ruined cardinal. A friend, who went to see him in a country house to which he had withdrawn, found him holding a lighted taper to his face at noon, and begging to be told if he did not look healthier than before. 'The victim's victim,' said Amandi, 'has to pay for everyone's sins!'

London, 1868

From Cesarini to Monsignor Santi:

> Monsignore,
>   Has it occurred to you that Miss Ella and you look remarkably alike? No? Well, the resemblance ends there. I loved her for qualities which you have not got. She incarnated the magic which the Church promises but fails to deliver. I thought Langrand-Dumonceau did too, but he, alas, is losing his powers – as you may see!

Enclosed were cuttings from Belgian newspapers. One from *l'Echo du Parlement belge* said: 'The Langrand companies are in their judiciary phase. Thanks to the courts, those accounts books so carefully kept from shareholders will now see the light of day and the scales drop from the eyes of small investors bamboozled by agents in soutanes!' Another clipping trumpeted: 'Now that the collapse of Monsieur Langrand's *Crédit foncier et industriel* has brought ruin to so many Catholic families, the clerical press . . .'

Nicola went cold. So the Pope had been right!

'I,' wrote Cesarini, 'never did know what went on in L-D's inner sanctum. Ignorance, though, may be no protection.'

He saved us, thought Nicola of Pius and skipped squeamishly on.

'. . . the Pope has come in for some harsh criticism, since the papal title was an endorsement of . . .' He did not want to read that. Turning the page, he found: 'The Princes Thurn and Taxis and Duke Cesarini as well as a host of other leading noble houses stand to lose . . .'

Contrary to the old compensatory law of fortune-telling – lucky in love, unlucky at the gaming table – Flavio had lost on all fronts!

'Miss Ella . . .'

It appeared that she and the former chaplain were living sedately somewhere in Louisiana. They had opened a riding school. The letter informing Flavio had come through a lawyer. He was not to disturb their peace. A *post scriptum* informed him that they had adopted a child.

Cardinal Amandi, having left the Pope's territory for Tuscany, could now write freely and his latest note gave details of an audience with Pius on the eve of his departure. He had requested it weeks ago so as to plead for d'Andrea. Pius, however, had divined and foiled this plan and Amandi had had to wait until after d'Andrea's awful reception for his own. The memory of that hung ominously. However, Pius gave him his hand – d'Andrea had been proffered a foot – and, asked:

'Is it true that you have a white cat called Cacanono?' Plucking coquettishly at his own cassock. 'As white as this? Does it mean "don't shit" or what? Is it a devil's name, Eminenza? Have you a predominant passion represented by this cat which has such an interesting name? It's a pun, isn't it? You must explain it to me. I like puns.'

Amandi, in a steady voice, said that the cat was an ordinary cat, Holiness, and not called Cacanono.

The Pope looked pained. 'I am often misinformed. I am an Argus with a hundred squints! What *is* your cat called?'

'Mangialuce, Holiness!' The cardinal, red as his robes, eyed Mastai who said, 'Another odd name!' and eyed him back.

'We both,' wrote Amandi, 'belong to that impoverished but resourceful squirearchy of the Marches. He knew I was rattling responses around my head and wondering which to risk. He was enjoying that but – I could see – the enjoyment was not malign. I was to be given a good fright, a tap of the crosier, then hauled back to the fold. The implications of Mangialuce's name were not construed. "Beware of scandal!" said he. "My ears have been burning, Eminenza. Be wary! So many people spy! Our poor friend d'Andrea wasn't wary at all! The poor man was never *papabile* material, wouldn't you agree?"

'If there is any message in all this,' concluded Amandi, 'it is that those who say he is senile have been hoodwinked. Here it is not Hamlet, the pretender, but the old king who feigns madness.'

Rome, 1868

Monsignore,

You will recall our compact whereby, once Girolamo Marchese Cardinal d'Andrea was restored to the exercise of his episcopal jurisdiction *in spiritualibus et temporalibus*, you would send me a certain file. I count on your forwarding it. Yours affectionately in Jesus Christ

Prospero + Bishop of Philippi

Nicola's dreams had been invaded by Sister Paola's. Towards the end, these had fractured into tantalising slivers which flew together under the magnet of his curiosity.

Images recurred: a mountain presbytery and a convent school. One was bathed in bright air and the other crammed with the dull impediment of women who expected little from the here and now. Fierce practical jokes leavened the drabness. A cripple's crutch was hung out of reach; a wigged bolster placed in someone's bed; a sheet sewn across so that the occupant couldn't get in; a spaniel bitch on heat was locked in a confessional so that canine hordes assailed the church. On that occasion, the chaplain demanded that the perpetrator, having committed a reserved sin, go to the bishop for absolution. Nobody did. Sister Paola recalled with a shocked giggle that the secret sinner had been more in awe of Monsignore than of hell and never owned up.

'You were a terror, Monsignore!'

Her voice, at such moments, grew young and old, innocent mischief animated her wrinkles. Her eyes were as bright as coins. He guessed her to be about fifty.

He came back and back again to see her, as she failed to recover or die, lingering perhaps until she had passed on her memories. He felt her intense interest in himself, her last listener, who was administering secular rites as well as the ones which the Church had taught him to give: a bonus to which she had every right since she herself had extended it to many. 'Useful' work was what nuns were expected to do by the Siccardi laws – called after the deputy who presented them to the Italian parliament – and that was what Sister Paola had agreed to do and did.

'Tell me,' he held her hand, 'what you look like.' He asked because her eyes were intermittently naïve with hope. 'You came back,' she had just said and he guessed that the 'you' she was addressing was not him. She bridled. 'Oh, I have long hair. Black.' Her fingers moved feebly towards the greying stubble on her cropped head. 'A river of it! I wear it in a coil. I would *like* a silk dress. I'm not sure if I'm pretty. Napoleon

Louis said I was. You never did!' She laughed. 'But I know you thought so, Monsignore!'

'Does it matter?'

'Of course it does! Pretty women are grateful to God and charitable to others! They're nicer people, hadn't you noticed? Even pretty nuns are! And statues of the Virgin are always pretty. That shows that pious people value prettiness even though they pretend not to. Have you ever seen an ugly statue of the Virgin?'

'Never.'

'See!'

'But we mustn't tell the ugly that. They would be too unhappy.' Absurdly, he flirted with this dying woman in her dotage. It was as if, beyond their roles as confessor and penitent, a connection had been established. They liked each other. There was something responsive in each to the other's temperament. Like magnets, they leapt into conjunction again and again. And then, one day, he decided to reverse their roles.

'Tell me,' he decided to ask. 'I know someone who perhaps had a son whom someone else now wants to find and adopt . . .' But this sounded confusing even to himself.

Her face closed like a frightened sea anemone. 'Why,' she asked, 'do you raise that – that bit of the past?'

'There may never have been one . . .'

'There was!'

'No, no, quite possibly, even probably, there wasn't. But this person – the one who wants to adopt – will, I suspect, find a boy anyway whom he can pass off as the lost one!' Nicola foundered, then decided to go on since, after all, he, like the barber in the old story of King Midas's ears, was really talking to himself.

'He says he wants to help the child – who, if it exists, is no longer of course a child – but his purpose may be . . .'

'What?'

'Sodomy.' He doubted that she knew the word yet used it anyway. It was like addressing the Delphic sybil, a pythoness in a cave, someone whose answer must be dictated by some force beyond her own understanding. 'Sin.'

She asked: 'Who are you talking about?'

'Cesarini. Flavio. Do you remember him?'

'Of course. Does he want to adopt the child?'

'Yes, if he can find it, but . . .'

'But how wonderful! Aren't you pleased? We will be able to know it –
her, him, without scandal. And it will be now be grown up, anyway, so
what harm can come of it?'

Nicola marvelled at her sudden lucidity. Sibylline intuition? Had she
a gift? Perhaps this was why Mastai – from what she had been saying –
had asked her about his infallibility! The boy, he told her, would be
eighteen now.

'No, no!' She argued. 'Thirty-six.'

Twenty-six

In the garden walked His Eminence and his cat, a creature which carried itself like an emblem.

'Gardens,' Prospero looked out the window, 'remind me of Jacobins and their Utopias.' He must, thought Nicola, be the last man left to call Liberals 'Jacobins'. Nose to tail, the cat seemed to be chasing an errant piece of itself. 'My father . . .'

He had died the year before and now Sister Paola too had slipped away in a dream which had, in the end, grown real to Nicola who could have mapped her uncle's presbytery. Copper gleamed there; ceilings were sooty, faience plates crazed, and a hand ran, with tenderness, over the soft bindings of books. The uncle had been a scholar, rusticated for reasons she never knew.

'Leniency,' Prospero tried to persuade himself, 'sells the pass.' He was remembering a guillotining seen in Rome last November in the piazza dei Cerchi. He had not planned to witness it. 'But, somehow, on the day itself, I felt I had to. D'Arbuez – our inquisitor saint – must have witnessed the deaths of the heretics he condemned. It was a test.'

'I would fail it,' said Nicola. 'I would feel that our beliefs aren't worth so much.'

Prospero's face thawed into passion. 'If they were worth Christ's death, how could they not be worth those of Giuseppe Monti and Gaetano Tognetti?' These were the dead men's names. They had been convicted of trying to blow up a papal barracks.

The guillotine had been on a small platform and in the end the headsman or an assistant had held up the heads. First one. Then the other. By the hair. 'One man's was short. He had trouble grasping it. The blood . . .'

466

'All right! All right!' It was Prospero's nausea which Nicola hoped to staunch.

'There was sawdust to soak it . . .'

'Prospero, it could have been your father!'

'That's why! Don't you see?' His voice was hoarse and his jaw clenched. 'One must confront things!'

'Let's have lunch. I'll send the footman to call His Eminence.' Nicola pulled a thick, prettily twisted woollen bell-rope, yellow and pink.

He had known, of course, about Sister Paola, having guessed from the first, but hadn't wanted, any more than she – surely? – could have done, to live through the recognition scene so familiar from opera *libretti*: '*My mother*!' cries the repelled and horrified Figaro, on being confronted with an ageing woman who has mistaken her maternal instinct for amorousness . . . Horror and farce! What other response, implies the librettist, could there be to such an untimely revelation? The timelessness of Sister Paola's memories were what Nicola had relished. The girl from 1831 was the one about whom he had wanted to know: unchanging, luminous and perfectly preserved. The remembering nun, lying there like a shell resonant with sea sounds, was best, for dignity's sake, treated as the medium she was. Neutral and unrecognised. Separate and, if possible, distanced from the story which both had come to enjoy remembering. He rejoiced in imagining her at fifteen, a radiant creature at its peak, aquiver like a cresting wave – soon to be ruined by his birth.

His father's identity was as elusive as a face on a spun coin. Libretto prince or incestuous uncle? Tenor or baritone? A ruthless man might have forced her to say – only to find, perhaps, that both masked the unbearable memory of an anonymous and multiple rape. Shrinking from that, he cherished uncertainty. As for her, the spirited old relic, he was as glad to have known her as that she had not known him. He genuinely mourned her now.

Amandi, reluctantly, agreed that they must hand over the La Salette file. 'How resist *his* overweening if we become Petrine in our own opinions?' His watchword, these days, was 'flexibility', and his hope that, even now, a way could be found 'to conciliate Revelation and Revolution'. Why not? Why *not*? 'After all,' he said, 'what is the Revolution but Charity grown impatient and turning to arms? It's not hard to

467

understand. D'Arbuez, in his day, stood for armed Faith. And *he*'s been canonised!'

At lunch none of this came up.

Nicola, seated between his seething friends, talked of the weather – a topic on which, said Amandi impishly, we must all learn to discourse! Not only was it the only one safe to discuss with H.H., it was also a challenge! How far could one spin out discussions of, say, wind? The sirocco and its properties. The *tramontana*. The winds of change! Gaiety seized His Eminence. 'Do you know *why* it's unsafe to talk to *him* of other things? It's because *he* blows the gaff on his informants! He can't help it! He gets carried away. That spiteful tale-bearer, Monseigneur de Ségur, got into hot water with his superior, Darboy, whom he had maligned secretly to Pius. When he got home Darboy knew every word he'd said!' The cardinal laughed.

'Was I being warned?' Prospero wondered later.

Nicola shrugged. Bickering unnerved him. He had handed over the file.

'We need men like you,' Prospero said as he left. 'By "we" I mean true Catholics. Liberal ones aren't true ones.' And with that he waved to his coachman and sped off in his well-sprung carriage.

Some months later, Nicola found this opinion spelled out in *La Civiltà Cattolica* and knew it to be policy. 'Catholics,' said the Vatican organ, unlike 'Liberal Catholics', hoped that the coming Council would dogmatise the Syllabus and define papal infallibility 'by acclamation'; in other words, that the assembled bishops would passively acclaim what was read out to them.

This roused great anxiety and by summer the European episcopacy was showing strain. Pro- and anti-infallibilists differed with decorum, as befitted men of the cloth. Yet there was harshness and some panic in the copies of pastoral addresses, sermons, newspapers and synodal letters which bishops living outside the reach of the papal censor were free to order. Amandi took them all and soon the stacks, pro and con, had to be moved from his desk to the floor where they rose to his waist.

'Pro' was hortative. The *Civiltà* and its following argued for a definition by acclamation on the grounds that 'the Holy Ghost needs no debate to make up His mind'.

In the other pile were the pained statements of men who knew their message to be unwelcome: historians who found that the doctrine, having been unknown to the early Church, had been later condemned as a heresy by one pope and discredited when another was branded a heretic by three ecumenical councils.

The Vicar-General was shocked. 'These things should surely be forgotten,' he argued, 'in the interests of . . .'

'. . . a career?'

Charity had been the first casualty of the pamphlet-war. It was unfair to goad the Vicar-General who found the sheer sight of the climbing piles of pamphlets troubling to his faith. Challenging authority had never been our way. 'We might as well be Protestants,' he lamented to Nicola, who promised that nobody would hold it against him if he followed his conscience. But the Vicar-General's conscience was a pendulum which had been given a push and whose giddiness tormented him. Extracting a paper, despite his better judgment, from the polemical 'anti-' pile, he learned that, as recently as 1826, the doctrine had been repudiated by the bishops of England and Ireland when their government questioned them about it on the eve of Catholic Emancipation. Had they lied then? If not, how could Manning now hold the opposite view? Anxiously, the Vicar-General circled the rising stacks and was to be seen sidling towards them with a crablike movement and a hovering hand which annoyed Mangialuce, who liked to sleep on them and had been known to hiss as the troubled cleric pulled out, then poked back in, papers in languages he didn't know. It distressed him that the Dean of the Theological Faculty of Paris had attacked the doctrine and that the papacy's old champion, Bishop Dupanloup of Orléans, advised against defining it. An unopened bundle of the *Augsburger Allgemeine Zeitung*, which nobody could read, was said to deliver a crushing historical criticism of the doctrine. This, though pseudonymous, was thought to be by the same Professor Ignaz von Döllinger as had fingered the new Saint Peter d'Arbuez. Peering at the devilish-looking German script, the Vicar General shook his head and, once, Nicola saw him put his nose to it, as if sniffing for sulphur.

But perhaps Mastai would *not* try to bring in the doctrine? His Bull convoking the Council made no mention of it. It was possible that, having tested the waters, he would judiciously desist.

*

469

Not every skirmish in the paper-war was represented in Amandi's files. Some news reached Imola only as hearsay, like the report of the secret letter which fourteen German bishops had sent His Holiness, warning that to dogmatise the doctrine would cause havoc in Germany, where Catholics had to live with Protestants.

Roman reactions to this were waspish – for why give thought to Germany when it was Rome which was in danger, Rome, the *caput mundi*, the head without which the limbs could not function?

Letters echoing the debates going on in presbyteries up and down the land went into neither pile. These Amandi burned from concern for his correspondents' safety and because of admissions which they might one day prefer to forget.

Noble motives mixed with trivial ones. Coveted privileges, such as the right to deck one's carriage horses with tassels, would be risible the day there was no court. Rome had seen the agony of too many courts – the Stuarts had ended up there as had several Bonapartes and the Bourbons of Naples – to be deceived on this score.

German abstraction got on Roman nerves. Abstraction, as anyone with pastoral experience knew, meant nothing to the body of the faithful, but the panoply of liturgy spoke to the heart and eye. And that included tassels! Absolutely! Yes! Ritual, a ladder to heaven, manifested the transcendent in ways the multitude could apprehend. A mirror in a dark shaft, it caught the light!

'But if we're found to be telling lies,' worried the Vicar-General, 'about history and so forth, might that provoke a schism?'

'You've touched the *hic*,' said Amandi, 'the *hic est quaestio*.'

All summer clerics discussed the odds. Might a strengthened pope even now save the city? Mastai was known to think so. Alternatively, might the Council offer a chance for reform?

'Think,' said Amandi, 'of all those churchmen from across the globe gathering here for the first time ever! Surely something unlooked for may happen? The Holy Spirit is not a caged bird.'

December slid damply in. It had been raining for weeks. The city gleamed like wrinkled silk and, outside Nicola's window, bright red unpicked persimmons rotted prettily. Reaching Rome late, he and the cardinal found their major-domo eager to let out rooms and arguing that there were fortunes to be made. Foreign bishops had come in unforeseen numbers and the *cerimonieri* were at their wits' end. Convents and private *palazzi* were brimful. To be sure, one must pick and choose. One foreign archbishop was said to have a ring in his nose and another had disconcerted his host by pissing on the floor! Council Fathers had come from places whose names, even mangled on Roman lips, had the ring of legend. Mexico, for instance, was where Emperor Maximilien had so wretchedly perished, and it was just three years since his demented Empress had trailed her folly through Vatican antechambers, imploring help for what had once been presented as a Crusade. The spectacle had disquieted a population attuned to omens and signs.

When Prospero called, he found the cardinal nursing a chill and his cat, shaken by the outrage of a travelling basket, crouching beneath a chiffonier. From here its offended amber eyes blinked suspicion at the caller.

He and Nicola went for a stroll.

The streets were crowded, vehicles entangled and a docile old horse, on being obliged to back and bump its rump, suddenly reared and rolled the whites of its eyes. Foreign priests leaned from the windows of their conveyances, crying '*Quid, quid?*' in a Latin so alien that people did not know it for Latin at all.

Prospero remarked that the Council too would be a Tower of Babel and the Fathers – over seven hundred of them – could come under the wrong influence. 'Democracy could raise its hydra head.'

They walked through fine rain. 'So the steam engine,' quipped Nicola, 'by bringing us so many outsiders has justified Pope Gregory's fears. *Chemin de fer, chemin d'enfer*! An infallible instinct? *Is* the doctrine to be defined?'

'Oh, its opponents saw to that! Their vehemence was a tactical mistake. Now, we *must* show the world that the Church is united.' Prospero laughed. '*Quod inopportunum dixerunt necessarium fecerunt.*'

'But they were provoked!' Nicola protested. 'The *Civiltà* said the doctrine should be defined by acclamation! That would turn the Council into a rubber stamp!'

'And they took the bait. Admit it was a clever move.' Playfully squeezing Nicola's elbow. 'Here's the man behind it.'

They had reached the piazza Scossacavalli and here, in the doorway of the Palazzo dei Convertendi, headquarters of the *Civiltà*, stood Father Grassi, who was soon speaking with such candour that Nicola guessed his own loyalty must have been vouched for. He felt discomfort but had no chance to say so. Time, it seemed, pressed, for the sheep, said Grassi, must be quickly sorted from the goats. Today there was to be a meeting at Archbishop Manning's to decide who should be voted onto the commissions which would manage the Council. No votes must on any account go to Liberal bishops – goats. To prevent this, Manning would draw up a single list of candidates for each commission, then get all our friends to vote for it.

'The meeting is at three and we have still to make a list of Spanish nominees.' Away he raced.

Prospero smiled. 'The English know how to spike democracy's guns. Grassi's taking lessons.'

The rain had grown heavier, so they hugged the wall. Pinned to a church door, a notice declared a book made up from the articles in the *Allgemeine Zeitung* to be on the Index. Lines were being drawn. Yesterday, early arrivals among the Council Fathers had been addressed by the Pope and a Brief read out, laying down the rules of procedure. Some, said Prospero over his shoulder, were upset. They had expected to draw up their own rules like at Trent. 'An absurd idea! Trent lasted *years* and we haven't got years. We're near my place. May I offer you lunch?'

Nicola accepted and the two walked up a spacious stone stairway which had lately been used as a privy. Escutcheons with the arms of the *palazzo*'s successive owners decorated the walls.

Over the meal, he learned that some foreign bishops had expressed resentment at the Pope's setting the agenda. Others jibbed at having to obtain permission before leaving Rome, at their post being censored, and at the ban on printing anything to do with the Council. What did they expect, exclaimed Prospero. 'It's not a parliament, after all!'

'But earlier Councils were more free!'

'Oh, Councils have a turbulent history, which is why we plan to keep this one in control.' It should not be difficult, explained Prospero, for about three hundred foreigners were to be the Pope's boarders, kept here at his expense. *They* would hardly bite the hand that fed them! Curial cardinals too would be reluctant to show disloyalty.

Then he made a suggestion. Nicola, whose opinions would be

assumed to coincide with Amandi's, should let people go on thinking this. It would be useful to His Holiness to have someone privy to the cabals of the Liberal Minority. 'Simply pretend to be one of them. To be sure,' Prospero admitted, 'voting will be public. But by the time a significant vote reveals your true allegiance, you will be able to claim that the Holy Spirit led you to change it. Indeed, this could usefully influence other waverers.'

'I am not a waverer, Monsignore!'

'I'm sorry. Look, Nicola, it was a *lapsus*. I only meant . . .'

'That you can handle me! You think that of the whole Council. You and your friends plan to run it by trickery. Well, perhaps you can, Monsignore, but I shan't help you.' Nicola, who had not meant to say any of this, felt his anger rising. As he stood up, his chair fell, knocked something over and brought things to a head, since now he must either apologise or storm out. He stormed out.

In the street, his temper was doused by the rain. Dodging from doorway to doorway, he had leisure to reflect that, not only had he said uncharitable things, he had made a tactical error. With hindsight, he should have accepted the role of traitor. After all, he need not play it. Instead, by staying friends with both sides, he could work for a reconciliation. The chance to do this had come his way – and must be got back. Painful or not, he must apologise. If he did not, some other bishop would be asked to betray the Liberals – and would do so. How, he wondered now, had he come to lose his temper? He had, just a while before, been feeling close to Prospero who had been speaking with passion and looking like his younger self. Humanity, he had warned, could be driven to despair. We were at the hub of things at a pivotal moment. 'It's like France in 1789,' he had argued over the *crostini*, then developed this analogy over the rice, the roast eel, and the veal in Madeira sauce. Look at the parallels! No money in the Treasury, the monarch seeking support from the notables and they, namely us, thinking of their own interests. 'You don't think, do you, that the devil talks with a devilish voice? He talks about rights and episcopal privilege. Lucid and persuasive arguments led to 1789 and we are approaching the 1789 of the Church.'

Nicola, granting that there might be something to this, let his friend work at winning him over and realised, as he felt himself expand in the glow of his attentiveness, how he had been missing their closeness.

473

Possibly, he had seemed more sympathetic than he was. Encouraged, Prospero, having lined up all his points, turned, at the pudding, to the latest pasquinades.

Their butt was Bishop Dupanloup whose entourage of seven priests and many mounds of baggage had astounded the papal Customs. 'He travels like an Egyptian bey and one can but wonder who pays. Could it be the French Emperor?' The guess was perfidious. Dupanloup was staying at the Villa Grazioli. 'He's miles from the centre, which isn't lost on the wags. "Who", runs a joke, "is the most ex-centric bishop? The furthest from grace?" They've Latinised his name to "De pavone lupus", implying that from a peacock vanity come wolfish ways or that he is the product of a mismatch . . .'

'This is *low*!' Nicola was indignant at the reference to the French bishop's being a by-blow of the House of Rohan. The 'wag', it struck him, was probably Prospero himself.

'I'm preparing you,' said Prospero, 'for the zoo which Rome now is – a place where the dove must deal with lupine peacocks.' Then he made his proposal.

Monsignor Santi to Monsignor Stanga:

> Monsignore,
>   I hope you will forgive my intemperance today. Your proposal caught me unprepared. Thinking it over, I see that mine was a worldly reaction and out of place.
>   Perhaps you will give me some days to think. Then I can give you a more pondered reply. Yours in J.C.
>
>   Nicola + Bishop of Trebizond

Rome, 8 December 1869

It was the feast of the Immaculate Conception: a day of rain and rising muck. Bells had pealed for an hour and the Council's opening had been announced by a roar of canon from the Castel Sant'Angelo, whose name commemorated an angel's appearance centuries before. The angel had been sheathing a sword and perhaps today's swords too might be sheathed? Not everyone hoped for this. The young and buoyant rather favoured the red shirts, but were ready, for now, to enjoy the current show.

Eighty thousand people had squeezed into the basilica where few could hope to glimpse as much as a mitre.

Rain had curtailed the ceremony, but the procession was impressive, as over seven hundred Council Fathers in silver copes assembled above St Peter's Portico, then descended the Royal Staircase. They were followed by the Pope, borne high on his *sede gestatoria* surrounded by fan-bearers. Passing St Peter's statue, they moved up the aisle – by now deep in a slush of mud – towards the high altar where the host was exposed behind the bronze columns of Bernini's *baldacchino*. God, ran a whisper, was doubly present: as Pius-Deus and in the consecrated wafer.

Mastai's revelling voice rang out in a strong chant; then the procession turned into the right transept which was to be the Council Chamber. It measured forty-five meters by twenty and through its opened doors the faithful glimpsed cushioned seats – green for bishops and red for cardinals – arranged lengthwise down the aisle.

Mass was celebrated. Then a bishop from Trent, site of the last Council, delivered a greeting. There was a rumour that he had been promised a cardinal's hat if he would urge his fellows to define the controversial doctrine. Straining to hear, they realised that the *aula*'s acoustics were nil. What had he said?

The Pope chanted '*Adsumus Domine*, here we are, oh Holy Spirit, gathered in Your name, though in the fetters of sin . . . Do not allow us to betray justice . . .'

The music thrummed on. How many hours more? A-a-a-a-a-a-a-amen and again amen! Seasoned in ceremony, did prelates here mentally hibernate? Certainly, their torpid minds feared lively ones – hence their dislike of Germans. Bishop Dupanloup of Orléans, by visiting Germany last summer, had incurred some of this. Just now, in the robing room, Cardinal Pitra, looking like a wizened choirboy, had sidled up to him to hiss in his face: '*Wissenschaft*, Monsignore! *Wissenschaft*!' Perhaps he took it for a vice or a disease? His teeth were black-veined and yellow like a clutch of wasps.

Dupanloup prayed for humility – yet, felt that politics could be forced on a man. Two months ago he had gone to see Louis Napoleon at Saint Cloud. The Emperor did not relish Mastai's bullying of French bishops. If provoked, he might again withdraw his troops and this time the consequences could be fatal. Feeling him out, Dupanloup had concluded that the threat was real. Paradoxically, this made it harder to stand up to Mastai. For how hand him over to his enemies?

Yet the Pope himself failed to see that public opinion in France must be appeased. Indeed once, when Dupanloup mentioned this, he had said, 'Ah, you mean the rabble? Do you suggest, Monseigneur, that God's Vicar should bow to their whims?'

'No, *Santità*, but in Paris . . .'

The Paris rabble, said Mastai, was worse than our own. Two Archbishops of that city had been murdered in the last twenty years! 'Things go in threes! You should warn your friend Darboy!' And, horrifyingly, the fat old pontiff had begun to giggle. 'The rabble may get *him* too if he tries using it against us.' It was heartbreaking. Was senility now the norm here? '*Wissenschaft*!' The spittly cardinal could have been cleaning his mouth.

The service was inaudible. Could the poor acoustics in this Council Chamber be deliberate? A way to muffle dissent and make us all harmonise like bells?

Now, with much shuffling and rustling, the Council Fathers filed up to kiss the Pope's hand, knee or – according to rank – toe. In the gallery reserved for lay dignitaries sat the ex-King of Naples, the Empress of Austria, the Czar of Russia's sister, the former Duke and Duchess of Parma, and other ornaments of old Europe. Glittering like amphibians, they were perhaps dreaming of a time when their kind had been secure in its own element.

Monsieur de Banneville was doyen of the diplomatic corps. The Emperor, who had for a while upset Pope Pius by sending him free-thinkers, now sent aristocrats – perhaps to satisfy in small ways a man he planned to throw to the wolves? Among whom, thought Dupanloup who knew his nickname, Pius is wrong to count me. He would know his friends better if he had laboured to more purpose on the political treadmill.

Dupanloup had learned about *that* when helping Prince Talleyrand de Périgord to make a Christian death. Thirty-one years ago now! The prince had been the most skilled of turncoats, and news that he had turned to God when *His* kingdom was about to come for him had aroused widespread hilarity. But the Abbé Dupanloup – who had been the butt of some of it – had not doubted a repentance rooted in what the old prince described as 'moral fatigue and deep disgust'. Politics had left the arch-politician with ashes in his mouth and the abbé had caught the burned-out effluvium. Talleyrand, ex-royalist, ex-revolutionary, ex-Bonapartist and ex-bishop, had in the end signed a paper repudiating the world's excesses and his share therein. This had satisfied the priest in Dupanloup but disturbed the man. Thinking of it now, he found more detachment in the great worldling than in himself – who was heartbroken to be seen as an enemy here, in a city which he loved. He was suffering too at Mastai's coldness for, entwined with his exasperation, he felt tenderness for the obstinate old pope and had been trying not to hurt him when he warned that to define the doctrine would be 'inopportune'. But the word was a red rag to the Curia.

The main body of the basilica was surmounted by a cloud. Many in the congregation had arrived soaked and, as the place warmed up, vapour rose, feet steamed like puddings and now, five hours later, it looked as though a locomotive had driven through.

'*Libera nos, domine.*'

Maximin Giraud was trying to do his Zouave uniform honour by standing as straight as the nobs from the Noble Guard, but was tormented by an itch. Fleas? Bedbugs? Lice? In a crowd like this there must be congregations of all three. He was shocked to hear the Zouave behind him parody the litany. Some chaps in the battalion were none too stable. Maximin, whose own stability had been put in doubt, recognised an alien brand of crackiness.

'Good Lord deliver us . . .'

A priest looked around. Maximin knew he was French by his neckband. He had thought of being a priest himself once.

'. . . from Bishop Félix Dupanloup . . .'

That Zouave was looking for trouble. The priest looked at Maximin who didn't move a muscle. His confessors had told him that he owed it to God and man to get respect. This, he argued, was a burden with which he needed help. 'But,' the last one had said, 'you're not easily helped, Maximin!' He'd got him into the Zouaves, though, and maybe something would come of that? There were bigwigs here today. One might take him up.

'Our Lady,' the last confessor had said, 'didn't show herself to you for your own sake. You bring hope to millions.' Humanity's worst fear, said the priest, was that God had forgotten it and so any divine message was a consolation, even a stern one. Maybe indeed stern ones were best? Prophesying plagues and penalties, Maximin and Mélanie had explained the potato blight, the failed walnut and cereal crops, and the famine. People were consoled by that. They preferred punishment to random bad luck.

The word stuck in Maximin's head. Had he, while delivering other people from randomness, got stuck in it himself? 'If I've to get respect,' he'd argued, 'wouldn't it be safer if . . .'

'Not money, Maximin.' The confessor was curt. 'You're getting no more out of me. It doesn't help you. I'm sorry.'

Maximin's hopes had been raised, then cruelly dashed. On his way here from France, he'd met someone who'd had the same experience. A former boy-soprano, the chap had had a taste of fame until he lost his voice and couldn't, he explained, take to anything else. Not after the professional satisfaction he'd known.

'That's *it*!' Maximin had never before met anyone who understood. They'd met in a Marseilles café and, by the evening's end, got as drunk as lords. Before that, the singer had tried, gravely and wistfully, to sing. Then he wept and Maximin almost joined in. The parallel with his own life was striking. *He* had been a famous visionary when he was eleven. He was now thirty-four.

When the singer passed out, the waiter explained that he was a castrato who had left Rome after losing his voice. 'The poor bastard lost the other thing when he was eight. He's one of the Italian exiles here. The police know him well. He's a Garibaldino.'

Maximin, who was joining the Zouaves to fight Garibaldini, left the place hurriedly . . .

There must be some row going on between bishops. Maximin wasn't surprised. Since the age of eleven, he had seen a lot of churchmen. They were what he knew best: churchmen, not God. God hadn't bothered with him again – if it *had* been God the first time – but churchmen took an interest in him and he, for the most part, kept his doubts to himself. After all – who cries 'stinking fish'?

'Beware of Doubting Thomases!' a priest had warned. 'They'll stick their fingers into the wound of your doubt. They did it to Christ, so you can expect it too.'

That was after he'd been caught out in contradictions by the Curé d'Ars whose questions had reduced him to saying he wasn't sure he had seen a vision, after all. There had been a terrible scandal then and threats of punishments for deceit and blasphemy. Luckily, the thing was patched up and Maximin told not to talk openly, even to priests. Holy things, he was told, should be mysterious. The hunt for precision was the vice of our time.

He agreed with that. Life was a cloudy business. Look at today! Hours of standing had made his head swim and brought on a kind of fever which, at moments, swept you up, only to return you later to the throb of back pain and the ache of a full bladder. Judging by the smells, some had succumbed to that.

6–7 January, 1870

At night now Cardinal Amandi was often agitated and couldn't settle. Instead, he rose, creaked open drawers and could be found riffling papers. Sometimes a desk-top banged. Courtesy and patience with the world were deserting him.

Tonight the papers rustled like restive doves: images of the Holy Ghost who was, Amandi had contended over dinner, 'mute and muzzled'. Archbishop Darboy with some of his priests had been his guests and they had sat up late, drinking sweet wine into which the cardinal liked to dip biscuits. There had been a special cake too, for today had been the Feast of the Epiphany.

Talk was interrupted by the scraping of metal, as the cardinal's knife encountered a miniature king, a reminder from the cook that the Epiphany was also called the Feast of the Wise Kings. Amandi put the effigy on the side of his plate.

Nicola tapped at his door. It was 3 a.m. 'A little opium?' he suggested, but Amandi ignored this. The Church, he declared, standing there in his nightshirt, was threatened from within! He tapped his forehead. 'He's put himself above the Council.'

'Eminence, what about a tisane?'

'Don't soothe me, Santi! Twenty-four years. It's the longest reign since St Peter's, which was twenty-five. Do you remember the old prophecy?'

'That if any pope's reign matches it the Church will founder.'

'No need to laugh. It's what the habit of power does to a man that's dangerous. Lord Acton is shocked by the form chosen for the conciliar decrees. Listen.' Amandi read from a paper. '"Pius, Bishop, Servant of God's Servants" – here, you read it.'

Nicola read, '". . . with the approval of the Sacred Council orders . . ."'

'Exactly! "Orders"! *He* does. Not the Council! So why summon it? To deceive the world? At Trent – Acton tells me – they said, "The Sacred Synod, etc., ordains . . ." And now the Prefect of the Sacred Archives, Father Theiner, has been forbidden to let us see the Trent agenda! *He*

479

doesn't want it known that our predecessors, in 1545, did their own ordaining!' Amandi's grimace smudged his face like smoke.

'You need your sleep.'

'We've *been* asleep.' Pouncing on papers, the cardinal's hand was a fox in a hennery. 'Read this.' His ring glinted like an eye.

It was headed 'Fetters placed on the Council's Freedom'. Vertical Roman numerals vibrated blackly. Nicola read on. '"One, bad acoustics; two, oath of secrecy; three, prohibition to print."'

'That only applies to us,' said the cardinal. 'The toadies can print what they like.'

Nicola read, '"Four, prohibition to meet in groups of more than fifteen."' The strokes of the numerals made a cage.

'Ditto,' said the cardinal. 'Only to us!'

'"Five, the Curia prepared the agenda before we got here."'

'They rigged the elections to the key commissions! His minion, Manning, did that. The Commission on Faith hasn't one anti-infallibilist on it! So now the Council is in his hands.' Amandi's eye pierced Nicola. 'Yet *the* doctrine hasn't been officially mentioned. Why? Are they planning a sudden move? To spring it on us? Have it passed by acclamation?'

'Surely, Archbishop Darboy put a stop to that?'

Darboy had let it be known that if such a move were attempted one hundred bishops would walk out 'and take the Council with them in their shoes'.

'It's whispered,' Amandi suffered a spurt of laughter, 'that Pius expects a celestial apparition to do the job for him.' His laughter turned to a groan. 'I've grown blasphemous! I'll end by damning my soul.'

Scenes like this – there had been many – kept Nicola in a state of distress. By now even innocent Liberal bishops were worried and the alert were on the rack. He, lying low as he had resolved to do, watched anger mount like a man watching a storm through glass. At least the fear of a definition by acclamation had, he assured Amandi, been warded off. The proof was that the infallibilists had got up a petition begging Pius to put the question on the agenda.

'And that means a debate and a vote.'

Since opposition within the Council had been all but throttled, battles were fought in corridors and alcoves and, on nights like this, in Nicola's head where Amandi and Prospero pulled in opposite ways. The wrangle was bitter. His view of himself as an *agent conciliateur* was proving over-optimistic and he knew that if his understanding with Prospero became known, Amandi would be deeply hurt. Yet his reason for not surrendering the role still stood – another agent would take his place – so he had to continue. Neither could he warn the Minority lest exasperation drive them to some excess. Meanwhile, his friends' minds were in a fume; they were angry with each other and each accused him of belonging to the ranks of the tepid whom Christ spewed out of his mouth.

Last Saturday, meeting Prospero on the Pincian Hill, he had assured him that the anti-Infallibilists did not, in their innocence, see any need to intrigue. To help that sink in, he added: 'Surely the Holy Ghost doesn't need a rigged Council?'

Prospero admitted that His Holiness had in fact favoured letting one member of the Opposition onto the Deputation on Faith. 'For the look of the thing. Manning, however . . .'

'Is he out of control?'

Oh, said Prospero, Westminster lacked Roman *suavitas*.

Close by a band struck up. Children were rolling hoops. Avoiding the din, the two bishops moved towards the parapet. Across the river lay the Vatican in a prospect of fields. Controversy, Prospero acknowledged, was quickening.

And the Minority, said Nicola slyly, had had a victory! A bill dogmatising the first part of the *Syllabus of Errors* had been sent back for redrafting. Bishops had described it as 'verbal dysentery' and 'fit only for a decent burial'. Pius, who had expected a docile Council, was said to be shaken and the Curia which had drafted the bill, stunned. No doubt, retorted Prospero, German bishops, knowing themselves tainted with Protestantism and related heresies, had acted from fear. Was Nicola *sure* no intriguing was going on?

Nicola, fearful of being replaced by a more hawk-eyed agent, promised to stay on the *qui vive*.

Prospero, meanwhile, declared himself unruffled by the Minority's victory which would surely be their last. 'If we change the electoral rules so that a bill can be passed by a majority of one, they will be unable to obstruct the Council's work. Why should two hundred men out of seven hundred and fifty be allowed to do so?'

Nicola protested that those figures were meaningless, since the Minority bishops represented great and populous dioceses such as Paris, Prague, Orléans and Cologne, while men like himself and Prospero represented imaginary ones. 'There are two hundred titulars voting with the Majority. We've been used to pack the Council. Half the so-called

Majority are Italians! Do you think we represent half the Christian world?'

'So that's the kind of talk going on!' Prospero's smile congratulated his friend for keeping his ear to the ground. Forget numbers, he advised. Or remember this one: almost two thousand years of continuity lay behind the Church. Were we to trade that for some trumpery notion of fairness? 'Bishops do not *represent* anyone. They are the successors of the apostles!' His hand on Nicola's arm propelled him gently through the throng of promenaders.

'There's your devil!' he murmured of a small, ascetic-looking prelate who was walking with a bearded gentleman. Manning of Westminster had been called 'the devil of the Council' because of his intrigues, and indeed had the look of a spider, being thin as a whip, with clenched jaw and a mouth like a slit. Nicola recognised his companion as the British agent Odo Russell.

'Conspiring?' he wondered.

'Oh I think it's the Minority who whore after secular governments. They have had telegrams to the effect that Count Daru, the new French Minister for Foreign Affairs, is "ready to be of service". The telegrams were seen, by the Post Office – and we know the sort of help France can give.'

'I can't think why you need me. *I* didn't know this.'

'Well, you should try to know such things! Monseigneur Dupanloup's friends meet in the Orangerie of the Palazzo Borghese and are called "the Orangistes". Join them. Find out whether Daru's appointment means that the Emperor will withdraw his troops.'

'No bishop would want that.'

'Who knows?' Prospero turned into a leafy side alley.

'They are more innocent,' Nicola insisted, 'than you think. I've met several who are amazed to be treated here as enemies. Amazed and hurt! These are men who think of this as their spiritual home. Who come from divided countries and . . .'

'Are contaminated?'

'No, are used to respecting people with whom they disagree.'

They had moved in under close-knit evergreens. There was only one other promenader here, Father Grassi, who caught and held Nicola's hands in the stemmed, pale chalice of his own. Prospero was gone before Nicola knew it – had this then been arranged? – and he was alone with the Jesuit in a seaweedy dimness so oppressive that a small boy,

482

running in after a ball, bolted like a rabbit which has found a ferret in its warren.

Darkness suited Grassi. Like celery, he might have grown in it, for he was now bald and his pate glistened. Swaying and rubbing Nicola's imprisoned hands, he explained that Prospero had not wished to appeal to their friendship. From delicacy. 'He felt you would find it easier to refuse *me*! We hope you will work with us.'

Pushing aside a branch, he made a window in the greenery to reveal Manning and Russell strolling in a contiguous alley. They were out of earshot. As the branch swung back, it sprayed drops on his cassock which reflected the purple at Nicola's throat.

That had been last Saturday and now here was Amandi too looking for a declaration of solidarity. Tremulous in his night attire, he made a show of tidying his papers and tried not to beg for this from Nicola whose holding back – due to scruples – he divined. 'Those who are neither hot nor cold . . .' He let out a self-deriding cackle. Today's ceremony had left *him* on the boil.

It was to have been the first Open Session designed to publish the Council's findings in the presence of Pope and public. But, having rejected the schema on the Syllabus, the Fathers had nothing to publish and were told that a stopgap ceremony had been devised wherein each must solemnly retake his ordination oath and declare his loyalty. They were being called publicly to heel and saw the humiliation as a signal from Mastai who had let it be known that he could *feel* his infallibility. The Catholic press was publishing similar claims and, back in their dioceses, every biddable Tom, Dick and Harry was encouraged to sign petitions urging the bishops to follow the Pope's line. Caught between grinding stones, episcopal consciences were being reduced to chaff.

'Well,' demanded Amandi at last, 'do you agree with me?'

Nicola told him he did and said, for good measure, as he had to Father Grassi, that he prayed for harmony in the Holy Spirit. Surely we could all agree about that? Well, no! Both Amandi and Grassi – at one in this – thought the Holy Spirit needed help.

'You disapprove of intrigue?' Grassi had asked. 'But should we not prevent others intriguing? Will you agree that whoever is sending information from inside the Council to a German newspaper – thus breaking his oath of silence – is a traitor?'

Increasingly insidious letters had been appearing in the *Allgemeine*

483

Zeitung of Augsburg. Stating the case for the Opposition more cogently than its members dared do, these rallied waverers cited Church history with knowledgeable brio and, most maddening to the Curia, reported secret and unedifying incidents, including the Pope's bullying of bishops who opposed his will. Worst of all, by disclosing what had been said in closed sessions, they made a mock of the ultramontane claim that Council matters were pitched at a level too high for the profane to discover or understand. The Council, *l'Univers* and the *Civiltà* had assured their readers, was immune to factionalism. But instead, as the *Allgemeine Zeitung* impudently revealed, factionalism was rampant, not only within the Council, but in the breasts of the Fathers and the bitter breast of Mastai.

The press, said Grassi, was the evil spirit of our time. We tried to fight it – but how triumph over the writer in the German paper who combined a theologian's erudition with the impudence of the gutter? It seemed that, like Faust, some German theologian must have sold his soul! His Holiness was heartsick. It could provoke another schism in that difficult country. 'We must,' Grassi urged, 'find the perjurer inside the Council!' Bishop? Theologian? Stenographer? 'You, Monsignore,' he insinuated, 'are well placed to find out!'

Did he think it was Amandi? Surely not!

As though guessing this thought, Grassi said that the cardinal, a noble soul, was naturally above suspicion. 'Perhaps you hold against me the fact that I once told you I would support His Eminence's candidature in the event of His Holiness's demise, then withdrew my support. But my dear Monsignore . . .' The priest paced and argued and the gist of what he said was that we served Eternity but lived in Time. A future pope could not receive present allegiance – think of the consequences! 'Not least,' he lowered his voice, 'in the mind of a suspicious pontiff who, from a laudable concern for stability, is at pains to prevent any appeal from this Council to a future one!' Pius knew – the Italians trumpeted it daily in their press – that half Europe hoped to reverse his policies once he was gone. He was counting on the doctrine of Infallibility to protect his legislation from change.

They had reached the end of the green tunnel. Grassi looked right and left, then, taking Nicola's elbow, walked him back through it. As far as the future went, he whispered, His Eminence, now that d'Andrea, poor turbulent spirit, had died, must be the first choice. Even his age spoke for him. Nobody wanted another long reign. Flexibility now was an asset and men lost that in office. A pope of one persuasion was best followed by one of the other. It kept our barque on an even keel. Meanwhile – Father Grassi became next to inaudible – we must bear our cross if the present pontiff was a little *too* concerned for the future. The Bull he had just published was provocative. It forbade the Council to interfere in the election of the next pope if he were to die during its tenure. In that event, it was to be suspended and the election left to the College of Cardinals, *unice et exclusive*. The Fathers disliked that. But, well, Rome had never liked foreign fingers in its pies. However, all this was a digression. The question now was, who was the perjurer? Suspicion fell naturally on Germans. Cardinal Hohenlohe and his theologian, Professor Johann Friedrich, were prime suspects but something, a sixth sense – perhaps a whisper from the Holy Spirit – told Father Grassi to look elsewhere. Was Monsignor Santi disposed to help at all?

They had again come out of their tunnel. Archbishop Manning and Mr Russell, whose trajectory now came close to theirs, bowed and were bowed to. Then each pair took off on their diverging paths.

'Acton!' Grassi hissed. 'Lord Acton! The other Englishman! You must have met him? He runs the Opposition and I think helps write the letters. He's ruthless! He stirs up governments. He is trying to poison Mr Gladstone's mind against the new doctrine!'

'New, Father Grassi? You concede that it is new?'

'New dogma! Old doctrine! Acton is a former pupil of Ignaz von Döllinger who is surely the "Janus" whose book is on the Index. The letters are in the same style. Or so German friends tell me.'

'So then you know?'

'No, no. Acton is a layman. The questions are, first, who tells him what is said inside the Council, and second, how are the letters sent from Rome? They do not go through the Post Office. Even if you incline towards the Minority, you cannot condone . . .'

'But I know nothing.'

'But may come to know!' Benevolence sparkled in Grassi's smile. 'There are rewards for loyalty. Fifteen red hats are to be bestowed. Who knows on which heads they may land!'

Twenty-seven

Father Gilmore's gaze was blocked by clouds as dank and shaggy as the udders of Romulus and Remus' foster-mother. There was no other view. He had been assigned a cell whose window-screen blotted out the middle ground. This, as it happened, had soft associations, for he had spent his boyhood under the protection of just such a censoring device. Being back was a privilege. Accommodation in Rome was as scarce as hen's teeth.

'Accept it,' was the advice of Cardinal Cullen, who had unflatteringly added, 'the last shall be first!'

Well, Gus Gilmore knew he was one of the last and least. Shaking ink from his pen, he wrote, 'Back in old haunts.' A drop jumped off the nib. Mopping it, he recalled Cullen's voice at the dinner table lambasting doubters. 'How but by obedience,' the cardinal had demanded to know, 'is the moral order to be protected – or indeed this city?'

Someone mentioned the French garrison.

'Pff!'

Cullen – sometimes known as 'the Grey-Green Eminence' – would give no colour to the jibe that Irish churchmen were 'politicos in priest's clothing'. Some blamed him, arguing that the Pope's recent condemnation of the Fenians could have been averted. But Gilmore, a mere dogsbody, had no such thoughts. He had installed a censoring device in his head which he hoped would be as effective as the one at his window. He was here to help our bishops with their Latin, and their lordships were tetchy. Big fish in their diocesan ponds, they didn't want to feel like minnows and disliked hearing *him* speak of his youth here in Rome. Perhaps they took it for boasting? Reminiscences of those years were now known as *quarantottate* – forty-eighteries – and this, he was mortified to see, caused them marked amusement.

486

'Hear that, Father Gilmore?'

Did they think him vain of his *Romanità*? Was he? Flicking back through his diary, he read: 'Old city lovelier than ever. Mons. de Mérode's improvements said to be every bit as clever as Baron Haussman's in Paris. Rode in an omnibus.'

He had paid three *baiocchi* to go from piazza Venezia to the Vatican, then come back on foot to piazza Navona which was so deep in rainwater as to recall the old practice of flooding it so that citizens might refresh themselves during the summer's heat. He imagined cardinals' coaches splashing through. Wheel spokes whirling. Urchins dodging. Though the ground had been levelled, the freak rainfall had flooded it again.

'This morning,' he reread, 'in a refreshment room off the *aula conciliaris*, I stood so close to Mons. Santi that our shoulders touched.'

'Liberal Catholicism,' said Father Grassi, 'is a nonsense!' How, he asked, have a dogmatic theology in a Liberal Church? His cassock lacked a button. Nicola was ashamed of disliking him. 'Pope Pius,' Grassi confided, 'is stalking God. Don John Bosco saw him three times in February.' Did Nicola know about Bosco? He received divine messages in his dreams. The most recent was that Pius must steadfastly pursue his course.

Nicola asked whether Father Bosco got any help with his dreams.

The Jesuit smiled. 'He's hard to harness.'

Again they were in a garden, this time that of the Villa Ludovisi. Music floated from illuminated windows. Nicola had been inside, partaking of refreshments, when word came that he should join Father Grassi out of doors. It was spring again and magnolia chalices broke apart in pink, fleshy segments.

'What I want you to do is spy, not for but *on* God.' By this, said Grassi, he meant that we must wait for a sign from Him and make the Opposition wait too, which might not be easy. They were headstrong men, but we must lead them back to simplicity. The vocabulary of prophecy, we might say, was indeed limited, but so were the trajectories of clocks. Could not God as easily make use of Don Bosco's tales of the French being reduced to eating rats as of a German intellectual stiff with *Wissenschaft*?

'Does he say the French will eat rats?'

'Yes. Louis Napoleon will fall and Paris choke with blood and burn like paper. It's unlikely – but so was what happened to Sodom and

Gomorrah. You and I,' said Grassi, 'must mend rather than make. We are close to power but have none. I am in the confidence of our General who, as you know, is known as the Black Pope.'

This was their second meeting. Suspended above the greenery, the reception indoors grew more visible as dusk gathered. Ladies in draped bustles and *illustrissimi* magnified by capes moved with sinuous ease. Light gleamed on pectoral crosses and on trays loaded with bright goblets. It must be warm, for an opened window, swinging to and fro, caught a blaze of light which at moments obliterated the entire, pretty scene.

Miss Foljambe had opened her apartment to the Opposition. Already, this afternoon, four bona fide members had taken refuge here from the biting *tramontana*. Not small fry either! Every cassock was violet-piped.

'The Holy Father,' said an English one, 'sent our Collegio a present of twenty-four woodcock.'

A lady whose name no one caught offered tea. 'India or China?' She might have been tendering slices of the globe.

Their hostess greeted Amandi and Nicola. '*Em-m-minenza! Monsignore!*' The sounds lolled on her tongue and she smiled at the *papabile* cardinal. They must, she urged, treat this apartment as their own. No need to fear she would disturb them. She had her private quarters down below. 'I know you'll need privacy for your discussions.' She was a woman grown androgynous with age and today, soberly fine in moire and amethysts, could have been an Anglican bishop, though what she actually was, as she was pleased to tell the company, was the only English Council Mother or, as that nasty creature Veuillot liked to put it, *Commère du Concile*.

'That means "gossip", does it not? Well, if I'm to be called that, I may as well earn the insult!' Lowering her voice, she told Nicola that she had a surprise for the company. Later on.

Her apartment, whose dominant colour was red, was quilted like a doll's cradle. There were several such welcoming houses now in Rome, for the rule forbidding more than fifteen bishops to foregather meant that countless coveys of them needed places to settle and consult.

And what was *his* allegiance, Miss Foljambe teased Nicola, who told her he counted himself a sturdy member of the Opposition.

'Sturdy!' cried the cardinal, almost spilling his tea. 'You've got him down off the fence!'

Nicola said, no, it had been the offer of a red hat.

Had it really been offered? The Englishman sounded titillated.

'Not quite offered,' said Nicola. 'Dangled.'

'We're giving scandal to the laity!' cried Amandi. 'Worse, to heretics!'

But Miss Foljambe protested that she was scarcely a heretic now, having become so Romish that her own Church kept expecting her to go the way of former Archdeacon Manning and convert.

A pity Manning had, murmured the English bishop. The Almighty did us a disfavour by calling Mrs Manning to Himself! If He had not, the worthy Archdeacon would, perforce, have stayed in the Church of England to be its scourge instead of ours! 'Ah well,' sighed His Lordship, 'whom the Lord loveth He chasteneth!' Smiling, he feigned shame at his malice, then spoiled the effect by saying that Westminster would certainly get a red hat for his work here.

Miss Foljambe asked whether it was true that the Council was so secretive that bishops might not see the shorthand reports of their own speeches?

Yes, said her compatriot, but there was hotter gossip still! Four bishops had been released from their oath of secrecy by the Pope himself. 'They are to keep friendly journalists informed so that they may refute the inaccuracies of the *Allgemeine Zeitung*.'

Nicola drew the Englishman aside. How sure was he of this? 'Very,' said the prelate. 'I myself surprised Archbishop Manning handing over notes on Council proceedings and, to prevent a scandal, he had to make a clean breast of it.'

'Handing them to whom?'

'To Mr Odo Russell. They meet,' whispered the Englishman, 'on the Pincio. Manning admonished me not to tell a soul, but I fail to see why I should accept his admonitions!'

Could Manning, the advocate of Council secrecy, be himself the source of leakage? He could, for was Russell not Amandi's friend too and Lord Acton's? Perfidious Englishman! He had too many friends – and a diplomatic bag to ferry letters past the censor.

Speculation was interrupted by the arrival of Miss Foljambe's surprise. It was Martelli, with an envelope given him by some Italian customs officers. They were friends, he explained, for he had fought beside them in 1848 and that sort of bond outweighed many differences. They heartily disliked cassocks and often boasted of playing tricks on priests. He had reproved them for this, which was why yesterday he had been treated to salvos of winks, before being handed proof of the 'cassocks'

489

duplicity'. The men had confiscated it from a Jesuit for a lark and on general principles, then, on examining it, decided to show it to him who, as a deputy, must know what it was about. To their noses it stank of subversion.

'But,' said Martelli, 'I saw at once, Reverend Friends, that the subversion was aimed not at our parliament but at yours.'

He gave a wad of papers to Nicola, who read: '"Insofar as error has no rights . . ." It's the Majority Party's battle strategy!'

Amandi read over his shoulder, '"There are turbulent spirits in the Council."' Reaching forward, he turned a page. '"To defeat proud heads, appeal to hearts. Preachers should dwell on the three weak things which conquered the world: in the manger a child, in the tabernacle a host, in the Vatican an old man." Mmnn!' Tightening his lips, he invited, 'Listen to this: "(1) To bishops whose board is paid by His Holiness, quote his joke: They may not make me infallible, but they will surely make me a *fallito* – bankrupt! Shame them into loyalty. (2) Frighten the vulnerable. (3) Make use of visionaries. Giraud from La Salette must be brought to tell the Council of Our Lady's wish that the Holy Father be declared infallible. The file in Mons. Stanga's possession will prove . . ."' Amandi's hand grasped Nicola's shoulder, then snapped forward to finger this. 'So what's why you gave it to him! I felt there was something!' His face was in spasm. 'You connived!'

Suspicion burned the air between them. Also pain. It was as though a window had opened and both had blown in to steam and scorch. Nicola's breath failed him.

Amandi hissed. 'I'd heard you had been seeing Father Grassi. I suppose Stanga brought you together? He uses his father's tactics against his father's ideals. Intrigue. Secrecy. I preferred the old count.' His wounded gaze contrasted with his words.

Nicola couldn't speak. Nothing he said now would seem credible. His throat closed and his brain felt like unmeshed gears. How had things turned so treacherous? Bewilderment worked in him like fever. Was *he* treacherous? Was that so bad? If so, was it because he was tepid or, conversely, because he felt things too much? Where, anyway, was the treachery since God was manifest in His Vicar and His Vicar's men – and both Nicola's friends were that! But now his painful, mental whirlwind changed course as he remembered philanderers confiding – it was their defining theme – about contradictory loves. They were most often shrugged at and seen as self-deceivers. *Was* there an analogy?

There was no time to ponder any of this for Martelli had produced a second document. 'There's more,' he told the company. 'Father Grassi hopes to found a network of spies within the clergy to report on the orthodoxy of their fellows and defend "integral Catholicism". He plans to call it the Sodalitium Pianum.'

'Pious Sods!' gasped the English bishop with an astounded laugh. He could not have followed the exchange in Italian, but anarchy must have reached him on a visceral level, for he blessed himself as though to ward it off, then, perhaps in the same spirit, blew his nose. Out with evil! Blow it away!

'So,' Amandi whispered coldly to Nicola, 'that's why they appointed you to be my Coadjutor!'

'I swear . . .'

'Please don't or I'll think you too have been absolved from keeping oaths! I am going. Don't come yet. I could not bear, just now, to hear cajoling lies.'

Miserably, Nicola watched him take leave of Miss Foljambe and her guests. In his black and scarlet, the cardinal looked as frail as a kite in high wind. Nicola felt a surge of rage against Grassi and Prospero, both of whom, if he'd had his hands on their necks, he could have cheerfully strangled. One outcome of all this, he told himself, was that now, at last, he saw the folly of trying to reconcile the unreconcilable.

A rum lot the Zouaves! Their founder had made his name by subduing the Dey of Mascara and, when he put his sword at the Pope's disposal, he'd remembered the blackies who'd fought for him then. Or other people had. Anyway, his Franco-Belgian riflemen came to be called 'Zouaves' and an officer, who must have gone too often to the Opéra Comique, designed their uniforms.

They saw themselves as sons of St Louis, but the life didn't suit Maximin. Just look at the chore he'd landed now! He was on guard duty at the mouth of a back alley with orders to stop people going in there to shit. *Défense de chier*! There were scarcely any public latrines, so alleys like this were used by those taken short. Up and down walked Maximin in his ballooning trousers, keeping an eye out for anyone whose fingers reached for their own. He glared. 'Thou shalt not shit,' said his glare. Anyway, not here.

For minutes he had been watching a lurker – hat down, collar up – whose hands moved under his coat. Maximin was considering asking him if he had no consideration for the dignity of the city in which the cream of the world's prelates were convened. Did the stranger think they wanted to drag their cassocks through his *merde*, caca, night soil, *stercus*? Maximin should have been told the German and Russian words too. The man's hand emerged bearing a paper. He was looking for a discreet place to go to confession. Ah, so the relief sought was spiritual! Just as well, then, that Maximin had not insulted him! Especially as, on closer examination, he looked good for a tip. Scrutiny revealed Dundreary sidewhiskers and well-cut clothes. A gentleman. What was he doing in a back alley? He was, it seemed, about to say. He had dismissed his carriage, wanted a priest but was avoiding fashionable churches.

'I am,' he confessed, 'well known.' Money was introduced into Maximin's hand. 'I need a simple confession priest,' said the gentleman who had a Belgian accent. 'Confession priests' were those who attended to pastoral duties. 'Yet,' said the Belgian, 'perhaps not too simple!'

He's afraid, thought the Zouave happily. Fear produced tips.

Garrulous now, the Belgian said he had been staying near Albano where the priest, a mulish martinet, was incapable of confessing a man like him. 'I wouldn't hire a cook in such a place. Why did I think I could use its confessor?' He had, he admitted, insulted the man and was now sorry. He needed God.

Maximin, wondering if the gentleman was in danger from an angry husband, said he didn't know any confession priests. Only the military chaplain who – but the stranger waved the idea aside.

'Take a message for me then,' he said.

'I can't, sir. Not until sundown. Then I go off duty.'

The Belgian cursed his own stupidity in sending away his coachman. He had been afraid someone might recognise his livery. As if anyone would have noticed or cared! People cared only for their blood kin. Only your kin stood by you, so why leave them destitute on the say-so of a priest from Albano?

The baffled Maximin shuffled his feet in a suspect substance – it stank – and agreed. Plainly the gentleman needed a listener.

A learned Jesuit, said the Belgian, who seemed not to notice the stench, had sent him a message to the effect that a bankrupt could sinlessly conceal his assets. To be precise, he had said 'those assets necessary for his survival'. But who was to compute necessity? What the priest in Albano considered necessary would not buy oats for the Belgian's horses, all of which, he confided, had white stars on their foreheads. For luck.

Maximin felt like a stray dog who meets an ideal master only to find that he too is a stray. Was this promising patron too far down on his luck?

There was a time, said the stranger, when the kings and Emperors of Europe had been ready to do favours for him. 'Yet I started out probably poorer than you.'

Maximin could not resist doubting this.

'Do you want to bet?'

Maximin, prudently, said he had no money.

'Ten to one,' cajoled the Belgian. 'Thirty to one! Done? Well, my grandfather was a *filius exposititius* brought up by the *Assistance Publique*! *He* became a weaver. My father kept a tavern for a while but died when I was ten, so I had to go to work. I peddled pencils through the villages of Brabant, then worked in a bakery and a brick kiln and later joined the Foreign Legion. I had to run away from that.'

Maximin mentally kissed goodbye to hope of employment. Any minute now, he thought, this chap will admit a crime and after that he'll not want to see me again! Morosely, he told him, 'I was poorer than that. I was a herder and slept with the cows. I slept on dry dung and was so lonely I used to moo back at them.'

'Ah,' said the gentleman. 'Muck for luck!' And coughed up the promised sum. 'Your cow dung is a poor omen for me.' Then he asked Maximin to go to the residence of Monsignor Nicola Santi and tell him that André the Baptist needed him. 'He'll know who it is.'

If the Pope was God's Vicar, Cardinal Cullen was His man in the Irish College. Lunch was an occasion for him to air his views, and having a Jesuit from the *Civiltà* at his table stiffened them. 'This Council,' he opined, 'will leave the nineteenth century's prime legacy! It's not for science that it will be remembered!'

Around the table, assent had the purr of a *placet*.

Gilmore was told to stay when the rest withdrew. Cullen tried to tell a joke, but it fell flat.

'*Traduttore traditore!*' said Father Grassi. 'Jokes travel no better than books on usury.' His laugh startled Gilmore for whom the subject was a sore one.

Some years before, just when Catholics were being urged to invest in bonds to save the Papal Treasury, Gilmore had, in all innocence, published a pamphlet spelling out the position of usury in Canon Law. His aim was to protect Irish tenant farmers, and both he and his bishop had been amazed by the wrath of Rome.

'It seems that your book was untimely! Money has been baptized.'

The bishop, an unworldly old man, had gazed in bewilderment at Gilmore. Shortly after that he was forced to retire and Gilmore was packed off to a parish in a bog so wet you could rarely tell whether its white stipplings were cloud-reflections or sheep.

Father Grassi asked, 'May I take Father Gilmore for a drive?'

The cardinal must have said 'yes', for in no time a dazed Gilmore was in a carriage bowling down the Quirinal Hill. At some point, while passing a dazzle of freshly disinterred marble, he was presented with his own diary. It had, said the Jesuit, been found in the street. Someone, seeing a reference in it to the Romano, had brought it there.

'But it never left my cell.'

Grassi shrugged.

On they drove, keeping pace with other carriages whose wheels could have been faceless clocks until, slowing to visibility, they changed to clock dials afflicted with a plethora of hands. A section of Gilmore's mind tried to recall what was in his diary but knew only that it was unfit for alien eyes. Mortified, he looked away from the Jesuit. On one side of the road, mauled earth made a ragged mound. A notice announced 'Temple of . . .' The Holy Father had been encouraging excavations in the hope that impressive finds might coincide with the Council.

Grassi fingered a paragraph in which its writer addressed his remembered, fifteen-year-old self: Augustine Gilmore, future priest. That was how he had known to whom to return it!

Reading with difficulty – his eye was blurring – Gilmore was dismayed to glimpse an account of how he had felt about Nicola Santi twenty years ago. His avowals were vague, and recognition of what they could be taken to mean would not have burst on him if he had been alone. But now he read with Grassi's eye, an eye not privy to the fog of unknowing through which Gilmore's faint self-awareness had dimly seeped – dimly until now. Now it glowed with misleading and lurid clarity. Gilmore felt a disagreeable flush swell the veins in his cheeks.

Santi had failed to even recognise him when, last week in the Council refreshment rooms, Gilmore passed him a plate of sweet *maritozze* stuffed with pine kernels.

Grassi's thin finger pointed to Gilmore's name: *An Giolle Mór.* 'I knew you were one of the *Hibernici*,' said he. 'I had a friend translate your name. It means "big servant", does it not? We are hoping you will render us a big service.'

On they drove. Once the horse paused to shed bright, steamy golden turds, then set off again past vineyards, grazing sheep and marble as grey as the sheep. Kitchen gardens, excavations, the Terme di Tito and the Colosseum sparkled in haloes of wet weeds.

Grassi was saying that the thought of sin could be more corrosive than any reality and the Irishman wondered angrily whether he must defend himself and why he should. The doodling words which the Jesuit had read were *private*! A clutch of reveries, they had flashed as briefly in Gilmore's mind as thrown confetti will flash before ending in the street-sweeper's midden. Even at fifteen, he had lived on memory-scraps: hollow of waist and ribcage. The graceful young Roman had focused the rather shambling Gilmore's notion of what he himself could be.

Rome, after all, was our pole-star.

But Grassi said, 'You were in love with him! *Caro padre* Gilmore, you mustn't mind my calling a spade a spade. Where's the harm? It was clearly innocent: a surge of fellowship brimming a tiny bit dangerously as it often will! I hope you feel some now. Rome needs that more than ever and in your case I have a favour to ask which may be more easily performed if you do feel it.'

What he wanted was for Gilmore to see Monsignor Santi, a man who could be of great assistance to the Holy Father if detached from some unwise allegiances. Gilmore, by reviving the glow of their joint past, might be able to effect this. 'Follow your heart,' instructed the Jesuit. 'He's an emotional man, tender and more easily reached by his own kind. I rub him the wrong way, which is why I am appealing to you. Will you try?' Grassi asked again, as he dropped Gilmore back at the Irish College.

'But what shall I say?'

'Follow your instinct.' The Jesuit leaned out of the carriage window. 'Remember that scruple can be a form of shirking. Act!' he recommended and snapped his fingers at his coachman.

*

Gianni, Cardinal Amandi's major-domo, had been doing nicely out of their stay in Rome and was collecting mementoes to sell to foreign pilgrims. Just about anything could be sold: bits of bone from the catacombs, bits of old vases, bits of captured red shirts, rosaries, shrapnel, papal hair-clippings, dust ... As a further bonus, he had become friendly with a widow living in the same *palazzo*: a source of joy. Everything was going beautifully – and then, out of a clear blue sky, *un finimondo*! Disaster! The cardinal said, 'Pack our bags, Gianni, we're off to Imola!' Why Imola when the Council was set fair to go on for months, if not years, and the widow planning a surprise for Gianni's birthday? Why were they going? Well, it appeared that it had to do with an audience which His Eminence had had with His Holiness where H.E. had told H.H. that the Opposition bishops felt he was sacrificing the rest of the world to Rome. 'Ah,' said H.H., 'the world!' And H.E. answered, 'I mean the Catholic world, Holiness!' Then H.H. had said that the only sacrifice he was making was of himself, and that he knew H.E. might be his successor and undo his work, but he knew how to put a stop to that. H.H. was very upset. 'Frothing at the mouth!' said H.E., though whether that was a manner of speaking Gianni couldn't say, for H.E. was frothing a bit himself and hard to hear through the keyhole. Anyway, *he*'d said if that's how you feel I'll go back to Imola and we'll think up some excuse to prevent scandal. So H.H. said 'Do!' and now it was 'Gianni, pack our bags'.

He'd only just had time to run and tell the widow that everything was off. Sorry. See you God knows when. Then back to the packing, while Monsignore and H.E. paced about like raging cats. They'd had a tiff which Monsignore had been trying for days to make up. Anyway, since it never rains but it pours, some lunatic Zouave chose that moment to ring the doorbell and ask to see Monsignore who had said he'd see nobody. Nobody, said Gianni to the Zouave. But, says he, an important man needs a priest to hear his confession! What's 'important'? asked Gianni, and nearly slammed the door in the fellow's face. Indeed he would have if another caller hadn't appeared just then, a foreign priest who also wanted Monsignore. Gianni, seeing that the man was shabby and of no account, told him that Monsignore was in Imola but that he should write down his name which Gianni would be sure to give him on his return. The priest did this and left, but the Zouave, a rougher customer, had his foot in the door. 'Say it's for André the Baptist,' says he. 'I'm not leaving till I get satisfaction.' So off went Gianni for less than a minute and when he came back, he gave the Zouave the foreign priest's bit of paper and said that Monsignore recommended the man whose name was on it to John the Baptist, or whatever his name was, as a confessor. That was two birds felled with one stone, thought Gianni, as he closed the door. If ever H.E. did become Pope he'd do well to keep Gianni as his *Cameriere Segreto*. Why not? The last Pope's barber had been the most influential man in Rome!

Sobered, he began to wonder whether the retreat to Imola was a setback to their joint prospects. He hoped H.E. had made peace with Monsignore. He'd need someone to be looking out for his interests here while he was away.

Nicola and the cardinal had, in fact, achieved a truce.

'Don't you see,' Nicola had insisted, 'that we can't part like this?' Then, having soothed Amandi's doubts and convinced him that he had neither spied nor lied, he asked how he was to explain the cardinal's departure.

'Say I've gone to Imola to perform some ordinations. *He* doesn't want me here.' Amandi was going through his papers, selecting pamphlets for Gianni to pack. 'He,' he said of Mastai, 'is in a euphoric mood. Mad with holy zest! Don John Bosco has been infecting him.' Bosco, he explained, had a curious brand of piety. 'He gathers outcast boys into asylums then, in his dreams, sees which are secretly committing abominations and chases them away. Lately, he has been seeing spiritual abominations in the Council and urging Pius to smite the perpetrators. Does my scepticism distress you? I try to resist it. Why, I ask myself, should not a visionary be a spy? Or the Pope mad? God may be testing our faith.'

'Mad?'

'Maybe it's my nerves speaking. Do you know where we keep the laudanum?'

Nicola didn't and there was no sign of Gianni who had taken to slinking off at odd hours and wore a long face. Perhaps, said Amandi, we should ask why. Servants were often the first to know things. Awkwardly, he confessed to a fear of ending like d'Andrea, whose troubles started when he left Rome without permission. Amandi had now been encouraged to leave – but had no witnesses to this.

'You need rest,' Mastai had said. 'Imola is, as I recall, a restful place.' An order? A trick?

'Had you heard that he tried to cure a cripple in the Roman streets

497

not long since? His head has been turned by lickspittles. Don Bosco calls him "God on earth" and says – I quote verbatim – "Jesus has placed the Pope higher than the angels! He has placed him on the level of God Himself!" Idolatry? *Folie à deux*? Anyway, he came on this cripple and said something like "Arise and walk!" Think of the wretched cripple. He knew his role. Tried to play it. Couldn't. He'll probably die of shame at letting down the Holy Father. Think of the epigrams!' Amandi laughed, then stopped.

'It's not,' he blurted, 'that I want to be pope!' A query bounced off the denial: should he *not* want to be? The two fell silent and the cat turned on them the full, unflinching beam of its amber eyes. Perhaps it sensed their fear of being cast out of the only institution which meant anything to them. Thaumaturges were taking it over. 'After 1789,' said the cardinal, 'it was said that God had sent the Revolution to punish men's pride of intellect. Has He now sent us a mad pope to punish the opposite sin: failure to think at all?'

'But thinking,' Nicola reached for a light tone, 'in the middle ranks undermines order. Only popes may safely think. If one is wrong his successor can rectify things.'

'Successors, if he is declared infallible, won't be able to!'

While waiting for the Zouave to come back, André Langrand-Dumonceau strolled around and came on a wine shop. It was a dingy place, smelling of mould, a Roman equivalent of the tavern his father had once owned. Backing away, he slid a hand into his pocket to feel the cap of Brussels lace which his grandfather, the *filius exposititius*, had been wearing when found. It was of surprisingly fine quality.

Omens mattered for he had not thrown in the sponge. On the contrary, he still hoped to defeat the forces now hounding him through the press and courts of Brussels and Brabant. Jews, Protestants and Liberals had made a set at him. Last year an assault on his empire had been made in the English Courts of Chancery and now press slanders were leading to a case in Belgium too. Mandel – the slanderer – had for some time been trying to provoke him to sue, but Langrand sat tight, knowing that if he sued his account books would be subpoenaed and all his secrets known. Unfortunately, his associates lacked his nous. The Belgian Attorney General and his colleague, the King's Attorney, having found for him in an earlier case, felt their honour impugned. Both were spoiling for a fight and so were collaborators whose activities up until now had been limited to lending his companies the lustre of their names. In short, Mandel was to be sued. A disaster!

Langrand had fled to Rome under an assumed name, after destroying what papers he could, but feared that his enemies would turn up something damaging. His wife kept forwarding letters from friends of the feudal sort who urged him to return, face the music and clear his name – meaning, to be sure, theirs! Honour, they repeated, their honour required . . . He tore their letters up.

When the Zouave brought news that Monsignor Santi was unavailable, the count's mind flicked to the nub of his concern: the assets which he had put beyond the reach of liquidators. Honour might be put aside but sin worried him. Loath to lose God's support, he desperately needed an understanding priest.

The Zouave, an elf with a yearner's grin, led him to the Irish College where, according to Monsignor Santi's major-domo, there was an excellent confessor. The count dismissed the elf, then waited in a chapel which reminded him of the one in the Jesuit house which was educating his sons. A priest from there had sent a professional opinion on the ethics of bankruptcies via Langrand's wife, whose letters referred to him by a code-name. Bobo, was it? Bobo or Bibi had said, if she was to be believed, that 'the conscience is not bound by penal laws, so we may hide all we can from the receivers'. Langrand, distrusting her, wanted a second opinion.

Turning, he found himself facing a gangling cleric who must be the Irish priest.

'Father Gilmore?'

This was he. Langrand did not give his own name but, to thaw the ice – the cleric looked cranky – mentioned Monsignor Santi and pretended to have just left his company.

'Monsignor Santi's?' The cleric sounded incredulous. 'You were with him *now*? Here in Rome? This evening?'

'Yes.' Langrand believed in using one's connections and thought nothing of a white lie. The priest's scowl had become alarming and, to soften him, he added, 'He says you're the ideal man to save a shop-soiled soul!' This did not elicit a smile.

'Ha!' snapped the priest in a disconcerting way.

He was, Langrand saw, unworldly. Never mind. This man was a mere medium and he, the penitent, must marshal his arguments for God – who, to be sure, knew them already, since they had appeared some years back in a pamphlet, commissioned and paid for by Langrand, entitled *Taking Usury – Is It A Sin?* The author, an agile cleric, had declared such scruples to be as archaic as those the Apostles had once harboured against baptizing Gentiles.

Priest and penitent now inserted themselves into the confessional and the count found that speaking without having to doctor his effects brought surprising relief. What he had been needing, he saw now, was not to argue his case, as his friends had wished, before the *Cour d'Assises* of Brabant, but to look coolly at it, as he had not hitherto dared to do. In the enabling presence of the invisible priest, he worked at putting his doubts into words simple enough to get past the brass screen and his listener's French.

A growl interrupted him: 'Recite the *Confiteor*.'

A stickler, thought the count. A growler and a stickler! But he was consoled by the ritual words: 'I confess to Almighty God, to Blessed Mary Ever Virgin, to Blessed Michael . . .' Empanelling this jury, which had undoubtedly seen worse, was a way of emancipating himself from the particular and perhaps inadequate presence – he could smell onions – of the growler who had begun to shuffle his feet. It was also a way to leap beyond his own temporal limits, and Langrand might have attempted this – after all he was a vaulter and an experimenter – had it not been for the abrupt and savage assault now made on his person. This did have premonitory signs. It was with a divided mind that he, who was adept through long practice at thinking of more than one thing at a time, cited the opinions on usury of the pamphlet which he had financed and those of Bobo/Bibi on bankruptcy. While so doing, he was mentally querying their value, biting them as he might have bitten coins, while monitoring the groans and growls which greeted his words.

Hearing the hissed imprecation '*Homo mercator!*', he craned from his own niche to where the red curtains on the front of the priest's part of the confessional mimicked – for the cloth was shuddering – a matador's muleta. Hands shot suddenly between them and, hurtling after them, came a cassocked fury with a stole around its neck. So speedy was the eruption that the confessor's door was still swinging as he reached the financier, hauled him from his niche and propelled him, feet skating beneath him, down the nave.

'Out!' howled the scourge and purifier. '*Fuori! Hors d'ici!*' Gilmore was driving the merchant from the temple. Langrand saw this at once. An omen-watcher, he had the answer for which he had come and, though a fit man, did not struggle. God would not help.

'Father Gilmore! Have you taken leave of your senses?'

A lacily surpliced figure had emerged from the sacristy and stopped the priest long enough for his victim to apply a trick remembered from the days in his father's tavern. Ducking quickly, Langrand broke his captor's grip, unbalanced him and fled. The new arrival was someone he had met before. Some English or Irish cardinal. Cullen, was it? He didn't want to meet him now.

Outside, finding that he had dropped his lacey talisman, his grandfather's cap, he took this as a conclusive sign: God and Mammon had forsaken him. He had lost his luck.

Twenty-eight

Cocky Nazareno, the valet who looked after Mr Russell, was himself looked after by certain gentlemen who represented Italian interests. They slipped him a retainer and paid for information supplied. Cocky sold them what came his way – old letters, used blotting paper, etc. without any qualms. Indeed, he suspected Russell of closing an eye and looking, like many another, to the future. Cocky was his stall, the diplomatist's diplomatist. That, anyway, was Cocky's guess.

So, when chance – or Mr Russell? – delivered into his hands a run of dispatches to England, plus a letter from Lord Acton which the diplomatic bag was helping on its way to Munich, Cocky copied extracts from the dispatches, noted the addressee's name on Lord Acton's sealed letter, and passed everything on to his paymasters.

Earl of C. to O.R.
Private.   F.O., 1870
I agree with you that this monstrous assault on the reason of mankind is the only chance of mankind being roused to resistance against being thrust back into the darkest periods of Church despotism, and cannot therefore regard the prospects of papal triumph with the alarm of Gladstone . . .

O.R. to Earl of C   Rome, 24 January 1870
Opposition leaders admit that their party could not have been organised without Lord Acton . . . I bow before his genius but adhere to my conviction that humanity will gain more in the end by the dogmatic definition of Papal Infallibility than by the contrary.
The Papal Condemnation of the Fenians will be . . . read from the Altar by every priest in Ireland . . .

O.R. to Earl of C.   Rome, 24 March 1870
Efforts at improving the acoustics in the Council Chamber have had no success, but requests for a change of venue are doomed by the Pope's

belief that powers emanating from St Peter's tomb will inspire the bishops with veneration for himself: a feeling which his conduct has all but eroded. He calls Opposition members 'mad', 'ignorant' and 'leaders of the blind' and sends out apostolic letters congratulating those who attack their writings. Meanwhile, a papal decree has ruled that a bill may henceforth be passed by a minority of one. Thus the ideal of moral unanimity is quite abandoned.

Bitterness has ensued. When Bishop Strossmayer, the great Opposition orator, urged that a Council lacking such unanimity lacked ecumenicity, there were attempts to shout him down, and when he said that Vatican policies towards non-Catholic sects were uncharitable and that there were Protestant writers whom Catholics might usefully read – there was a riot. Bishops yelled '*Hereticus*! *Hereticus*!' And when Strossmayer cried '*Hoc non est Concilius*!', 'This is no Council!', some five hundred rushed round the tribune shaking their fists and yelling 'We all condemn you!' 'Not all!' called his supporters. But the rioters drowned them out, yelling 'We *all* do! *Omnes, omnes te damnamus*!' Thereupon, the five presiding Cardinal Legates rang their five bells, the speaker was obliged to come down from the rostrum and the Council broke up. So much for freedom of speech! The consequences of this incident could challenge the legitimacy of the Council's decrees. *Hoc non est Concilius*?

Rome, 25 March 1870, Feast of the Annunciation

A ribbon of golden sand marked the route the Pope would take when he came to celebrate mass at the Minerva Church. Sun blazed. Banners floated and bells pealed. Behind Nicola someone murmured: 'All this to dazzle the riffraff and overawe bishops.' He thought the voice might belong to a member of the French garrison.

'The overawing,' said another voice, 'has turned to browbeating. Did you hear about the Bishop of Mainz?'

Clergy then! Only they – one must fervently hope – could know about poor Bishop Ketteler. Nicola had been at a meeting of the Minority when the bishop, fresh from a papal audience, had arrived in a state of shock. What had happened was that he, feeling duty-bound to enlighten the Pope, had armed himself with notes and precedents in the hope of persuading him that certain conditions were indispensable if a Council was to be a Council, and not what prominent bishops were now calling the 'robber synod' and 'the Vatican Farce'. It was a crime, thought the conscientious German, to allow a philistine pontiff to discredit the

Church. Accordingly, having rehearsed his arguments, he craved an audience, only to be floored by Mastai's opening gambit.

Ketteler – powerful chin, fine eyes, and a sweep of forehead from which his pale hair had retreated – *looked* like a pope. Noble but sensitive – there were delicate shadows at the corner of that firm mouth – he must have risen from kissing the pontifical hand so that for a moment the two were face to face: the troubled bishop and Mastai whose features had the contours of a currant bun.

'Do you love me?' was Mastai's greeting. '*Amas me?*'

Mainz said he did.

'*Amas me?*' Subtly, the repetition changed the query's thrust.

The bishop, submissively, repeated, 'Yes, Holy Father.'

'*Amas me?*'

It had now become a threat. It meant, if it meant anything, as the bishop later told his fellows, 'forget your precedents, your sheaf of notes, tradition and the law, and give me what I want'. 'Love,' here the German was overtaken by scandalised and near-hysterical laughter, 'is to conquer thought.'

'*Viva il Papa!*'

This signal that the procession was about to arrive was, as always, given by professional cheerers known locally as 'the hundred bald men'.

'Long live the infallible Pope!'

A catcall cut in: 'May he live somewhere else!'

Amused, the crowd altered '*viva*' to '*via*' ('away with him') which was dangerous, but not very, and it was a while before the '*Viva*'s won. By then the procession had glittered into view, manifesting the pomp and confidence which, at whatever cost to its Treasury, the Vatican needed desperately to show.

First – craning his neck, Nicola could just see the wagging of their swords – came a platoon of police, then a bedizened *batti-strada* followed by carriages full of officers and men on foot surrounding a cross-bearer on a caparisoned mule.

And now, arresting the cries of fritter-and-lemonade-vendors, came the Pope's coach. Adazzle with gilt, it was driven by postilions, for the coachman's box had been replaced by a brace of angels holding up a tiara. Inside it sat Pius facing two cardinals.

A dip rippled the crowd as people knelt, and Nicola sank too, prey to a clash of impulses as painful as if a knot were clamped around his heart. Exalting and at the same time casting him down was a contagion at which non-Romans, like Bishop Ketteler, might not even guess. The

Pope, murmured the tribal pulse in his blood, may be senile and sour, but he is ours and we, in a visceral way, are part of him, since he is our Vicar as well as God's with Whom we commune in this city where the whole world comes to worship!

'*Viva Pio Nono!*' The crowd was mesmerised by its own cry.

Rising from his knees, Nicola came face to face with Prospero who said approvingly, 'He knows how to win love!'

'He exacts it like a tax!' Nicola felt as if he had, somehow, let down Amandi and the Bishop of Mainz.

Prospero's nod ignored churlishness. There was a rumour that he was in line for major office. 'Love,' he said, 'is surely the essence of Christ's message.'

'Love of whom?' The last of the procession was passing, a platoon of sweating dragoons. 'The poor? The Germans say . . .'

'Oh don't quote them! Abstraction is all they deal in.'

'No, they can be specific. They say we complicate marriage laws so as to make them send us money for dispensations. When a woman trapped in a brutal marriage has none . . .'

'Germans always complain about money. Luther . . .'

'. . . she doesn't get one, no matter how good her case. Where's the love there?'

'Nicola!' Prospero's use of the first name had the thrusting intimacy of a kiss, 'has it ever struck you that civilisations are destroyed not by the foolish but by the clever? Any fabric has flaws and the clever pick at them until there is no fabric left!'

They had reached the door of the Minerva Church. Nicola decided to ask Prospero about the *Sodalitium Pianum*.

But the Pope, who had descended from his coach, was being cheered and again a counter-cheer cut in: 'The baldies are on duty! Long live the baldies!' The Pope and his entourage moved quickly into the church. A last half-laughing cheer triggered Prospero's anger. 'See the company you've joined!' he was exclaiming when an emollient voice intervened.

'*Cari Monsignori!*' Father Grassi slid between them, congratulating himself on finding such good, old friends together. Friendship was more precious now than ever. Even the Holy Father was showing strain and who could blame him! Had Christ not cursed the barren fig tree? Barren rhetoric was our torment! Poor Mainz, though! Grassi tittered. Germans don't like to be silenced. 'Which reminds me, I suppose neither of you have any tidings for me on this Annunciation Day? No? What a pity! If we only knew which German was divulging our secrets, we could stop suspecting them all. It would be a step towards brotherhood and reconciliation.'

O.R. to Earl of C.
Secret.

Count Daru, the French Foreign Minister ... also wrote a widely quoted letter saying 'We would be unable to keep our troops in Rome a single day after the proclamation of infallibility ... Public opinion in France would not allow it.'

Unfortunately for the Count, the Pope does not believe this. When Cardinal Antonelli advised prudence, he replied, 'I have the Mother of God on my side.' He is convinced that the Virgin's protection calls him to a special destiny.

News that the schema on Infallibility is to be brought forward out of turn has roused indignation and Count Daru received a Memorandum from the Opposition Bishops asking France to insist that the Council be prorogued to prevent a moral schism in the Church.

O.R. to Earl of C.

The fate of Count Daru bears out my belief that an Italian priest can always get the better of a French statesman. Following his efforts to help the Opposition, ultramontane bishops were sent to softsoap susceptible members of the French cabinet and remind them that in the May plebiscite they will need the Catholic vote. The outcome was Count Daru's resignation!!

O. R. to Earl of C.
Private and secret.

The Irish bishops are a hopeless set of humbugs! Cunning and deceitful as Neapolitans, they all declare themselves delighted with the stringency of the peace preservation law for Ireland and the suppression of pestilent newspapers ... But who can tell whether they are sincere?

Miss F and her companion are undoubtedly innocent, though their maid who is young and handsome may have been imprudent during their absence. Miss F often lent her rooms for meetings of the Minority which she did not herself attend. She also invited prelates to receptions, and the Holy Office or Inquisition, thinking these occasions too attractive for ecclesiastics, appealed to the Pope.

The 'enamoured priest' has no doubt been imprisoned in a convent where he may linger many years and, to save others from a like fate, the Pope has ordered the cause of the danger to be banished. Miss F's theory is that the 'priest' was an *agent provocateur* and the whole incident concocted to harass the Opposition and discredit her. She claims – a little

506

excitably, I fear – that this trick was played on her once before. Naturally, I cannot openly doubt the word of an English lady, and so my position has been difficult. At last, we have reached a compromise and I have managed to persuade her that, whatever the truth of her suspicions, there is nothing to be gained by airing them. Meanwhile, Archbishop Manning has been most kind and energetic and Cardinal Antonelli tells me that it is thanks to his intervention that the Pope will allow Miss F's maid to return to Rome.

The ladies are indignantly vociferous in her defence and not at all grateful to His Lordship whom they credit with the most Machiavellian of natures.

O.R. to Earl of C.   F.O., 2 May 1870
The Opposition bishops' reliance upon the non-ecumenicity of the Council, a modern notion, must make Pio Nono laugh. Acton & Co. have made a gallant swim in the torrent but have known for a long time past that it was carrying them away.

O.R. to Earl of C.   June
As Your Lordship knows, the Infallibility Schema has been brought on out of order despite protests. The Fathers have now met thirteen times to consider it and made so little progress that the discussion is expected to last into July. The heat increases. Bishops, many of them old and used to cooler climates, grow sick. The Pope resists requests to prorogue the Council. 'Let them croak!' he is said to have said. '*Che crepino!*' Some have. Others leave for their dioceses and when they belong to the Opposition the Vatican is glad.

Mr Gladstone, you remind me, thinks that if Opposition Bishops could join in a protest against Infallibility and leave Rome 'en masse' it would be a great blow to Ecumenicity. I think so too but fail to find in them that resolution which makes martyrs. The Roman Catholic Church is discrediting itself and should be allowed to do so. As for us, our good relations with the Vatican have led to the condemnation of Fenianism. We should not compromise them.

Since the Italians had no official representatives in Rome, Nicola had long guessed Martelli to be one of their unofficial ones, and was not surprised when he arrived with a copy of an English diplomatist's letter. 'Read this,' he invited.

O.R. to Earl of C.
Rumours of a war likely to interrupt the Council have thrown Infallibilists into a panic and revived the idea of a definition by acclamation. My source is Manning . . .

The plan is to get an acknowledged visionary to inform the Council of the Virgin's support for such a move. This, if well managed – and Rome does not lack *impresarii* – will lead the bishops to see themselves as the recipients of a divine message which, together with their bruised consciences and yearning for unity, will quite sap their resistance.

I shall not inform Acton lest he outwit a plot likely to discredit his Church in ways advantageous to ourselves.

'You see!' said Martelli. 'Her Majesty's unofficial agent even outfoxes his compatriots! Manning is his source and Acton his channel and, as the *Letters from the Council* appear in Germany, the Germans take the blame. It is the English, not we, who inherited the guile of Machiavelli and of the three, the Protestant is the coolest. Manning and Acton lack detachment and make mistakes, but Russell's dispatches are often on the edge of laughter. Perhaps his enthusiasm for amateur dramatics keeps him in training.

'We,' objected Nicola, 'put on dozens of plays at the Romano!'

'But it was all *ad maiorem dei gloriam*! Our consciences were never off duty! Nonchalance, Monsignore, is what refines intrigue.'

'It follows, then, that we nonchalantly let Manning go on damaging his own side by supplying information to Russell?'

'Indeed! But we must stop the plot to force a definition by acclamation which would grant Mastai a dangerously wide range of powers. Given modern means of communication, such a strengthened Rome could interfere in Catholic countries everywhere in ways unimaginable till now. I hope I need waste no time convincing you of the damage which he and his successors would be able to wreak!'

Imola

It was late afternoon when the cardinal laid down the copies of the English agent's dispatches. The sun had gone behind a clock tower and Martelli was keeping off mosquitoes by smoking a cigar.

'He's well informed,' said the cardinal. 'And his contempt hurts. Do you think . . .'

'Oh,' said Martelli, '*we* are not well enough informed to play guessing games. Italian bishops – Your Eminence being one – who are not rabid papalists have tended to boycott the Council and so we have few friends there to brief us.' There had, he noted, been only seven signatures on an anti-definitionist *postulatio* drawn up by Italian bishops. 'Eminence,' said Martelli, 'we need you in Rome.' Religion, he urged, was the woof of our national fabric. If we weren't to suffer the travails there had been in France, some understanding must be reached. Extremism bred extremism and revenge revenge. But if the bishops saw a likely moderate candidate for the succession, they might be heartened to struggle against the strait waistcoat now being prepared for future popes.

'You're asking me to confront intrigue . . . vilification . . .'

'And you're saying "Let this chalice pass". But you may be responsible for . . .'

'What? A divided country – possibly a divided Church?'

There was a silence. Then Amandi said, 'Leave me the dispatches.'

Martelli's departing carriage was a distant dust-puff, as small as blown thistledown, when Amandi gave his major-domo orders. They would leave tomorrow. Seeing the man's face brighten, he remembered that Gianni, a married man, had a woman in Rome and that this could be used against the cardinal himself. Memories of Amandi's own long-conquered flesh stirrings had no more piquancy than the memory of an old bee sting and, on the whole, this made him inclined to indulgence with others – but none could be afforded now.

'Tuscany,' he told his servant, 'is where we're going. Not Rome. I plan to visit the Abate Lambruschini.' The dimmed pleasure in Gianni's eyes was an offering to luck.

From the diary of Raffaello Lambruschini:

Winnowing through old letters, I am struck by the candour of my Tuscan friends. If a thing strikes one of them as bilge or a *coglioneria*, why that is what they say. Romans, on the other hand – but why marvel? They live at court and only men who have done that can guess what it does to the mind. How many people, I wonder, know that when the Pope sneezes, his attendant prelate must fall to his knees and cry *Eviva?* Well, readers of the *Augsburger Allgemeine Zeitung* do now, for their correspondent reports it in his letter for 18th June. It will shock in a way unimaginable to the Curia.

Amandi who, despite himself, is the Liberal candidate for the succession, came to see me ten days ago in great agitation. Absence from Rome has stripped away his courtliness and he has begun saying things baldly: namely, that he and I should repair the *coglioneria* we perpetrated at the time of the last Conclave when we interfered with the workings of the Holy Spirit and helped Mastai get elected.

'Do you mean,' I asked, 'by interfering a second time?'

He had no answer. Anything he says now must look either like shirking or ambition. Moreover, political motives animate his advisers whom he distrusts. Would I, a proven man of integrity, read some dispatches which had come his way and advise him? Politics, he confesses, disgust him now and seem incompatible with a priest's vocation. He has neatly exchanged positions with the Mastai of twenty-five years ago.

Doubts are contagious. *Am* I a man of integrity? I withdrew. Should Amandi? How? There is no formal candidature for the papal succession, so he has no way of stepping down. Anyway, should he?

I took him on a tour of my small estate and, as he sat next to me in my two-wheel trap, could feel his thoughts seethe and collide like wasps in a jar.

Yet the country was at its most soothing: still as a mosaic and bathed in those blue shadows from the acacia leaves which mimic pools of water on dry days. Relying on the courtesy which would oblige him to listen, I calmed – and bored – him with talk about the relative merits of husbandry and industry in our area, the prosperity – also relative – of my share-croppers and a new sort of coulter which Ridolfi and I devised some years ago.

A neighbour was waiting when we returned from our drive. He had come from Rome full of the latest scandal which he had been told in confidence. We assured him of our discretion and he told his story. It was about the Greek-Melchite patriarch, Gregor Yussef, a man of almost eighty who fears that if the treatment he received at the hands – or, rather, foot – of Pius were to become known in his own country, a schism could ensue. He and his fellow Eastern patriarchs defended their traditional rights on which Rome plans to encroach. Pius, who is minutely informed of what goes on in the *aula* and the committees, summoned him, and when Yussef kissed the papal slipper, pressed his foot down on his neck, then actually placed it on his head, saying, '*Mala testa*, Gregor!'

Amandi went pale. Interestingly, neither of us doubted the story – which turns out to be true – since we already knew of Pius's warning to the Eastern patriarchs against letting themselves be recruited by the Minority. He intervenes openly now in what he has described as a battle against 'myself and this Holy See'. His claims to neutrality are quite given up.

'The latest joke,' said our neighbour, 'is that the Inquisition has revived, for the heat is unprecedented and the Pope is roasting bishops.' I think he felt badly about this jibe, for he left soon after and next day sent us a gift of wine.

Since then, I have read the dispatches which Amandi brought but find him hard to advise, since he sees my retreat here as admirable and I cannot burden him with my doubts. We took more drives and my little mare supplied him with a metaphor. Pius and his minion, Manning, hope, he says, to arrest movement and conquer history. He waved at the buzz of light through which we were spinning to a rhythm of soft hooves – I keep the mare unshod.

'How,' he asked, 'arrest all this? It can't be done!'

Later, he said, 'At least your uncle, before becoming Cardinal Secretary, had been nuncio in Paris and knew what went on in Europe, Mastai and Antonelli are small-town men who have no idea of the trouble they will stir up in France and Germany. Mastai relies on *doctrina infusa*, so why should he bother informing himself?'

Then he told me of Martelli's plan.

'But,' said I, 'if it becomes known it will be seen to mirror what it aims to stop: intrigue.'

'Are you telling me to refuse?'

'How can I? I withdrew. I have no right to speak.'

'You're withdrawing *now*. Say something. Be indignant.'

'I can't,' I told him. I felt despair. My lack of faith is not only in this world. It is also in the next. The world as we knew it has ceased to work and the new world is not ours. I read about Acton and Gladstone and Döllinger and marvel at their energy, but lack the will to admire them. For me meaning has leaked from the struggle. As in a chess game, bishops now are not bishops nor knights knights. They are mere tokens whose deployment has no other aim but the play of skill. I cannot care about the skill. My last virtue – if a man with no faith can have any – lies in not disillusioning others. I cannot blame Mastai for his foolish self-delusion. He took on something which could not be achieved and is forced to pretend that he *is* achieving it. Amandi risks falling into the same trap, but I did not trust myself to warn him about this, lest my despair infect him too. So I repeated, 'I cannot help you.' I could see that he was disappointed.

In the abate's kitchen a discussion was going on about the relative merits of the *Lottery Dream Book* and the *Renowned Method for Winning*. The *Rinomato Metodo* said, quoted Gianni, that 'the country' meant number nine would come up.

But, said the abate's cook, *he* was always in the country and it couldn't always come up.

'It's come up in your mind now, though!'

'I'll need three numbers for a *terno*. What else shall I put?'

'And five for a *quinquina*. You win more with that.'

'I dreamed of a corpse.' The cook dismembered a hare with swift, expert strokes.

'Sudden death is fifty-two.'

'It was just lying there.' The cook examined his cleaver, 'Bleeding.'

'Mortal wounds means forty-nine.'

Darboy's face had shrivelled. The Council had aged him. Gripping Amandi's wrist, he said, 'You should think of yourself. No, not your soul! Your safety.' The Archbishop frowned.

They were in the Alban Hills in a villa belonging to a hospitable nobleman. It was cool at this altitude and the villa's owner had thrown it open to bishops who needed a respite from the city's heat. Greenery feathered slopes on which, said Amandi, snow was harvested in the winter. There were wolves here too.

'There are wolves everywhere!'

Amandi asked about the likelihood of the Opposition bishops walking out of the Council, but Darboy said it was hard to settle on a tactic. Even he and Dupanloup did not see eye to eye. Himself a senator, he lamented his colleagues' lack of parliamentary experience – and of nerve. Pius was informed every evening of what had been said and done during the day and cold-shouldered those who were undocile to his will.

'Neither Dupanloup nor I will be able to vote for you, Eminenza. We shan't reach the Sacred College while he lives.'

Before leaving for the capital – Amandi was to stay here a little longer – Darboy disclosed a secret. Word had come from Paris that if the Opposition could hold out, help would come from an unexpected quarter. He was unsure what was meant, but his source was a man close to the new Foreign Minister, the Duc de Grammont.

His last words were melancholy. 'It will be hard for us to run dioceses where everyone knows that we are loathed and despised by the Infallible Head of our Church.'

'So,' said Amandi, 'we'll fight. You, especially, had better. After all, it's not two months since you submitted plans for the reform of the papacy! You burned your boats!'

'*La furia francese*! It's expected of us!'

Twenty-nine

Attention was what Maximin Giraud missed from the days when he had stood with Mélanie on altars, rostra and the backs of carts. That hum from the crowd tingled your body and speeded your pulse. It made you more intelligent and was like nothing else – except, perhaps, being God! Indeed it was that touch of divinity which had descended on him after the fact which convinced him that the vision had not been just another of Mélanie's stories. As attention waned so did belief, but he expected both to return here in Rome where he had been told he was to take part in some event which would restore faith in God and himself *and* be one in the eye for Mélanie who took more than her share of the limelight.

Expectancy, having buoyed him up, again began wearing thin. Then, just as he thought he'd been forgotten, the signals started. Anonymous priests visited him; Monsieur Veuillot, a famous big pot, took him to lunch; then a lady came to the barracks to ask for him.

'Take him,' said the Colonel. Maximin, outside the door, heard every word. His ears were like bats'. 'Are you on the side of the good angels this time, Donna Costanza, or of the fallen ones?'

The Mérodiani, she retorted, were the fallen ones. The Colonel was one of those.

'Lazarus was raised from the dead,' said the Colonel.

'Well, if you're raised, think of me,' said the lady and, in a low voice, 'If Antonelli's people ask, no need to say where he is.'

'*Entendu.*' The Colonel opened the door. 'Here's Giraud. Giraud, Madame Diotallevi needs a bodyguard and I'm assigning you the task. Make sure you give a good account of yourself.'

So Maximin had come to live at the lady's apartment which was like falling into God's pocket. Only now did he let himself know how much he hated the regiment. Until joining it, he had thought his father a violent man. But violence for his father had been explosive and chancy, whereas the Zouaves dreamed of it as relentlessly as some men dreamed

514

of fornication. They were connoisseurs who would tell with a slow relish the ingenious things which had been done to priest-killers during the White Terror in France. Their dreams were ledgers glinting blackly with debts, and more than one had come here resolved to outdo a grandfather's role in that great blood-letting or at least bag a Garibaldino. They were sportsmen with a taste for human game. Yet, they could be as polite as women, played exuberant, even childish, jokes and went to mass every day.

Donna Costanza told Maximin that the reason she needed a bodyguard was because she had worked for Monsignor de Mérode when he was Minister for Arms. *He* was now so out of favour that, when he broke his leg, the Pope said it was a pity it wasn't his tongue. The barracks was a gossip-shop which must be why the priests who talked to Maximin had been tight-lipped, revealing only that he should be ready for 'the crowning moment of his career'. Coming from men with cold, clever eyes, that had a disquieting ring.

'Are you one of them?' he asked Donna Costanza, but couldn't say who he meant, since they hadn't given names.

Her apartment enthralled him. It was as soft as a tent with glinting brass and feathers and shawls from North Africa. Gifts from French officers? His friends, when he went to pick up his kit, had stories about her morals, but to him she was kind. She had a Savoyard maid, fresh from her mountains, who couldn't have been more than fifteen. 'This is Catherine. You can keep each other company,' said Donna Costanza and left them together.

'Help me shell peas, then,' said the girl.

This reminded him of his childhood and soon he had slit open a mound of pods and flicked the bouncing peas into a delft bowl. He asked if he could smoke and she told him to put his head out the window. Papal cigars, he told her, were known as *stincadores infamos*, but she was too ignorant to laugh. Then she said that she must take coffee in to the mistress and her guests who were very grand people. One was a bishop, a Monsignor Santi.

When she came back, she showed him the empty coffee cups. The Signora, she said, had offered to read her guests' fortunes in the grounds and the Monsignore's cup had a double cross in it. See it! That could be a death!

'Did she tell him?'

515

'He wouldn't listen. He said fortune-telling was forbidden by the First Commandment.'

Later, Catherine sent him down to the courtyard to the well and, through the window, he heard the voices of Donna Costanza's guests. 'A scandal,' said one, 'may be the only way!'

Sliding a dipper into glistening water, he drank from it. The voices from the window were now talking secretively in Latin.

Maximin wasn't surprised when the bishop sent for him and asked the usual questions and offered brandy. From caution Maximin said 'No', then grew sorry. Describing the vision had become harder, for he remembered how other listeners, especially the Curé d'Ars, a sharp-minded holy man, had picked at details and marvelled suspiciously at the Virgin's clothes – shoes with rosebuds, golden apron, robe with pearls – being identical to those worn by her statue in the wayside shrine which Maximin and Mélanie used to pass on their way to and from the pasture.

'Are you sure you won't have a brandy?'

This time he took it and felt relief as the sparky stuff pirouetted inside his mouth. We're on the same side, he reminded himself. The priests didn't want the vision discredited. Not after all these years. At the beginning, they had been leery because state officials were watching *them*. This had been explained to him. The officials were free-thinkers. He drank some more and thought of the first free-thinker to bite the dust: his blasphemous old man.

The bishop said, 'Tell me about your father. I never knew mine. I envy men who had fathers.'

'Envy!' Maximin almost spat out his last precious mouthful. Indeed a fine rainbow spray reached the bishop's cassock and shone reproachfully. Unnerved, he began to curse his venomous sire.

'Ah,' said the bishop. 'An atheist and a Jacobin? Perhaps it was for him the Virgin came!'

'What?'

'Her words were addressed to them. "Don't blaspheme! Don't desecrate the Sabbath!" Those were her words, weren't they?'

Maximin remembered then that he had talked to Catherine about his old man. He'd been stirring egg yolks and sugar. 'Wrist tired?' she'd asked, then stuck her finger in the mixture and licked it. 'Jesus!' she'd said blasphemously, 'it's good!' and he had recited the Virgin's words.

*

The bishop was remembering them too, for he had been watching through a perforated screen in the Diotallevi's dressing room.

'This,' she told him, 'is where the stenographer will sit.'

Reluctantly, for he found the arrangements distasteful, he put his eye to the screen and heard the girl ask '. . . tired?'

'Never too tired for action!'

'*Here's* where that's needed!' The girl set the bowl between the soldier's knees and dodged away, laughing.

The monotony of sexual play was a penance to spies. The bishop sighed. He had voiced scruples about the unseemly endeavour to Martelli and been withered by contempt.

'Monsignore!' Impatience whistled in the deputy's indrawn breath. 'You, thanks to my unseemly arrangements, can help your friends and mine. War may break out *any day now* between France and Prussia! If it does, the French garrison will leave and the Council have to be prorogued and then,' Martelli bit off each syllable as though it had been made of some brittle substance, 'bringing on Giraud may be your opponents' only hope of getting their dogma in time!' This hope can be nipped in the bud. Now. Here. Surely, in such a cause, a little unseemliness can be stomached?

Goaded by memory, Nicola reapplied his eye to the spy-hole and heard the atheist father described. A wheelwright, he had learned scepticism in Napoleon's army.

'My father hated priests.'

'Did he?' The girl dropped an unbroken apple peel over her shoulder, then turned to examine it. 'In my village,' she told him, 'this is how girls who know their alphabet learn the name of the man they'll marry.' It was a boast.

He ignored it. He was remembering one of his father's stories. It was about a chair falling from the sky.

That got her attention. 'A chair?'

Yes. He mimed the fall. Whoosh! It was a true story. A chair had landed in a village and the villagers were sure it must have come from heaven. What puzzled them was that it was badly made. Could heavenly carpenters be botchers? 'The Curé said one thing and the schoolmaster another. Then – can you guess?'

Catherine was rearranging the apple peel with her toe. Revealing a stretch of sturdy calf, she gave it a quick twitch. Nicola read 'M', but her slow swain failed to note it.

'It turned out that a balloonist had taken a chair up as ballast, then

517

thrown it out. My father loved that story.' Maximin laughed. 'When Mélanie and I saw the Virgin, he said what we saw might have been a hot-air balloon. The Curé said the only hot air around was in him.'

'And what did you think?' She was peeling a fresh apple.

'I think that if my father hadn't been a bully I might not have seen the vision.'

La Diotallevi's hand gripped the bishop's sleeve. *This* was what they were waiting for!

But the girl had cut herself. 'Oh, ai! Maximin, give me your handkerchief.'

'Silly little bitch!' said la Diotallevi. 'He'll say no more now!'

Earlier, she had said, 'No need to worry about impropriety, Monsignore. She's to be the good girl from his own mountains. That way he'll *talk*, which is, I understand, what's wanted.'

She herself was quite at ease. Intrigue was her métier and she attended to it without fuss. Martelli who had known her when she was a three-or-four-way spy, ferrying between rival groups in Rome, either had some hold on her or was paying her well. The bishop was glad to be left in ignorance. Amandi, who had consented to Martelli's plans, could surely not have guessed that they would lead to his Coadjutor spending time in the bedroom of the nearest thing to a madam one could find in a town where amateur courtesans kept professionals out of business.

Back in her drawing room, she explained that she had given her servants a holiday and told friends she had gone to the country. Catherine had been specially engaged.

Lightly touching on their previous acquaintance, she congratulated the bishop on escaping the wrath of Monsignori Pila and Matteucci, two stingless wasps whose venom had been drawn. She had herself feared for her pension when Mérode fell, but the arrangement was being honoured. And, yes, she had Italian connections still.

'That's why Signor Martelli engaged me.' Clasping plump hands with composure, she explained that she was a person who liked to help others, irrespective of party.

He knew he mustn't show distaste – but perhaps had for she was delivering an apologia, telling how she had started on her trade. First a lover had asked her to spy for the French. Later, she spied *on* them too. Why not? By then, her husband had been cashiered from the Army for debt and needed cash to set up as a photographer. It was shortly afterwards that the bogus photograph of the Queen of Naples was commissioned by the Democrats leading to more hullabaloo than could have been foreseen. 'What harm did it do *her* after all, Monsignore? Nobody believed it was she!' Instead, said the Diotallevi, the one harmed was herself who was given an ultimatum by Monsignor de Mérode: work for him or go to prison. And working for him had made her an object of odium – her, not him! That was how the world was. And now he was rich. '*Ricchissimo*, Monsignore! He bought up great stretches of the city out of his own pocket and had the roads widened and improvements made and when the Italians come here his investments will be worth a pretty penny! And don't think those who worked for him will benefit! Oh, yes, he granted me my tiny pension. Scarcely enough to keep body and soul together. Yet he's a great one for charity! Goes out in that hood the confraternities wear, shaking begging boxes under people's noses. Peering through the slits, recognising some but hiding his own identity, he defies them to refuse alms. But he gives nothing to those who jeopardised their souls in his service. Used spies, Monsignore, are thrown on the midden like dogs.'

The old complaint brought back an old image: a splayed body on the steps of the Collegio Romano. It made it harder for the bishop to dismiss the self-serving farrago being poured over him like slops from a balcony. It was ironic, declared la Diotallevi, that she should pretend to need a bodyguard. Because she had in fact received death threats. Notes had been slipped under her door and there had been whispers from masked faces at carnival. Last spring, an Arlecchino, pretending to kiss her, had made her feel his knife. 'There was a rent in my dress here!' She touched her navel. 'No, don't talk of an investigation. It could have been the police! Everyone hates me now. Users hate their spies.'

The reproach was to his cloth. He was its representative, facelessly confronting her like Mérode through the slits in his hood. He chid himself for believing that, as an individual, he would have behaved better. How know? Yet the rogue individual inside himself itched to settle an individual debt. Before he knew it, he had said: 'A penitent of mine – you may remember that he was the reason we first met – wants to make amends to a woman he helped push onto the downward path.'

Donna Costanza's soft descent of eyelashes opined that there was no such penitent. As one masker to another, he had an impulse to slough off deceptions, but owed it to his cloth not to.

A hand swooped and squeezed his knee. 'Monsignore, you wouldn't deceive me, would you? I mean in a way that matters?'

He flinched.

'Is it amends your penitent is after or revenge?' She removed the hand. 'The world isn't tender to women without protectors and hers is jealous. I tell you what, I'll send her to confession to you, Monsignore. Can you arrange to hear confessions here in Rome?'

It was two days later and here he was again in la Diotallevi's drawing room. In his hand were the notes taken by a stenographer who had spent several afternoons behind the perforated screen listening to Maximin talk to the unwitting Catherine.

The city had grown maggoty under the unrelenting sun and simmered with wrangles. Amandi was coming back to Rome but must not give any appearance of conspiring. He was to preach, say mass, be active in the Council but avoid private meetings. Nicola should not give any appearance of conspiring either.

Archbishop Darboy, whom Nicola had consulted in a cryptic way about his troubled conscience – he didn't wish to trouble *his* – agreed that preventing an intrigue was a salutary thing though never, he warned, easy. For instance, had Nicola seen what the Majority was up to now? In the *Giornale di Roma*? The paper had named several Opposition bishops as having declared their readiness to submit and vote for the doctrine. This was a lie. Yet, to issue denials and say they would *not* submit to the Pope's wishes took more courage – as the *Giornale* well knew – than most of them had. And letting the lie stand would dishearten their fellows.

Darboy groaned that our pity for this unfortunate pope was being used against us. He raced off then, leaving Nicola to his doubts and to the sheaf of notes handed him by the stenographer who was even now ruining his eyesight, recording trivia which he lacked the discrimination to leave out.

A note from Martelli warned, 'Giraud's Colonel says important men want to see him, men he can't put off.' Time was running out and Nicola, struggling through the stenographer's transcription, saw that Maximin had been wasting it in courting Catherine.

Stocky and bandy with the face of a man who has too often been soused, the Zouave had spent yesterday afternoon in la Diotallevi's laundry-room, talking of onion bouquets, while two forgotten smoothing irons of the sort tailors call 'gooses' glowed red, then white on the stove.

Onion bouquets? Reading more closely, Nicola found that in Giraud's village these were presented to a jilted girl on the day her suitor married someone else. To avoid such shame, men too, argued the Zouave, needed to be let know whether they had a chance before risking a rebuff. Stuck-up girls had hurt him in the past, starting – ah good!! – with Mélanie whom he had first known as a fourteen-year-old whose every other word was 'look'! Look what's in my hand, under my skirt! Look, oh look at the lovely lady!

'She's still at it and people listen! Just the other day a friend at the barracks showed me a newspaper with a piece about her. She says now that the Virgin told her there'd be an earthquake in Marseilles and Paris would burn down! Make a lie big enough, as my old Dad used to say, and people will swallow it whole!'

Back to the Dad! Nicola's eyes slid down the page and found that old Giraud had had 'ideas' and because of them never darkened the church door until the day when water from Maximin's lady's spring cured his asthma. That staggered his son. Think of it, he invited Catherine. Just imagine *him* admitting such a thing!

Maximin's mother had died when he was small and life with the widower had been a skulking hell as the child developed a bobbing right arm, ever ready to ward off a box on the ear. Then, one September when he was eleven, he was sent from his own village of Corps – thirteen hundred inhabitants, grim, muddy, poor – to the pasturelands above where he was to mind Monsieur Selme's four cows. Up there he was free as air and the air was luminous with cataracts and reflections from the Alpine peaks. Berries and mushrooms grew in abundance and you could think of heaven as spilling past the snow-line onto the cropped green slopes. Down in Corps, a huddled world, this heaven was unknown – until the miracle.

Maximin never got over that. Just picture old Giraud begging pardon of him whom he had walloped the day before for conniving with blackbeetles! Begging pardon of the blackbeetles themselves! *Mea culpa*! His asthma had cleared up and he roared the news so lustily that, blasphemous though it might be to say it, he sounded drunk. His new transports were not so different from the old. He aged after that and, though he let the priests show him off, his eye had the reddish, melancholy cunning of a circus bear's. Poor old sod! He reminded his son of the Good Thief – or was it the Bad Thief? He had been happier in his Jacobin days.

Mélanie, by contrast, throve on attention. She had been wanting it since before the nuns taught her French. Nobody in those villages talked it except the curés, which was why when townspeople came puffing up the track, having tired of jolting their bones in the carts hired to convey them, it was to the curés that they turned to translate what the children were saying. Maximin felt that that had been the start of his own troubles. The curés told the bishops who told the Pope and the story changed as it made its way down the slopes to Grenoble and over the Alps to Rome.

He had to keep up with it. Had to be careful. Especially now that there was money riding on the thing. He told Catherine how he had once retracted the whole story and then retracted the retraction. That was when the Curé of Ars got him mixed up.

'You mean,' the curé had asked, 'that it didn't happen like you said?'

Maximin said people had mixed things up.

'Was there a lady there at all?'

'There was a coloured light. In those mountains you see all sorts of things.'

'But a lady with satin slippers with roses under her feet and on her head a great golden crown. Did you or did you not see that?'

'Mélanie did.'

'And the message the lady gave you?'

Maximin said he wasn't sure. But, later, when the papers said he'd denied seeing the vision, he denied that. Because anything that could tame his father was worth believing in. And what would have become of him if he backed off now? Besides Mélanie *was* sure. Not for one solitary second did she doubt or take back a word. And now she was prophesying the end of Paris. The Zouaves said it was a judgment on France for what it had done to its kings.

'Did she speak French or *patois*?' asked the government official who, warned Monsieur le Curé, had been sent to trick them.

'She used,' said Mélanie sweetly, 'a language that spoke straight to our hearts.'

There had been no picture of *her* in his friend's paper, but he remembered how she had looked on the very first day when he was told 'This is Mélanie Mathieu. She minds Monsieur Pra's cattle. She'll help you get the hang of things.' Thin as string and pale as skim milk! Tart-mouthed! At home, she said, she slept with her sisters. Now she must make do with the cows and Maximin. She made him feel he ranked way below the cows.

He'd run off then to play with his dog, Loulou, and pretty soon she

522

was trying to lure him back. It was then that she told him of the stigmata, what it was and that she had it. 'Here, under my skirt!' Catching his hand, she slid it between her thighs, then showed him the blood. Later, she swore him to secrecy. If he breathed a word, she said, her father would skin her alive. That interested him and, comparing fathers, they became quite friendly. Then they watered the cows, ate their rye bread and fell asleep.

Waking, he ran up the slope after the cows and, on reaching the top, found her on the rim of a ravine. A freak mist was drifting in. 'Look,' she cried. It was like a screen reflecting the sun's globe. 'It's opening like a tabernacle. Look what's inside!'

So what *was* the secret message? asked Catherine. Was he going to tell her? No, said Giraud. Not yet. It was worth money, he explained. Enough to start a shop back in his village. 'I can just see you behind the counter, selling things. Would you like that?'

Monsignor Santi asked if Maximin would mind answering a few more questions and Maximin said right you are. Questions would be part of his mission which, he now knew, was to address the Council.

The trouble was, said His Lordship, that there were sceptics among the bishops, and it would be appalling if one of them were to confront Maximin with his previous retraction or with his sworn declaration, made some years ago, that the Lady's secret message, far from having to do with Infallibility, as he now claimed, had been that the Orleanist Pretender should rule France. There were contradictions here and a danger that he could be convicted of telling a lie *piis auribus offensiva, ingiuriosa, scandalosa* and apt to get him and his sponsors into grave trouble. Did he want to be handed over to the Holy Office, alias the Inquisition? No? Well . . .

The bishop looked sad. Naturally, he said, we had had to make inquiries before sponsoring your appearance in the Chamber.

While Maximin struggled to find some way out of this – the disappointment was too sudden and crushing to be accepted – the bishop talked of mountains and the odd phenomena to be seen on their upper slopes: circular rainbows, luminous reflections, mirages. Balloonists, he said, had told him of seeing things which the uninformed could mistake for a vision. An honest mistake was one thing, but a persistent attempt to deceive the Church . . . Here his voice grew coldly menacing. Then he talked of Maximin's father whose cure need not be of supernatural origin at all, though, to be sure, it must have made a strong impression on the small Maximin.

'You were, I think, eleven, whereas the girl was . . .?'

'Fourteen,' said Maximin. 'She's the one who should have known better. She made it up. She was always making things up.'

'Well, then it is your clear duty to sign a paper saying that. You see she's causing scandal with all these interviews and this might stop her. It would also prove to the Holy Office that it was never our intent to perpetrate a deception.' These, said the bishop, were difficult times. Strife had penetrated even within the *sanctum sanctorum*, but better say no more about that.

'Ah,' said Maximin, putting two and two together. Strife? Danger? 'Yes,' he decided, 'I'll sign your paper.'

The bishop had it ready and before Maximin could think twice, the thing was done.

Afterwards, he began to wonder whether he had perhaps dished himself. The more he went over the thing in his mind, the likelier this seemed. He needed advice. He needed the help of a cool, unbiased eye. Whose? Catherine's? No! She was too ignorant and, besides, might think him a fool. Avoiding her, he went into the empty drawing room and poured himself a stiff brandy. He would have confronted the Signora, but she had gone out. Had she, he wondered, helped trap him? – if he had been trapped. And if he was her bodyguard, why did she go out alone? Worried now, he had another brandy, then set off into the city where, needing a confidant, he headed for a café patronised by Zouaves.

There was a card game in progress in one corner and, at the bar, a discussion of the attempt, some years ago, on the Emperor's life. The mistake, it was concluded, had been in using bombs. It took more guts to use a knife. True, you had to get close to get it *into* the guts – but then you couldn't miss!

'Like this!' A man held a knife to the barman's apron, but the barman flicked it away and went on drying glasses.

Maximin had a drink, then, finding nobody he knew well enough to confide in, went back to the Signora's apartment. Walking in, he paused on the covered walk outside the drawing-room window. The Signora was inside, talking to Monsignor Santi. They were saying that some woman would go to confession to Cardinal Amandi's titular church tomorrow about four. Monsignor Santi would take His Eminence's place hearing confessions. That way, if her protector came to hear of it, he would think the confessor was Amandi who, being in his seventies, could hardly rouse his jealousy.

'All right?' asked Donna Costanza and the bishop said yes.

Maximin waited until Monsignor Santi came out, then followed him downstairs. He had changed his mind about the paper he had signed. Could he have it back, he asked.

'Why Maximin, it's for your own protection,' said the bishop. 'Besides, I haven't got it any more. I'm sorry.'

Maximin felt like hitting him and, bishop or no bishop, might have done it too if Monsignor Santi's carriage had not been standing there with two liveried footmen, one of whom had opened the door and lowered the step. After that, there was nothing for Maximin to do but go and get stinking drunk, which is what he did.

He awoke with a headache and an idea. He would go to the lodgings of Monsieur Veuillot whose card he had kept ever since the journalist had given him lunch. Surely, he could smooth things out?

Cardinal Amandi had been disheartened by the Abate Lambruschini's tactful silence when asked for advice. Tact carried a judgment. This, it said, is all you can accept: not truth, only this. It came close to pity and the cardinal was crushed.

Arriving in Rome, he had gone at once to the Council in whose anterooms were the usual loiterers, quidnuncs, pious sightseers, and touts. Seen afresh after an absence, they distressed him. Money, as all but the invincibly innocent now knew, was paid by surprisingly respectable people to equally respectable ones for tidbits of information. Agents were active, stenographers under siege and foreign bishops regularly invited to their embassies to be pumped – hence the frustration of the Italians who lacked such a resource – while the more illustrious were regarded as being 'booked' by such families as the Borghese, Doria, Aldobrandini and Caetani, in whose drawing rooms they could be approached with circumspection. Naturally, they did not – one hoped – break their oath of silence, but small indiscretions showed how the wind blew.

Seeing it all with Lambruschini's borrowed eye, Amandi blamed himself. Years ago, when Amandi first tempted him, Mastai had been an unworldly man. Intrigue and pride had been alien – or, if not alien, behind him. He might have devoted his life to orphans or lived quietly as a provincial bishop if Mephistophelian friends had not tempted him with a belief in the Church's need of his gifts.

So worldly had he then become, that he had sloughed off these friends, turning his coat, abandoning Liberalism, seeking increased power, creating this hive of bitterness, anger and intrigue . . . But whose fault was it? Who was to blame if the Pope had so destroyed his conscience that he mistook his own wilfulness for rectitude?

Amandi feared that a like fate could overtake Nicola, whom he had known as a shy, reticent boy and formed and educated so that his political sins, if he was committing any, must be all Amandi's fault. He too could turn into monster – especially under the tutelage of the slippery Martelli whom Amandi did not trust at all. Martelli had assured the cardinal that his aim was of the purest and that so were his methods. Amandi doubted this – which was why he wanted to see Archbishop Darboy who, Martelli had assured him, approved of his strategy. Amandi would ask the archbishop straight out if this was so. He was looking for him now and, hearing that he was expected, hung on, listening, willynilly, to the gossip all around. In under half an hour, he was made privy to more intrigues than would have animated several circles of Dante's hell, mainly those of the fraudulent, the faint-hearted and the choleric.

Several men welcomed him back, the Liberals with surprise. Their ranks were sadly thinned. Worn out by wrangling, by the heat and by the stacks of pamphlets which followed them to their lodgings – the more determined of those who had been prevented from having their say in the *aula* had had these printed in Naples – many had simply left. About six a week were now petitioning to be let go and, every day, the benches were emptier.

Then came the whispers. Had he heard about the Armenian bishops? They had acquiesced in Rome's encroachments on their freedoms, but then, unnerved by news of angry disturbances at home, reneged. Mastai promptly ordered them to a monastery to perform punitive spiritual exercises and sent his police to enforce the order. One man resisted and was supported by bystanders who started a small riot. After that the Patriarch of Antioch fled to Turkey with a fellow bishop and sent back a letter to the Council, explaining that in the face of imprisonment and his own ill health, he had feared for his life. A scandal. And there were others. Cardinal di Pietro was blackmailed. Told that if he voted with us that old story of the Spanish dancer and the threatened duel with the Russian General would be dug up. It went back twenty-five years to his time as nuncio in Portugal. But the Curia never forgets. Anyway, there's a vote we won't get. And poor Cardinal Guidi . . .

'Yes?'

A sad story! He was now under semi-house arrest at the Minerva and under pressure to recant. Yet on 18 June he had made a speech which had looked like reconciling all parties. Indeed, so hopeful were the bishops that when he came down from the ambo several rushed to kiss his hands and wept.

The Pope, he had argued, though not infallible in his person, could, with divine assistance, make infallible pronouncements when these reflected the views of the bishops and the tradition of the Church. Surely, here was the yearned-for peace formula? Joy. Tears. Embraces. No bishop *wanted* to oppose the aged, beleaguered Pope.

But, that evening, Pius, hearing of the speech, summoned the cardinal, threw a tantrum, and to Guidi's protest that he had spoken only as a witness to tradition replied, '*I* am tradition!'

'*Folie de grandeur*! Megalomania! He's unstoppable now! Like one of the old absolute kings!'

'Shsh!'

Yet was it not playing into his hands to intrigue? Should one not try for purity?

'You're swimming against the current,' Amandi was told. 'People are leaving, not coming back!'

What, he asked, about the idea of a mass walk-out by the Minority? Given up, said a bishop. How did he know? From his coachman. Someone jeered. *Ex cathedra*, then? From the box!

'Don't jeer! The coachmen have their own Council where the carriages wait at evening parties. They exchange information.'

'So what else are they saying now?'

'That Montpellier who left the city in disgust after throwing his conciliar papers into the Tiber . . .'

'That's stale news. He threw them in in May!'

'Well, they've been fished out and brought to the Vicariato. His name is on them. What do you bet that he'll lose his diocese?'

The jokes were a cover for fear, anguish and wounded loyalty.

When Darboy finally arrived, there was just time to ask him – discreetly and circuitously – what he knew about Martelli's activity. He knew nothing at all.

*

527

Amandi went straight to his palace where he told Nicola that trust was rotting, all trust. Trust between *them* and perhaps every chance of trust in the Council and the Church itself. Lies, he said, had worked like termites. They had burrowed through the structures. They had hollowed them out. He didn't blame anyone except himself. How could he? He too had played at the game of diplomacy and politics, had drawn fine lines and justified means by ends. Now he was unable to believe anything he was told. Pius too should disbelieve. When he asked the Bishop of Mainz did he love him, he was misusing the word and the answer he exacted was a debased formula. All words had been devalued and deformed. Therefore, he, Amandi, found it difficult to speak. He would have liked to tell his Coadjutor that he loved him, which he did. But how show the difference between his use of the word and that of Mastai? Shame gagged him.

He would have liked to tell Nicola that he did not want him to intrigue on his behalf, as he believed he had been doing and that he, Amandi, did not wish to be regarded as *papabile*. This was difficult to say because, under certain circumstances, he *would* be prepared to be so if only to undo some of the evil he felt he had done. But this sounded two-faced, self-serving, and was perhaps better not said.

Being unable to speak, neither could he credit what he was told. He did not want his Coadjutor, for instance, to hear confessions on his behalf this afternoon. The reason was that he believed him to be using the confessional as a hideout for purposes of conspiracy. Amandi didn't blame him for reasons already stated. But neither could he believe his denials. Sorry. No, Nicola! You are not to go there this afternoon. My name is on the box, so I shall be the one sitting there to hear confessions. Simplicity is the only route out of the mad maze in which we are strangling.

Maximin Giraud arrived at Monsieur Louis Veuillot's lodgings just as the journalist was setting off for lunch with a party of guests. Maximin must join them, he urged. Yes, yes, don't be bashful! We're not worldly folk! We won't ask for better company than the one chosen by the Virgin. So Maximin got into their carriage and drove with them to a restaurant where they proved to be in a merry mood and drank a lot of toasts. They had all heard of him and a balding Jesuit kept eyeing him as though keeping him under surveillance. Meanwhile, the rest of the company toasted his great moment and spoke of him as 'chosen', but though Maximin kept trying to get in a word, they were eating the pudding before he had a chance to mention the paper he had signed. The faces went tight. Ah, he thought, so it had been a mistake! He had hoped it might not matter and that Bishop Santi had, after all, been, truly, looking out for his good. Even now he hoped this.

For *whom* did he say he had signed it? asked the bald priest in an abnormally quiet voice. For Monsignor Santi? And could he not get it back? Maximin explained that he had tried and failed.

'But Padre Grassi,' said Veuillot to the priest, 'isn't Monsignor Santi a friend of yours?'

The faces were as smooth as marble. 'Only,' said the priest, 'when our loyalties do not clash. Cardinal Amandi is back in Rome. This is unlikely to be a coincidence.'

'Ah!' said Veuillot. 'The Pretender!'

There was some excited talk then and Maximin kept losing the thread. What he did grasp was that this cardinal would undo the Pope's work after his death if it wasn't made safe by the dogma which was our great rampart and bulwark. Maximin, said Veuillot, had let the Pope down and made it harder to get his dogma. Veuillot was all for fighting on even now but Grassi said better give up the idea. It had, he said, always struck him as too flamboyant and anyway, if the company would allow the expression, there was more than one way to skin a cat!

Give up what idea? Which? Maximin couldn't take this in. Did the priest mean the occasion in the *aula*? The announcement of the secret? The crowning moment of his life? The bright, multilayered pudding on his plate flared and dissolved into a coiled rainbow. For several seconds the visionary was blind.

'Tell me,' Monsieur Veuillot was asking when he came to himself, 'what exactly did the paper say?'

Maximin told him.

Padre Grassi said, 'I see the hidden hand. *La mano di Amandi*! Well,' he told Giraud, 'if you said that there was no vision and no secret, you must see that you can be of no further use to us. What could you tell the Council? You have denied your own news.'

Maximin was thunderstruck. 'But all I said was "maybe" . . .'

'"Maybe" is too much and you may depend on it that the paper will be cleverly written.'

By now they were out in the hot afternoon street where the light hurt the eyes. There were more headshakes, then Maximin's priestly hosts – even Veuillot seemed priestly – got into their carriage and left him standing, a discard for whom they had no futher use. His head swam, for he had drunk everything he had been offered, but still he ran after the carriage, shouting, 'What about my lump sum? Aren't you going to pay me?' At last, lacerated by a stitch in his side, he had to drop back. The footmen clinging to the rear of the carriage were laughing, so he picked up some dried horse dung and threw it at them hard.

He had been made a fool of! Even now he couldn't quite work out how. Distrusting his own eyes, he was startled by the blood smeared on his palms. He had clenched his fists so hard that his fingernails had punctured the skin. Too agitated to pause, he walked randomly through empty streets in tangling circles, raging against the city's mockery. Steely reflections dazzled him and once he nearly fell into a *mondezzaro*. God, he hated Rome. Hated siestas when everyone drew back into their own cosy lives and closed you out. He hated his own diminished life and bloody God. *Merde*!

Pausing in the shade of a church door, he saw a list of confessors and the languages in which they would hear confessions: Polish, Spanish . . . Confessions! Like a stung bull, he took off for the church where Monsignor Santi had told Donna Costanza he would be this afternoon at four. It was a little after that when he reached it and it seemed quite empty and dark as he thumped about, shocking himself by the sound of his own boots. 'The hidden hand'! Santi and Amandi! Where was that hand hidden now? Then he saw the name Amandi over a confessional, and just then a woman walked up the aisle and knelt in the penitent's niche. Putting her mouth close to the grating, she began to whisper.

Another conspiracy! thought Maximin and, on impulse, stepped up to the central section of the confessional and put his head through the curtains. He breathed in an odour of snuff.

'Monsignore!'

'*Che*! *Che*?' The irritable query from the oven-dark interior touched a sore nerve. '*Che*?' growled the invisible confessor again, as though Maximin were a passing annoyance. 'What is it? What do you want? Explain yourself.'

Maximin felt affronted, since an explanation was precisely what was due to *him* and he couldn't get his tongue around the buzz of questions raging in his head. What was happening? Why? And in what way had he deserved the mockery in which – it seemed to him now – he had been trapped since childhood. Trapped like a fly in *merde*! Angrily, he opened his mouth, but his voice would not come. His throat closed as though he

530

had asthma like his father. He was dumb, just as he had often been years ago, when he stood at the church altar in Ablandins to tell about the vision and found he needed a prompt. The old, smothering frustration choked him. It was the priests' fault, all of it, and now here was this one telling him to go away and stop blocking his light.

Which was he? The Eminenza or the Monsignore?

Almost without his volition, one of Maximin's hands drew a knife while the other reached into the box, seized the shoulder of the vociferous priest, and raised him so that the knife could reach his gut. Then, bracing himself against the side of the confessional, he thrust it in. For a moment it was arrested by bunched cloth, then he rammed it through.

Stepping away from the box, he looked across the nave to where the only two worshippers in sight seemed to have noticed nothing. And indeed there had been little to alert them, for the confessional was in a dark side chapel and the dying man's remonstrances had trailed off in a soft diminuendo sigh.

Maximin was about to leave, when the side door of the confessional flew open and out tumbled the woman penitent. Her mouth and eyes were rounded in panic. He had forgotten about her, but now the mouth's contagion terrified him. It looked so ready to launch a scream of alarm that for moments he thought he heard it. Whispering 'Hush!' he got his hands on her throat. '*Zitta!*' he urged. 'Just stay quiet!' Tightening, then loosening his grip, he pushed her back into the confessional, closed the door on her inert, slumping weight, and ran.

Nobody looked at him as he came out into the square, slowed, crossed it and walked at a funeral mute's pace down a wriggle of streets to another empty one in whose fountain he soaked his grey jacket to remove the blood. He was thinking that the woman had had a good look at him and must have noticed his uniform. Mechanically, he squeezed out his jacket. The sun would soon dry the damp.

An image of the alarmed woman's face danced before him and reminded him of an aunt who had defended him when he was small. She had been thin but resolute and he remembered her dodging behind his father's shoulder to catch the arms raised to deal blows. She could cling to the drunk's elbows just long enough for Maximin to race to the shelter of a neighbour's house. Then she had to let go. The Madonna too, it struck him, had said she was exhausted from holding back her son's arm lest he smite the world. Just like his aunt!

A priest stepped forth, then back into the crowd, as though playing some child's game like Nuts in May. Again! Third time lucky, he came up to Monsignor Santi and introduced himself. His name was Gilmore and they had been at the Romano together.

'I called a few weeks ago, but you were busy.'

Nicola tried to put the awkward man at his ease but couldn't follow his rigmarole. He was looking for Monseigneur Darboy and had an eye out for him even while they talked.

'You robbed me of an English passport in 1849!' This, though said jovially, made it impossible to walk off. Besides, Nicola now remembered the man.

'I hope you didn't get into hot water.'

'Oh, I'm rarely out of it.'

The bishop's laugh faltered. 'You're serious.'

The man, eyebrows horripilant and face atwitch, mentioned a book he'd written against usury. His Adam's apple gnawed at his Roman collar. 'It was condemned.' He laughed inappropriately. 'Because of your venture with the Belgian. Our fates seem intertwined!'

Nicola waited for an appeal. Then, still looking for Darboy, tried to speed it up. 'Is there something I can do for you?'

But the other said, 'No, no, Monsignore, I hope to help you!'

Nicola waited.

'You, I and Martelli were blamed for denouncing the Society.' Lowering his voice. 'But he didn't enter the Church and you had protection. I was hounded all my life. Mine is a small country.' Again that odd guffaw. 'Nowhere to hide.'

'I'm sorry.'

'No, I am. I shouldn't talk of myself. It's just to let you know why Father Grassi thinks he has me in his hand. He sent me. I'm to be an example to you. Something, I think, like a corpse on a gibbet. You might ask why I let him send me. Well, I wanted to see you. In friendship, if that's not presumption.'

The man's emotion was undiagnosable. Nicola waited.

'What they want is the paper you got Giraud to sign. He said you'd know what I meant. Otherwise they'll retaliate. I'm only a messenger but I'm at your disposal to help any way I can.'

'Forgive me,' said Nicola. 'Can you wait? I'll be back.'

Darboy had come out of the *aula* and was leaving. He was the most independent of the Opposition leaders and Nicola wanted him to have Giraud's retraction to use as he thought fit.

As it happened, Darboy was in a huddle of excited men, so Nicola handed over the envelope without any mention of Grassi's message which, anyway, was probably pure hot air. 'Keep it carefully,' he murmured, however. 'It's explosive.'

Returning to look for the Irishman, he didn't find him and was, anyway, distracted by a group airing some new rumour about the Prussians and the French. Walking home past the Minerva where Cardinal Guidi was now semi-confined, he wondered whether some bishops might secretly be praying for the arrival of Garibaldi.

Outside Cardinal Amandi's *palazzo*, Gianni, the major-domo, was directing two young footmen who were doing something with lengths of black fabric. On seeing Monsignor Santi, Gianni rushed up and began to weep.

'Monsignore! Oh Monsignore!'

'Gianni, what is it? What's happened?'

But the major-domo seemed to have lost the faculty of speech and could only sob.

Thirty

'Monsignore, we must implore you to treat this as a cross!'

Monsignor Randi, Governor of Rome and head of the Papal Police, was mortified at having had to send a subordinate to rush the bishop to Police Headquarters. He apologised in a voice deep with commiseration. Given a choice, he would have gone himself to the lamented cardinal's residence. An appalling loss! Such a holy man! Cut down when our hopes for him were verdant! But this, Monsignore, was a thorny business! The Governor fingered thorns, then wiped a forehead which may have felt crowned by them. It trickled sweat, and his handkerchief came away grimy. He put it in his pocket. Such a visit would have given rise to talk – or rather to more talk, for talk, alas, there would be.

Nicola was numb.

Randi mentioned a dead woman. With a vote due in the Council within days . . .

Woman? The bishop tried not to blink. When he did, redness engulfed him and he saw the cardinal as he had glimpsed him just now. Blood encrusted his cassock like tangles of surplus piping. Nicola had been fetched away before he could take it all in.

Randi consulted papers. If we let it be known that a prince of the Church had been found murdered next to a woman, the rabble would draw certain conclusions. So, for now, all this must stay *sub silentio*. Truth was elusive and though Monsignor Santi had given a version of events, frankly, Monsignore, nobody would believe it. Think, moreover, of the conflict of jurisdiction! The calumnies reaching close to the papal throne and . . . Patiently, Randi went over known ground. The Council Fathers' tranquillity of mind must be our first concern. And think of the foreign journalists. What a boon for their malice if this got out! No, we must give no quarter. His late Eminence would surely have agreed.

Nicola's numbness was wearing off and pain waiting to engulf him. Effortfully, as though building a dike of words against it, he asked,

'What about justice? If you give it out now that the cardinal died of a heart attack' – this was Randi's proposal – 'how open a murder investigation later?'

'Monsignore!' The Governor joined slim fingers in a steeple. 'Trust us. We know our trade.' The steeple became a probe. It nosed the air. 'We shall discover in due season, *after the vote*, that His Eminence's servants, moved by respect and other worthy motives, brought him home, bound up his wounds and concealed the scandal. As for our forgetting –' Randi smiled pityingly '– we have files in this office which go back a hundred years!'

But the bishop, a prey to delirium, rose to his feet and raved at Randi and at Rome where all truth was turned to lies. '*Menzogne!*' he groaned, then fell back in his chair.

Monsignor Randi walked to the door, signalled to someone, then, returning, stared from half-closed eyes at the afflicted bishop. Would he, he asked solicitously, like something for his nerves?

'Where is the Zouave?'

'Disappeared.'

'And the witnesses who saw him leave the church?'

'They don't know there was a murder. The sacristan, a man of judgment, sent for us at once. Then he closed the church. The cardinal's household can be made to hold their tongues. As for la Diotallevi,' the Governor looked thoughtful, 'her pension is paid by this office. For your own consolation, I can tell you that she confirms your story and was able to identify the second victim. She was a certain Maria Gatti, a woman who had been had up more than once before the Tribunale del Vicariato for her immoral life.'

Leaning forward, Monsignor Randi shot a sudden question, 'Who has the retraction?' The manoeuvre failed. Nicola did not blench. Randi sat back. 'If His Holiness were to have you confined to a monastery, it would be for your own protection.'

'Do you want me to sign something?'

But the Governor was all wounded courtesy, 'I merely want your word that you will collaborate with us until after the vote. The cardinal can meanwhile be decorously buried and you may go about your business: mourn, vote in the Council, intrigue even.' His smile was disillusioned. 'We are tolerance itself.'

*

535

So the ceremony of mourning unrolled its pre-ordained forms as the cardinal's corpse was laid out in falsified state. Its wounds were hidden and its face revealed a puzzled, perhaps faintly malignant surprise. It had been given out that his heart had failed: an act of God whose timing seemed to signify that Pius, whom Amandi had been expected to succeed, truly had God's ear.

The cardinal's household was in shock and the footmen on duty in their mourning livery shed real tears.

Mastai attended the Requiem Mass whose bleaker passages struck the congregation as heralding trouble in the near future rather than on Judgment Day. Rumours of coming turmoil had begun to seep through the censored post.

Gianni, the major-domo – never now to be a pope's right-hand man – was shaken to find that he had won a *terno* based on three numbers standing for surprise, blood and sudden death which he had picked for wholly fortuitous motives connected with a visit to a cousin who was a part-time butcher.

After the funeral, the bishop went to see Monseigneur Darboy to whom, until now, he had had time only to say: keep Giraud's retraction, but keep it dark. Its original purpose was now void – Giraud was on the run – but it could be useful if he was arrested. Nicola did not scandalise the archbishop by passing on a doubt planted in his mind by Martelli.

'How do we know?' the deputy had murmured between condolences, 'that Giraud was not inspired to act? By the Vicar's vicars?'

Darboy, as befitted the Emperor's chaplain and a senator of France, had rented a magnificent apartment in the via Condotti which aroused envy. 'Caesar's friends', murmured the shabby Italian bishops, 'enjoy the good things of this world: hangings, carpets, fires and a chef trained in the imperial kitchens who won't cook spaghetti!'

'Caesar, meaning Napoleon III, has protected their idle hides and kept them in spaghetti for over twenty years,' said Darboy coolly. He was an ascetic man of irreproachable morals, and if he made common cause with an Emperor whose morals were open to reproach – why, so did Pio Nono! 'Our best memorial to Amandi,' he told Nicola, 'will be to win the day for his policies. That, though, may take time.' Retreating from his earlier optimism, he was worrying about the *form* of the definition which was all anyone could hope to change for now. Zealots hoped for one so all-encompassing that Mastai would have the powers of an African witch-doctor. 'Westminster and Regensburg want to lock up thought.' The Archbishop's cool eyes rested on Nicola. 'They've got *le feu au cul*!
536

Their arses are on fire! Pius wants his definition fast before a war breaks out. The Council has a lot more on its agenda, but if he can get *that* he will let us leave Rome until the autumn. Then . . .'

'Then?'

'We shall come back and question its legitimacy.'

They talked of Amandi's death. Darboy did not believe that Randi intended opening an investigation now or ever. Even, said the archbishop, if the police were to catch and charge Giraud, the Zouaves would defend their man. They had done so in the case of Watson alias Suratt, a Zouave wanted in connection with the murder of Lincoln who, when the Americans made a formal demand for him, was let escape. Indignantly, President Grant had then sent an aide-de-camp to Rome and, to satisfy him, the officer responsible was retired – causing disaffection in the ranks. 'So you may be sure that Giraud will not be handed over.'

Gianni, the major-domo, had received an offer of a post in Paris in the household of the nuncio, Monsignor Chigi. This was rum and perhaps unsafe? His doubts grew when a policeman called to ask if he was going. No? Well, said the policeman, maybe he should think again. 'He said,' Gianni told Monsignor Santi, 'that I'd better go because I was known to be in correspondence with Garibaldini and could be gaoled if I stayed here. They showed me letters signed in my hand – letters,' said Gianni appalled, 'that I never saw in my life! They say they'll use them if I tell anyone that His Eminence was stabbed! They want me to take the first and second footman with me. The third can stay. He,' it struck him, 'must be one of *theirs*? *O Madonna santa!*' And Gianni wept, as he had been doing increasingly often, for his nerves were frayed to pieces. Paris was as alien as the North Pole.

Nicola tried to see Monsignor Randi but had to be satisfied with a subordinate who, though courteous and deferential, knew nothing of the case. *Was* there a case? He hadn't been informed. Making Rome safe for the Council was an overwhelming task. Had the bishop heard of the secret manufactory which had been discovered making umbrellas containing knives? Probably run by Masons! And how, asked the policeman, were things going at the Council now? Was the Holy Spirit's moment coming?

Nicola decided to go and see.

A 'trial ballot' was being held on the schema, *De Romano Pontefice*. A dry run for the Solemn Session on the 18th, it aimed to test resistance to chapters on the Primacy and Infallibility which had been amended and re-amended in meetings which Nicola had missed. The text on Infallibility was still unsatisfactory to the Minority. The one on the Primacy now ran, 'Jesus Christ established . . . primacy in Peter for the perpetual good of the Church . . . until the end of the world. Therefore Peter lives, presides and exercises judgment in his successors, the bishops of the Roman See.' Those in favour stood up, then those against, and it was clear that both texts had the required majority. Next came the vocal ballot when 'aye' was *'placet'*, no *'non placet'*, and those wanting an amendment said *'placet iuxta modum'*. Darboy had hoped for a hundred and forty *'non placet'*s, which would be a significant vote of dissent. However, there were only eighty-eight as seventy-six Opposition members, though still in Rome, felt unable to publicly defy the Pope's wishes and failed to turn up. The *'placet'*s were thus 451, with sixty-two *'placet iuxta modum'*s.

Next day Darboy went to see Cardinal Bilio in the hope of striking a bargain. His plea was that, if one counted the absentees and the *iuxta modum*s, the dissenters amounted to a sizeable group and he would recommend that they submit a solemn protest stating that, since the Council lacked moral unanimity, they did not feel bound by its decrees.

It was clear to Nicola that Bilio would not budge, for he knew Darboy's following to be neither resolute nor of one mind.

Returning to the apartment, he found Gianni looking sick. It had just struck him that a widow with whom he had been friendly must have given specimens of his handwriting to the police. She was illiterate and he had often written letters on her behalf.

A note from Prospero requested a meeting, but Nicola did not reply. He did not want to see anyone, though neither could he bear to sit in this residence which he had shared with Amandi and where he was a prey to streams of condoling visitors. Restlessly, he ordered his carriage and had himself driven about at random until this too palled and, remembering an address mentioned by Monsignor Randi, he found himself pulling the bell of the apartment in the Trastevere where Maria Gatti had lived.

The door opened a crack and a nose and mouth showed through. Sullenly, the mouth said, 'If you want my mother, she was buried days ago.' His mother? 'Yes,' raged the mouth. 'I am Signora Gatti's son, Pietro. She's dead. If you're one of her' – with a quick intake of breath – 'regulars, you can spread the word.'

'I haven't seen her for twenty years.'

'Ah.' Opening, the door revealed a boy who should have been good-looking but wasn't. He was too furtive, and the look seemed ingrained.

'May I come in?'

The boy stepped aside. Passing him, the bishop spied a quick grimace. Moving to a window which overlooked nothing, he mumbled foolishly about the view. Maria. Paralysis had seized him, for the young man was a living replica – though sulky and tormented – of himself twenty years ago.

Fine bones and figure. Slippery eyes. That reddish hair! Reflected in the windowpane against roof tiles and chimneypots were two quivering images. Old self? New son? Say nothing, he cautioned himself, then wondered if the advice echoed that made by and to his own father forty years before. Trapped in a trinity of ghosts, he took refuge in the ritual of condolence. His mother, he told the flinching youth, had been a lovely girl when he, Nicola, had known her.

The grubby apartment was a wistful imitation of Diotallevi's – and perhaps Maria Gatti had got her cast-offs? A Turkey carpet, too big to unroll, was half-bunched against a wall and a magpie scatter of baubles might, by candlelight, approximate Donna Costanza's opulent effects.

'Did your mother bring you up?'

No. The nuns had. He had only known his mother in recent years, after Signora Diotallevi got him work in a photographer's shop on the via del Babuino. Mother Church suckled us all, thought the bishop: me, Flavio, this youth. Furtively, he closed then opened his eyes to test his perception of the likeness. Had he imagined it? He was already less sure and his recollection of his young self seemed to melt like snow.

How, he asked Pietro Gatti, had his mother died?

'Strangled. The police favour the notion of a burglary.' He had not lived here himself, he explained. A neighbour found her.

'Here?'

'Where else?'

Nicola was back in the Governor's office at Montecitorio, where Monsignor Randi was striding about, punctuating his speech by short pauses and whirls which made his cassock bell.

'You,' said he, 'are suffering from a maggot of the mind! A megrim. It's understandable that while possessed by it, you resist believing this – but one has to tell you the truth and that, Monsignore, is that Cardinal Amandi died at home of a heart attack. Our last conversation in this office was held because his death was sudden and I wanted you to know that the doctor had established its cause. You are free to see the medical report and the minutes of our conversation. Your other memories are false. You must try to understand this and I pray that you will, since there is no other hope of your recovering your serenity. I have seen men in your state of shock before in this very office. I urge you to pray for resignation to God's will. Your fantasies, forgive my saying this, are a form of rebellion against it.'

Some time later, Nicola found himself in a small square, close to Montecitorio, seated on the rim of a well. He tried to recall how he had got here, but his vision was a cloud and his moiling mind only now recovering its ability to think. As it did, he marvelled at his restraint for he had not, it came back to him, raged at nor tried to throttle Randi. Instead, he had turned, walked silently from the Governor's office and, somehow, finding his way down dark stairs and corridors, reached the sunlight. This feat of self-control had left him numb. Yet where would have been the point in throttling the lickspittle, since the spittle licked must be Mastai's? Randi's impudence was inconceivable otherwise.

What had helped Nicola subdue his feelings was the memory of his conversation with Darboy. The Frenchman had stressed the need for prudence if they were to hope for an eventual triumph of the dead cardinal's policies. Darboy, bravest of the anti-Infallibilists, warned that precipitous action would play into Mastai's hands. Time and patience were our best assets. 'Later, much can be undone which is now being done, but only if we avoid exacerbating our differences with the Majority.' Then he asked Nicola to think of him as taking the dead man's place as a friend and adviser. The two could feel each other's emotion as they embraced. '*Du calme!*' murmured Darboy as they said goodbye.

Mindful of this, Nicola forbade himself to rile the unspeakable Randi who might yet – it consoled him to think – have to suffer his own share of humiliations, since the Italians, if they took Rome, would not be tender with men like him.

*

Gianni begged Nicola to forgive him if he didn't serve out his notice. He would forgo pay, but must leave now. He was a small man and had a family to look out for. 'Please believe me, Monsignore, if anything I said could help His Eminence, I'd say it. As God is my witness, I would! But it wouldn't, would it? Justice, Monsignore, is something we'll all see in heaven, please God!' Then Gianni began kissing the bishop's hand and weeping all over it. 'I'll pray for His Eminence,' he promised. 'I'll have masses said for his soul.'

Two footmen were leaving too. Having, like most of their kind, worked for tips only, they had no pay to forgo. Questions threw them into a mute terror. A third man who had been present when the cardinal was brought back denied having seen any sign of blood or foul play. None, Monsignore! Staring Nicola in the eye. Their departure was like a last funeral rite for, without the livery they had worn in Amandi's service, they dwindled to near-invisibility.

That same evening the news was that six more bishops had left Rome. All were members of the Opposition.

15 July. Evening

Darboy had gone to the Vatican with like-minded bishops – Mainz, Dijon, Lyons and the Primate of Hungary – to plead for changes to the form of the definition which would make it acceptable to the consciences of the Minority and secure a unanimous *placet* on the 18th.

'It's an olive branch,' his secretary told all who came for news. 'We must pray that His Holiness will not refuse it.' The Church was infallible. All agreed about that. But were there two infallibilities? Papal and ecclesiastical? Or, more reasonably, was the Pope infallible only when he had consulted his bishops and spoke as the voice of tradition?

16 July

The sun blazed. *Piazze* were griddles and jokes about the fires in which Pius was roasting bishops no longer amused anyone. There was a scum of sweat on the horses which drove Nicola to the Council, and when he pointed this out, the coachman was so surly that he feared he too might be about to give notice. He put off thinking about this, though, for the public crisis was peaking and by the session's end, when Prospero fell into step beside him, the two felt a precarious bond. Both were sick of strife.

This morning, each bishop had been handed the text of a protest, signed by the five Council Presidents, against pamphlets which impugned the Council's freedom. Cardinal d'Angelis then read it aloud with indignant relish. 'Calumnious', 'disgraceful', 'falsehoods' and 'filthiest lies' were the only official responses to the Minority's anguish. The bishops were then asked to stand up in token of approval and to sign and hand in their copies for the Vatican archives *ad perpetuam rei memoriam.*

Nicola, caught unawares, was already on his feet when he heard Majority members yell 'Anathema!' at those who had failed to rise. Only then did he see that the Council was being tricked into attesting to its own moral unanimity and that this was Mastai's answer to yesterday's delegation. Promptly, he sat back down and held hard to his seat when men next to him tried to wrestle him up.

'Don't be foolish!' called Prospero. 'It's too late!'

'All have stood up!' shouted a bishop.

'Not all!' protested several voices.

'All!' bayed the Majority, maddened by victory. And indeed the seated men were concealed by those who stood and their voices smothered by the roar.

When members streamed out, the younger men who sat on the lower benches were ahead. Prospero told Nicola, 'I said mass this morning for Amandi.'

'Do you believe he died of a heart attack?'

Prospero's eyes flinched. 'I won't pretend not to understand. I felt as you do when Count Rossi died. But, later, I saw that I had gone a little mad. Won't you come and talk about it? This evening?'

Nicola agreed gratefully, for he did feel a little mad. Also unshelled and lonely, so that the prospect of an evening alone was almost as bad as joining the Minority in their ingenuous huddles, where they would shame him by their surprise at the Curia's new manoeuvre, and by the pity or contempt or whatever it was that foreign bishops felt for men who lived here. Probably contempt. For why think their equation of *doctor Romanus* with *asinus Germanus* did not apply to him? Amandi, who had known the courts of Europe, had been one of themselves. What, without his patronage, could Nicola seem but a providentially strayed *asinus*?

So he looked forward almost with tenderness to the evening with Prospero and arrived full of expectancy of small, consoling intimacies and silences and ease: things for which he only now knew he had been aching. Even talking nonsense together would be cheering! Even being sad! But, almost at once, he sensed that Prospero was on, rather than off, duty and found himself wondering whether he had been invited from friendship or policy and whether he and Prospero were still friends. It would be hard if new associates thought him an *asinus* and old ones a renegade!

Cheated then of inconsequentiality and closeness, he had to listen to a defence of the *Sodalitium Pianum*, an experiment which, said Prospero, though shelved pro tem, must one day be revived. How else keep a check on the hordes of foreigners who now came here to vote? There was already talk of de-Italianising the Church! And in the name of what? As he spoke, Prospero kept looking expectantly at Nicola who only half listened and would not reply.

'Do you think men who disagree as much as we do,' he asked instead, 'can be friends? Or is friendship another "Liberal fallacy"?' Laughing, he held up his glass as though hoping for Prospero's body and blood or at least a toast to old cordiality. But all he got was Marsala which he drank too fast while his friend said something dampening about charity and how attachments could offend against it. Nicola, said Prospero, let his heart rule his head. Witness his mad suspicions over poor Amandi's death. 'You thought of him as a father, didn't you?'

We had too many fathers, groaned the needy and now slightly inebriated Nicola. And brothers in Christ. 'It's a stolen vocabulary,' he complained. 'Stolen! Even Grassi calls me *dilecte fili*! In his mouth it sounds like a lie. Everything does.'

'That's because Jesuit militancy envisaged persecutions of a simpler sort than those we see today. Grassi would make a splendid martyr but won't get the chance.'

'So instead he sacrifices others.'

'You are sour! Is it because you think Amandi was your father? He wasn't, you know. He wasn't your blood father.'

'I never – how do you know? What . . .? You were cousins. *Do* you know something?' Nicola felt strangely out of control. His body seemed to have got news which hadn't reached his mind. 'Blood father,' he repeated, and his blood effervesced while his mind viewed this phenomenon with surprise. At the same time, he felt annoyed that, having come to find a friend, he should instead be deprived of a father. Not that he had thought of Amandi as literally that. Especially not since learning about poor Sister Paola. That conjunction was not likely. But he had loved him like one and no mere begetter was going to displace the dead man in his loyalties – which must be Prospero's aim! *He* was on duty all right!

'Even if you do know something,' Nicola warned, 'it won't change my sense that Mastai and the climate he created were to blame for Amandi's death. And don't ask if I've lost my faith, because the faith we have now isn't in Christ. He was meek, but Mastai wants to win! Remember his foot on the Melkite patriarch's neck, and how the Armenian bishops had to flee from his police!'

Prospero came and held Nicola's shoulders. 'You're talking away faith,' he warned. 'You're like a man who needs cold water thrown on him. So I'm going to tell you something to give you pause. Mastai is your father, your spiritual father, but also your father of the loins. I wouldn't lie about this.'

Nicola made him repeat what he had said and felt the words tear at his flesh. He also felt something harden in his throat, then nausea. 'Wouldn't you lie about it?' he wondered slow-wittedly. 'I suppose not. Unless it's a parable? Is it? No?' There was a long moment of silence, during which the nausea got worse and he had trouble breathing. Then he asked, 'Have you proof?'

He didn't want it, felt befouled and humiliated – yet saw a symmetry here. It was as though the divisions and turmoil which had for years been moving closer to the city had now reached inside his own head. His skull thrummed. It was an assaulted belfry, a sickened aviary, and through its din he could just hear Prospero tell about 'pamphlets which ...' Distaste kept cutting off that voice. Then words slid through. He heard 'most were patent bosh', then the word 'censorship' pulled him up, for was he not engaging in it himself? He, like the sick body politic, was baffling off the inevitable. He started to listen then and learned, without surprise, that the Abate Gavazzi was Prospero's source and that, though he had not named Nicola in his pamphlet, Prospero's inquiries among his own aunts and cousins had supplied and confirmed the identification. 'After all, your mother was a connection of ours.' Prospero, though loath to root in the midden of scurrility, had had to take the Gavazzi pamphlet seriously, for professional ...

'Can I see it?'

'I destroyed it.'

'You can't have! You were reading for the *Congregatio Indicis*! Surely you're not allowed to do that!'

'What kind of a waxwork dummy do you think I am, Nicola? I destroyed it because of you! Putting books on the Index draws attention to them and I didn't want you ever to see this one. I couldn't foresee this conversation, could I?'

'There must be other copies?'

'In England? Maybe. Though the thing was ephemeral. Printed on paper destined to end up wiping bums. You *could* track Gavazzi down. But take my word for it, the story fits. As for your mother . . .'

'I know about her. Don't say anything!' Nicola was offended that Prospero thought of the secret as 'a midden of scurrility'. At the same time he felt something like this himself – but *not* because of poor Sister Paola.

'You know who she was?' Prospero clearly doubted this. He thinks, guessed Nicola, that I fancy it's some lady who does me credit: Donna Clara Colonna or the Countess Spaur.

'I know it was the nun.' This, he saw, had taken some wind out of Prospero's sails.

She, said Prospero, as though pedantically eager to establish that they meant the same nun, was in the news again. 'She is the object of a local cult and people are calling her a saint.'

Nicola closed his eyes and saw her palimpsest of a face. Greyed and roughened like salt cod, it used to glow as she reminisced. Sister Paola! Her he had accepted without difficulty, for an affinity had been growing between them even as he was reading his story into the tapestry of hers. He had not, it seemed, read it aright and her ramblings would have to be wrenched into a new pattern. Unless Prospero was wrong? Nicola prayed for this. Better the boy Bonaparte or even the incestuous uncle, both of whom were safely dead! She too, poor gallant creature, must have had felt this and confused the trail. She had brought him a new dimension of himself, a new Santi – though, to be sure, that name was false. Should it be Mastai? The mockery scorched him. The Pope's bastard! It was like the name of some obscene sweetmeat such as those cakes called Nun's farts or – stop, Nicola! Yes, he must stop – yet was intensely curious about his story and would later, he promised himself, put together the scraps he had in his head and find *his* truth. She – almost as if she'd known! – had given him the clues.

'One trembles to think – well, better not even to consider the possible ramifications!' Prospero was referring to the people's cult of the dead nun and how a makeshift shrine had had to be removed. 'I presume you know about what has been happening in Imola. Your Vicar General must have written.'

But Nicola had been neglecting the diocese and letters from it. The two fell silent, for the story was explosive and repugnant to them both. Turning to less charged matters, Prospero talked of his brother and of how he never visited the villa now. Why go to quarrel? 'If I couldn't stand my father's Byronic patriotism, how put up with Cesco's? Those rigged elections! Church property taken by fraud! No doubt, he knows on which side his bread is buttered! That's why I have always thought of you, Nicola, as my true younger brother. Personal ambition moves neither of us. I hope you believe that of me, and even,' smiling, 'of my friends.'

'I can't believe it of their leaders. Manning . . .'

But Prospero said the Englishman was dedicated to strengthening a Church which often, these days, could seem as frail as St Peter's did during the silver illuminations.

He was referring to that phase of festive evenings when the lanterns ranged along the basilica's contours first began to glow. Lit earlier but invisible until dusk, they emerged with the slow radiance of stars, and for moments this figured a heartbreaking fragility before being overtaken by a conflagration, 'the golden illumination' which pyrotechnists made to whirl along columns and cupolas in a river of fire. It was, of course, charged with meanings, for this was a city of symbols which of late had begun to say different things to different people.

What they said to Mastai was that he must prepare to be martyred. This, said Prospero, explained his harshness with the Opposition whose concerns could only seem petty to a man engaged in a dialogue with invisible powers. 'The external world can seem like an encumbrance. He deals with it summarily.'

'Including, if your story is true, myself.'

'We can't judge, Nicola! We can't imagine the circumstances. There are moments outside of time which, when time takes up again, reproach a man forever.'

'Amandi thought him mad!'

'It's only a word. Randi used it of you. It's late. I'll walk you home.'

They walked towards the river whose shrunken current gleamed like a lazy reptile. Reeds rattled in a pre-dawn breeze. Prospero pointed to some lighted windows. Plots?

'The Minority? Surely it's too late?'

But Prospero had been thinking of the Italians.

Nicola asked, 'If you found you had a son you'd never known about – it could happen – what would you do?'

Prospero thought about this. 'Nothing. It's usually the safest course. If he were in need I would do something for him. Anonymously. As we both know from that source of everyday knowledge, the confessional, this city is full of such cases. Blood is a materialistic fetish and significant only in your case because of your loyalty to someone you mistook for a blood relative. Mastai probably doesn't know about you.'

17 July

It was the eve of the final vote. Archbishop Darboy was ill and Nicola feared missing him altogether since the bishops would start leaving after tomorrow's vote if not before.

In the morning, he attended a meeting of the Minority leaders where, in Darboy's absence, the Hungarian, Haynald, urged a course of action of which he would have approved. This was that all go boldly to tomorrow's Solemn Session and, following their consciences, in the face of God, Pope and the representatives of the world's peoples, forthrightly maintain their '*non placet*'.

'Hear, hear!'

Haynald's infectious courage had carried the meeting, when Bishop Dupanloup came in late in a state of sickened scruple and argued that although having voted *non placet* five days ago, they could not vote *placet* now, neither could they vote *non placet* in defiance of a revered and threatened Pope. The Catholic world would be scandalised. The word, Nicola saw, worked like a 'close Sesame' on bishops' minds. Limply – for, with Lord Acton gone and Darboy absent, there was no one strong enough to ginger them – the very men who had been acclaiming Haynald's proposal now agreed to Dupanloup's compromise, which was to draft a letter to Pius and stay away from tomorrow's Public Session.

The letter, they agreed with relief, would register the Council's lack of unanimity and could be used, when it reconvened, as grounds for

547

challenging the decree. The fight could be deferred. Nobody need go out on a limb. It was the perfect middle way.

Leaving the meeting in angry disappointment, Nicola made for home. He seemed to be coming down with malaria and certainly *mal aria* was what all had been breathing, rather than the breath of the Holy Spirit on which Mastai was still counting.

Feeling increasingly feverish, Nicola was about to take to his bed when he received an unexpected summons. He was to go to the Vatican this evening for an audience with the Pope.

'Tonsured lackeys!'

The hiss mingled with the engine's steam.

The Opposition bishops were in full retreat and extra carriages had been hooked up to the train to accommodate those leaving Rome before tomorrow's Solemn Session. The *Stazione Termini* was filled with valises, trunks, boxes of china, books, bedding, favourite chalices and vestments donated by pious patronesses. In orbit around each departing bishop wheeled friends, servants, secretaries and commiserating sympathisers come to see them off.

'. . . lackeys!'

Monseigneur Dupanloup tried to think he had imagined that hiss, which was not impossible since he had lately grown very thin-skinned. Since coming here, he had been pointedly snubbed by Pope Pius, who was well aware of Dupanloup's personal fondness for him – not to say 'love'. That was a word often taken in vain, but Dupanloup, a fiery, tender man, had opened his heart to it. In France, where the great effort of his generation of priests had been to reconcile their country with their church, he had found souls tempered in that difficult combat and bound himself to them in ways which, it was sometimes said, smuggled some of the devotion due to God into relations with his fellows. But *was* it due only to God? What about loving one's neighbour? There it was again, sibilant and sour! This time, definitely, he had heard the hiss.

Addressed to whom? To all. To all the Minority bishops. This frivolous old city hated to be stirred up and would no doubt sing a gleeful Te Deum on seeing the back of De Pavone Lupus and his troublesome friends!

The jibe with its dig at his bastardy carried an implication that a bar sinister cut through his loyalties – which was quite untrue! For why in the first place had he entered the Church? He had been following his

548

heart! And it had led him to Christ, to the priesthood and to Pius IX! Love-child of a young cavalry lieutenant who had not acknowledged him – although relatives did help his career – the young Dupanloup had felt so needy for affection that charm became second nature and very soon – the quip was Renan's – made him into 'the most fashionable priest in Paris', with three queens sitting in at his catechism class at the Madeleine. He did like to be liked. Even as a teacher, he appealed to pupils' feelings and the method worked well for him. But it was not worldliness which ruled him. He was not divided. No. He was loyalty itself – and just now he was loyalty spurned.

Smiles. Melancholy embraces. Goodbye for now. See you when the Council reconvenes! *Deo volente.* Monsignor Haynald was travelling too. Did he think less of Dupanloup because he could not fling his *non placet* in the pontiff's face? Did Darboy? Dupanloup was glad they didn't know of a plea which he had sent secretly to Pius after the trial ballot. 'Mad!' had been Pius's reaction, which a third party promptly reported back. 'Either he's mad or he thinks I am!' And perhaps the Bishop of Orléans had indeed lacked sober sense. But how could a man of faith and feeling always gauge the possible? What he had done was to make a proposal and a promise never, if the pontiff were to adopt it, to reveal that it had been his. It was that Pius, now that he had won his point, should defer the definition until passions had cooled. Such sublime magnanimity would, urged the bishop, 'astound the world and excite universal gratitude'. Writing these words, his eyes had moistened. It was his last filial cry and elicited no response, because, he now saw, the idea was too French. He had appealed to Pius as to a character in a Cornelian tragedy exquisitely attuned to his own heroic virtue. *La gloire*! Honour! But neither Rome nor Pius could conceive of such a thing. *Noblesse oblige* struck them as vapouring vanity. Prideful! A showy fanfaronade if not indeed a sin!

Anxiously, Félix Dupanloup examined his conscience. Could Renan have been right? Had he been affected by the fashionable world to the point of confusing delicacy with morals? Grown feminine? Lost the virile resolution needed in a fight?

Georges Darboy too had heard the hiss. He made a moue.

He wished Haynald's plan had been carried but, as things stood, what mattered was solidarity. In a month the Council would reconvene. Meanwhile the fifty-five signatories to the letter must try to stand firm while being prepared for desertions. Even Christ in His agony had found His disciples asleep.

Our letter would no doubt end in the Vatican archives bearing, unlike Veronica's veil, no sign of the anguish which had gone into it. It ran:

Most Holy father,

In the General Congregation held on the 13th inst. we voted on the schema of the first Dogmatic Constitution concerning the Church of Christ.

Your Holiness is aware that 88 Fathers, urged by conscience and moved by love of Holy Church, voted *non placet*; 62 *placet iuxta modum*; finally about 76 were absent and did not vote. Others had returned to their dioceses . . . Thus our votes are known to Your Holiness and manifest to the whole world . . .

Nothing has happened since to change our opinion . . . We therefore declare that we renew and confirm the votes already given.

Confirming our votes therefore in the present document, we have decided to be absent from the Public Session on the 18th inst. For the filial piety and reverence which very recently brought our representatives to the feet of your Holiness do not allow us in a cause so closely concerning Your Holiness to say *non placet* openly and in the face of the Father . . .

We return, therefore, without delay to our flocks . . . Meanwhile . . . we are Your Holiness's most devoted and obedient sons.

This letter was to be handed to the Secretary of the Council before tomorrow's Session.

Monseigneur Darboy was returning to his flock with foreboding. He, more directly than any other bishop, had sought help from his government and saw its refusal as ominous. Why had it been so loath to interfere? A Christian king would have been less pusillanimous. Sixteenth-century ones had done their damnedest to interfere at Trent. The Empire was clearly in a shaky state and 'Napoleon the Small' seemed to be falling back on that great cure for domestic discontent: the quest for glory on foreign battlefields. His failure to find it in Mexico had, providentially, been far away. Next time the risks would be closer to home.

As the train pulled out, the Archbishop looked for Amandi's Coadjutor, but didn't seem him. A pity. The young Monseigneur was one of the few Italian bishops with any pluck. Darboy had wanted to assure him that the fight was still on, despite today's setback, and that he must not despair of our getting justice for poor Amandi. Terrible tragedies had happened as a result of this Council. Old, loyal bishops had seen their faith rocked and their hearts broken. Good men had been turned into cynics. We owed it to them to continue the struggle. Hailing a mutual acquaintance, he asked him to bring the Coadjutor a one-word message: '*Coraggio!*'

Nicola's audience with the Pope was stormy. Later, he supposed he must have been more affected than he knew by a dose of medicine taken to bring his fever down.

His Holiness wanted his *placet* at tomorrow's Solemn Session. 'You, Monsignore, are one of our own bishops from whom we expect more loyalty than has been forthcoming from some foreign ones.'

Though stern, he spoke with what seemed to be genuine feeling about the loss of poor Amandi. He was hard to resist. His confidence was electric, his gestures potent. He smiled with his whole face and his lower lip jutted as though a bee had stung it. Nicola thought, I don't look like him. Can there be anything to Prospero's story? It was as if there were two Piuses: the one here in front of him and the unlikely, shaming one who might be his father. He could not deal with both at the same time.

'He and I were friends long before you were born,' said this Pius of Amandi. 'His was a noble soul! How *sad* all these divisions are. I am glad you are loyal to his memory, Monsignore. It speaks well of you.' And the old pontiff shook friendly jowls and crinkled his eyes with such an air of understanding that the bishop felt softened and was thinking how hard it must have been for Amandi to defy old allegiances when it was borne in on him that he was being asked for Giraud's retraction. Monsieur Louis Veuillot wanted it, and he was a man, said His Holiness, whom he would not hesitate to defend against a bishop. Indeed, he had defended him in the past against their Lordships Dupanloup and Sibour – Darboy's predecessor in the See of Paris who had since then, poor man, been senselessly murdered by a mad priest. Such things happened nowadays, even within our own ranks! That was why a lay champion like Veuillot was worth his weight in gold. 'Gold, Monsignore! He's a brave soldier for Rome and Rome will stand by him. There are those who say that priests in France are refusing to become bishops because they fear he will have more power in their dioceses than they. I say it's just as well such priests do not become bishops. We have too many already who dislike bowing to our authority.'

Nicola saw that the moment was unpropitious. Time, however, was

551

short and he was unlikely to have another chance to make his request that the cardinal's murder should be investiga . . .

'Monsignore!' A gesture cut off the topic at such speed that His Holiness could hardly have been taken by suprise. Indeed, it now turned out that Monsiegneur Randi had told him of Nicola's delusions. 'Not another word! Have you got Giraud's paper?'

The bishop said he did not. The Pope said he should get it. The bishop said it had left the city because it would be needed to establish the truth. If Monseigneur Randi would only open an inquiry . . .

'Monsignore! Monsignore!' Mastai's headshake was ponderous but had an edge of humour to it, and Nicola saw quite suddenly that he was watching a performance so practised as to be second nature – but not nature itself. No, the play of whimsical mouth, compelling gaze, stern then complicitous grimace, was too well orchestrated to be spontaneous. Pius, Nicola saw, was an artist who evoked feeling but delivered none – which, after all, was his role. He was a Vicar. His dimension was mythic not domestic. He was nobody's father and his warmth of manner was a mere portent. All this was orthodox and if Nicola felt a sudden chill, well, he had malaria and could blame neither it nor his sense of desolation on Mastai. From a depth of himself opened by stress and fever, there welled up an intuition. Pius, after twenty-four years as pontiff, was a performer only. There was no humanity left in him.

If this was fever, Nicola prayed for more of it. Closing his eyes, he reflected that if he had managed to contact the departing Darboy – probably now at the station – he would have taken back the retraction from him and might now surrender it to Pius. As it was, he was being backed into rebellion.

'Monsignore!' The silvery voice had steel in it. 'Let me remind you that four days ago you and your brother bishops unanimously accepted the canon on the Papal Primacy decreeing that the Roman Pontiff has supreme jurisdiction not only in things pertaining to faith and morals but also in those pertaining to discipline and the government of the Church. How then can you refuse to give me the retraction?'

The bishop's head swam. He tightened his fists to keep from swooning. He was still on his knees, since the pontiff had not given him permission to get off them and, despite the risk of swooning, Nicola was determined not to ask for it. Yet his fever was gaining on him. Even the angle at which he had to keep his head was painful. And now, as he stared up at the fat, white shape above him he saw it levitate.

'Well,' asked the unsteady figure. 'Well, Monsignore?'

Later, it would seem to the bishop that he at this point uttered a somnambulist's warning to the fracturing whiteness. It was against deceptions like those now infesting his own head. Moths! Snow flurries! Paracletes!

'They're dangerous,' he told the skirted knees which were opening like those of a woman giving birth. Everyone, he thought, sees a different Pius – the saint, the martyr, the *perturbator ecclesiae*. But the knees menaced him like the white, age-smoothed heads of marble lions which flank church doors in towns like Imola. Changing back into knees, they were those of a woman in labour under a stretched sheet, flanking the cavity where doctors grope to deliver a child. Lion-kneed, the woman groaned about the ills of Mother Church and menaced Nicola with arrest if he did not hand over the paper.

Cunning in his delirium, the bishop said that in that case the paper would be printed in the French, English and Italian press.

'Ah, so the deputy has it! Martelli! You're a traitor, then, Monsignore! A traitor and a turncoat! A Judas!'

'I've been told that I'm the son of one!' was what he seemed to say next, before succumbing to a fit of malarial shaking. 'T-t-t-turncoat!' he remembered crying through teeth which chattered like castanets before being seized by a palsy so disabling that the audience had to be terminated.

On 18 July, the Council proclaimed the infallibility of the Pope. On 19 July, France declared war on Prussia and, on 19 August, withdrew her garrison from Rome.

'You were raving!' Prospero told Nicola when he came to visit him in the country, where he was convalescing. 'Delirious! Thank God this became obvious at the end! You're lucky!'

'What?'

Yes, said Prospero, because this furnished grounds for forgiveness. 'After all, you were sick, full of some drug and melancholy-mad over poor Amandi's demise. If you make your act of submission, declare your adhesion to the Constitution *Pastor Aeternus*, obtain and give up Maximin Giraud's paper and . . .'

'And what?'

'Apologise. It seems you were rather offensive in a mad way.'

'Unfilial?'

'Nicola, I want you to forget our conversation about . . . you know what I mean.' Prospero wiped sweat from his neck and forehead. He had driven a long way in unpleasant heat to make this visit.

'Tell me about the Solemn Session.'

Prospero was only too pleased to do so. None of the Minority had attended except for two rather obscure men, a Sicilian and an American, who, being unaware of the agreed strategy, had turned up and said *non placet*.

'Brave men!'

'No. Strays! They seem to have done it by mistake, or so they say now. Anyway, they submitted on the spot, crying *Modo credo*. They've shown the way all must go.'

'Hush. Don't gloat! Just describe what happened.'

The event had taken on the colours of legend. There had been a storm, a bizarre, blazing electric one which each side had interpreted as the voice of heaven signalling its anathema or – according to preference – sanction.

Prospero admitted that there was a divergence over detail. Reports differed as to whether a ray of light had pierced the darkness and lit the Pope's forehead just as he pronounced the definition. Prospero had not himself seen this. Conversely, had a windowpane shattered and fallen ominously near Mastai's head? In all the noise, it would have been easy to miss. All agreed that it had been hard to hear the *placet*s over the pealing thunder and that the crowd – smaller far than at the opening ceremony – had been distracted by the lightning darting about the *baldacchino* and flashing in at every window, down through the dome and around every cupola. 'In a way it added to the solemnity.'

'Lucifer's last signal?'

'Who can say? The storm was at its height when the result of the voting was brought to His Holiness, and it was so dark that a taper had to be placed beside him as he read and pronounced the definition: a light shining in the darkness that the darkness did not comprehend! Thunder and lightning were still raging. Then the Te Deum was sung, the congregation fell to their knees and he blessed them in that thrilling voice of his. It was deeply moving.'

'So his labour bore fruit. A new infallible self!'

Prospero ignored this. 'Meanwhile,' he said, 'a skeleton Council goes on. We've held two meetings. Both very sober. There are 120 of us left. We've gone back to the agenda which was put aside to make way for . . .'

'*The* question.'

'Yes.'

'Darboy reminded me that one of that word's meanings is "torture".'

Prospero did not demur. He was weary after his journey to this remote house where Nicola was keeping out of the way. Their host – Flavio – was doing much the same, for the collapse of Langrand-Dumonceau's empire was sending tremors through the world of the fashionable and the well-born. Pillars of old Europe had been shaken, as case after case dragged through the Belgian courts, revealing that the fallen Midas's collaborators – like the horses in his stables, most were thoroughbreds – must either have been cretinously ignorant of his fraudulent practices or have culpably connived. Indeed, said those who chose to think them cretins, he could as well have harnessed the blue bloods to his carriages and seated the horses in his boardrooms.

Slanderous charges in *La Cote Libre de la Bourse de Bruxelles* had turned out not to be slanderous at all, and Belgium's Royal Attorney and Attorney General had been dismissed for failure to recognise this, while its Prime Minister, a Langrand associate, was being challenged to resign.

Rome was a Limbo.

The French troops would not be back, for Prussia, contrary to predictions, was winning its war against France. Certitudes were collapsing. Yet here was Prospero demanding Nicola's submission to the doctrine of papal infallibility! Should he give it as a kindness to a crazed old man? He had neither the charity nor the cynicism.

Flavio admitted that the Belgian Courts were likely to charge him with embezzling sums which Langrand's books showed as having been paid to him. The truth was that they had been spent here in Rome. On bribes to churchmen – but how prove this?

'They don't give receipts.'

He also revealed that Victor Emmanuel had been ready to dismiss his ministers and govern by decree. If he had gone through with this – a royal *coup d'état* – his Finance Minister designate was to have accepted Langrand's plan to buy the Church property in Italy. The bribed churchmen would have secured Roman agreement and everyone would have been rich. The money Langrand and Flavio were being acused of taking would have multiplied, the ruined investors would be counting their dividends, and the Church would have its fourteen hundred million francs! 'It was all a matter of faith. I told you at the time. It was like St Peter walking on water! But Peter lost his nerve. And so, therefore, did the king!' Flavio kept repeating this in differing moods – drunk, sober, despairing, marvelling. Faith! Why had nobody had it?

'And what about truth?' asked Nicola on hearing this speech for perhaps the twentieth time.

'There's no such thing!' roared the duke. 'It's a discredited Voltairean notion! Reality is shifting, multiple and not to be relied on, yet Langrand and I are being crucified in its name. By Liberals. Liberals make a fetish of it because they don't understand the world. You'll see and so will they. Give them power for a bit and they'll begin to understand.'

Prospero said much the same thing. Now, he argued, was not the time for points of doctrine but for loyalty to the faith which could move mountains and stop armies! His Holiness was threatened by the Garibaldini who, now that the French were gone, could be expected at any moment. He needed the comfort of our support. Was Nicola going to give it? If he was, he should write his act of submission and let Prospero take it back to Rome.

Nicola temporised. He had promised fellow members of the Minority to hold firm until their return. But, said Prospero, the Garibaldini might be here by then. 'Ah,' asked the cruel Nicola, 'have you so little faith?'

A thought had struck him. If they did get here soon, then the judiciary would be in their hands and might seek Amandi's killer. But there was no time to ponder this, for he had to deal with Prospero who was grown emotional and hard to put off. Now, he insisted, when there was nothing to be gained from supporting the Church, was surely the time to support it.

'Give your *placet*. It's an act of loyalty. All the bishops are making it. Mérode has already given in and so have several of the fifty-five signatories who said they would hold out. Oh, don't be surprised! There are no secrets.'

'Were you sent or did you come?'

'Both. His Holiness says that all who oppose him will be struck down. So why wait for this to happen? Look, I know hateful things were said and done. But the Garibaldini will be more hateful. Radicals always are. Remember 1792! Remember Napoleon's treatment of Pius VII!'

'I won't. Pius IX has made too much capital out of it – yet his own worst experience was to be the house guest of the King of Naples. Why can't he forgive? The Church needs calling to acount, not loyalty.'

This, he now saw, was why he was eager to bring the wretched Maximin to book. He wanted clarity, a trial and a summing-up. A sad

556

ruthlessness stiffened him – he felt it in his body – as he groped towards a way to cut himself off from his own tradition. The confessional, an instrument for controlling consciences and inner motivations, was dark, curtained and forgiving. But the courtroom threw light on what people actually did.

Thirty-one

Flavio was encouraging his guests to drink up his best wines lest Italian looters soon be drinking them instead. Let this be a libation to a dying Rome.

This flippancy upset Prospero, who countered it with accounts of Mastai's prayerful serenity and the stir at Antonelli's office, which he described as awash in intercepted telegrams from foreign embassies. The same office was leaking false information – which came back to it in the telegrams! He laughed robustly. Human failure was grist to his milling faith.

Before leaving, he promised to obtain permission for Nicola to remain a while longer. 'For reasons of health. This will give you time to make your act of submission. Don't delay too long. Remember: the See of Imola won't be vacant long and won't go to a rebel!'

So Nicola stayed on with Flavio to whom, one polleny evening, bright with fireflies, he talked of Maria Gatti's son and the experience of coming face to face with an image of his youthful self. He did this to distract his host from the bulletins about the Langrand court cases which kept humming over the wires. The latest was that five directors had been declared personally bankrupt. Langrand himself was thought to be in hiding in London.

'He was here for a while,' said Flavio. 'In this house.'

It was a time of confidences. *Villeggiatura*: visits to neighbouring villas, drives, walks and mutual commiseration. They talked of Langrand and, one by one, Nicola learned the names of the Roman officials who had pocketed bribes. One was the man who had received him in Monseigneur Randi's stead and eluded his questions.

'Oh yes, he's bribable! *You* should have bribed him, Nicola! Not that he'd necessarily have produced the goods. He didn't for me.'

They were at a neighbour's, watching tennis balls skew off a bumpy court, when news came that the French Emperor had been defeated at a place called Sedan. He had been ill, suffering from a stone in the bladder, and was said to have rouged his cheeks lest his pallor depress his men. Yet, after the surrender, they turned their backs on him, and the Pope – the news came through Rome – greeted his protector's Calvary with a nursery pun. 'He's lost what? Sedan? *Ses dents*? Aha, he's lost his teeth!'

The chubby old man had the impulses of a spoilt child.

'Well, he'll soon lose his!' said Flavio.

'He doesn't think so,' said their informant. 'His new visionary tells him Rome will not fall, so he's serene!'

Thanks to the electric telegraph, news now came thick and fast. A republic had been declared in France and agreements made with the defunct Empire rendered void – which worried the Italian regime as much as it did the Pope's. For what if the French were to revive the old idea of setting up a sister republic in Rome? This could take over the peninsula! Alarmed, the Italian monarch sent an ambassador to Pius.

'The Jesuits at the Romano are burning papers,' said Flavio. 'The people say so. They always know. No doubt the police at Montecitorio are having a little bonfire too.'

He and Nicola were back in Rome.

'I'm going there!' said Nicola. 'Before they burn Amandi's file. Was what you told me about bribing that policeman true? I don't want to draw a blank at this late stage of things.' It was indeed late. Days ago, a notice in the *Gazzetta Ufficiale di Firenze* had announced that the King of Italy had ordered his troops into Roman territory and declared a state of siege.

At Montecitorio, Nicola learned that the man he was seeking had resigned from the police and been appointed chaplain to a convent. A clerk winked. 'He'll be safer there when the Italians come!'

Nicola took the address of the convent and set off again. All along the way French, Prussian and English flags flew on private *palazzi* whose owners had obtained the protection of foreign powers. Some doors were locked and barricaded but, by contrast and despite assemblies being forbidden, sightseers drifted about and a woman described a visit to the city walls, where an officer had allowed her up to view the defences. She sounded amused and so did youths who had climbed some scaffolding to take a look at the enemy camp.

The nuns were expecting the worst. A frightened doorkeeper interviewed Nicola through a fist-sized shutter and said she had orders to let no one in. However, when he claimed to come from Montecitorio, the door was opened.

'The Turks aren't coming!' he teased the two lay sisters who had opened it, but failed to raise a smile.

The chaplain, having shriven all the nuns, was restoring himself with hot chocolate. He was unshaven and his cup rattled as he replaced it in its saucer. The spoon fell. Nicola refused his offer of hospitality and told him that his friend, Duke Cesarini, was in a dilemma. He must account to the Belgian courts for monies spent here in Rome to promote his scheme to save our Treasury.

Dunking a piece of *pan di Spagna* in his chocolate, the chaplain avoided Nicola's eye and waited to hear more.

The trouble was, said Nicola, that the duke's notebooks listed the names of those who had received emoluments; but if these were turned over to courts which, alas, were in a priest-baiting mood, the emoluments would be described in the press as bribes. Scandal must ensue and careers suffer. 'I have been wondering how to advise the duke as to where his duty lies.'

The chaplain, grasping the nettle, asked what the bishop wanted and Nicola asked for the police file on the cardinal's death. 'We spoke about it once in your office.'

'Yes,' said the ex-policeman, 'but I can only repeat what I told you then. There is nothing at police headquarters. Nobody wants to keep compromising papers about and no file was opened.' He added, in a little rush, that as a proof of good will, he could offer the bishop a related item of information: 'Monsignor Randi knows that before Monseigneur Darboy left for Paris you gave him a certain secret paper. Now, as Randi has two audiences a week with His Holiness, he will certainly have told him this and Monseigneur Darboy will equally certainly be ordered to hand it over. That's all the help I can give you, Monsignore. Are you sure I can't offer you a cup of chocolate?'

Nicola accepted and the man rang for a second cup. Waiting for it, he fidgeted and, as Nicola drank the sweet, foaming draught, kept stealing glances at him. Close by nuns' voices were reciting a prayer.

'You want something else from me, don't you, Monsignore?'

Nicola observed that the Italians would soon be here. Some, having suffered at the hands of the papal police, might be vindictive with an ex-policeman who lacked protection. He had friends – he named Martelli – able to provide it.

The chaplain asked with some spirit if the Monsignore was leaving the ship even before it sank.

'I,' said Nicola, 'am not leaving. But I saw the result of a lynching back in 1848. A man called Nardoni. I saw his mangled body and hope you will help me avoid another such memory.' He laid out his demands. The ex-policeman was to go back to his office and manufacture a letter acknowledging payment by Duke Cesarini of an unspecified sum to the Governor of Rome for distribution to such charities as the said governor thought fit. The governor's seal should be appended and the date be three years old.

'But Monsignore . . . a forgery . . .'

'It is a short cut rather than a forgery. The duke *did* distribute large sums, as I think you know, but there is no time to solicit receipts from those who got them. As it is, this will have to be done today. The Italians . . .'

The chaplain gave in.

20 September

Two days later Rome was awoken by cannon booming from three different points. This then was it! It was 5.15 in the morning by the new way of reckoning and Nicola and the duke had, like many others, been up half the night. A rumour had got about that the invasion was for today and, sure enough, here it was. Would the people rise and give the Italians a pretext for coming in? No. The people, like themselves, were sitting tight behind closed doors, eating their stored provisions and perhaps killing time with card games and other indoor pastimes.

News of blood-letting in France was said to have upset the Pope and dissuaded him from authorising a last-ditch fight. It would have been a carnage. His men were outnumbered ten to one!

'The Zouaves will be furious! Maybe they'll persuade him to change his mind.'

'No chance. He'll let it go on just long enough to show that force was used and that he didn't give away God's patrimony!'

561

'A last pageant!'

At ten came news that white flags had been raised on the Vatican and the Quirinal – bed sheets in both cases. The duke insisted on going out. 'You stay here,' he warned Nicola. 'Priests will be in danger. I'll bring back news.'

But it was days before news could be sifted from rumour.

For a while, it was believed that Monseigneur Randi had been lynched in his office by the vindictive riffraff which had arrived with the Italian Army. Then it turned out that he had been lent a carriage in the nick of time and driven hell for leather to the Città Leonina, that small area bounded by the Santo Spirito Bastions, the Castel Sant Angelo and the Vatican Hill into which the Pope and his aides were now crammed like so many sardines in a barrel. Yes, that was all the armistice was leaving His Holiness! And yes, it had been signed. Needs must. Randi was safe but not everyone had been so lucky. Reports were murky but there had been savage scenes, and one who had had to be rescued from a lynch-mob was la Diotallevi. Martelli and some Italian friends had intervened at the last minute and spirited her away.

Nicola learned from the Zouaves' chaplain, Monseigneur Daniel, how, after the ceasefire, Zouaves had been insulted, spat on, and even killed by what the chaplain refused to believe were Romans.

'Look at the faces in the streets,' invited Daniel, whose own face was that of a man who had drunk vinegar. 'They're scum, Monsignore! Vermin! Trainloads of them are being imported gratis to vote in the so-called plebiscite! A sinister *canaille*!'

Enfevered by loathing, the chaplain described girls dancing with the invaders, and his horror on visiting General Kanzler in the single room which the Minister for Arms was obliged to share with his wife and small son! 'They put a screen around the bed!' he explained in shock. But no wonder God's servants had no place to lay their heads! The Italians were seizing Church property throughout the city. Even the Quirinal Palace had been seized in a scene – though the chaplain did not know this – orchestrated by Cardinal Antonelli. It had been agreed during the preliminary negotiations that it should be handed over. But when the moment came, the cardinal packed the place with the families of papal dependants and refused to give up the keys. The ensuing lock-picking and forced evictions provided a tale calculated to distress the faithful in distant countries and kindle energies in the papal cause. Christ had given Peter the keys of the kingdom – but then the lock-pickers came! A powerful parable!

562

Daniel's was a high-coloured face which one could imagine being painted by some unknown Maestro on a pocked wooden panel. Nicola had sought him out in the hope of learning something about the whereabouts of Maximin Giraud. But it proved impossible to wrench the conversation round to this. The chaplain was full of his last hours with Mastai. 'Daniel,' His Holiness had said to him, 'we are in the lion's cage!' And it was a double pun, for His Holiness was indeed caged up in the Leonine City. The chaplain's eyes were fierce but wet. How, he asked, had Nicola held on to *his* apartment?

It was private property, Nicola told him. It did not belong to the Church. Daniel looked as though the distinction astonished him. He brooded a while then burst out with the remark that disloyalty would surely draw down heaven's wrath. 'And sooner rather than later. God has already punished the absconding French. Has it escaped your notice, Monsignore, that Paris fell to the Prussians on the selfsame day as Rome did to Victor Emmanuel?' The chaplain's face, which was as raw as flayed meat, thrust itself close. His breath was sulphurous. 'Even if the Empire had not fallen, it might not have helped us, for Monseigneur Darboy is not loyal. There are Judases in the episcopacy, Monsignore! They too should be punished! We,' said Monseigneur Daniel, 'will have a tale to tell in France!'

Nicola, ill at ease, but unable to escape, had to hear of the Pope's last review of the Zouaves, when, preparing to deliver his blessing from a Vatican window, Pius found his voice failing and fell sobbing into his chamberlain's arms.

Monseigneur Daniel's voice shook as he described the shout from the piazza. '*Viva Pio IX*! Long live our king!' cried the chaplain, in imitation of the Zouaves' farewell. Then his control cracked and he wept into his handkerchief.

Rome, Autumn 1870

It was over. Rome was part of Italy and the new order settling in. Pope and Curia had shut themselves up in the Vatican.

Riffraff disported themselves in clerical cafés and priests who had been in hiding were starting to emerge. Some looked dazed. Others scoured the papers for signs of hope., One market day a peasant, indignant at the new taxes, had yelled a defiant '*Viva Pio Nono*!'

563

Flavio had gone to Belgium, taking his receipt from the Governor of Rome. This would save him from the embezzlement charge, but others, he now admitted, were pending. A legacy from Amandi had left Nicola financially indpendent, which was lucky, for the See of Imola had gone to someone else and he was in an administrative Limbo. This and the dwindled reach of the papal censorship left him free to join in the dispirited exchanges going on among the Minority bishops, many of whom now faced troubles at home.

French friends sent gloomy letters from their fallen country, often relegating to postcripts the question which had kept them so painfully on tenterhooks for eighteen months. PS

> The Bull proroguing the Council leaves our bishops in a worse case than ever, since pressures are being brought on those who have not submitted. The nuncio appeals over our heads to our priests with the result that Bayeux has had to go into hiding, and Autun's efforts to explain his *non placet* to his *curés* were drowned out by foot-stamping. PPS Monseigneur Darboy is shut up in Paris by the siege, so we have no news of his state of mind. As recently as last September, however, he spoke of the doctrine as 'inept' and the Church as run 'like a huckstery'. Burn this.

Repeated messages from Prospero reminded Nicola that his own submission was waited on.

In December Rome was flooded. The waters, as though rebaptizing the city, immersed it to the depths of three, then four metres, and gave King Victor Emmanuel a pretext for a first flying visit to comfort his new subjects and show his excommunicated face. Gossip claimed that he had tried to abdicate from very shame and that his ministers had had to stiffen him. To thwart them, Cardinal Antonelli, now a full-time *agent provocateur*, protested at the royal visit, as he had at the occupation of the Quirinal Palace and other iniquities. Formal protests dispatched to nuncios all over Europe were a way of affirming the Pope's surviving sovereignty.

Meanwhile, taking their cue from the Curia, some of the great Roman families sealed up their front doors as a snub to the new regime. But they were not greatly missed, as new arrivals from Turin and Florence were disembarking from every train. *Piazze*, lately as dreamy as cloisters, bustled, and the wild flowers which had adorned their cobblestones died beneath the heels of new citizens, while old ones complained angrily of the noise.

News kept reaching Nicola of Minority bishops who were still staunch and of those who had recanted. In the privacy of episcopal palaces

564

throughout Europe, struggles were painfully coming to a head. Stiffened by their country's victory, the Germans were resisting best.

By early February the last French bishops to hold out were Darboy and Dupanloup. Then, on the 18th, Dupanloup wrote his letter of consent, and on 2nd March, one month after the capitulation of Paris to the Prussians, its archbishop surrendered to the Pope. Some weeks later, a letter came from one of the priests who had been with Darboy in Rome. Its gist was that Monseigneur wanted Monsignor Santi to know his motives for recanting.

The Archbishop of Paris had not, said the priest, abandoned his principles. He did, however, feel obliged to postpone the struggle for them. As Monsignor Santi must surely guess, the decision had been taken after much agony of conscience. What he might not so easily imagine was the devastation here. This was no time for controversy. Events in France and Italy had inflicted wounds which it would be wicked to exacerbate. Unity was now the prime concern and Darboy believed that Catholics must be seen to work for it if they did not want religion to become hateful to their compatriots. Accordingly, despite his own links to the fallen Empire, he had ordered a hymn begging God's blessing on the new French Republic to be sung in all his churches and, in a similar spirit, made his submission to the Pope. Monsignor Santi must not despair. The justice he craved could be sought in happier times. For now, Monseigneur begged him to believe in his paternal love and in his loyalty to the memory of the late Cardinal Amandi. A postscript, written in the priest's own name, noted that Monseigneur's embrace of the new republic had angered many. Monarchists were especially enraged. 'The pursuit of peace,' concluded the letter, 'is a *via dolorosa.*'

There was no mention of Giraud's retraction. Nicola, who had been unable to request it while Darboy was besieged in Paris, decided to do so now. This, however, was delicate in the light of its controversial nature and Darboy's mood. He was pondering how best to couch his request when he received the following letter:

Monsignore,

I am writing on behalf of our unhappy archbishop in the hope that his Roman friends may be able to help him.

The rabble has seized Paris and the Government withdrawn to Versailles. The victorious Prussians, having signed an armistice, are letting us destroy each other and the rabble leaders – they style themselves 'the

Commune' – having taken Monseigneur and several other priests hostage, threaten to shoot them unless they can exchange them for a prisoner held by the Government, a certain Auguste Blanqui.

Adolph Thiers, Head of the Executive of the French Republic, appears reluctant to make the exchange. This baffles us and we are urging foreign diplomatists and other persons of rank and influence to intervene while Monsieur Thiers is parleying with the archbishop's envoy and there is still hope. I appeal to you most urgently, Monsignore, to bring to bear any influence you can.

The situation is grave and the mob enfevered. Having lost a war and endured the privations of a four-month investment by the Prussians, they want scapegoats. Unsurprisingly their rage has turned against their old *souffre douleur*, the Church. Communard newspapers are filled with ravings about monks found storing gunpowder, using bullets for rosary beads, etc.

Monsieur Thiers' motives are hard to fathom but we have indications that the archbishop could have fallen victim to ultramontane spite, which an appeal to the Holy Father could certainly disarm.

I have the honour, Monsignore, to express my deepest and most devoted respects, etc.

Nicola took this to Prospero. 'Your heart,' he hoped, 'will tell you what to do. If it does not, let me implore you to help. Unlike you, I have no influence here. Besides, I am going to France.'

Prospero was horrified. France? Was Nicola insane? What about loyalty at this time of trial? During the Pope's Calvary . . .

'Ah,' said Nicola, 'you choose to see him as Christ. But what if one saw him as Caiaphas?'

'Stop!' Prospero, picking up a poker, began to bang it against his coal scuttle.

'The Roman mode of refutation!' roared Nicola, trying to be heard above the din.

'What?' Prospero had deafened himself.

'You've just demonstrated it.' He stood up. 'I'm leaving.'

'No! Listen! Unless and until you give in your letter of consent, I shall not help Darboy, who is reaping what he sowed. He consorted with Liberals and is now in the hands of the Reds.'

'Are you offering me a bargain? Good! Write the letter and I'll sign it. But you must promise not to submit it until Pius has made an appeal on Darboy's behalf or Darboy has been released.'

'Agreed.' Prospero sat down, penned a few lines, dried them, and handed the paper to Nicola who read: '*Ego profiteor pure et sempliciter toto*

566

corde et anima adhaerere definitionis dogmaticis a Sanctitate tua prolatis die 18 juli habita.' He signed.

'Goodbye, then,' said Prospero. 'I hope I am in your prayers as often as you are in mine. As for the paper which I suspect you of hoping to recover from Darboy, it has no doubt been burned. The nuncio wrote that Darboy prudently burned a lot of papers connected with the Council during the Prussian siege of Paris.'

Nicola told him that he was thinking more of Darboy than of the paper. The living took precedence over the dead.

A week later he was in the drawing room of his friend the Abbé Delisle. The room, fragrant with the Sicilian blood oranges which he had brought as a gift, hummed like an apiary and showed signs that the unwary risked being stung.

A young woman cried, 'It's despicable!'

She was his host's sister or perhaps cousin. Nicola had not got this clear, for sisters, aunts, nieces and even a sprinkling of pious uncles had come in throngs to hear his news of Rome.

'I couldn't keep them away!' The abbé clasped his friend's hands and smiled in rueful amusement, for the guests, already oblivious of Rome, were embroiled in tussles of their own. 'Just as well,' he whispered, 'they're not of our way of thinking at all!'

All the guests had the same high colouring as their host, with bright blue eyes, hair like dimmed brass, and the forthright manner which had drawn Nicola to him when they met last year in Rome.

'There are Judases among the clergy!' cried the young woman.

'There may be an explanation!'

'There is: he's saving his neck!' She arched her own superbly slim-stemmed one, as though defying the guillotine. Her coiled hair flamed and Nicola thought of the Maid of Orléans. There was a combustive spark in her and Orléans was where they were, in the diocese of Monseigneur Dupanloup who, though a Liberal Catholic, was politically a royalist.

Getting here had been slow. The railways were disrupted by the recent war and progress through a wrecked but buoyant landscape – spring greenery was pushing through twisted girders – had made the traveller feel like a man doing the Stations of the Cross. All along the way he had seen maimed men and convoys of returning prisoners, gutted buildings and neglected fields. Yet the war's last act might be still to come and its victim could, said the abbé's guests, be Monseigneur Darboy whose Vicar-General, the Abbé Lagarde, had let him down and abandoned him in prison, apparently – but could this be true? – to save his own skin. Lagarde, a priest and the son of a baron, was a man whose word should have been his bond – and yet . . .

The Vicar-General, Delisle explained, had been released from the Paris prison, where he had been held with the archbishop, so that he might go to Versailles to negotiate an exchange of hostages with the Government. On leaving, he had promised to return at once, but two weeks had now passed without a word from him.

'And the rabble are making capital out of it! Listen.' The young woman took a newspaper from her reticule. 'This is one of their papers, *The Cry of the People*.' She read: '"It is our duty to put on record the fact that the French clergy in the persons of Monseigneur Darboy and his Vicar-General has betrayed an oath sworn on the archbishop's head. Let Paris judge on which side lie moderation, honour and justice and which must take responsibility for the outcome."' She dropped the declamatory tone in which she had been reading. 'He's let us all down.'

Watching a blush creep up her face, Nicola guessed that she was embarrassed at having lent her histrionic talents to the Commune's rhetoric. Poor Maid of Orléans, he thought. Her voices are garbled.

She had, however, found a more congenial topic. It seemed that a woman she knew had been slipping in and out of Paris, carrying letters from loyal priests to the Vicar-General in Versailles, pleading with him to keep his word and return.

Her listeners marvelled. A woman courier! How did she manage? The Paris stations were guarded and there was no longer a direct service to Versailles. And wasn't the Commune shooting anyone suspected of having contacts with that town?

'I naturally can't tell you how she does it – only that last time she saw the abbé, she flung herself at his feet, held up her crucifix and conjured him to return to his archbishop.'

'And what did he say?'

'Mumbled lamely about things he could not disclose.'

'How shameful – and how splendid of her!'

'Yes,' agreed the Maid of Orléans and gave Nicola her Communard paper as a memento of the trials of France. He wondered could the woman courier be herself?

When the guests had gone, he and Delisle talked more easily.

'Might they really shoot Monseigneur Darboy?'

568

'Yes,' said the abbé. 'Their hatred is visceral. They hate the Army because it lost the war and the Church because it abetted the Empire's twenty years of oppression – which it did. I was on eggs just now because to say so can start a war in one's own drawing room. People like my cousin, you see, think the Church was right.'

'The Maid of Orléans?'

'A good name for her. Only she would burn others rather than herself and now those others have Darboy in their hands. Forgive me if I tell you something distasteful, but Paris is not Rome and you should know how battles there are fought. What started the present turmoil was a squabble over cannons which the mob did not want turned over to the Prussians, despite the armistice. Well, it seized them and the French troops sent to get them disobeyed their general's order to fire. Chaos broke out. Two generals were shot and their heads beaten to a pulp, whereupon two women stepped from the crowd, squatted over their bodies, and urinated on them. I heard this from an eyewitness – an officer who was lucky to get away alive. That's to tell you the sort of rage which has been unstoppered. It is old and sour and goes back to the Revolution of eighty-nine and the revenge taken later on the revolution-aries. Its targets are ourselves and the Army: *couvent et caserne*. The Reds are ritualists. Why do you think they arrested Monseigneur?'

'To treat him as they did the generals? Then why offer to exchange him for this man What's-his-name?'

'Blanqui. Auguste Blanqui. Because that too would be a ritual, an exchange of the first priest of Paris for the man whose newspaper bore the slogan "War to the supernatural". Rigault, the Procureur, says he would happily strangle the last priest with the guts of the last king. It is as well to know these things.'

Nicola asked whether Delisle knew of *conservative* hatred for Darboy.

'Well,' said the abbé, 'Monseigneur is the devout, honourable, and ambitious son of a village grocer: a vexing mixture for the better born who have been obliged to play second fiddle to him. They too might relish his downfall.'

'But he's in the hands of the Left!'

'And it would be so easy to leave him there! There need be no plot. A climate of opinion is created and the thing goes from there. How?' Delisle shrugged. 'By reminding the faithful that he is in bad odour with the Pope and that, now that the Empire is gone, we need a less imperial archbishop. By chatter from people like the blind, blue-blooded Mon-seigneur de Ségur who has been spreading a story about the Emperor's having had a plan to found a schismatic French Church with Darboy at its head. It's slander, but mud sticks because Ségur was known to be Mastai's spy and the uncharitable say that Darboy slapped him when his tittletattle to Pius got back to him. According to some reports, the spy then slid to his knees and turned the other cheek! Don't laugh, Monsignore. This is all deadly serious, because those who peddle such tales do so as part of a scheme to bring back the Bourbons so that they, in turn, may restore the Temporal Power. Wheels within wheels! All things work together for the greater glory of the Comte de Chambord, known to Legitimists as Henri V. The connection escapes you? Wait. You should know that royalist bishops are circulating petitions to our new National Assembly, begging it to intervene on behalf of the Pope. Intervene how? With our ruined armies? While the Prussians are still in France? They know it can't be done but deceive their flocks so as to drum up support for Chambord who says that *he*, if restored, would do it. This manoeuvre is known as the Union of the Throne and the Altar! Does it not strike you that its supporters might prefer a new archbishop? Of course they would! Darboy always irked them, but he became intolerable the day he rallied to our new Republic and had hymns sung for it in the churches of his diocese. It was the patriotic thing to do since we were at war, but the *Domine salvam fac Republicam* stuck in monarchist gullets. It is hard though – in the ordinary way – to replace an archbishop!'

The abbé smiled mournfully. 'Do you think me fanciful? Look.' Rummaging in a drawer he took out a parcel tied with white ribbon. It contained two portraits. One was of Pius IX looking out through the bars of a prison. The other was of the Comte de Chambord. 'My cousin says it is the duty of every loyal priest to display these, and, as you see, she has provided me with them. A test? Very likely! Our so-called Government of National Unity is menaced from the Right as well as the Left and Monsieur Thiers will have to work hard to keep a balance. Darboy is a nuisance. Thiers claims that his refusal to exchange hostages is based on principle – one must not encourage hostage-taking, etc. – but for a different archbishop more might have been done. Not that Thiers need plot, you understand. His nickname is Foutriquet or Little Squirt. Little squirts do not plan crimes. They let them happen.'

'I think I shall go to Versailles.'

'Well, the nuncio is there and so are Thiers and Lagarde. I can give you a letter to help you find lodgings. Without help you won't get a room. There are suddenly 40,000 extra people in a town of 250,000. I, however, have a cousin . . .'

'You are well supplied with them.'

'They have their good points.'

At breakfast the abbé was glum with guilt over his lack of charity the night before.

'In school,' Nicola told him, 'the Jesuits told us it was all right to spy for God – so why not gossip for Him? What you told me was useful. I think they might absolve you.'

'We may have misjudged *them*.' The abbé, still in an atoning mood, had heard that the Jesuits in Communard gaols were being edifyingly heroic. A man he knew had gone to the Dépôt on the night of the great arrest – 4th April – and, passing a cell door, heard the rallying words '"*Ibant gaudentes*!" The martyrs went to their fate with a joy we may now hope to share!' It was Father Olivaint, the Jesuit Superior, trying to hearten those around him.

Fastidiously the abbé removed a cooling skin from his bowl of *café au lait*. 'I suppose,' he brooded, 'that if Jesuit zeal is now for sacrificing themselves rather than others, they may indeed find joy in prison!' With distaste, he considered then ate the dripping spoonful.

'It could be a legend!' said the cynical Nicola.

The abbé looked depressed. 'Maybe,' he wondered, 'a spell in prison would do us all good? Not that it helped poor Lagarde!'

Nicola asked what they should think of *him* and Delisle said his task might be impossible because the Communard press was provoking Thiers so as to scupper negotiations. 'You should see what they print! Accusations that Blanqui is being tortured and the like.'

'But why start negotiations then undermine them?'

'They're divided! When Paris falls, as it must, the moderates inside it will hope to save their necks while the rest will try to force them to fight on. To do that they must make surrender unthinkable. Kill Darboy and perhaps the Jesuits too.'

There was a silence. 'Do you suppose,' Nicola wondered, 'bigots make better martyrs?'

For moments, the abbé wore the look of a tempted man. Then he succumbed. 'Who,' he blurted, 'can say that martyrdom does good? It rouses a revengeful spirit and what good is that unless we, like inquisitors, make war on our own people?' He wriggled as though his

571

skin irked him. Peace was his ideal, and those threatening it made him bellicose. There were, he argued, better sacrifices. Had not Lacordaire argued that to become a priest was one in itself? 'He said that any man who can see through the aching envelope which cramps us to the undying image of God contributes to the blood spilled for salvation. "*Tu es sacerdos in aeternum*"! That's not about blood-letting! As you and I agreed in Rome, my dear Monsignore, it is better to reconcile than to fight!' Delisle's smile celebrated a precarious armistice with himself.

Nicola's experiences were leading him the other way. He remarked evasively: 'You have it by heart!'

The abbé's face was alight. 'For my generation, Lacordaire was the great influence. His message was to bring France back to the faith in ways she could accept, with tact and patriotism. He was the sort of man who makes this Pope see red: a Liberal Catholic like my bishop, Monseigneur Dupanloup, thanks to whose protection I am free to speak to you as I do. For now, a bishop in his own diocese is still strong.'

'Except for Darboy.'

The abbé sighed.

The Abbé Lagarde was a youngish man with a surge of black hair. Painted by Murillo, his might have been the features of a saint – or have had, in a livelier mood, the appeal of those youths in Baroque paintings who hold a piece of fruit between their lips. Today they looked pent and guarded, as though the Vicar-General were censoring his breath, and a grey smudging of the skin – poor health? Blunt razor? – had the dimming effect of a mask.

Nicola asked what hope he had of obtaining Giraud's retraction. It was a neutral question unlikely to catch the abbé on the raw.

Lagarde told him that the archbishop's papers had been seized by the Communards. 'Who knows why? Perhaps they are constructing a gospel acccording to themselves? That could be, for the last letter I received from Monseigneur was in duplicate. Odd, don't you think, that they should make him write two? My guess,' said the abbé, 'is that one copy had been intended for the press which propagates a gospel in which I am publicly dishonoured. Even Monseigneur must believe this version since, as my letters to him are intercepted, I dare not give him my reasons for lingering here. Forgive me. This is a long answer to your question.'

Nicola bowed and left. What else was there to say? As he went out, he saw a young woman waiting, and wondered whether she was the courier, come again to beg the abbé to stop being Judas.

His next call was on the nuncio, Monsignor Chigi.

'Welcome back!' cried His Excellency festively, but meant to the fold rather than to France. He had a copy of the latest *Osservatore Romano* containing a notice of Nicola's assent to the dogma. The bishop was the very last Italian to submit, said the nuncio, and to celebrate invited him to dinner this evening. We could talk then. Unfortunately, just now . . . Smiling with affable regret, Chigi sighed at the press of business with which he had to cope. Nicola left.

Had Pius made an appeal for Darboy? By the terms of Nicola's agreement with Prospero, the news in the *Osservatore* meant that the Pope must have done so. Else Prospero would surely not have submitted Nicola's letter of consent. Hoping to hearten the unfortunate Lagarde, Nicola returned to tell him this.

To his surprise, the abbé seemed already heartened. The bishop must have brought him luck. He had had news from Paris and, without wishing to divulge too much, could reveal that a plan – not the one involving Monsieur Thiers, but a parallel backstairs effort – was on the point of success. 'We must pray, Monsignore! We must knock on all doors.'

Nicola told his own news then, and the two celebrated modestly, as a footman brought in a decanter and a plate of *petits fours* with the compliments of the abbé's host, a Monsieur Perrot, who was, said the abbé, the deputy for l'Oise.

They discovered that they had mutual acquaintances and this so disarmed Lagarde that he began to tell of the obstacles encountered here in Versailles, where the Government was a distrustful of the hostages as of their captors. 'Monsieur Thiers,' he revealed, 'says that Monseigneur is now a blind instrument of the Commune!'

'Because he asked to be exchanged?'

'Because he acknowledges in his letters that the Communards have grievances. Unfortunately, he mentioned "barbaric acts" committed by our troops. Monsieur Thiers was indignant. Monseigneur could not have foreseen that passions here would be so inflamed and his charity seen as, well, frankly, cowardice. His old reputation as a friend of free-thinkers counts against him too. Indeed, I am as worried for his honour as his life . . .' Wearily, the abbé batted a hand across his eyes. 'You find me,' he confessed, 'in a weak moment. Hope softens me. Warmth after cold is treacherous. I must not burden you with dangerous knowledge.'

That evening at the nuncio's residence the first person Nicola saw was Amandi's old major-domo, Gianni, who was wearing Monsignor Chigi's livery and wept at the sight of him. Seeing Nicola also begin to give way, he drew him into a small room. Gianni was motherly. Have a little cry, he recommended. We can stay here a while – unless Monsignore would rather be alone?

'No, no!' Nicola felt overcome. *Famulus* was a servant, after all, and it was painful to remember how Cardinal Amandi's *familia* had broken up.

Gianni produced a glass of something consoling.

'Do you want me greeting His Excellency with brandy on my breath?'

'Thought of that, didn't I?' Proffering a peppermint fondant, Gianni dropped his voice. 'I have information which will interest your lordship.'

Nicola was amused. 'So you keep up your old ways! Isn't it harder to keep informed here, Gianni?'

Of course it was, whispered Gianni. Of course! Servants were worked harder, so how could they find time to swop information? It was astonishing how hard the French worked, though, lately, you could see the need for it, what with having to clean up after the Prussian pigs, if calling them that wasn't an insult to the pig, which was one of God's creatures and clean when you gave him a chance to be – unlike Prussians. *They* were dirty animals and so was their King Emperor who – Gianni had this from the footman who'd had to deal with the outcome – had shat in a window bay, *si proprio cacato!*, when he'd billeted himself on the Archbishop of Rheims, then wiped his bum on the curtains! So the French had been kept busy cleaning the stain on their honour, not to speak of their furnishings. They'd even cleaned the Paris streets after the Prussian victory march. With lye! Not but that they'd have to be washed in blood one day too. Redeemed, said Gianni, lapsing into a vocabulary redolent of his employers' calling. But to come back to French servants. Gianni was training a few likely fellows to pick up information. That was how he knew that Monsignore had visited the Abbé Lagarde twice today – 'Eh, Monsignore! Am I well informed?' –

which meant that Gianni's tidbit must be of interest. It came from the Préfecture where Monsieur l'Abbé and Monsieur Thiers used to hold talks. No more, though! Monsieur Thiers had *broken them off a week ago*. Lowering his voice further, Gianni whispered that since then the abbé had stayed here for one reason only: to fool the Communards who, if they knew the talks were stopped and they weren't going to get their man Blanko, would shoot the archbishop! *Pan!* Gianni laid a finger next to his nose and tapped it. 'You'd better go into the drawing room, now, Monsignore.'

Nicola was dismayed to find Louis Veuillot among the nuncio's guests. The journalist, however, behaved as though they were fast friends and drew him into an exchange with an Englishman who, having come to distribute food donated by the population of London, was one of the few people able to go freely in and out of Paris. 'Mr Blount is on good terms with the *Communeux*!' sneered Veuillot.

The Englishman retorted that, whatever their practice, some of the Communards' principles were admirable. Veuillot asked if it was true that Cluseret, their War Minister, had been General in Chief of the Fenians in England. Blount hadn't heard this.

'Scum!' said Veuillot.

At dinner, Nicola sat next to a frilly Polish lady who confided that there was a crusade among her countrymen to save the archbishop. 'Our gentlemen fight on both sides, so we have access to General Cluseret through Jaroslaw Dombrowski, the Commandant of Paris. Cluseret,' she lowered her voice, 'likes money!'

'Surely, Madame, we should not talk of such things?'

The lady looked surprised. 'But we are among ourselves!'

He remarked that there were servants in the room.

'Servants!' Her imagination leapfrogged past his. 'French Jacobins? In the pay of the Commune? Are we safe?'

He assured her that servants were rarely revolutionaries. But the lady kept looking over her shoulder and when a decanter slid past it, so forgot her breeding as to knock it away. The wine made a stain in the damask and the subsequent mopping brought a lull in which Veuillot could be heard defending his decision to reprint attacks made by Communard papers on the Abbé Lagarde.

These, objected the Englishman, must be painful to the abbé.

'That,' said Veuillot, 'is our hope!'

Observing the polemicist with interest, Nicola saw that his appearance was at odds with his bellicosity. His flesh was slack and his snub features had an air of *bonhomie*. The Englishman must have spoken in Lagarde's defence, for Veuillot cried that to show mercy to the sinful was to encourage sin.

'This cannot be sound doctrine?' Blount appealed to Chigi who admitted that zeal sometimes carried Monsieur Veuillot too far.

'Which,' the nuncio smiled drolly, 'allows *us* to intervene on the side of clemency and win hearts. Some say it's a Romish plot.'

Nicola asked whether Lagarde might not be keeping his own counsel for tactical reasons.

Veuillot fixed him with an eye untroubled by nuance. It was like a dog's eye. Did the bishop think, he asked, that the abbé was following up some clandestine intrigue? Nicola said he didn't know and wouldn't speak if he did. It was a time for prudence.

Veuillot pretended to flinch. 'An episcopal rebuke! What about freedom of speech? Our English friend will be scandalised to hear a Liberal bishop – sorry, sorry, Monsignore, the word slipped out!'

'The word doesn't frighten me,' Nicola told him.

'And it didn't frighten Darboy! Indeed, gentlemen, what we have here is a priest physically captured by forces which held him mentally captive all his life! What now are the odds?' asked Veuillot. 'Will he die well or will he cringe and . . .'

'I'm sure you'd offer him vinegar on a sponge! A good death is not in a man's control.'

'Oh, forgive me!' Veuillot feigned distress. 'Now I've reminded you of Cardinal Amandi's death which . . .'

Nicola left the table. He regretted provoking an incident, but anger was his barrier against grief. He had trouble containing a prickling in his eyes, as he stared down light shards which sprang, like the spokes of a monstrance, from mirrored chandeliers.

The Polish lady was creating a diversion at the piano, so Nicola seized his chance to ask Monsignor Chigi whether the Pope had made an appeal on Darboy's behalf to Monsieur Thiers.

The nuncio said no and that it would by unwise to call too often on the diminished store of good will now left to the Church.

'But I was assured before leaving Rome . . .' Nicola did not mention Prospero's promise.

Chigi took his arm. 'I wish I thought such an appeal would make a difference, Monsignore . . .' He made a helpless gesture. 'Let us comfort ourselves with music.'

The air was raw with woodsmoke and the sun, probing pocks and freckles in the dressed stone of Versailles, gave the town a look of old marzipan in a pastrycook's window.

Nicola's landlady had put a copy of Veuillot's paper, *l'Univers*, on her lodger's breakfast tray. She had circled an item: General de Fabrice, head of the Prussian GHQ at Soisy, had confidentially informed the Commune that if it shot the hostages, Prussia would punish the crime, 'in Europe's name'.

Thank God, thought Nicola. Then: might this threat, now that it was public, backfire and stiffen Darboy's captors? Anxious to hear Lagarde's opinion, he called at his lodgings and, failing to find him, drove to Mount Satory from whose summit one could see Paris. What was going on there? Should he go and see? What if, instead, he were to request a meeting with Monsieur Thiers and claim to have a message for him from the Pope? Would Monsignor Chigi deny him thrice? He would. It was a lunatic notion.

In the afternoon, he drifted into the château grounds, where a concert was in progress, and ran into Mr Blount, who asked if he had heard the news. What news? About Cluseret. 'Remember? The Commune's Minister of War. He's lost his command and been sent to Mazas prison.' The official explanation, said the Englishman, was that Issy, one of the forts held by the Communard troops, had been temporarily abandoned. But as Cluseret himself had promptly retaken it, this didn't hold water. No, the real reason had to be Cluseret's contacts with the Prussians and the fact that he had signed a paper – Blount claimed to have proof of this – agreeing to release Darboy. The contacts had been secret and would have remained so but for the item in *l'Univers*. 'If it was leaked when Veuillot first knew it,' said Blount, 'then *he* brought down Cluseret.'

And dished Darboy's chances?'

'Absolutely. The Commune has now appointed a Committee of Public Safety which will be hard to deal with because its members distrust each other. It has already repudiated Cluseret's order to release Darboy. Is there any reason,' asked Blount, 'to think the Vatican might prefer him *not* to be rescued? No? Forgive me. It was just a thought.' Before taking

577

leave, he invited Nicola to dine, later, at the Hotel des Réservoirs.

Calling again on the abbé, Nicola found him in a state of prostration over the failure of a plan, which had pivoted on the Prussian approach to Cluseret. Lagarde's go-between, the daughter of an aide-de-camp of the Tsar of Russia, had had to mobilise princely contacts, and it had taken weeks of manoeuvring up and down hierarchies of blue-blood lines and across enemy ones before the thing was done. Now – the abbé's groan had the knell of a death rattle.

'What about the Poles?'

Lagarde blenched. 'Can nobody keep a secret? How do you know about them?' A Polish group, he admitted, was trying bribery. For God's sake, Monsignore, don't let this go any further. Cluseret was gone, but some of the men contacted were still in place. What was lacking was the 60,000 francs that they wanted.

'Monseigneur,' said the unhappy Lagarde, 'cannot be told. He talks too openly to his captors, so it is safer to let him and others think I am saving my own skin and doing nothing.' In fact, though, the Poles' Communard contacts had already managed to obtain the release of the prelate's sister, Mademoiselle Darboy.

The Hotel des Réservoirs, once the pretty residence of Madame de Pompadour, was now so seething with customers that, without Mr Blount's invitation, Nicola could not have eaten there. Tables, he learned from his host, were booked from morning till night and, when the last diners left, table-cloths were replaced by mattresses and the dining room became a dormitory.

Mr Blount pointed out the English Ambassador, Lord Lyons, and other well-known people, then said, 'I have a surprise for you. An old friend of yours will be joining us.'

It was Flavio, who, though courtly as ever, had a tremor in his eyelid. He was still struggling with the aftermath of what the press was calling 'the Langrand labyrinth of swindles'. Thanks to Nicola's paper, he had come unscathed through the Belgian phase of court cases but a French one threatened and his present respite was due only to the fact that the prosecution's papers were in Paris and unreachable in the Palais de Justice. Langrand, facing personal charges of fraudulent bankruptcy, was likely to skip to America. 'It's hard to blame him,' said the forgiving

578

Flavio. 'He was a paladin of the imagination. His account books are a cross between dream books and explorers' charts. He was too good a Catholic to be a good businessman. His venture was a prayer.'

This sparked off a hope in Nicola's head. Could Flavio get his hands on the money needed to ransom Darboy? Langrand must have secret caches? From what the papers said, so much was missing that nobody would miss more, so why not use it in a good cause? 'It will bring you both luck,' he cajoled. *Ad removendam maiorem calamitatem*, one could, he saw, with shame, cease to care about shame. Briefly, he felt a flicker of fellow-feeling for Mastai.

Flavio, though surprised, agreed to provide the money.

The Abbé Lagarde was too agitated to listen to Nicola's news. He had had two letters from different groups of Parisian clergy. One summoned him back to Paris 'to avoid bloodshed', while the other said that if he were to return without an agreement for an exchange of hostages, the Communards would shoot the archbishop.

The abbé, looking wizened and twitchy, said, 'I pray for guidance, Monsignore, but how can I trust my judgment when others don't?' He was thinking of Darboy, who had sent a bitter letter ordering him to return forthwith, no matter how things stood.

'You must disobey him.'

'But he thinks I'm a traitor and a coward.'

'That's your cross. His is being in Mazas gaol. Besides,' said Nicola, surprising himself, 'it's a time when loyalty is best shown not by obedience but by the opposite.'

The abbé looked mildly cheered. He had a guest, a man in secular clothing. This was le Père Amodru, who had brought one of the letters from Paris. The Communards, said Amodru, were growing desperate. Cluseret's fall was a sign of panic. 'Which means,' he warned, 'that extremists are taking over and bribes harder to give.'

'We failed them!' groaned Lagarde. 'They were our flock!' But it was no time, his companions reminded him, for such concerns.

'Monsieur Plou, Monseigneur's lawyer . . .'

'Has he been allowed to see him again?'

'No, but when he did see him he found him unrecognisable. Monseigneur has grown a beard, lost weight, wears a wretched old soutane and black nightcap . . .'

Nicola, leaving them, walked out into the stately, ramshackle town.

579

Under the Empire, this seat of royal pride had been deliberately allowed to run down, and now houses were requisitioned and streets looked as though people had been picnicking in them. Passing a café, he found himself crunching oyster shells. Versailles! The name hissed like a sad cacophony of ghosts. Evading them, he tried to imagine the racy, energetic France of Napoleon III.

Prisoners, taken in the fighting outside the Paris walls, were being herded past. Former National Guardsmen, not drunk now, though they had allegedly been so for months on looted wine, they stared with unfocusing, furious, stunned eyes. They were hobbled together and had to be protected by their escort of regular soldiers from assaults. The abbé's lost flock! A soldier pushed aside a well-dressed woman who was spitting and the spit fell short.

Thirty-two

Flavio now disappeared to raise ransom money – or to abstract it from his creditors' grasp – and Blount brought back a copy of a proclamation which was posted all over Paris. It promised 'a new ... positive and scientific era in place of the old clerical world ... and of the militarism, monopolism and privilege to which the proletariat owes its servitude and the nation its downfall'.

'They may whistle for their new era, now,' said Blount. The city was being bombarded and he believed the Army could take it if it chose. 'Thiers,' he speculated, 'is drawing things out.'

In mid-May, exiled Parisians, observing their city from Mount Satory, were surprised to witness the fall of the pillar on the place Vendôme. It had been made from German cannon captured during the Napoleonic wars, so the watchers guessed the Prussians to be to blame and the Commune hand in glove with them!

'That,' said Blount, 'is a slander!'

Lagarde agreed. He was alert for slanders because of those spread about himself – for instance, that he had deserted Darboy from ultramontane spite. 'The Communards smashed the pillar,' he told Nicola, 'from hatred of the Bonapartes. They may shoot Monseigneur for the same reason. As the Emperor's man.'

'God's man, surely?'

'For us,' said the abbé despondently. 'Not for them!' Fresh danger signals had come from the city. The Red Virgin wanted the hostages shot. 'Louise Michel. I used to see her during the Prussian siege. She would march into our churches collecting money for the ambulances. Always with a red belt and a gun on her shoulder. Her father was a landed gentleman and her mother a chambermaid. The Commune's other virago, Elizabeth Dimitrieff, is a bastard too.' The progeny of mismatches, said the abbé, were forcing-pits for revolution. 'Topsyturvy-dom is policy now and such freaks are bloodthirsty.'

Nicola tried not to feel resentful. Personal feelings had no place here – and perhaps the son of the Baron Lagarde did not mean what he said. One must hope not, for his drift was woundingly clear: the viragos were viragos because they were bastards, and misfits aimed to tailor the world to fit themselves. But: was Monseigneur Dupanloup not the son of mismatched parents? And Jesus Christ? Both their sires had picked ancillary loves and left their sons a soft spot for underdogs. Hence Dupanloup's Liberalism and the Sermon on the Mount.

A Commune rampaged through Nicola's thoughts. Veuillot would have said he had encouraged it by dallying with Liberalism: a bastard creed. Would Lagarde? It was hard to know what he thought about anything other than his impugned honour, his archbishop's doubts of him, and his hopes of outwitting the Reds. Unity was fracturing and the air hazy with sunshot dust.

Meanwhile, Darboy was plumbing a humiliation custom-made for grocer's stock, as he tried to peddle an unwanted lot made up of himself and five fellow hostages. His last two pleas were delivered to Monsieur Thiers on Saturday and Sunday, 20th and 21st May. That same Sunday, government troops entered Paris and the news, which reached Versailles in time for after-dinner toasts, filled the archbishop's friends with dread. 'That's it then. Thiers won't negotiate now. And the Communards will fight like cornered rats.'

Wolves! Badgers! Baited bears! Over the next weeks, idlers in Versailles would enjoy the pleasures of zoo-visitors as they threw stones and dung at the convoys of captives who came hobbling in their thousands through their town. These, said Blount, were the lucky ones. Ferocious stories were leaking out of Paris.

The day after the troops went in, their advance was halted. Though welcomed in the wealthy western districts, they came up against a line of resistance stretching from the Batignolles, through the Gare St Lazare, across the river to the Chamber of Deputies and south to Montparnasse. East of this front lay Mazas prison where the hostages were held.

That evening, the sky over Paris was red; and next day stupefied Versaillais, many of whom owned houses in the capital, saw columns of black smoke rise, spread like the branches of an umbrella pine, then, erupting still higher, form a vast, red-tinged, glowing mushroom. The city was on fire.

Rumours clashed with counter-rumours. The Tuileries were burning and so perhaps was Notre-Dame Cathedral! What about the prisons? Had the bridges been blown up? The dry, windy weather was perfect for arson, and it was not until the Friday that rain came.

All week Nicola prayed for Darboy who, in his aching mind, fused with other figures visible in the shabby gloom of Versailles churches: stoned Stephens, Jeromes with their tamed lions, meek Christs. Remembering what the abbé Delisle had said about the uses of martyrdom, Nicola, even as he begged the Virgin to take pity on the hostages, fancied he saw a sardonic twitch to her lip.

Early on Saturday, 27th May, a manservant of Flavio's called at Nicola's lodgings with the 60,000 francs for the hostages' ransom. Although ill, the duke, said his man, had forced himself to travel. He had got here from Brussels last night but was now too sick with a fever to take the money into Paris, as he had hoped to do. Besides, it was too late. It would be foolhardy to venture into that furnace. The rules of war were being observed by neither side. Paris was a slaughter-house, but the duke wanted Monsignor Santi to know he had done his best. He had done it for *him* because he knew that he had come to think of the archbishop as Amandi's successor and must dread to see him, too, struck down.

The messenger left him staring at the useless money. Amandi and Darboy were his heart's elect, yet he, like one of the wailing women posted along the *via crucis*, must stand impotently by – must he? Surely, *this* time could be different? Paris was in chaos, but might he not hope to turn this to account? Convince the Army of the urgency of a rescue? Bribe a Communard official at the last, critical moment? Even this week, people had been into that hell and come back. Edward Blount knew some who had, but was refusing to repeat their stories. Hearsay, he claimed, was a factor in the vengeful follies being reported and misreported.

Blount! Might he help? He had contacts in the city and knew whom to bribe. Nicola would ask him for a loan of lay clothes – and maybe the Englishman would offer to come with him. Lagarde? No. Blount was the man, decided Nicola, and set off to find him.

*

Two hours later they were in the smudgy heart of ruined Paris. Like Virgil in the *Inferno*, Blount named wrecked, half-deserted streets, the rue Royale, the place du Carrousel. By now the Army had fought its way east and only the fire-brigade was left and, with the help of residents, was struggling to quench fires laid by the retreating Communards. Occasional gusty flames rose, were beaten back by the wind and seemed, at moments, to creep along the footpaths. Gutted ministries – just here were the Admiralty and the vast, devastated Ministry of Finance – had been doused with petrol and set alight. Arsonists, a resident told them, had been shot out of hand.

'We were in the cellars.' A *concierge* held her door half open, ready, if need be, to dodge behind it. There had, she said, been summary killings right here. First the *fédérés* had killed people and, when the regular troops came, *they* killed *them*. On the spot! Up against the wall. *Pan*! As if she had frightened herself, she closed the door and they heard her shoot the bolt.

'They can't believe it's over.'

'It *isn't* on the other side of the city. Hear the cannon?'

On their way here, the sky had been dotted with scraps of blackened paper which floated sootily for miles outside Paris. Here, at the ministries, was their source. Carbonised particles rose like black butterflies, were caught by the wind, whirled in gusty flurries, then fell back, often into one of the conflagrations still dully burning throughout the area.

Blount plucked a fragment from his sleeve and, reading '. . . nistry of Just . . .', noted that that must have come from across the river. 'The duke should be pleased. If the Ministry of Justice has lost its records, the evidence against him has gone up in smoke!'

He had a message from him, he remembered then. Indeed, he had intended telling it to Nicola this morning but, distracted by the idea of this expedition, had forgotten. 'He'd have written, but is too ill and it wasn't something he wanted to tell a servant. He told me last night at the station.'

'What is his message?'

'He wants you to know that he is adopting Maria Gatti's son. He wants an heir. It seems he's worried about his health. Did you know that? Apparently it's not good, so starting the adoption procedure couldn't wait. I gather it's a ticklish subject. Oh God,' Blount interrupted himself in shock. 'Corpses!'

They had a domestic, even casual look, as if they had just slipped out for bread or milk. There were too many for that though. Spectators or combatants in some skirmish, they had been piled, six feet high, under an arcade and three urchins were turning out their pockets. Nicola got a sour smell, as the two rushed past.

There was smoke everywhere and smells of burned varnish. Gutted buildings smouldered as they made their way down the rue de Rivoli towards the Hôtel de Ville, which had been the Commune's head-quarters. The sky showed lacily through its gouged façade, but the flames had been doused and a lambent phosphorescence glimmered from its shell. Dead horses. More bodies. Broken barricades. A hiss of water hoses everywhere, and all the time that distant rumbling growl of the cannon.

'Look.' Blount pointed across the river. 'Notre-Dame Cathedral! They didn't burn it after all.'

At Mazas Prison the Army was in control and the tricolour flying. The news was, however, that the retreating Communards had moved the hostages east to the prison of La Roquette which, though not far, was unreachable. Fighting in that area was intense, for the rump of the Commune was entrenched in the *Mairie* of the Eleventh Arrondissement which was just near the prison.

Blount said he knew some people east of here who might have news. So they pressed on laboriously, taking roundabout routes to avoid the rubble of barricades. His acquaintances were café owners who had closed their shutters and were reluctant to open them. In the end, however, they let the two in and agreed to give them a scratch meal. The Englishmen had made their acquaintance when distributing provi-sions bought by the Lord Mayor of London's Fund. He asked the *patronne* for news of the hostages.

'You didn't hear? They were shot in La Roquette prison on Wed-nesday. The men from the firing squad were in the wine shops after-wards, spending their fifty francs and talking their heads off. Besides, there were plenty of witnesses in the Place Voltaire when help was recruited.'

'You're sure they shot the archbishop? Darboy?'

Nicola felt dizzy with disappointment, but Blount put a hand on his. 'Don't despair!' he said. Most rumours were untrue. 'Remember Notre-Dame Cathedral? We just saw it intact, yet two days ago a man swore to me he'd seen it in flames! We'll go to La Roquette now. '

The woman came back with some preserved fruit. 'Life goes on,' she said, dishing it up. 'Just! This morning soldiers shot a child here in the street. A chimneysweep. They said he had gunpowder on his hands, so they shot him. It wasn't gunpowder. It was soot!'

The other side, she told them, was no better. They'd massacred fifty prisoners in the rue Haxo. Maybe more? Some were priests. That was yesterday. They'd taken them from La Roquette prison and, although Commune officials tried to rescue the prisoners and there was no proper firing squad, they were mown down by the mob. 'Shot like rabbits. Turned into human porridge.' That was what she'd heard from a man who had got a shaking fit while he was telling her. Anyone who had a gun just shot into the mass without taking aim or even lining them up. They did it because of what the regulars did to their own people. '"An eye for an eye," they said.'

Blount's eye held Nicola's. These are only stories, it signalled. On their way out, Nicola's attention was caught by a poster. It was a call to arms by the Committee of Public Safety. 'Citizens,' he read. 'Treason has opened our gates to the enemy . . . If Thiers wins you know what awaits you. Labour without fruit and poverty without relief . . . To arms. No pity! Shoot all those who might help the enemy. If you are defeated they won't spare you . . .'

'It's not all lies,' said the woman indecisively. She pointed to the words 'Woe to those caught with powder on their fingers or smoke on their faces'. 'I told you about the chimneysweep. A child! And you may be sure he wasn't the only one. That's Monsieur Thiers' justice for you!' Carefully, she unpinned the poster and, as they stepped out, locked her door. The sound of guns was close.

There was a cluster of marines within three hundred yards of La Roquette. They had captured a barricade and were sheltering behind it. Priests, they told Nicola and Blount, had tried escaping from the prison in small groups. Two had got this far and by now must be safely home in their presbyteries. They had reported that others too might try to get out, for the prison authorities had run away and the remaining guards were ready to defect. The danger was the die-hards fighting between here and the gaol. Already, several fugitives had been caught and shot.

Meanwhile, inside one wing of La Roquette, prisoners, many of them captured regular soldiers, had broken out of their cells and raised barricades against the mob which they feared might invade. The prisoners in the other wing were still locked up.

'What about the archbishop?'

The marines didn't know but noted that anyone making a run for it would wear civilian clothes. 'Your archbishop won't come out wearing his pectoral cross.'

At that moment a sniper picked off a marine close to them and the fighting started again. An officer ordered the two civilians out of the line of fire.

Blount thought they should approach the gaol from another direction. He had lost his hat, had blood on his jacket and smelled unusually high for an English gentleman. Nicola guessed that he too had a gamy tang. His clothes were sticking to him and the unaccustomed trousers felt tight around his crotch. As they moved off, the sniper fire grew fiercer and the marines retreated. The officer told them that the prison was unreachable for now.

'But,' asked Blount, 'might the Communards not burn it?'

The officer shrugged. 'We'll go in when we can.'

The sun had now set but a persistent radiance in the sky suggested that it might re-arise. Tomorrow was Whitsun, the feast when the Church celebrated the Holy Ghost's descent on the timorous apostles. Then, too, He had come in the form of tongues of fire. A marine told the two civilians that they should return to the safe part of the city. In an hour or so, the troops would have tightened their noose around the prison and might even have freed it.

So off they set, turned a corner, then another, and were in the line of fire. Confused, they bolted in different directions and, moments later, Nicola found himself confronted by four smudge-faced creatures with the white eyes of maddened horses.

'Aha!' cried a loose-toothed, hairless one and grappled him to his bony chest. Rubbing a blackened, stubby cheek to his cheek, he cried, 'Don Nicola, isn't it? A ghost? Or am I dead myself?'

He, he cried, was Don Mauro, alias Monsieur Maur! Remember? At Monsieur Lammenais' funeral? He was fighting with the Garibaldini who had come to help the Commune. Why not? At his age it would be a bonus to die fighting. Think of it! He had expected to die decades ago of tuberculosis and instead here he was. Better a bullet than consumption! Eh? Here, take a gun. What are you doing here? What a turn-up! We're all Italians here!

He waved at three other men, veterans all, he said, of 1848! 'Hunker down behind this. So you threw off your cassock in the end, did you? Ha!' cried Don Mauro, 'they're getting brazen!' And turning away he

587

began energetically shooting through a small gap at what, Nicola feared, must be the same troops as he and Blount had just left. 'Keep *down*,' scolded Mauro. 'You're not a combatant, I can see. What are you doing here?'

Nicola said he was seeking news of Archbishop Darboy. Was he dead? Yes, said Mauro. 'They shot him last Wednesday inside the prison. R.I.P. The Vatican won't be sorry, whatever they pretend.'

'Why do you say that?'

'Keep down, will you! Down!'

Bullets skidded off the top of the barricade and one of the others said, 'We'll have to leave here. Fall back to the *Mairie*.'

'The Army says you're surrounded.'

Don Mauro rose and peered over the top, then waved at an empty street. 'They've gone!'

'Tell me about Darboy.'

'He was shot by a firing squad. In revenge. Six National Guardsmen had been put up against a wall by the regular army, so their mates killed six hostages. They thought it would make more of an impression if they took Darboy.'

'What did you mean about the Vatican?' Nicola felt sick with foreboding.

Don Mauro winked. 'General Cluseret had ordered Darboy's release and he was within a whisker of being freed. Instead, someone told Cluseret's colleagues what was afoot and they arrested *him*. What you must know is that *that* someone was an agent of Monsignor Chigi's. And if you want to know how *I* know, I know the man. He's an old Garibaldino who turned his coat. We rumbled him years back but tolerate him lest they replace him by someone more efficient. When we're killed he'll be laughing – or maybe he'll miss us? Maybe he'll put flowers on our graves?'

The lull continued. One of the Garibaldini was sucking at a loaf of bread and Nicola wondered whether he dare move on. He had, however, lost all sense of direction. Sheepishly, he consulted Don Mauro, explaining that, apart from his interest in Archbishop Darboy, he belonged to neither side. Don Mauro was amused. 'Better not tell them!' he said, with a jerk of his chin towards his companions, who were using the respite to make themselves comfortable. One was reloading his gun while another relieved himself in a corner.

'It's Judgment Day on earth!' said the one with the bread and wrapped it in a blue check cloth. Putting it away, he squinted along the barrel of his gun. The moment absorbed them and Nicola thought, They've found eternity in the here and now. Just then, the one who had reloaded his gun climbed up to survey the street, stiffened, then flopped limply across the top of the barricade.

'*Merde!*' Don Mauro swivelled to point his gun the other way.

The shot had come from behind. The marines had them hemmed in.

'This gentleman is a bishop. I give you my word.'

It was the small hours. Four? Five? Nicola's watch had stopped. They were in La Roquette prison and Blount was arguing with a tight-lipped staff colonel. In the sky, a milky daylight was mixing with the incendiary blush. Dawn then? Earlier there had been arguments with lesser officers and, in between, hours of just sitting, first in an army outpost, then here in the prison registry which looked as though it had been vacated in a great hurry. Two gold-braided uniforms and a red scarf hung on a peg.

Blount explained again that Nicola had come to Paris in lay clothes and without papers for fear of falling into the hands of the *fédérés*. '*I* have papers,' he offered, but was waved away. The colonel knew who he was, having seen him, it turned out, on a platform representing the Lord Mayor of London's Relief Fund. And *he* had not been caught with a gun in his hands and powder on his face firing on our men. 'But . . .' began Blount and was interrupted.

The colonel, lean as a whippet and, under his steel demeanour, perhaps as tremulous, held up an arresting hand. 'Your countrymen give asylum to all and sundry. It is one of your quirks. Any so-called "political" murderer who reaches your shores receives it. Therefore, Mr Blount, we do not easily let them out of our hands and into yours. This story has neither head nor tail. Bishop of Trebizond, you say! An Italian! Trebizond, when I was in school . . .'

'It's a diocese,' said Nicola numbly, '*in partibus infidelium.*'

'*Infedelium?* I'd say that was where you were apprehended! And you say the other desperado who was shooting at my men is a priest too? I don't recognise such priests. We have heard horrors about what was done to real priests, including Archbishop Darboy, whom you claim you hoped to save. Sizeable bits of their brains are stuck to the wall out on the parapet walk. I have just seen them and they're one of the reasons why I am shooting all assassins.'

Did he mean, asked Blount, he was sending suspects for trial?

No sir, said the colonel. He did not mean that. He showed Blount a proclamation. It was the last one put out by the retreating Reds. 'I'll read it to you: "Order: destroy all houses from whose windows shots have been fired on the National Guard and shoot all inhabitants unless they themselves . . . execute the perpetrators of such crimes. 24 May at 9 p.m. The Committee for War." That's the sort of war we're fighting. So, no trial. However, though I shoot defrocked priests, I don't shoot real ones. And though I do not doubt your word, you must permit me to doubt you perspicacity. Can you prove that this gentleman is what you say?'

Blount asked whether the Abbé Amodru, one of the released prisoners, was still in the building. Very likely, said the colonel. Fighting was still going on and few prisoners had left.

'He'll speak for him. They met in Versailles.'

The colonel said he would have the abbé called and would himself be back shortly. He left and Blount picked a cassock from a pile left, presumably, by the priests who had worn lay clothes to escape. Put it on, he begged Nicola. Encouragingly, he shook it out as a valet might have done, or a tailor's assistant. 'Without it, Amodru mightn't know you. Besides, it will have a good effect on the colonel. He's ready to crack. I can tell. All that logical talk through clenched teeth is a form of frenzy. This conflict is doing odd things to people. I had an uncle who used to tell me about living through the Sepoy Mutiny in India and how people became quietly unhinged – looked perfectly all right, then suddenly ran amok. Useful to have uncles like that. Does it fit?'

Nicola was apprehending things as though through a slatted blind. 'Cracking'? Perhaps that was what it meant? Cracks in one's inner landscape! Did *what* fit? Ah, the cassock. It was a Jesuit one. Wondering whether its owner was now dead, he ran his hands over the matted and faintly sticky cloth. It felt like skin.

The Abbé Amodru came in. He was horrified that Monsignor Santi should be doubted and far more so by what had happened to Darboy and the Jesuits. Yes, three had been shot with Monseigneur, and their Superior, Father Olivaint, had been with the group taken to the rue Haxo. 'The warders are spilling secrets in the hope that we'll speak up for them. Turncoats of the worst sort! Yesterday, several changed sides more than once.' While the abbé talked there was a rattle of gunfire nearby. Rrrrrrr! He crossed himself. Another firing squad. He began to speak of Monseigneur's death, which had sounded just like that. 'We were all kneeling in our cells . . .' There was another sharp explosion.

'That's the *coup de grâce*. I'm afraid,' Blount told Nicola, 'that those were your companions in arms.'

'Three old Italians,' confirmed the abbé. 'I passed them on my way here.'

The colonel returned and took in the scene. Well, did the abbé vouch for His Lordship? His use of the title showed that he was now ready to be convinced. The abbé began to praise Monsignor Santi's devotion to the cause of Monseigneur Darboy.

'You've shot them!' Nicola's laggardly mind had just caught up. 'You shot Don Mauro!'

'. . . by no means defrocked,' the abbé was assuring.

'I am now!' Nicola wrenched off the cassock – it was choking and clinging to him like a dead man's skin. 'I don't want its protection. It's Judas cloth! Shoot me! Shoot *me* now as well!'

But the Colonel, embarrassed by such a failure of decorum in a senior officer of our spiritual army, had faded from the room.

From the notebooks of the noble abbot
Raffaello Lambruschini: *1873*

Chance reveals latent patterns. Nicola Santi's name has come up in connection with an inglorious little incident proving that the Church is secretly buying back bits of its lost kingdom. Since it may not do this legally, it uses laymen to hold the property in trust – at the risk that they may default. One who now has is Pietro Gatti, Duke Cesarini's adoptive heir. On the duke's death last year, Gatti nominally inherited a lot of such property which he is brazenly claiming as his own. State officials are amused, not to say cockahoop, since this must discourage fresh manoeuvres of the sort. They hint privately that, as Gatti is whispered to be the bastard of the Pope's bastard – Santi – he is conforming to old usage. *Plus ça change* . . .! The Curia, to be sure, is without remedy and, sooner or later, must learn to do without the temporal.

Oddly, Santi said exactly this to me when explaining why he had flung his cassock – as they say – to the nettles. 'The Commune,' he claimed, 'brought home to people the materialism of our spiritual arithmetic, which is why Darboy asked to be exchanged for Blanqui. He saw the coercive nature of the argument from martyrdom – not to mention how it begets violence.'

Why then, I asked Santi, did *he* ask to be shot? From shame, was his answer. 'The Temporal Power corrupts,' he argued and the staff colonel's assumption that they belonged to similar corps outraged him as much as he outraged the colonel.

Apparently, he went to pieces then and Amodru had to take him to his cell and give him laudanum. Nobody could leave yet because of the fighting. He went to sleep and when he awoke, hours later, the sound in his ears was the rattle of the firing squad. This time it kept pausing and restarting and was punctuated by the shots which he knew now to be *coups de grâce*. He was petrified. It sounded as though many hundreds of men were being shot. Wondering whether he was hallucinating, he stumbled from the cell and went looking for his two companions. The building baffled him. It seemed like a maze, though he realised later that its west wing, which was where he was, consisted of a double row of cells with a courtyard on one side and a double parapet-walk on the other. It was out there that he came on a great pile of freshly killed bodies smelling of faeces and urine. A fresh rattle of gunfire made him bolt back in and up a spiral staircase which brought him within earshot of Blount and Amodru, who were in what had been Darboy's cell. They had found words pencilled on the Judas hole in the form of a cross. These were *robor vitae salus mentis* which, said the abbé, if you read the cross as a word, spelled 'the cross is the strength of life and the salvation of the soul'.

Just then the gun-rattle took up again and Santi began shrieking. 'Don't start a new legend!' Alarmed lest he draw attention to himself again, they firmly frogmarched him out and into a carriage for which they had been waiting, and drove west across a Paris now entirely in the hands of the Army. Fighting was over but the 'expiation' was in full swing and the papers next day would describe the Seine as streaked with blood.

He learned later that what he had heard was the start of a great massacre of Communards. Nineteen hundred were shot in two days in La Roquette prison, and these were only a fraction of those killed in Paris that week, whose number some put at twenty thousand and some at forty thousand. The cross was no salvation at all and in many minds 'Bloody Week', as it came to be called, made it impossible to go on believing in the redemptive grace of Passion Week.

He went to England after that with Edward Blount, and only came back when he heard that his friend Cesarini was dying of consumption. He was with him at the end, then came to see me, on his way to Imola to give money to Sister Paola's old hospital. He set up a secular institution there modelled on those Blount had shown him in London. When he left, he sent me a letter explaining that what he loved in Christianity was the compassionate teaching of Christ. Since this had been sacrificed to the ruthless defence of the Institutional Church, he, from love of Christ, had left it.

I heard no more of him.

1881

Prospero Cardinal Stanga read Lambruschini's diary with close interest. It had reached him anonymously and, instead of deciding what to do with it, he lingered over familiar names and let memories of old friendships soften him. Prospero was not quite the man he had been, for he was on less good terms with the new regime than with the old one. The new Pope had turned down his plan to resurrect the Sodalitium Pianum and, gently, let him know that such intransigence had had its day. Grassi was dead. Another like-minded Jesuit from the *Civiltà* had had to go to America after an unfortunate confusion over the paper's funds and Prospero himself was being kept far from the levers of power. The effect of this was that he had grown mild, reflective and a little lonely. The diary's reference to Nicola reminded him of his own most recent glimpse of him which had been at Pio Nono's funeral, a troubling occasion where the sight of a face from happier times had flooded him with emotion. Nicola, dressed as a layman, had been standing among the crowd, watching the procession. Starlight gleamed on his silk hat and caught an expression which impelled Prospero to lower his carriage window and, taking advantage of a pause, whisper his name. They were within a foot of each other and he could see Nicola's cold face perfectly. '*Please*,' whispered Prospero, thinking that the renegade might need to be set at ease.

But it was one of those moments – they were near the Tiber – when the rabble wanted to assault the hearse and it is not easy at such a time to convey feelings of friendship or even of bygones being bygones. Moreover, he was aware of his coachman's anxieties lest the men close to the carriage have malevolent intentions.

'*Carogna!*' came the shouts. 'Pitch the carrion in!'

'Won't you shake hands with me? Or even,' he ventured, 'sit in the carriage for a moment?'

But his hand had not been taken and his carriage shot forward leaving behind that pale, cold face. Why? he wondered. And for most of the funeral, it was not the rabble's roar which bothered him, but that wounding personal rejection.

GLOSSARY

Carbonari: a secret political association active in the early 19th century. Their aims varied. In the Papal States, these included reforms, a lay administration and even secession from papal rule by the northern Legations.

Centurioni: a voluntary, part-time police force set up after revolution of 1831 by the then Secretary of State, to keep order and check left-wing secret societies. They were generally acknowledged to be thugs.

Chamberlain: an official attached to the personal service of the Pope.

Coadjutor bishop: one appointed by the Pope to assist a bishop suffering from specified infirmities.

College of Cardinals: the ensemble of seventy cardinals who assisted the Pope in governing the Church.

Conclave: a meeting of all the cardinals to elect a Pope.

Congregations: departments or ministries which assisted the Pope in governing the Church. At the head of each was a prefect, usually a cardinal.

Curia: the authorities and functionaries forming the entourage or court of the Pope.

Encyclical: a circular letter addressed by the Pope to all his bishops.

Fédérés: in the Paris Commune, those members of the National Guard who joined the Communards.

Legations: in the Papal States, the provinces beyond the Apennines under the authority of papal legates. Provinces closer to Rome were governed by delegates. Both legates and delegates were clerics. Cities of the Legations were Ferrara, Bologna, Imola, Ravenna, Forli and Rimini.

Legate: An ecclesiastic representing the Holy See. A legate *a latere* – always a cardinal – was an emissary sent, for instance, to govern the northern papal provinces.

Motu Proprio: A papal rescript whose provisions were determined by the Pope personally.

Prelate: After the cardinals, prelates occupied the first rank in the Roman Curia. All bishops possessed the dignity and so did prominent officials of the Curia. Various requirements, financial and otherwise, had to be satisfied by a man entering the prelacy, though he need not be a priest. Once accepted, he was addressed as Monsignore and wore violet.

Roman Republic: the first Roman Republic, set up by the French in 1798, lasted eighteen months; the second, proclaimed by an elected Constituent Assembly in February 1849, lasted until 2 July.

Titular bishop: one deriving his title from a former bishopric lost – often by Muhammadan conquest – to the Roman Church. Curial officials often received such titles *in partibus infidelium*.

Ultramontanism: the doctrine of absolute papal supremacy. So called because churchmen north of the Alps looked for orders 'beyond the mountains' to Rome.

Zelanti: zealots, bigoted papalists, anti-Liberal and anti-reform.

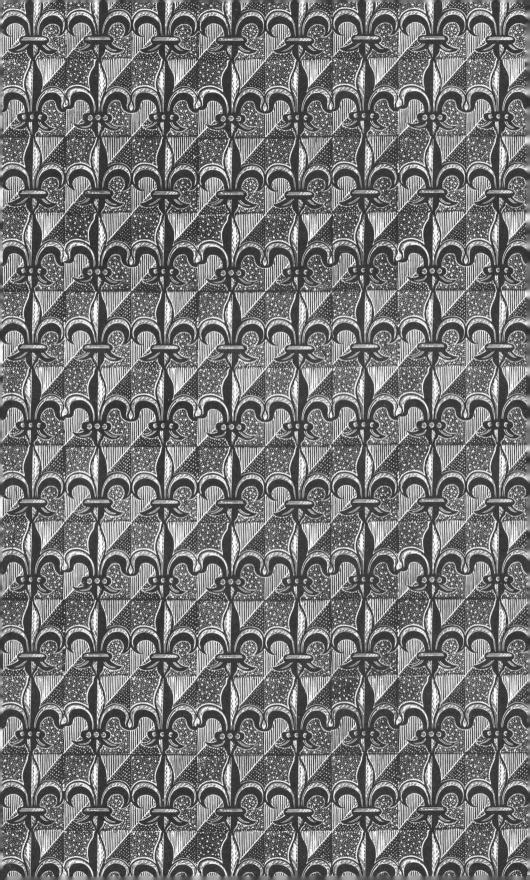